ALSO BY JEFF SHAARA
AVAILABLE FROM
RANDOM HOUSE
LARGE PRINT

A Blaze of Glory

A Chain of Thunder

The Final Storm

The Killer Angels

The Smoke at Dawn

THE FATEFUL LIGHTNING

THE
FATEFUL
LIGHTNING

A NOVEL OF THE CIVIL WAR

JEFF SHAARA

RANDOM HOUSE
LARGE PRINT

Copyright © 2015 by Jeffrey M. Shaara
Maps copyright © 2015 by Bob Bull

All rights reserved.
Published in the United States of America by Random House Large Print in association with Ballantine Books, a division of Penguin Random House LLC, New York. Distributed by Random House, a Penguin Random House Company.

Cover design by Tom McKeveny
Cover illustration © The Granger Collection, New York

The Library of Congress has established a Cataloging-in-Publication record for this title.

ISBN: 978-0-8041-9467-9

www.randomhouse.com/largeprint

FIRST LARGE PRINT EDITION
10 9 8 7 6 5 4 3 2 1
Printed in the United States of America

This Large Print edition published in accord with the standards of the N.A.V.H.

Dedicated to Patrick Falci and
Joan McDonough, and
Colonel Keith Gibson and Pat Gibson,
who, throughout the entire process of
researching and writing my seven books
on the Civil War, were always there with
support, assistance, and a kind word

CONTENTS

TO THE READER

This is the fourth and final volume of a series that tells the story of the Civil War in the "west." The first three, dealing with Shiloh, Vicksburg, and Chattanooga, featured a cast of characters that varied according to the significance of those men (and in one case, woman) and their roles in the story. In all three books, the one consistent character is Federal general William T. Sherman. Here Sherman becomes even more of a primary figure, as this story covers the campaigns from November 1864 through the end of the war in North Carolina, in late April 1865. Much of the book covers what we know today as "Sherman's March to the Sea," across north and central Georgia. But there is much more to this story.

In every book I've written, I agonize over just where the story should begin. Inevitably, the question arises, from letters and emails I receive, of why I did not include certain events or certain specific people. This book will be no exception.

This is not a history book. I never make any attempt to include the entire history of any campaign or battle, or to include every major historical figure. That is the job of the historian. My primary objective is to find what I hope is the best story I can tell, and by doing so, to bring the history to life. This is a novel. But the characters are real, the accounts based on as many original source materials as I could find, including the work of a great many historians who have dug far more deeply into these characters than I can. In addition, I depend on those readers who offer up pieces of their own family history, often including diaries, collections of letters, or memoirs that have never been published and thus have never seen the light of day. The extraordinary value of all of these resources creates the acknowledgments section of this book, found at the end.

The choice to begin this story in November 1864 was a challenging one. My last book, the third volume in this series (**The Smoke at Dawn**), dealt with the Chattanooga campaign of late 1863. What happens immediately afterward, continuing through the summer of 1864, most notably the vicious struggles around the city of Atlanta, is a book all its own. Though I make frequent reference to that campaign and to the campaigns that follow in central Tennessee (specifically the battles of Franklin and Nashville), this story begins with Sherman's march away from Atlanta, and features four principal voices and their experiences through the final six months of the war. To those who feel I have ignored or overlooked the significance of the events I have left out, I apologize. But I am restricted often by my publisher, who in this case was rather insistent that I not attempt to tackle six or seven books on this particular part of the war (or write one gigantic book that would make Harry Potter pale in comparison).

So, I'm hoping you will accept this book as my attempt to bring you the final chapter of the war, a chapter that to many is virtually unknown, especially compared to the more familiar stories of Robert E. Lee and Ulysses Grant in Virginia.

This story focuses on four primary points of view. One is Sherman, certainly. Two others are his adversaries General William Hardee and the young cavalryman Captain James Seeley, both of whom were introduced in the first volume (**A Blaze of Glory**) at Shiloh. Alongside these three soldiers comes a civilian, a very different kind of voice. He is a slave who discovers that, as Sherman's army makes its way through Georgia, the bullwhips and tracking hounds of his master have suddenly disappeared. Thus he joins an extraordinary parade, tens of thousands of men, women, and children who escape their bondage and follow along with Sherman's troops. I hope that the character of a man named Franklin offers you a perspective on this horrific time in our history that few have explored.

Regardless of your feelings about General Sherman (and I've heard a great deal about that), I hope you will find this to be what I intended: an engaging and entertaining story about a part of the Civil War that is often overlooked. As always, the history is as accurate as I can make it, and the interpretation of the personalities of these characters, along with their day-to-day dialogue, is my own.

This was a wonderful book to write. I hope you feel it is worth reading.

JEFF SHAARA

APRIL 2015

LIST OF MAPS

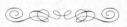

PART ONE

I propose to demonstrate the vulnerability of the South, and make its inhabitants feel that war and individual ruin are synonymous terms.

—WILLIAM T. SHERMAN

He has done either one of the most brilliant or one of the most foolish things ever performed by a military leader. The date on which he goes and the plan on which he acts must really place him among the great generals, or the very little ones.

—THE BRITISH ARMY AND NAVY GAZETTE

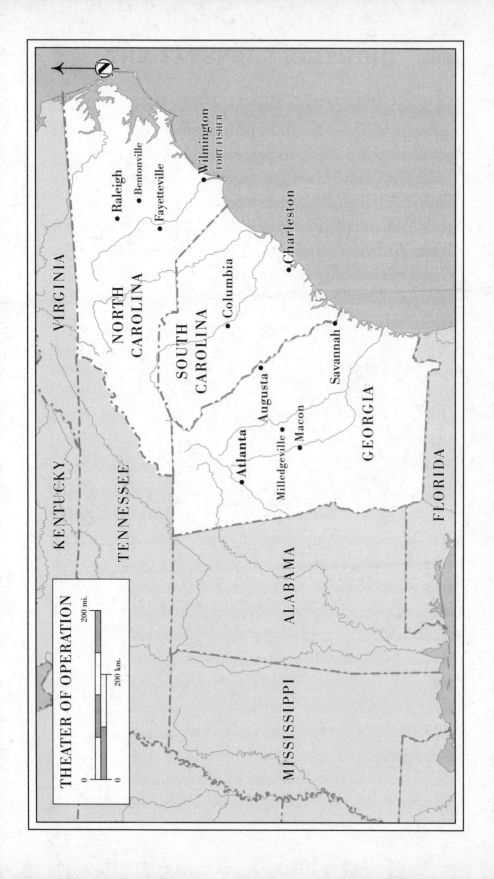

THEATER OF OPERATION

VIRGINIA

KENTUCKY

TENNESSEE

NORTH CAROLINA

SOUTH CAROLINA

GEORGIA

ALABAMA

MISSISSIPPI

FLORIDA

Raleigh

Bentonville

Fayetteville

Wilmington

FORT FISHER

Charleston

Columbia

Savannah

Augusta

Atlanta

Milledgeville

Macon

200 mi.

200 km.

0

0

CHAPTER ONE

SHERMAN

ATLANTA, GEORGIA—NOVEMBER 16, 1864

He halted the horse at the crest of a hill, pulled back on the reins, stared out westward for a long moment. The staff did the same, following his lead, spreading out to give him room, no one moving close unless he was told to. He heard the low murmurs, their reaction to what they were leaving behind them, the picture they would carry within them for the rest of their lives, the perfect portrait of absolute victory.

Sherman held the horse as still as possible, the high-spirited animal moving nervously beneath him, seeming to know there was much more to be done. He clamped his legs in tight, calming the horse, his focus now on the scene. He didn't try to see detail, absorbed instead the vast panorama, the entire city offering itself as a marvelous show-piece. He wrapped his mind around that, what this meant, what it would mean to Grant, to the War Department, what it would mean to all those whose homes were boiling up in black smoke. Pieces of the enemy, he thought. No, it is more. It is the enemy itself. All of it. Everything I can see, everything beneath the march of my army.

The sun was rising behind him, but the city was lit from within, the spreading fires blowing through the fragility of the wooden structures, homes, businesses, factories. He had no urge to destroy the homes, had surprised his staff the night before when he pitched in, trying to extinguish the flames on several small houses near his headquarters. Those fires were premature, without purpose, defiance of his orders that infuriated him. His hands were still smeared with soot, but he ignored that, the futility and anger now past. Throughout the night the fires grew far beyond what a few men attempted to contain. Those men were outnumbered, swarmed over by a passion fueled by alcohol and a lustful revenge. The first fires had been set by vandals, miscreant soldiers more interested in a cruel game than in waging war. But the game became more ugly very quickly, a contagious disease spreading among men who knew that Sherman's order would eventually come, that in time he would have given them permission to set the fires anyway. As the night wore on, the torches were thrown by not only drunken soldiers but even the sober, seduced by the raw power of the fires they could create. Those fires were indiscriminate, aimless, and Sherman was disgusted by that, had hoped instead to offer the rebels the message with clarity.

The order had been given to his chief engineer, Captain Orlando Poe, and Poe's men had been selective, had followed Sherman's instructions to leave nothing behind that the rebels could ever use again, nothing that could help anyone make war. The factories had been the greatest priority, whether munitions and powder plants or the simplest ironworks. The mills and cotton gins had gone as well, along with storage facilities for everything an army used, food and fuel, and any structure that aided transportation. But Sherman had seen this before. Atlanta was no different than Jackson, Mississippi, or any other town on the continent. Even the brick and stone structures had skeletons of wood, and so the slightest breeze pushed the destruction from the intended target to the random storefront, the house that happened to be downwind. He saw it now, a vast sea of red, the harsh glow of a hundred small fires uniting into a raging mass that swept away entire neighborhoods, ash and smoke billowing through every alleyway, the wider avenues bathed with clouds of gray and black, pierced by sharp fingers of red. The smoke rose high, columns of raw heat caught by the morning's breeze, drifting out over him, a light rain of ash filtering down around him, around the others. In the road, the soldiers marched, some of them staring back, a last glimpse, trying to see the amazing horror of it. But there were others who kept their eyes away, hard stares into the backs of the men who marched ahead.

Sherman knew there had been protest, some born of guilt in those men who saw the civilians for what they were: obstacles. Sherman had dealt with that as efficiently as he could, had issued an order to the city's authorities that the civilians simply leave, vacating their homes and businesses to avoid what might follow, what he knew **would** follow. The order was met with outrage, heated letters from Confederate commander John Bell Hood. Sherman responded with vigorous outrage of his own, wondering if any rebel leader thought it best that the civilians remain where they were, ensuring they would suffer from Sherman's occupation of the city. But Sherman had no intention of occupying anything, though he would never reveal that to Hood.

The order was pushed hard into the faces of the civilian leaders still in Atlanta, and the word had spread, much of the population accepting their fate. The refugees had boarded trains provided by the Federal army, some leaving in their own wagons. The scene had been as dismal for the civilians as any other time of the war, some knowing of the exodus from Fredericksburg two years before. But there was one very sharp difference. The citizens of Fredericksburg evacuated to avoid the inevitable fight that would sweep over their town. In Atlanta, the fights were over, the town held firmly in Sherman's hands. Whether or not anyone in Atlanta saw compassion in Sherman's order, he was certain it was the moral thing to do, that removing the civilians from the enormity of his newly acquired armed camp was most certainly in their best interests. He dismissed Hood's protests as the necessary quest for honor, that particular Southern trait, the gentleman's objection to the ungentlemanly. As though, he thought, we are spreading an indecent stain over their precious illusion of Southern sainthood. There are no saints in this army. Just men who know how to fight, who want to go home to their families with victory in their hearts.

He knew there would be protest even in the North, mostly from civilians with ties to Atlanta or those with political animosity toward President Lincoln and his generals. The word had come only the week before that Lincoln had been reelected, that the so-called Peace Party of George McClellan had been soundly defeated. Sherman received that news with smiling satisfaction. He had no doubt at all that the fall of Atlanta had ensured Lincoln's victory, that the citizens in the North could finally feel confident that the war was nearly won. But the newspapers wouldn't just let that pass; the enemies of Lincoln, of Sherman himself, were certain to raise a cry against the punishment of the innocent. He fought through the stench of smoke, thought, There is no **innocence** here. They have made this war, and no matter that the good citizens of this city choose not to carry the musket or fire the cannon, they are just as much my enemy. The mother who sends her boy away to fight, the wife who sacrifices so her husband can make war, the others who go about their business supporting the health of the South while their army does the dirtiest part of the work.

He chewed on the cigar furiously, had gone through this before, through every part of the South. The image flowed through his brain, so many fights, the chaos and horror. A soldier who has been in the fight . . . he knows of pain and tragedy, bloody wounds and the death of a friend. A man has brains splashed upon him . . . he knows what war can do. Now, there is pain here, and horror and punishment. And now these people, these civilians who feign outrage that this army has soiled their innocence, those **gentlemen** and Southern belles who dared send their sons off to destroy our flag, now **they** will know what their soldiers have already learned. War is absolute and when you innocent civilians started this, when you ripped and spit at my flag, you **invited** this. Do not speak to me of innocence or blamelessness. In war, there is no such thing.

He spit the cigar out, brought out another, stabbed it through his teeth, unlit, rolled it with his tongue, side to side, new thoughts breaking through his concentration. He was angrier still, thought, You cannot let this drive you. It is no one's doing. God's maybe. That's what Ellen believes, certainly. Why would God cause affliction to a child, to the truly innocent? Or is it the child's father that must be made to suffer?

He carried the note in his pocket, word coming in a telegram from Ellen, only three days before. His infant son, Charles, was gravely ill. Sherman struggled to keep that from his thoughts, had tried so very hard to dampen down the crushing sadness from the death of his oldest son, Willie, memories from a year ago stuffed in a place inside him he could never really shut away. Nine-year-old Willie had been something of a mascot to the troops, the young boy named **honorary sergeant,** his death casting a pall over Sherman's entire command. It had steeled Sherman against ever bringing his children anywhere near the war, which he knew was a useless gesture meant only to appease Ellen, his feeble attempt to ease her sorrow. Willie had been struck down by typhoid, a deadly enemy that had nothing at all to do with the war. Now it was baby Charles, Ellen not specific, perhaps not knowing just what the malady was. There was time for only one response, the rail lines and telegraph wires soon to be cut by his own orders, severing him and the rest of his army from any communication northward. The isolation he imposed on the army struck him harder than anyone around him, and so he could not tell them. He could only mask his fear: a hopeful note to Ellen, a show of confidence that the infant would recover fully. He had fought against seeing her in his mind, what kind of torture this was for a mother who has already lost one son, whose husband is a thousand miles distant. There was shame as well, the worry softened by a numbness that made Sherman more guilty than afraid.

Willie had been a part of Sherman's daily routine, a bright light suddenly turned dark. But Sherman had never seen Charles, had never held him, had fashioned a fantasy around the baby that one day he would rise up to assume Willie's place, capturing the affections of Sherman's men, that finally Sherman would know a father's joy at doing all those things that would make his son a man. Ellen's news only intensified the need he felt to end this war, to put aside the army and the duty and find a way to be a family. There had always been a low burn of conflict between them, Ellen's devout Catholicism just not Sherman's way. Throughout most of the war, the miles between them muted that conflict, but if there was luxury in not having her close to him, there was guilt as well, more so now that his selfish need to keep the peace with her meant burdening her alone with the care for her infant son, in the deepest agony a parent can have. Now Sherman had no choice. His attentions could be focused only on what lay close to him: Atlanta, the new campaign, the job he was expected to do.

He glanced at the marching troops in the road below, pushed thoughts of his family far away. There were faces looking up at him, a few hats in the air, muted cheers. Fourteenth Corps, he thought. Jeff Davis's men. Damn fool, that one. Jefferson C. Davis. By God, change your damned name. If those other fellows had a general named Ulysses Grant, he'd catch grief everywhere he turned. Davis seems oblivious, like he's proud to wear the same badge as that lunatic in Richmond. Too much temper for my taste. Killed a man, General Nelson, I think. Got away with it. Not sure that would wash today. Damn sure won't have anyone killing their commanding officer in **this** army. Bad for morale. Mine.

Sherman turned away from the troops, drawn again to the sea of fire, still thought of Davis. Maybe it's just bad luck that he shares that name. His mama couldn't know what she was doing to her boy. Well, Jeff, keep your pistol in its holster and do the job, and maybe you'll end up more famous than the other one. Maybe we grab those scallywags and Grant will let you do the honors. **President** Davis, meet **General** Davis. He's the one with the rope.

The voices caught him again, more cheers, and

he looked again to the road, another regiment passing by, flags in the breeze, smiles, waving hats. He
straightened in the saddle, acknowledging them,
heard the fife and drum, those men in perfect
rhythm, the march of the soldiers punctuated by
what passed for music. He saw the drummer, an
older man, no surprise there. Sherman had removed
the human baggage from the army, those who
took more in rations and care than the power they
could give to the fight. That man will fight, he
thought. Knows it, too. They all know it. No sick
men on this march, no feebleness, no one too weak
to keep up.

He couldn't avoid the surge of strength from the
column of men, the smiles only reinforcing what
he already believed. They have no idea where we're
going, but they know what I expect of them. Sixty
thousand men who know what the enemy looks
like, and what they have to do to him, what they
want to do to him. It's up to me to put them in the
right place, keep them ready for anything we find.
But look at the faces. They're smiling, for God's
sake. He clamped hard on the cigar, offered a slow,
deep nod to one group, knew the look of veterans.
Yes, by God, let's win this thing.

Another regiment passed, and now he heard
music, real music, a band, the tune clear, distinct,
joyful. He saw them now, moving up behind an
officer, the tune flowing through the column, carried on the voices of the men. It was "The Battle

Hymn of the Republic." He stared at the musicians, felt pulled into the moment more than their joy, their skills with the instruments. He didn't hide the smile, put one hand up, removed the shapeless hat, raised it just off his head, his silent salute. The soldiers cheered him again, but still they sang, the glorious words digging deep, opening a soft place Sherman couldn't show them. He jammed the hat back down, both hands on the reins, felt suddenly as though he knew them, all of them, each man a piece of who he was.

The band was past now, the notes softening, and Sherman felt the staff close by, knew they would expect orders, that he was too energized to stay in one place for long. He noticed the smoke again, the breeze picking up, the view of the city obscured by its own death. He pulled the reins, turning the horse away, patted the animal's neck, said, "Sam, you know what that stink is? It's the rebels' defeat. Rather enjoy that smell myself." He tossed a glance toward the staff, Hitchcock, Dayton, the others waiting for the command. He didn't hesitate, slapped the reins against the horse, his single spur digging into the flank. "It's time to go to work. I've had all the **Atlanta** I want."

He had divided his army into two wings, commanded by men he had come to respect. Oliver Howard was a veteran of the

fights in the East, had lost an arm and a great deal
of prestige by shouldering the blame for defeat at
Chancellorsville and the first day's debacle at Gettysburg. But Sherman saw more to Howard than reputation, and from all he could gather, it was more
often the poor quality of the men in Howard's
command who had failed him. Howard was a West
Pointer, and to Sherman, that alone gave Howard
the benefit of many doubts. Sherman had no use
for the more political generals, though his own
army fielded men like John Logan and Frank Blair.
He tended to rely on men who had been trained
to follow orders, not bathe in a glow of their own
making. The vacancy Sherman had to fill was a
difficult one for more reasons than simple command decisions. He had come to rely enormously
on General James McPherson, but McPherson had
been killed during the battles for Atlanta. The loss
was devastating for the army, and worse for Sherman himself. The men had become friends, a rarity for Sherman. In an army where Sherman had
learned to distrust so many, McPherson had been
a bright light, the keen mind of the engineer, with
a talent for making the good fight. In his place Sherman needed someone who could drive forward
with the same diligence McPherson had shown,
and the tendency toward obedience Sherman required. George Thomas had pushed Sherman to
consider Oliver Howard for the job. Though Sherman and Thomas had often clashed, Sherman

respected Thomas's judgment when it came to leadership.

Henry Slocum had been Sherman's choice to command his second wing. Slocum was another of the West Pointers who had experienced nearly every major fight in the East, including the brutality of Gettysburg. Like Howard, he had suffered a severe wound early in the war, had survived to earn the respect of every commander he served. When Sherman assembled his forces in Georgia, Slocum was in command of the posts around Vicksburg, what had now become a backwater of the war. Sherman appreciated that Slocum's talents were being wasted, and Grant and Halleck agreed. Now Henry Slocum had joined Oliver Howard as the two fists that Sherman intended to drive through the heart of the deep South.

Sherman's command now consisted of four corps, with Slocum's two as the left wing and Howard's as the right. The army numbered sixty thousand men, aided by five thousand cavalry commanded by Hugh Judson Kilpatrick. Cavalry had long been a weakness in the Federal army and Sherman had little enthusiasm for Kilpatrick. His first choice would have been Phil Sheridan, but after Chattanooga, Grant had whisked Sheridan off to Virginia, had placed "Little Phil" in charge of the entire Federal cavalry force operating against Lee's rebels.

Kilpatrick was an unruly, crude, and boastful man who seemed possessed of a need to make enemies. As Sherman had done with Oliver Howard, he pushed past the reputation, measuring ability first. In Georgia, Kilpatrick would be far from the view of Washington, which Sherman hoped would keep the man's ambitions in check. During the campaign Sherman had planned for Georgia, the eyes of his cavalry would be crucial. Sherman accepted that he had to stomach Kilpatrick's personal failings, including an amazingly vulgar boldness toward women, but Kilpatrick had shown that when confronted by the enemy, he at least knew how to fight. It was up to Sherman to disprove the rumors that flowed past his headquarters that Kilpatrick's various accolades, his abilities in the field, might have been trumpeted most loudly by Kilpatrick himself.

Sherman's artillery numbered only sixty-five guns, a purposeful lightening of the machinery his troops would have to haul. Though the army was supported by some three thousand wagons and ambulances, those loads were far lighter than what many had been accustomed to. Sherman's goal was to drive his troops fifteen miles per day, and with winter approaching, the unpredictable weather could be a hazard equal to anything the rebels put in his path. The easier it was for his men to march, the greater the chance that the most serious roadblocks would come only from what might be offered by the enemy. Sherman shared the confidence and enthusiasm of his men that any fights would be one-sided affairs. This was a veteran army, led by officers Sherman had chosen specifically for the job, whose commands had accomplished many of the Federal army's most resounding victories of the war. Sherman rode eastward fully appreciating that most of the men who marched with him had never lost a fight.

DECATUR, GEORGIA—NOVEMBER 16, 1864

He led the staff to the side of the road, scanned the town, saw faces peering out from half-opened windows. The men continued their attention to him, some calling out the name he had become accustomed to hearing: "Uncle Billy."

He pulled the spent cigar from his teeth, spit out a sliver of wet tobacco, drank from a canteen. The staff held their distance, as always, and he ignored them, had no interest in talking to anyone. But the intrusion came anyway, a horse moving up close behind him, and Sherman knew it wouldn't be any of his officers. In these moments, when he rolled through his own thoughts, they knew better. He waited for the inevitable, the greeting he had no interest in answering.

"Halloo, General. Perfect day for this, I suppose. Nice chill in the air. Has to be more comfortable for the men, wouldn't you say?"

Sherman closed his eyes for a brief moment,

fought the urge to just ride away. At one time
he would have done exactly that, but Grant had
changed that, had forced Sherman to accept that
it might be beneficial to be pleasant to a newspaper reporter. Sherman had carried a lustful hate for
those men through several campaigns, but Grant
had pushed him hard to understand that whether
or not the reporters would ever be his friends, an-
tagonizing them might destroy Sherman's career.
It had nearly happened already, early in the war,
Sherman's personal collapse, the overwhelming fear
and insecurity even he didn't understand. It had
been Kentucky, his first major command, Sherman
reacting to rebel movements northward not with
strategy but with panic, calling out publicly that the
Federal army was too weak, too inferior. The indiscretion had found its way to the paper in Cincinnati, a portrait of Sherman that emphasized what
must surely be madness, insanity, a brutal description that continued to dog him throughout the war.
His response had been to remove newspapermen
from his camp, and if they didn't obey, Sherman
had unleashed the occasional bodily threat. That
had been too much for Grant. The scolding was
harsh, a stern warning from Grant that Sherman
absorbed. In the campaigns since, the two men
had grown closer still, mutual respect in an army
where too often a man's ambition created enemies
instead of cooperation. Sherman accepted the lesson still, knowing very well that Grant's unflinch-

ing support was the only reason Sherman held this command.

The horse stopped beside him, a hint of soap and perfume reaching him. Sherman let out a breath, kept his eyes on his marching column. He waited for more, the man insisting on breaking the silent moment.

"I say, General, they are a fine-looking lot. Up to the task, as it were. Fourteenth Corps, I see. General Howard's people are down to the south a ways. Saw a bit of their column earlier."

Sherman accepted defeat, knew that the man would not leave him alone until he got some response. He glanced at the man's face, familiar. "Do you have a question for me, Mr. Conyngham?"

"I always have questions, sir. It's my job, you know."

"You're from New York, right?"

"Indeed, sir. The **Herald**. I must offer my appreciation to you for including me on this most ambitious campaign. My readers will appreciate that as well."

Sherman looked at him again, saw an ingratiating smile. "You sure?"

Conyngham seemed surprised by the question. "Well, most certainly, sir. Every officer I've spoken with has virtually erupted with enthusiasm for this adventure. Every one!"

The word rolled through Sherman's brain. **Adventure.** "Pretty exciting stuff for you, then? War? Blood, intestines, severed limbs? And dead horses.

Make sure you include that one, too. Make note of the stench."

"Sir, my apologies. I did not mean to suggest that war is anything . . ."

"Here's what I suggest, Conyngham. I suggest you pick up a musket, fix the bayonet, and wander out a ways away from this column. There's rebel cavalry out there watching every move we make. You'll find all the **adventure** you want pretty quick."

"Again, my apologies, sir. I spoke in error. I served with the Irish Brigade, in case you were not aware. I have witnessed a great deal of this war, and its cost. I do not intend to glorify anything this army accomplishes. Or you, sir. There is much to see here, much to experience."

"And all of that stuff will make it into your story?"

"It will. I have to ask, sir, do you know how long it will be before I can telegraph a dispatch northward?"

Sherman reached for a fresh cigar, kept his eyes on the marching column. "You know, that's the kind of question a spy would ask. You a spy, Mr. Conyngham?"

He could feel the reporter's frustration, felt a tinge of satisfaction.

"General, please. You know my credentials. Technically, I am a commissioned officer, with the rank of captain. Whether or not I actually command troops is of course up to you. It is not a responsibility I am seeking. You personally authorized me to accompany you, one of only a few men of the press allowed to do so. I am grateful for that. I only hope to be able to offer some account of this campaign when the time is right."

Sherman knew he was being outdueled, had no talent for wordplay. "I don't know, Conyngham. You not have a chance to send a story out before we left Atlanta?"

"Yes, sir, I did. The lines were severed only four days ago, and I was fortunate. We were given no warning of that."

"The warning went to the people who needed it. I gave the order. Sorry I didn't consult you news-boys first."

Conyngham lowered his voice, leaned closer. "Sir, I am well aware of your disdain for my pro-fession. I am not here to insult you, or humiliate you. I have no cause to soil your name. I accept my role as an observer, to chronicle this cam-paign. Is that not a good thing? For this army? For you, sir?"

Sherman let out a breath. "Suppose so."

Conyngham straightened. "Thank you for that, sir." He paused. "General, if I may ask, a number of the others are curious as well. Why did you not leave behind a force to defend our positions in At-lanta? Do you not fear the rebels might return to the city? So much effort to capture the place. And, if the rebels were to retake the city, would that not pose some hazard to this march?"

Sherman pondered the question, knew it had been asked in Washington as well. "A short time ago, there was a rebel cavalry raid in Tennessee. Place called Johnsonville. You familiar with this fellow Forrest?"

"Certainly, sir. Nathan Bedford Forrest. A scourge, no doubt."

"He's a hell of a cavalryman. Scourge, too, I suppose. Couple weeks ago, he waltzes his crew up the bank of the Tennessee River, fires a few artillery rounds into our depot there. Strong position, good many of our boys, a fair amount of artillery of our own. You know what happened? Our boys ran scared, scrambled toward Nashville like a flock of frightened sheep. Cost us, hell, maybe two million dollars. Why'd they run, you might ask? 'Cause it was Forrest. The **scourge**. That's all it took. Well, right now he's feeling pretty fat and happy. No doubt he'll hit us again, bust up the railroad, every supply line we have out of Georgia."

"You think he might move up behind us? Capture Atlanta?"

"No. Hood needs him in Tennessee. Hood couldn't keep us out of Atlanta, so he's gonna do the next best thing he can to save his honor. Richmond's howling about the loss of Atlanta, so Hood has to make it up to them, find salvation someplace else. Point is, he needs a victory. So he's marching north, probably aiming to hit Nashville."

"Right. But I don't understand what this has to do with Atlanta."

"Not a damn thing. We cut off all contact with Atlanta, and every other place that's not right in front of us." He raised a hand, pointed down the road toward the marching column. "That's where we're going. I don't care a whit about where we've been. It's a pure waste if I leave men in Atlanta. I'll not slice off a big piece of this army just so they can sit in earthworks, and maybe offer a target for Forrest or whoever else might be tempted. There's nothing in Atlanta right now to protect. Nothing to save. Nothing threatened. It's behind us. Just like your telegraph wires." Sherman looked at Conyngham now, saw comprehension on the man's face. "You'll just have to keep your stories to yourself until we find another telegraph." He paused. "You just a bit curious when or where that'll be?"

Conyngham shook his head. "No, sir. It will happen when you tell me about it."

Sherman knew a lie when he heard one. "Don't 'pleasure' me, Conyngham. It's gotta be killing every one of you reporters just what we're headed for, just what the plan is."

"I've given it some thought, yes, sir. Every man in this army knows your orders, your careful vagueness. **A special purpose, well known to the War Department and General Grant, a departure from our present base and a long and dif-**

ficult march to a new one. Well expressed, sir. The message is clear to all involved. The most effective way to prevent the enemy from knowing our intentions is to keep those intentions secret even from your friends. If I may, I only ask that, when time permits, you allow me to inquire and observe those things that are appropriate. You know that General Grant supports a free press, as does the War Department."

Sherman knew he was on dangerous ground now, felt a small simmering heat rise up in his chest. After a long moment, he said, "Any one of you newspaper boys writes anything that reveals anything useful to the enemy, I shall arrest you as a spy. I am no enemy of freedom of the press, but if you believe the press governs this country, then I would suggest you be the ones to fight this war. No reporter I have ever met understands the necessities of battle, not even one who claims affiliation with the Irish Brigade. Do you understand my feelings, Mr. Conyngham?"

Conyngham did not hesitate, kept his voice calm, no heat in his words. "I understand completely, sir. We are, all of us, on enemy soil. If we are confronted by rebel troops, your judgment and your weaponry will lead the way. As I said, sir, I am merely an observer. Your orders apply to me as they apply to those men in uniform."

Sherman felt disarmed, couldn't avoid the feeling that he actually **liked** this man. But he wasn't prepared to offer Conyngham any hint of that. "You can ask anything you like. But be aware, Conyngham. I am the king of this particular mountain. If that ever displeases you, you are certainly free to find another mountain."

Conyngham laughed, another surprise. "I am aware of the proximity of enemy cavalry, sir. Obviously, I have no place else to go. This mountain will do just fine."

CHAPTER TWO

GRANT

CITY POINT, VIRGINIA—
NOVEMBER 17, 1864

The bank was steep, high above the soft light reflecting off the river. He came to the over-look often, staring out at the enormous might of the Federal strength he had assembled, a vast armada of supply ships, the wharves below him never quiet, supplies and armaments and men all adding to his army, the army whose sole purpose was to destroy Robert E. Lee.

He glanced up at the moon, a clear night, chilly, a slight breeze rolling down across the wide expanse of the James River. Behind him, the construction had ceased for now, the row of headquarters structures mostly completed, the protection from the winter soon to come. There would be little such protection for his troops, something Grant never ignored. It frustrated him that Lee's army was still out there, that throughout the months of campaigning Grant could never really force the issue, could never drag Lee into the open, where the superior strength of the Federal forces would bring the war to an end. There had been great bloody fights in the spring, through the Wilderness, Spotsylvania. But Lee had been slippery, a master of maneuver, evading any full-on confrontation. There had finally been one grand opportunity in June, the Army of Northern Virginia halting just long enough to invite an organized attack. Grant had obliged with a frontal assault that rolled into utter disaster. The place was Cold Harbor, where Grant's army suffered thousands of casualties in a fight that accomplished nothing at all. It had been Grant's worst day as a commander, and five months later the images were still fresh, would haunt him as he planned every new fight. Worse for the army, for Lincoln, Cold Harbor had threatened to erase the aura of invincibility that the newspapers had wrapped around Grant, the great hero Lincoln had selected to finally crush Lee's army.

The loss at Cold Harbor had been as devastating to Lincoln as the loss at Chickamauga the year before, a stain that dampened the great successes

at Gettysburg, Vicksburg, Chattanooga, victories
that, for a while, boosted morale in the North. But
the public had short memories, and despite strategic advantage, especially the capture of the Mississippi River, the war still went on. By all accounts,
Grant and Lincoln both knew that the armies in
the South were reeling, with a lack of capable leadership, a collapse of morale, reports of rebel soldiers
simply walking off the line, going home to salvage
what they could of their lives. The successes Grant
had enjoyed west of the mountains had shoved rebel
forces out of every vital city and rail center, limiting
the Confederates to strongholds in Texas, Alabama,
and the Carolinas. But still, the great crushing blow
seemed so elusive, the resilience of Lee in particular
astonishing to Grant. With Lincoln facing reelection, even Grant knew that a weary Union might
opt to cave in, the Congress offering the South
what they wanted, if only to stop the bloodshed.
It infuriated Grant that George McClellan had
put himself forward as the candidate for **peace**. As
popular as McClellan had once been, few in the
army had cast their votes in his direction, most of
the troops sharing Grant's anger that the general
who squandered the opportunity to win the war
in 1861 would now claim no one else could win
it, either.

Grant searched for a cigar, had gone through
a pocketful already today, felt a paper in his coat
pocket. His hand stopped, fingers touching the note.

It was the final message from Sherman, the telegram received more than a week ago now. He had read the note often, the words still fresh inside him.

"I still have some thoughts in my busy brain. . . ."

Grant smiled. Yes, my friend, you always do. Good thoughts, mostly. Perhaps never as important as what you're doing right now.

T he arguments had begun as soon as the details of Sherman's strategies reached Washington. There was considerable doubt whether Sherman could command that entire theater of the war on his own. Grant insisted otherwise.

He thought of Nashville, Sherman's order sending Thomas and most of the Army of the Cumberland back to protect that crucial city. It was only one part of Sherman's design, inspired by what the Federal command now understood to be an amazing lack of discretion by the Confederate president, Jefferson Davis. Grant still marveled that Davis might seek to bolster the morale of his own armies by revealing in broadly reported speeches their strategy of maneuver and feint. The fall of Atlanta had certainly crushed Confederate morale, and Davis had reacted by traveling to various parts of his army, a mission of reassurance that **all would turn out fine**. But far beyond reassurances, Davis spoke

openly to vast audiences of John Bell Hood's attempts to draw Sherman out of Georgia by driving
northward into Tennessee, severing crucial supply
lines, drawing Sherman's army into utter destruction, if not by starvation then by the sheer might of
Hood's army.

Grant had been baffled by Davis's optimism,
since Sherman had soundly whipped Hood in
nearly every encounter around Atlanta. And Grant
agreed with the War Department that the remnants
of Hood's army, still a formidable force, should be
dealt with once and for all, and not just left to its
own planning. Sherman didn't agree, something
Grant knew to expect. Once Davis began giving
his speeches, Grant understood what Sherman was
insisting upon, that Hood would do what Davis
suggested and move north to threaten middle Tennessee. If Sherman pushed his pursuit of Hood
away from Atlanta, following him through Alabama
or Tennessee, that would accomplish exactly what
Davis had suggested publicly: Sherman would be
removed from Georgia. Sherman had already predicted that Hood would move away, would strike
out for new victories against a weaker foe, or some
vulnerable outpost. Nashville seemed the logical
place, and Sherman had addressed that supposition
by sending enough force with George Thomas to
defy any significant push from Hood. Grant had
assisted as well, ordering added strength toward
central Tennessee from Federal forces in every part

of the Union, including a vast new ocean of recruits.

The War Department still fidgeted, wondering
if Hood's hints of movement northward were only
demonstration, deception that might somehow en-
danger Sherman around Atlanta. But Grant knew
better. Davis would not stand up and lie to his entire army. It wasn't the man's way, would fly in the
face of Southern honor for their president to be
so publicly deceptive. And now Hood was shifting
northward, exactly as Sherman had predicted. It had
been one of the most convincing arguments Sherman could make that his own operations should
proceed as he designed them. Before Hood could
destroy Sherman's supply lines to Nashville, Sherman did most of it for him. It was Sherman's plan,
eliminating any possibility that a raid by Forrest or
anyone else could threaten Sherman from behind.

The last train northward from Atlanta had moved
out on November 12, the same day the final telegraph link was cut. With Sherman now in motion
east of Atlanta, he was opening up an even larger
gap with Hood's army, an army that Sherman had
already thrashed. By now it was clear that Davis's
speeches had been accurate, and Hood's intentions
were plain. From the Confederate base in northern
Alabama, Hood was intending to march north.

Grant smiled again, stared out into darkness. Yes,
Sherman, that will suit you quite well. Keep the
prying eyes away from your backside. Whatever

you're doing down there, they'll still be stewing up here, mouthing off their fears that your army is facing certain doom. The newspapers love that sort of thing. All those military geniuses wringing their hands how you're violating every textbook. Well, Sherman, I remember the old man doing the same. You weren't there, which is a damn shame, because you'd have appreciated what it meant to take ten thousand men into the middle of Mexico and push up against thirty thousand who sat behind big stone walls. And by God, it worked.

He thought of Winfield Scott now, the man who had brought a flock of young lieutenants right out of West Point and, with complete faith in their ability to command, had led them to victory in Mexico. We're not lieutenants anymore, Grant thought, and some of those boys are generals on the other side of this thing. Grant put a hand to the strap on his shoulder, the three stars, knew he was the only man since Scott to hold the rank of lieutenant general. Big shoes to fill, he thought. Thank you, Mr. President. More faith in me than I had in myself. Scott had to approve that, too. Lincoln wouldn't have made that kind of move without talking to him. He pictured Scott, a massive hulk of a man, heavy with age, well into his eighties now. I love that old man, he thought, as much as I love that skittery redhead in Georgia. A lot in common, and I'd wager Sherman would take that as a compliment. Probably Scott, too. But first Sherman's got to pull his army through the fire. Like the president said, we know what hole he went into. Just not sure which one he'll crawl out of.

Grant spun around, gave a glance toward the lanterns at his headquarters. He couldn't avoid a nervous shiver, was too used to having Sherman's ear, or advice, or just his cantankerous mood to crack through the tension. Now there would only be silence. He began to move back to his headquarters, a handful of his aides lingering in the darkness, moving with him. He flexed his fingers, fought the nervousness boiling up inside, turned to one side, changing course, still moving quickly. He wouldn't disturb Julia, not yet. The shakiness bothered him, the unavoidable fear that Sherman would join so many of the others, Reynolds, Sedgwick, McPherson. All good men. All dead. Even Winfield Hancock had come to Grant, suffering mightily from his wounding at Gettysburg, too crippled now to continue. Is that the first word I'll hear, that the redheaded fool stuck his head out too far, is lying in some ambulance somewhere? Or they buried him in Georgia? Not much chance of that. Dead or not, he'd not sit still for that insult.

He shoved away the thoughts, scolded himself. He's smarter than you are, Grant. Well, maybe. He's enjoying himself down there, and he'll not do anything to ruin that. You've got bigger problems, more to concern yourself with right here. He stopped walking, forced himself to focus on the campaign right in front of him. Lee's army was spread out in a line nearly thirty miles long around the rail hub at Petersburg. Grant hated the idea of a siege, something he shared with Sherman, but Lee's army was dug in hard, and a siege was the most effective way to avoid a mass of Federal casualties. He walked past a small elm tree, stopped, his fingers finding his last cigar. He lit it, the fire warming his face, and he knew now there was no separating Sherman from what Grant was facing in Virginia. Thank God for you, Sherman. The newspapers hate sieges as much as I do, and the president might have lost the election by impatience alone if you hadn't given us Atlanta.

He stared out past the headquarters houses, toward the distant lines of Lee's army. There's nothing else I can do here, not right now. All right, Sherman. We're doing it your way. It better work, or both of us will end up shoveling manure. I know I can't hear from you, not for a good while. But by God, I'll be worrying about you every day that passes. Can't help that. He thought of Sherman's words again.

"I will not attempt to send couriers back, but will trust to the Richmond papers to keep you well advised."

Grant chewed hard at the cigar, searched the darkness, saw one man alert, responding, moving closer.

"Sir? May I be of assistance?"

"Colonel Porter, at first light, send out riders to every camp along the siege line. I know there's trade going on with those other fellows, whether I authorize it or not. Provide coffee or bacon or whatever is required. A few of Lee's boys know how to read, and I want copies of every newspaper printed in Richmond."

CHAPTER THREE

SEELEY

ATLANTA, GEORGIA—NOVEMBER 17, 1864

The horror spread out nearly to the horizon, the low hills not disguising the astounding magnitude of the destruction, entire blocks of the city in smoldering ruins, thick black smoke in columns rising up in every direction. He felt sick to his stomach, stared down, took his eyes away from the skeletons of so many structures, most of them unidentifiable heaps of rubble. But the smells engulfed him, unavoidable, hinting of burnt flesh, or something close, cloth and lumber and so much more.

"Captain, bring your men out this way. There's folks here need a hand."

Seeley looked toward the voice, saw General Dibrell, pointing directly at him, motioning crisply,
as though it were some gesture made on a parade
ground. Seeley didn't answer, spurred the horse,
pushed past more of the rubble, the smoke watering his eyes. The horsemen tailed out behind him,
no more than thirty now, half what he had commanded only a month before. Some of those had
simply disappeared; some had been captured by
Sherman's cavalry, the ultimate indignity for any
man who had once ridden with Forrest. The squad
followed him down a narrow alleyway, pushing forward to reach the open avenue, where they might
escape the stink, breathe cleaner air. Dibrell waited
with obvious impatience and Seeley could see a
flock of ragged civilians gathering around the man's
horse, other cavalrymen unable to hold them back.
Seeley jabbed at the horse, moved closer, Dibrell
now offering him a shrug.

"See if you can handle these people. I have to locate General Wheeler."

"You there! Can't you help us?"

The words came from a woman, old, frail, soot
on her face, her dress caked with ash. Dibrell spoke
out again, and Seeley knew the man's habit, trying
to sound official.

"Help is aplenty, be sure of that! We shall ride
hard into the devils who did this! There shall be no
mercy! General Wheeler shall see to your salvation,
you can be certain of that!"

Dibrell seemed to exhaust his own bravado, and Seeley eased past a handful of the citizens, saw the eyes turning toward him now, no one inspired by the general's words.

"Sir, I have secured a single wagon back that way, past that church spire. There is corn, some sweet potatoes. With your permission, sir, these folks can take what they need."

He knew the wagon had been a treasure, gathered from abandoned cellars and larders that somehow escaped the claws of the Yankee occupation. His own men had already filled their pockets with anything that might sustain them another day. But Seeley couldn't deny the desperation of the civilians, and Dibrell seemed resigned to that, pointed toward the church, still the annoying bombast in his voice.

"Very well! Good people, we have come to your rescue. We will provide for you as long as there is breath in the Confederacy!"

Seeley turned his horse, the general's assurances meaningless, empty bluster. He rode past his own horsemen, the townspeople following, and he looked at the faces of the men he led, saw glimpses of optimism, some grabbing on to Dibrell's promises as though the next fight would turn things around, would rescue the people of Atlanta, would put the glorious city back to what it once was. Seeley held them up with his hand, said, "Half of you, come with me. We'll show 'em the way. There's bandits about. The rest remain here."

He knew which men would stay close to Dibrell, the ones who still held the fire, who still ached to rip into a column of Yankees. But there were others like him, worn-out, road weary, hungry. If any one of them thought his suffering was worse than that of any civilian, the gaunt faces of the citizens said otherwise.

Much of Atlanta was destroyed, the wider avenues lined with skeletons of buildings or piles of brick and stone, gutted houses that still smoldered. Smoke and ash coated everything, the hard streets beneath his horse's hooves or any structure that remained. The sights had inspired anger, some of those men who hung on Dibrell's ridiculous speech prepared to march into whatever hell the Yankees offered. Seeley had seen some of this before, on a half-dozen battlefields where a town happened to be in the way. But Atlanta was very different, if only for the scope of it, the sheer volume of the destruction. Word had passed beyond the city, reaching Hood's army in Alabama, and orders had come for the cavalry patrols to ease closer to the city, probing to see just what the Yankees were doing, whether or not Sherman was pushing out farther west in what would certainly be a fresh pursuit of Hood.

As the cavalry moved in, they expected skirmishers, scattered musket fire to keep them away. Instead they found a city devoid of soldiers, and whether or not Sherman intended a pursuit of Hood, all that Seeley knew was that they had marched away from Atlanta in another direction altogether. Now in their place came the civilians, some seeking loot, bandits and thieves that Seeley had been ordered to capture. But most of the people he saw now were simply returning to their homes, many finding no home at all. Already the roads were growing busier, cavalry scouts beyond the city reporting an odyssey of scattered wagons, even more civilians emerging from safe places in the countryside, some returning with their most treasured possessions. They seemed to be everywhere, their numbers increasing by the hour, some sitting slumped over in their wagons, staring at the wreckage of what might have been a grand house or an entire street of tall and elegant homes, now rubble and ash. For some the final insult had come from the Confederate cavalry, orders to confiscate wagons where they found them, to scrounge through the remains of the city for anything the Yankees might have left behind.

He rode slowly, the people from the square following, word spreading to a few more. The horsemen behind him herded them in the right direction, the church spire standing tall over the ruins of what had once been a grand place of worship. He glanced up, saw a shattered hole in the spire, the impact of a random artillery shell. Or maybe, he thought, not so random at all. Target practice. He tried to feel anger, was too weary, too sickened by all he was seeing. He rounded a corner, saw the wagon his men had filled, pointed, the civilians moving forward in a mad surge. His horsemen stayed back, held away by the simple command of his raised hand, the men understanding just how desperate these people had to be. They were mostly women, with a pair of old men, a flock of small children. As they reached the wagon, one younger woman climbed up first, tearing through ragged cloth bags, scooping corn into the folds of her dress. More were there now, the woman abruptly shoved aside, tumbling in a heap to the ground. Seeley felt a stab of alarm, would not let this turn into a riot. He put his hand on his sword, ready to do what he could to protect them from one another. But there was no energy for that, either, not from him or the people who fought weakly to empty the wagon. A young girl jumped down with a pair of sweet potatoes clutched to her chest, another older woman taking her place in the wagon, more sweet potatoes, the people taking all they could haul. Beside him the old sergeant, Gladstone.

"Wish you hadn't done this, sir. We'll be a-needin' them rations afore long."

Seeley kept his stare on the civilians, said, "We're supposed to be protecting these people. That's what this army is for. I'll not let anyone starve."

"Hope you're right."

Seeley looked at him, saw a stubble of beard, a rumpled hat, bare remnants of a uniform.

"Of course I'm right. These people are counting on us. Won't much matter if we win this war if we can't take care of the very folks we're fighting for."

There was a quiet moment, and Gladstone said, "You think we can win this war? Even now?"

Seeley had asked that question of himself too often, didn't want to answer it now. "General Dibrell thinks we can. General Wheeler, too, I'm guessing. I know Bedford Forrest is back home fighting like the dickens, and he wouldn't be doing that if he didn't believe."

"What about you?"

There was too much informality in the sergeant's question, but Seeley didn't care. The older man had been with him for more than two years now, since the bloody awful fight at Shiloh, and the devastation around them made military discipline seem out of place.

"I'll fight. Have to. We all have to. You remember that."

"Not what I asked you, Captain. I'll fight, sure enough. I'll push my saber through the guts of every Yankee who did this, even ole Sherman himself. But begging your pardon, I'm not certain anymore that we can win this thing."

Seeley took a deep breath, watched as most of the civilians moved away. One woman came his way, her skirt gathered up like a satchel, revealing a glimpse of her underpinnings Seeley tried not to see. She made a short bow toward him, said, "Mighty obliged to you, sir. Yankees didn't leave us with much of nothing. I got three little ones in my cellar down the street there. Breathed smoke for two days, but I kept 'em alive. You fight with General Hood, then? He coming back here, set this right? Yankees need to answer for this."

Seeley started to answer, thought better of it, a hint of military discipline emerging. "I've fought with General Hood. General Forrest, too."

"Well, sir, you tell General Hood or any of the rest of 'em, if'n they can't keep them blue devils from burning up our homes, ain't much use to keep fighting this war. Governor Brown done told us we was perfectly safe here. I seen the president, too, came through here on a train, all kinds of pretty talk about how we was whippin' the Yankees. They didn't look so whipped to me."

"Ma'am, please return to your little ones. The army is here now. There'll be no more problems with the Yankees."

The woman grunted, turned away, moved with a slow waddle down a narrow street.

One of his men eased his horse up close to the wagon, said, "Sir, there's nothing left. They took it all."

Seeley nodded. "We'll find more. That's our job, after all."

"Yes, sir. Reckon it is."

Gladstone was still beside him, said, "It's also our job to find out where the Yankees run off to. How many of 'em, what units, who's leading 'em. The general told us they was sure to hightail it to Tennessee, wouldn't let old John Bell out of their sights. I ain't no more than an old muleskinner, but even I figured out the Yankees done gone somewheres else. You agree, Captain?"

Seeley had spent most of the day on the ridges west of the city, the one direction where the smoke didn't obscure the view. The passes that led toward Chattanooga had been empty of any marching troops, even the railroad quiet. He had led his men close to several stretches of track, nearly all of it ripped apart, bridges burned and broken. That was strange at first, and he had assumed another cavalry squad had patrolled the same area, with the same orders. But the word had come from George Dibrell, ride straight into the city, there was no longer any danger from the Yankees. Seeley had ridden slowly, cautiously, convinced Dibrell was wrong, that surely there would be enemy pickets, outposts, or even stragglers still protecting the routes into the city. But all along the route, he had seen only wreckage, and when he found Dibrell, the man's first words had told the tale: The Yankees had destroyed their own supply line, had cut themselves off from any route back to Chattanooga, any route toward Hood's army at all.

Seeley rubbed his empty stomach, thought of the

sergeant's warning. We'll find something around here, he thought. Too big a place, too much bounty, even if the Yankees stole all they could find. He thought of the man's question now, shook his head. "No, Sergeant, they didn't go west, didn't go toward Tennessee. We should return to General Dibrell. I know he's itching to find General Wheeler. Maybe they know which way Sherman took all these blue-bellies. Too many of 'em to get far without being noticed."

"How many, if you don't mind me asking?"

"More than you and me. More than Wheeler's whole cavalry. Not sure what's gonna happen if we find 'em. Might depend on how many men the state of Georgia can still give to this fight."

"I'll ask you again, sir. You think we'll win this thing?"

"Any man thinks too hard on that, he's thinking about home. You intend on deserting, Sergeant? You best make good on it, get a serious head start. I'll hunt you down and cut you in two." The boast was needless, and Seeley felt ridiculous saying the words.

"You know better than that, Captain. Just wondering. If I'm gonna be shot outta my saddle, just want to know it's 'cause I'm moving forward, doing some good."

"We're all moving forward. Right now, it's to find General Dibrell."

Seeley pulled at the reins, the tired horse sluggish,

stumbling, struggling to right itself. He held tight, gripped with his legs, the horse now upright, obedient, moving with a slow gait. Seeley motioned the others to follow, led them back toward the square where the general had been, where there were certain to be new orders.

Seeley hadn't been to his home in Memphis in nearly a year now. He had first joined the cavalry late in 1861, inspired by Nathan Bedford Forrest, who had gathered up a legion of able men from that part of Tennessee and then all through northern Mississippi. But Forrest's command had been ripped apart, mostly by the efforts of Braxton Bragg, who despised Forrest. That feud had become legendary, but those who had pride in Forrest's refusal to tolerate what the commanders called the overripe incompetence of Bragg soon understood that Forrest's pride had come at a price. After Bragg's magnificent victory at Chickamauga, with Forrest serving as an invaluable asset, Bragg had stumbled into a horrific defeat at Chattanooga. Even then Richmond had sided with Bragg, agreeing with his demand that Forrest be sent away, given what amounted to an independent command in central and western Tennessee. But Bragg had jabbed Forrest with one last insult. Just prior to the defeat at Chattanooga, several of Forrest's prized cavalry units had been stripped away and placed under the command of Joe Wheeler.

Seeley had loved Forrest, had ridden close beside him through a dozen serious scraps, raids on Federal supply depots, confrontations with blue-coated cavalry where Forrest had nearly always prevailed. When Seeley had received the order to leave Forrest's command, his first inclination had been to disobey, to ride back to Memphis whether the army, particularly Bragg, wanted him to or not. But Forrest understood military necessity, had convinced those men to do their job for Wheeler as well as they had done it for him. Seeley had to accept that no matter the damage to Forrest's pride, it was a fair trade that several of his regiments would remain with Wheeler, while in return Forrest would have his precious independence. The order to Seeley had come from Forrest himself, a hand on his shoulder, that hard gleam in the man's eye, the stern words that convinced Seeley his duty would now lie with leading his horsemen anyplace Joe Wheeler needed them to be. As if the order hadn't been enough, Forrest had reminded Seeley what he already knew. Memphis was firmly in Federal hands, and no Confederate officer could ride back home and expect to pass unmolested into the city just so he could visit his young wife.

Seeley wrote to Katie as often as he could find paper, but mail delivery had become nearly nonexistent, the thorough interruption caused by Federal cavalry throughout Mississippi and northern Alabama. Now a handful of letters remained in his own saddlebags, waiting for the word that it might be worthwhile to send them along.

They had been married merely four months when he enlisted, and the rare visits home had been far too brief. One of those visits had come when the Federal naval boats shelled the city, a monstrous stroke of bad fortune for Seeley. He had been captured by a Federal patrol and sent northward to Camp Douglas in Illinois. But his fortunes changed. The desperate fear that his life would end in a Yankee prison had been erased by surprising news that he had been exchanged, could return home after all. He had passed through Federal outposts and past Federal strongholds on the Mississippi as though he had never been to war at all. But Memphis was still firmly in Federal hands, and though he had been allowed a brief visit, Forrest had sent word that his officers were greatly needed. Once more Seeley had kissed his teary-eyed wife goodbye and returned to the cavalry. Forrest rewarded him by promoting him to captain, but Forrest had already been stricken with the disease of Braxton Bragg, and very soon Dibrell's regiment, with its young Captain Seeley, was given wholly to Joe Wheeler.

Whether Wheeler was any closer to Bragg's affections, Seeley learned that he at least knew to keep clear of Bragg's erratic behavior. After Bragg's astounding failure at Chattanooga, the man who had alienated so much of his command was alienated himself, recalled by Jefferson Davis to Richmond. But the army reorganized, pulling itself together as quickly as possible to confront whatever new threat the enemy was planning. Wheeler continued to command the cavalry, including those units that had once ridden with Forrest. Seeley had become accustomed to the rugged landscape of northern Georgia, Wheeler's men doing all they could to follow the advances of Sherman's army.

During the first fights around Atlanta, Confederate commander Joe Johnston had seemed to appreciate Wheeler's understanding that cavalry had far more value as observers than they did leading some vainglorious charge. But then Johnston was gone, one more casualty of Jefferson Davis's penchant for managing the army based on who his friends were. Johnston had been replaced by John Bell Hood, and to the dismay of the cavalry, Hood seemed more focused on driving his army straight into Sherman's guns than on any maneuver where the cavalry might be most useful. Though Hood still held his command, the loss of Atlanta had been a blow no one in the Confederate army could easily accept. Now Hood was off on another campaign, as though conceding that Atlanta had become unassailable, a Federal fortress Hood dared not assault. If Davis seemed to accept that, Georgia's governor, Joseph Brown, most certainly did not. The political wrangling between Brown and Davis was far beyond what Seeley's horsemen would ever know, but the order had come down, what must have been some kind of compromise to appease the Georgian. Hood would drive northward, assisted by Forrest's horsemen. Wheeler's cavalry was to remain in Georgia, if for no other reason than to scout the movements of Sherman's forces.

Seeley was reluctant to ride with Wheeler. While Wheeler was a thorough and mostly diligent horseman, he carried none of the spark of Forrest, didn't have the man's aura, that invisible magnet that draws men to do the seemingly impossible. He seemed devoid of ambition, following orders because it was the right thing to do. In the immediate aftermath of the disaster at Chattanooga, Wheeler had stood tall alongside Patrick Cleburne at Ringgold Gap, holding the Federal army away while the Confederates succeeded in their retreat to northern Georgia. If the man lacked personality, Seeley began to appreciate that Wheeler at least knew how to lead his men against the enemy.

Wheeler was a West Pointer, and no one doubted his abilities in the fight. But the Confederate cavalry was now suffering from the same disadvantage as the army. Increasingly, the Federal commands were growing larger, with new recruits and better supplies, fed by the Mississippi and Tennessee rivers and the network of rail links spreading northward. Even as they fought to defend the southern-most states of the Confederacy, both the cavalry and the foot soldiers began to realize that any efforts to call upon new recruits for the army met with indifference at best. The cheerleading from the government seemed to point to a vast sea of untapped manhood, but the soldiers themselves saw little of the kind. If there were civilian men lurking in various corners of the Confederacy, in Georgia they seemed to have vanished altogether.

A problem equally damaging was the lack of rations and equipment. The numerous factories throughout Georgia had long sent the greater amount of their goods northward, mostly to Lee's beleaguered army in Virginia. Now, with Georgia suffering a direct Federal invasion, the people seemed to be holding closely to what they produced. Few civilian officials, including Jefferson Davis, ever expected that the Federal forces would drive so deep into Southern breadbaskets. Seeley only knew what the occasional newspaper said about Virginia, that Lee was valiantly pushing back against the overpowering forces of Ulysses Grant, forces that Lee would soon eradicate. Seeley knew better than to accept anything in the papers at face value. The latest reports all pointed to the inevitable liberation of Nashville by Hood. Men who had little to cheer latched on to those claims in a burst of optimism, a boost in morale that spread quickly through southern Tennessee. But not even the most optimistic of the men around Seeley seemed to grasp that Hood's crushing losses in and around Atlanta had cost the army more than just manpower they couldn't afford to lose. Atlanta was a crucial rail hub, had fueled Confederate armies in every part of the war. Now those rail lines were wrecked, the factories that supplied the railcars turned to ash. But Seeley couldn't dwell on a greater part of the war than what lay in front of his own horsemen. For now, those men who still rode with him had one duty: Find the enemy and drive them out of Georgia.

"Your men can accompany me. There might be a need for some security detail, should the Yankee stragglers make themselves known. I am not convinced that the enemy has completely vacated this city. It makes no sense that Sherman would walk away from such a prize. We shall redeem our army before this is long past. I am certain of that."

Seeley nodded, nothing else to say, General Dibrell seeming to offer speeches at every turn. He saw Wheeler now, standing on the veranda of an undamaged house, a cluster of officers moving around like bees at a hive. Farther away, a hundred horsemen tended to their mounts, buckets of water hauled by slaves from the wells the Yankees had left untouched. The horsemen looked as worn as Seeley's own, poor uniforms, dull boots, few wearing anything that could be called "clean." He led his own men closer to the house, glanced back, motioned with his hand the order to spread out. They complied, a single row taking position as a makeshift skirmish line, protecting the officers from whatever imaginary threat might suddenly erupt.

Wheeler was even more unimpressive physically than Seeley could recall, a short, slightly built man who moved with the quick darting motions of a frightened squirrel. But Seeley knew that what seemed to be nervous agitation was in fact a serious attention to detail, to all that surrounded the man. Seeley had never seen Wheeler laugh, the man never offering a joke, or even a hint of light-hearted banter. But when Wheeler led them into a fight, he pushed as hard as any man could, even to the point of outrageous risk. That was something Seeley was accustomed to, a trait shared by Nathan Bedford Forrest. They shared another trait as well, a kind of vicious fire that Seeley had struggled to find in himself. Wheeler and Forrest both believed that killing Yankees was the most important task they had.

But there were differences between Forrest and Wheeler that went far beyond appearances or Forrest's lack of West Point training. Wheeler was not yet thirty years old, not much older than Seeley, some fifteen years younger than Forrest. What Wheeler lacked in age he seemed to make up with aggressiveness, whether or not that was always the correct option. If there were to be fights ahead, Seeley had accepted that Wheeler might put all of them in a situation that could be disastrous.

Seeley dismounted, followed Dibrell toward the veranda. Wheeler scanned the men as they approached, glanced at the other officers, then moved with short, quick steps into the house. Seeley held back, waited for the more senior men, saw no one of his rank. He felt suddenly as though he shouldn't be here at all, had never taken part in anyone's council of war, if that's what this was. But the mood was too serious, too grim for anyone to pay much attention to this one captain. If he wasn't welcome, someone, especially Dibrell, could order him away.

The room smelled of smoke, some of it tobacco, some from the breeze that carried the stink of burning lumber from the next block, where one house still spewed out a column of black smoke. Seeley crept forward, a large sitting room, saw Wheeler pacing, his hand holding a single piece of paper.

"This came from Beauregard, who is right now . . . well, I have no idea where he might be. He's on his way here, that's all I know. All he'll say."

"Is Beauregard our new commander?"

The words came from one of the brigadiers, and Wheeler spun on his heels, stared at the man as though intent upon killing him.

"Possibly. For now anyway. There is also word that General Bragg is assuming command from a base in Augusta, Heaven help us. General Hardee is

supposed to be on his way toward Macon, to organize defenses there. General Johnston is no doubt
perched up on some pole somewhere watching this
with great amusement. A herd of generals, and none
of them are here, and all of them with the authority to tell me what to do." He spun again, paced a
few steps, his boots clattering on the wooden floor.
"Most of you have been with me in a great many
scraps. This army has the astounding talent of winning battles and then losing them, all at the same
time. Or perhaps we win the battles and lose the
campaigns. Never mind. We have orders to pursue Sherman's army, wherever they might be going.
We are to stay close, inviting them to delay their
march by forcing them to respond to our presence with vigorous aggressiveness. If there's a fight
to be had, we must have it. But we are not to attempt to bring on a significant engagement. The
fact is, gentlemen . . ." He paused, looked down.
"The fact is, there is no other army in Georgia to
lend us a hand. In this command we have four
to five thousand effectives. Sherman is leading ten
times that number, or more." He stopped, reached
into a pocket, withdrew a crumpled paper. "I suppose you should hear this. I was sent this order by
General Hood, just as he began his operations into
Tennessee. Allow me to quote. 'You must endeavor
to keep the Atlanta and Dalton railway constantly
cut, and should the enemy evacuate Atlanta, you
must destroy all the roads north of the Chatta-

hoochee, and constantly concentrating toward your left be prepared to join at any time the main body of the army. Should the enemy advance anywhere you will drive off all the stock in their front, and destroy all the mills within ten miles of their lines of march, retarding them as much as possible.'" He stopped again, held up the paper. "Four to five thousand effectives. We are to destroy every rail line that leads north, while we prepare to move to the west, all the while destroying the enemy's sustenance to his front, wherever that may be, and maintaining a ten-mile-wide path of destruction along the enemy's route of march. I have a solution to this 'interesting' problem offered us by General Hood."

Wheeler tore the paper in half.

Seeley heard an audible gasp from men in front of him, but Wheeler's hard stare silenced them. To one side Hannon spoke up, another of the brigadiers.

"Sir, it seems General Hood does not have a complete grasp on our situation. I for one will support your decision to pursue and do damage to Sherman. Do we know where he is going?"

Wheeler glared toward Hannon. "I believe it is our job to find that out. Every mayor in Georgia believes Sherman's army is breathing fire outside his front door. There's people in Pensacola convinced Sherman is moving that way. Macon is a ripe target, as are Augusta, Savannah, Tallahassee, the prison at

Andersonville, St. Augustine. How many more can I name? The only thing we actually know, that I have seen myself, is that the bluebellies marched away from here on four different roads, moving east and south, possibly to assault four different targets. With little to stand in Sherman's way, he has the luxury of choosing his targets as he feels inclined. All right, so here are **my** orders. At first light, you will drive your men out toward Macon and Augusta. I'll give you your routes of march then. Those would be the most significant targets, unless any of you believe Sherman's off to a vacation on the Gulf of Mexico." Wheeler continued to pace, seemed to ignore the others. Seeley looked around the room in front of him, saw nervous faces, no one making any attempt to speak out. Seeley felt a stirring in his empty stomach, the question burning inside him. It makes sense, he thought. Surely he knows this. Seeley took a long breath, said, "Sir, I believe either Augusta or Savannah would be his goal."

Wheeler tilted his head, looked at him with cold eyes, no other expression. "Why is that? Who are you, anyway?"

"Captain James Seeley, sir. I rode with General Forrest."

"Seeley. One of the bandits from Tennessee. Steal anything today?"

Seeley felt the weight of the stares in his direction, took another long breath. "Sir, if Sherman moves through Augusta, it would follow that he's intending on marching farther north to join the fight in Virginia. If he goes to Savannah, he will certainly find support from the Yankee navy. You said yourself, sir, there's very little army for him to fight here, and from all we've seen, the Yankees have cut themselves off from their supply lines. With all respect to General Hood's orders . . ." Seeley glanced at the torn paper on the floor. "Sir, General Hood must not be aware that the Yankees have already destroyed those roads leading north."

Wheeler stared at him, the eyes softening. "A great many ideas for a man who rode with Forrest. I was not aware General Forrest encouraged his men to think."

There was a murmur of laughter, but Wheeler kept his stare on Seeley, said, "I was born in Augusta, Captain. You know that? No, don't expect you do. But I agree with most of what you say. I also believe Macon is his target. Too many factories, valuable goods there. It's a crucial supply link for General Hood's advance." Wheeler paused again. "Captain, I started my army life as an Indian fighter. Most ridiculous, infuriating kind of war you can wage. The enemy never stays put, is never where you expect him to be, seems to rise up out of the ground when your back's turned. Right now we will become the Indians. Gentlemen, Captain Seeley might be mouthy, but he could also be right. Our duty is to harass Sherman from every direction, make him look over his shoulder every hour. Until General Beauregard or someone else in authority tells me different, I'm going to pursue the enemy with a special eye on both Augusta and Macon. We'll follow his trail, determine what he's planning to do, and make life as miserable for him as we can. Find plenty of axes. We may be cutting down every tree in Georgia to block every road he can use. Any other suggestions, Captain?"

Seeley felt the stares again, wanted to shrink away.

Dibrell spoke up now, standing tall beside him. "He's my man, General. Good fighter, certain to lead a division one day. Allow me to lead his men toward Augusta. We shall do all that is possible to prevent any harm from coming to your homestead."

Wheeler ignored Dibrell, paced again. "Return to your camps. Seek information from the slaves, from any citizens who might have seen or heard something important. Gather rations, wagons, do what you can for the health of your mounts. Find ammunition, and sharpen your sabers. Until someone decides to assist us with a few thousand troops, we're the army in this place. Let's find the enemy."

CHAPTER FOUR

SHERMAN

NEAR COVINGTON, GEORGIA—
NOVEMBER 17, 1864

The army will forage liberally on the country during the march. To this end, each brigade commander will organize a good and sufficient foraging party, under the command of one or more discreet officers, who will gather, near the route traveled, corn or forage of any kind, meat of any kind, vegetables, corn meal, or whatever is needed by the command. . . . Soldiers must not enter the dwellings of the inhabitants or commit any trespass. . . .

THE MARCH BEGINS / NOV. 15, 1864

Union
Confederate

0   100 mi.

0   100 km.

The army responded to Sherman's order with complete enthusiasm, every unit now offering up those men who were called **bummers,** every brigade commander designating those few soldiers whose job would be to move out far from the column, ahead or to the side, for the sole purpose of locating food and forage for the army. It was the only logic that made sense to Sherman: Even if the enemy made little effort to impede progress, if the army was to survive long enough to reach the coast they would have to live off the land.

This part of Georgia was lush, fertile, with vast farms and plantations where slaves toiled, where cattle and hogs had been gathered into enormous pens, and barns and pantries were full. It was one of those nagging worries, and Sherman knew that Grant had asked the same question, the most important question this army would ask itself: How would they eat?

The army brought cattle from the farms around Atlanta, several thousand head, along with those wagons Sherman had authorized, filled with whatever grain and corn they had pulled from close to the city. But Sherman had no expectation that anything they carried with them would last long enough for the kind of campaign he expected. He knew soldiers too well, that no matter the orders, a man given five days of rations would consume most of that in a single day. If the commissary officers believed the army carried a month's worth of food, Sherman knew it could be gone in a week. And even more important, none of those calculations had made any allowance for possible raids by rebel cavalry. Sherman had seen the cost of those raids firsthand, as far back as the planning for the assault against Vicksburg. Grant's entire strategy had been delayed for months by a raid against the enormous depot the Federal army had created at Holly Springs, Mississippi. The loss of supplies had totaled in the millions of dollars, damaging Grant's reputation in Washington. It had been carelessness, poor preparation and poorer performance by men who were charged with protecting such a valuable part of the army's offensive. This time there were no such depots, the lesson learned not just by Holly Springs, but by the ferociousness of rebel cavalry in every place Sherman had traveled. He knew it was certain to continue, mostly where the rebel army was pushing forward an offensive of its own, Hood's men driving northward toward Nashville. But that was a very long way from where Sherman was now, and farther still from his intended targets. In his wake would be nothing like Holly Springs, or Johnsonville. There were no stagnant depots to invite rebel cavalry at all. The wagon trains that trailed each corps were protected as well as the generals could provide, but Sherman had too much respect for the abilities of rebel horsemen and too little faith in his own commissary officers to believe his supplies were completely safe.

He saw the first wagon, overflowing with all manner of spoils, hams and headless chickens hanging from the side, sacks of corn and flour stacked high. The men were cheerful, great tales of their bravery against what seemed to be hordes of furious rebels, an army somehow brushed aside by this handful of heroic souls.

Sherman moved the horse toward them, eyed the wagon, ignored most of the talk coming from the men. But they saw him, and so the talk grew more fierce, the tales taller still, all for his benefit. He stopped the horse, leaned out, inspected the wagon, the men quieting now, waiting for his response.

"This all?"

The comment was purposeful and Sherman expected some show of indignation. The man driving the wagon obliged him.

"Um, sir, begging your pardon and all, but this here's every scrap of food there was at a farm no more than a half mile from this very spot. You want we should go out farther, well, that's fine by me. But there was rebel cavalry aplenty gathering up, and we might not have made it back a'tall."

Sherman looked at the man. "How much cavalry?"

He saw the man inflate, the question showing the rest of them that even the commanding general took him seriously. "Why, sir, there was a good hundred of 'em. Sabers drawn, ready to ride right down on us. I seen their eyes, I did. We was gonna stand and fight it out, but I knowed that the lieutenant was expecting us to strike it rich with this here kind of bounty, and make it back safe and all, so we's could have a good feed tonight. Fact is, I thought better of making the fight. But, General, if there's another chance, we'll send them horsemen scampering off, sure as fire."

Sherman looked toward the lone officer, said, "Fine. Lieutenant, I'll have your man here promoted to general. But please tell me how many cavalry **you** saw."

The lieutenant was very young, sheepish, seemed unwilling to contradict his own man. "Well, sir, we did see a flock of gray coats. I didn't have much chance to make a count. One of 'em took a shot at us."

Sherman had the picture now. "So a musket ball flies past, and you wisely give the order to haul that wagon back here quick as you could, thus saving the lives of your men and making sure this, um, bounty made it back here safely. All for the good of the camp."

The lieutenant smiled, readily accepting Sherman's explanation. "That would be about it, sir."

"Well, Lieutenant, I'd like you to accompany Major Dayton here to my tent. We should hear a good deal more about your heroics."

The man seemed to quake, put one hand on the wagon to steady himself. "By all means, sir. Right now?"

"Right now. Follow my adjutant back to where they're settling me down for the night. Major Dayton, escort the young lieutenant here off into those trees. I'll be there as soon as the tents are up."

"Yes, sir."

Dayton motioned with his hand, the lieutenant walking behind the horse like a small duck following its mother. Sherman looked again at the wagon, saw more officers moving up, salutes, low greetings.

"Gentlemen, your foragers made a good haul. That's **one**. We'll need a good many more of these every day. Keep these men on the move, keep them out in front of the column or as close by as you can." He looked at the wagon's driver. "What's your name, Private?"

"Jerald Guffney, sir."

"Well, Private Guffney, if there's hordes of rebels lurking out there, I don't want anyone doing something stupid enough to get themselves captured. You understand that?"

The man seemed to grasp that his particular show of heroics had run its course. "Yes, sir. No doubt about that."

Sherman's patience for the game had ended, and he turned, saw Major Hitchcock, motioned him closer, said in a low voice, "Let's check the next camp. That lieutenant can wait a bit. Dayton will know what to do, how to talk to that 'boy.' We'll find out just what these men saw out there, some real numbers. He'll be a little more forthcoming if he's away from these braggarts. Maybe I can teach him not to make heroes out of scroungers."

Hitchcock smiled, said, "Yes, sir. In your charge, sir."

Sherman jabbed the horse with the lone spur, moved quickly past the men still gathering around the wagon. Hitchcock caught up with him now, glanced back, the other aides following, the crowd around the wagon out of earshot.

"General, you think there was any rebel cavalry at all?"

"Yep."

"Really?" Hitchcock seemed surprised, stared out through the darkening trees.

"Easy, Major. There's a hundred of our skirmishers out that way, hoping for just that, a fat wad of horsemen trying to bust in here. We'll get plenty of warning."

"Thank you, sir. Just not all that familiar with such things."

"You will be."

They rode farther, officers coming to attention as he passed, their men calling out the salutes, more of the same, "Uncle Billy." Hitchcock said, "Sir, that not bother you? So much informality? I would think they'd show more respect."

Sherman stuffed a fresh cigar in his mouth, chewed on the tip, always enjoying that first bite into dry tobacco. "They're showing plenty of respect. Good for morale. They can call me anything they want, as long as they do the job. You see some general insist on his men calling him by his full rank, all of that nonsense, you can bet it's because they're afraid of him, or maybe they hate the man. They love you, they'll think up some kind of nickname. Always been that way."

Hitchcock seemed to ponder that, said, "Think they'll find one for me?"

Sherman couldn't help a chuckle, pulled the cigar

out, twirled it in his fingers. "Don't count on that.
Staff officers are usually pretty invisible. Supposed
to be that way. Only adjutant I know who insists on
being front and center is Grant's man, John Rawlins. Puts himself into Grant's business like some
cocky-ass rooster. Wouldn't put up with that here.
But Grant's good to his friends, and I guess Rawlins
is a friend. So Grant puts up with a great deal. He's
put up with me more than most."

He suspected Hitchcock didn't know much of
what he was referring to, could see the man absorbing every scrap of information Sherman was giving
him.

"I can see that you and General Grant have a
good understanding."

"You might say that."

Henry Hitchcock had been with Sherman's staff
for only three weeks, had come to the army from a
notable law practice in St. Louis, by way of the influence of his uncle in Washington. General Ethan
Allen Hitchcock had been a longtime acquaintance
of Sherman before the war, though Sherman had
no idea the old man had a nephew who aspired
to be a soldier. The word had come from the War
Department, the younger Hitchcock rejecting an
offer from Edwin Stanton to serve in the logical
position as judge advocate in his hometown of St.
Louis. Henry Hitchcock had determined that service in the army meant service close to the front
lines, and so the elder Hitchcock had appealed di-

rectly to Sherman. There was always room for more assistance, and Sherman had obliged his old friend, welcoming his nephew to camp in Atlanta. What he did not expect was that, unlike every other member of Sherman's immediate staff, Hitchcock was by their measure old. He was thirty-five.

Sherman appreciated the immediate discovery that Hitchcock could write well, and to the relief of Dayton, McCoy, and most of the other staff, Hitchcock assumed the role as an unofficial secretary. But Sherman had seen this kind of itchiness before, recognized that Hitchcock had that aching need to be a part of **something,** and if he were to miss it, he would regret that for the rest of his life. It was up to Sherman to make sure that Hitchcock didn't act rashly on that instinct, by putting himself into serious danger.

"So, how's the horse?"

Hitchcock reached down, gingerly patted the horse's neck. "We're getting along. He hasn't tried to toss me into any mud hole yet. I suspect he's tempted."

"Might find your own yet."

"Doubt that, sir. Reports were pretty specific that the **Belle Peoria** was captured by rebel raiders. My mount Ellis is likely under the backside of General Forrest right now."

Sherman made a small laugh, rolled the cigar back and forth, thought, His horse was named **Ellis**? One hand began fidgeting with a button on his coat, and Sherman said, "If you say so. Didn't know you were bringing a thoroughbred to camp. Reb cavalry boys are pretty particular about their mounts."

Hitchcock was silent, and Sherman realized he had embarrassed him. He had an instinctive respect for the man, beyond the fact that Hitchcock was far closer to his own age than nearly anyone around him. There was something serious in the man's sense of duty, even the most mundane task attacked with the kind of vigor that earns promotions.

"Heard you went to Yale. That path usually puts a man into politics. You?"

Hitchcock seemed to welcome the change of subject. "Oh, not really, sir. Missouri was a deadly awful place to go that route. Nasty in the extreme. I voted Whig until Lincoln came along, and so I changed over to Republican. Thought Lincoln was the only real choice we had. I've no use for those who preached rebellion, none at all. No use for those in Missouri who resorted to such violence." He paused. "I guess that seems a little silly. There's plenty of violence now. And here I am."

"Why?"

"Heard a lot of talk about the problems with the country, all the arguments. Saw that it was very easy for a man to come down hard on any position he chose, if he didn't have to die for it. Not intending

to die, of course. But this war is too important for
me to spend it arguing law cases in St. Louis. I just
couldn't remain safely at home making money and
enjoying a comfortable life while others were doing
the fighting. And of course . . . dying. I rather expect that's why you're here. I took you for a Lincoln
man right away. You rose quickly in this army, a
man who fights for the right causes. Pardon me for
the observation, sir."

"It's not an observation. It's a guess. And I never
said anything of the sort. Don't talk much about
my politics, don't intend to start. I care not at all
for the side issues in this war. Does no good, on
any account. There's one reason I'm here, Major.
Those people out there, whether they carry a musket or wear a skirt, they have undertaken to rebel
against and destroy my government. They will stop
this war and return to the obedience of our laws or
my government shall destroy **them**. I am presently
employed by my government, and I'm rather good
at following orders. Usually."

Hitchcock stared at him. "Well put, sir. You
should argue the law."

"Tried that. Do a better job of . . . this."

They approached another camp, an Illinois flag
planted high, only one walled tent, as Sherman
had ordered it. He saw horsemen now, moving
his way on the road, led by a familiar face. The
man pushed his horse faster, his small staff trail-

ing behind. He reined up, offered Sherman a crisp salute.

"How very good to see you, sir. Might I be of service? We're making camp in this clearing, and the skirmishers have been deployed."

Sherman felt washed over by the man's energy, the annoying combination of high rank and youth. He returned the salute, said to Hitchcock, "This is General Mitchell, one of General Morgan's brigade commanders. Ohio lawyer. You a Yale man by any chance, General?"

"Yale? Oh, my, no sir. Kenyon College, in Gambier. Didn't spend any time at all outside Ohio until the war."

Sherman leaned closer, shook his head. "How old are you, General?"

The man hesitated, as though the admission might be costly. "Um . . . twenty-six, sir."

Sherman looked at Hitchcock, pointed toward the young man. "See what you missed? If you'd have joined up sooner, you might have made general by now. Twenty-six, and this man doesn't have to show me any more courage than he already has. Used to command the 113th Ohio. Lost a hundred men at Kennesaw Mountain. Hell of a scrap, that one."

Mitchell still seemed hesitant, any hint of a smile now gone. "That's correct, sir. Thank you for the mention."

"I don't usually mention my bad days, General.

Major, his division commander, General Morgan, slammed his men straight into Cleburne's people. Bloody mess. Good thing for us that less than a month later, we had taken Atlanta. If we didn't do that, Kennesaw Mountain might have cost all of us our commands." Mitchell seemed ready to protest, but Sherman held up a hand. "Enough **then,** General. Let's talk about **now.** Your foragers having any luck?"

"Quite, sir. There are plantations in every direction. It's growing too dark now, but the smoke over that way was giving us a pretty good sign that my boys had found what they were after."

"What smoke?"

"The boys couldn't hold back, sir. Ran into some old rebel woman who cussed them something awful. Rode that way myself, heard the most obscene language you can imagine, sir. The boys decided to raise her spirits up a little more. Cleaned out her hog pens, her chickens, everything else they could load up, then they burned the place."

Sherman stared that way, nothing but darkness. "I gave no order to burn anything, General."

"I know that, sir. Several officers made the attempt to put out the fire, but it was too late. Didn't stop her cussing, though." He paused. "Should I arrest those men, sir?"

Sherman ignored the question, his mind filling with the "appropriate" response. But he kept silent, stared past the man, the darkness swallowing the open field, watched the men sliding beneath their shelter-halves, some laying out in the open on their blankets. There were scattered campfires, the smell of coffee now, bacon frying, laughter and singing, one man with a harmonica. Sherman looked skyward, no stars, the day heavy with clouds.

"Might rain tonight. Could muddy up the roads. There's a river ahead . . . Yellow River."

"Yes, sir. Bridge is burned away. We'll put the pontoons out, make it across in short order."

"Any sign of enemy cavalry?"

"One squad, came in for a look, took off pretty quick. They're just watching us, sir. So far, anyway."

Sherman nodded, his mind drifting past the brigade, the smell of their cooking bringing him back to Atlanta, a very different smell. He turned the horse, said to Mitchell, "Offer my respects to General Morgan. I'll be at my field headquarters, should he need to find me. Good night, General."

Sherman spurred the horse, Hitchcock keeping up, awkward in the saddle, the unfamiliar horse tossing him clumsily side to side. Sherman's mount slowed to its usual quick-stepping pace and he kept his back straight, heard the cheers, the nicknames, acknowledged them by not acknowledging at all.

Hitchcock gained control of his horse now, and Sherman heard the man's breathing, Hitchcock seemingly nervous. After a long silence, Hitchcock said, "Sir, what of the burning? You ordered no trespass. A helpless woman?"

Sherman knew this would come, wanted to ignore the man, but he respected Hitchcock, knew the questions wouldn't go away until he answered them. "No officer in this army can control men who are out there on their own. This is dangerous ground, Major. Enemy cavalry is being cautious, but they have orders, too, and we'll start hearing some musket fire pretty quick."

"But, sir, a woman?"

"Probably a widow. Or maybe her husband or son is off fighting with General Lee. And if there is no son, she's making this war on her own."

"What do you mean? I don't understand, sir."

"I'll not coddle you, Major. This army must sustain itself, and that requires doing what is necessary. I will not accept that just because we are shoving a big damned army through their backyards, we are to believe that, my goodness, they have always supported the Union, that all they want is a gentle peace. Suddenly we have made the war 'inconvenient' for them. Well, Major, if they wish this war to be gone, then they may choose to stop it." He reined up the horse, felt the full anger now, stared into darkness, his eyes caught by a distant campfire. "I do not expect this to be a peaceable campaign, Major. I expect blood and death and sadness. These men are in the best of spirits right now. That is the most important part of this campaign. These men believe we are winning this war. I will not stand in the way of that. That spirit will prevail over any number of rebel cavalry, or any number of hot-tempered Southern ladies. It **has** to be so. It **has** to be!"

He felt his hard grip on the reins, loosened one hand, snatched a fresh cigar from his pocket, stabbed it between his teeth. Hitchcock seemed subdued, kept silent, and Sherman was surprised by his own fury, had tried to keep that away, to focus on the duty, the campaign, the well-being of his men. He had seen that tonight, that so far all was well, the march, the advance, the progress. And the foragers were doing their job with perfect success.

"Major, I will not excuse criminal behavior. But I will not punish those men who find the need to punish our enemies. Anyone complains to you about a fire, about their homestead being molested by our men, you can believe there is more to that than one arsonist in our ranks. The men know exactly what I know, and I will tell anyone who wishes to hear it. **We** do not burn anything, Major. **Jefferson Davis** has started these fires. Only **Jefferson Davis** can put them out."

CHAPTER FIVE

SEELEY

Despite Seeley's suggestion that Augusta was the most likely target, Wheeler's cavalry had focused more on the southerly movement of Sherman's right wing, a route that would indicate an attempt to capture Macon. In the state capital at Milledgeville, barely thirty miles east of Macon, Governor Joseph Brown had echoed what many of his constituents were feeling, that Sherman was certain to make efforts to capture any place the Georgians themselves considered vital to the war. Those who had once dismissed the danger from Sherman's "ragged band of Yankees" now changed their descriptions completely, word spreading that this savage mob was certain to occupy every town and village while laying waste to every structure in its path. The rumors, fueled by deep-rooted hatred of the Yankees, began to expand into something far more dramatic, tales of outrageous acts each more devastating than the last, heated stories of violence against the civilian women, as though Sherman's entire army were no more civilized than Mongol hordes, raping and burning their way with all the savagery of Genghis Khan.

In Milledgeville, Governor Brown was wrapped in a panic of his own, the state's legislators convinced that Sherman intended to engulf the capital with the same kinds of destruction said to be ripping through the farm country. Since the unexpected collapse of Atlanta, Brown had sent desperate pleas to Richmond, urgent requests for additional troops and armaments, but so far the responses had been mostly rhetoric, the Confederate government only too aware that any significant reinforcements would have to come south from Virginia, where Lee's forces were already stretched much too thin against the army of Ulysses Grant. It was clear to Wheeler's cavalry that Sherman was carefully disguising his intended routes of march. If Richmond could offer little in the way of reinforcements, it would be up to Wheeler's men to strike wherever possible, to delay or disrupt the overwhelming force Sherman was spreading across Georgia. Wheeler's reports had reached the Confederate War Department, where Sherman's actions were still being met with surprise. None of President Davis's advisors could seem to fathom why Sherman had severed himself completely from any support, either from Grant in Virginia or George Thomas in Tennessee. Davis himself continued to insist publicly that Sherman had played right into Confederate hands by "isolating" himself and thus was certain still to be crushed. The strategists in Richmond were eager to agree with their president, loud predictions filling the newspapers that Sherman had made a monumental and possibly fatal blunder. That optimism finally inspired Davis to shift a number of his senior commanders from their far-distant posts, hastening them to Georgia in the hope of organizing a heavy force that would blunt the tide of Sherman's advance, and possibly destroy it altogether.

Despite Richmond's optimism, Governor Brown seemed to grasp that a gathering of generals might add to Georgia's morale, but unless those commanders were accompanied by great masses of troops, there was little hope of stopping anything Sherman might try to do. If they considered that problem at all, the War Department in Richmond seemed to have no answer.

By the third day after Sherman's columns abandoned Atlanta, a new challenge swept over this part of Georgia. The rains came, a soaking, relentless chill spreading over the country roads and woodlands, a blanket of muddy misery that spread through both sides of the fight. The Southern horsemen were forced to ease up on their exhausted mounts, the soft mush of the trails taking a toll on the strength of the horses far more than it affected the men. But the mud also slowed the Federals, most notably Sherman's right wing, under Oliver Howard. Howard had reached the west bank of the Ocmulgee River, a formidable obstacle to any march eastward. The Federal engineers set to the task of bridging a turbulent river now swollen from its banks by the addition of so much rain. With Wheeler's Confederate cavalry keeping a discreet watch, Howard's men began constructing a pontoon bridge, the only available means of crossing the river. From their perches in distant woodlands, the cavalry quickly learned that Howard's progress was being slowed considerably, that any crossing of the river would be a tedious affair. It was the first piece of good news the Confederate commanders had heard in the many weeks since Sherman occupied Atlanta.

It was no surprise to Seeley that his suggestions to General Wheeler had been tossed aside, that Seeley had been ordered to join a far greater force of cavalry that rode more to the south. Though Federal cavalry patrols seemed to appear in every part of Georgia, Wheeler had become convinced that with so much effort being made to cross the Ocmulgee only thirty miles above Macon, that city, with its

foundries and armament shops, had become Howard's primary target. For now, Richmond seemed
to agree.

Along with the greater part of General Wheeler's
cavalry, Seeley had kept up his patrols in the dismal
weather by helping to form a tight screen across
Macon's northern perimeter. Should the Federal
cavalry shove toward them, the horsemen could
at least offer the feeble militia at Macon some
warning. Near the village of Planter's Factory, the
troopers continued to observe Howard's sluggish
construction of the Federal pontoon bridge, while
west of the river, Howard's two corps could only
suffer in the rain. With so many Federal troops
close by, there was little the Confederates could do
to stop Howard's engineers from completing their
task. Equally as discouraging, no one in Macon
could be certain just what he intended to do once
he had made his crossing.

South of Planter's Factory, the river ran straight
southward into Macon, which seemed to show that
the Federal forces would make any advance toward
Macon along the east side of the river. At the very
least, this observation allowed Wheeler to consoli-
date his cavalry to that side of the river, eliminating
the need to keep up patrols westward. In Macon itself, the local militia and the few Confederate regulars there began to focus most of their attention on
strengthening their defenses to the north and east,
which helped to narrow their area of vulnerability.

Under the wary eye of Wheeler's observers, with the occasional sniping skirmish to keep the Federals on their toes, Howard continued the tedious task of constructing the bridge.

Whether or not Howard was indeed aiming for Macon was still only speculation. Milledgeville lay east of the Ocmulgee as well. Despite the panic in the state capital, Wheeler had to concern himself with what seemed to be the most logical military target for Sherman's army. But by crossing the swollen river in such miserable weather, Howard's troops had strung themselves out for a good many miles. There was no illusion among the Confederate horsemen that they had any hope of containing a major thrust by close to thirty thousand Federal infantry. But at the very least, the rain had accomplished what Wheeler knew his horsemen could not. The muddy roads and turbulent river had effectively slowed the Federal advance in a way that gave valuable time to the Confederate forces, time Wheeler could use to make an attack of his own.

MACON, GEORGIA—NOVEMBER 19, 1864

TO THE PEOPLE OF GEORGIA:
Arise for the defense of your native soil! Rally round your patriotic governor and gallant soldiers! Obstruct and destroy all roads in Sherman's front, flank,

**and rear, and his army will soon starve
in your midst! Be confident and resolute!
Trust in an overruling Providence, and
success will crown your efforts. I hasten
to join you in defense of your homes and
firesides.**

GENERAL PIERRE G. T. BEAUREGARD

The optimistic entreaty had reached Macon from
Corinth, Mississippi, where Beauregard's journey eastward had been slowed by poor weather
and crippled rail lines. Though some newspapers
continued to portray Sherman's army in desperate
straits, and all but ignored what the Federal troops
had done to Atlanta, Beauregard's message seemed
to acknowledge that attention was being paid, that
someone in the Confederate hierarchy at least knew
what was going on.

While Beauregard struggled with feeble lines of
transportation, the senior commanders available
had gathered in Macon to weigh their limited options. Wheeler had brought a half dozen of his cavalry commanders together, those who were nearby,
the fortunate few who had brought their men out
of the miserable weather. The word had come to
Wheeler that finally, in response to the urgent pleas
from the local commanders in Macon, assistance
would be sent their way from outside the state
of Georgia. For Seeley it was pure chance that he
was closer to Wheeler than his own brigade com-

mander, General Dibrell. Whether or not Wheeler disliked Seeley, he seemed at least to respect his ability to lead men on horseback. For now it meant that Seeley and most of his men had come in out of the rain.

They gathered in a stately home, kept warm by a glorious fire at one end of a large sitting room where a half dozen of Wheeler's officers waited. Seeley was convinced that Wheeler knew exactly what was going on, but it was Wheeler's way to keep the most important orders and information to himself, to parcel out to his officers only the small details he required them to know.

As they were waiting for more men to appear, Wheeler had read Beauregard's note aloud; he handed the paper to Seeley now, said, "Pass this around, let everyone see it for themselves. Make sure General Dibrell is informed. You can read, Captain, is that correct?"

Seeley had become used to the edge that crept through Wheeler's taunts, knew it had only to do with Seeley's service to Forrest. "Yes, sir. Been reading now for a week or two. Learned how from one of **your** men."

He knew Wheeler wouldn't respond to any attempt at humor, Wheeler now focused on the others in the room. The talk was quiet, urgent, most of the observations about the Federal river crossing already well known, the rains dampening the enthusiasm for any of the troopers to keep out in the open for long. From the front of the house, Seeley heard boot steps, a chorus of voices, and Wheeler turned abruptly, said, "I wish it was General Beauregard. But perhaps we'll get some orders. Or answers."

Two officers entered in a flurry of rainwater, followed by a cluster of aides, all of them unwrapping from heavy raincoats, the aides taking them away, too late to prevent a puddle from spreading across the floor of the grand parlor. The gauntlets were off now, low comments to the aides, who quickly made their exit. Seeley saw a tall, handsome man, the rank of lieutenant general. He was older, with a tight beard on a face that showed experience. The other man was shorter, thick-waisted, beardless, a major general, his uniform unsoiled, none of the frayed cuffs and split seams the rest of them couldn't hide. Seeley saluted, others in the room doing the same, and Wheeler said, "General Hardee, your presence is most welcome."

Hardee returned the salutes with a simple gesture of his hand, scanned the room. "Maybe. Have you been introduced to Georgia's former governor, Mr. Howell Cobb? Forgive me. **General** Cobb."

Cobb was the shorter man, looked at the cavalry officers with undisguised pride. "Not at all. I am grateful to make the acquaintance of General Wheeler, as well as his distinguished officers. I appreciate the presence of professional soldiers, men who have 'seen the elephant.' I am entirely in your debt. Georgia is suffering as it has never before done in this war. No one shall doubt your bravery or your sacrifice on our behalf."

Hardee seemed to suffer through the brief speech, looked straight at Wheeler, said, "The 'general' here has organized the militia and the transportation as effectively as possible. He has also issued a call for every capable man to rise in defense of his state."

Cobb seemed oblivious to Hardee's sarcasm, said, "Oh, well, thank you, General Hardee. But I must offer my appreciation to Senator Benjamin Harvey Hill, who watches our predicament here with a hard eye. Even from his office in Richmond, the senator is certain to inspire native Georgians to cast out the foe."

Cobb pulled a paper from his pocket, straightened it with a flourish, read, " 'You have now the best opportunity ever yet presented to destroy the enemy!' Well, there's more, but he concludes with a cry that must reach the ear of every Georgian: 'Be firm! Act promptly, and fear not!' "

Seeley saw a slight frown on Hardee's face, and Hardee held up his hand, said, "Yes, very well, Governor. How many militia have you been able to bring together in Macon?"

Cobb seemed to deflate, his words softer. "Some fifteen hundred, sir. I had hoped by now to treble that number. It might still happen. General Gustavus Smith . . . I believe you know him. He is in direct command of those forces and has taken to training them as quickly as possible."

Hardee kept his eyes on Wheeler. "Yes, well, we shall keep up our hopes. General Wheeler, if Macon is to be assaulted, how many men have you at hand?"

"Two thousand effectives, perhaps more. Scouting parties are scattered a good bit, but even in this rain, I am able to summon most of them. I have kept a sizable force farther north, observing the track of Sherman's more northerly advance, anticipating that he might move on Augusta. If you will allow me to continue on that course, sir, I believe we must observe from every vantage point. The enemy has given us no real information as to his intentions. And our cause is not helped by this weather. I regret that a good many of my men are performing their duty even while carrying illness."

Hardee moved to a chair, the cavalry officers making way. He sat slowly, stretching a stiff back. He seemed to ignore Cobb now, kept his focus on Wheeler. "I brought two hundred men from Charleston. Two hundred! Not even an adequate headquarters guard. The enemy is marching with four corps, so I've heard. You confirm that?"

Seeley had already heard Wheeler's estimates of the numbers, stood to one side, saw Wheeler hesitate, as though uneasy with the question. Seeley's eyes were drawn to Hardee, the man's calm, the firm tone in his voice, what Seeley had always thought a **commander** should look like. Hardee waited for Wheeler's response, and Wheeler glanced downward, then straightened, spoke slowly. "It appears that is accurate, sir. I have identified the Fourteenth, Fifteenth, Seventeenth, and Twentieth corps. My scouts in Atlanta suggest Sherman left the city with near sixty thousand men."

Hardee stared down, nodded slowly. "Others suggest fewer. No one seems to know how many Federals moved north into Tennessee. Sherman would not abandon Nashville to a mere skirmishing force. General Thomas is up that way, that much we know. The Federals are sending considerable reinforcements toward Nashville from several directions." He paused. "General Sherman's campaign has been sanctioned completely by General Grant, and the Federal War Department is responding by shifting troops to allow for General Sherman's absence. Any bickering that has taken place in Washington has apparently been silenced."

Wheeler glanced around the room, lowered his voice, as though being discreet. "Forgive me, sir, but how do you know these things?"

Hardee looked up at Wheeler with a hint of a smile. "One advantage of having been commandant of cadets, General. There are a good many West Point officers on both sides of this war, and even the ones in blue can be persuaded to reveal what they know. Occasionally."

Seeley marveled at that, thought, Spies? He has spies in the Yankee army?

Wheeler seemed to understand far more clearly than his young captain, responded to Hardee's revelation with a slow nod of his head. Hardee leaned back in the chair, rubbed a hand through his beard, said, "With all respect to you, General Cobb, our current governor, Mr. Brown, tells me that the state of Georgia will soon furnish us as much militia as we can arm. I suggested that twenty thousand would be helpful. He suggested they might produce several hundred."

Wheeler glanced at Cobb, who had withdrawn toward a corner, seemingly out of place. Wheeler shook his head, said, "With all respect to General Cobb, and to Governor Brown, I do not believe local militia, boys and old men, will be of much value."

Cobb sputtered the obligatory protest, but Hardee silenced him with his hand, said with a hard frown, "Would you prefer they remain on their farms? I respect General Cobb's zeal, if not his strength of manpower. He knows these men are fighting for their own homes."

"Certainly, sir. As they fought for every other city that now smells of blue."

Seeley waited for some explosion from Hardee, but the man kept his composure, seemed to accept Wheeler's grim assessment, no matter the insult to any of Georgia's political leaders. Hardee stood slowly, moved past Seeley, a hint of stale perfume blending with the wet wool of the man's uniform. Seeley followed him, watched as he picked up a decanter from a small round table. Hardee looked at Seeley now, as though for the first time, said, "This is brandy?"

Seeley stiffened. "Not certain, sir."

"We'll see. Care for some?"

Seeley shook his head. "No, sir. Thank you, though."

Hardee sniffed the contents of the bottle, poured a small amount into a fragile glass, sniffed again. He sipped the brown liquid, his face curling, handed the bottle to Wheeler. "Here. Pass this among your men. Your aide here seems to have a good instinct for the quality of spirits. Nasty stuff."

Wheeler took the bottle, sniffed it himself, seemed to approve. "The captain here is not my aide, sir. He commands a company of my horsemen. He's a Forrest man, actually. But, as with the militia, these days we cannot choose our comrades."

Hardee studied Seeley now, said, "Well, Captain, welcome to Georgia. Regardless of General Wheeler's prejudice against your former commander, I would much prefer General Forrest be right here with us. We could use every fighting man we have. Even General Wheeler would agree that Bedford Forrest is a good man with a saber."

Seeley saw a hint of friendliness in Hardee's face,

felt more comfortable now. "Yes, sir. I'm certain General Forrest would be here, if duty allowed it."

Hardee moved back to the chair. "'Duty.' Yes, I am certain he is performing great deeds for General Hood. Just what kind of duty General Hood is performing, I cannot say. But he is my superior now, and of course, respect must be offered. No doubt, once he advances farther into Tennessee, he shall fare much better than he did with the assaults he tossed into Sherman's front lines. But General Hood has no failings in the eyes of our president, and we must agree with the instincts of our president."

There was no humor in Hardee's indiscretion, no one responding. Wheeler seemed to pulse with impatience now, said, "Sir, the enemy is in force north of this city, laboring to cross the Ocmulgee River at Planter's Factory. I believe there is opportunity, if you will authorize it."

"Oh, I'll authorize it. Until Beauregard or Taylor gets here, I am in command. What is the enemy's deployment?"

"Taylor?"

Hardee shrugged, nodded. "Oh, yes, indeed. You were not aware? No, there would be no reason for Richmond to inform our cavalry just who was coming to take command. My apologies to the president, and anyone else who believes we are in a position of strength. Yes, gentlemen, Richard Taylor is on his way, fully cloaked in the legacy of his illustrious father. I would offer everything I own just to observe Zachary Taylor confront our situation as it is today. Sherman would not enjoy that at all. But lest we be disrespectful of his son, Dick Taylor carries the legacy of his **own** great deeds, all those decisive victories in the Trans-Mississippi. Forgive me if I cannot name them. You do know that General Beauregard will soon be gracing us with his presence, as will General Bragg, on his way even now to take command of the garrison at Augusta. It is possible that Bragg will venture to Macon, if he can avoid capture along the route. The president has determined that even those generals who have once embraced failure might be assets to us down here. Regrettably, none of these commanders are accompanied by any quantity of troops." Hardee paused, and Seeley felt the gloom spreading among them, could see a glare of anger emerging in Hardee's expression. "Forgive my impudence, gentlemen, but in my efforts to understand the president's strategy, I have concluded that Richmond believes we should confront Sherman's army with as much 'brass' as can be mustered. We can 'general' them to death. I prefer you take this fight to his army any way you can. Unless you see an alternative?"

Wheeler glanced at his other officers, said, "Sir, the weather, added to the difficulties in fording the river, has strung Howard's columns out for at least twenty miles. There is opportunity."

"What of Federal cavalry? They'll be screening those columns."

Wheeler made a fist, shook it in front of him, the most animated response Seeley had seen from the man. "Hugh Judson Kilpatrick! Forgive me, sir, but Kilpatrick's screen is of no concern to me. I embrace the opportunity to confront such a scoundrel."

Seeley was surprised by the outburst, a surprise shared by Hardee. "I was aware Kilpatrick commanded Sherman's cavalry. I wasn't aware you had . . . a relationship with him?"

"You could call it that, sir. We were classmates at West Point. Surely you must recall, sir. We feared your authority more than anyone there."

"Of course, yes, I recall. It's the commandant's job to be feared, General. Your compliment is accepted. You were a year or two ahead of him, as I recall."

"Yes, sir. I will say, sir, he is the worst kind of man. I assure you, I will treat his horsemen with the same contempt I feel for him. How he rose to such heights of command, I do not know. But he shall pay for whatever lies he has told, or bribes he has paid, or whose wife's virtue he has soiled."

Seeley saw a smile on Hardee's face. "Then go about your business. But be aware that if the Federal infantry pushes hard toward Macon, you must assist us here. Screen the city as best you can, and make your assaults accordingly. Be prepared to fall into a line of defense."

"Of course, sir."

"You are dismissed. God go with you, General. And your horsemen."

Wheeler saluted, Seeley doing the same, Hardee nodding them onward. Wheeler handed the decanter back to Seeley without speaking, Seeley suddenly facing a new responsibility. They moved out quickly, the others trailing behind, the horses waiting for them in the rain. Outside, Seeley's company emerged from various shelters, leapt to their mounts. He saw the older sergeant, Gladstone, and handed Gladstone the bottle as he moved past him. Seeley climbed his own mount now, saw others coming together farther out in the rain, all of them waiting for Wheeler to give the order, leading them out into muddy darkness.

CHAPTER SIX

SEELEY

NEAR PLANTER'S FACTORY, GEORGIA— NOVEMBER 20, 1864

They had kept a careful eye on the Federal cavalry, but the men in blue seemed eager to complete their crossing, slogging farther from the river, making way for the infantry behind them. Even through the dismal darkness, Seeley could hear the orders, Federal officers barking hoarse profanity, prodding their men to make fast tracks across the bouncing pontoons. Seeley slipped forward, closer to the edge of the wood line, wet brush slapping his face, rain dripping from the brim of his soggy hat, every part of him soaked to the skin. Behind him, others followed his lead, moving forward, no one speaking, the Federal column not more than a hundred yards to their front. He shivered, tried to hear the orders more clearly, could never be calm so close to the enemy. The Federal cavalry had surprised him, had not seemed to care if anyone was observing the crossing, no significant patrols sweeping through the nearby woods, the woods where Seeley had brought his men. It was arrogance, he thought, perfect certainty that nothing any rebels could do could hold back this unstoppable caravan of strength. Surely there had been scouts late the afternoon before, a veil of protection out east of the Ocmulgee, making certain no wayward Confederate artillery batteries might be positioning themselves to embarrass the pride of the Federal troops as they made their crossing of the river. They don't believe we can hurt them, he thought. Surely that's it. We have no real army here, and every bluebelly general is puffed up with worship for Sherman, just how "perfect" their plan might be. He thought of Forrest, somewhere out in Tennessee, those glorious assaults against surprised Federal outposts that so often just melted away. He would know what to do here, Seeley thought. General Wheeler, well, probably. He's just so . . . what? Miserable? Grouchy? Doesn't much matter to me, regardless. It's my job to follow him, do what he says, no matter how much he needles me. I'm still in charge of these boys no matter

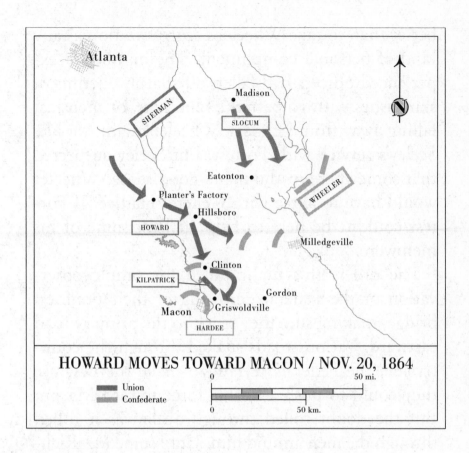

HOWARD MOVES TOWARD MACON / NOV. 20, 1864

how much he dislikes me. And now, more besides them.

It was a surprise to Seeley that Wheeler had added to Seeley's small command, increasing his lone company by more than a hundred men. It was necessary for Wheeler that his troops be organized as efficiently as possible, that Wheeler maintain careful control over the various patrols and observers. There were just too many Federal troops to be careless, too much to lose if the Confederate horsemen stumbled clumsily through their tasks. Seeley knew better than to take Wheeler's reorganization as any kind of personal compliment. The number of experienced officers had fallen off sharply, victims of skirmishes with Kilpatrick's bluecoats, or men just falling away from sickness. Wheeler might not like Seeley's service with Forrest, but Seeley suspected that somewhere in the man's good sense, Wheeler would have to agree with General Hardee. If Forrest couldn't be here to help, at least some of his men were.

The orders this night called for simple observation of the Federals' crossing of their pontoon bridge, making sure they stuck to the primary road eastward. Various roads snaked through the countryside, the Federals certain to make the best use they could to push a sizable force toward Macon. But the doubt rolled through Seeley, as it rolled through the men around him. Until someone, Richmond perhaps, managed to strengthen Wheeler's hand with a formidable number of infantry, there was little the horsemen could do but watch as Sherman moved his people anywhere he intended them to go. For now Macon seemed secure, but no one around Wheeler had any expectations that the forces manning their earthworks could withstand a powerful thrust by two Federal corps.

The boasting from Southern newspapers had become absurd, the quotes from President Davis strangely unreal, some of the men close to Seeley daring to ask if their president really had any idea what the war had become. Seeley could only hold on to his optimism; despite the shocking indiscretions from General Hardee, Seeley had to believe Richmond would not allow Georgia to be swallowed up by the Yankees without a serious fight. But just who would make that fight was a question Seeley couldn't ask. The only enemy he had any involvement with were those troops across the muddy field, trudging their way over their pontoon bridge.

The bridge had been completed now for several hours, but Kilpatrick's cavalry led the way, what seemed to take another good hour for the horsemen to make their way across the bouncing span. Seeley knew to expect that, that certainly Kilpatrick had his orders to push out east of the river, screening the advance of their main column. Seeley could see them moving past, low lantern light reflecting off the wet horses, the slickness of the troopers' rubbery coats. He had thought of keeping a count, and for the past hour more than two hundred of them had come off the bridge, that number telling him that his wisest move would be to remain exactly where he was. As more of the cavalry moved out along the road to the east, Seeley understood just how precarious his situation was. If Kilpatrick's scouts were suddenly to surprise him from behind, or if the march of their main body suddenly changed to spread through the woods where he sat now, Seeley could be swallowed up without any kind of fight.

He kept his stare on the lanterns, watched the

movement off the bridge, saw a pair of artillery pieces moving away with the cavalry. He understood that, knew that Federal cavalry would haul their own fieldpieces, if only a few. A wagon followed, then another, and for a long minute no one came off the river at all. He kept his stare through the rain with curious intensity, but now more horsemen appeared, a cluster of men keeping close to the bridgehead. Foot soldiers were spreading out now, guards being posted, and Seeley watched those men as they spread into position, knew those would be the men most likely to learn he was there. The officers on horseback seemed in some sort of council, and Seeley thought, Brass, certainly. Probably trying to figure out how to get dry. There's a few houses farther out on the road, but I bet that Kilpatrick fellow's grabbed those.

He could hear orders called out, more infantry spreading out along the road, some of those men slogging closer to the brush line, the hiding place where Seeley had placed his men. He felt the instinct to back away, but his men were spread out all along the thickets, and no orders could be called out. His heart began to beat harder, a stab of nervousness, not helped by the wet chill. No, he thought, if they move right into our line, we'll have to hit them. Sabers. The powder might be wet. We sure as blazes can't have fistfights breaking out.

The Yankee foot soldiers settled down in an uneven line halfway out in the field, no more than fifty yards in front of him, most of those men curling up into some kind of makeshift cover, their own bedrolls, or shelter-halves. The chill of the rain was relentless and Seeley was shivering now, knew those men would be as miserable as he was. No one wants a fight out here, he thought, not in this. It'll be morning soon, and they'll make a camp here, add a bunch of men to these few. Fine by me. I'll be long gone.

He looked past the row of Yankee skirmishers, heard their low talk, griping mostly, curses toward the weather or the officers who had given them this duty. Seeley didn't smile, was too nervous still. Some of the men new to his command were complete unknowns, and he had to trust that no one would be tempted by the enemy being so close to do something abominably stupid. So far his men had been as silent as he was, obedience to his own order he appreciated. He knew what he was seeing, the advance of what was surely an entire Federal corps. The shivering grew more intense, hard cold in his chest, the column shoving forward under the shouted curses from the men on horseback. Seeley had never crossed a pontoon bridge, wondered just how that felt, especially in the cold black of the rain. You slip, stumble, and you're in the river. And dead. They might not even notice. No wonder those men are in a hurry.

The rain had settled into a hard, hissing drizzle, thick and misty, masking the sounds of the marching column. Seeley could make out the muted clink of canteens and mess kits, bits of grumbling from the skirmishers close to his front. Beside him Seeley heard breathing, a hand on his shoulder.

"Cavalry all gone? What the dickens?"

Even in a whisper he knew the voice of Gladstone.

"Not certain yet. They could come back."

"Captain, sir, those bluebellies have done skedaddled out of here to find someplace to keep their bedrolls dry. Those officers right out there is cussing up a storm to move those troops over this here river. Those bluebellies have been on their feet for most of the day, waiting to go somewheres, anywheres a'tall. The only **happy** Yankees out there are the engineers who built that stinkin' bridge. They're drinking their whiskey in some house in that nothing little town. Which reminds me, I didn't properly thank you for that bottle you tossed me. Not bad."

Seeley was still nervous, didn't need a conversation with the older man, not now. "Courtesy of General Hardee. Thank him."

"Well, by crackin', I might do that." Another man moved up behind him, another whisper.

"What now, Cap'n?"

Seeley ignored the man, and Gladstone said,

"Seems to me if the bluebelly cavalry done gone, those foot soldiers is mighty alone. We got the whole company right here, another out to the right. Might be a good time, bustin' right in on 'em."

Seeley thought of Wheeler, the man's stern orders issued to all his commanders, **Seek opportunity**. He stared hard, tried to ignore the rain in his eyes, studied the column, at least a full regiment already across, and now, a gap in their column, more officers riding on the bouncing bridge, harsh words, and Seeley felt the hard stir in his gut, had been through this with Forrest, the same orders. **Seek opportunity**. And attack it.

He turned, a handful of men close by, others sitting low in the brush to both sides of him. He kept the whisper, spit out as loudly as he dared. "Back to the horses! Formation!"

He led the way, the others responding to his quickness, the entire line backing away, tracing their steps through the thickets, the trees taller now, holding away the rain. He could see the gathering of horses, one-fourth of his men left back to keep them together, the cavalry's protocol. Another company had moved closer as well, and he saw a man up on a horse, knew by the man's posture it was Dibrell. He moved close, still dismounted, said in a harsh whisper, "General! Captain Seeley, sir. We should attack the bridgehead! The Yankees don't know we're here. Their cavalry has moved away!"

"Captain, mount up. There will be no attack here. Move your men out with the rest of the brigade. We're moving south, toward Clinton. General Wheeler's orders."

Seeley stared up at the man's silhouette, faint shadows against the high treetops. "Sir, are we not to attack where the enemy—"

"Mount up, Captain."

Seeley felt an aching helplessness, glanced back, saw his own horse brought closer, one of his troopers handing him the reins. He wanted to protest the order, but Dibrell had little tolerance for dissent. Without a word, Dibrell moved away, other men moving into line with him, the woods alive now with the dull slurp of muddy hoofbeats. Seeley turned to his horse, caught the usual stink of wet hair, patted the animal, put his foot up in the stirrup, and hoisted himself into the saddle. There were low voices around him, and he saw shadows now, a surprise. He turned, saw a harsh glow of light coming from the river. Men were pointing, some calling out, no one seeming to care about the closeness of the Yankees. He stared with them at the harsh light, blinding in the darkness, the misty rain not disguising what the Yankees were doing. They were burning the town.

NEAR CLINTON, GEORGIA—
NOVEMBER 20, 1864

He knew the expression, had seen it far too often. This time he couldn't say anything. The scolding had come first from Dibrell, but now it would come from Wheeler himself.

"You were going to attack the bridgehead? With a hundred men? Were you planning on charging right onto the pontoon bridge itself, toss those Yankees right into the river? You know how many. Yankees were on that bridge, how many would have grabbed your horse before you could fire your pistol?"

"No, sir."

"Well, Captain, neither do I. But I'm guessing several hundred, and the men who had already gone across would have done just what?"

"I imagine they'd have turned around."

"That's a good guess. And so, young captain, where would you be now? I'll tell you. Your whole force would be wrapped up in ropes, hauled behind General Howard's column out there. You figure that would do me any good? You may be as stupid as a pine tree, but I need every saber I can put on a horse. Even stupid ones."

Wheeler turned away, spoke to an aide, called out to another, sent the men riding off, the fast gallop spraying Seeley with mud. He waited for more, could see other officers keeping their distance, thoroughly enjoying the scene. Wheeler turned toward him again, said, "Take your men down that road, line 'em up in the woods off to one side, where the best cover is. Keep 'em down and quiet. The Yankees are marching on this road, and it won't take 'em long to walk right on by this very spot." Wheeler paused, let out a long breath. "Captain, I intend to find out just what kind of iron holds your guts together. Forrest made you a captain, so I'm going to see if he was as stupid then as you were this morning. You get your men into place. If you see a squad of Kilpatrick's bluebellies, and they don't see you first, you hit them hard. But don't stay around like it's some parade. Do your damage and withdraw. Is that understood, young captain?"

"Yes, sir."

He saluted, Wheeler returning it with no flourish at all. Wheeler moved quickly away, and Seeley ignored the low laughter coming from the other officers, those men now getting orders of their own.

His men were in line along one side of the wide, muddy lane, and Seeley pushed the horse their way, felt himself sweating, the chill of the light rain adding to the miserable embarrassment of the dressing-down from Wheeler. As he moved closer to his men, he saw the faces, but there was no laughing, no taunts at his expense. He was surprised, curious, scanned the familiar faces first, veterans of a hundred scraps. He scanned the others as well, the men he didn't yet know, the troopers Wheeler had added to his command. They watched him as he rode closer, and he saw looks of disgust, felt the shame of that, as though they were cursing him for the idiocy that inspired General Wheeler's embarrassing lecture. He stopped the horse, no one talking, eyes on him, and Seeley had a sudden fear that these men wouldn't listen to him anymore, would take the general's lesson to heart, that their captain might have gotten them all killed. Now one man saluted him, the others responding the same way, one of the privates, Horner, loud, brash, the man spitting out the words.

"Ain't right, sir. We shoulda gone after 'em, like you wanted. Had 'em right in our sights we did. No cause for the general to chew your behind like that. We'd have done some good."

The others made low sounds, nodding in agreement, even the new men taking some umbrage at Wheeler's lecture. Seeley felt a sudden flood of pride, his doubts erased by the outrage he was hearing from his own men. He held up a hand, tried to quiet them, said, "No. General Wheeler was right. Surprise or not, we were outnumbered ten or twenty to one. We'd have done some good for a few minutes, but they'd have shot us out of the saddle. Not every fight is the right one to make."

Horner spoke up again. "Then what are we doing out here, sir? I ain't been in a 'fair fight' yet. If we ain't outnumbered, it just ain't fun."

The others joined in a chorus of agreement, and Seeley let them talk, glanced back toward Wheeler, but the others had already moved away. He held up his hand again, looking them over, most with only bare hints of a uniform, ragged bedrolls strapped to worn saddles, the horses as poor as the men who rode them. The roll that morning had counted one hundred twenty, the new men mostly from other companies that had been devastated by the fights around Atlanta. They were paying more attention now, the griping exhausted, and Seeley said, "We've got orders. Move out and keep to the left of this road. There's a good stand of trees a half mile back, a farm trail back of it. We'll settle in there, keep an eye on the main road. You boys want an **unfair fight,** well, General Wheeler thinks we might get one."

The Yankee skirmishers came by first, some of those men treading carefully into the woods close to Seeley's front, then out again, as though they would detect any threat by some instinct alone. Seeley had held his men more than a hundred yards off the road, could see enough details through the trees and brush to know that the men in column on the road were infantry. If there was cavalry at all, they had taken some other route, or had already moved far beyond where Seeley had placed his men. The only horsemen seemed to be the various commanders, keeping watch on the march of their foot soldiers.

With the daylight had come a slackening in the rain, enough to add confidence that the powder in their pistols and carbines might actually fire. But Seeley kept General Wheeler's scolding in his mind, knew that he was seeing a force far larger than anything Wheeler had anywhere around them. But still . . . he knew what Wheeler wanted him to do, had thought long about Wheeler's hatred of Kilpatrick. No one had explained just why Wheeler despised his adversary with so much vigor. The depth of Wheeler's passion for a fight with Kilpatrick seemed almost irrational, the kind of fire that leads to bad decisions. But now Seeley huddled low in the wet brush wondering just what Wheeler would say if the only enemy to his front was Federal infantry.

"Sir! There's a gap. No one out there!"

Seeley followed the man's pointing hand, raised his head a few inches, could see the road more clearly now. One wagon rolled past, another, then a pair of horsemen. But there was no infantry. He felt a jolt, listened as well as watched, none of the usual sounds of a column, no voices, no clanking of metal. More men were rising up from the brush, most looking toward him, waiting for . . . something.

He stood, full view now, felt the surging thrill of what he was seeing, the very opportunity his orders called for. His brain was working, spilling out guesses. Muddy road, slow march, wagon wheels bogging down back there. He waved frantically, Gladstone, other sergeants coming close now, and Seeley said, "Mount up! Follow me out onto the road, and ride hard into the column that just passed! Grab the wagons, or anything else!"

He turned quickly, scampered back through the muddy woods, reached the horses, his men doing the same, responding with the same energy. Seeley climbed up in the saddle, waited impatiently, watched as they came together, pistols checked, some men already drawing sabers. He hesitated a full minute, the men falling into formation, as impatient as he was, horses bucking slightly, responding to the hard grips on their reins. He turned toward the road, a single path that led through the thickets, pointed his own sword, made a hard shout, "Go!"

They followed him through the dripping woods, the hard spray of drizzle ignored now, swept aside by manic energy. He reached the road, saw the last wagon, the officers in blue, the men turning suddenly. Seeley rode that way, sword in the air, the men spurring their own mounts, a fast gallop past the wagon. He rode hard, reached the wagon, pointed the sword at the teamster, the man jumping down, a panicked run into the woods. He pushed forward, the second wagon, the driver calling out, but his hands were in the air, one of Seeley's troopers holding him motionless with his pistol. Up ahead the column of soldiers was scattering, turning, an officer furiously putting them into line. He rode straight toward them, saw muskets being loaded, men fumbling with equipment, too slow. He was there now, swung his sword down hard, impact on a man's shoulder, kept moving, right past them, more of the Yankee column trying to respond, some fleeing into the woods. But Seeley's men were all among them, swords and pistols aimed, scattered shots, his eyes finding a blue-coated officer firing his pistol, the man suddenly cut down, other Yankee horsemen riding quickly away, leaving their men. The Yankees were in complete confusion, and Seeley halted the horse, waved the sword in the air, shouted out, "Surrender, bluebellies! Surrender or die!"

The order was foolish, childlike, but for the single moment he didn't care, the burst of victory swirling around him. Men still ran away, but others kept to the road, his own men herding them with their horses. The muskets were dropping now, hands in the air, some of Seeley's men dismounting, gathering the Yankee prisoners together, leading them quickly toward the captured wagons. Seeley kept the sword high, his breathing hard and hot, heavy pounding in his chest. He looked down the road, concerned now with more than prisoners, saw a mass of blue moving toward him, the Federal column formed into a battle line, stronger now, organizing, officers in control. He searched through his men, saw the prisoners, at least two dozen, and he called out, "Put them in the wagons! Now! Get them up quick!"

The captives seemed to understand, prodded hard by the swords, one officer cooperating, pointing, ordering his men up to the wagons. Seeley rode that way, drew his pistol, a gesture he enjoyed, the glorious power of the moment.

"You are my prisoner, sir! Order your men to cooperate and we won't abuse them."

Seeley saw the shoulder straps of a lieutenant, the man very young, terrified, nodding profusely, his stare on the muzzle of Seeley's pistol.

"Yes, sir! We are your prisoners, sir!"

The shouts were growing up the road, the musket fire coming now, whistles and sharp whines past Seeley's head. His men were on their mounts again, the prisoners mostly heaped together on the wagons, and Seeley glanced toward the Yankee infantry, close enough to see faces, a heavy line moving toward them, a hundred yards, closing quickly.

"Let's go! Take the trail!"

The road through the woods was just wide enough for the wagons, but the mud was deep, the horse's hooves pushing down into soft goo. He watched the wagons lurch crookedly into the trees, bogging down, and he wanted to shout them through, but there was little hope, the mud too deep, the wagons too heavy. His frustration fueled into raw anger, and he pounded his saddle, waved his men into the woods, most of them pushing their mounts tightly past the heaped wagons. He looked down the road again, the Federal line closer still, more musket fire, a ball whistling through the side of his coat. And now there was a new sound, from the thickets on the far side of the road. He heard the sound of horses, saw the blue mass emerging from woods, pushing through the brush toward him, one flag, then another. It was Federal cavalry.

He yanked hard on the reins, turned the horse, the wagons abandoned, the Yankee prisoners scrambling down, making their escape. The Federal horsemen poured out onto the road, and Seeley drew his pistol, saw another squad farther down, pushing past the line of blue infantry. The Yankee horsemen halted, a frozen moment, barely thirty yards away, eyes on him, his pistol motionless. He focused on their carbines, and he heard the orders, the silence broken now, spurred the horse, the animal responding with a lurch. He followed his men into the woods, the wagons clogging the trail, offering blessed cover, blocking the Federal fire. He skirted around the wagons, the carbines rattling in a chorus of fire like nothing he had ever heard. His head was low, the horse obeying the urgency of his spurs, his eyes on the men in front of him, **his** men. They kept up the gallop, mud flying, the wet branches slapping past Seeley, the men still riding hard. They reached an open field and Seeley shouted out, some of the men halting, then more, coming back together, the immediate danger past. He drew them into line, the sergeants riding behind them, straightening the formation, and Seeley stared back into the woods, expected to see the blue horsemen in close pursuit.

"Make ready! Aim low!"

The men were silent, waiting, the agonizing tension spread through all of them. Seeley stared out down the trail, strained to hear, but there was nothing, only the hiss of more rain. Beside him was one of the new men, a corporal.

"They ain't coming. They think they just chased us off."

Gladstone was there now, the old man spitting a stream of tobacco juice close to Seeley's horse. "They did chase us off, boy. You hear them damn carbines? Eight-shooters. Ten-shooters. Whatever the hell they got now."

Seeley absorbed that, knew Gladstone was right. He had seen that before, in Tennessee, the Yankee horsemen with their new weapons, one man able to shoot as quickly as half a squad of Seeley's own. He had actually captured some of the repeating pieces, but they were useless to his men. The ammunition they carried didn't fit.

He felt his breathing, the hot anger at losing the prisoners, the prize of the wagons, whatever goods they might have carried. But there was nothing else to do. He felt a sudden enormous sadness, the image of so many blue troopers planted in his mind. Had to be twice what we've got here. And those carbines . . .

He slid the sword into its scabbard, called out now, "Let's ride back to Clinton, find General Dibrell. We're not doing any good right here. We stick around, those Yankees will figure that out."

The men were grumbling, but no one offered any real objection. The sadness rolled through him still, an aching impotence. He spurred the horse, the animal sweating beneath him, but still obedient, as were the men. He led them back along the trail they had first come, back to where Wheeler would give them another task, put them into someplace where there might be another "unfair fight."

CHAPTER SEVEN

HARDEE

MACON, GEORGIA—NOVEMBER 22, 1864

"You certain, Lieutenant?"

"Quite so, sir. The telegraph operator proved most efficient. His discretion should be rewarded. Once he was aware that his communication was no longer private, he cut off all transmitting. Certainly the Yankees were intercepting our wires, possibly for some time. But the line is now dead."

Hardee walked slowly, felt a sudden dread, the uncertainty of being cut off from communication with anyone who could help him. He kept it inside, wouldn't let that show to the young officer,

stepped through a crust of frozen mud. Beside him
the lieutenant moved with a precise march to his
steps, as though Hardee were leading him on parade. Hardee had grown used to that, the younger
officers treating him as much with fear as with the
respect due his rank. He knew that kind of behavior had been spread by the West Pointers in the
army, the men who knew Hardee first as **commandant,** the man most responsible for discipline
at the academy. At first that had flattered him,
Hardee hoping that the respect they showed him
came from his creation of the army's field manual.
But few paid much attention to that now, and his
reputation for discipline carried more weight than
even he would prefer. He often thought of those
in the North, had even kept up some correspondence with them throughout much of 1861. But
that wasn't practical now, might even be considered
collusion with the enemy, a perception he knew
Braxton Bragg would have embraced with a vicious
glee. Still, there were the friends, the very discreet
network of men who offered to trade information
in return for his advice on tactics. Most of that was
worthless, in both directions, but Hardee knew to
keep trying, that occasionally a nugget would slip
through, something even the man in blue wouldn't
realize had value. Hardee was far more careful, kept
his missives cloaked in the veil of friendship, pride,
and loyalty toward the good student, the promising
young officer, no matter the color of his uniform.

The men closest to him now were loyal indeed,
but West Point had nothing to do with that. They
had endured what every Confederate commander
had suffered, whether the heavy hand of Jefferson
Davis or the ridiculous abuse of authority by generals who Hardee knew had no business leading an
army.

He continued to walk, the air colder still, a flurry
of damp snow swirling around him. He glanced
up, the sun sinking low, and he moved closer to the
earthworks, could see that the men who had once
occupied the works were mostly gone. The lieutenant beside him kept up his rhythmic pace, splashing
through the icy potholes in the street, and Hardee
stopped now, turned to the young man, said, "Will
you please avoid the parade ground drill, Lieutenant? There is no one here to congratulate you on your
precision, including me. Your report is accepted.
You may return to Major Roy, and request he assign you to . . . something else. We must prepare to
leave this place, and I don't want fanfare about it.
Do you understand?"

The man seemed crestfallen, as though accompanying Hardee was the most useful task he could
perform. Hardee thought, He might be right about
that.

"Yes, sir. I shall report to Major Roy. With your
permission . . ."

The young man slapped up a perfect salute, and
Hardee returned it with as much enthusiasm as he

could muster. The man moved away now, Hardee letting himself sag, turning again toward the earthworks.

The telegraph line had been the last one that was useful. There had been a game of sorts, Federal cavalry most likely, Kilpatrick's men tapping into the line to hear whatever messages might still be on the wire. The latest word from Beauregard had been more annoying emptiness, Beauregard still far away, hampered by the condition of the transportation routes. Beauregard's last message had been directed more toward General Wheeler's cavalry, the painful reality for Hardee that no one else under his meager command would have much effect on the Federal troops bearing down on Macon.

My views are that positions should be defended only so long as not to risk safety of troops and materials required for active operations in the field. Remove to safe locality all government property on line of enemy's march, and consume or destroy all supplies within his reach.

Hardee had passed Beauregard's order along to Wheeler, but there was little enthusiasm for what Hardee knew was one more piece of instruction from someone too far away to understand just what was going on. The only piece of the message that Hardee took seriously was the need to remove troops who were likely to be crushed by whatever forces Sherman was pushing toward them.

Beauregard will get here eventually, Hardee thought. And then he'll know exactly what I know. We would have defended this place as best we could, and we would have cost the enemy some heavy casualties. But the men here would never have stood for long. No matter the nonsense the newspapers trumpet over our heads, we were never strong enough here to keep Howard's two corps away. It was only our good fortune that General Howard made the decision to avoid us. I just wish I knew why.

Those few men who still held the ground saw him coming, salutes and hats in the air, no more than a few dozen of them now. He searched for their officer, whoever that might be, had no patience for anyone not at his post. He climbed up on a dirt embankment, freshly dug, and so a heap of soft mud. The men kept their distance, respect he appreciated, and he steadied himself, stared out through the wisps of snow. I should have sent them out with a more experienced commander, he thought. Zealous generals kill men, usually their own. Like Pleasant Philips, a man who knows nothing about leading men in the field, and so he decides to impress us all by making his own battle, as though by leading his untrained militia against anyone he found, he would become a hero.

That fight had been a few miles outside Macon,

a small town called Griswoldville. Hardee had only ordered reconnaissance, most of that in the hands of Joe Wheeler's cavalry, and Wheeler understood clearly that if opportunity presented itself, he could strike the Yankees at will. But Philips had been sent out on another mission entirely. It was Hardee's intention that Philips's militia avoid contact with the Yankees and seek out a functioning railroad farther east or south that might transport those troops away from Macon altogether, along with Hardee himself and the various other units still in place.

By preserving as much troop strength as he could, Hardee kept alive his own optimism that the Georgia troops, and anyone else sent to bolster their ranks, might be placed into some advantageous position, a strong defensive line where they might actually accomplish something useful. The railroad was key to that plan, but General Philips had interpreted Hardee's order as though a fight was desirable. Philips had stumbled into a dangerous confrontation, the inexperienced brigadier taking it upon himself to launch his two-thousand-man force into what he must have believed was the unprepared rear guard of one of Oliver Howard's columns. Instead Philips had sent his ragged and disorganized troops into the repeating rifles of a well prepared force. The results were no surprise to anyone but Philips. It was a disaster, more than four hundred casualties, from a command that couldn't stand to lose anyone at all. If there was one positive from Griswoldville, it was confirmation that Howard's columns were moving away to the north and east of Macon, the Federal troops granting a mysterious reprieve to the town that Howard most likely could have grabbed at will.

Hardee wiped the chilling wetness from his face, stepped carefully down to level ground, stood alone, still examined the works. We'd have made a good fight of it. I have to believe that. Georgians fighting for Georgia. Perhaps the Yankees feared Wheeler, the threat of a fight with good cavalry. Howard's probably under orders from Sherman to keep clear of any significant fight. The question I cannot answer is: Why? He must know the kind of weakness we have here. No, if Sherman had wanted Macon, he'd be here, right now. He expended great energy to convince us . . . hell, convince **me** that he was coming. I suppose that was the point. We sat here and waited for him, and all the while, the other half of his army was somewhere north of here, maybe driving right into Augusta. Or maybe he doesn't care about that place, either. Maybe he's going all the way to the ocean. And there's not a thing Richmond can provide us that will stop him.

He walked toward the groom holding his horse, saw his adjutant, Colonel Pickett, a handful of aides on horseback. He kept his eyes on Pickett, expected some kind of news, something bad yet again. But Pickett offered a simple nod toward him, the casual friendliness that marked their relationship.

No, there is no news at all, he thought. No orders, no absurd hurrahs of encouragement. The Federals control the telegraph, and so all we have here is silence. Not even the cavalry can tell us what's happening beyond a few miles from here. He stood for a long moment with his hands on his hips, the cold, wet air piercing him through his coat. Silence. I hate silence.

William Pickett was older than anyone on his staff, had come to Hardee out of Alabama, served as his adjutant general. He was a veteran of Mexico, a rarity among the officers around Hardee now. It had not escaped Hardee that most of the younger officers who led the men around this new command had no idea what a victory felt like. At least Pickett has that inside of him, he thought. The question now is whether or not I can recall that myself.

Pickett and Thomas Roy had served Hardee through the worst of the controversies Hardee had suffered throughout the war, most often the clash of personalities with men like Braxton Bragg and more recently John Bell Hood. Hardee appreciated their loyalty, had felt fortunate that nearly all of his staff had kept with him even as he was moved into various new commands by the clumsy maneuvering in Richmond. The latest move had come at the urging of Hood, even as Hardee served under Hood in attempting to hold Sherman away from Atlanta. As Atlanta fell into Federal hands, Hardee was sent east, to take command of the garrison at

Charleston. Richmond cloaked that assignment in
all sorts of meaningless compliments, but Hardee
knew that Hood simply wanted him out of the
way. Hardee had seen too much of this in the army,
most notably with Braxton Bragg, the year before.

He despised Bragg, the animosity mutual, but
Bragg could not avoid the blame for the disaster a
year earlier at Chattanooga. When Richmond accepted Bragg's resignation, command of the army
had then been offered to Hardee. He accepted, but
very soon he knew it was a responsibility he simply
didn't want. Though he worked tirelessly to rebuild
what had been shattered at Chattanooga, Hardee
had pulled away from the weight that army command required. To the astonishment of Richmond,
and particularly Jefferson Davis, within three short
weeks Hardee relinquished the command, urging
Richmond to appoint Joe Johnston in his place.
Hardee had no doubts at all that Johnston could
do a better job, could inspire the army and the citizenry, and would be a more effective strategist. A
stunned Jefferson Davis had reluctantly accepted
Hardee's recommendation, and Johnston had been
given the command. But even Hardee knew that
the longtime friction between those two men could
have no pleasant outcome. Like Beauregard, Johnston had a talent for irritating the president.

Once Sherman pushed his Federal army deep
into Georgia, the president had all the excuses he
needed. Predictably, Davis removed Johnston and

replaced him with John Bell Hood. Hardee had often been frustrated with Johnston's tendency toward retreat, but in the face of overwhelming odds, Johnston reacted with careful strategy, had always shown he preferred maneuver to all-out assault. Hood seemed to understand that Davis expected him to perform with far more aggression, even so far as to contradict every strategy Johnston had recommended. But Hood took his authority beyond aggression into outright recklessness. Johnston had been roundly criticized for retreating in the face of Sherman's advance, and so Hood did the opposite. The results had been devastating for the army, and for Atlanta. But Davis continued to support Hood in his command, the amazing talent the president had for ignoring his own errors in judgment. Now Hardee was convinced that Hood's pursuit of some new glory in Tennessee would result in one more nail in the lid of the Confederacy's coffin.

Hardee had no idea if anyone in Richmond appreciated Georgia's importance to the Confederacy, the state supplying critical supplies to Lee's army in Virginia. And yet, he thought, Davis seems to believe every state is its own kingdom, invincible, that one by one, we shall throw the invading bluebellies out, as we march proudly toward some heavenly conclusion. And so, what is your duty, General Hardee? Would you not prefer to return home to your new bride? The thought stopped him, made him smile.

He knew there was talk, even among some of his staff, that his recent marriage had been viewed as a distraction, that his focus was on the perfumed skirts of his beloved Miss Mary. She was his second wife, his first—the mother of his three children— passing away more than ten years before. Charleston is a lovely place, he thought. Suits her, as it suits the children. If they would only listen to me, and remain out of harm's way.

It was his daughter Sallie who insisted that her place should rival his own. During the battles for Atlanta, Sallie had served as a nurse in every make-shift hospital she could reach, and even now Hardee knew she would continue to serve the army whether he wanted her to or not. She will not follow orders, he thought. At least, not my own. But I can hardly prevent her from doing such work, when we have so much need for it. But still . . . Charleston. A wonderful place for a family. Yes, Miss Mary, I have had enough of this. But there is still so much more to do. And so many fools to suffer along the way.

Hardee had served John Bell Hood with as much conviction as he had always brought to the field, but during the fights for Atlanta, Hardee began to accept what Hood would not, that Sherman's vastly superior force of arms, as well as the quality of his generals, could not be swept away simply by throwing troops directly into Sherman's guns. Inevitably, the fall of Atlanta required a scapegoat, and Hood had singled out Hardee for many of the failures against Sherman, an accusation Hardee could not completely contradict. Rather than subject the army to a lengthy game of approbation and courts of inquiry, Hardee accepted the transfer to Charleston, where he now commanded the garrison. Until Beauregard or Richard Taylor reached Macon, Hardee was the ranking commander, had traveled southward into Georgia with the clear understanding that halting Sherman's advance was still the higher priority, even if Hood thought there was greater glory to be found in Tennessee. It continued to surprise many in the War Department in Richmond that Sherman had not chased after Hood, had instead seemed perfectly content establishing a military base out of Atlanta itself. And now, Hardee thought, Sherman is pushing toward . . . where? But that is an answer I am expected to know already. And they provide me with what? Wheeler's cavalry, and a few thousand war-weary troops or conscripts who have no experience at all, led by men like Pleasant Philips, who still believe they can find glory in killing men for no good reason.

He fought through the gloom, brushed wet snow from his shoulder, took the horse's reins from the groom. He climbed slowly into the saddle, forced his back straight, blew out a breath of white fog. Pickett moved closer, said, "I expected the Yankees this morning, General. Still thought they'd drive right through here."

Pickett was pointing out past the earthworks, and Hardee ignored that, had been through this already in his mind. The only real push toward Macon had come from Kilpatrick's cavalry, a noisy assault that was clearly designed to attract attention, a loud show that served only to terrify the untested troops. But the infantry never came, those columns of blue instead marching eastward, still strung out from the miserable weather, and so still offering Wheeler some possibility of an opportunity. Hardee thought of the telegraph again, thought, We're an island, drifting in a sea. At least there is Wheeler. Word could come, some great victory over the Federal horsemen, or even more, a crushing blow against Howard's infantry. I would hear of that, for certain.

"Anything from Wheeler, Colonel?"

"No, sir. Not since this morning, early. They're keeping close to the enemy's movements. If there was a problem, he'd tell us."

Hardee nodded slowly. "We squandered an opportunity here, Colonel. We have troops garrisoned at Augusta, Savannah, Charleston, and more spread out through outposts everywhere in between. If we had brought them here, a united army, General Howard's forces would have been in serious trouble."

"You could have ordered them to assemble here, sir. It was in your power."

"You know better than that, Bill. Dick Taylor's set to ride in here anytime now. This will be his command, until Beauregard gets here. I can see it all. Clean shirts and preening staff officers, gathering in front of some glorious fire in some citizen's cozy hearth, poring over maps, still holding on to Richmond's fantasy that Sherman has doomed himself. I prefer to prepare for what must still come."

"I don't understand. You mean . . . winter?"

Hardee glanced up, the snow light, breezy. "No. Sherman's not halting for any kind of winter quarters. He's marching his troops all over God's creation, spreading his people into columns miles long, on roads not fit for a plow horse. All we're doing is watching, reacting, hoping for something positive to happen. No matter what Beauregard tells us to do, or what the president believes, we're not in control of anything here. I have one option, and if my new superior officers allow it, I'll do what I believe to be the only maneuver that makes sense. If Sherman intends to strike Augusta, he's going to run straight into our gallant Braxton Bragg. I have my own prediction how that fight will go. From here there's nothing at all we can do to help, even if Bragg would admit he needed it. But if Sherman marches for the coast, Savannah, Charleston, his columns could be vulnerable. There are rivers he must ford, and the weather is unpredictable. There is always the chance we can hurt him."

Pickett stared at him, knew Hardee well, wouldn't interrupt, Hardee still forming the words in his mind.

The snow came heavier now, and Hardee looked toward the staff, the aides shivering, ragged coats on thin frames, the ribs of their horses too plain.

"Bill, order the men to prepare our movement. If General Philips is capable of following orders, have him push on to the next rail station that Sherman hasn't yet found. Beauregard can establish his headquarters here if he wishes it, and if he tells me to march to hell itself, I'll obey him. But Sherman's moving away from us, and right now it's time to gather up every unit we can muster and find a way to stop him."

"Where should we go, sir? The staff will want to know where your headquarters will be. General Wheeler must know as well."

Hardee stared eastward, pictured the maps in his mind. "If Sherman is planning to advance to the coast, his likely target is Savannah. Unless I'm ordered elsewhere, that's where we need to be."

CHAPTER EIGHT

SHERMAN

WEST OF MILLEDGEVILLE, GEORGIA—
NOVEMBER 22, 1864

The orchard was whipped by the wind, the trees bare of leaves. The staff was spreading out through the narrow rows, seeking some kind of shelter from the stiffening chill, while behind them, Sherman wiped at the watering in his eyes, cursed the cold. In the distance the staff was drawn to what he already saw, a glow of firelight in the distance, a blinking eye from a small cabin. The aides pushed their mounts that way, Sherman following, and he could see now small structures, crude, in something of an organized row. Slave quarters, he thought. Better to sleep there than put a fool tent out here in the open.

His headquarters guard had already swept through the cabins, anticipating his order of this night's resting place. He rode closer, saw guards at each, more firelight through small windows down the line.

Major Nichols rode toward Sherman now, one hand holding his hat on his head, fighting off the wind. Nichols was red-faced, shivering, said, "Sir! There's good shelter over there. Not much for grandeur, but it'll get us clear of this infernal cold."

Sherman said nothing, clamped his teeth on the cigar, the tip missing its fire, extinguished by the relentless breeze. He moved the horse past Nichols, saw the aides dismounting, anticipating his approval. Can't argue with that, he thought. He glanced toward the nearest rooftop, a ramshackle layering of timbers and flat wood, tree limbs matted together, the patchwork of a generation of inhabitants. Above was a broken-down chimney, a drifting column of black smoke. Through the window, the firelight grew more inviting, and Sherman dismounted, said, "This will do for tonight. I assume no one's putting up a fuss about it."

Hitchcock was there now, blinking hard through his glasses, hatless, disheveled. "General, these people seem most friendly. Some are anxious to make your acquaintance, and all of them have offered their homes for our use."

"Where's your hat, Major?"

"Not entirely certain, sir. Blew off a minute ago. One of the aides is fetching it. With the general's permission, might we venture indoors? I swear, sir, I've not seen this kind of weather since I joined your staff."

"It's called winter, Major. Even in Georgia."

Sherman was as weary of the windy cold as his staff, had ridden through gusts of snow flurries and dropping temperatures throughout the afternoon. He glanced at his pocket watch, just after four, said, "Long enough. Hope for better weather tomorrow. What distance we make today, Major?"

"Near twelve miles, sir. Best as I can tell. Captain Poe mentioned that a ways back."

Sherman nodded, looked again at the light through the window of the cabin. "Good engineers keep track of that sort of thing. I'll take this first one. Let's see who's at home."

He handed the reins to a waiting groom, the staff gathering quickly around the door of the cabin. He pushed past them, knew they were as cold as he was. A guard stood at the door, saluted him, said, "All clear here, sir."

"I assumed that."

The guard pushed open the rickety door, and Sherman smelled the fire, the scent of tobacco and soot. He stepped inside, saw one old black man sitting at the fire, the man's eyes locked on Sherman.

"Hello, old man. I'll be using your cabin for tonight."

The man kept his eyes fixed on Sherman's face, and Sherman saw a missing leg, a rag of the man's pants leg rolled up to the knee. The man's skin was deep black, his eyes a dark yellow, the stare rigid, serious.

"You welcome in my home, good suh. They tells me that Genil Sherman done come heah. You knows him?"

Sherman pulled the cigar from his mouth, handed it to an aide, who moved cautiously toward the fire, relit it, eased back toward him, the cigar quickly back in Sherman's teeth. "What do you know of General Sherman, old man?"

"De Lawd Hisself done sent him heah. He's come to free all us folk."

"Could be."

"Yes, suh, I suppose he's up de road, at de mas-suh's house. Or mebbe he's done come to this place right heah. You suppose? Mebbe that be you, then?"

Sherman saw the man's game, smiled. "I'm Sherman. We'll not injure you. Your fire is an invitation I can't ignore."

The man slapped one hand against his good leg, a broad smile of his own, gaps in yellow teeth. "Ha! I knows it, fo' sho!"

The man struggled to stand, Sherman motioning to the nearest aide, McCoy, who went to the man with a helping hand. But the old man was up on his own, pushed McCoy away. "Don't need no hep. Been without this leg for years. If'n I can, suh, I'd like to take myself a closer look. Dese ole eyes ain't so good now."

The man moved toward him, leaned close, no more than a foot away, the man's scent overpowering, sour breath, more soot and tobacco. Sherman felt awkward, the man studying him, scanning the uniform, then straightened up again, took a step backward.

"They tole me you was with horns and such. The divil hisself. I ain't seein' no horns. What I see is . . . de Lawd's gift." The old man slapped his hands together, looked around his small room at the gathering aides, pointed to the open door. "If'n you don't mind it, suh, could you'uns please shut dat ting? Took me a good hour to get out the cold. Ain't easy to keep up the fire with no hep."

Sherman looked toward the door, the guard watching him, and Sherman didn't need to give the order. The door closed abruptly, a half-dozen aides packed in close around him, all of them looking at the old man. Sherman pointed to the door. "Close it from the outside, all of you but Nichols and Hitchcock. We're not having any damn council of war here. Out!"

They obeyed quickly, Sherman enduring the blast of cold while the cabin emptied. The old man still watched him, seemed extremely pleased at Sherman's authority. He pointed toward Sherman now, still the beaming smile.

"I knowed it, fo' sho. I knowed you was tellin' the

truth. There won' be no sleep in this house tonight, no suh. I done seen the king of the worl'."

The man backed away, his eyes still on Sherman, felt his way to his chair, but didn't sit, a show of respect. The smile gave way to a new look, a surprise, the old man's eyes filling with tears, rough fingers sweeping them aside. Sherman looked down, wasn't prepared for this kind of reception. Beside him, Nichols said quietly, "Sir, this man said there's a house up ahead. The guard confirms that. It's a grand home. A plantation house. Must be this man's owner."

The old man nodded. "That'd be it, suh. Massuh Cobb. He done gone, fo' sho. His gals gone, too, some of his hands go wid him. Some just run off. I'da gone, too, but this heah leg slow me down. Don't do no good to get catched up wid cavalry."

The word caught Sherman's attention. "What do you know of rebel cavalry?"

The man sat slowly, the smile gone now. "I knows that Wheeler is on the prowl round heah. Everywheres. Don' do for none of us to be catched on the loose. They's good wid the bullwhip. Massuh Cobb got his dogs, too. Hounds, they say. Sniff out a man from any hole. One of dem hounds caught good hold of this heah leg. Chewed hard on my foot. Bad day, that. Near bled out. Massuh Cobb had the doctor take the leg off, jus' so. No use for dem hounds, no suh. It ain't jus' the hounds that keeps me close to home. See heah, suh."

The man turned in the chair, one hand pulling up his loose shirt, his back now bare. Sherman stared at the marks, welts, old scars crisscrossing the man's black skin.

"The cavalry did that to you?"

The shirt came down again, the old man facing Sherman. "No, suh. That'd be Lucky. Boss man for Massuh Cobb. Massuh Cobb, he's a good man, most often. Don' care much for Lucky. He's done gone, too."

Hitchcock leaned forward, closer to the old man. "You mean this Lucky fellow whipped you. He's the foreman, then?"

The old man shrugged. "Calls him what you like. He's the one wid the whip. You find him, I'd be mighty pleased you tell me about it."

Hitchcock looked at Sherman, furious outrage in his voice. "Sir, this is everything I've ever heard. The cruelty against these people is—"

Sherman held up his hand. "Enough, Major. We know our duty here. What's your name, old man?"

"Henry, suh. Or Buck. I gots a few names."

Nichols spoke up now, hesitant, soft words. "What'd your mama call you?"

The old man looked at Nichols with a soft smile. "Wish I'da knowed that, suh. Not never seen what you'd call my mama. Old Bess cared for me, till she done gone to the Lawd."

Sherman was growing impatient with this, said, "Gentlemen, let this man be. We don't need any lessons here on the curses of slavery. Old man . . . Henry. You have something to eat?"

The man hesitated, pointed to one corner of the cabin. "My boy, Franklin, done put some bacon in de flo. It's your'n, I suppose, you need it."

Sherman shook his head. "No, it's yours. We have plenty. I'll not leave anyone to starve behind us. We'll be here tonight, out of your way at dawn." He paused. "Where's your boy now?"

The old man stared hard. "You certain you'd be Genil Sherman now, ain't that so?"

"I'm Sherman."

"Franklin's out yonder, in de fields. Hidin' low. We done been fooled once, by cav'ry sayin' they was Yankees. We called out to 'em, **hally-yoo**. Then they done come with de bullwhips." He paused, looked down, then over to the fire, a shower of sparks from a settling log. "Dey whupped Franklin good. Kicked him till he couldn't breeve. If I'da had the whip, I'da kilt me a man that day. Franklin had a knife, and I prayed to the Lawd he not try nothin'. De Lawd answer. Franklin done lived that day. But he ain't gonna be whupped no mo. Scares me when he talks like dat. He'll be heah, when he sees you is Yankees fo' sho. He never gon' believe I seen Genil Sherman, that you done been in this here house. He thinks I'm addled anyways."

Sherman ignored the others, could see now that this man had more behind his eyes than Sherman usually saw. "I don't think you're addled. I think you know how to help us. Rebel cavalry is close by, right?"

The old man nodded. "Out past dem trees. Dey's a deep cut, a crick. Dey's hidin' dere, mebbe. Come outten de dark like ghosts. You be careful, Genil Sherman, suh. Dey be comin' for you, fo' sho.'"

Sherman smiled. "Don't you worry about that. We'll take care of any ghosts that come out of these woods. They don't have enough bullwhips to scare my boys."

The door opened, the cold air blowing in, and Sherman saw Dayton, red-faced from the cold.

"Sir, begging your pardon, but there's a grand house up the road a piece. There's a few officers there now, but I would suggest, sir, it might be a bit more comfortable as a headquarters."

The old man pointed toward Dayton. "I done tole you! Massuh Cobb's house. You go on dat ways. Dat house be fine. Bluecoats done been through dere all day, but you's be welcome, too, I reckon." The man smiled the gap-toothed grin again. "Dat would be a fine happenin', ain't it now? Massuh Cobb makin' way for Genil Sherman. De Lawd done His work heah, dat's for sure."

Sherman rolled the name through his head. "Cobb. That's Howell Cobb? The governor?"

The man kept the smile wide. "One and the same, Genil, suh."

Sherman glanced toward the officers. "Well, my apologies to you, sir. We'll be moving on. Some of my people will wish to use your fire. No harm will come to you, I'll see to that. Your boy, neither."

"I knows, suh. De Lawd done sent you heah."

The tears came again, and Sherman felt embarrassed, couldn't leave the old man with such thoughts. "I'm not here from God, old man. Just President Lincoln."

The old man wiped his eyes, sat again, still the smile. "One's good as t'other, suh."

Cobb's house was everything Sherman expected, a grand mansion overlooking a vast plantation, wide fields where a bountiful crop of corn and cotton had long been harvested. But the barns and outbuildings were mostly intact, showing only hints of vandalism from the foragers who had certainly been through earlier. Even now, another band of those men were moving up from the road, a handful of wagons, coming from the column marching behind Sherman. They had their orders, followed them as Sherman watched through the tall window, loading up as much as the wagons would hold. He watched for a long minute, the darkness settling on the scene, the fire in a wide stone hearth behind him reflected on the glass. He turned, the officers watching him, could smell the cooking of some kind of meat, saw Nichols emerging from a back room, holding a newspaper.

"This is Cobb's place, all right. Found linens with

his name on 'em, one silver spoon on the floor in the dining room. Probably dropped by a thieving forager. There's engraving on a teapot, same as this. 'HC.' I talked to some of the slaves. They say this place is called Hurricane. And, General, it seems he keeps souvenirs. There's a newspaper here from Macon, mentions a speech he gave, not so long ago. Seems 'General' Cobb is calling on all the good men of Georgia to attack us from every direction."

There was laughter, the half-dozen officers enjoying the moment, the warmth of the fire, each man holding a cup of something Sherman assumed was whiskey. Hitchcock was moving toward him, holding his own tin cup, held it out toward him.

"A taste, sir? Not too awful, considering. Mighty sweet, though."

Sherman took the cup, sniffed, the raw power of the alcohol stabbing through his nostrils. He sipped slowly, the sweet sugary liquid burning its way down his throat. He took a breath, let it out, took another sip. "Corn whiskey. Had this in Tennessee, once in a while. Probably the best they've got in these parts. Only reason why Cobb would have it in his house. Probably makes it himself." He sipped again, handed the cup to Hitchcock, who seemed anxious to have it back. "Don't worry, Major, I'm sure they have more."

"Um, no, sir. That was the last bottle. The bummers made it through here pretty early today, cleaned out most everything worth having." He looked at Nichols. "I guess what they couldn't haul away, they just dropped."

"You'll survive, Major. They grow a great deal of corn in this country, and only **eat** some of it."

Behind Sherman, boots on the hard floor, a voice, Major McCoy.

"Sir, Captain Heaney is here, from General Howard."

Sherman looked toward the door, saw Heaney, a short, stocky man, the man Howard used most often to convey messages. Sherman liked the man, always a smile, eager to do the work, something Sherman appreciated in his own aides. Heaney stepped in briskly, held up a salute, which Sherman returned, but there was no smile this time, no paper in Heaney's hand.

"Something wrong, Captain?"

"My apologies, sir. The ride was difficult. But General Howard insisted that you be informed immediately. There was a good scrap today, sir, the town of Griswoldville."

Sherman felt that familiar sting of alarm, as though something awful was coming. "What kind of 'scrap,' Captain? How bad?"

Heaney stood firm, took a breath, said, "General Walcutt's brigade was engaged completely. The enemy had a strong force. Except . . ."

Sherman had no patience for this, took a step toward the man, felt his fingers locking up into fists. "Except **what**?"

"Sir, General Walcutt made a good fight of it. He held his position against superior numbers, and drove them away."

"Then what's so damn serious, Captain?"

"Sir, General Howard insisted I inform you of the casualties. Not ours, I mean. General Walcutt reports the loss of barely a hundred men. But the enemy sustained heavy losses, sir. Several hundred."

The men at the fire had been silent, but broke into cheers now, the cups raised. Sherman kept his stare on Heaney, saw nothing there to cheer about.

"Is General Howard not in a celebratory mood, Captain?"

"Oh, certainly, sir. He offered his respects to General Walcutt, no doubt. But sir, General Howard wishes me to inform you that those casualties, the rebels . . . well, they weren't really soldiers, sir. They were boys mostly, some old men, too. General Walcutt reports that his men took possession of the field, and found no regulars at all. The dead and wounded were a tragic sight, sir."

"Dead rebels are never a tragedy, Captain!"

Sherman looked toward the voice, one of Jeff Davis's staff officers, already staggering from the effects of the whiskey. Sherman turned again to Heaney, said, "What does General Howard know of those troops?"

"They had to be local home defenses, sir. Militia, as it were. The general is pleased with General

Walcutt's victory. But General Howard will not celebrate the death of boys, sir."

The men at the fire were more subdued now, wilting under Sherman's seriousness. Sherman respected Howard as much as any commander he had, knew he was devoutly religious, would never resort to empty bravado. He looked toward the increasingly drunken officers. And, he thought, he'd never tolerate **this**.

"No, Howard wouldn't celebrate anyone's death. They were militia, though. No doubt about that?"

"Yes, sir. Certainly, sir."

Sherman stared away now, toward the darkened window, nothing to see outside. He imagined the scene, a flood of untrained troops, charging with flags unfurled and manic screams into the well-positioned guns of a veteran enemy. So now, he thought, that field is covered with so many gallant corpses. **Boys**.

"There's a military academy in Macon, right?"

"Yes, sir. I believe so, sir."

Sherman ignored the men at the fire, who were beginning to ignore him, engulfed in their own celebration. He stepped closer to the window, stared at his own reflection, a dark silhouette. There were too many of those kinds of fights, he thought. Young men rushing forward full of piss, enjoying it, all of that excitement. They thought they were going to destroy the enemy in one mad rush, until the guns started. Until the blood came. And none of them

ran away, you can be sure of that. Too young to
be scared, the foolishness of the inexperienced. So,
they had their wonderful taste of glory. Until they
started to die.

He did not look at Heaney, his mind still far away,
the question emerging, and he said, "Walcutt's men
have repeating rifles?"

"I believe so, sir."

Sherman nodded toward the darkness, another
horror for boys who know nothing of war. "Hope
his men know how to use them. Never thought
those things would make much difference. The
damn cavalry crows about how valuable those rifles
are, but when a man has a single shot, he takes his
time, aims, finds a target. A man has a half-dozen
shots, he fires them all, quick as he can. I've seen
that too many times. Waste of ammunition, doesn't
hit a thing. Makes a hell of a racket, though. Maybe
that'll scare hell out of the enemy. That's something,
I guess."

"Yes, sir. I suppose so, sir."

Hitchcock was standing to one side, his empty
cup hanging limply in his hand. He moved closer to
Sherman, away from the noise from the men at the
fire. "Sir, if they ventured out of Macon with militia,
that has to mean it's all they had. They wouldn't hold
their veterans back."

Sherman looked at him, brought himself back
to the room, the heat from the wide hearth swallowing him. His eye settled on Hitchcock's head,

still no hat to cover the man's mess of hair. "I see you're learning, Major. The rebels finally figured out we weren't going after Macon. If there's any real army left down there, they'll be scrambling out of there like rats, finding some good ground, someplace where they'll wait for us. It's the only plan that would make sense, the only plan that might actually work. But I haven't told **this** army exactly where we're going, so they don't know, either. No matter who's out there, they can't stop us if they don't know what we're doing." He paused, the thought of that lifting his spirits, the image of the fight at Griswoldville swept away. He felt a burst of energy, a slight stir in his brain from the corn whiskey. He smiled at Hitchcock, said, "That's the **fun** of it, Major. The enemy's guessing, stabbing in the dark. They've got cavalry lurking in shadows trying to learn what we're up to, and so far, the only fight they can make is no fight at all." He clenched his fists, rolled the cigar rapidly along his teeth. "That's why I do this job, and why Grant lets me do it my own way." He pulled the cigar from his mouth, tossed it toward a brass spittoon, perfect aim. He pulled a fresh cigar from his coat and handed it to Nichols, who moved quickly to the fire, lit it in the low flame. Nichols returned, and Sherman stabbed the cigar into his mouth, pulled hard, felt the hot smoke drifting all through his mind, his thoughts.

He turned to Heaney again, had already forgotten about the short man, who waited patiently, his demeanor pleasant, obedient. "Tell General Howard I congratulate him for his progress, and for General Walcutt's triumph. Keep his columns drawn up as tightly as he can, and avoid any significant confrontations. Wheeler's cavalry is all around us, so remain vigilant. Oh, hell, Howard knows that. But he needs to be aware that what the rebels tried to do to him today was an act of desperation. Or just blind stupidity. Both can be dangerous. We don't know who's leading those boys to their deaths, but no doubt, they'll try again. Damned fools."

Hitchcock seemed uncomfortable now, and Sherman said, "Something to say, Major?"

"Well, sir, I just . . . if they're sending boys and old men to fight us, I can understand why General Howard would not celebrate. Boys might be foolish, but dying in a hopeless fight . . ."

"It's not the militia who are the fools, Major. It's the men leading them. The blood belongs to **them,** anyone who claims the authority to kill his own people without any good purpose."

The thought rushed into his brain, and he called out, the officers bleary-eyed, some effort to turn toward him. "Are we certain this home belongs to Howell Cobb? Governor and 'General' Cobb?"

He saw nods from the sleepy faces, Nichols speaking: "Quite so, sir. It was confirmed by the slaves."

Sherman looked again at Hitchcock. "Politicians who become generals. That's who started this war, and that's who bears the blame for the death of boys." He turned again to Nichols. "Major, send word to General Davis. When his corps completes their march through this place, tell him to burn everything, every structure that's standing. Spare nothing."

Hitchcock said, "Sir, what of the old man . . . the slaves? Their cabins?"

Sherman felt a tug of frustration, couldn't escape the old man's emotions. "They'll likely leave here. Can't control the men once they get their lust up for a fire." He saw the despair on Hitchcock's face, the silent protest. "Major, we can't be that careful. It just has to be that way. I'm not going to stand around and watch every man with a torch." He paused, a new thought, the old man's missing leg. **Hounds**. "If it makes you feel any better, Major, pass out the order that we shoot every damn hound dog we find."

Hitchcock seemed surprised at the order, nodded. "Yes, sir. That ought to make those people rest easier."

"I'm more concerned how much 'easier' we can make it for this army, Major. I want a knife stuck in the hearts of these people. Burn it all, everything that has value. If that son of a bitch Cobb doesn't have a conscience for killing children, perhaps he needs a different kind of lesson in **pain**."

CHAPTER NINE

FRANKLIN

HURRICANE PLANTATION, NEAR
MILLEDGEVILLE, GEORGIA—
NOVEMBER 23, 1864

He had no idea how late it was, knew from the moon it had to be after midnight. He couldn't stop shivering, crept slowly toward the row of cabins, eyes on the vast field of campfires, shelter-halves in long lines spread out in every open place. More than one guard had crossed his path, but there had been no trouble, those men seemingly staring right past him, as though his dark skin made him invisible in the chilly night air. But he was still anxious, the long hours hiding in the swampy ground stripping bare his nerves, the animal instinct for danger. Now, as he moved back toward the cabins, he tried not to seem elusive, as though on some furtive mission, and walked upright, a slow, even pace, always with his eyes on the cabin at the far end of the row.

He moved to the closest cabin now, the home of the Pitts family. Old Billy Pitts was allowed to share a home with his wife and their infant son, a gesture seen by some as generous. Franklin saw the arrangement as little more than a miniature breeding ground, where Pitts could father an addition, and many more, to the Cobb family of slaves. But that kind of talk was never tolerated, not even by his own father, and so Franklin kept it to himself, a habit he had learned, taught most effectively by the bullwhip of the foreman, Lucky.

The cabin was dark, the family there certainly asleep. No, he thought, they won't leave. They're too scared. Pitts has a baby, after all, and the cavalry will rip the child right out of their arms if he gives them the chance. He moved past the next cabin, dark as well, the home of the four men that Lucky called the "monkey boys." Franklin had worked beside them for several years now, the youngest of them his own age, the others older. They were large, broad-chested, the kind of men who brought the higher bids at the slave market. Franklin could remember when they arrived, silent, angry, no one even sure if they spoke English. But gradually one, then the next had begun to open up in the quiet of the cabins, tales of tedious journeys, the loss of a wife, then another, the men now certain to live out their lives working the fields with little chance of ever knowing the affection of a woman of their own. They spoke of a mother, something Franklin had only imagined, a woman to care for the injuries, to soothe the vicious pains dealt out by the overseers, the bloody bites from the dogs. Franklin's own mother had died giving him birth, a story that even now could bring emotion from his father. When he was young, any questions about his mother would throw the man into deep sobs, the worst sounds a boy could hear. Until the leg.

The boy had seen all of it, the attack by the hound, a sadistic beast who kept the slaves in the fields by sheer terror. Franklin had been barely twelve, sent to work beside Henry when the master believed the child old enough to haul the baskets, to dig with the spade. Henry had protested, a father's outrage at the abuse of his son, a disastrous mistake. Lucky responded by unleashing the dog, and Henry had reacted in the worst way possible, by running. The dog had toppled the old man like a cornstalk, a ripping clamp on his ankle, the animal's head whipping back and forth as the blood poured out on soft soil. Franklin's screams had spread across the wide fields, the boy's horror slicing through the heat of a July day, bringing other slaves closer, curious, just as horrified. But their helplessness was absolute, no

one daring to grab for the dog, all of them knowing there could be no aid, no one questioning the
punishment, to stand up to Lucky at all. When the
dog was finally pulled away, the boy had run to his
father with more screams, had seen the awful damage, the lower leg ripped to sinews below the knee,
the blood unstoppable, flowing over the boy's arms
as he tried to wrap small hands over the worst part
of the wound. But then Lucky had come, a dirty
cloth tied tight, the bleeding stopped, and the others who watched accepted what they all knew, that
Henry was valuable property, that Lucky, after all,
would answer to the master, and the master was
tight with his money.

The master, Cobb, had come soon after, and
Franklin had heard the argument with the doctor,
the medical man with no interest in caring for one
of **them**. But Cobb's influence prevailed, the doctor kneeling low, ripping away the cloth, the saw
slicing through the leg bone with a sound Franklin
still heard in his dreams. Henry had been given a
swig of what the boy guessed to be whiskey, but his
father could not ignore the pain dealt out through
the carelessness of the doctor's work. Those sounds
were there as well, the father's desperate screaming,
even now, deep in some hollow place in his son's
brain.

Franklin had grown into a young man holding
tightly to the memories of that horror, a promise to
himself that if he was to remain forever at the Cobb

plantation, the opportunity would come one day. He would kill the dog, then kill Lucky, and since the price was his own head, then he would wait until Henry was dead, would never let the old man hear any cries or see the blood that Franklin carried in his own veins.

He moved past the narrow gaps between the cabins, stared into the darkness, could never escape the terror of the dog, who seemed to attack the black men for sport. Even with the Yankees about, the dog could be anywhere at all, waiting only for him, to complete the job he had begun when the beast took the old man's leg. Franklin sensed that the dog knew he was a threat, that one day there would be opportunity for Franklin to set things right, but the dog was old now, had no fear of him, would watch the men working the ground, carrying the baskets, all the while watching Franklin with a look that dared the man to make good on his vow. It was the same with Lucky, the man's hideous smile opening across a slit of dark teeth, one hand always on the bullwhip coiled at his belt. There were other overseers as well, men with big mouths who smelled of whiskey, who seemed to fear their own foreman as much as the slaves did. It was another fantasy Franklin kept alive, that one day the dog would turn on **them,** an act of God's justice. But the fantasy was only that, the dog seemingly eager to obey the commands of any white man, while holding a special viciousness for the slaves.

He heard voices now, another cabin, firelight
through the lone window, a surprise. He peered
in carefully, saw men in blue coats, no one else.
The cabin was occupied by Gordon and Sam, older
men, and a pair of boys in their teens, new to the
plantation. But there was no sign of anyone but
the soldiers, and Franklin felt nervous, wondered if
they had carried out their plan to run away. Lucky
and the overseers had gone away abruptly, as the
first of the blue soldiers appeared. These men had
reacted with outright glee, backslapping joy, as they
pledged to join the vast horde of "Missuh Lincom's
boys." He hesitated at the window, a half-dozen soldiers huddled close by the fire, a conversation about
the march. He backed away, turned toward his own
cabin, saw firelight there as well, no surprise, the
old man not needing to be up so early, unable to
work the fields. And so, while Franklin fought to
find sleep, the old man would stir, hobbling around
the small cabin fiddling with some chore, something to keep him busy. Franklin had thought of
moving to another cabin, but that would require
some kind of perverse permission from Lucky, and
Franklin would never speak to the foreman unless
spoken to first. Even then there would be nothing
more than a polite response, his head down, hands
at his chest, an act of humility that stirred a storm
of anger in his gut.

"Hey! You, boy. What you about?" He jumped
at the voice, turned, saw a bayonet, the sleek blade

reflected in the firelight. "I said, what you about, boy? You got business out here? I think you don't."

He assumed the pose, his head down, had no idea how to respond. He had barely spoken to any white man but the overseers. "I'm just walkin', sir. I live there, with the old man."

"Well, boy, you get on home. No army business for you to be worrying about."

"Yessir. Thank you, sir."

He still eyed the bayonet, couldn't see the man's face clearly, but the blue uniform held his gaze, brass buttons, his eyes moving back to the point of the bayonet.

"Go on, boy. I'll not hurt you. Just don't need no spying going on here."

Franklin turned quickly away, deliberate steps toward the cabin. He reached the door, was surprised to see another soldier, the man as surprised to see him.

"Whoa, there, darkie. What you doing here?"

"My home, sir. My papa is inside. One leg."

"Well, there's some officers in there, and they might not care for company. The old man your father, then? Strange old coot. Makes a fellow laugh. Even General Sherman liked him pretty good."

"Can I see him, sir? I live here. A soldier with a bayonet told me to go to bed. That's right here."

"All right, go on in. But it's a mite crowded. Damn, but you smell like the swamp. They toss you out of there, find you a creek and wash off.

Course, you'uns seem all to smell like that. Comes with the hide, I guess."

"Yes, sir. I'll keep to myself."

The guard pushed open the door, and Franklin blinked through the light of the fire, saw the white faces turning toward him, no expression, one man with gold straps on his shoulder, older, sitting in the lone chair.

"What you want, boy?"

"I lives here, sir. The old man there, my papa."

He saw the old man sitting up now, from a matted blanket on the floor. "My Gawd, Franklin! I done gib you up fer dead. These heah is Genil Sherman's boys! Dey done chased the massuh clean away."

The soldiers ignored him now, and he moved closer to his father, knelt, felt the old man's hard hands in his, spoke softly, "You sure, Papa?"

"Sure as sunrise! You done give me the frights somethin' awful, runnin' off. It's aw right now. Everythin' be aw right."

Franklin sat close beside his father, felt a sudden wave of exhaustion, hadn't slept in more than two days. He lay flat, stretched his back on the hard floor, one arm folded behind his head. He stared up, the crude roof, rough-hewn beams, heard low talk from the soldiers, who seemed to be cautious with their words.

Franklin rolled over slightly, looked at his father. "General Sherman. You see him?"

"Yep! Hee! Seen him raht heah. Done talked to

him. This is de Lawd's work, Franklin. Mebbe now you can work dese fields fer yer own sef. Dere's happy times comin'. You got no need to run off'n fer dese boys."

Work the fields. He tried to feel the old man's excited optimism, but the weariness was overwhelming him, the hard floor softening beneath him, like some thick, deep mattress, feathers and layers of blankets. He spoke, low soft words, "I ain't gonna work no damn fields, Papa. There's more to this world than dirt."

"Huh? What you say?"

He didn't answer, his voice trailing away, the sleep pouring through him, the heat from the fire soothing, cradling him, no energy for words, thoughts rolling through his mind, what he had already seen, a vast sea of blue soldiers.

He awoke with the soldiers, the first man rising from Franklin's own straw mattress. Franklin watched him in dark silence, the man stumbling slowly toward the dull light that came from the coals in the small hearth. The man leaned low, stirring the ashes with an iron rod, but the fire was done, the man cursing. He stood upright, stretching his back, one foot prodding another of the soldiers.

"Rise up! The camp's up and moving! Let's find some coffee."

The man sat up, another curse, said, "Dang it all, Captain, we shouldn't have been up so late. It five o'clock yet? We in some kind of hurry to get . . . where? Ain't no one told me yet where we're marching to."

"And they ain't gonna. You go right on and tell Uncle Billy how he needs to tell you all about his plans. I'll sit back and watch while the guards haul your hind end to the stockade."

The man rose to his knees, sneezed, then again, the captain standing tall above him.

"Don't you try and tell me you're sick, Lieutenant. Not hearing that. Ohio's a heap colder than anything they got down here. Get up. Wake Hankins. Hey! Ugly! Up and moving! Now!"

The third man rose silently, the closest to Franklin, glanced toward the two black men, still said nothing. All three men were on their feet now, coats and hats gathered up, the captain at the door, pulling it open, the blast of cold wiping away the last hint of warmth from the dead fire. Franklin rolled over, fought through the stiffness in his back, rubbed a rough hand on his arm, working the hard muscle, the limb that had been his pillow. He looked at the shadowy form of his father, the old man unmoving, thought, He can sleep through thunder and lightning. No need to wake him up now.

Franklin stood, eyed the last hints of light from the ashes, thought of the woodpile outside the cabin. He moved out through the door, absorbed the numbing cold, stepped to the side of the cabin. The light was faint, sunrise not for a while yet, but he could see clearly enough. The woodpile was gone. He looked out to the distant fires, the Yankee army coming alive, warming itself with fence rails and tree limbs, and, of course, the woodpiles from the slave cabins. He slipped back inside, rubbed his arms together, closed the door, saw the old man sitting up.

"Dey done gone?"

"Yeah, Papa. I suppose the army's got plenty to do. They're in the enemy's own ground. I guess it's smart of them to be careful."

"Dere's bacon in de floor. Genil Sherman done made sho we got 'nuf to eat. I didn't say nothing to dose boys dere. Dey not as kindly as Genil Sherman."

Franklin looked toward the corner of the cabin, moved that way, knelt, raised up a loose floorboard. He lifted the cloth bundle, the smell reaching him, a dull rumble in his gut, raw hunger. He unwrapped the bacon, didn't hesitate, took a hard bite.

"Heah, boy, let's cook dat. It'd be better."

"There's no firewood. Soldiers took it all."

The old man said nothing, and Franklin pulled out a small knife, sliced a corner off the bacon, reached it out to the old man.

"Here. Eat this. Best thing I ate in days."

"Only ting you et, most likely. Where you go off to?"

"The swamp. The cypress hole I used to play in when I was little. Seen some cavalry out that way, kept my head down. Those boys seemed as jumpy as me, trying to watch the Yankee camps and all. Wish't I'd a had me a musket."

"Don' talk dumb, boy. They'da strung you up."

Franklin knew his father was right, thought now about the cabin down the way, soldiers, no sign of Gordon or Sam. "What you know about those boys down the way? Looks like Gordon's gone. Rest of those four, too."

"Don' know nothin' and you best not, neither. Always the trouble wid you, Franklin. You ask questions, wanna know stuff. Massuh Cobb done let you learn to read, and it's blowed up your head. Just take it like it is, boy."

He thought of Cobb, that day long ago, when Franklin was barely five. It had been Cobb himself who came to the cabins, the teacher in tow, a man who carried books and paper. The lessons had been long and unforgiving, but the teacher was nothing like Lucky, had shown patience, seemed to actually care that the few black children learn to read. The Bibles had come next, of course, a heavy dose of religion, the teacher doing the duty that Cobb had assigned him, planting the seeds of a civilized life into the slave children. Franklin had adored the teacher, had seen a kindness in the man that no white man had ever shown him. But when the job was complete to Cobb's satisfaction, the teacher had moved on, and in his place had come the Sunday school teacher. There was little kindness in that man, the lessons full of terror for what God would do to them if they ever sinned. Franklin still wasn't certain just what kind of sin he might have committed, wondered if the white men understood that any better than he did. But those seeds were planted as well, a healthy fear of the devil, an eternity in a hell that seemed to stretch beyond the imagination of a child.

And so Franklin had stopped fearing the lessons, had instead read the Bible just to read, had soaked up the stories mainly from the Old Testament, an angry God who punished the enemy, who chose his favorites and helped them slaughter the rest. It had been intensely curious to him if the slaves were the enemy, if God had put them to work for the white man, punishing them for some misdeed that had happened long ago. But there was no religion in the cruelty of Lucky, in the slobbering jaws of the dog. If there was a true devil, Franklin had begun to wonder if he had seen him, in the face of the foreman. And if there was a true hell, had Franklin felt just a bit of that from the hard slap of Lucky's bullwhip? Those thoughts rolled through him in the fields mostly, the endless hours of handwork, whether the corn or the cotton. He had wondered about the others, if these kinds of thoughts festered in them as they did in him, if any of the older men could read at all. The women had been kept mostly in the house, doing work that Franklin couldn't guess. He saw them once in a while, a carriage taking the white girls to town, the black girls carrying the bags. The carriage was driven by an older slave, a man called Albert. Albert stayed close to the Cobb mansion, was never in the fields, another question for Franklin. Why was he different? Would the old man do that job one day? He glanced at his father now, sitting in the chair, staring into dark ashes. He can't do much else. They know that. But he can drive a carriage.

"You seen Albert?"

The question seemed to surprise the old man. "Nah. Massuh left, Albert wid him. The gals, too. Whole house done gone off. Genil Sherman go dere las' night. Slept in Massuh's bed, I bet. Dat put a smile on dis ole man's face, fo' sho.'"

"Lucky's gone, too?"

"I done tole you dat las' night. Dey done runned off when de Yankees come."

Of course they did, he thought.

He felt his brain waking up, the bacon sitting hard in his stomach. "I'm going outside. It's gettin' light. I wanna see the Yankee camp."

The old man seemed to jump, pointed his finger. "Don' you go close to none of dem! Dey got no use for you'uns. It be time to go on to de fields."

Franklin stared at his father, felt a jolt of concern. "Papa, there's no work to do. The master's done gone. No crops to tend."

"Don't make no matter! You gots to stay out of de way! Dey all be back. Cav'ry come, too. You keep to where you need to be! Stop thinkin' so much!"

Franklin stared at the old man, saw raw fear on his face, heard the tremble in his voice. He understood now that the old man would never leave this place, that no matter what the Yankees were here to do, the old man was just like Billy Pitts, his family too afraid of what might happen next, too afraid of anything different than they had ever known before.

"You're wrong, Papa. It don't matter if Master Cobb comes back. The Yankees have changed everything. There's a war been going on, and if General Sherman is here, it's because Master Cobb's people are losing. Look outside. Look how many of them there are. Thousands, in every direction. The cavalry's too scared to do anything to 'em, and that ain't gonna change. I seen barely a hundred horsemen in the swamp. That's all. A hundred. In the back cotton field, there's a hundred Yankee horses eatin' Master Cobb's corn. Hundreds more all over their camps. And the foot soldiers. Papa, there's flags spread out over that big cornfield like it's some kind of celebration. Only they ain't celebratin' nothing. They're going to work. They're going after Master Cobb and whatever army he's done run off to." He paused, saw the old man shake his head. "I'm not addled, Papa. And if the Yankees have come, it's because Lincoln sent them. We're gonna be free. That's the first thing that's gonna change."

"Ain't no talk like dat in dis house. Massuh Cobb's been good to you. To all us."

"Papa, Master Cobb sits up in that big house, and sends Lucky out here to mind what we do. What happened to your leg?"

He regretted the question, but the old man didn't react, kept his stare on the dead fire.

"Dey all be back. You be goin' back to de fields. It's de way. It's de only way."

Franklin lowered his head, knew this was an argument he couldn't make, understood now that the old man was simply too afraid of what **change** might mean. "I'm sorry, Papa. I don't know all that's happenin' in this war. But I got to see it for myself. I got to know what's out past these dirt fields. You said General Sherman was sent here by the Lord. Well, I don't know about that. But if there's more for us colored folks than being scared of some dog, or settin' still while some white man holds the whip . . . well, no sir. This army's gettin' ready to march on, that's for sure. I'm sorry, Papa. But I'm going with them."

CHAPTER TEN

SHERMAN

MILLEDGEVILLE, GEORGIA—
NOVEMBER 23, 1864

He saw the smoke first, the usual scene as his advance foragers pushed ahead of the army into every town they had passed. But this was different, Sherman and his staff riding with an edgy sense of the important, as though this day, and this march, would be something different, something more meaningful.

Sherman had been careful with his orders, had sent specific word to Slocum that the state capital not be laid waste, at least not until Sherman had examined the military objectives that the rebels might have left intact. But it was routine now that the men who led the way took far more liberties with his instructions than even their officers could control. As the first column of black smoke came into view, he was annoyed, knew that the complete destruction of Milledgeville would be a stain on his reputation not only in Richmond, but in Washington as well. Symbols still mattered, whether Sherman cared for that or not. And with Georgia sliding further beneath the boots of his army, the necessity of obliterating symbols became meaningless. This was still a war, the enemy capable of inflicting a deadly surprise, and no matter the soaring morale of his troops, Sherman couldn't avoid the nagging fear that somewhere out there, a few miles ahead or along some distant river, the rebels had somehow created a significant barrier to block his way. If their defenses were strong, as they had often been around Atlanta, the cost in casualties would blunt the enthusiasm Grant had offered him. If Grant lost confidence in Sherman's plan, all of Washington might react with loud condemnation, a far cry from the hopes Sherman still held in his fantasies that when this was over, there would be great raucous celebrations, with himself at the head of some glorious victory parade. It was a tonic for the other fantasies, the dark gloom that he could not avoid, infuriating doubts: that there would yet be some calamity he could not predict.

Sherman had never escaped that private war, but

Grant had done all a commander could to provide Sherman the crucial spark of confidence, the marvelous gift of pushing forward his strategies on his own, so far from the eyes of Washington, from the telegraph wires of the newspapermen that Sherman considered little more than traitors. But still, the shakiness inside him would come, annoying bouts of neuralgia, aches in his joints, his arm stiffening even now, a sharp pain in his elbow that he kept to himself. The weakness infuriated him, so much like the shuddering fears that had plagued him since the very start of the war, the panic at Bull Run, his failures at Shiloh, and even the struggle at Chattanooga. Around him, the veteran army seemed to have forgiven him his faults, or even better, they had forgotten all of it, his officers and senior commanders believing that this new campaign to sweep the rebels aside would be carried out with few problems at all. So far the enthusiasm for the march was plainly evident, the men treating each day's progress as one more step toward inevitable victory. The only real conflict with rebel forces had come from scattered cavalry assaults, clearly meant for show, accomplishing little more than keeping Federal skirmishers and rearguard troops on alert. The damage had been minimal, the casualties often resulting from those few men in blue who lagged behind. Many of those lost had been scavengers, seeking loot from the destruction of plantation houses or what treasures might still be hidden in the small towns already passed. For Sherman there was a level of justice in that, no matter how angry his officers had been. Ultimately the stragglers were the responsibility of their commanders, and if any of the men were so undisciplined as to keep their eyes more on booty than on the orderly march, Sherman couldn't help the feeling that those men were receiving their just deserts.

They had started at dawn, a few hours before, and he rode at the head of his staff, the headquarters guard spread out to the front, what had become the daily routine. He could see the fog of their breathing, men and horses both, and he pulled at his own coat, the icy wind still seeping through. The cold had been surprising, but Sherman tried to ignore whatever suffering was going on around him. He knew the South, knew that this kind of weather was temporary, regarded it as more of a nuisance than anything to slow their progress. For now the rains had ended, the roads hardening and the flurries of snow brief, the skies finally opening up to a delicious blue. There had been little to occupy the staff that morning, and so they rode together, silent mostly, few messages coming to him from the corps commanders. Beside him, the color bearer rode just a step back, and on the other side, the always present Henry Hitchcock.

Sherman had begun to appreciate that Hitchcock's observations came from life outside the army, the man only there now because he had suffered from the guilt of being a civilian. Sherman respected the man's conscience, whether or not he always agreed with Hitchcock's lack of enthusiasm for the more difficult parts of army life. He reached for a fresh cigar, thought, The **major** should try the picket line. Especially on a day like this. At least the horse beneath him offers some warmth. Let a rebel take a shot at him from some hiding place and that shivering will get a whole lot worse.

Hitchcock caught Sherman's glance, eased his horse closer, slapped his gloved hands together several times. "I say, sir, it is a brutal morning. Coldest so far, I believe."

"Could be."

"You see those columns of smoke, sir? That has to be the town. Shouldn't we send someone up there and be sure there's not too much mischief going on?"

"I can't stop every act of 'mischief,' Major. We'll be there soon enough. General Slocum's men know their orders. They won't take it too far."

"Can you be certain of that, sir?"

"It's my job to be certain of everything we do, Major."

Hitchcock blew on his hands, useless effort through thick leather gloves. Sherman saw the grime on his gauntlets, unusual, said, "A bit casual today, aren't we, Major? I thought you preferred looking the part of a prim and proper staff officer."

He saw a deliberate shiver in Hitchcock's shoulders,

felt it himself, kept it hidden, and Hitchcock said, "Just too cold this morning, sir. There was a crust of ice on everything in my wardrobe. My trunk was left somewhat in the open, it seems. My uniform and outerwear were regrettably wet. It was a carelessness I will not repeat."

Sherman knew better, had seen McCoy slipping into the headquarters wagon with a look of the kind of devilment befitting a schoolboy. It was custom, whether or not Sherman approved, that the newest member of the staff be the butt of some kind of misplaced humor. McCoy seemed especially prone to that kind of idiocy, something Sherman had usually ignored. But he had begun to depend on Hitchcock for more than the usual staff routine, respected the man's abilities with the pen, his efficiency in transmitting orders where they needed to go. It helped no one if Hitchcock was the most miserable man on his staff. Sherman turned in the saddle. "Major McCoy, here, if you please."

McCoy rode forward, seemed intent on ignoring Hitchcock. "Yes, sir? May I be of service?"

"It seems Major Hitchcock's baggage suffered from the effects of last night's damp cold. I observed a bit of snow."

"Yes, sir. I observed that myself."

"I will have no one on this staff suffer more than myself. Thus, since you seem reasonably comfortable in your coat, I would suggest you offer it to the major. For a while at least, until he stops his infernal shaking."

McCoy seemed to droop, and Sherman knew very well that his officers understood the meaning of Sherman's "suggestions." McCoy knew better than to argue, pulled the coat over his head, had another lighter cloak beneath it, and Sherman waited, watched as McCoy slowly handed the outer garment to the wide-eyed Hitchcock.

"For how long, sir?"

"An hour, I suppose." Sherman looked toward Hitchcock. "You think an hour with a coat that heavy should warm you up a piece, Major?"

Hitchcock eyed McCoy nervously, seemed to understand that Sherman was dishing out some sort of punishment. "Absolutely, sir. My appreciations to the major. Most generous."

McCoy huffed, and Sherman caught the glance, McCoy's acceptance that his little joke had swung against him. Sherman turned toward the front again, called out, for the benefit of the others, "One hour, Major. That should be enough."

There was already a shiver in McCoy's voice, a low, husky response. "As you order it, sir."

Sherman looked to the side, Hitchcock still not certain why Sherman had offered such a gesture. "Warmer, Major?"

"Most certainly, sir. But I fear for Major McCoy's discomfort."

"Don't. You ride with me long enough, you'll find out a great deal about discomfort. One hour, then you give it back to him. After this, you'll be more careful with your baggage. Major McCoy will see to that."

The smoke above the town was drifting off to the east now, caught by the stiff wind, and Sherman studied the skies all across the open ground, another cloud of smoke hanging low to one side. Some plantation, he thought. But so far, no one's burning much more than a barn. Slocum knows what I want. Davis and Williams, too. Any corps commander ignores me . . . The thought drifted away, a waste of energy. They know better. This is too important to leave affairs to . . . what do they call them? Bummers? I'm not in the mood to relieve generals from their responsibility. But if they can't control their people today, if they inflict more damage on Milledgeville than I instruct them, I'll toss them all in the stockade together.

He pushed that away, had no reason to be angry with anyone. It's just this damnable weather, he thought. Louisiana was never this cold. Ellen would say this is God's warning, some kind of sign. Be careful, do nothing evil. He pictured her in his mind, pretty and stern, the pleasant smile rolling into a scolding lecture. It's that Catholic thing, he thought. She loves reminding me how I'm the eternal sinner, and she's destined for glory. Well, there's glory here, too. Just not that kind. If she was here, she'd be telling everyone who'd listen that this cold is punishment from the Almighty, as though I should be reminded that I'm not really in command here. That's an argument I'll never win. His mind drifted, thoughts of Grant. He keeps Julia close by, when he can. I suppose he has his reasons for that. I rather prefer doing things this way. Ellen can stay in some warm safe place and confess my sins for me. Tell the priests how bloody arrogant I am, how this war has made it convenient for me to avoid their sermons. It's the truth, whether she believes it or not. I'd rather fight this war than kneel in her church. I don't need anybody reminding me how fallible I am. Like right now. Damn this cold.

Beside him, Hitchcock moved closer again, and Sherman waited for it, thought, He hates it when I'm quiet. Must think I'm conjuring up reasons to put a musket in his hands.

"No firing this morning, sir. Not yet. The cavalry is having an easy time of it, it would seem."

Sherman didn't require the observation, had learned to ignore the small bursts of distant fire, knew that Kilpatrick's men had fanned out into every farm, every kind of hole where rebels might be staging an ambush. No, he thought, the enemy's pulling back, keeping their distance. Rather they didn't do that. It would be useful to know how many they are, and what they're going to do about this little parade of mine.

He glanced to the side, open fields, a distant

farmhouse, nothing at all like the grand mansion where he had slept the night before. There were blue-coated horsemen there, a cluster of men doing their job, but the silence told Sherman exactly what Hitchcock had observed. No one's home. So, he thought, where might they be?

"Oh, my, sir. These appear to be the enemy's works. All out through the fields there."

They rode past felled trees, a gathering of earth that someone had piled high, clearly meant as a defensive position. Hitchcock seemed to animate, the man's usual show of excitement when he saw something that smacked of combat.

"I would say they chose not to make a stand, sir. These works have not been used at all, from what I can see."

"Nope."

They rounded a bend, the headquarters guard making way, and Hitchcock said, "There it is, sir. Seems we've arrived."

Sherman kept his stare ahead, the larger buildings and church steeples now in full view, the wide streets, the prominent buildings spread along an avenue lined with shops and smaller homes. The smoke was still there, but only a few fires from several blocks away. In front of him, clusters of blue troops began to gather, seemingly watching for him. Hitchcock said, "It seems they're intending to give you another salute, sir. If I may, sir, it's appropriate."

Sherman didn't respond, kept his stare straight ahead, one hand inside his coat, a fist twisting on a brass button, the nervous gesture he tried to hide from anyone else. He felt the tension growing in his gut, his heart beating faster, and he eyed the larger buildings, scanned quickly, saw it now, the Stars and Stripes, waving in the brisk chill, high above the most prominent building.

Hitchcock seemed giddy, his horse responding by dancing to one side, beyond the man's control. Sherman kept his eyes on the large building, heard voices behind him, McCoy, Dayton, the others, telling him what he already knew.

"That must be the State House, sir."

Sherman tried to respond, but there were no words, a sudden choking emotion he clamped down. Hitchcock was there again, the horse brought under control. He heard a low cheer coming from the man, a strange childlike glee, but he knew Hitchcock was right. This was the capital city after all. Since the fall of Atlanta, Sherman's goal had been to subdue Georgia, to crush the spirit of the men who would defend it, and if necessary, to use his army to crush any rebel troops who stood up to him. But there was no resistance here, none of the nagging scattershot firing endured by the cavalry, no sign of rebels, of militia, of anyone to stand in their way.

There were citizens in view now, and Sherman eyed them, saw mostly women, old and young, and along the way, scattered throughout, scores of black faces. The cheering grew louder, aimed at him, at all the officers on horses, what these people would know of authority, of just who commanded the hordes of troops who had preceded these blue-coated officers into the town. He could see what was typical now, that the cheers came only from the slaves, while throughout the crowds, the white faces seemed mostly emotionless, sullen, some staring at him with silent defiance, the only protest the people dared to show in the midst of so much power. From the early campaigns on Southern ground, the cries and calls of the Negroes had surprised him, and even now made him uneasy. Sherman never could quite believe that those people had any real sense of what the war was about, what this army had come to do here. He had no special mission in mind to free slaves, had never thought of this campaign as some glorious act of liberation. His job was the war, to wipe away the rebel army with as much brute force as the task required. But the black people he saw now, as he had seen before, seemed to understand that the men in blue carried with them a different kind of power. Their joy was absolute, spilling out into the street, some of the people held back by the guards. Others made it past, and Sherman felt that first stab of concern, the unavoidable caution that disorder could explode into something unmanage-able, something dangerous. But that fear vanished quickly, and he saw it in their faces, so many smiles.

They came closer, grabbing at his horse, cries and laughter, many calling out the one word he always heard: **Lincoln**.

The troops were cheering him as well, some in formation, guided by officers, and he acknowledged them with a brief nod, tried to push past the increasing throng, his guards doing their best to clear a path along the wide avenue. Hitchcock was close to him now, and Sherman knew he was smiling, would always smile at whatever success flowed through this army.

"First act of this drama well played, sir!"

Sherman didn't look at him, moved the horse with care, past the outstretched hands, the voices, the faces, tears, and toothy smiles. By damn, he thought, we're really here. This is the capital of Georgia.

"Yes, Major. You are correct. The first act is played."

GOVERNOR'S MANSION,
MILLEDGEVILLE, GEORGIA—
NOVEMBER 23, 1864

Sherman paced furiously, waited for his officers to enter, knew only that there had been a considerable ruckus at the State House. The two majors were there now, hesitant, as though expecting Sherman to pounce on them. They came to attention, waited for him to speak.

"What happened? Who did it?"

McCoy glanced at Dayton, both men seeming to hope the other would respond. Finally, McCoy said, "From all accounts, sir, the 107th New York and the 3rd Wisconsin."

"How bad they wreck the place?"

McCoy seemed eager with his answer. "Oh, no, sir. Not at all. There were papers strewn about, of course, but much of that had happened before we arrived. The cavalry had already reported that the legislators and other officials had left the town in some haste, sir. They even hauled away their state seal. Too bad about that. It would have been a nice prize. As it is, we captured no civilians of any import."

"My orders were explicit, Major. The State House shall not be destroyed."

McCoy seemed surprised at Sherman's reaction, and Dayton said, "Nothing destroyed, sir. Certainly not. There was some revelry, at worst. The men had found some spirits. Well, sir, you know how things can get out of hand."

Dayton offered a smile, but Sherman was not amused. "How far out of hand?"

Dayton couldn't help a stifled laugh. "Well, sir, the men engaged in a meeting of the Georgia state government."

Sherman saw smiles on both men, knew they wouldn't make light of his orders, and he couldn't help feeling a hint of their joviality, the heat of his anger softening. The questions rose now, more curiosity than fury. "A meeting?"

"Well, sir, not exactly. They called the legislature into session. Quite a spectacle, sir."

Sherman was confused now. "You said the legislators had left town."

McCoy responded. "Oh, my, yes, sir. Our men deemed themselves capable of substitution. They elected one of the brigade commanders, Colonel Robinson, as president. It was actually quite orderly, sir. One of the newspapermen, Mr. Davis, accepted the position as page, or sergeant at arms, or something appropriate to the event."

Sherman's eyes grew wider. "A brigade commander? There were officers present?"

Dayton nodded, still smiling. "Quite a few, sir. I would say, with all respect, that our men made a most suitable assembly. They passed various ordinances, issued decrees, all quite in step with protocol."

Sherman turned away, paced slowly, his hands behind his back. "Not my protocol, Major. It sounds as though they located more spirits than I was first informed."

McCoy looked down, the joke passing. "Yes, sir. It seems so, sir. Things grew more subdued as the bottles were emptied. Many of the, um, lawmakers settled in for a nap beneath their desks."

Dayton looked at McCoy, then said, "Uh, sir, I do have to mention, that as events proceeded, there were others involved in the festivities."

Sherman knew there was something unsaid in Dayton's description. "Others. Name them."

"Well, sir, the cavalry arrived, and joined in. They added considerable energy to the proceedings."

"Names, Major."

"Um, sir, General Kilpatrick assumed command of the affair. He was most . . . entertaining. At least for the short time we saw him."

Sherman closed his eyes, fought the anger, knew too much of Kilpatrick's ridiculous habits already. He turned toward the men, spoke slowly. "I assume General Kilpatrick was also infused with spirits?"

McCoy tried to stifle the smile again. "Quite so, sir."

Sherman's patience had run dry, and he moved to a tall window, stared out from the mansion, the streets filled with throngs of his troops. "Is General Kilpatrick of any use in his current condition? I mean, right now?"

Dayton said, "I'm not certain what you mean, sir."

Sherman spun toward them, his voice louder. "Is he capable of reporting to me without falling down?"

Dayton stiffened, the joke now over. "I shall retrieve him, sir. I'm certain General Kilpatrick would gladly offer you his report."

"Then go get him. Lay him across his saddle if you have to."

"By all means, sir."

The two men saluted him, then left quickly. Sherman paced again, ignored the scenes outside, stared at the bare floor beneath him. Stripped the place clean, he thought. Their esteemed Governor Brown chooses not only to vacate his home and his state-house, but he decides to take everything that isn't fastened in place. He took his furniture, as though I should not be allowed to sleep in his bed. Does he think I am some sort of barbarian? Well, yes, I sup-pose he does. I shall oblige him, then. I'll sleep in this grand place with my own bedding, no matter that it might soil his perfect floorboards. Perhaps bring the horses inside, allow them to feed in his parlor.

He paced again, felt an odd frustration. What kind of war has this become? We conquer without conquering. Have these people no pride in their own homes? Will they not fight to protect what is theirs? They made such noise over the right to keep their slaves, and now they scamper off and leave them behind, free to move about as they wish. The thought stopped him, and he looked toward the street again, black faces moving with the troops, like some kind of grand party. How much control did they really have over those people? I have never believed the Negro would make a good soldier, or that there is some sort of destiny to him working the fields. Where else did God intend him to be? Ellen would quote scripture, quite sure of that. Her priests would "educate" me, as though a Bible would tell me how to fight this war. He rubbed a hand on his chin. A man should be paid for his labors, and I suppose that's the point. Those damned rebels insist the Negro is happy where he is, suited for this life. Chains and bullwhips. From all I've seen, those people don't seem happy to do anything but leave those damned plantations. That old man at Cobb's plantation . . . Henry, whatever the hell he said. I guess he seemed happy enough. Crazy old bird.

He saw a group of soldiers circling around a pair of black children, the children now starting to dance, some sort of jerking silliness, the soldiers clapping, shouting them on. That old bird might be out there, too, he thought, if not for his leg. Dancing like some dervish, entertaining us with music and some other foolishness. Is that what they do, when they're not at labor? Or is it, maybe, that they're just happy we're here? And how many of them will there be? How many will flock to the roads and follow us to . . . where?

He thought of Mississippi, the Vicksburg campaign, the first time he had marched through the plantation country, the throngs of slaves gathering up in some kind of parade behind the troops. That wasn't too good, he thought. Had to feed them. Still have to. Maybe easier now. This countryside has a good deal more to offer. Nobody's going to starve, no matter what the damned rebel newspapers say. But if there's a fight, if there's something hard in front of us, these damned Negroes are in the way.

So, what then? Protect them? Any of these people bow down to us, then go back to their shacks, some rebel cavalryman will butcher them for disloyalty. So, I suppose it's my job to keep that from happening. That's what Washington will think. Maybe Grant, too. Well, at least we can keep 'em fed.

"Sir, General Kilpatrick."

Sherman turned, curious as to what kind of state his cavalry commander would be in. McCoy stood aside, and Kilpatrick was there now, hard boot steps on the wood floor, a hefty salute. Sherman saw a slight tilt to the man's stance, let it go, returned the salute, said, "I'd have you sit down, General, but our host carried away his chairs. You'll have to endure like the rest of us. You fit?"

Kilpatrick feigned indignation, another slight wobble, said, "I am always fit, sir! Always in your service!"

McCoy stepped closer, said, "Sir, General Slocum is expected presently. He has made his headquarters at the Milledgeville Hotel. I shall inform you when he arrives."

"Fine."

He moved again to the window, his eye caught by a black woman in a flowered dress, a flock of soldiers moving with her as she paraded past. That's either spirits, he thought, or lust. Plenty of both in this army, apparently.

Behind him, Kilpatrick said, "Sir, I wish to report that the rebels have withdrawn any defensive forces

to the east side of the Oconee River, and appear
unwilling to make a stand. I believe we shall have
little difficulty crossing beyond the town. Have you
heard from General Howard, sir?"

Sherman turned, saw the annoying smugness that
always seemed to inhabit Kilpatrick's expression. "If
I require you to know of General Howard's situation, I will inform you. As it is, he's doing much the
same as we are here. Things are mostly quiet in his
front. Rebel cavalry is showing itself in minor skirmishes, but nothing more. I would have thought
your own people would have told you that."

Kilpatrick made an exaggerated nod. "Oh, most
certainly, sir. I regret that we have chased that bantam rooster right out of the country. Truly a shame.
I had hoped to wipe him from the map with one
good stand. My men are prepared to give those
other fellows exactly what they deserve."

Sherman thought, Wheeler. This is like some kind
of game, whose pants carry the heavier load. Knights
in shining armor. Neither one of you is much larger
than a bantam rooster.

"I would expect that General Wheeler's cavalry is
intending to do the same to you. Keep to your vigi-
lance. I do not wish to hear of surprises, General.
Joe Wheeler is capable of causing damage wherever
he goes, including our camps. I will have none of
that."

Kilpatrick seemed wounded, puffed up again.
"With all respect, sir, Wheeler's bandits will not

cause your command, or mine, any trouble. I would take serious exception to anyone who claims differently."

Watch yourself, Sherman thought. Intoxication doesn't excuse insubordination, no matter how much I need you.

"Just do your job, General. And try not to forget that **your** command is also **my** command."

Kilpatrick seemed to ponder that, nodded agreeably. "Of course, sir. I am honored to be in your service."

"Do the job. That's all the 'honor' I require. You'll have orders in the morning. Captain Poe is providing me with maps this afternoon, and I will instruct Generals Slocum and Howard on the routes I intend them to follow. Your men will continue to patrol the army's perimeter, and you will report to me any enemy activity that could be seen as any threat to our progress, or to our supply trains or encampments, wherever they may be. I will instruct you on a route of march that will move you closer to Augusta. I want the railroad between Augusta and Millen destroyed. I have no intention of delaying around this place any longer than is required to bring the army together, and that includes your horsemen."

"Sir, my men will be prepared to ride on the morrow. I shall continue to perform with conspicuous gallantry."

The words were slurred, and Sherman had seen

enough of Kilpatrick for now. McCoy was there again, and Sherman looked past Kilpatrick, said, "Slocum?"

"No, sir, not just yet. However, this boy has requested entrance. He claims to be—"

Kilpatrick spread out his arms, another burst of bombast. "My nephew! Yes, by all means, Major, show him in. I wish him to make the acquaintance of the great General Sherman!"

Sherman winced at the volume in Kilpatrick's voice, saw the boy now, hesitant, peering in, and Kilpatrick wheeled around, grabbed the boy around the shoulders.

"Sir, this is William Kilpatrick, my nephew. All of fourteen and soon to be a hero in your service! My boy, I told you I'd put you in the presence of our commanding general. Pay your respects!"

The boy stared at Sherman, who felt completely uncomfortable.

"I am honored, sir."

The words came out in a nervous stammer, and Sherman ignored the boy, focused on Kilpatrick's annoying expression of pride.

"You brought your nephew along on this campaign? My orders were that no unnecessary personnel accompany this march."

Kilpatrick seemed wounded again, put his hands on his hips, as much defiance as anyone would offer Sherman. "I assure you, General, this fine young boy is destined to make his mark in this army. You'll see!"

The boy stood slack-shouldered, his mouth hanging open, his eyes locked on Sherman. Sherman fought his annoyance, said, "I do not anticipate this war lasting long enough that this boy shall be forced to don a uniform."

Kilpatrick turned serious now, his eyes in a squint, moved a step closer, the air around him ripe with whatever intoxicant he had been drinking. "Oh, sir, I just recalled a matter of utmost importance. I wish to report that we have discovered that the enemy is murdering prisoners. It is an outrage, sir, a moral and human outrage! With your permission, I shall endeavor to return the favor."

Sherman saw the boy lean closer as well, wide-eyed, soaking up Kilpatrick's grotesque report. He understood now, this was Kilpatrick's idea, impressing the boy with his perfect knowledge of all the dastardly deeds the rebels would do. "What prisoners are you referring to?"

Kilpatrick seemed satisfied with the impact of his message, crossed his arms at his chest. "None of my men, of course. I would assume our stragglers. Those gray devils skulk about in the darkness, looking to pluck any poor soul from this army who fails to keep up with his unit. We have found bodies with throats cut, sir. Ghastly, and quite unchristian. I shall make them pay for their wickedness, sir."

Sherman had heard nothing of this kind of atrocity, studied Kilpatrick, wondered if the liquor had inspired exaggeration. "You will do no such thing.

If I am satisfied that Wheeler's men are committing such acts, then I will order the appropriate response." He paused, saw disappointment on Kilpatrick's face. "Am I clear about that, General? My orders will dictate yours."

Kilpatrick glanced back toward the boy, who still nervously eyed Sherman. Kilpatrick seemed disappointed now, his grand show ruined. He lowered his voice, said, "Most clear, sir. I shall keep you informed."

Sherman looked for a chair, the instinctive need to sit down, but there was nothing there. "Why in hell did he take his furniture? Major McCoy, locate a chair from some neighboring house. This is absurd. I'll not sit on the floor with my knees under my chin. General Kilpatrick, have you completed your 'report'?" Sherman didn't wait for a response. "Good. Return to your men. When they are assembled and their mounts are fit, I shall have orders. Until then, perhaps you can show your nephew what a rebel city looks like. And no more **parties,** General."

He took his own advice, left the horse behind, a dozen of his guards keeping a careful lookout on the buildings he passed. Hitchcock had come along, had done a poor job of hiding his displeasure at the raucous behavior of the men who had staged their mock lawmaking

session. Sherman couldn't help feeling that Hitchcock was becoming something of a conscience, had
not been comfortable with the destruction Sherman's men had spread throughout the countryside. Worse, Hitchcock had pushed harder than he
should have by suggesting that Sherman himself
wasn't making much effort to enforce his own re-
strictions on the men. It was subtle, but Sherman
had learned to read the man, could hear it in his reports, a marked disapproval of Sherman's generals,
who weren't completely following instructions not
to lay waste to so much of the countryside. Sherman tolerated Hitchcock's indiscretions, as long as
the man did his job. But Sherman felt little need for
another conscience. He had left his own behind, in
the form of his wife.

They walked with purpose, Sherman insisting on
touring the town, seeing for himself just what the
Georgians considered a suitable place for their capitol. He had passed that building already, a thick,
squat rectangle, the roofline fashioned with what
could pass for battlements, like some kind of Eu-
ropean fortress. So, he thought, where did they go?
Grabbed anything of value and just vanished into
the woods. Or maybe to Augusta. Hardly matters.
There's a good many targets here we'll deal with
anyway.

He moved down a side street, the guards spreading out further, some inspecting the homes that lay
in his path. There were citizens there still, women

mostly, and whether or not they recognized him, they kept mostly silent. Hitchcock moved with more energy, typical, and Sherman said, "What of these people, Major? You see anything special? Anything to justify starting a war?"

"Not certain what you mean, sir."

"Never mind. They're just people. Wrongheaded, no doubt about that. That's my job, you know. Show them that. Their legislature, all those fine-suited gentlemen, scurried out of here like so many mice and left their women behind. Some gallantry in that, wouldn't you say?"

"They certainly assumed we would not harm the women, sir."

Sherman knew he was right, a trait Hitchcock had that was becoming tiresome.

There was commotion ahead, the guards responding quickly, a handful running forward. Sherman waited, had no need to walk into some kind of turmoil, but the guards were looking back at him now, their lieutenant trotting toward him.

"Sir! Come see!"

Sherman hated mysteries, but the young lieutenant was already gone, returning to whatever was drawing the attention of even more soldiers. He led Hitchcock down the street, saw a gathering crowd of men in blue, most of them forming in a wide circle, an officer on horseback now riding up, familiar, one of Jeff Davis's staff. The officer saw Sherman, saluted, said, "Sir! I just heard about them. Look what we have here!"

Sherman pushed past the soldiers, saw now a dozen men, ragged clothes, filthy, thin, some of them on their knees, tears and cries, one man hanging his head, heavy sobs. Sherman moved closer and Hitchcock moved with him, said, "Rebel prisoners?"

One of the men looked up from his knees, stared hard at Hitchcock, then saw Sherman, seemed uncertain, said in a hard whisper, "We're prisoners, sir, but we ain't rebels. We've done made a hell of a march. If this ain't heaven, then please, sir, tell me it's Sherman's army."

Sherman scanned the clothing, hints of blue. "Where did you march from? Wheeler have you?"

The man seemed barely able to speak, shook his head slowly. "Don't know no Wheeler, sir. We heard there was a great army marching 'cross Georgia. We made our way best we could. Couple of us was grabbed up. But we made it, sir. Had to try, and I s'pose the Lord was smiling on us. Unless I'm dreaming, sir, we was able to get here after all."

"From where?"

"Sir, we come from Andersonville."

Sherman let the word drive into his brain, studied the men, and other soldiers around him responded, questions and salutes. Sherman heard Davis's officer order coats for the men, rations, water, anything they might require, and Sherman stood silently, nodded in approval. He stepped forward, put one hand on the man's shoulder, felt bones beneath what remained of the man's shirt. "I'm General Sherman. You made it, son. We'll take care of you."

The man looked up at him, seemed not to believe him, but there were tears on the man's face, and he lowered his head again, both hands flat on the dirt street. "Heaven enough for me, sir."

He had wondered how many more might be wandering the countryside, but there was nothing he could do for them now. The Confederate prison at Andersonville was far to the south, and Sherman knew that if there was to be any liberation, it would have to come later. The men had been taken away, the soldiers receiving them with vengeful pledges, curses toward the rebels. But Sherman wouldn't hear that, not now. His goal had not changed. If there were Federal prisoners to be found along the route, he was pleased for that. But someone else would have the glory, or experience the horror, that might come from smashing down the fences of a place as gruesome as Andersonville was supposed to be. As he continued his tour of the town, he couldn't avoid feeling the man's emotions, what kind of craftiness and determination it had taken for those men to find his army, and just what kind of thankfulness they would feel for him now.

He moved slowly past shops, faces staring at him through curtained windows. I'll not make them fight again, he thought. We'll doctor them, get them fit. I'll take no credit for their liberation. Where are those damned newspaper reporters now? Write about those men, not about me.

Sherman looked ahead, saw another grand building, the streets around it blanketed with debris. Hitchcock moved ahead slightly, the guards standing in place, waiting for Sherman to catch up. Hitchcock said, "What you suppose happened there?"

The question rose up inside Sherman as well, and he saw the guards spreading out in a larger square, doing their job, still watching the surrounding homes. Hitchcock was out in front, began kicking slowly through the wreckage, reached down now, picked up a bundle of papers. He looked toward the main building, held the papers by his side, then back at Sherman, said in a low voice, "My God, sir. It's a library. They destroyed the library."

Sherman walked out into the square, stood surrounded by the remnants of what had once been books. He looked down, scanned the paper, felt a surprising helplessness, a dull ache. He reached down, picked up what was left of a single book, the spine ripped, half the pages gone. He tossed it aside, moved with slow, automatic steps to the entrance of the library, ignored the caution of his guards, stepped inside. There were no soldiers, no one there to offer any sort of explanation, anything of value either stripped away or simply destroyed.

"Did you order this, sir?"

He didn't need Hitchcock, not now, ignored the question. "We must order the officers to be more attentive."

Hitchcock moved past him, farther into the main hallway, bent low, eyeing the ripped pages, scattered manuscripts. Sherman moved back out into the cold sunlight. The breeze was blowing through the papers now, scattering the debris along the street. He pulled out a fresh cigar, turned away from the wind, lit it, stared out to the other buildings nearby. Someone will write of this, he thought. We will be labeled barbarians. He thought of the history lessons, long ago, some classroom at West Point. Did this not happen to Rome? To Alexandria? This is the kind of thing that gives newspapermen goose-flesh, and by God someone will glory in this. Waxing poetic at my expense. Damn them. And damn the officers who cannot control their men.

Hitchcock emerged now, and Sherman wouldn't look at him, knew there was outrage, a sputtering need to condemn those who would create such useless destruction. Sherman wouldn't hear it, said, "Major, return to the Governor's Mansion. I will draft a new order regarding our course of march. The arsenal and any accompanying structures shall be burned. I have been told there is a penitentiary here. That will burn as well. Rail depot, telegraph office." He paused. "Newspaper office."

Hitchcock hesitated, and Sherman looked at him, was surprised to see raw emotion on the man's face.

Sherman turned away, stared out, his eyes rising toward the crystal blue above, his brain pushing away the sight of the destruction. "You have your orders, Major."

Sherman stood for a long moment, rolled the cigar in his hand, made a final glance over the papers now drifting with the breeze. He stepped out into the street, moved away, low words for no one in particular. "Dammit. It's war."

CHAPTER ELEVEN

FRANKLIN

OCONEE RIVER—NOVEMBER 24, 1864

The army had been moving out of town all morning, columns of troops and their wagons, some of those filled with whatever goods the foragers had confiscated from the civilians. The citizens had responded to the march by emerging from their homes, some lining the streets as the formations of troops passed, aware that whatever nightmare the blue soldiers had swept into their lives might actually be ending. For many that nightmare was nothing like they expected. The greatest fears had come from the rumors of what had already occurred, that Sherman's devils had left a vast swath of utter destruction across their state, no home spared, every larder stripped bare, every stick of furniture destroyed. But the marching columns were now moving out of Milledgeville in good order, past guards that manned the entryway to dozens of homes, stern-faced men who had been assigned to prevent any further looting, or any mindless use of the torch. As they passed through, some of the men were calling out to the women who watched them, big words that carried little threat beyond impolite flirtatiousness, even more of them offering a dose of good cheer. The women mostly kept silent, regarding the soldiers with the same contempt they had felt when the men in blue first arrived. Many of the civilians did not understand the level of morale that had spread through the ranks of the soldiers, that the destruction of Milledgeville or any other town was not the reward for these men, but merely one of their tools. The fires that lay in their wake, and those still to come, were mostly aimed at any kind of industry, buildings, or factories that had the potential to provide the Southern armies with any sort of assistance.

It was not up to the officers to explain that to the civilians, and so they usually said nothing at all. But the exaggerated rumors spread far more rapidly, and made a much greater impact on the expectations of the civilians, than the flames themselves ever could. By now the men in blue had marched through far more towns and plantations than most of the people of Milledgeville had ever seen, and when the fires had come, it was often the work of the bummers, heedless to orders, heedless to the kind of decency and tolerance that the officers had been instructed to monitor. The soldiers knew that the greatest reward for this army would come with a victory. Burning a plantation provided short-lived entertainment; hauling away chests of silverware might enrich a man for the short time he could conceal it. But the vast majority of Sherman's troops gave little thought to the question of whether or not Milledgeville should be torched. If fences and barns were dismantled, it was more for the necessity of firewood than any thoughts of revenge. Whatever Sherman's ultimate goal might be, so far the men understood that this march had been one of conquest without the accompanying horrors that so many of the veterans had seen before. Sherman was already respected by his men, and increasingly that respect had evolved into the kind of affection that drives men to accomplish any deed their commander asks of them. Not even the foot soldiers believed that this campaign would continue without some massive effort by the rebels to stop them, but none of those men shared the quiet dread as deeply as their commander, Sherman's inescapable fear that some disaster might still occur.

As had happened through every town and every large plantation, the Negroes gathered to follow the army in a joyous parade. The men in blue seemed used to that by now, whether they considered the crowds with annoyance or amusement. For some of the troops, the focus was on the women, and by now some of the younger black women were recognizing how that kind of attention might be of great benefit. Many more of the gathering throng were families, strong-backed men with wives and flocks of children, some too young to walk. But the duty for the officers was to keep their troops in line, and to move them at a hearty pace, Sherman ordering the men to make fifteen miles per day. If the Negroes chose to come along, they would have to keep up as best they could. When it came to water and sustenance, until they gathered at the nightly bivouacs they would mostly have to fend for themselves.

Franklin had fallen in with a group of older men, but all around him more Negroes continued to emerge from houses and fields, many more than he had ever imagined existed. It was a question he had asked himself, just how many men like him there were, and how many of the white masters lived in the grand mansions, like Cobb, the men who had once held control over the lives of every man Franklin saw now.

Learning to read had opened new worlds to him, stretching his imagination. But most of that was still biblical, the more modern world around him still with so much mystery. Now he was begin-

ning to see it for himself. For years he had heard
much about the war, most of that in loose talk from
the overseers, absurd reports of the massacres that
had all but obliterated the Yankee armies. Even
if his father took that for fact, Franklin hated the
overseers enough to assume anything they said was
a lie. With his world suddenly overrun by blue-
clad troops, he was certain of it. As he walked the
street, carried by the sheer momentum of the men
and women around him, Franklin was beginning
to feel a terrifying combination of fear and regret,
that somehow this celebration of freedom would
suddenly end, that the guns would come, aimed at
the slaves, that the dogs and the bullwhips would
find them again, that this mighty blue horde was
only a fantasy, a fragile dream that would suddenly
fade away.

And yet . . . he heard the voices, the astounding
joy in the people near him, the calls to the soldiers,
ongoing salutes toward Sherman, to the godlike
man they all knew as **Lincoln**. This was more than
escape from the fields, more than a furtive glimpse
into some other life. This **was** life, new and frightening, and yet so many of the people around him
seemed to forget what their lives had always been.
There were too many experiences, pain and sadness
and the agony of unending labor, a mindless existence fueled by discipline and routine. But Franklin had tasted something far beyond that, had asked
questions, if only of himself, where the new slaves

came from, where the old ones went when they died, and even more mysteriously, what happened to a man if he made good his escape?

It had been taught to every slave, from the time he was old enough to walk, that running away meant death or something far worse. As a young boy, Franklin had listened to his father's lessons with perfect obedience, but then he would be astounded by the men who would still try, slipping away through stands of corn, or just disappearing in the night. But then the dogs came, and in short order the man would be brought back to face the lustful wrath of Lucky and the overseers, the other slaves called to watch as the whips sliced the man's skin until blood sprayed the ground. With the loss of his leg, his father had seemed more afraid than anyone Franklin knew, and so the lesson was driven hard into him, never think of it, never concern yourself with what lay beyond. It had been another mystery to Franklin that no matter the horror of the whippings, the screams and blood and the agony of a wife's tears, **some men still tried**. And now they were all out here, all moving in unison away from everything they had known, away from the whips, the great fields, leaving behind their shacks. Going . . . where? He had no answer to that, thought now of his father, a man always afraid. He will die there, Franklin thought. I should have stayed with him. He will fear for me, believe the worst. But this is not just **escape,** and if the punishment doesn't come, if these men in their blue uniforms with all those muskets are truly as strong as they claim, then this is . . . deliverance.

His brain continued to absorb all that was happening around him like the pages of a book, each new sight turning a page, another memory, strange, bizarre, and still frightening. He had said nothing, hadn't joined the singing, the cheers for the blue guards who watched the throng from the side. There was a new feeling growing inside of him now, an unexpected sense of guilt for the old man he had left behind, his father seemingly locked into a world that was no more than the old man could see, barely past his own hands. By numbers alone, the black families who followed along with the procession had opened Franklin's eyes to a fascinating reality. The crowds around him had grown to several hundred, more of his own kind than he had ever seen, more than he ever knew were alive. His mind had already begun to see the mathematics of that, that the simple ciphering the Sunday school teacher had taught him had begun to expand, the numbers rolling through his head, just what a **hundred** actually meant, his brain counting people instead of kernels of corn. But there were many more than that, and he struggled with his own ignorance, had so many questions about all he was seeing now, if it was possible that there was some number even larger, just how big this world could be, just how many people, how many soldiers might there be.

Where were the men from Georgia, from anywhere else the war had spread? There were other
questions as well, spawned by the town itself, his
eye studying the buildings, houses and shops,
nothing like the Cobb mansion. There was another
stark mystery as well, that those whites who cursed
them as they passed seemed to be so few, and so
powerless. As for the blue army, their sheer mass
had overwhelmed him, men and horses and wagons, and with them those enormous guns, his eye
settling on each cannon as it had rolled past. Their
crews had responded to his gaze with joyous pride,
answering his openmouthed stare with cheerful
boasting of the sheer might of their weapons.

As he moved out of the town, columns of smoke
rose up behind him, a glimmer of fear rolling
through the procession that the fires might be pursuing them. But the panic was fleeting, the river
looming large, the troops leading the way across a
hard bridge, flags flying, men on horseback. With
the soldiers mostly across, the way was clear for the
great crowd of Negroes, some of them reaching
the far side only to embrace the ground with their
hands, as though crossing the river meant passing over to some new and wonderful land. On the
far side of the bridge, Yankee cavalry held court,
a row of horsemen who watched the black horde
with amused curiosity, some of those men calling
out a casual obscenity, suggestions for what they
would do to the various women, words that Frank-

lin didn't really understand. But he understood
the tone of their comments, saw that their smiles
weren't friendly, and even the most outgoing of the
women seemed to slip more tightly into the protection of the parade. It punched a hole through
the fantasy, the caution rising inside of him, that
these men might be salvation, but not all of them
were there to help. And there was destruction to
come. The Negroes had mostly made their crossing
in safety, spurred on by raucous shouts from men
none of them knew were engineers. With the wave
of humanity on the east side of the river, the torches
came out, the blackened timbers of the bridge soon
falling into the muddy waters of the Oconee.

He stopped to watch the flames, felt an instinctive sense of safety in that, the blue army protecting
itself, and him, from some sudden surprise by rebel
cavalry. As the men with their torches had gone
to work, a civilian had scrambled among them, a
small fat man that Franklin eyed with curiosity. The
cavalry had gathered as well, and from everything
Franklin could hear, the man was making claim to
the bridge, as though it belonged only to him. If the
soldiers heard him at all, nothing of the man's fury
halted their work. With the rubble of the bridge
now washed by the flow of the river, the men with
the torches had resumed their march, no differently
than any of the soldiers Franklin had already seen.
He had marveled at that, an act of war that required
no muskets. As he moved farther from the river, the

thoughts rolled through him, if the fat man was a rebel soldier, if that's what the men of Georgia were doing to make a fight. It seemed ridiculous that any man would stand up to this army, all those muskets, swords, men on horseback, just to protect a bridge. The fires had been . . . to protect an army. It was a concept that Franklin embraced, a bit of knowledge he took pride in repeating to himself. He had seen a piece of the war.

To one side of him now, people were slowing, gathering with noisy enthusiasm around a small group of blue cavalrymen. The horsemen were tossing papers, scattered by the breeze, fluttering out over the outstretched hands of the Negroes. Franklin moved closer, curious, reached out, plucked a single piece of the paper from the air. It was fragile, thin, something he had seen before, what his father said was **money**. Franklin had never felt the notes, wasn't completely certain what any of it was for, had seen only what the overseers had done, offering piles of the paper in exchange for something they wanted, or using it for what he was told was wagering, some kind of game with small colorful cards. But the cavalrymen were letting loose bundles with loud-mouthed glee, the people responding by snatching up every piece they could grab. He studied the paper in his hand, recognized the number one, two zeroes, his eye settling on a vignette, a portrait of slaves working in a field, men bent low, weeding cotton, something he had done since he was a small boy. He stared at the image, had seen a portrait in the Cobb house, what his father said was a painting. But this was very different, a scene familiar to him, as though someone had frozen a moment in time. There was an odd peacefulness to the scene, a strange beauty, someone's handiwork with a pen perhaps, someone who had been in those fields. There was another portrait, low on the paper, a white man, stern, and to one side, a woman, standing tall, draped in some sort of gown. He turned away, knew there was punishment for looking too long at white women, but the boisterousness of the crowd swept that away, and he looked again, his eye on the men working the cotton. Why would someone draw this? he thought. It was another mystery, in a day that was now bursting with them, confusion rolling through him that the white people who regarded the slaves with such authority, such cruelty, would use their labor as something to adorn their currency.

He looked up at the horsemen, the game over, their bundles now spread over the sea of eager hands. Beside him, a man gripped a wad of the paper, held it out toward him, said, "Whooee. I gots me a treasure heah! I be buying the whole worl'."

Franklin glanced again at the vignette on the note in his hand, thought, They wouldn't be giving us this if it had value. He held out the note to the man, said, "Here. Take it."

The man eagerly accepted it, then hesitated, said,

"Hey, now. You oughta keep it! We be needin' all manner of vittles and such. Dey's a great land up ahead. Heaven itself done come down. We's been delivered by de Lawd Sherman. He might be a-wantin' us to pay him."

Franklin said nothing, watched as the man stuffed the paper into his pocket. He looked at the man's eager smile, pondered the strangeness of his words. "If we're bein' delivered, God won't be needin' none of this. I ain't seen nothing in the Bible about tradin' paper to get into heaven."

He turned away, moved back out into the road, saw even more people in the procession, some of them singing, a disjointed chorus, a mishmash of songs from Sunday school lessons, some just non-sensical. He moved with them again, ignored the ragged attempts at music, studied the faces close to him, an older woman, tears, clapping her hands in some kind of rhythm, and she looked at him now, smiling, held up her hands to the sky.

"Is a glorious day, young man. We's free."

He didn't know the woman, saw her dress, something far more grand than suited her, the garment too large, taken from her mistress's wardrobe. He nodded, polite, moved away, quickened his steps, couldn't help thinking of the overseers, the punishment for theft. Is it stealing now? Is that what it means to be free? What happens if the army leaves us behind, abandons us to those other men, those **other** soldiers on horses? There's cavalry out there, still. Has to be. And Lucky's not done with us. Not Master Cobb, neither.

The blue cavalrymen had moved off, the parade resuming, and Franklin walked again, keeping pace with those around him. He stared out to the side of the road, brush and trees, distant fields, a farmhouse, nothing as large as Master Cobb's. He looked upward, the sky a rich blue, the air cold, energizing, thought of his father again. I'd have carried him. But he's just like an old mule. Won't go where he don't want to. The woman's words rolled through him. **We's free**. I don't know what that means. If we don't work the fields, what else are we to do? What else am I to do?

He kept walking, moved forward through a flock of older women, past the young men like him, strong backs, thick arms. He felt a strange energy, began to run, slow, methodical steps, slipped his way past more of the throng, faster now. He eased out to the roadside, his pace quickening to a full sprint, up past the parade. There was a wagon in front of him, soldiers, heads turning toward him, and he ran past them, ignored the shouts, fought through the painful jabs in the soles of his bare feet, ran until he saw the backs of the men in blue, another wagon, men on horses, guards with guns eyeing him as he passed. The questions in his mind had stopped, replaced by something new, a fire that pushed aside the doubt, the fear, the mysteries. He wanted to know more about these soldiers, to do what they did, to stand up and fight the men like Master Cobb, like Lucky. The joy in the people around him had been overwhelming, and the thought that the bullwhips and the dogs could take that away made him cry, tears smeared across his cheeks, sadness blending with a growing fury. If the men in blue were indeed his salvation, he had to know that, had to know why, had to know **how**. And he had to help them.

"He says he wants to join up. Told him ain't no use in asking. We ain't got much use for darkies here, sir. We wanna put them into a battle line, there's a whole damn army following along behind us. That ain't happening, I'm wagering."

The man laughed, the officer across from him smiling. The officer looked at Franklin, said, "What makes you special, boy? You like all these blue uniforms, then? Wanna march around and play soldier?"

The man's tone was infuriating, but Franklin kept silent, knew these men could do whatever they wanted with him, no different than any white man before.

The soldier who had him by the arm spoke again. "Want me to toss him back out with the flock, Captain? We're passin' out hardtack to 'em right now.

Hey, boy, you hungry? Don't wanna miss out on General Sherman's generous feast."

Franklin felt the churn in his stomach, hadn't eaten anything since the night before. "I'm hungry, yessir, General, sir."

The officer motioned to the man, who released his grip on Franklin's arm. "Sergeant, get him a piece of hardtack."

"Sir."

The sergeant moved away, grumbling something under his breath, and Franklin kept his eyes low, wouldn't meet the officer's eyes, felt his power, the authority in his voice.

"I'm Captain Gorman, boy. No generals here. You're with the 113th Ohio. Lucky you weren't shot, running through here all hell for leather. What's eating you? Soldiering, I guess. That it?"

Franklin kept his head down, pondered the question. "Not sure, sir." He paused, tried to choose his words carefully. "Sir, if you don't mind me asking you. They's plenty of folks back there, saying you've freed us from the masters, that we ain't gotta go back to them anymore. I have to know, sir, is that the truth?"

Gorman sat back, folded his arms across his chest. "Well, now. Can't say I've ever had a darkie ask me a question. Didn't know you boys knew of such things. You speak pretty well, better'n most I've heard. Can you read?"

Franklin saw the opening, the captain's expression changing, the question serious. He stood straight, a quick glance into the man's blue eyes, nodded. "Yessir. Been taught by Master Cobb. The Bible mostly. Know all about Jesus and Mary. Cain and Abel. King David and Mr. Solomon. I can do ciphering, too. Count to a hundred, and take away, too. Subtract and whatnot."

The sergeant returned, held out a flat piece of bread, a small square. "Here, boy. It ain't roasted beef, but for Thanksgiving, it's better than starving."

Franklin took the bread, put one corner into his mouth, tried to bite, the bread breaking off. The sergeant laughed, and Franklin felt tricked, the soldier playing some prank. He stood tall again, looked at the officer, tried to hold his anger. "I can't eat this. Not as dumb as you think. I guess you don't care if we go hungry a'tall."

The sergeant said, "Well, listen to that. This army's rations don't suit these folks. You'll feel different, boy, by morning."

"Sergeant Knight, you may return to your post. I'll take care of this boy."

The sergeant saluted, the laughter passing, the man giving him a last quick look, nothing friendly in the man's eyes. Franklin looked at the hard piece of bread in his hand, said, "Sir, if I done wrong, I am sorry."

The captain laughed now, said, "You haven't had any of our delicious hardtack before. Go on, you can eat it. It's just a cracker. Won't kill you. Takes a while. Your spit will soften it up. They call it hard-tack for a reason. If it was any good, they'd call it soft . . . something. It sure as hell ain't my wife's Thanksgiving dinner."

The word rolled through him, two words, **thanks . . . giving**.

"Sir, what's that mean? Thanks, giving."

The captain stared at him, a silent pause. "You don't know about that. Not surprising. These damned rebels not about to give you anything to be thankful for. Last year, President Lincoln set aside a day for us to celebrate, well, everything we wanted to. We give thanks for everything good around us. I've got three boys at home. I'm thankful they're not old enough to be in this war. I'm thankful for General Sherman. He's gonna whip these rebels, and then we can all go home. You have heard of General Sherman?"

"Yes, sir. He was in my papa's house back there a piece. Master Cobb's plantation house, too."

"That's General Cobb, boy. More likely, he'll be Prisoner Cobb before long. Either way, he's just another rebel. So, he was your master? Guess you don't have to worry about that anymore."

"If that's what you say, sir. I'm scared that might not be true. There's some bad men work for Master Cobb. They probably kill me for being here a'tall. I'd feel a whole lot better if I knew you were right. I'll do anything you need if I can help out."

Gorman stared at him for a long moment. "Captain Jones's not likely to let me have a servant. There's no colored regiments hereabouts, or I'd send you there. Here, they'll not let you fight. Won't give you a uniform, if that's what you're thinking." He paused. "You read **and** cipher?"

"Yes, sir."

"Where'd you learn to speak well? Half the slaves I run into, I can't hardly make out what's being said."

"Sunday school, I reckon, sir. Read the Bible out loud most days. Some of it was . . . hard to figure out. But I learned most of it. If I got a word wrong, a man's name, like Job, well, the teacher would slap my hand with a stick. Didn't much care for that."

Gorman was smiling now, pointed to the hard-tack in Franklin's hand. "Eat that. The sergeant's right. You'll wish you did later on. Tell you what, boy. What's your name, anyway?"

"Franklin, sir."

"That your first or last name?"

It was a question he had never considered. "Both, I suppose, sir."

"Don't tell people that. You'll never stop being a joke. There's more inside you than just some ig-norant slave, isn't there? No need to answer that. I want you to come with me. Captain Toland Jones is the regimental commander. I'll bet he can put you to some use."

The smells pouring out of the tent drove a hard stake into Franklin's hunger, the one piece of hardtack doing little to stop the rumbling in his stomach. He followed the captain to the edge of the tent, heard voices inside. All out across a wide field, soldiers were bedding down, campfires spread out as far as he could see, more smells, someone singing, the sound of a banjo.

"Stay here."

He obeyed, watched Gorman slip into the tent, heard the talk, tried to hear the words. The captain emerged again, and behind him, another man, gold on his uniform, then two more men behind him. The first man said, "This him, eh?"

The captain seemed to stiffen, was suddenly uncomfortable, a surprise to Franklin. "Yes, General."

The man looked behind him, said, "Captain Jones, do what you can. If it helps, more the better."

Franklin felt a sudden bolt of excitement, the words bursting out. "You be General Sherman, sir?"

The man looked at him, and Franklin heard low laughter, stood silently, was suddenly afraid.

"No. I'm General Morgan. General Sherman's . . . elsewhere. Captain Gorman says you're a lot smarter than the usual darkie. This fellow here is Captain Jones. For now, you're in his command. You do what he tells you, prove just how smart you are, find out what we need to know, then maybe you'll get to meet General Sherman."

"Or the Almighty, if he talks too much. Rebs catch him, they'll carve him into pieces."

The voice came from another of the men, and Franklin was learning to tell the ranking officers by the tone of their voice. This one was young, mouthy, ignored by the others. The man introduced as Jones said, "Come in here, young man. There's food going to waste, and you look like you're about to drool on my boots." He looked at the mouthy man, said, "Lieutenant, you're done with supper, right? Good, he can use your plate."

The lieutenant started to protest, clearly knew better. General Morgan moved away, and Franklin saw the soldiers near the tent saluting him with their hands, with words of respect, one man calling out, "Happy Thanksgiving to you, sir!"

Franklin felt his head spinning, tried to absorb all that was happening, the sounds and smells, new words, so many white men.

Jones moved into the tent, and Captain Gorman slapped Franklin on the back, said, "You're getting a big opportunity here. Don't make me look bad."

The man moved away, and Franklin turned, saw the open tent, stepped forward, bent low, hesitated, caught the smell of meat, saw Jones sit in a small chair.

"It's all right. Come in here. The captain says your name's Franklin?"

He leaned in, still nervous. "Yes, sir."

"Well, eat something, Mr. Franklin. Sit down, there. You any idea what a scout is?"

"No, sir. Not directly."

"Well, that's what you need to learn. Here, there's some chicken in this stew. Potatoes. This gravy's not bad. Cook found some salt pork, too. Helps the flavor. Bread's a little hard, but it's the best we've got."

He stared at the food, felt the warmth from the soft light of a lantern hanging to one side of the tent. Jones pointed to a small stool.

"It's all right. Sit down."

Franklin moved that way, sat slowly, felt hesitant, still not certain what they wanted him to do. But the food was engulfing him in smells now, a large pot of brown liquid, lumps of chicken, so much more. Jones handed him a plate, said, "Use that spoon. There's plenty. Had about all I can hold." He paused. "I'm wondering if you know how to act stupid." Franklin stopped, looked at him, felt a stab of anger, another joke at his expense. "What I mean is, a stupid man attracts the right kind of attention. A fellow like you passes for stupid, you can find out a great deal by just listening, as long as you act like you're too dumb to understand anything. You're, well, harmless. Somebody makes fun of you, you just take it. Somebody kicks you, calls you names, you don't react to it. That's not always easy. But we need to know things about the people out here, farmers and whatnot. There's rebel cavalry, too, and that's the most dangerous part. They think all of your people are stupid, and they'll kill you for being out by yourself. Doesn't do us much good if you let that happen. There's more, but we can talk about it on the march tomorrow. I've got orders to keep an eye on your people, at least for now. You might help us there, too. You're not some criminal, some misfit, are you?"

"No, sir. Done nothing bad. It's not smart, what with the overseers and all."

"Well, maybe you can help us keep your people in line back there, tell them that if they're going to follow us, they need to keep up with us. We can't protect them, and there's people around here who'd like to see you strung up. All of you. You can make sure they understand that. I assume . . . **you** understand that?"

"Yes, sir. Very much understand that, sir."

"Good. As for the rest of it, you think you can get out there and talk to the slaves still on those plantations, find out where the rebels are going, what they're doing?"

"You make sure, sir, that there's more vittles like this?"

Jones laughed. "Better than that. You'll get paid for whatever information does us some good. I'm guessing you haven't been paid anything before."

Franklin remembered the paper money now, thought, I should have kept that. "No, sir. There was some of your cavalry passing out money back at the river. That's about all I seen of real money."

Jones was curious now, seemed to explain it to himself, nodded. "Yes, well, you don't worry about that. Rebel money won't even light a good cigar. You do the job, you'll get paid with something you can use. Gold, probably."

Franklin wasn't sure what the captain meant, but he was beginning to understand even more why the soldiers had tossed so much rebel money to the people. To this army, it was just so much garbage. Jones leaned over to a small desk now, picked up a pen, scanned a paper, motioned to Franklin without looking at him.

"Go on. Eat your fill. Just some work I have to do."

Franklin began to feel light-headed now, the glow of the lantern reflecting off the sides of the tent, embracing him in a blanket of warmth. He scooped out a spoonful of the stew, slow and careful, poured it onto the plate, his stomach howling with his brain at the marvelous smell. He picked up a piece of chicken, meat falling from the bone, slid it into his mouth, swallowed quickly, then another, filling his mouth completely. Jones glanced at him, seemed amused, then set the paper down, sat back in his small, low chair, watching him. Franklin stopped, wiped his mouth with his sleeve, thought, Something wrong, I've done it wrong. But Jones still watched him, said now, "Go on. Eat it up. It'll be slop in the morning."

Franklin obeyed, drank from the plate, then more chicken, tore a piece of bread from a heavy loaf, wiped up what remained of the gravy, the plate more clean now than it had been before. He caught his breath, the food falling into one massive lump in his gut, and he tried to relax, to keep the extraordinary feast inside him. He took long, slow breaths, tried to calm his stomach, looked around, saw the desk, a layer of papers, a narrow, low bed, a sword in its scabbard leaning up to one side. The warmth was rolling over him, his mind wandering, the exhaustion of the day's march taking over. He thought of all he had seen, the joyful parade of people, knew they had to be settling down into camps of their own, out somewhere beyond the army, fires and singing, some of those people probably entertaining the soldiers. He was beginning to understand now what the others seemed already to know, that their joy had been real, honest, that something was happening that was changing everything in his world. The people who were following the army had seemed to lose their fear, seemed to understand more than he did about what this army was doing for them, what was to follow. But now he was in the midst of it, a part of it, still uncertain, still nervous. He pulled off another piece of bread, heard a low laugh from the captain.

"We don't usually eat this well, Mr. Franklin. Special day for us. You know what Thanksgiving is?"

Franklin swallowed, saw the kindness in Jones's expression, was finally at ease, comfortable, allowed himself to feel a hint of excitement for what might lie ahead, for what this army was allowing him to do.

"I believe I do, sir."

CHAPTER TWELVE

SHERMAN

SANDERSVILLE, GEORGIA—
NOVEMBER 26, 1864

He had seen the rebel cavalry himself, as much as a brigade, firing on the advance troops as they pushed near the town. But those men left quickly, making good use of their horses to escape the rapid advance of much of Sherman's Twentieth Corps. The few rebels who dared to continue the fight had used the town itself for cover, especially the courthouse, the town's most prominent building. But the fight was short-lived, even the most stubborn rebels bowing to the over-whelming pressure of the growing number of in-fantry who had moved into the town.

Sherman was already in a foul mood. Even be-fore the action at Sandersville, he had ridden up on a significant obstacle at a narrow waterway called Buffalo Creek. What should have been a simple crossing had been delayed for several hours. De-spite the cavalry's precautions, someone had burned the lone bridge on the primary road, whether rebel troops or simply rebel sympathizers among the local civilians. Either way, the delay had infuriated him. The repairs had begun immediately, and with bet-ter than half the day wasted, the men had resumed their march. Sherman recognized his overreaction, had crossed the rebuilt bridge with the clear under-standing that thus far he had been spoiled. Even in the miserable weather of the week before, the march along both wings of the army had consis-tently measured his prescribed fifteen miles. The left wing, Slocum's men, had often gone farther than that, inspired perhaps by Sherman's presence. He had grown used to that, that the men were as dedicated to this campaign as he was, and he knew what every field commander knows, that a goal as ambitious as fifteen miles per day is rarely achieved. And yet, with so little interference from the rebels, he had grown accustomed to plotting his prog-ress ahead of time, anticipating just where his next headquarters would be.

The burned bridge had been a stark reminder that this country was not yet his, that even with the cavalry's patrols, the rebels were capable of surprise. In Sherman's mind, there was meaning to that beyond the military concerns of the men who led the way. It was simple geography, that every day he pushed his columns forward, the enemy that lay ahead was in tighter quarters, less room to maneuver, fewer places to make a stand. Buffalo Creek was one of those places, as was every creek, every river, every swamp. It hadn't yet come to pass, the crossings contested most often by squads of rebel cavalry who scurried away at the first volley from infantry who had no intention of granting the rebels a bridgehead. Those few places where the rebels had made a stand, they had been outflanked, the Federal troops spread out along the waterway in far greater numbers and along a far greater front than the rebels could hope to contain. The results had been predictable. The rebels had simply run away.

He knew by now that Hardee had traveled to Savannah, knew as well that Braxton Bragg had come south from Richmond to take command of the rebels now ensconced at Augusta. Both men commanded forces that separately could not hope to stand tall against either of Sherman's two wings. The scouts and spies had estimated that Bragg had ten thousand men at Augusta, Hardee not quite that many on the coast. Together, united, they could put up a scrap that Sherman would have to take seriously, one that, if properly executed, could seriously cripple Sherman's efforts. Sherman's strategy to prevent that was simple: Convince the rebels that he might strike either city, or both. At the very least, keep them totally in the dark about just what his intentions were at all. It had worked at Macon, and Sherman had no reason to believe it wouldn't work now.

He rode forward with the staff through the outskirts of the town, saw the guards moving up alongside infantry, the men on foot slipping into the houses, cautiously searching for any lingering rebels. He stopped, motioned to his staff to hold up, letting his men do their jobs. He thought of dismounting, but an itchiness kept him on the horse, another nagging sliver of worry that something might yet happen, the lone sniper, the suicidal rebel who just might make himself a hero. He thought of saying that to Hitchcock, Dayton alongside him, but it was hardly necessary, none on his staff with any enthusiasm for wandering headlong into a field of fire.

The houses were small and pleasant, with very few signs of opulence. That kind of finery and grand architecture was still reserved for the plantation houses far outside what he could see now was little more than an extended village. But the delay at the bridge had dug hard at him, pushing up a kind of anger he hadn't felt in a long while. He didn't need to say anything, the staff sensing his moods, keeping their distance, something he preferred. The anger came from some odd place, as though one part of himself had allowed him to forget about the war, that this campaign was so perfectly successful that the sudden intrusion of an enemy had been an annoyance far beyond the labor required by his engineers. He knew that was a mistake, that the burned bridge was a symbol of rebel stubbornness, an infuriating tenacity that seemed to infect every part of the Confederacy.

"They're being **squeezed**." He spoke to no one in particular, Dayton the closest to him.

"Sir?"

Sherman realized now he had spoken aloud. He glanced toward Dayton, the others, shook his head. "Ruminating, Major. The enemy is being squeezed backward, growing stronger in a limited area. It makes him more dangerous every day. We must be on our guard, do all we can to confuse him. Have we any word from Kilpatrick?"

"Not this morning, sir. His main force is close to Augusta, we know that. He will not keep you in the dark, sir."

No, Sherman thought, he won't. He will not just wander away without telling me about it. Hell, he'll tell everyone in this army about it. But this isn't a lark, General. You're pushing toward Augusta the same way you jumped all over those roads to Macon. I need you to convince Braxton Bragg that I'm marching right up his pants legs.

Dayton moved his horse closer, Sherman ignoring that, knew there would be **talk** now.

"Sir, there has been cannon fire, perhaps to the north. Very hard to tell the direction. Major Hitchcock believes it's coming from the south. I would expect some word from either direction if there was a problem, sir."

He had heard the faint rumbling himself, knew what Dayton was referring to, that often artillery fire at great distances could play tricks on your ears, distort just where it was coming from. He thought of Bragg now, the image of a man who never smiled, who sucked the joy out of every room he entered.

"We are certain that Bragg is at Augusta?"

"Oh, yes, sir. He has been seen often, and the papers there speak of little else."

"I would rather ride up there myself before I believe anything in the papers. I suggest we pay more heed to the quality of our observers."

"Yes, sir. Be assured, sir. General Bragg is in Augusta."

He imagined Bragg in a Confederate uniform, no more pleasant now than he had been years before. Sherman had been surprised each time he had learned the man had been put in command anywhere at all. Damnedest way to run a war, he thought. We whip him completely at Shiloh, wipe him completely off the field at Chattanooga, disgrace him for all the world to see, and now . . . here he is again. If that were me, if I failed that miserably, Grant would have my scalp, and Stanton would make sure it hung from the rafters of the War Department. But that's not how Jefferson Davis runs his army. We have been too weak for too long, made far too many mistakes on the battlefield, or that son of a bitch would have been hanged. That's my job, by damned. Grant knows it. But . . . Bragg?

"Major, how do you think Bragg got the job?"

Dayton eased the horse closer still. "Not sure what you mean, sir. In Augusta?"

"Well, yes. Augusta. But anywhere else. I knew him, you know. Rather well. He actually had dinner in my home in New Orleans. The most disagreeable fellow I've ever met. Well, rebel, anyway. There's a few in Washington." He paused. Keep that to yourself, even around your staff. "Only thing Bragg liked to talk about was Mexico, his personal glory. He did something grand, got noticed, apparently. Made fast friends with Jefferson Davis. Claimed he was Zachary Taylor's favorite boy. I suppose some of that is true. The part about Davis, anyway. That's the only reason I can see why he's in charge of anything beyond a slop detail." He paused. "Knew a lot of them back then, Louisiana. Some fine gentlemen. Some not so fine. He's the one I recall the most. A complete jackass."

"Yes, sir. You think we'll face him?"

Sherman had pondered that question since he had first learned of Bragg's presence. "Nope. Hates every general in the reb army, and they hate him right back. Nobody wants to do anything for him, with him, or under him. And he has to know the newspapers hate him. He'll be careful. Probably too careful, fight like hell to stay put in some mansion up there, giving orders to people who don't need them, all to impress the local dignitaries that he's necessary. But if anyone under him thinks they ought to venture out a ways, push us, maybe find our flank . . . well, that damned Kilpatrick had better do his job. Keep those fellows right where they are."

"Oh, he will, sir. He's a firecracker, for certain."

Dayton had answered too quickly, an annoying tendency to toss out glad tidings just to brighten Sherman's mood.

"Major, I had a firecracker go off in my hand once. Still got the scar. I don't like the man, not one bit. Too many bad habits, too much energy spent seeking glory. He's done the job, so far. But Wheeler's a firecracker all his own, and just as likely to go off. The reb cavalry is following every move we make. All I want from Kilpatrick is a good demonstration close to Augusta, just like he did at Macon. Throw a little fear into the townsfolk up there. Keep Bragg's people sitting still. Keep all of them sitting still. Hardee, too. Best weapon in the world, Major, is confusion. Bragg is ripe for it. Hardee, I'm not sure. But he hates Bragg as much as any of the rest of them. Likely he'll find a way to stay put in Savannah."

"Pardon me asking, sir, but your orders . . . do you still intend to march to the coast?"

Sherman cocked his head, looked at Dayton, saw the others inching closer. "Rumors, eh?"

"Quite a few, sir. Some of the generals still aren't certain just what you intend them to do."

"Good. Generals have staffs. Staff officers have servants. There are big mouths in every corner of this war. The less they're certain of right now, the better. If I can keep **you** guessing, the rebels won't do any better. My Order 127 was very specific, Major. The corps commanders know what routes I intend them to follow, and I am more interested in the destruction of the railroads than any confrontation with rebel skirmishers. If we must slow the march to accomplish this, I will order that as well. Without railroads, nothing can move anywhere around us. Where this army finds itself in the future is not a concern for anyone but Grant . . . and me."

He kept his gaze on the town, saw his guards returning, Lieutenant Snelling leading the way, a quick salute.

"The town is clear of rebels, sir. The cavalry squads chased away those few who did their mischief. It cost us one killed, a dozen or so wounded."

Sherman stared ahead, saw the first of the ambulances rolling forward. The anger returned, and he looked again at the homes, a pair of shops to one side. There were citizens now, faces in windows, coming up from the safety of the cellars, the usual mouselike cautiousness as the blue soldiers moved through their towns. A voice came, a woman, from the open doorway of a house.

"You cowards! You have no cause to be here! Scoundrels and vagabonds, the lot of you!"

Sherman watched her, saw age, gray hair, a drab gray dress. The guards moved that way, their usual caution, and Sherman had heard too much of this already, moved with them. The woman stood defiantly, arms crossed, a hard scowl on her face, the words spitting out.

"You come to kill me now? You choose to harm the innocent? We've done nothing to you, nothing at all!"

Sherman moved out beside the lieutenant, saw the man's hand on his pistol, waved him back. "It's all right, Lieutenant. I don't believe she's carrying a weapon. Tell me, madam. Where are all the young men of this town? Don't see any."

The woman kept her stance, her chin now raised, one more hint of her defiance. "Why, they're all off with the army, that's where!"

"And where might that army be?"

"Anywhere you bluebellies dare to trespass! There will be justice served, soon enough!"

"There were some of them right here, a short time ago."

"You'd be mighty smart for a Yankee. Yep, and they'll be back, sure as rain. I seen what they did to

you boys. I seen their muskets, I seen your men falling like so many sticks, right out there in the street!"

"And they made good use of your courthouse for
their protection, I suppose."

"And they'll do it again!"

"No, madam, they won't." He turned to the staff,
Dayton closest. "Major, send the order to General
Williams. They made this place a battleground,
made that damned courthouse their fort. Now
they'll know the cost. Burn the thing."

He had made his camp in a home north of
the town, thoroughly infuriating the two
women who lived there. He kept away
from them, a mother and daughter, the mother
more prone to outbursts of fury that he left his staff
to absorb. It had been that way even in Atlanta and
everywhere since, the more elderly women with
the lack of discretion, the daughters usually terrified what these soldiers might do in response. Occasionally the outbursts were humorous, not at all
what the old women intended. But Sherman did
not require entertainment, not now. His mood was
blacker than it had been in days.

"You certain of this?"

Hitchcock stood with his hands at his back,
blinked through his glasses. "Quite so, sir. We were
able to rescue the paper before the old fellow had
the chance to burn it."

"The **Chicago Times**?"

"Indeed, sir. The gentleman must have had a close acquaintance in Illinois who wired him the news. The account was quite detailed, including our direction of march, and offered names of the senior officers, down to the division commanders, at least."

Sherman stared down from the hard chair, his eye following the tight seams in the floorboards. His fists were clenched, a useless gesture, and he tried to breathe, to sit back, the anger holding him in place. "We march out of Atlanta, and a Northern newspaper provides anyone who cares to know just what kind of force we have, just who commands it, and perhaps, just where we're going. What am I to do about that, Major?"

Hitchcock seemed to stammer, no response adequate. "Not certain, sir."

"I hate them, Major. They have no courage, no discipline, no integrity. They lie when it suits them. And, apparently, they commit treason as well."

"Sir, if I may . . . Mr. Conyngham seems a decent sort. I can't think of him doing something to damage this army, or you, sir."

Sherman sniffed. "Mr. Conyngham is here at my pleasure, protected by the guns I command. For now, he knows just who is keeping him alive. As soon as he goes back to New York City, there's not one thing I can do to influence what he writes." He rubbed a hand on his rough beard, gripped a cigar in his teeth, his other hand now gripping the edge of the chair. "I've a good mind to resign as soon as this campaign has concluded. You cannot carry on a war with a free press."

"Sir, I do not wish to defend that Chicago paper. But from what I have observed, no harm was done. We have ample numbers of Southern papers who continue to make incredible pronouncements, sir, each one more fantastic than the last."

"Anything recently?"

Hitchcock seemed to jump at the chance to defuse Sherman's mood. "Yes, sir. If you will allow . . ."

"Go on."

Hitchcock slipped quickly away, and Sherman heard the order to the aides, a scramble of footsteps. He couldn't help a smile, thought of Hitchcock. He's still afraid I'll stick a musket in his hands.

Hitchcock returned now, held a folded paper in his hands, seemed out of breath. "If I may, sir."

"Go ahead."

"We received a copy of the Augusta **Constitutionalist,** calling upon all citizens of Georgia to lay waste to the countryside, to starve this army by burning everything in our path. The **Columbus Times** claims we'll be swallowed up by the swamps to our front. Let's see, this is the **Savannah News.** They claim the people of Georgia are outraged and insulted by your presence and all of Georgia will soon take to the forests as bands of guerrillas. We will be . . . um . . . utterly annihilated, sir."

Sherman worked the cigar in his teeth, nodded. "I like that last one. These old women would make interesting guerrilla fighters. Not sure who'd arm them, train them. And if they burn all the food stores, not sure how they'd eat. What do you think, Major?"

"I think we're doing quite well, sir."

"Me, too. There's a great deal of noise, that's for certain. But we've accomplished something none of them will ever admit. We've pierced the heart of the Confederacy, and that's more dangerous to Jefferson Davis than any field of battle. We've proven to one and all, North and South, that this nation, as they would call it, is a mere shell. Crack through, and it's hollow inside. Whatever 'cause' those damned rebels claim to fight for is nothing but illusion, planted in them by slaveholders and politicians. And newspapermen. They spit out their words as smooth as oil, and get their young men all fired up to fight, even if they don't know why. These women have sent their men off to die, just to prove that their cause is the right one. We are proving them wrong. Simple as that."

EAST OF SANDERSVILLE, GEORGIA—NOVEMBER 29, 1864

The landscape was changing dramatically, the lush greenery of the rolling hills giving way to flatter land and sandy roads, scrub pines, and stunted live oaks. The plantations had changed as well, far fewer of them, and those farms they came across were mostly hardscrabble, the people as ragged and poor as the land they worked. It was a curiosity mainly to his staff, and those soldiers who had never really seen the poorest parts of the South. Sherman knew it well, had seen this kind of land and its people in Louisiana and Mississippi. The biggest challenge of this change would come for the foragers, who were learning quickly that the bounty of the farmlands behind them was mostly gone, the wagons often returning to the camps with far fewer luxuries than the troops had become accustomed to. Each division had its own supply train, but very soon their vast reserves were diminished, the men forced to make do with whatever the foragers could find. Instead of the mountains of hams and bacon, stores of molasses and honey, the enormous flocks of chickens and turkeys, more often the foragers were settling for potatoes and cabbage. The herds of livestock were often as poor as the people who owned them, and even the foragers seemed to grow unwilling to strip bare the poorest people most of them had ever seen. But the necessities of the army had priority. Sherman had no ill will toward the poorest citizens of Georgia, had met them along the trail as he had met the wealthy ones, women mostly. But the change was dramatic, these people far more ignorant of the war, of what was happening anyplace beyond their meager farms. And a great many of them knew only the faintest of rumors about just who these blue-coated soldiers were, and why they were marching past their homes.

There were exceptions, of course, those few who made the unwise decision to strike out at the bummers first or the cavalry patrols who rode past. The threats and curses came as they always had, and the bummers, free from the oversight of their officers, reacted as they had since the beginning of the march. Houses and barns were torched, fences and livestock pens wrecked, those few cotton gins destroyed. Sherman passed by the destruction without expression, knew that Hitchcock and others among his staff were outraged at the lack of obedience to Sherman's orders. But the reality had settled upon all of them, that the men who chose to disobey were a fact of life in this army. Sherman's officers still attempted to rein them in, punishing those who committed the most outrageous acts. But more often, a burning home or the blackened timbers of a barn offered no evidence just who had committed the act. It only added to the trail of destruction that Sherman knew spread out behind him. If he had any serious misgivings, the reality was always in his mind that the swath of ruin he was creating would convey a very clear message to anyone who believed the rebel army was capable of winning this war. First, they would have to put

a stop to Sherman's march, and so far, no one had
seemed willing to offer the fight.

They camped in a grove of trees, many of the
men creating cover from their canvas shelter-halves,
offering some protection against the cold night
breezes. Sherman's staff had found him a house,
nothing like the grand mansions to the west, but
a wooden floor and solid windows that would at
least offer him warmth. It was one part of the turmoil he seemed to carry with him every day, and
every night, the inability to sleep for more than an
hour or two. His staff knew that during the day,
when the columns took their brief rests, Sherman
was just as likely to dismount the horse and find
a soft bed in a tuft of grass, grabbing a nap that
might only last a few minutes. Once in camp, he
allowed the staff their sleep, wouldn't plague anyone with that ridiculous habit some officers had of
working all night just to prove they were capable
of it. Driving a staff to such lengths might impress a
superior officer, but Sherman knew it did very little
good if your aides were so exhausted, they tumbled
out of the saddle.

The night was clear, and around him the fields
were speckled with campfires, the men huddling
up for another cold night. It wasn't as bad now
as it had been over the past week, and Sherman
knew they were pushing ever closer to the coast. He
understood enough of the weather to know that

proximity to the ocean meant milder temperatures, especially in winter. As long as no violent storm rolled in from the sea, the worst the men would have to contend with were the enormous swamps that spread all along the coast.

He stood beside the twisted limbs of a live oak tree, smoking a cigar, a cup of coffee in one hand. Behind him the house was alive with lantern light, the commanders offering their couriers to report on just what kind of activity the rebels might have tossed up in front of them. Little had happened over the past few days to give him real concern, and if the troops felt relief at that, it just made him more cautious. The ground to the east would offer the rebels ample opportunity to make strong defensive stands, the waterways more spread out into swampy marshes than steep-sided rivers. The going would be slow, the men forced to wade through muddy wetlands, and Sherman thought now of Vicksburg, the months before the great siege, when Grant's engineers had tried to plow their way through the Louisiana swamps by digging a canal. The men had suffered mightily for it, exhaustion and sickness, the entire project finally collapsing. The campaign had to be executed once more from scratch, a severe embarrassment for Grant, his reputation salvaged only by the extraordinary success once the army had found a more intelligent way to cross the Mississippi River. Sherman had been an enormous part of that, though he had argued with

Grant about the tactics, as much as anyone could. In the end Grant's plans had been nearly perfect, and their relationship had grown stronger still. Sherman still believed that the army had conquered Vicksburg only because he had worked alongside Grant, instead of against him. There were mistakes to be sure, always, in every campaign, but Sherman had no patience for any kind of blunder now. So far, he knew his greatest achievement had been planting uncertainty in the enemy's commanders, but his greatest asset was still the power of his army. Losing men to disease was simply unacceptable. And the sick, just like the wounded, could not be left behind.

He heard boot steps on the porch of the small house, waited for the intrusion, took a hard pull on the cigar, enjoyed the final moment of uninterrupted warmth. The voice came now, Hitchcock.

"Sir, sorry to intrude. My work has concluded for the day, and I was seeking permission to retire. Do you have any further need for me?"

"What time is it?"

"Just past eight, sir."

"Fine. Nothing now."

A horse broke through the low sounds from the camps, and Sherman felt a bolt of alarm, the man riding quickly in the darkness, a certain sign of urgency. Hitchcock said, "Courier, sir. I'll check with him."

"Go."

Sherman watched through the haze of cigar smoke as Hitchcock trotted across the open yard, the courier dismounting, his loud voice breaking through the quiet darkness. Sherman moved that way, the lantern light from the nearby windows revealing a young lieutenant, too much excitement in his voice.

"The general reports that the enemy was vanquished from the field entirely! It was glorious, sir. The general has outdone his own achievements by this outcome. He bade me convey that to General Sherman himself."

Sherman was closer now, emerged from the shadows. "I'm right here."

"Yes, sir! Oh, my, permit me." The lieutenant stood straight, snapped a salute, which Sherman returned. "I am honored to be the bearer of such news, sir. I have been instructed to communicate the general's pleasure at this day's victory, sir. The general hopes that you will agree that his men deserve only the heartiest praise from the entire army!"

Sherman's expression locked into a hard frown, and Hitchcock leaned closer to him, said, "General who?"

"Kilpatrick, sir."

Sherman put both hands on his hips, the cigar clamped in his teeth, stepped closer to the young man. "What the hell happened, Lieutenant? Numbers, the location. Save the happy celebrations for the men who earned them. Did he burn the damned bridge?"

"Uh, sir, what bridge is that?"

"The bridge I ordered him to destroy. Brier Creek, north of Waynesboro. His orders were to demonstrate toward Augusta, wrecking railroad lines and burning that bridge."

The man hesitated, and Sherman felt an uneasy stirring in his gut.

"I'm not familiar with those orders, sir. General Kilpatrick was making plans to drive on Augusta when we were met by a significant number of the enemy's cavalry. General Wheeler was no doubt among them. It was a glorious affair, sir. I am ordered to tell you that General Kilpatrick secured the field in a most gallant fashion."

Sherman felt the words flowing out of the man like a river of soft manure. "Drive on Augusta? Intending to do what? Attack the city? Enough of this, Lieutenant. I'm wondering if I should ride up there myself to deliver my orders to his face."

There were more horses moving closer now and he saw a cluster of men, a flag hidden by the darkness. They were led by one of his own guards, who pointed to the house. Sherman watched an officer dismount, recognized him, stepped that way.

"I'm right here, Captain."

The man seemed relieved to see Sherman, snapped a salute of his own, but there was no joy in the man's expression. "Sir, General Baird sends his respects and wishes to report that his brigade was successful in rescuing General Kilpatrick's men from a serious predicament. General Baird reports that General Kilpatrick is safe now, though it was a nasty situation. With your permission, sir, the general insists I offer you his dismay that the cavalry did not entirely complete their assigned mission. The enemy's horsemen were in considerable force, and without the support of General Baird's infantry, we might have lost him."

"Lost Kilpatrick?"

"Yes, sir. I was there myself, sir, when General Kilpatrick made it to our lines. The rebels were hot on his trail, as it were. Our muskets drove them off. General Baird is most distressed, sir, as he was informed by General Davis of your orders regarding the protection of our flank toward Augusta. We were assigned to support General Kilpatrick should the need arise. General Baird orders me to report, sir, that the need did . . . arise."

Sherman chewed hard on the cigar, shredding it, spit it out in a wad, turned toward the lieutenant, who seemed to hide behind Hitchcock. "So. You have anything to say on behalf of your commander?"

The young man emerged, kept back far enough that Sherman couldn't actually see his face. "I was not informed by General Kilpatrick as to any other report, sir. I was ordered to communicate . . . what I said."

The captain stepped forward, as though anticipating some sort of challenge, said, "Who's this fellow, sir?"

Sherman saw it clearly now, had too much respect for Absalom Baird to believe there was any exaggeration in his staff officer's report. "Captain, this fellow has been sent here by General Kilpatrick. His version of events differs from yours."

The captain took a step closer to the lieutenant, who seemed to quake slightly, and the captain said, "General Sherman, I was present when Kilpatrick's courier reached our lines requesting immediate aid. We were told that Wheeler's cavalry had surrounded General Kilpatrick with a superior force, and that our presence was urgently required. We were told that General Kilpatrick's men had exhausted their ammunition, their horses were broken down, and that if we did not respond with haste, all would be lost. General Baird did respond, and from all we could determine, Wheeler's cavalry was driven away. I saw it, sir. I was there."

"Where is Kilpatrick now?"

The question was aimed at the young lieutenant, who seemed to slump.

"At his new headquarters, sir. I don't have a map. Close to Waynesboro. To the south of it, I believe."

The captain stepped closer to the young man, his voice rising. "Is he still accompanied by his Negro concubine?"

Sherman held up a hand. "No more, Captain. I

will get full reports from both generals tomorrow. I want a precise report, Lieutenant, as precise as I can expect from General Baird. Am I clear?"

"Certainly, sir. Should I return to General Kilpatrick tonight, and pass along your request?"

Sherman felt something snap inside of him, a rising heat, worked to control the words. "It is not a 'request,' boy."

The lieutenant saluted again, backed quickly toward his horse, was up and away. Sherman watched him until he faded into the darkness, turned now to the captain.

"You, too. General Baird will make his report to General Davis, and both of them will report to me. If it is not too much of a bother, I wish to know just what happened." Sherman paused. "He has a Negro concubine?"

The captain looked down, took a long breath. "Sir, when the infantry arrived, the rebels had been attacking General Kilpatrick's forces for several hours, well before dawn. There was considerable confusion, and General Kilpatrick became separated from his men. I personally escorted a considerable number of his troopers through our lines to safety. I was told . . . with some certainty, sir, that General Kilpatrick had been asleep in his headquarters when the rebels attacked. There was considerable, um, talk, sir, about the general's Negro female. The civilians of the house where he made his bed were most outraged. That's all I should offer, sir."

"That's plenty, Captain. Return to your camp, advise General Baird of my orders for a full report."

The captain saluted, returned to the other riders, four men, one color bearer. Sherman thought, He wanted to make sure I knew the man was authorized to be here, not some lone wolf rider coming in here spouting off rumors. That's Baird. He knows when he's treading quicksand.

Behind him, Hitchcock eased closer, said, "What do you make of this, sir?"

"I make of it what it is, Major. What we have in this campaign is all we're going to have. I must put these people to the best use I can, including Kilpatrick. Apparently, this morning, that was not done." He paused, pulled out another cigar. "Go to bed, Major."

"Sir."

Hitchcock moved toward the house, and Sherman stared out down the road, could still hear the hoofbeats from Baird's staff. He thought of Kilpatrick, had heard hints and suspicion that the man tended to twist his reports slightly toward his favor. Well, it seems he might be more proficient at that than I thought. Tomorrow I'll send him orders again, tell him that I assume he didn't understand things the first time. Save face for him, prevent any huge smelly mess from erupting where I don't need one. He's the damned eyes, and I've no one else to depend on. All I wanted him to do was burn a bridge.

CHAPTER THIRTEEN

SEELEY

NORTH OF WAYNESBORO,
GEORGIA—NOVEMBER 30, 1864

The fight had been magnificent, the kind of roaring surprise that cavalrymen lusted for. They had hit Kilpatrick's men just after midnight, striking hard through the darkness into stunned horsemen who made what fight they could from their makeshift camps. Even after Kilpatrick's men had been alerted, the attacks continued, Wheeler's men rolling in throughout the early dawn to drive the bluecoats back in utter panic.

Seeley had no idea just how successful they had been, the confusion too great on both sides. But when the Federal infantry appeared, the cavalry knew their good fortune had passed, that no matter how badly they had whipped Kilpatrick, they could not hope to ride hard through waves of Yankee infantry, and the heavy guns that supported them.

At least part of the spoils of the fight was plainly evident now. Seeley rode at the head of a column of nearly two hundred Yankee prisoners, surly men who carried their hatred for the Confederates in every glance, every word they spoke. They marched first through the town, the citizens reacting as Seeley knew they would, answering any Yankee's show of disgust and shame with a viciousness that made Seeley uneasy. Already there had been reports coming into Wheeler's camps that some of his men had levied their own kind of justice on the Yankees they had scooped up, one band of Sherman's bummers unceremoniously dumped along a roadside, throats slit, where Sherman's scouts were certain to find them. Wheeler had stopped short of accusing anyone in his command of such an atrocity, but Seeley couldn't help asking himself if Wheeler could have authorized that, the general's animosity toward Kilpatrick seemingly a force stronger than any passion Wheeler had shown merely for fighting bluecoats.

There had been orders passed along to Seeley and the other commanders, that even with so much abuse of the citizenry from Sherman's scroungers, no quarter should be shown to any prisoner captured while raiding any civilian homestead. That troubled him even more than Wheeler's devout hatred of Kilpatrick. For days now, Seeley had been forced to participate in the same kinds of raids, the Confederate horsemen desperate for food and fresh mounts, so much so that horses had been taken from civilian plantations at gunpoint. The original orders given Wheeler by Beauregard had been specific: that all manner of supplies and forage be destroyed before Sherman's men could take those supplies for themselves. But the civilians had no greater inclination to hand over their animals and empty their pantries for Wheeler's men than they did for the oncoming Yankees. If the Confederate horsemen were to eat, and keep their horses in condition for the necessary journey, the cavalry had no alternative but to take what they needed. If money was to be exchanged, so be it. But currency seemed to carry far less value these days than it had during the fights in Tennessee, and even then, it wasn't the purchase price that made the civilians uncooperative. More and more, they simply wanted to be out of this war. Certainly the people hated Sherman, hated any man in blue who arrived on their doorsteps to pillage whatever he chose. But Seeley had experienced the same kind of hostility toward his own men, which even now was a mystery.

His entire company was serving as guards, lining one side of the road, easing their horses alongside the walking prisoners. Many more brought up the rear, men half asleep in the saddle, some of those tossing rude insults forward to the men they guarded. It was more force than required, but the orders had come from Wheeler that the Yankees should see that the Confederate cavalry had plenty of men to spare for such a duty. Whether any of the prisoners would ever escape to make such a report, Seeley had no idea. He had no intention of letting any of these men slip away. But Wheeler seemed to believe that Kilpatrick might attempt some kind of rescue, that Kilpatrick's pride was so fragile that he would go to any lengths, no matter how foolhardy, to bring home his men. It was one more part of the chess match between the two men, though Seeley had begun to wonder if before this was over, the two generals would stand up to each other in some field, surrounded by their two commands, whether a duel with pistols or a battle with fists, as their men cheered them on like some sort of schoolyard brawl.

The victory the morning before had been a stroke of grand tactics, but the celebrations were muted by the clear understanding that the Federal forces had done exactly what was necessary to pull Kilpatrick's bacon out of the fire. If the cavalry had been swept off the field, the infantry most certainly had not. The fight that came so close to bagging Kilpatrick had simply settled into another one-sided skirmish, with the Confederates forced to pull away from overwhelming odds.

He led the prisoners through a crossroads, saw a

small gathering of civilians, a half-dozen women, two old men, their gaze mostly on the men in blue, one woman calling out, "Ye'll burn in hell, ye will!"

No one responded, and Seeley focused more on the old men, saw plain civilian clothes, homespun coats, meager protection against the day's chilly winds. Beside him, Sergeant Gladstone spit a stream of tobacco juice between their horses, said in a low voice, "You'd think they'd be a-cheerin' us just a bit, now, wouldn't ya?"

Seeley kept his eyes on the civilians, heard nothing that anyone would describe as a cheer. He raised his hat to the women, saw no response beyond a hard glare from a girl, no more than fifteen. The girl called out now, "Why you spoil our country so? Why not just leave here?"

The girl's mother snatched at her, silencing the child, a whispered word to the girl that Seeley assumed was caution. He wanted to offer them something, couldn't just leave her words unanswered, called out, "We're General Wheeler's men. Whipped these boys yesterday. They're our prisoners. There's more to be had. Put your faith in this army."

The words had no energy behind them, and the civilians looked at him with no change in their expressions. The girl shouted toward him now, "Shoot 'em all! Hang 'em! Where you going anyway?"

One of the old men spoke out now, his words weak, barely audible. "Go back where you come from. Don't need none of you hereabouts."

Seeley didn't respond, their hostility digging at him, and Gladstone said quietly, "Told ya. They's hatin' us more'n the Yankees. Damn strange of 'em. Weren't like that in Tennessee. The people knew General Forrest, loved him for all he did."

Seeley tried to recall that, happy civilians, but it was rarely like that, no matter what memories Gladstone held. "Nobody's loving this war. They're as sick of this as the rest of us. This whole place just wants to be done with it all. Put down the muskets and bring their men home. Can't say I blame them."

"You goin' soft on me now, Captain?"

Seeley didn't answer, turned in the saddle, looked back at the column behind him. He ached to be done with this duty, to dispose of the prisoners at the temporary depot that had been prepared closer to Augusta. The railroad tracks farther south had mostly been destroyed, the work done by the Yankees before Wheeler had found Kilpatrick's camp. That was common now, the cavalry who trailed Sherman's columns accustomed to riding past wreckage of wood and iron that seemed to stretch for miles.

He saw a gathering of horsemen ahead, another intersection, a squad now riding toward him. He felt relief, allowed himself to feel tired, sagged in the saddle, the men approaching with too much enthusiasm, theatrics that seemed designed to scare the prisoners. Ridiculous, he thought. They know how bad it's gonna be for 'em. Don't need us to make a show out of it.

An older officer reined up, held up his hand, halting the others. "Captain Seeley, I'm Captain Riles. You're to leave these men here. The stockade is down that road to the east. General Wheeler is up ahead, another mile or so. He orders you to join him with your company. There's likely a good fight coming. The Yankees are aiming toward Augusta, sure as hell. We'll finally get our chance to gather up a bigger lot than this bunch."

The words carried more volume than necessary, another part of the show. Seeley knew the man, Alabama, a veteran who carried a deep scar on his neck from a nasty wound at Shiloh.

"They're all yours. Thank you, Captain."

The man seemed to recoil at Seeley's politeness, a self-conscious glance toward the prisoners. "I've been ordered to execute anyone who doesn't keep in line."

The man's words were louder still, and Seeley had no patience for the dramatics, turned, waved to the men spread back along the column.

"Assemble up ahead. Let's ride."

The men seemed as relieved as he was to be shed of their walking cargo, Captain Riles's men moving out to replace them, sabers drawn, a show of menace toward men who had no fight left to give. Seeley waited for his troopers to fall into line, looked again at Riles, saw a smirk directed toward the prisoners, thought, Would he do it? Would he shoot these men down . . . just because he can?

He wanted to say something to Riles, but the man was already moving away, walking his horse along the column of blue-coated men, more curses and taunts that Seeley tried not to hear. He waved his own men forward now, a color bearer moving up behind him, the column pushing their mounts up the dusty road.

Wheeler was in a worse mood than any Seeley could recall, sat on his horse in the middle of the road with a handful of officers gathered close. Seeley motioned his column to keep back, rode ahead alone. Wheeler waited for him to move up, said, "Your duty completed, young captain?"

"Yes, sir. The prisoners have been delivered to Captain Riles."

"Anyone escape along the way?"

Seeley felt the sarcasm in Wheeler's question, heard a low laugh from some of the others. "None, sir. They're not happy to be in our hands, but they appreciated the fix they were in. I kept a tight rein on 'em."

Wheeler seemed completely uninterested in the report, said, "Well, young captain, I'll tell you what I told these men. Seems we have been given the gift of another commanding general who lives in a world of dreams."

No one spoke, and Seeley knew there would be more. He pushed against the aching weariness in his back, the long, slow ride that seemed to weigh him down in the saddle. But he pushed upward, tried to show enthusiasm for whatever Wheeler needed him to hear. Wheeler stared out across a wide field, and Seeley reached down for his canteen, took the last swallow, Wheeler ignoring him. All across the open ground, horsemen were tending to their mounts, to campfires and anything they had to eat. Seeley looked back to his own men, motioned to Gladstone to lead them there as well. No need to keep them in the road. Nobody else seems much concerned that we're having a fight today. He turned, was surprised to see Wheeler looking at him.

"So, young captain, you much of an acolyte of General Bragg? Your General Forrest didn't have much good to say about him. I had hoped they'd fight a duel, maybe shoot each other dead, save this army all manner of complications. Perhaps another day." Wheeler pulled a paper from his pocket, pointed it toward an officer standing off to one side of the road. "That fellow there brought this. Says General Bragg offers me his 'respects,' and this young fellow is 'pleased' to offer us General Bragg's orders. Allow me to read this again, gentlemen, for the young captain's benefit.

"The general commanding wishes you to impede General Sherman's progress

by covering the enemy's front, retarding, whenever practicable, his lines of march."

There was nothing new to the order, the words similar to what they had been told to do by General Beauregard. Wheeler did not wait for a reaction, said, "General Bragg is offering us plain evidence that he has no real idea just how many roads Sherman's troops are using, nor does he seem to have any idea just how wide his 'front' might be. According to that fine young adjutant, General Bragg is commanding an enormous number of reinforcements at Augusta and his command extends to Savannah, where General Hardee is well supplied for troops as well. It seems not to matter to General Bragg that his vast army is sitting still, while his orders call for us, and **just us,** to retard Sherman's advance on either place. Or, perhaps, both at once. I'm not certain what General Bragg intends to do with those troops if we are successful. Perhaps there will be a parade in our honor. I will send that fine fellow back to Augusta with my request that General Bragg consider marching all those troops out into the field, offering us some assistance. Perhaps General Bragg could lead them himself, a gallant charge into four corps of bluebellies. That should provide General Sherman at least with some entertainment."

Another man spoke, one of the officers from the

Georgia regiments. "Do you really expect him to march out here?"

"Of course not. No, gentlemen, we're on our own. Word of yesterday's activity has already reached Augusta, and I am quite certain it will enliven the conversations among the city's dignitaries as to our next assault, which will no doubt sweep Sherman's hordes out of this country. That's what the newspaper is already saying. Did you know that, according to them, we have his entire army surrounded?"

Seeley felt too tired to keep silent, the annoyance of yet another absurd order overwhelming his discretion. "How are we to stop Sherman's advance, sir? Our orders are to retard his progress, not destroy him."

Wheeler looked at him, seemed ready to pounce on Seeley from his own saddle. "Bold question, young captain! I am just a bit uncertain as to the answer, despite General Bragg's confidence. Did you not observe the enemy's infantry yesterday? We crushed Kilpatrick, sent those boys scrambling back to their mamas. I would say that we successfully retarded Kilpatrick's mission, whatever that might have been. And for what? So that half the Yankee army could remind us what we already know? They have ten guns to our one. Time was, young captain, that every newspaper called out with perfect glee that one lone Confederate could whip ten Yankees, and have the muscle to whip a general or two in the bargain. Time was."

Wheeler seemed to run out of energy, looked toward Bragg's adjutant, who seemed eager for some new orders. The man came closer now, the clean uniform of a man who never sees the enemy.

"Do you wish me to return to Augusta, sir?"

There was an urgency to the question, and Seeley could see now, he had no interest in lurking about in this countryside. Wheeler removed his hat, ran a hand over his thin mat of hair. "You don't care for life among the cavalry, Lieutenant? Well, no, I suppose this isn't as comfortable as the headquarters of the 'general commanding.' You may return to your comforts. If General Bragg can bring himself to march down this way, it might be of value. Or it might not. We don't know precisely what Sherman intends to do. I shall keep him informed. That won't satisfy Braxton Bragg. He'll wish to see reports of great victories, vast numbers of enemy casualties. We shall do our best on that account. Offer the general my extreme courtesy and the assurances that his orders will be carried out with the same sincerity with which he offered them."

Seeley watched the man, who seemed puzzled by Wheeler's sarcasm.

"Yes, sir. Thank you. I shall return at once."

The man ran slowly toward a horse, mounted clumsily, spurred the animal, who responded with a high kick of his front legs. The man fell forward, wrapping his arms around the horse's neck, a valiant effort to remain in the saddle, the horse now

galloping away, the man clinging desperately to
the horse and its mane. There was laughter from the
troopers, insults and taunts, but Seeley was too tired
to join in anyone's frivolity. Wheeler watched the
man depart, said in a low voice, "There it is. A perfect portrait of the Southern army, in all its glory."

One of the others spoke up now, a major Seeley
knew from the fights in Tennessee. "Sir, might I
tend to my men? Our mounts are in poor shape. If
we don't find some fresh animals, I fear I won't be
able to put more than a company in the field."

Wheeler acknowledged with a scowl. "All of us
are in that state, Major. Send out patrols to the east
and north. Go into Augusta if you have to. If there's
better horses to be found, bring them in. Bring in
every wagon of forage, every sack of flour, every
ham and every chicken. What we don't take, Sherman will. Whipping Kilpatrick was the most fun
I've had in this entire campaign, but he's still out
there, and he'll be looking to save his honor, and
maybe his hide, from Sherman's anger. When Sherman finds out where we are, he'll push hard our
way." He paused. "I had always believed this command could accomplish something truly glorious,
a great victory we'd be remembered for. If any of
you believe that to be possible, I salute you. Right
now, I'm just satisfied to be the thorn in a lion's
paw."

The men separated, Seeley pulling the horse
around, aiming toward the makeshift camp his

men had spread out in the field. He didn't say how we're to find all those supplies, he thought, or the fresh horses. Do we just . . . take what we need? What will we leave behind? How will the people respond to that? The war hasn't come to Augusta yet. They should welcome us. They **all** should welcome us. Instead they blame us, just as they blame the Yankees. So we'll make that worse by stealing everything we require. How can that help us?

He dismounted, one knee buckling, his hands gripping the reins, keeping him upright. The pains of the long ride shot all through his body, and he closed his eyes, tried to loosen the agony in his joints. Gladstone was there now, held out a canteen.

"Easy, sir. Here. There's a spring back in those far trees. Ain't much, but it's better'n goin' dry."

Seeley took the canteen, drank, the water cold and perfect and energizing. He wiped his mouth with his sleeve, handed the canteen back to the sergeant, said, "Rest the men as best we can. General Wheeler's right. We punched Kilpatrick square in the face yesterday. But it's not a done thing. It's like smacking a hornet's nest. We'll have to keep to the saddle tomorrow, find a way to do it again. If Sherman's going to Augusta, we need to stand in the way, give him the best fight we can."

"If'n you say so, Captain. I'm just happy to grab me a Yankee by the shirttail. That little mix-up yesterday, well, sir, I never heard a baby squall like that bunch did. They ran like we was straight outta hell. Kinda makes you believe we can win this thing."

Seeley looked at the older man, saw the yellow teeth locked in a broad smile. He glanced down the road where the prisoners had been, the men gone now, taken to wherever Riles had wanted them to be. I don't like that man, he thought. Could do something really stupid. We treat their boys that way, they'll do the same to us. No need for it, none at all.

He let out a deep breath, took the canteen from the sergeant again, another drink, saw smoke rising from the first fires. He returned the canteen once more, said, "I suppose we'll be needing fresh mounts."

"That we will, Captain. The horse meat out there ain't worth much a'tall. Four of 'em dropped dead soon as we tied 'em up."

Seeley thought of Wheeler, the order, "take what we need." If patriotism or money won't convince the civilians to help us, then the general's right. There's only one other way. He looked down, put a hand on the scabbard of his saber, saw the grime on the butt of his pistol. God help them. But first, He's gotta help us.

CHAPTER FOURTEEN

FRANKLIN

WEST OF LUMPKIN,
GEORGIA—DECEMBER 2, 1864

He knew better than to make any ventures too far from the protection of Federal skirmishers. No matter Captain Jones's suggestion that **stupid** would ensure his safety, Franklin had heard too many stories of the brutality from rebel cavalry. Jones had seemed to agree, at least for now. There hadn't been any tasks for Franklin beyond the routine that most of the senior officers required around the camps. Whatever the captain's definition of **scout** was to be, Franklin had to wait until Jones decided to tell him.

Franklin heard the orders, the officers passing along word of the army's next significant objective, a town to the south called Millen. The soldiers began to speak of a Confederate prison camp, that the army could enjoy the opportunity to liberate a number of captured Federal soldiers. That kind of talk seemed to energize the troops, men speaking openly of an **eye for an eye,** that if Millen was anything like Andersonville, any rebels they encountered along the way would feel the sharp wrath of this army. There was an air of viciousness to the talk, men around campfires speaking more of vengeance, making less of their usual idle chatter. It had once been about home, a woman left behind, children. That had been no different than what he heard from the parade of Negroes, some of them already longing to return to whatever kind of home they had abandoned, the only other life they knew.

That some of the freed slaves would become homesick was odd to Franklin, that anyone might want to go back to life under the overseers, no matter how "kind" their master might have been. But the new sort of enthusiasm from the soldiers rattled him, some of their wrath seemingly pointed toward him, that this Negro now in the service of Captain Jones was a symbol of just why they were here, what had happened to so many of their comrades, and what they intended to do to set things right. Franklin tried to understand their anger, could see now that hatred of the rebels extended not just to those other soldiers, the men who wore the gray uniforms, but to everything about the South. That of course included the slaves. Franklin knew better than to engage a group of soldiers on his own. The soldiers seemed far more interested in the kinds of entertainment they could draw from the slaves, the spectacle of children dancing like some kind of happy dervish, or old men offering up a song they had learned in some faraway Sunday school. Franklin could see for himself how that kind of entertainment had grown stale to some of the soldiers, replaced by a hostile curiosity about just what a Negro actually was. Those debates carried a menace of their own, the stares toward him carrying a message Franklin had seen before, from the men with the bullwhips. No one seemed to resent his presence in service to the captain, performing various duties that none of the soldiers seemed required to perform. For Franklin, even menial tasks around the regiment's headquarters were preferable to the frivolity, the attention that some of the black children seemed eager to receive.

The women who had accompanied the march had become a different matter altogether, performing the kind of service Franklin didn't understand at all. Around the plantation, the white men had often taken the slave women behind closed doors, a cautionary word coming to Franklin from his father that no black man could ever interfere in anything the overseers or any of Master Cobb's guests wished to do with the women. Franklin had never seen just what was happening, and the women rarely spoke of it, though more than once he had seen tears and blood. But now, around the camps of these soldiers, there were slave women who seemed to welcome the attention. Franklin had stumbled into one encounter, odd noises coming from beneath a shelter-half, cries and groans that sounded like agony, as though someone might need help. Instead, he saw the shocking sight of a bare black leg, the hulking body of a soldier seemingly crushing the woman. The confusion of that had backed Franklin away, more scared than outraged. The soldier was a gruff sergeant, Coleman, a man who had no use for Franklin at all. The thought of stepping in, giving assistance to the woman, brought back those lessons from his father, that no slave could ever touch a white man, that if Franklin did anything at all, it might cost him . . . well, he didn't really know what it would cost. But he backed away from the gut-churning scene in silence, feeling the shame of what he saw, shame as well for the woman. He saw her afterward, prancing casually through the camp, displaying what seemed to be an evil smile, and more glimpses of a bare leg, offering compliments to the soldiers as though there had been no assault at all. The sergeant had been there as well, had returned to the campfire to a slap on the back, low happy talk from his fellow soldiers that Franklin tried not to hear.

The menace he saw in some of the men in blue was a lesson he scolded himself not to forget. They were, after all, white men, and in that they were no different from the overseers. And if he was to enjoy the protection of the army's guns, he was entirely vulnerable to whatever they wanted him to do, and however they wished to treat him. So far, the least threatening of them had been Captain Jones. But Franklin could feel that it was an even trade. The man commanded most of the men that Franklin encountered, what the flags showed was the "113th," and for now they did exactly what the captain told them to do. The other officers commanded respect as well, the notion now clear to him that officers were just like the bosses, Lucky, the others. They carried authority, and if it had not come from Master Cobb, it most surely had come from Abraham Lincoln. But not all the officers welcomed his presence the way Jones did. The captain he had first met, Gorman, eyed Franklin even now with a hint of suspicion, as though Franklin had to prove every day that he had some value to justify the food they gave him. Franklin understood that if Captain Jones in particular told him to do something, anything, Franklin would certainly oblige him. It was an odd change for him, to obey a man without threat of punishment, accepting the authority that came from the man himself, some piece of gold cloth on the man's shoulder. There were no chains or bullwhips, no dogs to threaten Franklin if he did not perform. But there was a threat still, that Jones or any of the rest of them might suddenly have a change of heart, that the parade of slaves, or just Franklin alone, might suddenly be sent away from this army, forced to return to any part of the lives they had known before. That possibility terrified him.

The captain's small staff had made use of another of the slaves, an older man called Poke. Poke was bent-backed, rough, leathery skin, spoke with a crude dialect Franklin hadn't heard before. Most of it was English, in a fashion, but Franklin often had no idea what the man was talking about. He had one great asset, though, something Franklin could not fake. Poke was always smiling, always had a kind word for anyone who approached him. As well, he seemed to have a talent for handling horses, and Captain Jones made use of that, putting Poke to work as a groom. It was perfectly reasonable to Franklin that until Jones gave him some specific job to do, he could pass time by helping the old man tend to the mounts.

He carried a pair of water buckets, the kind of job difficult for the older man, moved with as much smoothness as he could. The creek was a great distance away, the buckets heavy, and Franklin had wondered why the captain would camp so far from it, until he actually saw the creek. There more tents were pitched, more men in those ornate uniforms, gold buttons and embroidery on their sleeves. It

was Jones who had educated him why he outranked Captain Gorman, a detail Franklin tried to
grasp, the "date of his commission." But then Jones
told him an obvious truth. Generals outranked
captains, and those men usually had the better
camps.

He had made four trips across the field, saw Poke
waiting for him again, standing with four horses
lined up in a neat row along a taut strand of rope.

"Heah, boy. Po' it in de big trough again."

Franklin poured the water into a wooden trough,
nearly full now, and Poke led one horse to drink,
then another, then pointed out toward the far distant creek, toward a small house perched just beyond it.

"Mebbe one mo. Go on. Dey mus' be mighty
powerful folks in dat house dere. Is fool not to put
dese horse no closer to water."

No more fool, Franklin thought, than for me to
go fetch it. He started back across the field, saw the
campfires growing, the men gathering closer, their
muskets stacked in neat cones, bayonets locked at
the top. There were bugles blowing, discordant
sounds that rolled out over the ground, through distant patches of scrub woods. He glanced up, darkness coming quickly, the usual chill settling down
over them as the soldiers prepared for one more
night under the stars. Best hurry up, he thought.
You want more than those crackers, you get done
with this. Never seen any man eat as fast as those

soldiers can, and they'll clean a pot quicker'n any one of us.

He jogged now, the ground rough with sticks, tufts of thick grass, sandspurs that quickly coated his pants legs. In a long minute, he reached the creek, dipped each bucket, filling it, started back quickly, avoided staring too long at the men gathered around a large tent, pitched to one side of the house. There were horses there as well, tied up far beyond a roaring fire, which reflected off the faces of a dozen officers. He stopped, his curiosity overwhelming his judgment, eased closer, saw the men eating, a bottle passed around, some of the talk punctuated with laughter. The voice startled him.

"Hey, you! What you doing here?"

Franklin heard the edge he had become accustomed to, kept his head low, turned. "Workin' for Captain Jones, sir, over thataways. Waterin' his horses, sir."

He saw the man's uniform, an officer, the voice young, shrill. "How long you been standing here, boy?"

Another man was there now, hatless, glasses. "Never mind, Lieutenant. I've seen him in the 113th's camp. Go on over there, boy. Nothing for you to see here."

There was a kindness in the man's words, and Franklin kept his gaze low, said, "Thank you, sir. Much appreciated."

He turned, the buckets heavy in his hands, moved

back out across the field, saw Poke waving at him, a manic display that made Franklin quicken his steps. He saw an officer by the horses now, thought, I'm in trouble. Took too long.

He moved straight to the trough, emptied the buckets, dropped them, faced the officer, saw now it was Captain Gorman.

"Sorry, sir. I had to haul the water clear across—"

"Mr. Franklin, come with me. Captain Jones has got something he wants you to do."

He saw a civilian first, then Jones, sitting at a table outside Jones's tent, his eye settling on an enormous ham set between them. Franklin smelled the ham, a glorious sight, saw the white bone protruding, the meat half gone. Beside him Gorman said, "As you requested, sir. He was helping that old fella, Poke, water the horses."

Jones pointed to the ham. "Grab a piece, Captain. Plenty left. Not sure how many more of these we'll find. Mr. Conyngham has made the observation that the farther east we go, the worse this country gets. The scouts have confirmed that."

"Thank you, sir." Gorman moved to the table, pulled a knife, sliced off a large chunk of the ham, looked back at Franklin, then again toward Jones. "I assume, sir, you'll allow Mr. Franklin here . . ."

"Of course. Grab a handful. There's a sack of turnips over here. Can't say I'm too fond of those things, but if you're hungry, beats hardtack."

Franklin eyed the civilian, realized he had never seen a Northern man who wasn't a soldier. The man was watching him carefully, studying him, no smile, no expression at all. Franklin focused on the ham now, moved closer, the smells of the smoked meat churning up the emptiness in his stomach. He pointed to the knife in Gorman's hand.

"If you will allow me, sir?"

Gorman held out the knife, and Franklin felt the heft of the blade, the grip fitting perfectly into his hand, something far more dangerous than the small folding knife Franklin had always carried. He had kept that hidden deep in his pocket, had no idea if the army allowed anyone to carry any kind of weapon, no matter how small. Gorman's knife was heavy, a blade wider than two fingers, the kind of weapon no slave would ever dare to wield. He admired the knife for a quick moment, then stabbed the ham, sliced off a small piece, felt self-conscious eating in front of the officers, saw the civilian watching him still. He stepped back, slipped the ham into his mouth, a quick swallow. The strong smokiness was overpowering, as wonderful as the pot of chicken from days before.

"Thank you, sir. Very kind."

Jones laughed. "Mr. Franklin, you've got to learn that in the army, when you get the chance, you eat till you bust open. Cut off some more, and take some of these damned turnips."

Franklin moved forward eagerly, ignored the civilian, sliced off another piece of ham, saw the cloth sack beside the table, reached down, pulled out a pair of the purple bulbs. He felt awkward now, his hands full, held the knife out to Gorman, who took it, wiping it off on his pants leg. The turnips disappeared into the lone pocket in Franklin's pants, the ham into his mouth. Gorman slipped the knife away, said, "By your leave, Captain. I'll return to Company A."

"Dismissed. Get some sleep. Get them up at five. According to General Morgan, we'll be on the march by seven."

Gorman was gone now, and Franklin eyed the ham again, but an orderly was there, the ham scooped off the table. He fingered the turnips in his pocket, a treasure he had rarely been allowed to enjoy. He looked toward the civilian again, who leaned back in the chair, said, "Franklin, is it?"

He felt hesitant, still no smile on the man's face. He was suddenly afraid, thought, An overseer. They're sending me back. He looked toward Jones, thought of the small knife in his pocket, buried now by the turnips. He thought suddenly of escape, a mad dash away from these men, a rising animal terror inside him. But there are so many . . . they'll shoot you down. He saw kindness in Jones's face, the same as it had always been, and he brought his hands together, like a prayer, his words coming out in a burst of fear. "Don't sen' me back there. Please, sir. I'll do better. Please. I promise you, sir."

Jones seemed puzzled, said, "Calm down. No one's sending you anyplace 'back there.' This fellow might not be a favorite of General Sherman, and these fellows usually make enemies, but he's not after you."

There was still no menace on Jones's face, and Franklin tried to believe him. The civilian seemed concerned now, said, "It's all right, Mr. Franklin. My name is Conyngham. I'm a reporter from New York City. I write for a newspaper. Do you know what that means?"

"I seen newspapers, sir. Master Cobb had a mess all the time. The overseers read 'em."

"You read?"

"Yes, sir. Mostly."

"Well, maybe you'll read something about yourself one day. The captain has been gracious enough to suggest that you and I take a trip into Millen tomorrow."

Jones held up a hand toward Conyngham. "He doesn't know about Millen."

Franklin felt the tug of yet another mystery, and Conyngham said, "Certainly, I understand. That's your department, Captain. I'm just to observe."

Jones said, "You'll do a great deal more than that, unless you're careful. Mr. Franklin, I want you to walk with Mr. Conyngham on the main road toward Millen. You'll cross the Ogeechee River there, though that shouldn't be any trouble. The cavalry is about, in some force, and there has been no fighting in that area to speak of. All we know is it's a nasty place for some of our boys. The rebels have a place there we're aiming to destroy, and in the process, we hope to rescue some of our men who might still be held captive there. But there's more for you. I need to report to General Morgan, and my corps commander, General Davis, and tell them just what the citizens there know of the rebel troops, and that includes citizens both white and black. Mr. Conyngham can easily pass for your master. If any one of us tried to do something like that, and the rebels captured us without our uniforms, we might be shot for it. And Mr. Conyngham has something of a silver tongue. He might be a natural at the spying business. The two of you will claim to be refugees from back west of us, and if you spread enough of that manure around the town, you might grow some daisies."

The words flowed over Franklin in a flood of confusion. "I'll do what you want, sir. I'm not sure what that is."

Both men laughed, and Conyngham said, "Forgive me, Captain, but I'm fairly certain whoever it was taught him to read probably neglected to include a lesson on metaphors. Mr. Franklin, you and I will make a show of being slave and master, making our escape from the Federal army. I'll see what

I can observe among the white citizens, find out what I can about the movement of the rebel army, that sort of thing. You will mingle with the Negroes there, see what they might know. Very simple, really. Just . . . talk to the people you meet. Show a little fear, spread a few rumors about how this army has destroyed everything in its path, how the people of Millen are in serious danger, all of that. The army needs to find out just what the rebels are planning to do to stop General Sherman. If the white people there won't tell me much, their slaves might talk more freely to you."

Jones was serious now, a hard stare at Franklin. "Can you do this?"

Franklin felt the weight of the man's tone, felt a surge of excitement. "Will it make sure I can stay?"

Conyngham said, "Stay?"

"With you all, sir. You won't be sendin' me off nowhere else?"

Jones said, "We're not sending you back to any master, Mr. Franklin. We win this war, and I promise you, there won't be any more 'masters' at all."

MILLEN, GEORGIA—DECEMBER 3, 1864

They crossed a wide river, moving alongside bands of soldiers, men in blue who mostly ignored the civilian and his servant. The air was heavy with smoke, the black tar stink of burning pine that

Franklin had smelled often at the Cobb plantation. He didn't ask any questions, kept behind Conyngham.

There seemed to be very few civilians, the town swarmed by soldiers. Many of them carried bundles, were loading wagons, all manner of clothing and linens, some with kitchen pieces, pots, pitchers, others hauling boxes and crates. Nearly everything went into the wagons, sacks of what Franklin assumed to be flour or corn. In front of him, Conyngham stopped, halting Franklin with a slight wave of his hand, and Conyngham said, "Not many citizens. We're a little tardy, it seems."

"What's the smoke, sir?"

"Let's go see for ourselves."

They walked that way, and Franklin saw blue troops on horseback, a hundred or more, spread out through the houses. Conyngham tugged his arm, a silent motion toward what seemed to be a shop of some kind, words on the window glass that Franklin didn't know. Conyngham led him toward the doorway, and through the window Franklin saw the faces of women, hard, angry stares toward the cavalry. Conyngham pushed through the door, Franklin keeping close behind him. They were inside now, mostly ignored, and Franklin saw three women, two of them older, one most likely a daughter, holding a baby in her arms. Behind them, sitting on a staircase, was a young black woman, no older than Franklin.

Conyngham removed his hat, spoke in a low voice, as though fearing he might be overheard. "Excuse my intrusion, ladies. We are from near Milledgeville. Seeking shelter from the ravages of these monsters. Is there a man here we may speak to, someone who owns this establishment?"

Franklin saw tears on the younger woman's face, all of them shaking their heads. One of the older women said, "Sir, you best leave here. Those devils are killing anyone they don't care to see. It is only by God's grace that they spare the women."

"Have they harmed any women here? What dastardly crimes have they committed here?"

"I don't know, sir. Those men there, the cavalry I suppose, they done burned the prison."

Conyngham raised his voice just slightly. "Were there prisoners?"

The younger mother stepped forward, looked at Franklin, who lowered his gaze, glancing at the black girl at the rear of the room. "Our boys marched them out of here last week. Gone to Savannah, they did. That cursed Sherman won't be helping those boys, no, sir. But the soldiers done left, too, run out of here like they was leaving for home. Nobody here to protect us. Like Auntie Annabelle said. God's grace is the only protection we have."

The other old woman had said nothing, and Franklin saw a scowl on her face, a hard stare at Conyngham.

"How you get here?"

"We were most fortunate, madam. My boy and I kept to the woods, mostly. Moved at night."

"And you didn't think to go somewheres else? South Carolina ain't but eighty miles to the north of here. You go south, there be no Yankees at all, I suspect. How'd you cross the Ogeechee? Yankees holding on to every crossing. No way for none of us to go west. Only way out from here is the railroad, or the road to Savannah."

Conyngham hesitated, then glanced back at Franklin. "We were most fortunate, madam. God's grace, I suppose."

"General Sherman's grace more like it. You're a Yankee, sure enough. My whole family's in Milledgeville, been there every month or so my whole life. Never seen you before. Who's your kin?"

Conyngham kept silent for a long second, then said, "I will not be questioned by you, madam. I am fortunate to be alive."

"Then you best be moving on, keep yourself a step out front of this army. Or maybe, go back to General Sherman and tell him we ain't leaving here on no account."

The first woman spoke now, seemed shocked by the comments. "Carrie Louise, don't you be so rude to this man. Sir, I must apologize for my sister's harsh words. It's been a tryin' time hereabouts."

The other woman kept her stare on Conyngham, then Franklin, who kept his eyes low. "He's no man, Annabelle. He's a Yankee. You best leave now, sir."

"Wait. Please." The words came from the black girl, a short, thin figure in a dull plaid dress. She moved toward Franklin now, made a short bow toward Conyngham. "You be Yankees, sho?"

Conyngham looked at Franklin, shrugged his shoulders, looked at the older woman. "I admire your powers of observation, madam. But I am not a soldier, nor this boy, either. I am a civilian from the North."

The hostile woman looked at Franklin. "This boy's not from the North. He's nothing but a field hand, done made good his escape. Look at his hands. If our soldiers was still here, they'd string you up. Maybe both of you."

Franklin felt a cold shudder, saw the raw hate in the woman's eyes, backed away a step, silently urged Conyngham to do the same. But the black girl was close to him now, said to the woman, "I ain't stayin' no more. I been talking to those cav'ry men. They says I can go with this army." She looked at Conyngham again. "Please take me with you, sir."

The old woman reached out, grabbed the black girl's hair, yanked her hard to the side. "You ungracious, ungrateful little monkey, I'll kill you before you leave this place!"

Conyngham pulled out a pistol from his belt, pointed it at the woman. "No, I don't think you will. Release her."

The woman obliged, still the hate in her eyes.

Conyngham took the black girl's arm, pulled her

back toward Franklin. "Take her outside. I'll be along."

Franklin obeyed, his hands shaking, cold in his chest. The black girl had a hard grip on his arm, fear of her own, and he pulled her out into the cold air, the door closing behind him. The smell of smoke rolled over him, the girl holding close beside him, her thin frame still soft, pushing hard at him. He tried to pull away, but she had a grip that he couldn't break, and she said, "I'm Clara. Don't leave me here. Please. You can take me with that army?"

Franklin saw her tears coming now, looked again to the window, could see the women there still, Conyngham talking to them, still at the point of his pistol. "I s'pose you can come. That's what I done. There's a bunch of us, whole bunch. They say we're bein' freed."

"Oh, Lawd, God bless you. I been seein' the coloreds coming through, days now, some of them caught up by the dogs, other cav'ry. They hung one man down at the river, say it be a lesson to the rest of us. I hate bein' here. This blue army, they say we bein' saved. Is that true? I can go with you?"

He looked at her face, saw rich brown eyes, her skin as smooth as water. She was crying, the fear still in her, shaking as she held tight to his arm. He felt embarrassed, wanted to pull away, could feel her through her dress, had never touched a woman like this. He looked again at the shop window,

Conyngham still talking to the women, Franklin broiling up with impatience now, fear of his own, had to believe there were many more of these white people still lurking in this town, too much of the kind of hate he had seen before.

"Yes. I'll take you to the army. Don't worry. There won't be no more masters. They done promised me."

Conyngham emerged from the shop now, backing away, still watching the women, who kept their stares on him through the window. He moved out into the street, motioned for Franklin to follow, putting distance between them and the shop. "Nasty little group, that was. No offense, Mr. Franklin, but if they'd have decided to fight us, not sure the two of us could have held them off. I'm just grateful that old bird didn't have a pistol of her own. And I'm pretty certain there's someone in the cellar. Heard the bumping around. Probably a man, maybe a rebel soldier."

"We oughta tell someone."

"We will."

"Why'd you stay and talk to 'em? What they say?"

Conyngham laughed now, surprising him, made a quick glance at the girl beside him. "I asked them a few things. Names, whatnot. I might be a terrible spy, Mr. Franklin, but I'm still a newspaperman."

Franklin saw the butt of the pistol protruding from Conyngham's waist. "Newspapermen carry those things, too, I reckon? Didn't know that."

Conyngham put a hand on the weapon, nodded. "Just in case, Mr. Franklin. Just in case."

A line of horsemen moved along the street past them, the flag Franklin was getting used to seeing. Their officer halted them, some of the others moving up, their horses forming a tight half circle around them, the officer with a hard look at Conyngham.

"You live here?"

"No, sir. David Conyngham, reporter for **The New York Herald**. I come here on orders of Captain Toland Jones, the 113th Ohio. I have a letter here from General Sherman, giving me passage."

"Do you, now?"

Conyngham held up the paper, and the officer took it, read, his eyes widening.

"Well, now my hat's off to you, sir. I recognize General Sherman's handwriting. I'm Colonel Spencer, 3rd Brigade, Kilpatrick's cavalry. I didn't expect to see anyone like you. They belong to you?"

He pointed toward Franklin, and Conyngham said, "They're working with me, Colonel. That's also part of Captain Jones's orders. We were on something of a scouting mission, but it seems we're too late. You've done our work for us."

"Scouting? If you say so. You might want to keep off the streets. We're cleaning up things hereabouts. Shouldn't be any rebels, but there's always somebody feels like fighting their own war."

Conyngham pointed toward the shop. "You're correct on that count, sir. You had best search that place. The women there aren't too hospitable, but there's someone in the cellar, seems to be hiding out."

"That's what they do. Young girls, mostly. Scared what we're gonna do to 'em. Damnedest stupid people. Think we're demons." He turned, called out, "Lieutenant Conley, take a half-dozen men, search this building. We'll spread out, do the whole block."

Franklin watched with wide eyes as the Federal horsemen dismounted, pistols emerging from holsters. They moved past him into the shop, no hesitation, no pleasantries. There was shouting from inside, the women protesting in furious tones, and Franklin heard the one hateful woman above the others, her fury digging deep into him, no different than if she had held the whip.

Conyngham said, "Excuse me, Colonel, but are we certain there were no Federal prisoners remaining here? I know General Sherman was most hopeful we could offer them rescue."

"Rebels carted off the prisoners on the railroad before we could stop them. We've already got men out on the rail line, wrecking the tracks. My orders are to burn the place."

"So, that fire is coming from the prison? I say you've carried out your orders admirably."

"Not yet I haven't. I said I'm to burn the place. Not just the prison. The rail depot, the warehouses, the whole damned town."

CHAPTER FIFTEEN

SHERMAN

MILLEN, GEORGIA—DECEMBER 3, 1864

"They dug their own shelters, looks like."

Sherman stared down from the sloping hill, past the smoking remnants of the log walls. "I can see that. No other shelter there at all. Holes in the damned ground."

Dayton pointed out toward the hills to one side. "Rebel fort there, sir. Guess that's where the guards stayed."

"We grab anybody at all?"

"Sorry, no, sir. They skedaddled out of here when the cavalry came in. Citizens say the prisoners were hauled out of here on railcars. General Kilpatrick reported that as well. His men just missed them."

"Naturally."

McCoy came trotting up now, pointed down the hill. "Sir, we've found what seems to be a cemetery. Several hundred graves, most unmarked. I'm guessing it's our own men, sir."

Sherman didn't respond, stared at the smoldering wreck of what had been the prison's walls. The logs were thick, long, charred timbers that told the story he didn't need from his staff officers. It had been rumored to be the largest compound of its kind, larger than Andersonville, larger than any place rebel prisoners were housed in the North. The fire had already consumed most of the structure, but there were remnants of outbuildings, warehouses, shelter for what the civilians said was grain and supplies. But within the log walls there was no shelter at all beyond the burrows and holes he saw now, dug by hand, muddy pits where men had lived. And died.

There was smoke rising out close to the railroad, Kilpatrick's orders sanctioned by Sherman himself, nothing that would service the Confederacy would remain standing. The rail depot had been impressive, the town growing up at a junction of three rail lines, and so an important cog in the transportation machinery throughout Georgia, and beyond. Already much of those rails had been wrecked by Sherman's men, the cross ties burned, the steel rails twisted by the heat of enormous bonfires, what his troops still called **Sherman's neckties**.

McCoy stood beside him now, breathing heavily from the climb, said, "What do we do about that place, sir? We can dig up the bodies, see what we find. But it has to be our own men, sir. The graves are haphazard, no stones."

"And then what, Major? Haul a few hundred corpses along with us? You want command of that detail?"

"Um, no, sir. Guess not."

"We'll get them back, one day. Nobody in this army will forget what's here, what these damned rebels have done to these men."

He stopped, kept his words to himself. *I suppose this is their notion of total war. Nothing too cruel, no reason to take humane care of prisoners. But the next man who suggests that I'm the savage in this fight . . . well, I'll send him here.* He was growing angrier now, thought of the rebel papers, their ridiculous propaganda. *It's in the Northern papers, too, I'll wager. Someone somewhere up there is probably twisted in sobbing knots that I'm* **hurting** *these people. Well, hell, I didn't invent the idea. There were Orientals torturing each other a thousand years ago, Huns and Mongols and God knows who else cutting off heads, burning villages. Anybody in Washington starts bitching at me for what we've done to these kinds of towns, I'll bring them here, too. This is one more part of the war,* and there's plenty of that on both sides. I could be doing a hell of a lot more to wipe this country clean, every town we've been through. Damn these savages. I've been generous, compared to this kind of obscenity.

"How many graves?"

McCoy said, "Several hundred. Not all easy to see. Some probably stacked on top of others."

Dayton said, "Wonder if Andersonville is this bad?"

Sherman had no more patience for this kind of chatter, moved away, McCoy following. "Get the hell away from me, Major. Both of you, any of you curious about Andersonville or anyplace else, I'll figure out a way to get you there. I'm 'curious' about one damned thing, and it's not what kind of bastards the rebels assign to guard duty. All I care about right now is how long this is going to take. We'll not remain in this damned place overnight. I want the men up and moving by this afternoon."

Dayton was there with McCoy, held back a step, both men knowing Sherman too well. Sherman turned away, looked out over the town, saw Hitchcock riding clumsily up the hill toward him. Sherman felt a new anger, impatience that Hitchcock was still not comfortable on the horse. He reined up now, seemed eager to dismount, and Sherman tried not to shout the words.

"You want to be a damned officer in this army, Major, you'll learn how to tame that thing!"

Hitchcock glanced at the others, saluted Sherman with wide eyes, said, "Yes, sir. My apologies, sir. The horse is not the most cooperative. . . ."

Sherman saw him look again toward Dayton, knew without seeing it that Dayton was motioning him into silence. **Don't explain**. "What the hell do you want, Major? More good news? We find a hundred thousand rebels between this place and General Howard? We surrounded, like that damn newspaper says?"

Hitchcock let out a breath, still held the salute, which finally Sherman returned. Hitchcock said, "Sir, we found something quite different. There's a citizen here whose slave cabins were hiding a considerable amount of cotton. The owner, he's quite a pistol, sir. German, I believe. Full of cuss words like I never heard. Says he needs to see you, and fast."

"Why?"

"He says he's from Philadelphia. Union man through and through. Says he intends to send the cotton north, as soon as he can. Not sure I believe him, sir. His story is somewhat inconsistent."

"How much cotton?"

"Near a hundred bales, sir."

"In the slave cabins?"

"Not in. Under. Someone went to a great deal of trouble to disguise the storage. He says he was hiding them from the rebels. Hard to imagine his neighbors didn't see everything he was doing."

Sherman felt a new weariness, said to Dayton, "Where's my damned horse?"

The groom appeared quickly, never far away. Sherman took the reins, climbed up, said, "Lead the way, Major, if you can keep your ass up in the saddle. I haven't heard any good cussing in a while."

"Oh, there, sir, he's coming up the hill."

Sherman watched the man with dread, was in no mood for complaints from civilians. The man was out of breath, and Sherman saw age, leathery skin cut with sharp wrinkles.

"Ah, you be General Blair, then? I was told there be guard for my home! I am Herr Myers."

The accent was there, but not as thick as Sherman had heard before.

"I'm not Blair. What do you want with him?"

"I was told to find him. I require a guard! Protect my house, my wife is there. They want to burn it all!"

Hitchcock stepped forward, closer to Sherman, said, "General Blair ordered the cotton be burned, sir. There should be no harm to this man's wife." Hitchcock turned to the man, said, "You still insist you're from Philadelphia?"

"Ya! Of course! I am loyal to Lincoln. To Union. Always!"

Sherman had heard too much of this before, as though every plantation owner was secretly behind the Union, unending claims how their allegiance to the Confederacy was forced, the only way they could protect their family. Sherman had long ago stopped believing that this much of the South held tight to their loyalty to Lincoln. Too many of them had boys off in the war, and those men didn't wear blue. Sherman looked off down the hill, saw a new fire, ripping wildly through a row of small shacks. He motioned that way with his cigar. "That be your place?"

The old man turned, seemed paralyzed now, and Sherman said to Hitchcock, "You get his coloreds out of the way?"

"I would assume so, sir. General Leggett was there, making a count of the cotton. He knew General Blair's orders. He told me he was going to burn the cotton unless he heard differently from you."

"He is burning the slave cabins?"

"That's where the cotton was buried, sir. Huge cave, the cabins built up right over the top. Captain Poe would have liked to see the place. Quite a bit of engineering went into the design. It's been there quite a while, sir."

Myers put both hands up on his head. "You would burn my cotton?"

Sherman felt a slight twinge of doubt, said to Hitchcock, "You certain of this?"

"Sir, I questioned the slaves. Mr. Myers has been doing a great deal to assist the rebel soldiers, the prison, the railroad. There was no suggestion, sir, that he is a Union man at all."

Sherman felt the guilt drift away. "Well, then,

Mr. Myers, you may return to Philadelphia any-time you prefer. Little to hold you back. I must ask. Why did you bury it so?"

Myers kept his stare on the distant fire. "To make it fireproof."

Sherman could see soldiers gathered around the fire, men on horses moving away, thought of Blair, no hesitation about meting out justice when it was due. Sherman had an instinct for liars, had no reason to trust this man's stories any more than so many he had already heard. He tightened the reins on the horse, said, "Now, why'd you go to all that trouble? Who'd want to burn all that cotton? Well, no mind. Seems it didn't work."

He turned the horse, rode out along the ridge of the hill, one more look at the wrecked prison camp, smoldering, a vast field of black timbers. Behind him, Myers was still shouting at Hitchcock, and Sherman tried to ignore that, thought, The more we destroy, the more they will hate us for it. Not much I can do about that. Only problem is, the more they hate us, the harder it'll be to whip them. There is no solution to that. Well, there's one. Don't just whip them. Crush them.

General Howard had come up from his wing of the army's position to the south of Millen, sat now with Sherman on the porch of a small house, just outside the limits of the town. Already the men were up and moving, no need to delay the march. Those who remained were wrecking more of the rail lines, carrying out Sherman's orders to destroy everything connected to the prison or the railroad.

As the reports came to him of the various troop positions, Sherman had been extremely pleased that the marches had been coordinated so well that the two wings had moved closer together, a more compact fist that Sherman would now push toward Savannah. Howard seemed restless, what Sherman recognized as impatience for chatter, for being so far from his command. It was a trait that Sherman shared. They had enjoyed lunch, courtesy of a slave who had eagerly revealed his master's hidden treasures. Sherman rubbed a hand on his stomach, had already forgotten what the meat had been, his mind far out to the south and east, imagining the distance and the land they would still have to cross. Howard watched him light a cigar, and Sherman did not offer another, knew better, Howard's habits as clean as anyone Sherman had ever met. After a long moment, Sherman said, "I will leave here very soon. No need to delay any more movement. The railroad is being wrecked far out to the north. I just wish we had been able to rescue our captives. Did you see the conditions in that damned prison?"

Howard sipped from a china cup, his usual serving of tea, said, "No, sir. Heard plenty, though.

Human tragedy, no doubt. We'll find them soon enough." Howard seemed to recoil from a wisp of cigar smoke. "Your Captain Poe has delivered the latest maps to my command. My men are prepared, sir, to make the march with the same vigor we have shown thus far."

Sherman saw McCoy to one side, waiting for the command, and Sherman motioned to him. "Maps, Major."

McCoy said something to a waiting aide, the man disappearing around the house, then returning quickly, a roll of paper under his arm. McCoy took the roll, moved to the table, spread the maps out for both men to see. Sherman ran a finger along the lines of roadways, said, "Hard to know if this is completely accurate. No fault of Poe's. Best damn engineer in the army." He saw the wince on Howard's face, the usual reaction to any kind of profanity. Sherman scolded himself briefly, continued. "The Fifteenth is . . . here. Right?"

"Yes, sir. We're close to overlapping our marches, if that's a problem."

"It's the opposite of a problem. There are still four main roads. General Blair will move the Seventeenth along the railroad, and I shall accompany him. General Davis shall march the Fourteenth along this route . . . here. The Twentieth and Fifteenth will use these remaining routes. I want good time, General. We have reached the point where Augusta is over our left shoulder. There is no longer

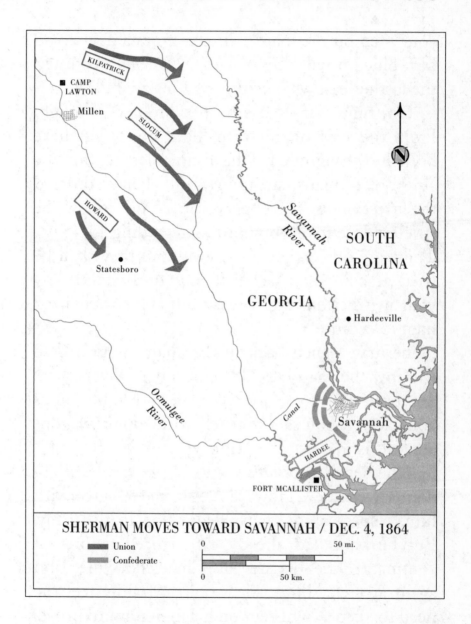

SHERMAN MOVES TOWARD SAVANNAH / DEC. 4, 1864

Union
Confederate

0   50 mi.

0   50 km.

any need for confusion, for deception on our part. Once they realize we've passed by Augusta, the troops there might push out toward us. I'm not giving them the luxury of time, Oliver. They want to stop us, they have to catch up with us first. Put

your men on the march, fifteen miles a day, if you
can. Slocum will do the same. It's rough country,
the farther east we go. Your wagons are full?"

"Oh, quite, sir. It has been a problem, though.
From the start of this campaign, my orders have
been mostly ignored. I have no tolerance for the
abuse of civilians, sir, none at all. I have ordered
the arrest of any scavengers who do not follow the
strictest intent of your orders regarding foraging.
There are officers guilty as well, and they shall be
tried at court-martial. I do not understand why
your instructions are so very difficult for civilized
men to execute."

Sherman leaned back in the chair, motioned to
McCoy, the map quickly removed. "Oliver, there
are some things you can control, and some things
you cannot. You said yourself your supply wagons
are full. Is that not the priority?"

"Obedience to orders would be preferable."

Sherman knew Howard would never agree with
him, respected the man's dedication to the army.
But Howard had already experienced failures of
command, the disaster at Chancellorsville, and
again at Gettysburg. He would certainly feel the
need to keep a tight rein on his men now, to prove,
at least to Sherman, that he was capable of managing a successful campaign. Sherman would never
mention the past collapses, knew the stain Howard
carried with him as boldly as he wore the rolled-up
sleeve over the stump of his missing arm.

"If you insist on carrying out the courts-martial, that's your choice. I would prefer that it wait until this campaign has concluded, whenever that may be."

Howard reluctantly nodded. "A stockade is not practicable, sir. There will be time for discipline later. I assume there will be much the same with General Slocum's troops. I have heard all manner of reports of the so-called bummers and their abuse of the citizens throughout this wing of the march, as well as my own. Mind you, I place no blame with General Slocum. But from all I hear, he suffers from the same lack of discipline that has plagued my command."

Sherman thought: Kilpatrick. No one else would pass such gossipy nonsense between my senior commanders. Certainly not my staff. And that damned Kilpatrick has spread enough of his own abuse across this countryside to ignite his own private war. He tugged at the cigar, a hard grip in his teeth, tore off the tip, more than he intended. Howard seemed not to notice, and Sherman tossed it aside, said, "General Kilpatrick's cavalry shall remain somewhat to our rear, to cover us from any possible advance by the rebel forces at Augusta. I do not anticipate any danger there, but unless rebel cavalry suddenly appears to our front, he will do us far more good watching our rear and left flank."

Howard finished his tea, set the cup to one side. "I prefer him in that position, sir. Rather unruly fellow, and he is not a good influence on the men."

"I don't care about his influence on anyone but the rebels. For that, he's adequate."

McCoy was there again, waited for a quiet moment, said, "Sir, we have just received word. It is confirmed that General Bragg is in Augusta."

Sherman looked at him, annoyed. "I thought we had already 'confirmed' that."

"Well, yes, sir. But several scouts have returned to General Kilpatrick's camp, having seen General Bragg at close range."

"Were any of them able to get off a shot?"

Sherman heard a grunt from Howard.

"Really, sir, I don't believe this army should be employing assassins."

"No, sir. No assassins. But we also received word that General Wade Hampton has arrived in Augusta, with some additional cavalry."

Sherman digested that, looked at Howard. "Well, Oliver, that should make you happy. Hampton's a gentleman, is he not? Wheeler's not much more than a bandit in a gray uniform. Maybe he'll add a little chivalry to this fight."

Howard was frowning, looked at Sherman, rubbed his hand on his face. "Are you not concerned? Hampton could have brought a considerable force of cavalry with him. Could make General Kilpatrick's job that much more difficult."

"Good. Keep his attention where it should be. If Hampton brought more horses with him, it means he weakened the cavalry presently assigned to General Lee. At the very least, our **problem** would be to General Grant's benefit."

McCoy pointed, said, "Sir, who's that?"

Sherman saw his guards escorting a group of men, civilians, watched Lieutenant Snelling step out in front, holding the men back. Snelling approached the porch now, saluted, said, "General, these men claim to have made an appointment to visit with you. I can remove them, if you wish."

Sherman looked at the civilians, who seemed uneasy, staring back at him, some with ragged clothes, one man older, well dressed. "No, they are correct, Lieutenant. I authorized them to come. Might be useful to us."

Beside him, McCoy said, "Sir, they're Negroes."

Sherman nodded to Snelling. "My staff has a talent for observation, Lieutenant. Bring them up. Let's see what they have to say."

There were six men, the oldest gray-haired, a stoop to his walk. His clothing stood out, what could pass for a well-fitted suit, something Sherman had rarely seen on a black man in Georgia. The rest carried themselves like so many others, homespun pants, ragged work shirts, the thick chests of men who worked the fields. They approached the shallow steps of the porch, stopped just short, and Sherman said, "You wanted to see me. What's your purpose here?"

The older man stepped forward, hesitated at the bottom step, held his hat now in his hands. "We are mighty grateful for your time, sir. We have seen that your army is followed by a great many of our people. I have been told by several of your soldiers that this has been a problem. We had thought of coming along with you. Is it true that we are not welcome?"

Sherman heard education in the man's clear diction, another surprise. "No one said you are not welcome. Not in this command. However, it is difficult for us to care for your people in such great numbers."

The old man bowed slightly. "We have decided it is best that most of us not go with you, sir. I myself suffer with the rheumatics. Some of the others have ailments of a sort. Some lame, sickly. The women with the small children cannot so easily travel with you. If you offer wagons, that would be welcome, sir."

"Don't have the wagons to spare. I believe you are making the correct decision to remain behind. We will permit the able-bodied to follow, if they choose to. No one will be forced to leave his home, or made to stay. If they can work for us, they shall be paid. Some orderlies and such have been with us for a great while."

"Some will follow you, sir. I will not. There is much age in these bones. I will hope that those who remain will work to make their peace with this land."

"What of your masters? Are they gone? I will hear

nothing of retribution against your people. My cavalry will be ordered to patrol this country with purpose, once this campaign is complete. For now, that's the most I can offer."

The old man smiled now, nodded, glanced back to the others. "I am thinking they'll come back, when the fighting stops. But it can't be like before. Those that don't go with you, well, we choose to stay to home because it's our home, too. But we have been praying for deliverance, and I am strong in the belief that it has come by your hand, sir. The war done changed everything. We are certain of that, sir."

Sherman looked toward McCoy, said, "Bring out another chair. My back's hurting just watching him. There's age in these bones, too."

"Yes, sir."

The chair came now, the old man climbing the steps slowly, more hesitation at the chair.

"Go on. Sit down. Tell me, what do you know of this war?"

"I know the North will win. I know that Mr. Lincoln has done been reelected, and that General Grant is whipping General Lee. Or, he will soon. I know what happened at Chancellorsville, at Fredericksburg, at Vicksburg, at Atlanta. Many men have died to make this war. There will be a reckoning for that one day. God will not let this pass without some calling. I know that slaves have freed themselves by your victories."

Sherman stared at the man, impressed. "What do you know of the rebels, right now?"

"Desperate men, sir. Many of the soldiers know the war is lost, just like the people around here. But they have to fight. No man can go home a coward. They'll try to stop you. They're awful scared what's coming. You've done changed everything they know. Just like you've changed me. All of us. Colored folk like us already been a part of every war this country fought. We was the ones who told General Jackson how to win the great fight at New Orleans. It was a colored man who told the general to use cotton bales to stop the British cannon. You know that, sir?"

More of Sherman's staff had gathered on the porch, keeping back, all of them focused on the old man. Sherman ignored them, said, "I have not heard that. Forgive me for doubting that just a bit."

"Best not do that, sir. I was there. I piled up the cotton. Strong back in those days."

Sherman couldn't help a smile now, saw nothing in this man that hinted at dishonesty. "You knew General Jackson?"

"Fought the British, sir. It was a high time."

Sherman saw a smile on Howard's face, a nod toward the old man. Sherman looked past the man, at the others, saw sober looks, the men keeping a respectful distance. The old man seemed to catch his eye, said, "They pick me to speak up for 'em.

Old age, I s'pose. I been readin' books most of my life, and it kept me inside, working for Miss Johnson. She owns this house, you see. These boys work the land. We'll work it again, stayin' here. I hear that you been killin' the hound dogs."

Sherman still watched the others. He saw scars now, one man's arm forced into a tight curl. He looked again at the old man, nodded. "I ordered it, yes. The president ordered you all to be without bondage. It seems you understand what that means. No more dogs."

"Then we'll go back to the fields, no matter if the masters come back. These boys will work if'n they can work for themselves. They'll fight, too."

Sherman had a thought, pointed at the old man with a fresh cigar. "I have to ask you, sir, something of great mystery to me. Why do the poor white men, here and everywhere in the South, why do they fight to keep slaves they do not own?"

The old man smiled now. "When the war broke out, the rich folk told the poor folk that if they win the war, they can have the land up north, and all the coloreds they want. The poor folk around here put faith in that. It ain't worked out quite like they was told."

"Do you know of Jefferson Davis calling on the government to put arms in the hands of slaves? To fight us?"

The old man laughed. "Tell you what, sir. The day the Confederates give us arms, that's the day the war ends. We'll take care of the work so you boys can go on home."

They rode away from Millen with the sun at their backs, passing the wrecked rail lines, the thick scent of smoke rolling past. Sherman kept the old man's words in his head, an experience that had surprised him completely. Educated man. Didn't say how. Or why. Some of the slave owners maybe did the right thing once in a while. Or, maybe they needed the old bird to teach their own children how to read. That makes more sense. Too lazy to do it themselves. Maybe too stupid.

He knew that was unlikely, had known too many Southerners whose education would compete mightily with anything he had learned at West Point. He knows of the dogs, though. They all do, I suppose. Nobody enjoys being a slave, no matter what some of those Louisiana fellows tried to tell me. Never thought I'd talk to one like that, though. God put them in the fields for a reason, simple as that. Seemed to work well enough, for a while. Lincoln's got other ideas, and he's using this army to change all of that. Not for me to question any of it. And, by damned, they sure do like us. Thousands of 'em, still following along with us. Gotta do something about that. This isn't over, and some of 'em are gonna have a problem with reb cavalry, or worse. They could get caught in some crossfire, a bloody awful mess, and sooner or later, some jack-ass reporter will make sure that story finds print in some newspaper up north. Explain that one to Lincoln, General Sherman. No, you've got some responsibility here, like it or not. That old man was telling you that, in his own way. He fought for us, Andy Jackson, no less. I'd like to hear more about that. And by damn, he knows more about this war than most of the white people I've met down here. None of that stupidity they spread around in Atlanta, how Yankees are just cannibals, eating the slaves for dinner. Somehow he sees through all the big talk, the newspapers and their fantasies. He'll tell others, too. That was the point, that's why those other boys followed him. That's gotta help us, once the fighting's over. I just wish I knew when that'll be.

The ground to the front was flat now, scrub oaks and thin stands of pines, the road sandy beneath his horse's hooves. He knew enough of this land to know that a good march would put them outside Savannah within a few days, and that between this army and the salt marshes along the coast, it was rice country. That's different, he thought. Seen that in Louisiana. Water and green grass. These boys will have to figure that out. No more cornfields lying out there like some Land of Plenty. And the closer we get to the marshes, the closer we get to whatever's waiting for us in Savannah.

He felt the excitement of that, the chilly breeze

blowing the smoky air past him, the symbol of where this army had been, what they had done, and how little trouble the rebels had given them. That will change, he thought. It has to. There's still a hell of a lot of those bastards out there, digging big damned ditches around Savannah. And just like that old man said, these rebels can't go home with their heads down, cowards can't face their wives or their fathers and tell them how they just ran away from us like a flock of birds. One man stands up to fight us, they all will. I just wish it would happen **right now**.

CHAPTER SIXTEEN

HARDEE

SAVANNAH, GEORGIA—DECEMBER 8, 1864

He had designed the defensive lines around Savannah himself, semicircles of earth-works and cut trees that spread out for more than ten miles from the center of the city. Adding to his efforts were additional troops, some of those coming in on the rail lines from the north, garrisons in Charleston and Augusta. But still the numbers were woefully inadequate, and even his carefully planned defenses could not be manned with enough force to hold Sherman away.

Hardee had ordered General Lafayette McLaws to take command of a force of some four thousand

men, mostly Georgia militia and green troops, min-
gled with those few veterans McLaws had under a
command of his own. It was Hardee's hope that
those men make some kind of effective stand well
out from the city, along Ogeechee Creek, a hard
defensive line that would at least delay Sherman's
advance, and possibly punch a hard fist into the
vanguard of Sherman's forces. McLaws was a capable veteran who had served under Lee at Gettysburg. But he was first a Georgian, and when
McLaws suffered the clash of personalities in
Longstreet's command, an event far too common
in the Confederate hierarchy, McLaws had chosen to return to his home state. Whether or not
he got along with his peers, McLaws was an asset
to Hardee. But more, once McLaws saw the vulnerability of his position along the Ogeechee, he
requested that Hardee allow him to withdraw eastward, to a strongpoint much closer to Savannah.
Hardee had no alternative but to agree. He understood what McLaws was observing in the field, that
a significant flanking movement by Sherman's advance might swallow up those troops completely, a
loss that would reduce Hardee's overall strength by
nearly half. Hardee had already accepted that the
troops he had on hand would likely be all he would
be given, even if Richmond or General Beauregard
promised otherwise.

As Hardee maneuvered his meager force into a
coherent defense, he was given a gift, one of the few

strokes of good fortune that the Confederates had received since Sherman left Atlanta. With Wheeler's cavalry still dogging the heels of Sherman's flanks, a Federal courier had stumbled into Wheeler's men. The message the man carried was the first indication Hardee or the rest of the Southern command had received that clarified Sherman's intentions. The courier carried orders and detailed planning intended for General Slocum, but instead those orders were carried quickly to Hardee. Though Hardee had concluded for himself that Savannah was to be Sherman's ultimate target, the orders now confirmed that. Word was sent immediately to Beauregard, who had finally arrived at Augusta. Hardee had every reason to expect that Beauregard would now order those ten thousand troops garrisoned there to be sent by whatever practicable route necessary, to strengthen his lines at Savannah.

But the chaos of command still plagued any efforts at coordination. Before Beauregard's arrival, Braxton Bragg was in command of the overall theater, and in a gesture that Hardee was forced to appreciate, Bragg had allowed a small portion of those troops to travel to the coast, adding to Hardee's force. But with Beauregard now replacing Bragg's authority with his own, caution once again prevailed. Though Beauregard had wired Richmond with a detailed report of the desperate situation in Georgia, he had seemed equally as concerned just how his reputation might suffer for what was becoming rabid impatience with John Bell Hood, whose vainglorious campaign in Tennessee was technically Beauregard's responsibility. Hardee had no interest in anything happening now beyond his own sphere, and if Beauregard was to understand just what kind of danger Hardee was facing, Hardee knew that Beauregard would have to travel to Savannah himself. The request had gone out, as urgent a call as Hardee had dared offer his superior. To his surprise, Beauregard, who had moved from Augusta to Charleston, agreed to do just that.

The earthworks were still not fully completed, but the labor was ongoing, men who worked their shovels in shifts, aided by every Negro Hardee could secure from surrounding plantations. He knew the outermost lines were indefensible, a loose configuration of artillery posts and rifle pits that spread in an organized pattern well beyond Savannah's limits. But he had focused more of the work on the positions closer to the city, an arcing defense that extended barely five miles from the center of town. Here earthworks were made stronger by flooded fields, the marshy ground claimed for growing rice. Now those watery plains were meant as a barrier, Hardee's desperate hope that the Federal forces would be funneled onto the higher ground of roadways and earthen dams, far easier for his limited number of troops and artillery pieces to defend. The final line hugged the perimeter of the city itself, a far stronger position, aided by the massive coastal guns that had once faced the sea. The men seemed to draw inspiration from that, though Hardee knew that once Sherman's artillery was in range of that line, no response Hardee could offer would keep the Federal army away for long. At the very least, the last line might offer Hardee's troops valuable time, enough perhaps to allow an evacuation of the city by any passageway that might yet exist.

They cheered him still, men sweating in the cold, some of them shirtless, strong backs to rival the strength of the slaves. He tried to acknowledge them, offering a tip of his hat, or a feeble wave, the most energy he could muster.

He was achingly tired, his eyes heavy with lack of sleep, had ridden along much of the defensive positions for a long afternoon, followed by several aides and a pair of staff officers. He kept pushing the horse, would not stop to chat with any of the officers along the line, felt the weariness in every joint, knew that this night would be like so many before. It was not just the responsibility, all those civilians and their fears, complaints about shortages or panic over just what kind of army was headed their way. Hardee had been kept awake as much by the torment in his own mind, if there was something more that he could have done, if there was some flaw in his planning, in the strategy that his own instincts told him were utterly futile in stopping Sherman's advance. As he read the reports from McLaws, from Wheeler, it seemed to engulf Hardee like a terrible dream, the bone-chattering fear that comes from absolute helplessness. In the darkness, his fitful sleep would give way to wide-eyed staring, a frustrating vision of some bizarre contest, a duel where only one participant carried a weapon. When daylight came, he could not just sit in his headquarters without knowing just how much progress the men were making on the earthworks. And so he rode, as he had ridden today, oddly surprised that his presence seemed to give them energy when he had none at all inside himself.

In the waning days of Bragg's authority, Bragg had kept Wheeler's cavalry between Sherman's army and Augusta, still believing that Sherman would make his move in that direction. Hardee hadn't believed that in more than two weeks, even before his suspicions had been confirmed by the captured courier. But Bragg was no longer any authority at all, and Hardee knew that a newly arriving Beauregard would know little enough about Sherman's actual maneuvering. Hardee had taken it on himself to move Wheeler where the cavalry might be more effective. Thus far there had been more skirmishes with Kilpatrick's bluecoats, nothing gained but a scattering of casualties on both sides. And for at least a short while, Hardee had pondered if the Federal courier had been a ruse, if

Sherman had sent the man into Wheeler's troopers with false information. But now Wheeler's tracking of Sherman's march had made him confident that Sherman's columns had put Augusta to their rear, and so there was little need for Wheeler to keep his invaluable strength so far behind where Sherman was now moving.

Hardee pulled the horse back, turned away from the earthworks, looked out toward the tall spires of Savannah's many churches, made brighter by the glare of the sun setting behind him. He stared for a long moment, thought of the civilians, knew that the churches had become more than a Sunday destination. They will be gathering there soon, he thought, after their evening meals. Seeking news, information, word of great victories, the foolishness of the newspapers, or anything that comes to us from Richmond. They will seek guidance, inspiration, hope. I can find no fault with that. They cannot know all that I know. They see guns and troops and stacked muskets and believe in us, believe that we bring great power to protect them. He looked down, blinked through the heaviness in his eyes, thought, What might I find there? Is there some priest who will take my hand and assure me that all will be well? It had been a significant change in his life, accepting the doctrine of the Episcopal Church, inspired by his friend and fellow commander, the army's most notable Episcopalian, Bishop and General Leonidas Polk. But soon after

Hardee's conversion, Polk had been killed outside of Atlanta. That devastating blow had resulted from a single round of artillery, blasting through the man like the fist of God, as though some great price had been exacted from a man who had inspired more religious fervor in this army than any other.

It was a devastating blow to Hardee, as much as to the rest of the army. His military mind agonized to understand how such a thing was allowed to happen, and he could not just absorb his friend's death with faithful acceptance, as Polk himself might do. He had been angered by it, examined the event by the only tools Hardee had, the mind of a strategist, weighing the mathematics of it, the raw odds of an artillery shell cutting through not just any one man, but **that** man, and if there had been a Hand of God in that, Hardee had convinced himself that for one brief moment, a flicker of time, God had looked the other way. There was no other explanation that satisfied Hardee, and now none was needed. As horrific as that news had been, what he had just learned was much worse, his mind grappling still with the greatest sadness he had felt since the war began. Hardee had learned from Bishop Polk to place his faith in a just God, but now that faith was not just tested, it was nearly torn away.

The telegraph line that ran to Charleston was still intact, allowing information to pass down the coast from Augusta and far beyond. And so word had reached him of an immense fight at Franklin, Tennessee, more than a week before, the bitter fruit sown by John Bell Hood's attempt to drive the war northward, deep into Federally controlled strongholds. Franklin had been a disaster for Hood's army, and Hardee couldn't help an angry grief that it was a disaster for everything decent in a world growing more indecent every day. Among the dead was Patrick Cleburne.

Cleburne had served Hardee with a tenacious and valiant effort throughout the campaign at Stones River. But Cleburne's star rose far higher at Chattanooga. He had been the single spot of bright light in a campaign dominated by what Hardee knew to be the unbending incompetence of Braxton Bragg. Despite Bragg's continuing missteps, a grossly outnumbered Cleburne had held off a number of powerful assaults from Sherman's own forces, had held out until the darkness silenced Sherman's guns. It was the only success in a day of catastrophe, the rest of the Federal army sweeping up and over the high ground far from Cleburne's enormous triumph, wiping away Bragg's entire army in a defeat as absolute as any of the war. Hardee had seen Cleburne throughout that remarkable day, had silently applauded the man's heroics. But in the end, Hardee had been forced to order his best subordinate to back off the ground he had won, Cleburne assigned to protect the army as it made good a desperate retreat. Cleburne not only accomplished the task, he bloodied the triumphant Federal pursuit completely at Ringgold Gap, a pass through the north Georgia mountains, which allowed the remnants of Bragg's army to escape. Even Richmond seemed to recognize what Hardee already appreciated. Cleburne was a true hero, earning an official "Thanks from the Congress of the Confederacy," a rare accolade in an army where few had earned it.

After Chattanooga, Cleburne had continued to show the kind of tenacity the army had not seen since the days of Stonewall Jackson, serving Hardee as well as anyone in the efforts to prevent Sherman's capture of Atlanta. But Hardee could not control the whims of Richmond, and so when Hardee had been ordered away to Charleston, he had lost command of what he believed to be the best field officer in the army, and even worse, he lost touch with one of his closest friends. Cleburne had been ordered to continue on with Hood, had been a part of what Hardee had always believed to be an astounding waste of effort and manpower. Even Beauregard, who could have prevented it, had allowed Hood to venture off on a quixotic quest for redemption, as though by striking out toward Nashville, Hood could excuse his loss of Atlanta. Now, Hardee thought, Sherman is right out here, coming this way, and the only man I know who could hope to stop him . . . is gone.

He tried to hold in his emotions, knew there were men watching him, the men with the shovels, his own staff close behind him, Major Roy and Colo-

nel Pickett. He held the horse still for a long mo-
ment, kept his eyes on the soft orange glow drifting
over the city, pushed hard to erase the image of
Cleburne, tried not to hear the man's self-conscious
Irish brogue. I should speak to a priest, he thought.
Try, anyway.

The emotions wouldn't leave, choking away his
voice, and he nudged the horse forward, ordered
the men to follow with a slow wave of his hand.

HARDEE'S HEADQUARTERS, SAVANNAH, GEORGIA—DECEMBER 8, 1864

He watched as Wheeler flexed his fingers, as though
scratching at the air, his mind occupied in some
place Hardee hesitated to disrupt. Wheeler looked
at him now, as though suddenly struck by the flash
of an idea.

"We're cutting trees everyplace there are trees to
cut. That will help."

"Possibly."

"Sir, we know that the Yankees are moving this
way, and there is no confusion as to their target.
Would you have me make any effort to impede
him? General Bragg—"

"Bragg isn't an issue here, Mr. Wheeler. General
Beauregard is in command now. You know that, of
course. He has agreed to come here, at my request.
So we will answer to him now."

Wheeler showed no change of expression, seemed to ponder the news. After a silent moment, he said, "Does that mean there are new orders, sir?"

"For you?" Hardee thought a moment, had gone through this in his mind all day. "Your men have been assigned to the destruction of everything of use to the enemy, everything that lies between the city and his current position."

"Yes, sir. Much of that has been accomplished. It was not a pleasant affair, sir. The civilians, as usual, have been carping at my men about their sacrifice. Who among us is not sacrificing? I have no patience for any of that. None."

Hardee had heard a litany of complaints from civilians, as hostile to Wheeler's men as anyone Sherman had in the field. It was an unanswerable question, how to fight this war and leave the civilians unaffected.

"I know of your efforts. If I intended to court-martial you for horse thievery, I would have done so long before now."

He expected a response, knew that Wheeler's men had tormented as many civilians in Tennessee as they were now doing in Georgia. Wheeler shrugged.

"My men require supplies. As does the enemy. Is it not advisable that I empty this country of anything useful to the Yankees? That was the order I was given, as I understood it."

"Yes, it was. Still is, I regret to say. The people of

this state are appropriately surprised that this war has suddenly entered their front yards, as though our struggle over the past three years has suddenly become a nuisance. Are you aware that their governor, Mr. Brown, has suggested that the state of Georgia engage in her own efforts at peace?"

Wheeler arched his brow, the most visible change in his expression Hardee had seen. "By themselves?"

Hardee nodded. "It is Governor Brown's position that each state in the Confederacy can withdraw their allegiance at any time. Since Georgia is now feeling the sword, he seems to believe his voters would prefer he do exactly that. You are aware that several South Carolina regiments have exercised the same privilege? Instead of assisting us here, they are safely ensconced at Charleston. Every state may now feel free to fight this war on their own terms."

"My men will hear none of that, I assure you. What of the Georgia regiments in other theaters? At Petersburg? Are they intending to just . . . resign?"

"I expect not." Hardee held up a hand. "General, do not concern yourself with this. Governor Brown is in hiding somewhere, best I can tell. Once the enemy took Milledgeville, he took the state government under his wing and flew off."

"He's in Augusta."

"If you say so. Hardly matters."

Wheeler shook his head. "Treasonous. Ungrate-

ful. I shall feel no reservations about what may happen to the loyal people of Georgia."

Hardee thought, When did you before? He let it
go, stood, tried to stretch away the sleepiness. He
moved to the window, his eyes searching through
bleariness, caught by the flickers of lantern light
down the street. Wheeler still mumbled something
about Brown, and Hardee ignored him, his eyes
rising to the black sky, a brief moment of peace.

Wheeler spoke out now, erasing the calm, the
words coming out in a boast. "It appears General
Forrest has equipped himself no better in Tennessee now than before."

Hardee turned, saw the maddening blankness on
Wheeler's face. "If you are referring to the fighting
in central Tennessee, the engagement at Franklin,
yes, I know of that. We lost a great deal more than
the prestige of General Forrest."

There was heat in Hardee's words, and Wheeler
seemed to grasp that he had stepped into a tender
place.

"I have had something of a competition with
General Forrest, sir. I meant no disrespect."

"Like hell you didn't. I know all about your dis-
taste for Bedford Forrest. But you will keep that little feud to yourself. The army lost a decisive battle,
and a number of capable field commanders. Thus
far I have learned of five generals who were lost,
Mr. Wheeler. **Five**."

He saw a hint of surprise on Wheeler's face.

"You did not know? General Adams, Granbury, Gist, Strahl. And General Cleburne. There could be others." Hardee's voice broke, and he stopped, was suddenly furious at Wheeler.

"Very sorry, sir. I was not aware of the extent of our losses."

Hardee again fought the emotions, but the words burst through, hot and loud. "There will be more, Mr. Wheeler. A great many more! There is no replacing these men. Do you understand that?"

Wheeler didn't flinch, said, "And Braxton Bragg sits in some mansion enjoying the luxuries of lofty command."

"I do not concern myself with Bragg!"

He was shaking now, closed his eyes tightly, fought for control. He could hear the faint boot steps, knew the staff had come, would be close by, whether he wanted them or not. He opened his eyes, was surprised to see Wheeler standing.

"Sir, I shall carry out your orders. We shall do what we can to empty the countryside to Sherman's front. We shall cut down as many trees as we can, to impede his progress on the roads."

Hardee saw the face of Pickett at the door, concerned, waiting for some kind of reassurance from Hardee. "It's all right, Colonel. General Wheeler will be leaving."

Hardee looked at Wheeler, felt some calm returning, pushed away the thoughts of Cleburne. "At your discretion, when you feel you have done an adequate job retarding Sherman's advance, you will move out once more to his left flank, and resume your harassment."

Wheeler seemed to absorb that, said, "That will eliminate any protection for the city beyond your defenses now in place."

"We do not have the strength to prevent the enemy from forcing crossings at any point along the creeks and rivers he chooses. The Ocmulgee, the Oconee, the Savannah, are not obstacles we can defend. The Federal engineers are making excellent use of pontoon bridges and so can ford anyplace that suits them. I had hoped to make a strong defense farther out from the city, but General McLaws was adamant that he could not hope to hold Sherman back. I agreed, and repositioned his troops nearer the city. General Beauregard has agreed to come here, to see our situation for himself. I cannot ask more than that. I am certain that if there is to be a stand at all, it will be in the works we are fortifying right now, closest to the city. I have ordered the larger coastal guns brought westward as well, placed where they might deal a blow to the enemy's advance."

"The coast is now undefended? What of the Yankee navy? Could they not be a threat?"

Hardee was in no mood for lengthy explanations, especially not to a cavalryman. "Sherman serves at the pleasure of General Grant. They are, at the very least, comrades. Friends, if you will. Grant will not let anyone else take thunder from Sherman's triumphant march. Unless we can injure him, and badly, I'm certain the Federal navy has orders to remain out of the way, unless Sherman requires their help."

Wheeler seemed to understand that Hardee had a peculiar knack for finding information no one else seemed to know. "Then, sir, if you will permit, I shall return to my men. We may not be capable of causing him great injury, but we shall cause considerable inconvenience, sir. As much as possible."

HARDEE'S HEADQUARTERS, SAVANNAH, GEORGIA—DECEMBER 9, LATE NIGHT

"Sir, the Richmond paper has arrived. It is only a few days old. Remarkable that it got through this quickly."

He looked up from his desk, Roy offering him a smile.

"Why are you not in bed, Major? It is late."

"Not while you're here, sir."

"So, Major, you would ingratiate yourself to me with blind loyalty. I suppose it works."

"Blind loyalty is still loyalty, sir. You might wish to examine the paper. There is word there about Sherman."

Hardee had had his fill of newspapers, already knew what kind of bizarre optimism was being

spread throughout Georgia, if not the whole Confederacy. He took the paper, "Sherman" catching
his eye, and read:

**Sherman's campaign, daringly conceived,
has been dimly prosecuted. He seems to
realize his peril, and is now concerned
only with making his escape. The great
hero has turned fugitive.**

Hardee glanced at the banner. Richmond **Senti-
nel**. He handed the paper back to Roy, who seemed
nearly giddy.

"See there, sir? If it's being said in Richmond, it
must surely be true."

"Go to bed, Major."

"Only after you, sir." Roy was serious now.
"There is nothing to command here while the rest
of the city sleeps, sir. Is it not best if you awake
with them?"

"There are men at labor in the defenses, Major,
even now. No hand can be spared, and whether it
be day or night, the work must go on. Or is that a
new idea for you?" He had no reason to scold Roy,
but the exhaustion had taken over, his eyes heavy
again. "Is there any coffee about?"

Behind Roy, a voice, Pickett now at the door.
"Sir, a wire for you, from Charleston. It's in cipher,
sir. Should I decode it?"

"Only if you wish me to read it, Colonel."

"Certainly, sir."

Pickett was gone, and Roy moved away now, said, "I will attempt to find coffee, sir. We had exhausted what was here. Perhaps there is a cooperative neighbor."

"No. It's near midnight. Leave the people be."

He couldn't avoid curiosity about the wire, looked toward the door, heard Pickett talking to an aide, the scratching of a pen on paper. He stood, started to move that way, a useless exercise in impatience, knew there was little he could do to hurry them. Pickett met him at the door.

"Here, sir. This seems accurate."

Hardee took the paper, the familiar penmanship of his friend. He moved back to the desk, sat, read:

Having no army of relief to look to, and your forces being essential to the defense of Georgia and South Carolina, whenever you shall have to select between their safety and that of Savannah, sacrifice the latter. Pierre G T Beauregard, Lieutenant General, Commanding.

Hardee set the paper down, and Pickett said, "Does that mean we are not to defend the city, sir?"

"That is exactly what it means. You will say nothing of this to anyone. Do you understand that?"

"Certainly, sir. It would be most distressing to the civilians hereabouts."

"I cannot concern myself with civilians right now, Colonel. Our task is to make it as difficult as possible for Sherman to complete his advance, and we shall offer as much of a demonstration as might convince him we intend to fight to the last. That kind of display might be the only effective weapon we have."

"If we abandon the city, where shall we go, sir? General Beauregard does not offer any specifics."

"I suppose I shall ask him that directly. He is supposedly on his way here. The only alternative may depend on Sherman's tactics. We must do all in our power to maintain a route of evacuation, most probably into South Carolina. If I were Sherman, that would be my goal. If he captures Columbia, he will most likely continue his conquests northward." He paused. "Even if Sherman is content with what he has gained thus far, he has swung a sword through the heart of the Confederacy, a wound we cannot hope to heal."

Roy was there now, showed the same concern as Pickett, who said, "What do we do now, sir?"

"You do what you wish. Both of you. I am going to bed."

CHAPTER SEVENTEEN

FRANKLIN

NEAR SPRINGFIELD,
GEORGIA—DECEMBER 8, 1864

He carried a written order from Captain Gorman, sanctioned by Captain Jones, a precaution Franklin took seriously. The paper authorized him to accompany the bummers on their next venture outward, what would be another sweep through the countryside that was growing more dismal by the mile. The swamps seemed to spread out in every direction now, marshy fields, thickets of enormous cypress trees, black water, mud, and every kind of insect. The plantations were fewer, most abandoned, and the bummers continued to ignore the authority handed them by Sherman's order at Atlanta. The complaints and entreaties from the Southern civilians had reached every headquarters in all four of Sherman's corps, but with food likely to be much more scarce, it became more important for the bummers, or the black aides like Franklin, to make the friendly effort to convince the slaves to even greater efforts toward helping the passing army. So often, when the plantations had seemed stripped clean of any useful goods, the slaves had led the way, revealing hidden treasures in underground larders, root cellars disguised by any means the white owners thought would help. The bummers had become expert at seeking out those hidden pantries, but much more, they had focused enormous energy at rooting out more than just rations. The hunt for some kind of treasure had not changed at all, the bummers growing skilled at identifying carefully disguised hiding places, freshly turned soil that might lead to a trove of silverware, or some other valuable booty. But there were far fewer opportunities for the bummers now, and so the urgency for befriending what slaves there might be seemed important enough for Jones to hand Franklin over to Gorman, both men recognizing that a Negro offering a kind word might be more persuasive in convincing any slaves that this army was not about pillage or suffering. There were too many rumors of that already, some ridiculous, some regrettably true. And by far, the greatest outrages had been committed by the bummers. To the officers who actually cared about the consequences of that, who took Sherman's orders seriously, it made sense to reach out to the civilians with a softer hand. But Franklin's officers also knew that some of the bummers had become uncontrollable, ignoring anyone's authority but their own muscle. It was a fact of life that as they spread farther across Georgia, more and more of the men regarded the foraging duty as a means of enriching themselves at the expense of any well-to-do civilian. It was infuriating to those officers who cared, and not all did. Franklin had heard plenty of that from his own captain to understand that too often, when the bummers moved out past the skirmish line, they left the authority of their officers behind.

It was a risk for any Negro to move across this land by himself. But Franklin's job on this day was not only to assist in the foraging efforts, but to observe just what kind of misbehavior the bummers themselves might engage in. He carried a nerve-rattling fear that if these men decided his company wasn't welcome, or if there was some certainty that he would return to camp only to pass along reports of their misdeeds, he might not return to camp at all.

Franklin welcomed the opportunity to meet other slaves in this different kind of countryside, the curiosity of that helping allay his fears about the soldiers he traveled with. He understood that his job was to offer a smile, convincing the slaves that helping the army also helped them. It seemed simple enough, that certainly a man with black skin could gain more cooperation in finding what might be hidden.

One part of Jones's instructions wasn't written on the paper now carried in Franklin's pocket. As persuasive as he might be in passing along the army's good intentions, he was also charged with persuading the slaves not to leave their homes. That made his task that much more challenging, especially if the slaves turned against those masters who might still be around to mete out punishment. For some time now the army had been suffering a heavy burden from the needs and the security of the followers who trailed behind them, some officers estimating their number to be in the tens of thousands. Some of those officers looked the other way as mothers rode with small children in wagons meant for something more military, and some ignored soldiers who made efforts to assist the lame and feeble. But many more of those commanders knew that Sherman's latest orders called for a march as rapid as possible, that the goal, now clearly defined as Savannah, was not too far to their front. With decent weather, it was relatively easy for the men to make their prescribed fifteen-mile march. But with so many Negroes in tow, every company commander knew he risked the ire of his general, who might hear it from Sherman himself. Sherman's anxiousness about reaching Savannah had filtered down through the entire army, no longer any secrets, nothing vague about their intended goal. The closer they drew to Savannah, the more cumbersome the great long tail of Negroes would become. Once the shooting began, something every soldier now expected, even the most benign officers knew that the Negroes would likely be on their own.

Franklin walked, picking his way over the rocky trail, while ahead of him the soldiers rode, a pair on horseback, the others up on an empty wagon. Their goal was simple and direct: by nightfall, fill the wagon with something for the army to eat. That task had been assigned to several teams of foragers, spreading out in various distances from the march of the army. This one numbered a dozen men, led by the enormous sergeant named Knight.

They mostly ignored Franklin, though Captain Gorman had emphasized to the group that Franklin was to travel with them by orders of Captain Jones, and that Gorman himself would hold them all responsible should some misfortune fall upon Franklin. But Franklin could see now, that once clear of the camp, these men seemed to change completely, the only kind of order and discipline coming from the massive fists of Sergeant Knight.

Franklin had seen Knight many times in the camp

of the 113th, a man who enjoyed confrontations, who relished the occasional big mouth, offering Knight an excuse to shatter a man's jaw in the name of discipline. Even the officers seemed to keep clear of the man, an odd contradiction to Franklin, in an army where so much authority seemed carried by those few men like Jones, just because they wore the fancier uniform. But watching Knight exact authority by brute strength had been a lesson learned, and even now Franklin kept his distance. From the start of this day's duty, Knight barely looked at him, a blessing Franklin took to heart. It was very clear to Franklin that, so far from anyone else's authority, Knight could do whatever he wanted.

The two-mule wagon bounced high, struggling with deep holes in the muddy trough of a road, an advantage for Franklin, who kept up a steady pace, keeping close enough that he could hear their talk, most of that a storm of cursing that passed back and forth through the men like some kind of game, made more dangerous by the weapons they carried. For most of the journey, he kept his eyes to the side, peering past the thickets of briars, the small black-water ponds, ringed by enormous cypress trees, their limbs draped in curtains of Spanish moss. He studied the water first, knew those places as the home of alligators, and the fat black snakes they called the **cottonmouth,** the creatures that Franklin had only seen in the deepest holes in the farthest corners of Cobb's plantation. He felt the warmth in the air around him, the brutal cold now days behind them, and he knew very well that the warmer weather meant the creatures would be here, as though rising up from the dead. They were never seen on the colder days, what he considered a fair trade for suffering through those days of bone-chilling temperatures. On those frigid days, a small boy could warm himself by exploring the wet ground in a rapid run, passing through the swampy places without fear. But when the air turned warmer, the creatures seemed to rise up from the mud itself, often seeking the brightest sunlight, spreading out on grassy banks, only to lurch violently into the water if the boy stumbled upon them. As a child, Franklin had found those encounters terrifying enough, the stuff of nightmares. Now he welcomed that those amazing beasts might be close by, infesting the black water. If there were bands of roving rebel cavalry, Franklin had to believe that those fellows would avoid those swampy holes for the same reason he did.

Two men rode ahead of the wagon, and he saw a hand go up, heard the call, the others reacting with a slap of the reins on the pair of mules. Franklin could see another cypress pond, and beyond that a house. It was nothing grand, two stories with a small wraparound porch, curtains billowing softly with the warm breeze. In the yard he was relieved to see a quartet of small black children, watched as they stopped whatever activity had occupied them, the four of them scampering away, dropping down behind a large azalea bush. He saw the muskets come up from the wagon, the men hopping down. An older white woman emerged from the house, a drab dress, her hair pulled tight into a small bun. She stood on the porch, scanned the men, then focused on Knight, who walked up close to her, climbed the step, an act of intimidation that backed the woman away. Franklin moved into the yard, ignored by all but the children, who eyed him from their leafy fortress. He offered them a smile, but their attention was grabbed now by Knight, who shouted out, loud enough for anyone in the house to hear, "Hey, now, missus. You be the lady what lives here? Any men about? Any soldiers, waitin' to take a shot at us?"

Franklin saw fear on the woman's face, so very different than the defiance of the shopkeeping women in Millen. He eased closer, felt the menace of the sergeant's bullying voice, but one of the other soldiers held out a musket, holding him back, the barrel hard across Franklin's chest.

"Easy, boy. We got work to do. You keep out of the way. We done this plenty before."

Franklin said nothing, backed up a step, the soldiers now spreading out, careful, weapons up, and Knight said again, "I say, old woman. You dumb? Just want to know who's hereabouts."

She was visibly shaking, said, "Please don't hurt us. We have nothing."

"Ah, then! Who would be the other half of that 'we'?"

"My daughter is inside, and she is quite ill. I have four darkies, plus those little children. Soldiers came through here yesterday, took everything we had, frightened us near to death. My daughter, Lou Ann, took to her bed."

Knight turned to the others. "This is what happens when you bring up the rear of the march. Damn it all anyway."

Franklin moved away from the soldiers, peered out around the side of the house, called out, "Sir, she says there are slaves. I'll talk to 'em. Where might they be, ma'am?"

The woman looked at him, the fear taking on something far more ugly. "You don't speak to me unless I speak first." She looked back toward Knight. "What kind of people are you? You let your darkies tell you what to do? Let them run about as they please?"

The sergeant looked toward Franklin, waved him past the house, said, "He's 'runnin' about' at my pleasure, missus. But he's gettin' wages for it. That's gotta be worse'n a horse's fart to you, ain't it?"

The woman's disgust was aimed at Knight now, and she crossed her arms, shook her head. "So, you would be more of those rude devils. You'll find nothing here. We've lost every bit of food, every piece of linen, every fork and knife. My late husband's watch, my own rings. They done stole every piece of anything I hold dear." She paused, and Franklin saw a change in her face, all her fear slipping down into something angrier. "Any one of you touches my daughter, and I promise you, Yankee, you don't have enough men to keep me from killing you."

Knight laughed, the others joining in. "Well, now, we got one with spirit! Look, missus, all we want to do is fill this here wagon with rations. Hams, chickens, anything else you got. Excuse me for calling you a liar, but we've done this before, seen places supposed to be all cleaned out, and then, just like that, we find more rations than we can carry. So, if you'll just stand aside now." He turned to one of the others, said, "Four of you, go on in. No need to mess with her gal. If she's sick, I ain't wantin' to carry nothin' of that back to camp." He pointed to a small outbuilding. "Looks like a chicken house. If there's a floor, rip it up. These damned people have a talent for hiding the good stuff. I'll keep my eye on the missus here."

Franklin saw Knight motion to him again, a silent order to move out around the house. He knew what he was looking for, saw it now, a pair of shacks along the edge of a small cut cornfield. Two adult men seemed to wait for him, standing tall in front of the shacks, eyeing him with suspicion. Behind them were a younger boy and a young woman. One of the men stepped forward, chest out, clearly trying to protect the others.

"What you want with us? You bring them soldiers here?"

"They brought me. I work for the army. General
Sherman. We're just getting vittles, anything you
can spare."

"Spare? There's been plenty of Sherman's men
come through here already, done took every scrap,
everythin' we gots to eat. Done taken Miss Harley's silver. Dishes and spoons and bed linens, done
busted up furniture jes for fun. Drove the young
miss to the sickbed. Why they need to do that? You
ain't eatin' none of that. Just thievery, that's all. Evil.
That what you aim to do? You too late."

Franklin saw more anger than he expected, shook
his head. "No, it's all right. I can't talk for nothing else that's happened. But the army's gettin' rid
of the masters, done killed a pile of track hounds,
every one they can find. Overseers have mostly run
away." He weighed his words now, knew what the
captain wanted him to do. But these men were
strong, big-chested, could help the soldiers with
any kind of heavy work. "You all, if'n you want,
you can come along. Work for the army. You'll be
paid. We're bein' freed."

"Freed from what? Why'd we wanna do that? We
got no cause to leave home. Got crops to plant,
greens goin' in the ground next week. Those little
ones gettin' bigger, need more to eat. Miss Harley'll
be needin' us. All I seen of this army is destroyin'

everything. Done took all we got. How we supposed to feed the chil'ren?"

The other larger man pointed out toward the muddy road. "You go on, get yourself outta here. Take them soldiers wid you. We got nothing for you here."

Franklin felt overwhelmed by frustration, as though these people were refusing to see what he had finally taken for granted. "You can stay here, all right. But the war will be over soon. The generals, they're all sayin' that. Mr. Lincoln has freed all of us. Ain't you heard about that?"

The first man still stood tall, still facing him. "All I know of Mr. Lincoln is he's far away somewheres, someplace no colored man ever goes. Don't know nothin' 'bout no war, 'cept that Miss Harley tole us her boy ain't coming home. Kilt by Yankees. That be you, then? You done take her boy away? Miss Lou Ann ain't never been right since. She's sickly all the time. Worse now. You done scared her too bad."

Franklin felt a surge of urgency, an aching need to make these people understand. "I'm not a soldier. I was a slave, just like you, Master Cobb's plantation, miles back. This army is freein' this whole country. We got no need to stay put, to work this land just 'cause they tell us to."

The man shook his head. "You talkin' nonsense. You go on, get outta here. Take them soldiers. They doin' no good right here."

Franklin stared at the man, then looked at the others, saw no comprehension, none of the joy he had seen so many times before. He backed away, said, "You'll see. This war ends, it'll all be different. No more cavalry, no more hounds. It'll be better. You'll see."

The man turned away, the others moving back toward their shacks, and Franklin saw the girl looking out past the side of the main house, horror on her face.

"Oh, dear Lawd! Dey's diggin' up my baby!"

Franklin looked that way, saw a pair of soldiers hoisting a small wooden box from the soft soil. One man called out, "Hey, Sarge! Something here, all right."

One man struck the box with the tip of his shovel, the box shattering, and Franklin stood paralyzed, knew what lay inside, and close behind him, the young woman was hysterical, screaming, "Tha's my baby! Oh, Lawd!"

Other soldiers were gathering at the small grave site, another shovel poking at the small bundle, the shovel coming up now, lying on the man's shoulder.

"Nothing here. Damn these people, anyway."

Franklin moved that way now, fists clenched, saw Knight moving closer, looking down at the shattered coffin. Franklin saw one of the others squat down, pushing through the rolled-up cloth, then standing, a shake of his head.

"Nothing. I'd a bet it was something good."

Franklin was there now, one fist swinging hard into the man's jaw, his other a sharp blow to the man's gut. The man absorbed the punches, bent low, falling backward, but the others had Franklin's arms now, hard grips yanking him back. Franklin shouted out, "What's wrong with you? It's just a baby! It's a grave!"

He felt the fist punch hard into his side, his knees giving way, his face coming down hard in the grass. He was pulled up again, gasping for wind, hands under his throat, the face of Knight close to his.

"I could shoot you, boy. Might, before we get back."

The hurt soldier stood slowly, rubbing his jaw, pure hate in the man's eyes. "Go on, Sarge. Kill him. Any darkie hits me, he oughta be cut in two."

Knight seemed to weigh the man's words, but he released Franklin, who dropped to his knees, gasping for air, the sharp pain stabbing through his ribs.

"Nah. Have to explain that to the captain. We still ain't filled this damned wagon, and these people ain't helping a bit." He looked up, bright sun overhead. "It's after noon. We best get moving."

Franklin felt his air returning, the pain in his side still cutting off every breath. The others began moving away, the sergeant still looking at him.

"What the darkies tell you, boy? They hiding anything?"

Franklin fought through the pain in his ribs,

heard the screaming of the young girl, looked back toward the shacks, saw the two black men holding her, staring hard at the soldiers. He shook his head. "Soldiers been here before us. Took everything. They got nothing left."

Knight grunted, kept his eye on the two big men, his musket pointed at the ground in their direction. He called out, "You all stay back. No need for nobody to get hurt. We'll do what we need, and move on." He looked down at Franklin, said, "The house has been busted up pretty good. They're right. Somebody's beat us to it. Come on. Get up, boy."

Franklin stood, and Knight stayed close beside him, while the others resumed their futile search. The older woman followed a pair of soldiers out of the house, was on the porch again, saw now the churned-up earth. She shouted toward Knight, "You find what you wanted? Defiled a grave, you did. You'll burn in hell, every one of you."

Franklin looked down at the broken coffin, the bundle of cloth disheveled, soiled with loose dirt. The sergeant ignored the woman, said in a low voice, "Ought not have done that. Didn't like this, and don't you think for a minute I did. God won't like it, neither. Damned stupid. It's that Dunlap, crazy fool. Thinks these people are rich with gold and jewels, every damn house is a palace gonna make us all kings." He paused. "Boy, you ever hit a soldier again, and captain or no captain, I won't hold 'em back. They'll hang you for it."

Franklin was surprised, Knight's words still low, the fierceness of the man's size masking what Franklin could feel was unexpected kindness.

"Thank you, sir."

Knight spoke louder now, still eyed the angry glare from the slaves. "Those coloreds back there got nothing? You think they hiding something? Seem pretty damn kindly to this old rebel woman. Don't trust that."

"They got nothing, sir. I believe them. They're stayin' fixed, right here."

The sergeant kept his eyes on the young black woman, and Franklin saw regret on his face, but there were no words, no apology that would matter. The woman seemed inconsolable, heavy sobbing, was still held firmly by the larger man, who said to Knight, "They's too many of you, or I'd a kilt me a man today." He pointed to Franklin. "I done tole him, and I'm telling you. Get gone from dis place." He paused, a break in his voice, and Franklin could see he was sharing the emotions from the woman he held.

Franklin said to Knight, "We oughta bury the body."

The black man stepped closer, hard anger through tear-filled eyes. "You done enough. Get gone from here. I done buried my boy one time. I'll do it again."

EBENEZER CREEK,
GEORGIA—DECEMBER 8, 1864

With the darkness, the rains had come, a soft, steady spray that softened the roads even more. They had returned from their expedition by passing through the skirmish line, soggy, hopeful men, who met the wagon with cursing anticipation. Franklin moved past them, was ignored again, the guards more focused on the haul of sweet potatoes, the only hint of treasure the men had found.

He followed the campfires toward the new camp, thought of the captain, knew he had to tell Gorman what he had seen, how meager the pickings had been. But he agonized now over the grave, an image he couldn't shake, what little piece of a child he had seen in the bundle of cloth. Sergeant Knight's sorry for that, he thought. There was no cause for it, and he won't let those boys do nothing like that again. He put a hand on his sore ribs, thought, You're maybe one stupid man. You go and punch at a white man like that. He flexed his sore fingers, shivered, the wetness from the rain soaking through his clothes. They woulda killed you if it weren't for the sergeant. Best keep away from all those boys. Maybe they'll forget about you. But I ain't goin' out with them, that's certain. Gotta tell the captain that, anyway.

He had begun to understand the anger he saw in so many of the soldiers, that this entire army seemed driven by some kinds of experiences from long ago. He still wasn't sure what happened in a war, listened to their talk around the campfires wondering if they were doing just what his father used to do, tall tales meant to scare a young boy. They spoke often of bloody fights, of men in pieces, of burying rebel dead in mass graves. Some spoke of facing the bayonet, the blasts of artillery slicing a man to pieces, while others kept silent, staring into the fires with hard anger. The talk seemed focused on the rebels, on what they would have to do to those men to end this war, and how some of them hoped for all that bloody fighting to come again. He thought of the soldier today, the man Knight called Dunlap. **I'll cut you in two**. He would. Best believe that. Believe that if these men have gone through the worst kind of fighting and killing, one stupid black boy don't mean a thing. That grave, though. That gal, she'll be seein' that forever. Maybe me, too.

He shivered again, moved toward a fire, a few men milling about, a coffeepot passing around. He searched the darkness for Poke, the makeshift corral of horses. He crossed the muddy road, passed through a gap in a marching column, a surprise, men on the move after dark. They're going somewhere important, he thought. Guess so, anyway. Maybe trying to put the creek back there behind 'em. Guess we all need to be on the same side of the creek, in case the rebels come.

The voice found him, a high-pitched call that

stopped the talk of the soldiers, men turning to find the source. He saw her now, Clara, the girl from Millen, running alongside the column, calling his name, a frantic wave, a tearful squall that made his heart turn cold.

"Franklin. You gots to come! Come now!"

He didn't ask why, watched as she turned, still looking at him, her arms in frantic motion, crying, pleading. "Now! Come now!"

He ran after her, his feet slogging in the muddy slop along the road, soldiers calling after him as he passed them, crude remarks he ignored. She stumbled, and he was there now, held her up by the arm, saw frantic fear on her face, said, "What's happening?"

"Come! You gots to come!"

She began to run again, and he followed, most of the column now past, wagons, horses passing, and he saw lanterns, to the rear of the column, men on horseback, more soldiers moving out from the creek, some carrying pieces of the pontoon bridge the men had built. There were more men at work, ordered about by an officer on horseback, something Franklin had seen often before. But now he heard a different cry, on the far side of the creek, another lantern there, soldiers in a line at the far end of the bridge, and all out through the swampy woods, a vast crowd of Negroes.

He followed Clara to the edge of the creek, and he stopped, out of breath, tried to absorb what he saw, what it meant. She shouted to him now, "They leavin' 'em behind! They ain't lettin' 'em cross over!"

He could see it now, the far side of the creek, the soldiers pulling up the planks of the bridge, a chorus of shouting, some of the boatlike pontoons carrying the soldiers as they moved out from the bank. More men were on the bridge itself, doing the same, the planks up, brought to the near shore, tossed into wagons. She was still screaming now, calling out to him, "What they doin'? They leavin' 'em! They tole me none of us is comin'. I beg 'em let me cross, run on the bridge, few of us come over before they stand up with guns and such. Now they stoppin' everybody! Why? What we do?"

Franklin saw the men on horseback, the flag, recognized authority. He ran that way, heard one officer calling out, "Let's go. Get that bridge up!"

Franklin moved up closer to the officer, a guard suddenly in his way, the man's musket across Franklin's chest.

"Back away from here, boy. You made it across, just move on. You can't help the rest."

Franklin pushed against the man, had to speak to the officer, but the guard held him fast, the officer now joined by another horseman, hard words, close above Franklin.

"Captain, who authorized this? General Baird knows nothing of this!"

"Major Connolly, my orders came from corps headquarters, straight from General Davis. I'm to pull this bridge up as quick as our men make it across. There's rebel cavalry back there, pushing to get up with us. There's another creek up ahead on that road there, Lockner, I think. We've got another bridge there, and we're to get the men over, then pull that one up, too, quick as we can."

"Captain Kerr, you will do no such thing! I've heard nothing of any rebel cavalry close to us, no confrontations at all! You cannot leave those people across the creek!"

Franklin felt the pressure from the guard slackening, the musket coming down, the man watching as he did, caught up in the argument raging between the two officers. Franklin eased forward, wanted to say something, anything, a protest, looked again across the creek, the lanterns now coming closer to the near shore, the vast sea of screams and shouts still across the way. Above him, one of the officers said, "Major, I have my orders. I don't like this, either, but General Davis's instructions were definite and very specific."

"I will report this to General Baird! You cannot just leave those people behind us!"

"My orders, Major."

The major swung his horse around, galloped away through the rainy darkness, and Franklin looked up at the captain, saw the man looking out over the creek, staring, as though he were paralyzed.

Franklin called out, "Sir! What are you doing? Those people . . . they're bein' left behind!"

The man looked down at him, a flicker of the lanterns reflecting on the grim sadness on the man's face. "Nothing I can do, boy. I have my orders. You made it across. You're lucky. Now move on, get across the next creek. We're taking that bridge up quick as we can."

"But, those people over there!"

"Get moving, boy!"

The captain turned his horse away, calling out more orders to the men on the bridge, the planks and pontoons coming ashore quickly, filling the wagons. Franklin moved to the water's edge, stared across, could see the surging mass of people, heard splashing, the water churning up, arms flailing, realized people were coming across on their own. He stepped forward, the cold water to his knees, but he had never tried to swim before, felt sick, his heart racing, heard the screams still, the splashing coming closer. One man was there now, arms grabbing the muddy bank, and Franklin dropped down, reached for the man's hand, pulled him up onto the shore. More were finding the shore, men calling out, some jumping back into the water, helping others as they made their way across. There were women coming ashore now, but not many, sobbing as they fell into the arms of any man who would help them. Franklin waded along the bank, had a desperate fear of the water, felt empty, helpless, the water alive with foaming splashes, arms flailing all across the wide creek. People were crying out all around him, more of the screaming, and he saw arms waving in the water, coming close. He moved that way, tried to step out, deeper, the water to his waist, his arms reaching out closer to the hands, a desperate grab, the hands suddenly gone, the water close to him empty, quiet. He reached down into the water, his face submerged, searching blindly with his hands, but the man was gone. He stood again, coughed out the bitter water, searched with frantic motions, saw others doing as he was, helping hands. Some of them were in uniform, the soldiers who dismantled the bridge now trying to help. But the lanterns were moving away, the darkness spreading over the sounds, the splashes, the cries, still a great chorus of voices on the far side, calling out, desperate and terrified, so many people left behind by the men they had trusted to save them.

Throughout the night, more of the freed slaves made good their crossing of Ebenezer Creek, but many more did not. There were makeshift rafts, some using logs to float their way over, aided by those who could wade out to receive them. The soldiers who stayed behind could not remain long, the next bridge already being dismantled, those men ordered to pull away, to make their way across Lockner Creek. Along that bank, the scene was repeated, those Negroes who had survived the crossing over Ebenezer Creek now faced with another barrier, another black waterway. But still they tried, exhausted, terrified people, plunging into the water in the driving rain, some, the most fit, making it across, while so many more did not. The helping hands were there as well, black and white, Franklin doing all he could even as he slipped deeper into the muddy bottom of the deadly stream. By morning, those who remained stranded beyond Ebenezer Creek were suddenly faced with a new terror. Rebel cavalry appeared, and for those who could not run, who could not escape into deep woods or treacherous swamps, the cavalry did their work. Those who tried to fight the rebel troops were mostly cut down, sabers and pistols, while others, the old and infirm, the women and young children, were grabbed up, only to be returned to the plantations and masters they had left behind.

CHAPTER EIGHTEEN

SHERMAN

NEAR POOLER,
GEORGIA—DECEMBER 8, 1864

The house was modest, something Sherman was used to now, but more than ever, he suffered from the sleeplessness that not even a decent mattress could cure. Outside, the campfires had mostly grown dark, faint hints of embers spread out through thin pine woods, the various units of Frank Blair's Seventeenth Corps spread apart, divided by patches of swamp, watery sandpits, and thickets of cypress and thorny brush.

He did as he had often done, easing the misery of sleeplessness by taking a walk, stepping down

quietly from the headquarters toward the nearest
fires. He rarely dressed, wore mostly his nightclothes, his brimless hat clamped down on his head.
There would be one cigar, no pockets to hold any
more, but it would do, offering a hint of warmth
for those few minutes until that too fell dark. He
stepped carefully, avoiding the occasional briar,
the stinging nettle or even the prickly pear cac-
tus, the unfriendly hints that the countryside had
changed completely. It was all familiar to him, so
much of it like Louisiana. But most of the men
around him had never been in anyplace like this,
and throughout the past few days, they had begun
to react with a raw energy he could feel spreading
through the entire army. It didn't require maps to
understand that this army was drawing closer to its
goal, that somewhere out across the flat plains of
swamp and rice fields lay the city of Savannah.

He stopped, took a deep breath, cool and wet,
the rains settling into a gentle drizzle. The winds
were from the east, unusual, but with that came
the scent of salt air, that first sign that the marsh-
lands were soon to change again, the black water of
the swamps giving way to brackish pools, and then
to the wide, grassy flats of pure salt water, where
oysters and crabs would be found. It had already
spread through the army, those men who knew the
coast anxious to reap this new bounty, something
they didn't have to take from the civilians. Most of
the men had begun to rely on a diet mostly of sweet

potatoes, the rich variety of treasures that grew in central Georgia now behind them. The supply wagons had brought forward most of the surplus, but after so many days on the march, even the vast oversupply of goods was draining low, more wagons empty now than full. As they passed the rice fields, the cooks and commissary officers had to be taught just what to do with the reedy plants, how to shake and pound the tiny grains from the wet greenery, and then, how the grains could be made edible. But the men were learning quickly, taught mostly by slaves, and already the army was experiencing a new kind of hardtack, or a pressed cake made very differently from the awful flour they knew so well. But hardtack was still hardtack, and more of the men now spoke with enthusiasm of the salt water, what new treasures could be found. Sherman was gratified to hear just how many of his men shared his love of oysters, other shellfish, and the proximity of the ocean had added considerably to the morale of an army that, for the first time in the campaign, was beginning to experience hunger.

He moved to the nearest fire, picked up a stick, prodded the faint embers. The ground around him was soggy from the rain, the fire nearly extinguished, but he poked harder, deeper, the embers growing brighter. He was determined now, searched the darkness for something to add to the flame, some kind of kindling, saw a stack of small sticks, covered by a canvas cloth. He pulled out a single stick, smelled it, the delicious scent of fat pine, used that to prod the embers until the heat ignited the stick. He let the flame crawl upward toward his hand, tilted it away, then added the fat pine to the glowing embers. He retrieved another, creating a new fire from the old one, the flames growing, the warmth on his hands comforting, the black smoke swirling past him even more pleasing than the cigar. He stood, his eyes still on the flames, his minor victory, and he looked across the camp, the men nearly all silent, unaware that their commander found so much joy from the simple task of building a fire.

Behind him, a whisper. "Sir. Excuse me."

Sherman kept the groaning response silent, knew it was Hitchcock. "What is it, Major?"

"Sorry to interrupt, sir. I'm finding it difficult to sleep. I know you usually take a walk. Hope you don't mind just a bit of company."

Sherman shrugged. "If you insist."

There was a silent moment, Hitchcock absorbing Sherman's hint. "Oh, sir, forgive me. I'll be going. I should return to bed anyway. Very late."

Sherman turned to him now, saw the man's hair tousled, the glow of the small fire reflected on Hitchcock's glasses. "No, it's fine. I don't usually have companionship out here. Can't sleep, eh?"

"No, sir. I keep thinking of what's ahead, Savannah and whatnot. Very exciting, to be sure."

"The skirmishes are growing hotter. Rebels aren't

just going to lie down and let us walk in. I'd rather keep my mind on what we have to do about that. It could get nasty, Major."

"I understand that, sir. But look how far we've come. They'll hear of this up north, soon enough. The newspapermen will get the word out, once we can find a wire northward."

Sherman saw Hitchcock staring at the small fire, marching in place, a slight rhythm back and forth, warming himself from the wet chill. "Don't really care what the newspapers say. Grab a couple of sticks from that pile, over there."

Hitchcock obeyed, added the fuel to Sherman's fire, the flames rising again. Hitchcock held his hands out over the low flames, said, "I understand, sir. But there will be some commotion at the War Department. They can't know yet just what we're doing, where we are. Must be a great deal of uncertainty about that. But with the news from Tennessee, I'm certain the president will have heightened expectations of our campaign as well."

Sherman knew of the great fight at Franklin, had been surprised to see detailed accounts in copies of a newspaper from Savannah, captured from rebel skirmishers. The accounts were extraordinary, especially for any Southern paper, the casualty counts clearly favoring the Federal army, what seemed to be portrayed as a one-sided fight, the newspaper not hesitant to describe the battle as a horrific defeat for John Bell Hood. Sherman had read those accounts with puzzlement, had to believe that if the Savannah papers were revealing a fight so clearly against Hood's army, the actual numbers were likely even worse for the rebels. **We should have chased him**. He rolled those words through his mind, thought of the doubters, Halleck for one, all that fear, the infuriating lack of confidence in Sherman, finally silenced by Grant's approval for the campaign. A whole rebel army running loose in Tennessee and I go the other way, he thought. He smiled now, staring down at the fire. I knew Thomas could handle it. Hood's no match for someone who sits tight in a strong defense, and Thomas knows all about defense.

He picked up another stick of fat pine, rolled it over in his hand. Hood throws his people away like kindling in a bonfire. He repeated the words to himself, dropped the stick in the fire, thought, You should write poetry, maybe. Well, no. You'd just say something stupid again, get yourself in trouble. Grant's pants. Lee's knees. Hardee's party. Might be easier than you think to make up rhymes. He thought a moment. Nothing rhymes with Thomas. All right, Sherman, let it go. Vermin Sherman. Yep, that's what they'll say. Just keep your mouth shut and fight the damned war.

Hitchcock added more fuel to the fire, the flames now high enough to warm them both. He reached into his coat pocket, retrieved a scrap of something Sherman couldn't see. "Oh, sir, look here. Picked up a piece of this Spanish moss. Good keepsake. I've seen it before, in Alabama, but not in such an abundance as they have here. Did you know that when it gets wet, it turns green?"

"I am pleased you find time for souvenirs, Major. It's not exactly rare. There will be a great deal more ahead of us. You got the itch yet?"

Hitchcock reacted by scratching his arm. "Itch . . . yes, sir. All day. How did you know that, sir?"

"The moss. Some kind of bug lives in it, I think. I tried sleeping on a bed of the stuff once. Never do that again. Spent half a day sitting in a creek bed, trying to get the bug bites to go away."

Hitchcock held out the small piece of moss, tossed it now on the fire. The smoke grew thick, and Sherman waved it away with his hand.

"Dammit, Major, it doesn't burn worth a hoot. Not wet anyway."

"Sorry, sir. At least I know why I've been scratching."

"Better than snakebite. Plenty of those to be had out here, too."

He heard an audible shiver from Hitchcock, couldn't help a smile. Step lively, Major. Or stay on your damn horse.

The rains had stopped, the breeze blowing colder, and Sherman heard men stirring, curious about the fresh fire. He said in a low voice, "Don't really want to draw attention, Major. Let them sleep. Move away."

"Oh, certainly, sir." Hitchcock stood back from the fire, followed Sherman out through the darkness. Sherman began to miss the cigar, felt the chill on his bare legs, remembered he was in his nightclothes. All I need now is for that Conyngham fellow to show up. He'll want to tell the world how I run this army in bedclothes.

After a long moment, Hitchcock said, "Sir, are you intending to inquire of General Davis what occurred tonight?"

"What are you talking about?"

"Oh, dear. You were not informed? That is my fault, certainly."

"I don't like mysteries, Major."

"Sir, we do not have all the details, but General Baird was most disturbed by reports from his staff that General Davis ordered that at least one column of the Fourteenth Corps cross the creek a ways back, and when the troops were across, General Davis ordered that passage be refused the Negroes."

"What do you mean, 'passage be refused'?"

"According to General Baird, sir, General Davis removed his pontoon bridges before the Negroes could cross. A great many of them were left behind. General Baird intends to seek some official remonstrance against General Davis."

Sherman closed his eyes, shook his head. "Is the Fourteenth Corps in its camps, in position for our march tomorrow?"

"Yes, sir. I believe so, sir."

"Then General Davis did what he had to do to get his people in the right place, including Baird's division. In every column, the slaves are strung out like threads from a worn pants leg. We cannot slow our progress just to accommodate them. I made it plain to every senior commander that the Negroes be encouraged to remain at their homes."

He was angry now, felt a nagging annoyance at Absalom Baird. He trusted Baird, actually liked the man, knew that Baird had been one of Sherman's most accomplished generals in the fights around Atlanta. But Baird was one of the three division commanders in the Fourteenth Corps, who answered directly to Davis. He held some respect for Jefferson Davis as well, though Davis was not a West Pointer. And he's got a crazy-assed temper, Sherman thought. He stopped at another smoldering fire, tried to feel any kind of warmth.

"Davis killed his commanding officer, you know."

"Sir?"

"William Nelson. After the start of the war, in Louisville. Took offense at something Nelson said to him. I heard it was the kind of thing that men fight duels over, but Davis decided to go the shorter route. Shot Nelson with a pistol, in a hotel hallway. Killed him dead. Got away with it, too. I guess nobody much cared for Nelson."

"Sir, that's awful! How did he keep his command? And how—"

"He's a good soldier, good leader. Stupid name,

but I can't hold that over him. As long as he handles his corps like he's done so far, I can't drag him down for some Negro matter. No time for that kind of thing, anyhow. Baird wants to pursue it later, I suppose he can. Somebody should warn him to stay out of hotel hallways."

Hitchcock held his hands out, feeling for the rain. He walked in silence for a long moment, then said, "Hope there's not more to it, sir."

"What do you mean?"

"The newspapers and all."

"To hell with newspapers, Major. When are you going to learn that? Those people are not your friends, will do everything they can to sell a story to a public that swallows their nonsense whole. I've got more important things to concern myself with, and it's right out there, about ten miles away. It's up to Slocum to handle his generals. If they want to fight a duel, that's Slocum's problem. My problem is all those damned rebels out there. The Negroes insist on following us, they can handle themselves."

Hitchcock seemed agitated now, and Sherman had no interest in another lecture of conscience. Hitchcock seemed to choose his words carefully, something Sherman was used to. "Sir, you must acknowledge that, when the time comes, the president will welcome the reports of so many freed slaves. These people are . . . well, sir, they are **worshipping** this army, they worship you. I apologize, sir, but I don't know of a better word for it."

"I'm not out here to be worshipped, Major. I'm out here to rip the guts out of this state, and the people who still intend to fight for it. I don't need my staff officers soaking up sympathy for the Negroes. I didn't ask them to follow us, and I can't pretend they're like my children. We're busting their chains to pieces, we're killing hound dogs every damned day, their owners are scattered to the winds. But I didn't plan this campaign around emancipation. This is an army, not some damned tent revival."

He was walking faster now, even more annoyed at the interruption from Hitchcock. He noticed the major falling back, heard his voice trailing away.

"Sorry to bother you, sir. I shall return to bed."

Sherman felt a hint of guilt, knew how much value Hitchcock had brought to his staff. He stared out into darkness, the breeze picking up, thought, It will be a cold one tomorrow, sure as hell. He thought of Davis, knew the man had been something of a copperhead, rarely had a kind word to offer toward Lincoln. Well, damn you to hell, General. Lincoln's been reelected, and he's in charge of this whole damned affair. I've got enough problems with Washington without one of my corps commanders stirring up a bee's nest. Maybe, just maybe, this won't blow up into something ugly. Best way to avoid that is to find some damned rebels and give the newspapermen something better to write about. Meanwhile, Sherman, just keep your mouth shut about all of that, and make sure these men do their jobs.

DECEMBER 9, 1864

"You can't burn me out! You can't do nothin' like that! My man'll be back! He'll tell you what I done told you! They made him go! Came and took him, just like that!"

Sherman heard the woman from down the road, saw a cluster of soldiers around her porch. Beside him, McCoy said, "Think it's a problem, sir?"

"It's always a problem, Major. Go on, see about it."

McCoy rode forward, an aide in tow, and Sherman tried to skirt the far side of the road, avoiding the confrontation. He dreaded the presence of his color bearer, knew that it would draw her attention. He wasn't wrong.

"You there! You a big general and such! They burning me out! I love the Union! I love Lincoln!"

Sherman tried to ignore her, but an officer moved out into the road, a hearty salute.

"General Sherman! Uncle Billy, sir! It is an honor! Your authority is most welcome!"

Sherman stopped the horse. "Why?"

"Lieutenant Phil duBois, sir. 43rd Ohio, Colonel Montgomery's brigade. We took musket fire from a pretty good bunch of rebels, back behind this house. When we returned fire, several of them scooted out of her cellar. We nabbed four of 'em, but the rest got away. According to your instructions, sir, this house is to be burned. But this woman says her husband was pressed by force into rebel service."

"You haven't heard that before, Lieutenant?"

"Can't say I have, sir. You think maybe she's lying?"

"Don't you? She's hiding rebels, and they bushwhacked you. What the hell are you waiting for?"

The woman came out into the road now, spit a stream of tobacco past Sherman's horse with surprising force. "Now, you look here! My husband was made to fight agin you. Made to! Didn't wanna go, no ways. We love the Union!"

Sherman watched as she seemed to assemble another mouthful of spit, was suddenly fearful she was going to aim it at him. "Madam, gather what belongings you wish, and keep out of the way. I've heard your story in every town in Georgia. It seems that the entire rebel army is made up of men who didn't want to fight. Well, madam, if that were true, this war wouldn't have come to much, would it? And sure as rain, there wouldn't be any need for me to be here, now would there?"

She spit again, down under his horse. "If he was here, he'd show you what it means to fight!"

Sherman had become too accustomed to this, though he was impressed with the velocity of the woman's spittle, thought, Even the women around here know something of marksmanship. Lying, too.

"Lieutenant duBois, continue your work."

He spurred the horse, the woman letting go of a stream of cursing, Sherman hurrying the horse out of range. McCoy rode up beside him now, said, "She was a real pistol, sir."

"Guessing she had one in her undergarments, Major. I bet her husband's right up there in Savannah, waiting for us."

He heard musket fire, spreading out to one side of the road, held up the horse. A burst of cannon fire came now, two heavy thumps, then two more, and he yanked on the reins, his eye caught by Hitchcock, the major's horse bucking wildly. Hitchcock calmed the horse quickly, a self-conscious glance at Sherman, who focused now on the stretch of road to the front. There were swampy patches to both sides, the road slightly elevated, someone's labor at keeping it clear of high water. He had already crossed a half-dozen small creeks, eyeing the work of Captain Poe's engineers, the men who were charged with clearing so much of the felled timber that lay across the roads.

There was more cannon fire, and he ignored the effect of that on Hitchcock's horse, stared ahead, saw troops moving up from the swampy fields, pushing forward. An officer emerged on horseback, now another coming out of the trees to one side, moving that way. There was a color bearer, the man's small staff pointing toward Sherman, an aide turning quickly toward him. The man rode at a gallop,

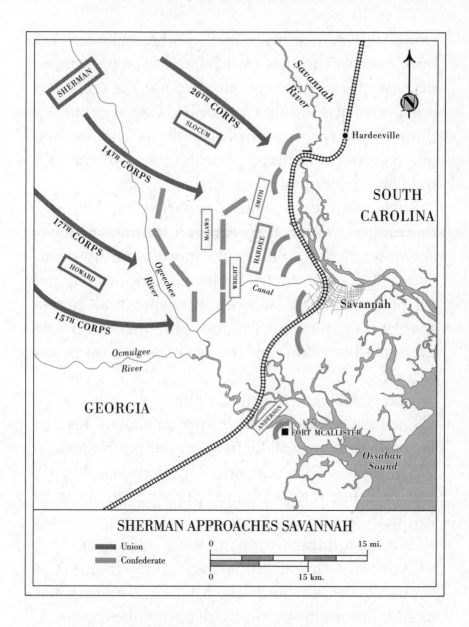

SHERMAN APPROACHES SAVANNAH

Union
Confederate

0   15 mi.

0   15 km.

reined up, Sherman still watching beyond, where more soldiers flowed across the road.

"Sir! Best stay back! There was a rebel guard post or something in the trees just there! We've got 'em on the run. More rebels to the front, dug into some works right across this road. Captain Drake ran slap into 'em, but they fired wild. Couldn't a been more than twenty or thirty of 'em. We put the men into line pretty quick, two companies. Cavalry came in from that way, hit 'em on the flank, and we had one battery unlimbered pretty quick. Did the job, sir. The rebs took off that way!"

There was more musket fire, farther to the right, shouting now, the fire scattered, fading. The officer returned to the road, moved toward him, said, "Welcome to our little celebration, General! All morning long. Reb outposts spread all across anyplace there's high ground. But there's no real strength. They don't seem to want to put up much of a scrap, sir."

"You're Alabama Cavalry, right?"

The man responded with a proud smile. "Yes, sir! 1st Alabama Cavalry! Lieutenant Jerome Novey, sir. We're hauling some prisoners, probably grabbed a few more just now. Colonel Spencer is up ahead, if you wish to speak to him."

"Not now. How strong are those earthworks?"

"Not very, sir. Even if they were, there's not enough rebels to hold 'em for long. Infantry has spread out to both sides, flanking the position. Rebs know they can't stand up to that."

Hitchcock was there now, said in a low voice, "Alabama?"

The lieutenant heard him, and Sherman knew what was coming, interrupted Novey's inevitable show of pride. "There's good Union men in every part of the Confederacy, Major. Unlike that lying female back there, these boys made a choice to fight for their country and not their state."

Novey sat straight in the saddle, a sharp nod. "That we did, sir!"

"Lieutenant, I want to see what kind of rebel position we've run into. If you'll lead us that way?"

"Certainly, sir. Please follow me. We'll move out off the road, in case of rebel artillery, sir."

Sherman followed, the staff falling into line behind him. His guards moved out with the cavalryman, Lieutenant Snelling spreading them out through the thin woods, tall pines, sandy soil, patches of soft and soggy ground the horsemen knew to avoid. They rode for several minutes, and up ahead, more musket fire began. Sherman listened with one hand gripping the reins, stared up past the horsemen, expected to see the rebels, some attempt to drive his men away. But the firing was almost all one direction, aimed away from his own men. Around him, more troops were coming into line, pushed forward by their officers, adding more strength to whatever confrontation lay ahead. Now the whoops and cheering came, the men recognizing him as he passed by. He eyed the officers, saw good order, none of the chaos of a major engagement. He felt relief at that, allowed himself to hear the cheers, saw officers with swords held high, some of those calling his name. The horsemen led them through a four-gun battery, those men cheering Sherman as well, the ever-present cries of "Uncle Billy." He was relaxing now, pulled out a cigar, was cheered even for that, an odd surprise. He lit the cigar, kept himself straight in the saddle, acknowledged the men with a brief nod, fought to hide the smile. Behind him, he heard Hitchcock, the words aimed at one of the others.

"God, but they do love him."

Sherman kept his gaze to the front, pondered those words, thought, If they love me, it's because we're winning the fight. One time, just one time, it goes badly, all that might change.

Up ahead, the cavalryman quickened the horse's pace and Sherman saw Lieutenant Snelling turn toward him, pointing out toward the road. There was a cluster of men, gathered up on the wide stretch of the sandy road, and he heard shouts, furious anger. The guards led the way, Lieutenant Novey now off his horse, down among the men. Sherman dismounted, stepped forward, Snelling coming toward him with his hands out.

"Sir! Please stop here! There is considerable danger."

"What kind of danger?"

"Torpedoes, sir!"

He pushed past Snelling, moved up onto the road, the men making way for him. To one side was a horse, its belly ripped open, the animal a fountain of blood. The men had gathered around the rider, and Sherman saw another man, bloody flesh on his leg, the bone stripped white, the foot completely gone. Another officer was there, Hickenlooper, a familiar face, no time for friendly greetings. Novey was bent low, looked up at Sherman now, red fury on the man's face.

"It's Lieutenant Tupper, sir. Our adjutant."

Hickenlooper was manic, angry, said, "There was a torpedo in the road. Killed the horse, and when we moved in to see, Tupper stepped on another one! Oh God, is he dead?"

Novey shook his head. "No. Bad wound. Get me a blanket, cover him up."

Sherman saw them both looking at him now, saw the anger, the sadness on the face of every man there. **Tupper**. The name wasn't familiar, and he watched as the blanket was laid over the man, only the face still showing. Sherman saw youth, his eyes open, but there was no crying, no screams, the man just shaking slightly. Novey was talking to the man now, soft words, encouragement, and Sherman looked away, saw other men gathered around some piece of hardware on the ground. He stepped that way, Snelling out in front, and one man said, "This here, sir. This is what done this. The rebs bury 'em just below the sand. These wire things, can't hardly see 'em. Man steps on 'em, they blow to hell, begging your pardon, sir."

"Sir! Rebels!"

He turned, saw a dozen ragged men under guard,

pushed forward by blue-coated guards, men with bayonets. One of the guards moved toward him, saluted, said, "Sir, I'm Lieutenant Jasper. Orders from General Blair that these prisoners are to clear the road of the torpedoes, sir. The general was most outraged, sir."

The response came slowly from Sherman, a deep growl. "Damned right he is. Carry out your orders."

The prisoners were halted, most of them eyeing him, no recognition beyond the uniform. Sherman walked toward them, the road now lined on both sides with men in blue, no one speaking. He faced the prisoner at the front of the line, pointed toward the young lieutenant Tupper.

"You know what wounded this man?"

The prisoner showed no defiance, seemed to understand his predicament. "No, sir."

"You know what a torpedo is? Maybe you helped bury the things on this road."

The man showed awareness now, looked down at Tupper, shook his head. "No, sir. Not me. Not none of us here. We was up that ways, at the outpost."

Sherman felt his fists clench, tried to hold his anger, pointed toward the torpedo his men had pulled from the ground. "Your people chose to bury those things to assassinate our troops, instead of standing up to a fair fight. We shall remedy that." He looked past the first prisoner, saw the others all looking at him, a new fear. "You men will remove these instruments from this roadway."

The first prisoner was wide-eyed, panic in his voice. "Sir, I don't know how to do that. They could explode."

"You'll do it the way it has to be done. I would suggest you be careful." He looked toward the lieutenant of the guards, Jasper. "You have your orders, Lieutenant. Put them to work."

The prisoners began to protest, cries of fear, and Sherman turned away, walked back toward the wounded man, Novey and Hickenlooper still by his side, a hand on the young man's head, his face ghostly pale. Behind him, one of the prisoners called out, "Sir, please. They could explode!"

Sherman moved down off the road, an aide waiting with the reins of his horse, and he stopped, looked back at the prisoner. "I don't give a good damn."

He climbed up, saw the guards pushing the men forward, the prisoners now down on their hands and knees, sifting slowly through the sand. He pulled on the reins, turned the horse, saw Hitchcock looking at him with wide eyes.

"You have some **problem** with my orders, Major?"

Hitchcock shook his head. "Oh, no, sir. It's just . . . I haven't heard of such things before. Torpedoes?"

Sherman thought a moment, tried to calm himself, knew he couldn't be angry at Hitchcock. "Heard of 'em a few times. Virginia peninsula, I think. The rebels used them mostly around fortifications, a damned nasty way to sound a warning if someone's coming at night. I suppose I can understand that. But this . . . damn it all, Major, these cowardly sons of bitches call us 'barbarous Yankees.' But this? This is nothing but murder."

They kept well off the side of the road, Sherman focusing on the sounds of fighting to the front, those rebels still making a stand in their works gradually pulling away. By now the officers in command of the fight knew he was there, and couriers came back every few minutes, their officers eager to keep Sherman informed. But there wasn't much to report, beyond the retreat of the rebels, who were far outnumbered by the troops pushing out and around them.

His engineer, Captain Poe, had come up quickly, word reaching him of the torpedoes on the road. Poe had walked about with childlike impatience, waiting for the prisoners to complete their work, the men unearthing seven more torpedoes, which had been spread in a single line across the road. The torpedoes were crude artillery shells, twelve-pounders, filled with black powder, ignited by the weight of a man's footstep. Poe had offered him even more details, but Sherman had little interest. The rebels' intent was obvious, to kill no more than a few men, or perhaps only one, the leading officer of a column.

As the fighting pushed farther forward, Sherman

moved with it, saw the rebel earthworks for himself, a stout fortification that could have caused far
more difficulties than it had. He knew that they
had been led by officers with experience, who
understood that the Federal forces, even the single
division led by Absalom Baird, were far stronger
than the rebels could hold away. The fighting continued, but in small bursts, all of it driving back
along a wide, sandy causeway that sliced high above
swampy fields and soggy pine woods. Farther along,
Sherman and his staff reached the small depot of
Pooler, a rail crossing where his men expected to
begin their usual job of wrecking the tracks. But
instead they were ordered to construct a heavy line
of log works, a precaution against a sudden assault
by the reorganized rebels. It was the first time his
men had taken a defensive line seriously, the understanding, even without any specific order from
Sherman, that the swampy ground to their front
might very well become a battlefield.

All through the swamps, both Slocum and Howard were driving their two halves of the army into
a more compact front, the men suffering through
waist-deep water, pushing hard to link their positions. Sherman established his headquarters at a
house near the Pooler crossing, could see clearly
that this rail line extended straight into the city.
As he waited for his two wing commanders to join
forces, Sherman was still uncertain just what kind
of strength the rebels had in Savannah and just how

much of a fight they intended to make. The concept of a siege had never appealed to him, but an all-out frontal assault against strong earthworks could cost more casualties than what they might gain. Sherman respected Hardee, knew that if Hardee had any strength at all, there was a hard fight yet to come. For now Sherman pulled together the links of his own chain, drawing them tightly around Savannah.

To make that effective, there would have to be assistance from the Federal navy. The maps showed him what the naval commanders already knew well, that, from the south, the Ogeechee River was the primary deepwater avenue into Savannah, and it was strongly protected by a formidable obstacle, Fort McAllister. With no direct communication with anyone at sea, Sherman had to assume that the navy would be reluctant to assault McAllister directly, since the position had certainly been designed with heavy armament, a sufficient strongpoint that the navy could not bypass without heavy losses. If McAllister was to fall into Federal hands, it would have to be done from the land side, a challenge Sherman was already beginning to plan.

As Sherman fielded the reports from the sporadic fighting in front of him, there were still questions, uncertainties, mysteries. But one fact began to burn in his brain. Since leaving Atlanta, the campaign had been simple and direct. No matter the complexity of his army, the various commanders, the unwieldy lack of discipline of Kilpatrick's cavalry, for three hundred miles the army had never been stopped, had never been forced to spread into vast lines of battle, had never faced an enemy who would meet them on equal terms. So far the entire campaign had been a lengthy **march**. Now, barely ten miles from Savannah, that march had ended.

CHAPTER NINETEEN

HAZEN

DECEMBER 12, 1864

He had convinced himself not to be intimidated by a meeting with Sherman. It wasn't working.

Hazen had commanded troops since early in the war, his first contact with Sherman coming at Shiloh, in April 1862. Hazen didn't serve directly under Sherman, or even alongside him, had been a part of an entirely separate command. At Shiloh there had been two Federal armies engaged, the first belonging to Grant, which was then aided considerably by the arrival of the second under the command of Don Carlos Buell. Hazen served Buell, knew only that when his troops reached the fighting, the victory over a tough and dominating rebel force was mostly under way. It was an astonishing turnaround for Grant's army, who had been rolled back by a surprise attack that nearly shoved Grant into the Tennessee River. Buell's men had arrived after the first day's fighting, what Buell himself considered to be a valiant rescue of Grant's defeated forces. But Grant, and most of the men in Grant's command, including Sherman, saw Buell's added forces as mere window dressing, that the Confederates had whipped themselves with poor decisions, brought on by the death of their commanding general, Albert Sidney Johnston. Grant's view had finally prevailed throughout most of Washington, Buell still fuming over the lack of credit for pulling Grant's bacon out of the fire. But Buell was long gone now, replaced first by William Rosecrans, whose subsequent collapse at Chickamauga a year later was one of the Federal army's blackest days. Soon after, Rosecrans was gone, replaced by George Thomas. In the changing hierarchy of the Federal command, Thomas had fallen under Grant's authority, and then, with Grant moving east, promoted over the entire army, Sherman had been elevated to Grant's former command. Thus Thomas was now under Sherman. Sherman had taken those changes mostly in stride, supported mightily by his friend Grant. Thomas, who seemed not to befriend anyone, had at least earned significant respect from his subordinates, Hazen included. Another subordinate, John Schofield, had just crushed John Bell Hood at Franklin, Tennessee.

It was what many of the brigadiers, Hazen included, had come to expect, that the War Department seemed to manage this war by shuffling through bad commanders, until, by pure chance, they stumbled on a good one. At Shiloh, Sherman had failed to impress anyone in Buell's army, Hazen included. But as the campaigns rolled forward through the western theater of the war, Sherman's star had risen, and with it the respect of the men who served him.

Hazen had done well under Rosecrans, and continued that under Thomas, especially during the magnificent victory at Chattanooga. With Grant now taking overall command, Hazen understood who Sherman's friends were, and so there was little surprise when Sherman, and not Thomas, had been named to fill the vacancy left by Grant in the West. Whether or not George Thomas was the more deserving general seemed to matter little to Washington.

At first Hazen had accepted Sherman's promotion with reluctant dread. Despite Grant's faith in him, Sherman's reputation was one of recklessness, a hot-tempered man who often talked too much, who was not yet suited for a serious command over such a substantial part of the Federal army. But many of those voices had been silenced, even Sherman's foes accepting that the Atlanta campaign had, for the most part, been superbly executed, even if the rebels opposing him, Joe Johnston and then Hood, had provided Sherman with most of those opportunities. But Hazen was surprised to learn that, unlike Don Carlos Buell, Sherman had no hesitation offering praise to those who earned it, and not just to those men who had marched under Sherman's own flag. When Thomas was sent north into Tennessee, Hazen remained in Atlanta by Sherman's order, the brigade commander now promoted to command of one of the four divisions in the Fifteenth Corps, part of Oliver Howard's wing of Sherman's newly organized army. That had been a pleasant surprise to Hazen, who fully expected to remain with Thomas.

What Hazen had learned by serving close to Sherman was the value of Sherman's instincts, something that could never be taught at West Point. With Atlanta under Sherman's belt, coupled with the decision not to chase John Bell Hood across Tennessee, Hazen had formed a far different view of Sherman from what had been portrayed in the newspapers. Hazen had become confident that as long as Sherman had Grant's support, he was capable of an independence rarely seen in the Federal army. The decision to march eastward out of Atlanta had caught most of Sherman's commanders by surprise, Hazen included. But now, with Thomas holding off Hood in Tennessee, and the lack of Confederate opposition in Georgia, Hazen's confidence in Sherman seemed justified. The man was not in fact some loose cannon, with delusions of his own abilities. Hazen had admitted to himself and his own subordinates that Sherman's army had accomplished thus far in Georgia a campaign that was not only successful, but possibly historic. There would be doubters still, always the harping from some rival commander, some reporter with his own axe to grind, that the rebels had allowed Sherman his success, that little had been sacrificed. But those voices were few. Strategically, the march toward Savannah hadn't really accomplished much more than wiping clean a vast swath of Georgia plantations, draining the state of an enormous supply from this year's harvest. But Sherman's goal had been to rip the heart out of a crucial area of the Confederacy. So far, that was exactly what he had done. If there was a greater success to be had, it lay ahead, what Hazen knew could be a far greater challenge than skirmishing with cavalry and frightening civilians.

With the army so close to Savannah, Hazen was as confident as the generals he served that the fall of Savannah was inevitable. What Hazen didn't expect was that Sherman had singled him out, much as he had done in Atlanta. This time Hazen was to be given a very specific duty. Lost in the reorganization of Sherman's forces was the quiet fact that Hazen now commanded the same units Sherman had overseen at Shiloh, and as part of the Fifteenth Corps, Hazen now marched at the head of the troops Sherman himself had led throughout the siege of Vicksburg and the brutal fight at Chattanooga. Hazen was being singled out not just because he was a capable leader, but because he commanded veteran troops who had become accustomed to pleasing their Uncle Billy.

The order had come to him first through Oliver Howard, and Hazen had obeyed by marching his division toward a prominent crossing over the Ogeechee River, nearly fifteen miles south of Savannah. He knew little of the geography of the area, beyond what his men had already seen. This was rugged, marshy country, dotted with deep swamps and water-soaked rice fields. Already his men had slogged their way through far more misery than he had ever expected, soldiers often pushing wagons and guns through mud and bog holes, the men themselves forced to march through water up to their chests. There were roadways, dry stretches of sandy causeways, but the men learned quickly that those routes were secured by rebel outposts, where a single artillery piece might make any narrow stretch of dry ground far more dangerous than what lay in the swamps.

KING HOUSE,
OGEECHEE RIVER—DECEMBER 12, 1864

He couldn't avoid the hard stare from Sherman.

"It has been suggested by General Kilpatrick that

his cavalry make this assault. I chose to defer to General Howard's view that this should be done with experienced infantry."

Hazen glanced at Howard, saw a brief unsmiling nod, and Hazen looked at Sherman again. "Yes, sir. I appreciate your confidence in my men. As you know, this division brings a great deal of experience. We are prepared for any assignment you consider appropriate."

He caught a frown from Howard, thought, Easy on the genuflecting. You're not some corporal, being chewed out for spitting on Sherman's shoes. Relax.

Sherman seemed to ignore Hazen's discomfort, focused now on a map, unrolled for him by one of Sherman's aides. Howard drank from a teacup, and after a silent moment, Howard said, "General, do you think it would be proper for General Hazen to have use of a chair?"

Sherman didn't look up from the map, waved his hand, another of the aides responding by bringing a heavy chair from some other room. Hazen was surprised, his two superiors seated on hard wooden chairs, this new one plush, a soft flowery cushion. The aide set the chair down with a heavy thump, backed away, and Howard pointed. "At ease, General. We could be here for a while. There's much to discuss."

Sherman looked up from the map now, stared past Hazen, pulled a cigar from his pocket, lit it casually, seemed lost in thought, then seemed to see

Hazen for the first time. "No. Not all that much. You are to capture Fort McAllister. Not much more complicated than that. Here, take this map. Pay attention to the path of the Ogeechee. General Howard's engineers are right now repairing whatever damage the rebels have done to the bridge. King's Bridge." Sherman looked at Howard now. "You certain it will be ready for tomorrow?"

"I have confidence in my engineers, sir."

Sherman pulled at the cigar, smoke rolling up around his face. "I am counting on that." He looked at Hazen again. "How many effectives in your division?"

"Today, sir, approximately forty-two hundred."

"Good. You will march them across the bridge first thing tomorrow, keeping to the right bank of the river. The map shows the fort to be roughly six miles downstream, if the river was a straight line. It's not. I trust Captain Poe to have calculated his figures correctly, but you will have to cover more than a dozen miles."

"Sir, will we confront any rebels along the way? Are there outposts, strongpoints we should be aware of?"

"Kilpatrick says no. On this occasion, I will trust his judgment." Sherman paused. "Know this, General. The fort is a strong position, but I believe it can be taken with a rapid assault from the land side. Most certainly, the larger siege guns positioned there face the water. The element of surprise should be maintained until the last possible moment. Kilpatrick says there is ample cover within a few hundred yards of the fort."

Hazen felt the stirring in his stomach, saw Howard watching him, as though expecting some kind of protest. Hazen looked purposefully at the map, saw the Ogeechee as a winding snake of a waterway, the fort positioned to guard against any waterborne intrusion upriver. The question rolled through his mind. Is that dry land behind the fort? Or will we march through swamps over our heads? He looked at Sherman, was surprised to see Sherman staring at him with a hard glare in his eyes.

"General Hazen, this assault may very well determine the outcome of this entire campaign. A lengthy siege of Savannah will be nearly impossible if we cannot feed this army. If we cannot make juncture with the navy, we are not in the kind of country where we can readily sustain the men. I have no intention of turning us around and marching back to Atlanta."

Howard seemed impatient, nervous, waited for Sherman to finish, then said, "General, we are even now making efforts to contact any Federal ship that might be close to the shore south of here. But we cannot depend on any assistance from navy gunboats."

Hazen knew nothing of any attempts to reach the navy, had wondered if there was a sizable force anchored offshore, as eager for some word from Sherman as Sherman was for them. Hazen thought, Careful, they don't have to tell you everything. But his curiosity was pushing the question. "If I may ask, sir, what kind of efforts?"

Howard didn't hesitate. "Scouts. It's all highly secretive, of course. If they're captured, it won't go well for them. In addition, General Kilpatrick is moving his men far to the south of Fort McAllister, seeking some other deepwater channel or harbor, and with some luck, he might find a vessel he can communicate with. We do not believe the navy has any idea just where we are, or what our intentions are."

Sherman kept his stare on Hazen. "The best way to tell the navy anything is to blow the hell out of Fort McAllister. The navy'll notice that one, pretty sure."

Howard seemed unamused by Sherman's declaration, said to Hazen, "It is certainly possible a naval vessel will observe any assault on the fort. The smoke alone should indicate our efforts."

Sherman stood, walked across the room, then back again. Hazen could see the man's hand twisting a button on his coat, still staring past him. Sherman said, "Plan well, General. Use your best people. There's artillery support coming. DeGress's battery, some Missouri artillery. Six guns. Put them to good use."

Hazen expected more, Sherman still pacing, Howard sipping from his cup of tea. Hazen looked again to the map, saw faint lines showing roadways, stared for a long moment, thought of the ordeal of the men already, the watery marshes, the struggle to move any column with much speed.

Howard seemed to read him, said, "Tomorrow morning, first light. General Sherman and I will find a vantage point, most probably at Cheves' Mill, there, on the map." He paused. "God be with you, General."

Sherman still paced, and Hazen could feel the weight of their expectations, had thought there would be more to the planning of the assault, which regiments should be employed, their exact route. That was the kind of detail he had seen from George Thomas, as much caution as preparation. But he could see from Sherman's brooding silence that the details were to be his alone.

He struggled to stand, freeing himself from the soft lushness of the chair. "With your permission, sirs, I shall retire. My men will be on their feet by five."

He wanted to say more, some grand pronouncement of just what a valiant effort his men would make. But that was foolishness, and for the first time, Hazen understood why there were voices of dissent against Sherman, why there were some commanders, if only a few, who groused quietly about Sherman's style. We're expected to do the job, he thought. That's all. It's not just West Point, what kind of pedigree we carry. We're here because he trusts us, and if he loses that, we get sent someplace else. And right now, at least for tomorrow, my place is here.

KING'S BRIDGE—DECEMBER 13, 1864

They were marching across the bridge well before dawn. The work by Howard's engineers wasn't completely finished, the bridge missing any kind of guardrails, the engineers simply running out of time. But Hazen's men kept in line, no one making the miserable plunge into cold, black water.

He had told no one of the assignment, beyond his three brigade commanders and the men who led his seventeen regiments. Of those, he had chosen nine to lead the assault. There would be others in reserve, a sizable force. Hazen knew the textbooks well, had been taught that ample reserves were essential when facing so many unknowns. And Sherman's message had been clearly received. Regardless of what kind of opposition Hazen faced, this operation was, in Sherman's mind, a linchpin to the entire campaign.

He knew that word had filtered through the ranks, as it always did, that some grand operation had been planned, his aides reporting even before the march that men were being told they were opening up a **cracker line,** seeking a route toward a fresh supply of food for the entire army. It was a phrase they had heard before, what Grant's troops had accomplished in breaking the rebel siege at Chattanooga. A year later, it was the stuff of romance, adding a mystique to Grant's reputation. Hazen knew that planting that kind of seed in his men could drive them to accomplish far more than they might expect, no matter the obstacles they might face.

As he marched across the bridge, he saw men standing back in the shadows, a cluster of officers, too dark to identify faces. But one man seemed to stand out, in front of the others, pacing slowly, the speck of light from a cigar. Hazen had said nothing, no acknowledgment, knew from experience that Sherman was likely as nervous as he was.

By seven in the morning, the division was entirely across, the march on mostly dry packed sand, blended with decades of spent oyster shells. They walked with the river on their left, the flat marsh grass seemingly endless, broken by clusters of timber, thicker woods that held the swamps. As the sun rose, he could see the clear blue above, a soft breeze off the distant ocean, a day for sleeping in soft grass, memories of a boy growing up in Ohio, leisurely picnics along peaceful waterways. But Hazen kept the daydreams away.

They passed watery rice fields, and he had been surprised by the civilians who occupied the land, a strange mix of Negroes and mulattoes, who emerged from their wet ground or crude huts, lining the road as though this were some kind of peaceful parade, wide-eyed wonder at the army that passed them by. They offered pleasant waves and greetings, something Hazen appreciated. What seemed to be innocent friendliness was certainly a boost to the morale of his men, who returned the waves with cheerful talk, as though in this part of the world, there was no animosity at all.

With the rice fields behind them, the roadway spread away from the river, deeper woods. As they marched closer to the fort, Hazen was relieved by this new cover, that any dust from the march would be hidden by the trees, great drooping oaks arcing overhead, their limbs intertwined, casting cool shade on the white road. Among the oaks were massive magnolias, all draped with Spanish moss. Spread beneath the trees were patches of palmettos, the fanlike blades of green usually marking the edge of the soggier ground, most of that in low places farther away from the side of the road. Hazen knew of the legendary tale from the Revolutionary War, Fort Moultrie, at Charleston, the men there building their seaside walls using the soft fibrous palmetto logs, frustrating the British warships, whose artillery shells embedded or thumped uselessly against the soft wood. He had wondered about Fort McAllister, if the rebels had done the same, but as they marched farther along the route, the lookouts could begin to see details of the fort, what seemed to be a mass of earthworks, the kind of defense the rebels seemed most comfortable building, one that required far less time and manpower than the great stone fortresses farther down the coast.

With a gap in the trees, Hazen had walked out on a high perch, had used the field glasses, seen it for himself, the fort a thick, hulking mound, still too far away, but between the fort and the deeper woods behind was the open ground he expected to see, saw grass for hundreds of yards, the gauntlet his men would have to cross.

They had reached an intersection, what the map showed was the route toward Genesis Point, the roadway that would lead them directly to the fort. Waiting for Hazen's men was a squad of cavalry, led by Judson Kilpatrick himself.

Hazen had no real ill will toward Kilpatrick, knew what most of the army knew, that he was a capable leader with some indiscreet personal habits. But right now Kilpatrick offered Hazen something he had not yet received: a scouting report.

Kilpatrick seemed to wait for Hazen to draw closer, Hazen not sure if he should salute the man. Hazen was a brigadier, was outranked by Kilpatrick, who wore two stars. As he eased the horse forward he was surprised to see Kilpatrick saluting **him,** an informal lift of the man's cap.

"Ho there, General. Fine day for an assault."

Hazen followed Kilpatrick's lead, stayed up on his horse, saw Kilpatrick's staff gathering closer, clearly a part of their conversation. Hazen glanced behind him, his own staff hanging back, the usual courtesy with senior commanders. Hazen said, "We're marching as quickly as possible. The weather helps." Hazen wasn't sure just what Kilpatrick was doing there, wasn't sure he should ask.

Kilpatrick answered the question for him. "After scouting this ground, I drew up a plan to assault the fort directly, a quick strike that might catch the enemy looking the other way. My superiors . . . **your** superiors thought differently. They preferred you make the assault and leave other duties for my horsemen. No doubt they believe their decision is the proper one. I can offer you some information, unless you have received all you require from General Howard."

There was a hint of sarcasm in Kilpatrick's tone, and Hazen realized for the first time that Kilpatrick might have pushed Sherman hard for this mission, and for reasons known only to Sherman, Hazen's infantry had been chosen instead.

"I welcome good information wherever I can find it, sir. I am not completely certain just what kind of attack this will be. I am unfamiliar with the ground."

"Yes, you are. I, however, am not. I seek no glory for myself in this affair, and my orders are to drive my men farther south, seeking contact with the navy wherever we may find them. That is my intention. I can tell you that you have a clear path of march to within a mile of the fort. Once clear of the timber, the going will be a challenge for foot soldiers, a great deal of tall grass, several shallow creeks, and patches of low water. The enemy shall have the opportunity to inflict considerable casualties, should they recognize what you're trying to do. However, there is a good stretch of forest within artillery range of the place. You did bring artillery, I assume?"

"Six guns."

Kilpatrick rubbed a hand on his chin, showing approval. "Good. That should be very helpful. The rebels cleared themselves a good field of fire for the first half mile or so out from the fort, but in their confidence that no enemy would ever assault them from the rear, they ceased cutting the timber far short of where they should have. Call that a gift to your cannoneers. I would suggest, if you will allow me to offer such a thing, that you make use not only of your artillery, but of your best sharpshooters. The fort was designed by someone who was not terribly concerned that the heavy guns there would ever receive fire. The works are designed **en barbette,** as it were. You're familiar with the term?"

There was a hint of arrogance from the younger man, and Hazen wasn't certain how to respond. He had no need to get into some sort of snot-fest with this man. "I am West Point, sir. Class of 1855. I know the textbooks. I was taught that term to mean that the enemy's artillerymen are exposed to fire."

Kilpatrick glanced at his officers, then back to

Hazen. "Yes, very good. Class of 1861 myself, but I assume you know that. Yes, poor design on the backside of the fort. No notches for the cannon barrels at all. Those guns that are positioned to fire in this direction are in fact set in place with their aim over the tops of the walls. Sharpshooters can play havoc with their gunners' ability to maneuver or load their pieces."

"How many pieces?"

"Our best estimate is two dozen, though most of those face seaward, as you might expect."

Hazen was enormously grateful for everything Kilpatrick was telling him, the plan for how he would advance already forming in his mind. Kilpatrick seemed to scan his staff officers, as though asking a silent question. One man spoke.

"Sir, shouldn't we advise General Hazen of the enemy's preparations closer to the fort?"

Kilpatrick nodded, turned to Hazen again, said, "Ditches, wide and deep. Abatis, certainly. As for the enemy outposts, they are lightly manned, if at all. The enemy seems to prefer mounted patrols. I suggest stealth. You might bag the lot of them before they can tell anyone in the fort just what you're up to." Kilpatrick paused, as though trying to recall any other pertinent piece of intelligence. Then he shrugged, said, "May good fortune go with you, General. I have no further purpose here, and I assume General Sherman is awaiting word of your success. Perhaps before this day is over, I shall find success of my own. Or at the very least, a fine homestead where my men can gather some acceptable rations. I am rather weary of rice. I will ride in this direction. You will go . . . that way. I assume you know that."

"I have a map, yes, sir."

Hazen saluted now, but Kilpatrick had already turned away, his men filing out quickly down the road that led southward. Hazen shook his head, his color bearer now moving up closer to him, anticipating the order to continue. Hazen looked at him, the always smiling face of Sergeant Lewis. "What do you make of him, Sergeant?"

"Odd one, sir. Rather enjoys being in command."

Hazen nodded. "Good observation. He wanted this to be his assault, that's clear. He could have been much more stingy with his information. But he seems to have taken his orders in stride. It's fortunate for us that he chose to be helpful, and keep his pride to himself." He turned, his aides waiting for the order to resume the march. "No bugles. Give the order to proceed by word of mouth." He looked at his watch now, thought, It's after noon. General Sherman will twist every button off his coat wondering how long this will take.

He looked again at the map, the column now moving past him, heard the low talk among the men, some joking, salutes offered in his direction. He looked at their faces, saw smiles, fists in the air, surprising enthusiasm from men who had al-

ready marched more than eight miles. He rolled up
the map, slid it into his saddlebag, held up a hand
toward the staff. "Move with the column. I will ride
forward. I wish to speak to the skirmishers."

Hazen spurred the horse, was quickly past the lead
of the column, saw scattered men in the road to his
front, the lead scouts stepping aside, making way for
him, others spread out through the woods to both
sides of the road. He reined the horse, searched, saw
their officer, a young lieutenant, moving out toward
him. The man saluted him, and Hazen let him catch
his breath, said, "Lieutenant Sherfy, we should have
about three miles to go before we can position ourselves for the assault. But rebels could be on the
prowl anywhere. Keep your men well off the road,
and proceed as rapidly and as quietly as you can. I
want no surprises, and any ambush against the head
of this column will cause us considerable difficulty.
Be the hunter, not the hunted."

Sherfy smiled now, just what Hazen expected. "My
platoon is known for their soft steps, sir. There's a
great deal of Indian in these men."

"Put that to use, Lieutenant."

It was after two, and Hazen was feeling the
pressure of that, avoided looking toward the
sun, now dropping off to his right. The men
were still moving as quickly as he had hoped, the
roads still good, no swampy obstacles yet in their

path. As he rode forward, his mind pulled them with him, urging them silently to keep up the pace. He thought of Sherman again, the man's legendary impatience. That man's smoked a hundred cigars since this morning, and probably chewed out every staff officer he has.

He saw men in the road to the front, hands waving, several of Sherfy's men. He motioned to an aide, said, "Move. See what they want."

There were more men walking into the road, emerging from the thickets to one side, horses in a cluster, one of them now coming toward him at a gallop. It was Sherfy.

Hazen felt a bolt of alarm, but Sherfy was smiling, reined the horse up clumsily, saluted him, said, "Whooee. General, we grabbed a pile of 'em."

Hazen was looking at the horse, thought, Cavalry? "Explain. Grabbed who?"

"Sir, there was a group of mounted infantry, a scouting party or some such. We crept up on 'em and nabbed the whole bunch before they could spit! Took the opportunity to liberate one of their mounts. Fine-looking beast, eh, sir?"

"Now is not the time, Lieutenant. You can make use of the horse elsewhere. I need you walking. There could be more patrols farther down this road."

"Oh, no, sir. Not likely. We're bringing in some prisoners, one in particular you should meet."

Sherfy turned now, looking back down the road,

and Hazen saw a trio of his men with a prisoner between them. Hazen pushed the horse forward, Sherfy keeping beside him, the prisoner now pulled to the side of the road. Hazen stopped, saw a rough-looking man, no uniform, shoeless, and Sherfy said, "Sir, this here is Private Tommy Mills. He sure hated being captured and all, but he done us a big favor. Tommy, old boy, why don't you tell the general here what you told us?"

Mills tipped his ragged hat, seemed surprisingly friendly, none of the usual surliness Hazen had seen so many times before. He made a slight bow, said, "Good afternoon, General. Seein' as this here lieutenant of yours done promised me a fine meal, meat and all, I will offer you some advice."

"What kind of advice?"

"Well, General, that road up ahead, it leads straight to the fort out there. I'm guessing that's what you boys are doing out here in the wilderness and all. So, if you are intendin' to provide me with a good feed, I'm happy to return the favor. That road, or causeway, or sandy trail, whatever you Yankees call it, it's chock-full of the best danged torpedoes our engineers could make. A whole passel of 'em, too. There's more torpedoes, too, all around the fort. I hate seeing legs and feet and such blowed off. This war's been hateful enough, and those buried things just don't seem like the way things ought to be done. I offered your kindly lieutenant here to show him where they's buried. Some ham might be good. Beef if you got it. They're eatin' much of nothing in the fort. Rice cooked fourteen different ways."

Hazen tried to read the man, but there was no reason for him to lie about the existence of torpedoes. "How many men in the fort, Private?"

"Nigh two hundred. Major Anderson's in charge. A good fellow, when he gets his sleep. If you folks go on and grab the place, I hope you'll be good to him. I ain't never believed none of those stories 'bout all the evil you done inflicted on the country folks hereabouts. Y'all just look like regular folks. Better uniforms than what they give us. They ain't give us much a'tall, tell the truth. But I ain't inclined to see too many more of us kilt. We's all gettin' pretty sick of that, sir."

Hazen saw obvious pride on Sherfy's face, the lieutenant leaning closer to him.

"Like I said. Indians, sir. Grabbed the whole bunch of 'em without a shot being fired."

Hazen knew Sherfy was fishing for a compliment, knew that the prisoner's information was crucial. But Hazen knew better than to be seduced by a willing captive, and he kept his tone serious, turned to an aide, said, "Captain, take the rest of the prisoners to the rear. Make sure they receive whatever rations we can spare. This fellow here, Mr. Mills, is it?"

"Tommy Mills, sir."

"Yes, Mr. Mills will be fed as well, but not just yet. Mr. Mills, you will assist our men in removing those torpedoes from the causeway. I assume you're willing to do that?"

Mills frowned, seemed resigned to the task. "I suppose, yes, sir. It's only fair. I seen some of 'em buried, helped out with a bit of that. Ain't hard to get 'em up, if you're careful."

Hazen turned to Sherfy now. "Leave the horse with my staff, Lieutenant. Keep your men off the road. We'll get you some help."

The order went back, and the officer responded, moving forward quickly from the column. Hazen saw Colonel Theodore Jones, in command of the first brigade, the man who would lead three of the designated regiments. Jones saluted, eyed the prisoner, said, "Are we to continue forward, sir?"

Hazen pointed to Mills, said, "Not just yet. Send a dozen or so men forward to accompany our new friend here. We have a dangerous problem on the causeway to our front. Go as far as the cover extends, then report back to me." He paused, knew how important his commanders were, men who had served Sherman, men who now would depend on him to put them in the right place. He lowered his voice, away from the prisoner. "Teddy, we're mighty close. I want the artillery brought forward as quick as the road is cleared. Time is our worst enemy now, and I don't intend to have my ass chewed on by angry generals."

The tree line ended just as Kilpatrick described it, a wide, grassy plain that led straight to the fort. Hazen had found a house, owned by a family named Middleton, quickly established a headquarters, and with the columns gathering up, he organized the assault. With the fort now plainly in view, Hazen pushed his men out into an arcing formation, sending three regiments out to each flank, with the final three holding the center. By three o'clock a single line of sharpshooters were sent forward, picking their way quickly through the wiry grass, stumbling through shallow creeks, the men driving forward to less than three hundred yards from the fort. There the poor planning of the rebels provided an enormous advantage. Where the trees had been cut, the ground was now spread thickly with stumps, offering each man protection as he drew bead on the walls of the fort. As Hazen watched from the tree line, the sharpshooters settled into their low cover, began firing at whatever targets the fort was offering. For the men in the fort itself, the musket fire accomplished just what Kilpatrick had predicted. The artillerymen defending the rear of the fort found that working their guns was deadly.

As Hazen feared, the ground he couldn't readily scout was proving difficult for his men, especially out to the right, far from his view. With nearly three thousand men flowing out into unknown terrain, the fears came, anxious glances toward the setting

sun, aides scampering out into thickets only to disappear without offering any real word just what
kind of progress the men had made. Besides the saw
grass, men were stumbling through head-high stands
of cane, briars, and mud holes, meandering soft-
bottomed creeks that sucked the shoes from men's
feet. With daylight starting to dim, Hazen became
desperate for word that his men had reached their
starting point, that more than just the men to his
front were waiting for the order they expected to
hear, the order to step off, to move quickly toward
the fort.

He strained to see through the field glasses,
the puffs of smoke few, the cannon fire
from the fort mostly ineffective. He
couldn't see the rebels themselves, but Kilpatrick's
description was accurate, the walls on this side of
the fort topped with a smooth line of earth, his
sharpshooters waiting patiently for any target.

There was commotion in the woods behind him,
more men moving up, the reserves, and he paced
through the trees, stared again through the glasses,
looked skyward, the sun low over the woods. There
was a sharp voice now, and he turned, saw his aide
running, stumbling through a thin curtain of vines.

"Sir! The signal post has made contact!"

"With who?"

The man was breathing heavily, and Hazen looked

past him, a futile stare toward the edge of the river, where he had ordered a lookout and signalmen posted.

The aide caught his breath, said, "They say it's General Sherman himself, sir. He's about three miles off, across the river. The general's signal officers sent a message, sir." The man was still breathing heavily, as much from the run as the weight of his sudden responsibility. "Here, sir. General Sherman says that he expects the fort to be carried by this night."

Hazen closed his eyes, let out a long breath. "So do I, Corporal."

He moved quickly toward his horse, thought better of that, the musket fire from the fort scattered, but any man on horseback would draw every rebel's aim. He searched the staff, saw men running up toward him, more of the couriers. He was out of patience now, glanced at his watch, past four, shouted out, "Report! Have the men reached their positions?"

The first aide dropped his hands to his knees, exhausted, shook his head breathlessly. "Don't know, sir! Thick as dog hair, sir. Couldn't find Colonel Jones. The 116th Illinois is in line, but they didn't know more than that. No word from the 6th Missouri at all!"

Hazen ground his teeth, knew that the Missouri men were the far right flank, well beyond anyplace he could see. He looked again toward the river, the signal outpost, tried not to see Sherman in his mind, thought, Howard is certainly beside him, both men pushing their eyes through field glasses, straining to see anything out here at all.

He stared out to the skirmish line, the men still firing at will, specks of smoke as they peppered the fort, the return fire very light. That could change, he thought. We have to have the entire force moving together. But I cannot control any of that. He searched the officers close by, saw a bugler, shouted to the man, "Sound attention!"

The man obeyed, the bugle slicing through the woods, men in line out to both sides. He had already given the order that none of the regiments be bunched up, that they move in a single line, shoulder to shoulder, no more than a heavy skirmish line. The men were falling into line now, officers close to him eyeing him, expectant, tension in their faces. Hazen tried to fight through the hard knot in his gut, looked again at the bugler, hesitated, thought, There is no time to wait. If you want to fight for Sherman, you've got to **fight**.

"Bugler! Order forward!"

The bugler completed his task, the men responding by stepping out from the trees, a long, snaking line, pushing through the tall grass. He expected heavy firing from the fort, a massive volley from heavy artillery, saw only specks of smoke, not much more than it had been already. He stood high on a stump, field glasses up, stared out over the backs of his men, guessed the distance one more time, six hundred yards.

He spoke out now, to no one, to them all. "Go! Don't stop! Don't slow!"

His heart pounded heavily in his chest, more firing coming from the fort, but the sharpshooters kept up their own fire, and very soon the main body had reached them, swallowing them, the sharpshooters rising up, moving forward with the thin blue wave. The fort responded, scattered artillery fire, but no massive burst, his men still in line. He stepped down from the tree trunk, saw his staff watching him, knowing just what was happening next.

"Time to go, gentlemen. I expect to see the inside of that fort pretty quick."

He walked out clear of the trees, stepped more quickly, felt the crushing weight of the order he had given them. He jogged slightly, trying to keep up, thought, No, not this way. He turned now, shouted out, "Bring my horse! They need to see me! Move!"

The groom appeared, leading the animal quickly toward him, and Hazen climbed up, stared out through the glasses again, the line of blue much closer to the fat earthen walls. Men were dropping away now, out of sight, and he thought of Kilpatrick, the description, ditches, abatis. There were blasts at the base of the walls, nothing like artillery, and he drove the horse through the grass, pushing closer, saw a blue mass gathering in clusters, some men firing up at the enemy. There were more blasts to one side, odd sounds, and the words drilled into him now, the words of the prisoner, legs and feet. He cursed aloud, saw the men gathering along the ditch, helping hands, knew it was the torpedoes, some of the men too anxious to avoid the deadly misstep. He spurred the horse again, saw more of his men coming out of the saw grass to the left, that flank hugging the river. They were nearly at the wall, and he thought of the torpedoes, some kind of warning, but they were firing up at the rebels along the walls, no time for anything but the advance, still moving, those men dropping down into the ditches.

He heard a single thump, out to the right, saw a wisp of smoke, glassed that way, a huge mortar, out away from the fort, worked by a handful of rebel gunners. Now the fire was returned, the gunners gone, punched down, more of his men emerging from that way, flags, the men from Illinois. He gripped the field glasses, one hand clenched in a hard fist, punched the air above his head, glanced toward the river, to where Sherman would be, where the smoke of the fight could clearly be seen. We're there, General. We're going in.

He looked again to his men, drove the horse closer still, saw the assault pushing right up to the walls of the fort, men scrambling through loose dirt on the earthworks, the enemy above, but the blue were too many, and they were up and over the wall.

He turned toward the trees behind him, saw the reserves in line, watching, waiting for the order. No,
he thought. Not yet. Not now. But be ready. It can't
be this simple.

He turned to the fort again, the horse close to the
wide ditch, clusters of tree limbs blocking the way,
some of that tossed aside by his men, some still in
place. He jumped down from the horse, dropped
low, saw a group of men, pulling a wounded man
back, bloody legs, the smoke heavy now, most of that
from the musket fire of his own men. He pushed
down through the ditch, the dirt walls in front of
him difficult, one man lending a hand, pulling him
up the steep slope. The smoke was drifting past, and
he glanced back, saw men in blue down, but not
many, wounded men crawling back, seeking cover,
others closer to the ditch, more blasted limbs, the
effects of the torpedoes. Damn them, he thought.
There will be punishment for that.

He was at the top of the earthworks now, the
fort a bath of smoke, but the firing was slow, scattered, his men swarming through, surrounding the
big guns, the musket fire now silent. Around him
the voices came, the men understanding what they
had done, that they were inside the fort, the rebels
whipped, men gathering prisoners, the piercing
screams of the wounded, troops on both sides. Beside him men rose up to the crest of the earthworks,
the walls of the fort, standing tall, waving, cheering. It was over.

"There were torpedoes, sir. Pretty thick, all along the base of the wall, just outside the ditch. We lost a few men there. Captain Groce was killed, sir. Musket fire."

Hazen saw the gloom in the colonel's eyes, put a hand on his shoulder. "I know about that. I want casualty counts by tomorrow. Plenty to do right here."

He looked toward the prisoners, saw an officer, the bandaged head, the man seated on a wooden crate. Hazen stepped that way, stood close to the man, said, "Major Anderson, my apologies for your rough treatment."

Anderson looked up at him, said, "It's war, General. But your men should respect a sword when it's offered. Fellow clubbed me with his musket."

"Heat of battle, Major. Not everyone is a gentleman." Hazen looked across the cluster of rebels, some bloodied. "Two hundred men, it appears. My report was accurate."

"You have excellent scouting, sir. We were never strong here. It was a mistake, to be sure. My men gave it their best, I assure you. Captain Clinch is among the dead. He fought a most gallant fight. These men were not prepared to **give** you anything."

Hazen had seen for himself that the surge over the earthworks had not stopped the fighting. Even now

bodies were being pulled from various nooks in the
fort, some of the rebels making a stand anywhere
there was cover. He walked away from the prisoners, climbed up beside one of the seaward guns, an
enormous forty-two-pounder. He glanced around,
had confirmed for himself what his men were saying, thought, Twenty-four guns. A good day's haul.
He stood tall, stared out through a darkening sky,
tried to see the place where Sherman would be,
where they all would have seen the fight. He wouldn't
expect grand compliments, didn't really know if
Sherman went for the boisterous salutes, a toast
with spirits. There are dead men out in that grass
still, he thought, as there are right in here. Anderson is right. I prefer to salute them.

The sun was nearly gone, the air now filled with a
rising chorus of creatures from the wetlands around
them, frogs and birds, and other things Hazen had
never seen. I will not miss this place, he thought.
He recalled Sherman's words, the great weight of
responsibility Sherman had placed on his back. I'm
not sure if the entire campaign will ever depend on
what these men did here, he thought. But if capturing Savannah required us first to take this place,
well, General Sherman, it's yours.

CHAPTER TWENTY

SHERMAN

CHEVES' RICE MILL, THREE MILES FROM FORT MCALLISTER—DECEMBER 13, 1864

He saw the Stars and Stripes go up the flag-pole at five, kept his gaze on the flag for a long minute.

"By God, Howard, they've done it! The whole assault lasted no more than thirty minutes!"

Howard was next to him, his single hand holding field glasses of his own. "Fifteen minutes, sir."

Sherman heard the boastfulness of the words, knew that Howard had been right to send Hazen, and not push for Kilpatrick's cavalry to make the attack. He glanced around, two signalmen behind him, the only other men on the roof of the mill.

"Hardtack tonight, gentlemen! Hardtack tonight!"

The signalmen seemed confused by Sherman's outburst, but he ignored their reaction, looked again at the flag, felt like a tub overflowing with perfect joy. He dropped the glasses, walked to the edge of the roof, saw his staff gathered below, expectant, broad smiles. Sherman thrust one hand out toward the fort, shouted, "He's done it! By God, it's ours!"

"Sir, what of the gunboat?"

Sherman had forgotten it completely, wiped away by the manic excitement of Hazen's success. He looked out down the river, saw the boat that had been there for most of the afternoon. The signal had come to him before the attack, a simple question whether or not McAllister was yet in Federal hands. Sherman was fairly certain the captain of the vessel did not expect a response directly from Sherman himself, a simple "No. Attack under way."

"They saw the fight. Have to know we've got it. Doubt Hazen even knew they were there. River snakes around too much. But he'll know shortly. I want to get over there quick as we can. There's an oar boat down there in the grass. Will it do?"

Behind him, one of the signalmen said, "I believe so, sir. We took a look at it earlier. Seems sound."

"Then we'll make use of it, and right now, before it gets any darker." He reveled in the excitement, most of it coming from him, knew Howard and the others were taking that in. Yes, he thought. **Victory**. There is nothing better. He slapped his hands together, then wrapped his arms tight against the chill of the evening breeze. He looked at Howard again, couldn't avoid the bursting energy, the most excitement he had felt since he had marched into Atlanta.

"This is a grand thing. A grand thing! Savannah's ours!"

"Yes, sir. Much to do, still."

Howard seemed cautious, a damp rag tossed across Sherman's enthusiasm. But Sherman had no interest in caution now. There was time later for careful planning. He rolled those thoughts over in his mind, what his priorities were, what had to be done first, said aloud, "The navy must be notified. They must know just what we've accomplished here, where my command is, what kind of condition this army is in." The words began forming in his brain now, all the dispatches still to be sent, all those messages that would go north. He called out again, more of the childlike enthusiasm. "I want to get over there, see the place, see just what we grabbed. Going with me, Howard?"

Howard seemed to ponder the question, a quick glance at the signalman, who said, "I believe the boat will hold at least four or five passengers, sir."

Howard absorbed that, said, "Well, then, sir, I wouldn't miss it."

Sherman ignored Howard's hesitation, paced the rooftop, still manic, frustrated that the ground was too far below, that making the jump from the roof was likely a bad idea. "I'm going down, Howard. Order some oarsmen to make ready. The moon's up already. It ought to be a glorious night. More glorious now."

He made his way off the roof, climbed down through the inside of the mill, his staff still waiting, men asking each other just who those passengers were going to be. Sherman burst into the open yard of the mill, one of the signalmen with him, the man trotting out to the edge of the water, working with the boat. Sherman moved that way, thought of the gunboat. I should get to that thing, find a way to communicate with whoever's out there. The navy has to be going mad with questions, watching that assault. They're not just going to sit out there and hang fishing poles.

His staff was gathering close now, following him to the river, one man with a lantern. Sherman stopped close to the boat, said, "I'm going across this damned river, give Hazen a handshake he won't forget. Major Nichols, you will accompany me. Howard, you require company?"

Howard motioned to his own chief of staff. "Colonel Strong, you should join us."

Sherman was moving about, aching impatience, watching the men chosen to man the oars. "I expect speed, gentlemen. Darker by the minute."

He had a sudden thought, the rest of his army, the men spread out along the causeways and swampy thickets all to the north. Those men had been engaged in steady skirmishing most of the day, pushing close against whatever rebels were manning their defenses. He looked for Hitchcock, the man with the good handwriting, no sign of him. "Where the hell's Hitchcock?"

Dayton responded, "Sir, he chose not to make the journey here. Said he had some work to catch up on."

Sherman shook his head, thought, What kind of a soldier chooses to miss watching a battle? Especially a good one.

"That is his misfortune, Major. I want a dispatch sent immediately to General Slocum. Tell him we have been successful here, and that the navy is now free to assist our efforts. As well, the way is open for rations, other supplies as we might need them." He paused. "Tell him that this day calls for a good big drink, that once he imbibes, he should take a good deep breath and yell like the devil."

Howard appeared now, moved past Sherman, examined the boat. "Not much of a craft, sir. They call it a skiff, I believe."

"I don't care if it's a hollowed-out tree stump. You going with me or not?"

Howard smiled, a rarity. "I wouldn't miss this, sir."

He arrived at the fort well after dark, had been gratified to find Hazen in his new headquarters, the McAllister House, sitting down to supper, a meager feast of Confederate stores, which suited Sherman just fine. With the tension of the planned assault, he had barely eaten all day. Sherman had been pleased to see that Hazen's dinner included one chair for the captured fort's commander, Major George Anderson, an appropriate gesture for a man who, from what Sherman could see, had been left out to dry by his superiors in Savannah, men who should have grasped the value of the place. But that was a topic for another time. With the meal concluded, Sherman had found a soft place in one of the bedrooms, had bedded down in a state of near collapse, the pleasing end to what had been a magnificent day.

"Sir! Are you awake?"

"Who?"

"Major Nichols, sir. Sorry to disturb you, but there's a dispatch from downriver."

Sherman blew the fog from his brain, blinked into the lantern light, saw the paper in Nichols's hand. "What the hell's it say?"

"It's from General Foster, sir. He's requesting in the most urgent terms that you board the gunboat **Dandelion**. He wishes to see you with all speed.

He says he is commander of the Department of the South. I'm not familiar with that command, sir."

"I am. Foster's one of those who enjoys bellowing just to hear the echo. But he commands whatever troops are garrisoned along the coast. He wants to see me right now?"

"He doesn't specify, sir, though he seems rather insistent."

Sherman sat upright, reached for his coat. He had little respect for loud-mouthed generals, and Sherman counted Foster among them. But Foster had friends in influential places, most of those in Washington. Sherman knew that ignoring the man's urgency might be a mistake that would return to bite him.

John Gray Foster was another of the West Pointers who had made a reputation in Mexico, serving later as an engineering instructor and commander at the naval academy in Annapolis. Before the war, he had been one of the army's primary supervisors for the construction of forts along the New Jersey coast, but when the war erupted at Fort Sumter, Foster had earned at least one more dubious honor. He was **there,** serving under the fort's commanding officer, Robert Anderson.

Sherman stood, fiddled with the buttons on his coat, said, "Engineers. Everything happens by the ticking of their clock. He wouldn't have sent the damned message in the middle of the night if he wanted me to wait till next week. The **Dandelion**?"

"Yes, sir. She's supposed to be a few miles downstream. The message mentioned Admiral Dahlgren, also most interested in meeting with you."

"Impressive. The whole damned Atlantic Ocean just woke up to us being here. How the hell we supposed to get there? They send a boat?"

"Doesn't say, sir."

Sherman completed buttoning his coat, saw Howard now in the shadows, and Howard said, "Anything you require of me, General?"

"Your presence, if you wish. We're taking that skiff downriver."

"Now?"

Sherman was already in motion, moved out into the open air, a breezy chill. Hazen was there now, scrambling to put on his coat, and Sherman said, "Our visit is brief, General. I need some oarsmen. A few strong backs would be appreciated."

Hazen shouted out an order, guards and other staff officers emerging, and Sherman moved out toward the river, could see the silhouette of the fort in the moonlight. Troops were gathering, Hazen making the selection, one of those men now moving past Sherman, standing at the edge of the grassy yard, and the man said, "Uh, General? Just one word of caution, sir."

"Not interested in caution, soldier."

"Begging your pardon, sir, but I'd advise it. There's

still torpedoes out here, scattered all over the edge of the river. We ain't had time to dig 'em all up yet."

Sherman moved beside the man, stared out at the moonlight on the river, saw the patch of sand that led down to the skiff. "We made it up here once, soldier. We can do it again."

Sherman started out, paused, heard the men following behind him, heard a low groan from Howard. He studied the sand, a hint of their footsteps from the first trip, said, "Step carefully, gentlemen. I don't intend to offer the rebels any reason to celebrate."

He appreciated the reception from the **Dandelion**'s captain, a pleasant man who had ordered his crew to welcome Sherman aboard with a rousing cheer. But the boat was nothing like the larger gunboats Sherman had boarded before, especially during the prelude to the siege at Vicksburg, and its commander seemed to read him, other officers stepping closer, all of them with smiles.

"Sir, it is my honor to be your host, if only for a brief while. Captain Horace Williamson, at your service, sir. This is Lieutenant George Fisher, Ensign Jarvis, Ensign Lofton. This craft is a tender for the gunboat **Flag,** anchored at the mouth of the river. I offer my respects from numerous officers hoping to meet you as quickly as your schedule permits. I should mention that during your most impressive assault on that fortress, I put this craft into motion, and made a quick journey downstream, notifying all the boats who were near of your triumph. There is considerable celebrating of your presence here, General."

"Captain, the pleasure is mine." Sherman was overwhelmed by the naval officer's manic enthusiasm, rivaling his own.

"If you will follow me, sir. I have a small cabin below. Something of a luxury on a craft this small."

Sherman followed the man belowdecks, Howard following, Williamson leading them into a small office, soft chairs, a narrow cot to one side. He retrieved a bottle from a small wooden cabinet, poured a deep golden liquid in three glasses, what Sherman assumed to be brandy. He glanced at Howard, knew the man wouldn't partake, thought, His loss, certainly. Leaves more for the rest of us. The captain motioned to the chairs.

"Please, sirs, we require no formality here. This is an occasion I shall recall to my grandchildren one day! I salute you both!"

Sherman took the glass, saw Howard doing the same, watched as Howard kept the glass in his lap. Sherman took a long sip, the pungent alcohol rising up through his head, felt the raw burn sliding down his throat. He coughed slightly, saw a frown on Howard's face. "My apologies for General Howard."

Howard seemed to jump, said, "I mean no impo-

liteness, Captain. I do not partake of strong spirits.
Please do not be offended."

"Oh, my, well, no sir. Not at all! Might I offer
you anything else? Fresh water, perhaps? I assure you,
it did not come from what flows beneath us."

"Nothing, thank you."

Howard put the small glass back on the captain's
desk, and Sherman eyed it, took another long sip
from his own, his eyes watering slightly.

"Fine offering, Captain. The people of Georgia
tend not to create such quality. A great deal of corn
whiskey, mostly."

The young man smiled, held up the glass, as
though studying the brew. "We do take pride in this
fleet. Much of our spirits comes from down south,
the West Indies. Some we capture from blockade
runners, so it tends to have superior pedigree to
something made in a barn."

Sherman emptied the glass, still eyed Howard's.
Howard said, "Do not hesitate on my behalf, General. This is a day for celebrating, certainly."

Williamson saluted Sherman again, another sip,
and Sherman reached for Howard's glass, another
strong taste. Once his throat had cleared, Sherman
said, "So, Captain, what are we to do now? You're
in command of this situation at the moment."

"Oh, my orders are to make acquaintance with
you, sir, and inform you that Admiral Dahlgren
is most anxious to greet you. You must know that
there has been considerable anxiety as to your

situation. We had little to draw upon but Southern newspapers. Hardly a reliable source." He looked at Howard now. "General, I assume you are aware that the three scouts you sent our way did reach their destination. They reached the shore yesterday morning, made themselves known to us, and thus were we informed that the army had reached your present position. That only heightened our anticipation that you would make yourself known in considerable force."

Howard looked at Sherman, surprised. "We could not know they had made contact with you. Those men embarked on a most hazardous mission, dressed as rebel miscreants. It was a risk at best that they reach anyone but a rebel firing squad. I am greatly relieved to hear they are safe."

"Oh, quite safe, sir. They of course were not aware what might occur today. Most impressive, sir. Most impressive."

Sherman slapped Howard on the shoulder. "Impresses the hell out of me. What were their names, General?"

"Captain Duncan, Sergeant Amick, and Private Quimby, sir."

"Write that down for me. They deserve promotion. Anyone volunteers for a mission like that deserves recognition for it. Or, an award for complete stupidity."

Sherman could see that Howard wasn't certain if he was serious or not.

Williamson seemed to wait for the conversation to break, then said, "General, I am also charged with offering you any news you may wish to hear, events that you might not be aware of. The army has achieved an impressive victory at Franklin, Tennessee, over their General Hood."

"Know all about that. Well, some of it. That was one piece of information we picked up from the Georgia papers."

"Very good, sir. As well, General Grant is confident that his siege of Petersburg can only result in victory. The enemy troops there are reportedly in a dire situation." Sherman nodded, finished the second glass, and Williamson touched the bottle. "More, sir?"

Sherman shook his head, tried to clear out the creeping fog moving through his brain. "Any notion what General Foster is so anxious about?"

Williamson's expression changed slightly, a hint that not every relationship between army and navy was as cordial as this one. "The general will of course make a report to you. Admiral Dahlgren wishes you to know that General Foster has landed a considerable force of men, perhaps a division, on the South Carolina side of the Savannah River. He has made considerable comment about driving his men inland, destroying the railroad nearer the coast."

Sherman perked up now. "Has he?"

"Destroyed the railroad? I do not believe so, sir. I

only know what Admiral Dahlgren has stated, and that was given me in confidence, sir. General Foster is not the most, um, open of fellows. The admiral believes the troops are having some difficulty carrying out General Foster's planning."

Sherman absorbed that, no surprise that Foster would keep his plans to himself. He realized now that a naval officer might consider a single division to be an enormous force.

"I should wait for General Foster's report, Captain."

"Certainly, sir. I did not mean to speak out of turn."

"You didn't. But putting people inland north of the Savannah River could be of enormous benefit. The enemy has a force probably exceeding ten thousand in Savannah right now. It is my intention to nab the lot." He thought again of Foster. Engineer, and so he will spend time on details. That could be an asset. Or not. Sherman felt his impatience returning, annoyed with Foster, no matter the aid the man might be giving the campaign. He tossed that over in his head, thought, Careful, here. You've been all alone out here, running this thing your own way. Now there will be eyes watching you. Important eyes. Damn it all. "Captain, it is essential that I make contact with the War Department, and with Grant. They will expect full reports of our campaign. As for Savannah, very soon we shall have every piece of our artillery within range of the city.

THE FATEFUL LIGHTNING 423

General Hardee is in command there, and certainly
he will appreciate the nature of his emergency. Once
our guns are in place, I intend on notifying him of
that situation." Sherman paused. "Notes, yes. Do
you have paper and pen?"

"Oh, of course, sir."

Williamson leaned low, retrieved both from a
drawer near his feet. He laid the paper on the desk,
turned a silver inkwell toward Sherman.

"Very nice, Captain. Appears to be valuable."

"Solid silver, sir. Liberated it from a British fellow
who tried to run me through with his sword. Such
are the dangers of confronting blockade runners.
Thank you for noticing. The admiral allows us to
keep some prizes, though it does remind one of pi-
rates."

Sherman caught the humor in the man's words,
thought, Every sailor in the fleet thinks about pi-
rates sooner or later. It's in their blood. Sherman
moved the paper close, thought a moment, the others keeping silent. "First thing, I must send word to
General Halleck. He will certainly pass that along
to the secretary, and perhaps the president. Love to
be there for that. A great deal of hand-wringing,
you know. Some of those people in Washington expected this to end rather poorly for my command.
It's a pleasure to correct that impression."

He wrote now, the other two chatting amiably,
Williamson rising, offering to give Howard a tour
of the small craft, Sherman sensing that there were

others gathered just outside. Howard obliged, both men aware that giving Sherman a few minutes alone was the right thing to do. He wrote feverishly, his enthusiasm returning, but he didn't hide his caution that Savannah was not yet in his hands. He focused first on the army, the condition of his men, knew the newspapers would care more about that than anything Sherman had accomplished. He had no problems with that, the report stating it simply and directly, "The army is in splendid order, and equal to anything."

He stopped, pondered the words, his hands quivering with the weariness, the excitement, the effects of the brandy. He tried to focus again, completed the letter, thought of Halleck, Stanton, like so many frightened birds. Well, sure as hell, this will calm them down.

He heard a commotion now, men calling out, and in a short minute Williamson was there again, hesitant, said, "Sir, excuse me for interrupting. Word has come from a tender for the cutter **Nemaha.** Admiral Dahlgren is on his flagship, the **Harvest Moon,** anchored presently in Wassaw Sound. He offers his warmest congratulations, sir, and expresses his wishes that you join him, possibly tomorrow. I am to return you to McAllister tonight. As well, General Foster hopes to make contact with you on the morrow. Or rather, later this day. It is well after midnight, sir."

Sherman said, "Will you run us up on this boat? Make a much easier voyage than that skiff."

He saw gloom on Williamson's face. "Very sorry, I cannot, sir. There are numerous torpedoes in the river, one part of the enemy's barricade upstream. You shall have to use the skiff, I'm afraid."

Sherman looked down at the notes, spread now across Williamson's desk. "You will see that these are dispatched?"

"In the morning, sir. With all haste. It is the least I can offer you, sir. Washington must know where you are, just what you've accomplished."

The thought burst into Sherman's brain like a bolt of lightning. "One moment, Captain. Before we depart. I seem to have overlooked the most important commander I have."

"Sir?"

"As long as you're in position to dispatch these, it is probably a good idea that I write a letter to my wife."

CHAPTER TWENTY-ONE

HARDEE

SAVANNAH—DECEMBER 14, 1864

Beauregard had arrived on December 9, his inspection lasting the better part of a day. But he was now back in Charleston, and for Hardee, whether or not his superior was looking over his shoulder made no difference at all.

They had disagreed about the course of action, Hardee still hoping to hold the line against Sherman by severely limiting the access the Federal troops would have into the city. Already dikes had been cut, rice fields heavily flooded, the avenues into the city now confined to five causeways, where Hardee had placed the larger coastal guns. But the open fields were not impenetrable, merely shallow lakes, usually waist-deep. If the Yankees could not be stopped, the best Hardee could hope to do was to slow them down.

To Hardee's dismay, Beauregard had little interest in making any real effort to stop Sherman at all, Hardee surprised at what seemed to be a spirit of defeat. Even if Beauregard was right that the evacuation of Hardee's troops was the only alternative, Hardee had planned on ferrying his men across the Savannah River. Once across, the men could be marched northward farther into South Carolina. But Beauregard overruled him, ordering the building of a pontoon bridge across the river, whether or not Sherman's artillery allowed them to complete it. The plan called for defensive assistance from the Confederate gunboats, already patrolling the Savannah River, as well as good defensive firepower from a floating battery, making use of several of the enormous guns that had once faced the sea.

Hardee had faith in his engineers, though he understood that completion of the bridge depended far more on just how quickly Sherman moved his artillery within range of the city itself. Even now, as he patrolled the earthworks that faced the oncoming Yankees, men were at work, hurriedly hauling rice boats that were lashed side by side, serving as the pontoons. More men worked to wreck the wharves themselves, some of which had stood strong for more than a century, their timbers to serve as wooden planking atop the long, thin boats.

North of the river lay the critical rail depot at Hardeeville, its name the kind of coincidence that some men took for meaningful symbolism. To Hardee, the name of the place was far less important than its function: From that point, the rail lines ran farther up the coast, serving as the primary links to Charleston and other rail lines there that fed into Columbia and then on to North Carolina. With the rail line went the telegraph line, and Hardee knew that protecting both provided Savannah with their only links to Beauregard, as well as any other garrisons of troops that might be needed. To that end, Joe Wheeler's cavalry had been ordered north of the river. Already Federal troops were reported to have landed along the South Carolina coast, a surprising threat Hardee had not expected, those men certainly put ashore by Federal transports. Hardee had immediately pushed troops out that way, hoping to destroy or at least contain the Federal incursion from that direction. But pulling those troops away from the defenses facing west merely weakened a line that was too weak already. Hardee had to consider the possibility that if Sherman was to alter his primary drive toward Savannah and shift a sizable portion of his men north of the river, any force Hardee could put there would likely be crushed, along with the railroad and any communication north of the city. Holding tight to his defensive lines was a gamble Hardee had to make, that despite Beauregard's seeming disregard for Savannah as a place worth defending, Hardee was not yet willing to order his men to abandon the place, at least before any hope of halting Sherman had evaporated.

He kept to the horse, read the dispatch as he rode, the courier trailing behind, held back by his staff. He had anticipated that Sherman would attempt to open a passage up the Ogeechee River by assaulting Fort McAllister, the one waterway virtually devoid of any Confederate gunboats.

He halted the horse, let the reins drop, his shoulders sagging. Pickett was there now, said, "It is not good, is it?"

Hardee handed him the paper, said, "The fort has fallen. I expected a tougher fight. The enemy clearly chose to make that a priority. There isn't much we can do about it."

Pickett read, stared at the paper for a long moment. "What now, sir?"

Hardee kept his gaze downward, stared at the horse's mane, the horse dropping its head, nibbling at a tuft of greenery at the edge of the street. "He has no idea what is happening, what we must confront. His entire world is in that mouthful of grass. He's a beautiful animal, Bill. We should all be allowed to experience that kind of bliss, nothing to concern us but what we're to eat. It probably doesn't taste like much, but he doesn't care about that, either."

"You all right, sir? Do you have orders?"

Hardee looked at him, saw concern on his friend's face. "Bill, there isn't anything more we can do, not now anyway. Sherman has opened up the Ogeechee to their navy. We're cut off from any roads going south. Strange, though. This says it occurred last evening, but I didn't hear the guns. It's pretty far, but I would have thought we'd have heard that."

The rumble of closer cannon turned Pickett's head, and he said, "Hard to hear anything else. They're pushing in closer, sir. No doubt."

"Of course they are. Sherman didn't make his jaunt across this state just to admire our shoreline. It was his plan all along. We spread this army all over Creation, running around like madmen, anticipating him to turn off in some other direction, and all the while he kept up a straight line of march, right toward Savannah. We allowed him to avoid any real fight, did him a favor by not inflicting more than a few casualties. We debated and argued and speculated. And Sherman just . . . marched. Now he's ready for the next act in his masterful play. The spoils of war, in this case. Quite the prize."

"He hasn't gotten us yet, sir. We're strong."

Hardee glanced at Pickett again, saw Roy, the others easing forward. "We **were** strong. Now we are waiting for the inevitable. Do you believe Sherman will march straight up to our heavy artillery?" He didn't wait for an answer. "No. He will employ his navy, he will dance around our perimeter, he will maneuver and jostle until his artillery is capable of rendering this city into rubble." He looked at Pickett again, then Roy. "Have we heard anything more from the gunboats?"

The two men looked at each other, and Roy said, "Nothing, sir. If they are not lost, it appears they are upriver, with the enemy preventing their movement back into the city."

Hardee shook his head, slapped the horse gently. "They are lost to **us,** Colonel. That's all that matters."

The two gunboats were the **Macon** and the **Sampson,** invaluable craft that Hardee had hoped to use to protect the evacuation, and at the very least prevent Sherman from attempting to move on the city from the north, across the Savannah River. Besides protecting the construction of Beauregard's pontoon bridge, the two boats added substantial firepower to the land-based artillery. But as they patrolled farther upstream, the two boats had been caught by surprise by a mass of Federal sharpshooters and several well-placed artillery pieces, forcing their captains to retreat farther upriver, and farther from the wharves close to the site of the pontoon bridge. The loss of the two gunboats added to the strain of Hardee's predicament and only increased Beauregard's determination that Hardee leave the city.

The rumble from the cannon continued out to the west, some of it impacting much closer than anytime before. The staff seemed nervous, men speaking in hushed tones, Hardee ignoring that, focusing instead on the sounds. He glanced up, clouds obscuring the sun, no hint of rain.

"What is the hour?"

"Near ten, sir."

He kept his gaze westward, could see smoke drifting above faraway trees, the thumps and thunder rolling out in both directions. He felt the familiar stab of concern, searched the roads for couriers, for some information, his mind asking the inevitable question: Is it time? He turned to Roy, said, "Send an aide to General McLaws. I must know if he is under direct assault. If it is more of the skirmishing, I must know that as well. Explain to General McLaws that I cannot be in three places at once. Send an aide down to General Wright. If McAllister is in enemy hands, I need to know if Sherman is driving a strong force up from that direction. Have we heard anything further from General Smith?"

The questions betrayed his anxiousness, and he stopped, held that in, knew his staff officers would understand the urgency. He had very little confidence in two of his three commanders, McLaws being the most experienced. But good generals made little difference in a fight against a force as large as what Sherman was pushing toward them. He had told Beauregard that Sherman likely had thirty to forty thousand men, but the reports that reached him from both flanks seemed to show many more than that. Is it exaggeration, he wondered, or is it that we have been wrong from the start? Even Wheeler could never give us numbers that matched what the civilians claimed they saw. Do I trust them? How? Perhaps Beauregard is right. That thought jolted him. Beauregard's reputation for timidity was legendary, as far back as the vicious fight at Shiloh. His timidity cost us that battle, he thought. Now it will cost us Savannah. And yet there is no argument I can make.

"Sir! Riders!"

He brought himself back to the moment, saw colors, following a small staff, Gustavus Smith. Smith was experienced in the field but had never displayed the kind of leadership that won admiration. Now he commanded the right flank, anchored against the river. But Smith's troops were the least reliable, those remaining Georgia militia, as well as the greenest troops Hardee had in the field, no more than two thousand men.

Smith rode close, saluted, called out in a voice louder than Hardee needed to hear, the voice of panic. "Sir! The enemy has embarked troops onto the islands, taking up positions all down the river. They are moving on my flank, and I have no means to prevent that. What are your orders, sir?"

Hardee stared at Smith, could read fear in the man's eyes, a disease that no doubt infected his entire command, men who had no place being in line against Sherman's army.

"Have they reached the railroad bridge?"

"They are close, sir. My skirmishers have attempted to halt their progress, but last night they must have used boats, and put men even farther downriver."

Hardee lowered his head. "They did not swim, General." He stopped, fought his temper.

Smith still called out, his voice piercing, the man no more than a few feet away. "What am I to do, sir? The enemy has pushed us hard into the lines just beyond the limits of the city. His artillery has come up. You can hear that now, sir. They are moving men closer to our position right through the swamps and wetlands, sir. I admit, that was a surprise to me. I had hoped they would advance into the chosen avenues, confront our largest guns."

"We all hoped that, General. Sherman is not a man preparing for suicide. He will continue to advance his troops through any means he has. If that means wading up to their necks in swamp water . . . that's what they're doing."

"Yes, sir. It seems so, sir."

Hardee thought of the railroad, the communications to the north, Beauregard, Richmond, any troops that might still come to their aid. But his tactician's mind swept that away. No, he thought, what we have now is all we are to have.

"General Smith, order the railroad bridge to be burned. Once that is under way, withdraw your men into the lines at the city's edge. Preserve your artillery. Your men are not veterans. I do not wish to see a stampede. Orderly withdrawal, do you understand?"

Smith appeared ready to cry, and Hardee turned away, had no use for weakness, not now. Smith moved away, called out orders to his staff, more of the urgency none of them needed to hear. Hardee spurred his own horse now, thought of Ambrose Wright, commanding those troops positioned on Hardee's far left flank.

"Gentlemen, we should inspect our position to the south. If the Federal navy intends to make itself known to us, we should be prepared."

Pickett moved closer, said in a low voice, "How? What can we do to prevent them?"

Hardee moved the horse, no response, the single word in his mind.

Nothing.

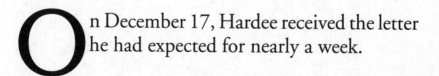

On December 17, Hardee received the letter he had expected for nearly a week.

You have doubtless observed ... that
seagoing vessels now come through the
Ossabaw and up the Ogeechee ... giving
me abundant supplies of all kinds, and
more especially heavy ordnance necessary to the reduction of Savannah. I have
already received guns that can cast heavy
and destructive shot as far as the heart of
your city; also I have for some days held
and controlled every avenue by which
the people and garrison of Savannah can
be supplied, and I am therefore justified
in demanding the Surrender of the City
of Savannah. . . .

                              W. T. SHERMAN
                              MAJOR GENERAL

CHAPTER TWENTY-TWO

SHERMAN

HOWARD'S HEADQUARTERS,
NORTHEAST OF FORT MCALLISTER—
DECEMBER 18, 1864

He read the note with undisguised anger, one line shouting out to him from the paper.

Your demand for the surrender of Savannah and its dependent forts is refused.

W. J. HARDEE / LIEUTENANT GENERAL

Howard sat close to the dying fire, a small white pipe in his mouth. "Did you expect anything else?"

Sherman folded the note with a harsh slip of his fingers, caught himself before he tore it into pieces. "I should keep this, I suppose. Others may want to see just what kind of dreams General Hardee is nurturing."

"Richmond, no doubt."

Sherman glanced at Howard, felt a surge of fury, fought to keep his voice below the hearing of Howard's entire camp. "I don't care a whit for Richmond. I don't care what kind of pride Hardee must display. He lies, all through this ridiculous letter. Lies. He is 'in free and constant communication with his department.' We have destroyed miles of rail lines in every direction. We have men wiring themselves into any telegraph line still standing, and if there are messages going back and forth, we'll hear them. He behaves as though we're barely a mosquito, buzzing around his horse's backside, something to be swatted away."

Howard kept his stare on the fire, and Sherman knew that Howard rarely showed excitement at all.

"Do you ever get angry? Does this not dig one big hole into your brain? The damned rebels took your arm, for God's sake." Sherman paused, felt a stab of guilt. "Sorry, Oliver."

"It is a fact, General. I cannot pretend to have what is not there. The fortunate thing is they did not take both. To be sure, that would be something of an inconvenience."

Sherman jammed the note into his pocket, focused his anger again toward Hardee. "The arrogance of the man, the arrogance of the entire rebel nation, their damnable cause, their insistence that all things Southern must be preserved against the Mongol hordes from the North. I'm sick of this, Oliver."

Howard looked at him now, the pipe still clamped in his teeth. "So. What would you change? Do you expect Hardee or anyone else to just throw up their hands and admit that this entire enterprise was one great error? Do you expect Jefferson Davis to call on Lincoln and offer a hand, apologizing for all the trouble he caused? You know what this will require. You know, better than anyone in this army that **guns** change minds, **guns** alter history, **guns** erase pride. We have plenty of guns, General. Big ones, little ones. We're moving them into position by the hour, and when you give the order, we'll drop shells anywhere Hardee thinks he's safe. That note isn't for you. It's for the civilians who are crowing at him every minute of the day. They're scared to death. They think he's their salvation, and he has to make a good show of it. It's for posterity."

"To hell with posterity. Hardee can offer reassurances and apologies all day long to the good citizens of Savannah. Doesn't change a damned thing. If he insists on standing up to us, then we shall oblige him, and a great many of his men will die. There's posterity for you."

He had slept for more than an hour, a luxury he had tried to enjoy. But the tent flap had stirred him awake, a low voice, one of Howard's aides.

"Very sorry to awaken you, sir."

"Who's that? Frasier?"

"It's Colonel Woodhull, sir. None of your staff are present, and I had no choice but to awaken you."

"Why?"

"An officer has arrived, just now, sir. Says he is Colonel Babcock, from General Grant's staff. He has made this journey to convey a message from General Grant."

"Orville Babcock? Here?"

"That's what he says, sir."

Sherman was awake now, stared out through the open tent flap, only shadows beyond. "Bring me a lantern, Colonel. And I suppose you may bring Colonel Babcock as well."

He sat up, grabbed his coat, pulled it on quickly, his mind racing. Babcock? What the hell for? The tent flap opened again, the lantern light blinding him, and Sherman covered his eyes, felt for a cigar, the pocket empty. The lantern was hung above him, and Sherman felt a hard dig in his insides, a stab of caution. Babcock was there now, offered a crisp salute, which Sherman returned.

"Long way from home, Colonel."

Babcock was never one for chatter, and Sherman

could read the man's seriousness, hints of arrogance that Babcock always carried.

"General, I bring you a letter, from the pen of General Grant. It is imperative that you read this without delay. There are two letters, actually. The first is less formal, composed by General Grant on December third. You may of course read that one first. The second was composed December sixth. There are orders for you, sir."

Sherman felt his heart racing, all thoughts of his independence erased by Babcock's haughtiness, something Sherman had seen before. Babcock was a brilliant young man, had graduated third in his class from West Point, had now earned an appropriate position on Grant's staff as secretary. He reached into a small leather pouch, produced a piece of foolscap, then another, kept his stance at attention, handed the paper toward Sherman. Sherman took both papers, fought to keep his composure, thought, He's congratulating me. Has to be. Why send Babcock? Sherman glanced at the headings, saw the dates, chose the latter one, Babcock's word punching him. Orders. He struggled with his sudden burst of nervousness, tried to keep his composure in front of a man who would notice every flaw.

"I haven't seen you in a while, Colonel. Since Vicksburg?"

Babcock's expression didn't change, still the formality. "Knoxville, I believe, sir."

"Yes, Knoxville. If you say so."

Sherman fingered the papers, had a gut-stirring uneasiness, was annoyed by the show of stiffness from Grant's officer, left him standing at attention. He opened the second paper completely, slow, deliberate, tilted it toward the lantern light, began to read.

I have concluded that the most important operation toward closing out the rebellion will be to close out Lee and his army. . . . My idea is that you now establish a base on the sea-coast, fortify and leave in it all your artillery and cavalry, and enough infantry to protect them, and at the same time so threaten the interior that the militia of the South will have to be kept at home. With the balance of your command, come here by water with all dispatch. Select yourself the officer to leave in command, but you I want in person. Unless you see objections to this plan which I cannot see, use every vessel going to you for purposes of transportation. . . .

U. S. GRANT, LIEUTENANT GENERAL

He stared blindly past the paper, felt a hard edge of nausea rolling up through him. "Leave me, Colonel."

"Sir, I am ordered to await your response. . . ."

"Get out of this tent, Colonel. You shall have my response in due time."

Babcock vanished, a surprise, and Sherman lay back on the bed, dropped the paper beside him. I am to leave here, to go to Virginia. He cannot see any objections to that. Grant, what are you doing? Am I not to be allowed to complete this task? Savannah is . . . right there. She sits waiting for us, her defenses certain to collapse, Hardee's army expecting capture. Why would you do this?

He rolled to one side, stared at the back of the tent, saw his shadow as a soft, uneven mound, raised a hand, watched the shadow moving with him, wiped the hand through his hair. I will not do this, he thought. It cannot happen this way. Grant is getting pressure from Washington. That has to be it. He is being shoved hard from behind to get Lee in his grasp, and my army will make that inevitable.

He rolled back, faced the lantern, his hand fishing for the paper beneath him. He pulled it up to his face, caught the lantern light, read it again. Now he saw the second piece, the date three days earlier.

Not liking to rejoice before the victory is assured, I abstain from congratulating you and those under your command, until bottom has been struck. . . . Since you left Atlanta, no great progress has been made here.

So, he requires my help. But he's **Grant,** for God's sake. He knows what to do, how to whip Lee. It's the damned newspapers, their traitorous headlines, surrounding Stanton like so many horseflies.

He read further, his eyes wide.

> **I do not intend to give you anything like directions for future actions. . . .**

He lowered the paper, stared into the yellow light of the lantern, thought, So, three days after he writes that, he changes his mind. Or Washington changes it for him. They read the sewage that flows out of Southern newspapers, all about our starvation and certain destruction, and someone up there believes every word of that. I have to be "saved" by leaving this place. Damn them. Damn them all.

Hitchcock sat to one side of the tent, paper on a board in his lap. "I'm ready whenever you are, sir."

Sherman was speaking to himself, words blowing through his brain, sentences, phrases, hot and fiery, condemnation and fury. But that would stay inside him, a hard fist holding on to the certain reality that Grant was his commander, his friend, and if Grant needed him in Virginia, there was a good reason for it. He stared at the floor of the tent, had mostly ignored Hitchcock, said aloud, "I won't do it. It's a mistake. A very bad mistake."

Hitchcock seemed to read his mood, kept silent, waiting for Sherman to look his way. The words kept flowing, Sherman forcing himself to slow them down, to ponder the meaning, the message, the tone. He looked at Hitchcock now, saw concern.

"Do you wish me to stay, sir? I can return later."

"Sit still."

Hitchcock nodded, the pencil in his hand, his voice barely audible. "Yes, sir."

"You got the heading?"

"Yes, sir. Lieutenant General U. S. Grant, Commander in Chief . . ."

"I know who he is. So does he. You don't have to read it to me."

"Yes, sir."

Sherman fought through his thoughts, the torrent of anger, the twisting frustration. "I have to convince him he's wrong."

"Yes, sir."

Sherman looked at Hitchcock now, as though for the first time, the kind face behind studious glasses. "How do I do that, Major?"

Hitchcock seemed surprised by the question, his mouth open slightly, words forming. "Well, sir, I would inform General Grant of our accomplishments. Nothing anyone can say will substitute for what we **did** here. It is not enough to suggest that we are in fine fettle. Offer him details, sir. This campaign has been more than a success. It has been a triumph. We must complete it."

Sherman was surprised, rubbed a hand on his chin. "You been talking to the others?"

"Yes, sir. Is that not appropriate?"

"It's fine, Major. You're my staff. I expect you to know what's happening. The rest of them feel like I do?"

"Sir, if I may suggest, the entire army feels as you do. No one here wishes to see you depart this command. None of us wish to depart. This is **your** army, sir. This is **your** campaign."

"I cannot disobey him, Major."

"Then you have to convince him. But not just that. You must offer the general an alternative that will accomplish the same goal, the goal of defeating the enemy. Ending the rebellion."

"You're an intelligent man, Major. Give me just a moment. We'll at least try."

The words came now, flowing out from Sherman through the hand of Hitchcock, the letter spread through several pages, lengthy recounting of the successes, the goals, the state of the army, the condition of the enemy. Through it all, Sherman relied on the one line in Grant's note, the single opening, that if Sherman had objections to Grant's plans, Grant would at least hear them. He kept Hitchcock's advice close at hand, that it was not enough to gloat, to feed the newspapers with glorious headlines. This was Grant, after all. Grant would understand exactly what Hitchcock suggested. If Sherman had plans that were better than anything Grant ever suggested, he had to tell him just what those plans were.

. . . With my present command, I had expected, after reducing Savannah, instantly to march to Columbia, South Carolina; thence to Raleigh, and thence to report to you. . . .

CHAPTER TWENTY-THREE

HARDEE

SAVANNAH—DECEMBER 18, 1864

Beauregard had returned to Savannah late the night before, a journey that mystified Hardee. The trip itself was hazardous at best, avoiding wrecked rail lines, skirting the Yankee patrols that extended both from the coastline and the islands upstream in the Savannah River. But Hardee had done what good subordinates do, greeting Beauregard with the respect due the man who would bear the ultimate responsibility for informing Richmond just what was certain now to happen. If Beauregard needed to see the state of affairs in Savannah, Hardee had no objection to that at all.

The Yankees had made solid advances toward the city from upriver, earthworks and log works rising up on Argyle Island, what Hardee knew could be Sherman's jumping-off point for a strong movement either toward Savannah or into South Carolina. There had been efforts to hold those Yankees back, but any kind of muscular assault would mean a weakening of other parts of the line, where every outpost faced increasing masses of blue.

They walked swiftly along the water's edge, Hardee laboring to keep up with Beauregard, a surprise. For so long Beauregard had carried some kind of illness, some debilitating ailment that drained away his strength, especially when his strength seemed most required. But now it was Beauregard with the energy, pacing manically along the riverfront, hands clasped behind him, observing the work ongoing to build the pontoon bridge.

"Three bridges? You need three?"

Hardee expected this, knew there could not be the kind of speed with the construction of the bridges that Beauregard had hoped for. "It is the best way. Three short spans, making use of Hutchinson and Pennyworth islands. If we attempt to build a single span bypassing the islands altogether, it could be vulnerable from as little as a single artillery shell. As it is, the longest span is near eleven hundred feet in length. We must make use of what the situation offers us."

Beauregard stopped, looked at him, and Hardee wondered if the man was grasping just what Hardee was telling him. But Beauregard seemed angry now, said, "General, I instructed you to construct a bridge for purposes of evacuating your army. Does that order not imply haste?"

"Sir, we have had difficulty locating sufficient numbers of boats."

Beauregard turned again to the water, hands on his hips, then pointed out to the river. "Yes, what are those craft, anyway? Peculiar construction."

"Rice boats, sir. We have a few shallow-draft barges we can use as well. We no longer have free passage up the rivers, in any direction. That has limited the number of those craft we could bring here."

Beauregard spun toward him again, seemed to search for any reason to be angry. "And just how were those rivers lost to us? I can understand the enemy moving troops up, anchoring one flank against the banks of the Savannah River. But now I hear that the Ogeechee is open to him as well, that he is able to support himself with fresh supplies from the Federal navy's armada of transport ships. Just how did that happen, General? Did we not have a substantial fortress to prevent just such an occurrence?"

Hardee suspected that Beauregard already knew

those details, part of the game Beauregard liked to play, as though it were insight and intuition that gave him his conclusions, and not old-fashioned rumor and intelligence.

"I erred in believing that Sherman would consider Fort McAllister a priority. He had to know it was well fortified. Their navy had never made any real attempts to bypass the place. I did not anticipate Sherman's willingness to take risk."

"Yes, well, in this war, General, the most successful commanders make their way by taking risks."

The response burned through Hardee's brain, his jaw clamped shut, the urge to puncture Beauregard's arrogance: **When did you ever take a risk?** He kept control, Beauregard turning away, as though his criticism should be the last word. Hardee looked down for a long moment, heard men out on the pontoons calling out toward them, recognizing just who these officers were. He glanced back toward his staff.

"Be certain Captain Stiles understands the urgency of his mission. Do we know where he is?"

Major Roy pointed to the nearest island. "I observed him on Hutchinson a short while ago. They are beginning to lay pontoons on the far side. The **Savannah** is anchored just beyond our view, sir. Her captain is concerned that the Yankees might still try to move onto the island."

Beauregard looked at him again. "The **Savannah**? Ironclad, yes?"

"Yes, sir. It is the one advantage we have in the river to this side of the city. The Yankees have made no effort to engage her. It would be a costly fight, no doubt."

"Hmm. No doubt. We should have had an entire fleet of ironclads, here and everywhere else the enemy has sealed up our ports. No one in Richmond would listen to me."

Hardee had never heard of any controversy about the navy, had no idea if Beauregard was being truthful or not. At the very least, it was one more hint that Beauregard was aware just how out of favor he was in the Confederate capital.

Hardee stared out over the water, saw another gunboat well away, said, "We have the **Firefly** and the **Isandiga** out on the far shore. They are assisting to hold away any Yankee approach. That should assist in the completion of the bridge. The **Georgia** is downstream, closer to the mouth of the river. The Federal navy is not making any attempt to contest this river."

Beauregard nodded slowly, seemed satisfied with Hardee's confidence in the naval guns, giving the first sign of any kind of enthusiasm for anything Hardee was doing. "They will pay a price in blood, no question. They cannot prevent us from making a successful retreat."

Hardee thought, They have yet to try. If Sherman knows of this bridge, surely he will do something about it. "There are forces north of the river, sir.

We are doing our best to push them away, but it is troublesome. General Wheeler's cavalry has lent some assistance, occupying the enemy's attentions on that side. I have urged in the strongest terms that the road toward Hardeeville be kept open. It is our only hope of keeping this army intact."

Beauregard spun around, pointed a finger into Hardee's face. "So, you see? You agree that we must withdraw from this place. I knew that. There were others who believed you would fight to the last. Foolishness, always has been. This country does not require martyrs. We have plenty as it is. How prepared is the army to begin the withdrawal?"

"The order has not yet been given to the men."

Beauregard turned to him again. "Good Lord, why not?"

Hardee hesitated before answering, chose his words. "Your orders are that we abandon this city to its inhabitants rather than risk the destruction of this army. I called a council of war last evening, before you arrived. I wished to know the feelings of the men who will command that withdrawal. There are engagements ongoing all down the line, from the far left to the shores of this river. If the men know they are to pull away, they may begin doing so prematurely. There is some sentiment in this army still to make as strong a fight as we can, damage the enemy severely. The morale of the men is better than I had hoped. I did not see any reason to remove any hope they might have."

"So, the men feel this is a fine time to stand up and face Sherman's guns, eh? Were they adequate to that task a month ago? They allowed their backs to be pushed against the wall, so to speak, and now they wish to show courage?"

"Morale is always a good thing, sir. Mass desertion or a wholesale surrender benefits no one but the enemy. Is it not my duty to prevent that from happening?"

Beauregard was shaking his head, stepped closer to the river, stared out again to the workers at the island. "If we could prevent any of this, don't you think we would have done so? It hardly matters anymore what the men believe will happen. We do not operate on **hope,** General. The plain fact is that the order I gave you was approved in its entirety by Richmond. There are no illusions as to what will happen here. I have seen plenty of evidence that the enemy is pushing hard up against whatever defenses you have constructed. He outnumbers us by a wide margin, and I regret that the quality of the fighting men we have here does not match up with his. That has been a problem for this army for the better part of this past year. You are not the only one suffering from that disease, General."

Beauregard paused, as though swallowing hard for what would come next. Hardee was curious, thought, What new disaster is he not telling me of? Has Lee been taken at Petersburg? Has the enemy moved into Richmond? After a long moment,

Beauregard said quietly, avoiding the ears of the lingering staffs, the laborers along the near shore of the river, "There has been an engagement at Nashville. General Hood's troops did not prevail. Hood is in retreat now, as far as we know. He left behind him the heart of his army."

Hardee had never expected anything positive to come from Hood's campaign, but he did not expect what sounded like an all-out disaster. "How bad were his losses?"

Beauregard seemed not to hear him. "That was my command, you know. Richmond entrusted me to put the right people in the right place, make the proper decisions. But I cannot be asked to do the impossible, no matter who is doing the asking. I am to govern a man who has shown himself to be ungovernable. General Hood is a favorite of Richmond, and so Richmond expects him to perform miracles, while I must stand aside and offer my approval. Then Richmond offers me nothing to see these miracles through, no men, no guns. All I receive is criticism. If Hood was victorious, all would be well, those who worship heroes would have their day. And still, no one would consider my place, my authority. Unless, of course, he failed."

For the first time, Hardee realized just how much authority Beauregard had been given, that Hood's entire campaign was approved through Beauregard's headquarters. If Hood was indeed Beauregard's responsibility, why did he not order Hood to strengthen his army right where he was, make some new effort against Atlanta? Now he claims . . . what? He didn't want to get in Hood's way? Hardee knew that Hood's decision to invade Tennessee seemed at best to be reckless. And so, he thought, because you would not give Hood a firm order, good men like Patrick Cleburne are dead. Is this what the president empowered you to do? He realized now that Beauregard had not used Davis's name once. Of course not. They despise each other. Why should that be any different now? Why should this army, this war be managed any differently now than it has always been?

Hardee stepped away, black anger flowing through him. He stared out at the labor ongoing toward Hutchinson Island, tried to keep his mind on the job he had to do, the right way to do it. I cannot tell him the truth. He would not hear it anyway. But certainly, he knows he will garner all the blame, for Tennessee, for Savannah. He must surely know he cannot keep this command. Davis will find any excuse to remove him, as he has done already . . . three times in the past? And so, Savannah is his last command, and surely everyone in Richmond, and everyone in Beauregard's headquarters, knows that.

"It is so terribly unfair, you know."

Hardee was surprised by the change in Beauregard's tone, but he knew exactly what Beauregard meant. Be tactful, he thought. He is not yet your enemy.

He forced his voice into calmness, said, "Sir? Forgive me, I'm not sure what you are referring to."

Beauregard looked at him, deep gloom on the man's face. "This war is very close to a conclusion. That is not a legacy I wish to embrace. I have served my government as best I could. Well, we all have, certainly. I do not mean to place myself above anyone else. But you see it, don't you?"

"I see what I am authorized to see, General. Savannah is my command, and I must consider the problems that we have right here. My greatest concern is that we cannot stand tall when we are outnumbered five to one in both men and guns."

"Do you not see how much of the Confederacy is now occupied by Yankee commanders? How am I . . . are we to reverse that?"

"I do not know, sir. If I am ordered to assault Sherman's troops to my front, I shall do so. Is that not how a soldier learns to fight? Perhaps General Hood believes that as well. He must certainly have believed he could have recaptured Nashville."

"And then what? General Hardee, you are either incredibly naïve or you are mocking me. We couldn't hold Nashville two years ago against a ragtag bunch of blue-coated misfits. It is an indefensible place, especially from the north."

Hardee held the question to himself: Then why did you allow him to go there? Why did you not order Hood to remain in Alabama? Why did he not pursue Sherman out of Atlanta?

The night before, those questions and many more had been thrown about his council of war, and the answers then were no more useful than the answers now. He turned away from Beauregard, thought, Would it have mattered, after all? If Hood had pursued Sherman, there was still Thomas, and Thomas would certainly have ridden hard against Hood from the west. No victories, and many more casualties.

Hardee had to ask, knew it would all come out eventually. "How bad was it for Hood? How severe were the losses?"

Beauregard shrugged. "Six thousand, perhaps. Hood says not that many, but Hood will lie to protect his reputation. He had possibly thirty thousand engaged. From what Hood claims, he was outnumbered by more than half." Beauregard looked at him now. "What of it, General? How does any of that affect what you are failing to do here? I ordered this bridge to be completed with extreme speed. When will that happen?"

Hardee looked again to the workers, saw men peering back at him, Beauregard's words flowing across the choppy water. "It shall be complete when the men have completed it. My commanders are all convinced that we have no good purpose to serve by remaining here, and sitting still under Sherman's avalanche. I agree with that view. So far I have made every effort to prevent the frontline troops from knowing what we intend, but that cannot last."

Beauregard paced again, slow, steady steps, Hardee following, keeping a step behind. The rumble of big guns came now, far out to the left, down toward the position along the Little Ogeechee. Beauregard stopped, and Hardee said, "Those are siege guns. Quite certain the Federal navy is offering Sherman any assistance he wishes to have."

Beauregard looked around, as though studying the city itself. "They have not shelled the town, the civilians."

"Not yet."

Beauregard looked at him now, as though genuinely surprised. "You believe he will?"

"I believe he can. Whether or not he will make this another Vicksburg will depend on us."

"It will depend, General, on how quickly you get that bridge built."

SAVANNAH—DECEMBER 19, 1864

Hardee stood in the parlor of the grand house, could smell the aroma from the small pine tree. The branches of the tree had been cut away in layers, to allow for gifts to be slid into the tree itself, each limb adorned with a candle, those to be lit on Christmas Eve. The tree was crowned with a small white angel, what the woman of the house had told him was her own doll, a toy from long ago, makeshift pieces of lace cut into wings, adhered to the doll's back. Beyond the tree, above the fireplace, one long stocking hung low, wide stripes of black and white, what Hardee guessed to be a child's optimism, that somehow, through all that was happening around this city, the stocking could be made full. He walked closer to the tree, eyed the water bucket nearby, the permanent precaution in the event any one of the lit candles should suddenly twist, or burn down, what could easily ignite the tree. That kind of tragedy occurred nearly every Christmas, in every town Hardee had been. He felt a stab of emotion, thought, No, that is one thing we cannot have here. Savannah shall not be burned. I will not oversee such an act, and I cannot believe that Sherman would commit such an outrage. If there is no danger to him here, if there are no guns, no sharpshooters, surely he will not inflict punishment on the innocent.

He thought of the cotton now, knew that throughout Savannah there were enormous stores of cotton bales, gathered throughout the fall, now waiting for the merchants to make the dangerous effort to deliver them to their clients in London, or anywhere else they could be sold. There is little chance of that now, he thought. So, do I destroy it? Those bales are gathered and stacked in every barn, every outbuilding in the city. If I burn one bale, it could erupt into a hell that would sweep through the entire place. And how many deaths would there be? He looked at the fragile tree, noticed the wood carving, a small manger scene placed close by. How much of this, how many Christmases would be consumed by a fire that I ordered? Sherman would get the blame for that, I suppose. The newspapers would certainly wish that upon him. But I would know, and I will not be responsible for such destruction. These people have done nothing to deserve any such cruelty, have not earned such disaster. There are forts here because we built them. There are soldiers here because I command them. And very soon, that will change. It has to change. Savannah will become what it once was, no matter what color uniform the soldiers wear. We cannot make a war in these streets, any more than I will make a war in Charleston. My family will not become victims of this evil. The war will end, it must end before reasonable men allow everything Southern to be rendered into ash.

He moved to a window, peered out, daylight fading, saw the river, one of his gunboats moving slowly past. That should be a fisherman, coming in with his catch. Or a merchantman, coming to load that cotton. His eye moved to the house across the street, one of several makeshift hospitals. There were ambulances parked in a cluster, one man climbing down, a man in a white gown moving toward the rear of one, more men now assisting. Hardee blinked hard, thought, Just skirmishing. There are always wounded, even if there's no real fight. But the fight is coming, and if there is a general engagement, every house in this city will become a hospital. I know what Sherman's trying to do, and I cannot stop him. It is one thing for him to gain his footholds on the islands, but he could yet put a great many men into South Carolina, more than Wheeler or anyone else could hope to contest. It's what I would do, sweep around the flank, sever all communication, all routes of transportation, pen my enemy up inside a neat box. No, General, I will not allow that. I have my orders, and I know what must happen. There can be no delay while my generals offer **opinions,** or make their arguments over the only option we have.

He knew the bridge was nearing completion, that even if it wasn't sound from an engineer's point of view, it would suffice to get the men and a good many of the smaller field guns out of the city. If it could be tonight, he thought, that would be ideal. The enemy is pressing us hard, but he does not seem to appreciate our urgency. Perhaps he has little urgency of his own. Why should he? He must assume we are staying put, intending to fight it out, protecting the honor of the city more than the lives of my army. There are some in this army who would still do that. The time for such foolishness is past. I suppose General Hood knows that as well as anyone. I wonder if anyone in Richmond is paying attention.

He backed away from the window, caught the fragrance of something cooking, the floor below him, the family still using their house. Gracious hosts, he thought. There is meat, still. Bless them for that. I will not see them destroyed so that we can claim some sort of useless victory over Sherman, even if all we gain is a single day. No, it is time, and if it is not tonight, it will be tomorrow. We shall take what remains of this war elsewhere.

He looked again at the hearth, the lone stocking, heard a rustle in the next room. There were staff officers there, and he heard the tiny song in the voice of the child, had heard it every day since he had been there. The owner of the house had one small boy, barely four, and Hardee had avoided him whenever possible, the necessary business of the army, and more, the necessity of keeping the face of children away from all the planning for war. The boy was one of so many, civilians with their families, with their routines, their jobs and careers and daily chores, the wealthy with their maids and nannies. But this family had no stately grandeur to their home, no real wealth to flaunt toward their neighbors. Hardee knew there were cotton bales in the barn, a half dozen maybe, sacks of meal, rice, what would supply the family with sustenance through the winter. Now the Yankees will come, he thought. Will they see the child and push right past, and steal everything of value, everything a young boy has to eat? I would stop that, if I could. But there is nothing I can do. And so the best that anyone can do is to move this army away, and perhaps those other fellows will choose to pursue us, and not pillage this harmless place. Perhaps Sherman has enough decency in him that he will not destroy a beautiful place just because he **can**.

He caught a glimpse of the boy now, a peek around the open doorway, the hand of an aide capturing the boy before he came in. Hardee called out, "No! Let him be. This is his home, after all." Hardee looked again to the small pine tree. "This is his Christmas. We are merely intruders here."

The boy entered, eyes locked on Hardee, and he moved quickly toward the tree, peered up into the gaps between the neatly trimmed layers, no gifts, nothing yet to see. Hardee couldn't avoid a smile, watched now as the boy eased close to the hearth, fingered the stocking, which was longer than he was. There was disappointment on the boy's face, and Hardee chuckled, said, "Too soon, boy. Not time for that yet."

He realized he didn't know the child's name, but he saw a sparkle in the boy's eyes, so familiar, the same kind of gleam he had seen from his daughters, too many years ago.

The boy studied him, a hint of fear, but his curiosity clearly outweighed the intimidation from Hardee's uniform. "When's it be time, Mister? Mama says Santa Claus will come. You ever seen him?"

Hardee knelt low, the boy unafraid now, and Hardee took the tiny hands in his. "My girls knew him well. When they were young, they put feed out for his reindeer."

The boy seemed confused, said, "What's reindeer?"

Hardee felt a pinch in his throat, didn't fight the smile. He sat down on the floor now, could see his staff watching him with wide eyes. He motioned toward them, **go away,** sat the boy down beside him. "You ever heard the story about Saint Nicholas?"

The boy shook his head.

"I used to tell this to my girls every year." He paused, memories flooding through him, the words coming now, and he looked at the boy, saw the wonder of a child's innocence. For a brief moment, the war seemed very far away, and he smiled again, lowered his voice to a soft whisper, said, "'Twas the night before Christmas . . ."

CHAPTER TWENTY-FOUR

SHERMAN

DECEMBER 19, 1864

He had left specific orders with both Slocum and Howard, to continue pressing their men hard against the defenses that faced Sherman's entire position. Already Howard was anchored down to the right against the Little Ogeechee River, an unassailable position. Slocum had continued to insist that he be allowed to push a vast force north of the Savannah River, but Sherman held him back, agreeing only to a single brigade. It had to be a surprise to Slocum, and to anyone in Sherman's command, that Sherman was suddenly showing great care, uncharacteristic caution. What he would not discuss with anyone was his roaring anxiety over Grant's reaction to his letter, his pleading response to Grant's order. No matter Sherman's classic impatience, it would be several days before he heard a reply.

It was entirely possible, even likely, that Grant would still bow to whoever was urging him to pull Sherman out of Georgia and simply repeat his order that Sherman put the bulk of his army on board the flotilla of transport ships. Grant's staff officer had been specific about that, the armada steaming toward him even now. If, on the other hand, Grant were to allow Sherman his wish, and authorize him to proceed with the capture of Savannah, the last thing Sherman needed to do now was make a ridiculous mistake. Any serious assault on Hardee's defensive lines could prove far more costly than Sherman would want to explain to Grant, and would no doubt justify Grant's order in the first place. Worse for Sherman, if Grant was being pressured from above, a blunder by Sherman could force Grant to do the worst thing possible for Sherman: relieve him of his command. The order to Sherman's generals made very clear that there was to be no direct confrontation with Hardee's lines. The skirmishing would of course continue, picking and prodding, seeking weaknesses that Sherman might still exploit. Once Sherman had his reply from Grant, he knew his generals would be fully prepared to launch a major assault.

From their first meeting, Sherman had been impressed with Admiral John Dahlgren, a man who took his job seriously and brought a level of expertise and sobriety that Sherman respected. That respect had only been enhanced by Dahlgren's offer of gunships to go along with the supply transports. Dahlgren had seemed fully aware that cooperation between army and navy was an asset for both of them. Though Sherman preferred any strategy other than a siege, he understood that Dahlgren's assistance could close the ring around Savannah completely, what would likely be an unbreakable seal. Dahlgren also favored a combined operation in assaulting the city itself, suggesting that the navy could drive gunboats and possibly several companies of marines up the Ogeechee, adding power to whatever attack Sherman intended to make. Sherman appreciated the admiral's enthusiasm, and planning for a siege wouldn't seem to contradict Grant's orders, at least for now. But until Sherman received Grant's response, he felt a different kind of urgency: the aching need to sit tight. Unfortunately, it would be Sherman's job to convey that message directly to Admiral Dahlgren.

There was another significant reason for Sherman to go to sea. Dahlgren had generously offered Sherman transport north toward Hilton Head Island, where General John Gray Foster was anchoring his own Federal presence along the shore. Sherman was increasingly elated by the prospect of a hard-charging invasion along that part of the coast, that Foster's troops could do significant damage to what the maps showed to be Hardee's last remaining avenue of escape. That route was called, ironically, Union Causeway, leading away from the city on the north side of the Savannah River, the route toward the rail depot and roadways at Hardeeville. But Foster's men had failed to advance as Sherman had hoped, no explanation given for their timidity, or why there was any delay at all. If Sherman was to shove Foster into action, he knew there was no substitute for meeting the man face-to-face, emphasizing just how important Foster's mission might become.

ON BOARD THE **HARVEST MOON**— DECEMBER 19, 1864

There was a small burst of lantern light, Dahlgren emerging from the ship's main cabin, moving toward him.

"We should arrive at Hilton Head at dawn, or thereabouts. The tides are somewhat in our favor."

Sherman stood with his hands pressed against the rail, his thoughts far away, his fingers caressing the damp wood, polished smooth. He suddenly realized Dahlgren had spoken to him, said, "Dawn, you say? Sorry, Admiral, my mind is elsewhere. Something about the water after dark, the moonlight flickering. The lights of Savannah seem brighter out here than anything I've seen from the other side. Rather peaceful, actually. All of that . . . takes my mind to other places."

Dahlgren chuckled. "Indeed. That's why many of us go to sea. There is always work to do, always those details of command to attend to, but then there are the times like this. Quiet moments. Thoughts of family, of home, one's wife, I suppose. These are happy times for some of us, I'm sure. Not all, I'm afraid."

Sherman knew only the slightest details of Dahlgren's son, Ulric, killed earlier that year. He was said to be a Northern spy, involved in a plot to assassinate Jefferson Davis. Ulric's capture and subsequent execution made rich fodder for the Southern newspapers, something Sherman almost always ignored. He looked at Dahlgren's face, saw a father's emotion, was suddenly struck by his own, stared out to sea again, tried to hold back the memories, his eyes dancing with the shimmering moonlight.

Dahlgren settled in beside him, leaned out as well, a silent moment between them, the only sounds the rhythmic chug of the steam engine beneath their feet, the soft splashing of the paddle wheels to each side of the ship.

Dahlgren was older than Sherman by more than ten years, the age showing itself in the man's lean and drawn face, a receding hairline with a healthy dose of gray. The man seemed stern, rarely smiled, but Sherman had seen moments of warmth, hints of melancholy, and more, had felt the man's respect for Sherman's command, a prize all its own.

The breeze seemed to shift slightly, a chill against Sherman's face, the ship turning, and Dahlgren said, "There are Confederate forts out from those lights, two miles or so, several heavy shore batteries we try to avoid. No need risking any chance encounter with a lucky rebel gunner. Once we're past Savannah itself, there won't be any problems."

Sherman studied the low line of faint lights, the shoreline blending together, nothing that showed him a fort. "Not sure how many men they have in those forts. Hardee's stretched pretty thin. I have to believe that."

Dahlgren seemed to ponder that, said, "Once we start bombarding those places, it won't much matter how many people they've got. I understand your need for delay. But I promise you, General, it will be a grand show." Dahlgren paused. "Your plans seem to have been well designed. My compliments again."

"Thank you."

"Doesn't always happen like that. Even good plans can take a tragic turn. My son, Ulric. He was part of a plan to liberate the prison camps near Richmond. He didn't plan on getting caught. Now the rebels are claiming that he was the linchpin of some kind of ridiculous plot, calling him an assassin, as though anyone should be condemned for killing Jefferson Davis. All my boy did was the job he was assigned. He paid for that with his life and then, his honor."

Sherman said nothing, felt awkward now, scolded himself for his own arrogance, allowing himself to feel pride in his campaign, blissfully unaware what kind of emotion might accompany Dahlgren's hearty slap on the back. He fumbled again with the cigar, no attempt to light it, stabbed it between his teeth. "Very sorry."

"Thank you. He was a soldier, and sometimes soldiers die. The tragedy is that he was only twenty-one. He'd have made a fine commander."

"Like his father."

"That's not necessary, General. I often feel his presence, as though his sword fights with me. If only in spirit. I would hope he's in a better place. Forgive my rambling, General. I am aware that you carry tragedy of your own."

Sherman was surprised, rarely spoke of the death of his son, wondered now how Dahlgren knew about it. "He was just a child. They die as well. Sickness, typhoid fever. Some say a disease like that is just misfortune, chance. I never considered **bad luck** to be a curse for the young." He paused. "My son Charles, just an infant. I've never actually seen him. Heard from my wife before we left Atlanta that he was quite ill. No day passes without me thinking of that, not knowing if he's well now, or . . . anything else."

"Very sorry to hear that. You should be hearing of his recovery very soon. The mail packets are already delivering their cargo up the Ogeechee. Certainly, all will be well."

Sherman had tried not to think of the baby, appreciated Dahlgren's kindness. "My wife, Ellen. She would put all of this business in God's hands. I am to be punished for my sins, or misdeeds, or profane thoughts, and so God carries away my firstborn. Very biblical."

"You don't sound convinced of that."

Sherman had no idea of Dahlgren's religion, didn't want this kind of discussion, not now. "Ellen is devoutly Catholic. I suppose . . . I'm not. If I'm wrong, then I'll find that out one day. I have too many things to concern me in **this** life."

"Indeed."

A voice came from forward of the ship, "Admiral? Your presence, if you please?"

Dahlgren extended a hand toward Sherman. "Please excuse me, General. I have a few matters of navigation to attend to. These moments rarely last."

Sherman took the hand, and Dahlgren turned away, moved slowly toward the bow of the ship, past the enormous paddle wheel, the figure fading now into the faint lights. Sherman felt the emotion again, his son Willie, the boy's face never truly out of his memory. Nine years old, he thought. Wanted only to be a soldier. Even more than I did. So, what about that, Sherman? You enjoy this, you're damned good at it. Maybe it's like the admiral says, you're making the fight for both of you.

That had not occurred to him until now, and he put one hand on the wooden rail again, the lights of Savannah nearly gone. So, we shall punish them doubly hard, he thought. Willie, if you're here, somewhere, well, fine. If I have to carry a sword for you, so be it.

He turned away from the water, shook his head, felt oddly uncomfortable. If my boy's a ghost, I sure as hell don't want him sticking his face into my tent. No, stop with that. There's no spirits fighting alongside you. How about a few thousand casualties, but then, there's a few thousand of those other fellows, too. They can have their own war, fight it out all over again. No one's here on this damned ship but you. And if the enemy's to be punished it'll be by my hand, and it'll be done the best way I know how. They deserve it. Let Ellen worry about where my boy is now, what kind of man he might have become. I just want this war to end.

HILTON HEAD,
SOUTH CAROLINA—DECEMBER 20, 1864

"I assure you, General Sherman, we will not fail. I have ordered my men to begin a rigorous patrol of the enemy's routes of escape. If anything, we shall succeed in crushing the rebels by crossing the river ourselves. With your troops to their front, old Hardee won't know what's driving up his backside."

Foster was a rotund man, an explosion of whiskers bursting from the sides of his face. Sherman absorbed the man's bluster, fingered the buttons on his own coat, couldn't avoid noticing that Foster's coat was stretched nearly to the breaking point. Sherman tried to keep his eyes off the man's face as well, couldn't ignore the thought that Foster looked exactly like a pumpkin.

He waited for Foster to finish, though after the first blathering sentence, Sherman had ignored half of what the man said.

"Your intentions are profoundly appreciated, General. However, **my** intention is that you secure the enemy's primary route of escape, the road from Savannah to Hardeeville."

Foster was still puffed up, nodded with exaggerated approval. "Certainly, yes, indeed. That is our goal as well. Tell me, General, have your men made a substantial crossing of the river? That pathway to the enemy's flank could be even more approachable, more vulnerable from your side of things."

Sherman didn't want to pour out the details of Grant's order, was already regretting this journey. "General Foster, I have restricted General Slocum to the movement of one brigade north of the Sa-

vannah River. We are facing heavily fortified works
all across the inland side of the city. I had hoped
your foray into this situation would be as an **addition** to our efforts. The railroad south of the
Savannah River is entirely in our hands, as is the
Ogeechee River and Ossabaw Bay. The enemy has
some power nearer to the city, on the Savannah itself, at least one ironclad, possibly two. There are at
least two wooden gunboats and floating batteries,
and it has been reported that he is attempting to
construct a pontoon bridge. It is clear to me that
Hardee understands the gravity of his situation,
and is seeking some means to avoid the sacrifice of
his army in a hopeless cause."

Foster nodded again, as though approving Sherman's description. "Yes, certainly. But their cause is
hopeless by many miles, General. Once the president issued his emancipation order, it played precisely into my hands. We have gone to great lengths
to establish colonies of freed slaves. Quite a feat in
the middle of a war, wouldn't you say?"

Sherman had wearied of this conversation, and
worse, he wasn't certain that Foster recognized
Sherman's authority at all. As it was now, Foster
had held command of this part of the coastline
for some time, and other than a brief command
in the Department of the Ohio, Foster's personal
kingdom seemed to be where Sherman's army had
now arrived. Sherman wasn't even certain if Foster

might outrank him. He brushed that thought away as quickly as it dropped into his mind. It was one thing to swallow a distasteful order from Grant. Foster could keep his orders to himself.

Sherman fiddled with the cigar now, his temper spilling over, his hands too shaky to light it. He kept a hard grip on his impatience, chewed hard on the end, biting an inch of cigar clean through. He spit the tobacco to the side, fought to control his voice. "I have studied the maps with great care. I strongly suggest, General, that you deploy one division, perhaps under General Hatch, and march them immediately across the Broad River. There should be very little opposition in that region, beyond some cavalry. Occupying the Union Causeway would seal the door, as it were. Hardee would have no alternative but to attack us, which would be certain suicide. Or he would be forced to surrender. I prefer the latter."

"Oh, I agree. A surrender would be most gratifying. And I see you've been going over my roster of command. Very good. Yes, Hatch is a good man, fine officer. He could do the job, definitely. I shall look into that possibility immediately."

Sherman waged a battle still with his own temper, ran a hand across his rough beard, the words rolling through his brain, pouring out now, more heat than he intended. "General Foster, just how soon is **immediately**?"

ON BOARD THE **HARVEST MOON**—
DECEMBER 21, 1864

The voyage southward was interminable, Sherman spending far more time in agitated pacing of the decks than in gazing across dark water. In a journey that had encompassed three days, he had gained nothing of substance from Foster beyond the man's assurance that all would be dealt with appropriately, Sherman sensing that Foster was perfectly content to have his command remain exactly where it was. For all Sherman could tell, the enemy in Savannah was only the latest inconvenience to Foster's routine.

Dahlgren had sensed his mood, kept mostly away, tending to the duties of his flagship. But throughout the journey, the coastline was clearly in view, Dahlgren keeping closer in an effort to give Sherman at least a sense of proximity to his own army. More, Dahlgren made as much steam as he could, regardless of the timing of the tides. As the **Harvest Moon** finally wound her way into the mouth of the Ogeechee River, her eight-foot draft gave Dahlgren every sailor's greatest headache. She ran aground.

The labor had gone on for more than an hour, the tenders working to pull the ship free of a muddy bottom that refused to yield.

Sherman paced again, another circuit around the open deck, working the cigars in his teeth until his jaws ached. The **Harvest Moon** was a seagoing vessel, more than five hundred tons of steel and wood, and as he prowled the decks, Sherman pondered that figure, wondering how so much heft could actually float, realizing that, clearly, there were times when it didn't float at all.

He felt himself sweating, the warm salt air working through his coat, made warmer by his mood and the unwanted exercise. He moved inside the common area, peered out through one of the deckside windows, felt stifled for air, moved out again through an entryway. He caught the stink of smoke from the stack high above, glanced up, then staggered slightly, caught off balance by the sudden tugging from one of the tenders to the stern, the smaller boat coming up to full steam, a valiant effort to free the larger ship. Men were yelling all around him, and he knew they shared his frustration, working the various ropes, doing all anyone could do to slide so much weight through the gumlike mud. Dahlgren was at the stern, leaning out, surrounded by men tending to heavy ropes, and Sherman moved the other way, keeping to himself, knew that his temper was magnified by every officer on the ship, and most probably by Dahlgren himself.

Sherman was at the bow now, stopped, stared inland, vast seas of saw grass, a narrow channel, and beyond, open water. He understood that this was for him, that the admiral had taken a different route toward the mouth of the Ogeechee to save time. He felt embarrassed himself now, thought, Dahlgren has to be humiliated by this. Keep your talk to yourself, Sherman. No joking about this to anyone. He looked down into muddy water, saw the current flowing toward the ship, the Ossabaw still leaking tide. That will change, he thought. The tide will change, rise, and in time the ship would free herself without all this damned work. He wasn't sure how much time, a matter of hours, probably, and he knew Dahlgren would have a chart somewhere. He left the bow, moved his way toward the small cockpit, saw Dahlgren approaching him, nothing pleasant in the man's demeanor.

"Ah, General. I've made different arrangements. If you don't mind a bit less pomp, I have ordered my barge put off. She's lashed now to the starboard side. Quite a bit easier to maneuver over these marshes. If you don't mind, please follow me, and we'll resume our journey."

"As you wish, sir. This is your command. I am merely a passenger. A bothersome one at that."

Dahlgren still didn't smile, moved past him, Sherman following. He peered out over the rail, saw the flat-bottom craft, men with ropes, what he had already been corrected to call **lines,** holding her tight to the side of the ship. He followed Dahlgren down the ladder, men below assisting, and Sherman descended as quickly as he could without tumbling off, dropped down to the small deck, saw all eyes on him, Dahlgren included. Dahlgren said, "Hold tight, General. She's not very stable. But we'll slide through this grassy flat in no time. Get you where you need to be."

Sherman realized they were all studying him, a distinctive air of fear in the men. He felt guilty now, all this labor on his behalf. He held up his hands, tried to show approval. "Yes, thank you. This is perfectly fine."

Do they think I'm some sort of demigod, he thought? I haven't shouted at a single one of these fellows since I boarded this ship. Perhaps my staff has been a bit indiscreet, told them a few things they shouldn't have. Or perhaps these sailors can tell I've been on water too long. Yep. Get me back to my damned army.

They pushed through the channel, past thick saw grass, Ossabaw Bay opening up before him. Yep, that's exactly what he did, Sherman thought. Took a shorter route to get to the mouth of the Ogeechee. He took a chance and did me a favor, and it bit him. Remember that. I don't imagine too many admirals embrace the idea of running aground.

From the bow, one of the crew raised his hand, called out, "Sir, a boat. She's signaling."

Dahlgren was there now, motioning Sherman to join him. "Yes, General, she's signaling for you by name. This should be a better ride for you. That's the quartermaster's tug, **Red Legs**."

The two craft came together, lines tossed, an officer on the tug shouting out toward Sherman, "Sir! Letter for you, sir! For both you and the admiral. Most urgent!"

Sherman felt the familiar cold jab, his mind rolling through so many possible disasters, images of every kind of bad news. He thought first of Grant, the response, thought, He's not interested in my ideas. He's ordering me to go to Virginia.

He raced past that to new thoughts, something much worse, a great fight, considered the possibility, the most likely place, the enemy surprising Slocum, perhaps turning the army's left flank along the Savannah River. He wanted to send troops northward, Sherman thought, and I stopped him. Bad mistake. Foster didn't do a damned thing, and Hardee attacked us where we weren't expecting. Those ironclads, they could have chopped our boys up on those islands.

The officer was on board the barge now, saluted Dahlgren, pulled the paper from his pocket, an identical one handed to Dahlgren. The man looked at Sherman, seemed desperately relieved to see him.

"We weren't certain where you would be, sir. Major Dayton prepared a letter for each of you, in the event we couldn't find you."

Sherman tore through the folded paper, frantic glances, forced himself to slow, to absorb each word. His knees began to weaken, and he moved to a wooden box, felt his way down with one hand, sat

THE FATEFUL LIGHTNING   483

slowly. Dayton's words struck him hard and deep, a heavy punch in his stomach.

> **General, I have sent you two dispatches via Fort McAllister in hopes of reaching you. General Slocum reports enemy gone from his front and he had got eight guns—this report at four A.M. General Howard reports General Leggett near the city and no enemy. General Slocum is moving and General Howard the same, and I have no doubt both are in Savannah now. I will ride with General Howard at his request, and leave our camp until the matter is more definite and you make orders. Maj. L. M. Dayton, Adjutant General**

There was a second piece of paper, official stationery, and Sherman saw the seal of the state of Georgia. It was addressed to him.

> **Sir,**
> **The City of Savannah was last night evacuated by the Confederate military and is now entirely defenseless. As chief magistrate of the city I respectfully request your protection of the lives and private property of the citizens and of our women and children. Trusting that this**

**appeal to your generosity and human-
ity may favorably influence your action,
I have the honor to be, Your Obedient
Servant,**

R. D. ARNOLD, MAYOR OF SAVANNAH

He stared straight through the paper, tried to feel
anger toward Dayton, toward all his staff, toward
Foster or Dahlgren, all the reasons why Sherman had not been there. He thought of Slocum,
so many men on those islands, and they did not
know what was happening? An army retreats across
a bridge and no one **hears** that? The question came
now, a voice inside of him from that place he hated,
the dark hole where the doubts lay, the fears. What
about you? What would you have done? Would
they have slipped out from under your own eyes?
Explain that to Grant. To anyone. You had to go
out and play in a damned boat.

He felt a bony grip on his shoulder, heard the
voice of Dahlgren. "Well, sir, my deepest apologies
to you. Had I made better steam, or taken a better
route . . . well, I cannot change what has happened.
But I am deeply sorry. It appears you have arrived
somewhat late to your own party."

Sherman kept his gaze down, the words on the
papers now a blur, Dahlgren's strong hand still on
him. He tried not to feel angry at Dahlgren, knew
the decisions had been his alone, the need to see
Foster, to make something happen that could not

happen at all. His words came now, a low, quivering voice. "I let him escape. We pushed him all the way to the sea, and then we allowed him to slip away."

Dahlgren removed his hand from Sherman's shoulder, sat down close beside him. "General, I know very little about such things, but if I may suggest, General Hardee is a problem for another day. By his absence, he has given you a gift. Or rather, you have done all that was necessary to earn one. Allow me to offer you the first of what will be many, I'm sure. Congratulations, General. You have captured the city of Savannah."

PART TWO

To His Excellency President Lincoln, Washington, D.C.:
I beg to present to you as a Christmas gift, the City of Savannah. . . .

—WILLIAM T. SHERMAN

The Confederacy seemed suddenly to have changed, a glory had passed from it, and without acknowledging it, we felt the end was near.

—MARGARET CRAWFORD ADAMS,
COLUMBIA, SOUTH CAROLINA

CHAPTER TWENTY-FIVE

FRANKLIN

WEST OF SAVANNAH—DECEMBER 22, 1864

He had spent most of his time now with the other freed slaves, a part of their community, and Franklin was surprised to learn that his voice was one of those that seemed to draw attention. Since the horror of Ebenezer Creek, many of the army's black followers had begun to see the army in an entirely different way, some of those former slaves choosing to pull away from the celebratory parade. Franklin understood their sentiment, that what had happened at the creek was seen by many as a betrayal, a promise broken. He heard their nervous talk, that so many of the slaves had accepted their liberation as a great gift offered by the men in blue, a gift that could be torn away from them anytime the army chose. Most of the freed slaves knew very little of any other life, and now many had spoken out about returning to the only world they knew. No matter how deep his anger, Franklin saw Ebenezer Creek as a decision made by one very bad man, that there were others in this army who genuinely cared for what these people were trying to do. It was a hard task convincing himself that his ignorance wasn't leading him into some kind of hell, that there could be many more blue-coated generals who didn't care whether the slaves were freed or not. But Franklin would not lose that faith, not yet, had no reason to think back to the Cobb Plantation as his home. Those horrors were permanent, something that ran deeper through him than what he had witnessed at the creek. He had tried to spread reassurances to the others, and some did listen, some agreeing with him that what happened at Ebenezer Creek was just a part of this war, that the Yankee soldiers had mostly been generous, even kind, and if there were bad men in blue, most of the former slaves knew enough of life in the fields to accept that bad men could be found anywhere. Ebenezer Creek had taught Franklin, as it had taught many, that being free meant looking out for yourself, that liberation meant there was no longer a master at all, whether on the plantations or with this army.

Even now, close to Savannah, Franklin faced a challenge convincing many of the fearful that the world they had left behind was gone completely, erased, and it infuriated him that so many would not listen. Some had lost a family member at Ebenezer, had become separated from everyone they knew, facing a terrifying world with more than just uncertainty. They were alone. If the blue army could not be counted on for protection, those few would seek protection in the familiar, whether or not they would be punished for returning to the only homes they knew. That sentiment carried great weight, hundreds of the slaves drifting away, groups large and small, accepting that they would likely be captured by rebel cavalry, men with whips, men who would happily take them back to their chains.

With the army now encamped in a wide arc around Savannah, the Negroes who remained were allowed to go pretty much where they pleased, and Franklin took advantage of that, but only to a point. He still held to the fear that a lone black man was vulnerable. Adding to his fear was his new companion, that someone might mistake Clara for those among the Negro parade who traded their flesh for some benefit. Clara had kept close to Franklin since the horror at Ebenezer Creek, and for the first time in his life, Franklin had begun to feel a soft bond with a girl, something the overseers might never have allowed him to do. At the plantations, the slaves were put together for purposes of breeding, and whether or not a strong healthy man cared for the woman he was to impregnate made little difference to those masters hoping to profit from their valuable offspring. Once the army had allowed the slaves to abandon their plantations, the men in blue seemed not to care what kinds of bonds the Negroes might have with one another. And so Franklin had allowed himself to see past the frightened girl he had pulled from the grasp of a nasty mistress in Millen, to realize that Clara was much more like him than he had realized. They were roughly the same age, though neither of them could be exactly certain of their years. Both knew the hand of the master, had felt the whip. To his surprise, Clara had listened to his stories of the dogs not with horror, but with teary empathy. It was the first time he had grasped the notion that he could share every kind of feeling with another person, whether pain or joy. And as they grew closer, she had begun giving him a great deal of joy.

The troops of the 113th Ohio had seemed to recognize that, and their abuse had poured out, the usual crudeness of soldiers, something Franklin had become accustomed to. But when it had been directed at Clara, it twisted something inside him that he saw as dangerous. She would never be one of **those** girls, and if a soldier was to suggest something so vile, or make an offer that Franklin found obscene, he might do something about it. But the warnings had buried themselves deep inside him, the enormous soldier,

Sergeant Knight, the man's strong advice that striking a white man, any white man, was still a foolish and possibly deadly mistake. Franklin's new bursts of anger had been a dismaying surprise all its own, and within days after Ebenezer Creek, he had pulled Clara away from the camp, farther from the eyes of the soldiers and their officers, and settled more with the black families who still trailed behind the army. If Captain Jones required him for anything, he would certainly answer. But with Savannah so close in front of them, the activity throughout the army was all about skirmishing, the men driven forward through deep swamps, increasing musket and artillery fire against an enemy Franklin never saw. There was little for him to do but help old Poke water the horses and assist the others in cooking the new rations of rice and sweet potatoes. Franklin realized quickly that those kinds of rations tasted far sweeter when he could share them with Clara, alone in some quiet place.

They shared a makeshift tent, and he met the dawn with a foggy-eyed stare at her, as she still slept. He was used to being up with the army, well before daylight, and it was no different now. But there was noise, a commotion that seemed to spread all through the camp, voices, men calling out. He stepped clear of the tent, wouldn't wake her, saw several of the older men moving past. He knew them all, had become close to a gray-haired man named Baxter. Franklin saw him waving toward him, moved that way, and Baxter seemed out of breath, said, "Oh, Lord, boy, you gots to get up and moving. The army's done moving out of their camps, marching into the roads."

"The roads are dangerous. Cannons."

"Not so now. Somethin's done changed. The soldiers is moving toward the city. Best be up wid 'em."

Another man came close now, Jeremy, more gray hair on a balding head. "Mr. Franklin, it could be bad, real bad. They's said to be rebel cav'ry movin' up behind us, or worse, a whole rebel army. The Yankees might be runnin' scared."

Baxter put a finger into Jeremy's face, his voice loud. "No, now dang you, don' go tellin' such things! Nobody's seen no rebels in a while."

Franklin had sparred with Jeremy often, the man prone to outrageous speculation. He looked at Baxter, said, "Let me go talk to Captain Jones. He'll know. He'll tell me."

"You go on, then. But he mighta done left this place."

The men began to squabble now, a familiar argument, Baxter seeming to understand truth more than Jeremy. He glanced back toward the tent, saw Clara looking at him with a hint of fear. He moved toward her, said, "Sorry to wake you. I have to go to the army camp. Something's happening." He couldn't avoid the ongoing argument between the two old men, others gathering, an audience that seemed entertained by the two men as much as they absorbed the concerns.

Clara grabbed his arm. "Don' leave me alone."

"Just a little bit. Let me talk to the officers. This foolishness is getting everybody all stirred up. Could be nothing. But I have to know."

She let her hand slip off him, and he touched her face, soft fingers, turned quickly, ran past the growing crowd, ignored the calls, the fears, the rumors now exploding into panic. He called out to them as he passed, "Stay here! Nobody's getting us! I'll find out what's happening!"

He moved into the road, could see men in blue everywhere, wagons pulling out of the clearings, men limbering their artillery pieces, some breaking down tents. He felt a rush of excitement, didn't see fear on any soldier's face, saw men joking, back-slapping laughter, and he moved past that, aimed for the cluster of tents he knew well. One had come down, horses gathering, the old man, Poke, tending them, keeping them together with a handful of reins. Franklin thought of asking him, knew better, Poke seemingly eager to stay out of everyone's way, embracing his own ignorance. Franklin was out of breath, stopped in front of the captain's tent, hesitated, saw Jones now, off to one side, a cluster of officers, what Franklin knew were the company commanders, Captain Gorman among them. Gorman saw him, waved him closer.

"Come here, boy! It's a good day!"

Franklin was there now, most of the captains ignoring him, but Jones said, "Mr. Franklin, we have been successful. The army is advancing into Savannah. The rebels have abandoned the city!"

Franklin heard the words, tried to decipher their meaning. "The rebels done left?"

The officers laughed, and Jones said, "That's exactly what they done. I imagine General Sherman's not altogether happy about that. They skedaddled north of the big river, probably headed deep into South Carolina. You ever been to Savannah?"

Franklin pondered that, wasn't exactly sure just what Savannah was. "No, sir."

"Well, gather up your people. Once we've set up the guard posts, made sure the city is free from any troublemakers, we'll all be making camp there. You, too, if you want."

The others began to move away, a final order from Jones, pushing them to get their men into columns. Franklin tried to feel their joy, was just as mystified by all of this as he had been many times before. The question came to him now, what he had wanted to ask Jones for some days, cutting through the loose talk and ridiculous rumors that festered in the Negro camps.

"Sir, can I speak to you?"

Jones pointed to the tent, said, "Come in. I've been putting my trunk together, what little there is. General Sherman made us leave most everything we owned back in Atlanta. I've got a whole world of goods sitting in some supply depot in God knows where. My adjutant's off at General Morgan's head-quarters, over by the creek, trying to find out just where they want us to go. This is quite a day, Mr. Franklin. Quite a feather in our caps."

Franklin wasn't sure what Jones meant, didn't see any feathers at all. He followed Jones into the tent, saw a pile of papers covering the captain's small camp desk. Jones stacked the papers, put them into a leather box, and Franklin felt like an intruder, still wasn't certain why the troops were so happy.

"Sir, is the war over? The rebels whipped?"

Jones laughed, looked at him. "Not yet. A big step for us, though. Word is, it's bad for the rebels everywhere right now. All I really know is what's in front of us."

"They be any soldiers going back?"

"What do you mean?"

It was the question that had burned inside him since the awful night at Ebenezer Creek. "To go back, try to find them that got left behind. It ain't right to just go off and leave those folks. Some was drowned. I saw it."

Jones stopped smiling. "Mr. Franklin, there will be no marching back there. Those people, the ones who didn't make it across, they're gone by now. I hope to God most of them made it to some safe place, maybe back to their homes, the towns we passed through. But you can't expect anyone to still be at the creek. Rebel cavalry went through there more than once. I'm sorry."

"I'm sorry, too, sir. There's bad feelings about that."

"More bad feelings than you know. General Davis is not a man who listens to counsel, and the only men in this army who can do anything about what he did are General Slocum and General Sherman. I don't expect you to ever respect General Davis, but he's my corps commander, and I follow his orders. Just like my division commander, General Morgan. It's just the way the army works."

"Pardon me, sir, but that night, at the creek, the army wasn't working a'tall."

Jones seemed frustrated, and Franklin began to feel as though he was going too far, expected Jones to order him away. But Jones sat at his desk, looked down for a long moment.

"You lose anybody there? Family and such?"

"No, sir. Not that I know." He thought of Clara now, her panic that took him back to the creek. "Might have gained something, strange to say."

"The girl?"

Franklin was surprised. "You know about Clara?"

"Didn't know her name. But when you left the camp, I had Sergeant Knight check on you. He said you had, um, found a friend."

"Yes, sir. Did that. I'm sayin' we're a little more than being friends."

"Well, that's your business. Some things have

a way of turning to the good. There is no excuse for what Jefferson Davis did at Ebenezer Creek. But maybe you got something from it. It's another way the army works. I've seen men killed, only to miss out on a great victory, as though there was some kind of trade handed down by the Almighty. Men were killed right out on this causeway, and today we're taking the city. It's a great triumph, and men died for us to get here. Not sure how else to explain it."

Franklin absorbed what Jones was saying, thought of Clara, the power of those feelings. "Don't seem fair I should be happy."

"It never seems fair. General Davis may or may not ever be punished for what he did back there. Nothing you nor I can do about it."

A new question rolled up through Franklin's thoughts. "Sir, if you don't mind me askin', I thought Jefferson Davis was the master head rebel and all. Up in Richmond. I heard Master Cobb mention him, the overseers, too. How'd he get to be a general in this here army? Didn't somebody ask what he was doing here?"

Jones laughed. "The whole army has wondered about that, Mr. Franklin. Fact is, they're two different people. You're right about that fellow in Richmond. I know for a fact that General Sherman wants his scalp. General Jefferson C. Davis just happened on that name by an accident of birth. You'd have to ask his mama where that came from. I bet he feels pretty miserable over that every day, knows very well that his own men make jokes about it."

Franklin moved toward the opening in the tent, men in blue moving past, more wagons in the distance. "Sorry, sir. He ain't been miserable enough."

Franklin and Clara had followed the soldiers into the city, the jubilation of the army finally spreading through the Negroes, a vast parade that could finally gather up in close proximity, a joyous crowd that now filtered all out through Savannah's streets. Joining them were servants and slaves from Savannah itself, many of them taking leave of their masters, whether the masters allowed them to or not. The infectious cries of liberation continued to spread, the streets and avenues, the docks and waterfront massed with black faces, mingling with soldiers attempting to bring order. Throughout the city, shops and merchant houses were coming apart, doors opened by force, both white and black looters helping themselves to food or anything else they could carry. The soldiers took part as well, many of them men who had served as scavengers now finding themselves in a race with the civilians to secure anything of value.

As the army gradually filled the town, the white residents had seemed to welcome them with at least a hint of happiness, cautious though they might be, staring at marching columns of men with muskets.

To the surprise of many of the soldiers, some of
the townspeople threw out their welcoming cheers
as though the army were a force of liberation. To
be sure, there were still a great many in the town
who regarded Sherman's army as an invasion force,
who feared the worst kinds of brutality. The rumors
flew, as they always did, sparked by the fires from
the rebel forts, or the flames swallowing the boats
on the Savannah River. What the rebels could not
carry, they had torched, including the wooden gunboats. The columns of black smoke were spread all
across the waterfront, but the rebels had been careful, had restricted the fires to those goods, ammunition, and other equipment inside their fortifications.
But still there was fear from the civilians that their
own homes would be next. As the army established
order, guards were posted along most streets, provosts patrolling every neighborhood. Even the most
hostile citizens, those who wisely kept their protests
indoors, began to see that this was not yet an army
bent on total destruction. Whatever enthusiasm the
soldiers put on display began to be infectious as well.
If it was a marvelous day to be a Federal soldier, it
was not quite so bad for the citizens of Savannah.

In a world seething with new experiences, Franklin was engulfed in yet another scene he had never
witnessed before. In every town the blue army had
marched into, crowds of gleeful black faces were
common, but in Savannah, many of those who so
welcomed the army were not slaves at all. Franklin

had focused mostly on the black men in the crowd, some of them dressed in finery that exceeded what their white neighbors wore. They were merchants and businessmen, some in their own homes, raising families out from under the boot heel of any white master. As he walked behind a company of troops, he caught the cheers, nothing unusual there, but the accents from some of these Negroes was very different, foreign tongues, foreign clothing.

He wandered about with little restriction, the army's guards moving to intervene in whatever angry protest might erupt, carefully searching for the straggling rebel soldier, always a danger in a newly occupied place. There were attempts to bring order to the looting, bayonet-wielding soldiers forcing crowds of both races away from the wreckage of warehouses, smashed storefronts, the crowds mostly accepting that whatever they had been able to grab thus far might be all they would get.

With Clara by his side, Franklin had begun to explore in a way he had never dared before. They moved through crowds of soldiers, past homes, staring at faces that stared back at them. The smoke from the fires drifted all across the town, adding the pungent odor of pitch and pine to the smells from spilled molasses, broken kegs of liquor. He knew to keep far from that, that spirits might turn a man into something evil, the young girl by Franklin's side a target that Franklin knew he would die to protect. They moved instead along the waterfront, staring out at the broken pieces of a pontoon bridge, most of that lying against the near shore. Already Federal soldiers were at work, boats moving back and forth to an island offshore, what Franklin guessed to be engineers. The bridge was being rebuilt, serving some purpose that Franklin did not yet understand.

Clara was holding his arm and he pointed across the river to the burning hulk of a boat.

"Has to be a rebel gunboat. They had to burn it, keep it outta our hands."

He knew she'd be impressed by his knowledge, had laid special emphasis on "our hands."

She pointed out, past the gunboat, said, "What's that, over there?"

He looked at the far shoreline, more blue-coated soldiers on the river, swarming close to the water, their labor increasing. "The captain said we were going to South Carolina. Maybe that's what that is."

"Why?"

"Don't really know. If the rebels went that way, the army will be wantin' to catch 'em, likely. Captain Jones says the war ain't over."

They stood together, watching the men in blue laboring, the ropes hauling the strange thin boats together, wagons coming up through the town, more pontoons, a stab of familiarity Franklin tried to ignore. He had a dark thought, The pontoons. Same ones they pulled up from the creek? He wouldn't say that to her, kept his eye on a squad of men unloading them, more men sliding them into the waiting hands of men in the water. She prodded him, said, "They seem to want to get over there quick as they can."

Franklin looked around, soldiers in every direction, not all at labor. "I don't know all about what the army does. But they sure building that bridge. Some of these soldiers making camp here, that's what the captain said. I guess we will, too."

There were voices now, a large building along the waterfront, soldiers gathering, excited calls. He pulled her that way, curious, and she seemed to accept his need to know everything that was still so foreign to both of them. He held her arm in a soft grip, moved behind one group of soldiers, saw them staring up, hands and hats in the air. He could see now, a man on the roof, more men, blue uniforms, one man with hands on his hips, staring out toward the far side of the river. In front of Franklin, a soldier called out, "Hooray for Uncle Billy!"

More joined in, and Franklin looked up at the man, a ragged red beard, a stub of a cigar in the man's mouth. There were more cheers, and Franklin was cautious, didn't want to disturb the revelry. But Clara reached out, touched the soldier's arm, the man turning with a smile. "Sir, please, who's that up there?"

"Well, Missy, only the most important man in this here country. That's General Sherman!"

CHAPTER TWENTY-SIX

SHERMAN

CUSTOM HOUSE,
SAVANNAH—DECEMBER 22, 1864

"They wrecked the pontoon bridge, I see."

Dayton was beside him, said, "Yes, sir. From all accounts, the last man reached the far shore by midnight or so. It was our skirmishers who figured that out. You know what it's like for them, sir. They make friends on the other side, all that trading nonsense. I suspect that at some point, some of their friends didn't answer the call. A few officers pushed their men up close to the rebel works and found them empty. That started the flood, so to speak."

Sherman kept his stare far across the river. "They'll gather up everyone they can over there. Whatever troops can be scraped up. They don't expect us to stay here, not for long. If I didn't have to wait for Grant, I'd have us over there right now. South Carolina started this war, and Hardee has to know there will be punishment for that. He has no choice but to haul in every last man he can, put up as much of a defense as we allow him to. Damn it all! I hate delay!"

Sherman paced the roof now, ignored the cheers of the soldiers in the street below. Dayton kept silent, McCoy as well, Sherman's thoughts drifting far to the north. He wondered what Grant was doing, if he had read Sherman's response, if there were Washington bigwigs surrounding him with all of that "advice." He retrieved a cigar, said to no one in particular, "What time is it?"

McCoy responded. "Just before ten, sir."

"Cold day. No rain. Rebels will make good time moving north. We'll need fresh maps. Put Captain Poe to work on that." He didn't wait for a response, watched the men working in the river, the pontoon boats being strung together, as Poe's men had done along every stretch of water since Atlanta. He pulled at the cigar, tried to feel some comfort from the heat, turned now, looked back over the city, mammoth oak trees, wide streets cut by squares. There were statues, war heroes from long ago, some of the town's squares adorned with fountains. Beautiful place at one time, he thought. He tried to remember just when he had been stationed there, recalled his rank, captain, the homes he had visited, flirtatious women, all the gentility of Southern aristocracy. He said aloud, "It all seemed so quaint then. Charming, even. Everybody bowing, all the women in their damned hoops. Wonder what happened."

Dayton glanced at McCoy, said, "The war happened, sir."

Sherman kept his eyes on the tumult in the streets, blue columns in motion, more of his army making their way to new camps, some of those in the forts once held by the rebels. "They didn't really suffer the war here. No damage I can see. This city was always the center of so much. I suppose the damned rebels used it just like the army did back in the early days, shipping, warehouses. Hell of a good place to start a business. Any fool could get rich."

He heard commotion, the doorway to the rooftop opening, low voices, Hitchcock now.

"Sir, we have some figures. You need to hear this, sir."

Sherman looked at him, saw Hitchcock with one hand on his glasses, staring at a piece of paper. "Hear what?"

"Sir, the provosts and commissary officers from General Geary's command are estimating that there are twenty-five thousand bales of cotton here."

Sherman pulled the cigar from his mouth, cocked his head toward Hitchcock. "You certain of that?"

"Well, sir, General Geary seems certain of it. His men were the first into the city in any force, and they took stock pretty quick of what was in the warehouses, and anyplace else there might have been rebels hidden away. All they found was cotton. Bags of rice, of course, other provisions. Pardon me for asking, sir, but how much is that worth?"

Sherman tried to picture the sight of that much cotton brought into one pile. "More than you or I can tally, Major. Where is General Geary now?"

An aide spoke up, a low voice to Hitchcock, and Hitchcock said, "He's coming this way, sir. He wishes to offer you a formal greeting."

"Why?"

"He was here first. I suppose—"

"I suppose he wants credit for capturing the place himself. I shall disabuse him of that notion. This army deserves the credit, not any single division."

"Sir, look there." Sherman followed Dayton's gaze, saw the men in the river setting markers, red and white flags. "Wonder what that's for? The bridge is pointing off that way."

"Hell if I know, Major. I don't ask too many questions of engineers."

At the riverfront, Sherman saw Poe now, the man directing the activity, and Poe noticed him, a hearty wave. Sherman called out, "Captain, here if you please."

Poe responded with quick steps, a beaming smile, stopped at the steps of the Custom House. "Sir!

We'll have the bridge toward Hutchinson Island put back in place by nightfall."

"Fine. What are those men doing with those flags?"

Poe looked over, his expression changing. "They're marking torpedoes, sir."

Sherman stared that way, saw the flags in a haphazard pattern, spread all across the river. "They're marking a hell of a lot of them."

"Regrettably, yes, sir. The enemy had secured any deepwater approach into the city from the sea. We'll be removing them with all haste. I shall keep you informed."

Sherman thought of the maps he would need, the roads that snaked all through the rice marshes and swamps across the river, felt his usual impatience, a hard burn in his brain to put this army back out on the march. "Clear those damned things away, Captain."

Poe saluted him, moved back along the riverfront, resuming his work. Sherman kept his stare on the small flags, said to Dayton, "It's fortunate Admiral Dahlgren didn't just shove his flagship up that channel. We'd be picking sailors out of those rocks down there. Nasty business. I'm getting very tired of the enemy's willingness to ignore the rules of war."

"Yes, sir. Too bad they didn't leave anybody behind. Prisoners, I mean. We could put them to work."

Sherman planted the cigar between his teeth again. "They did. There have to be some around here somewheres. Find out. And see if they can swim."

He stepped up into the lobby of the hotel, the Pulaski House, the guards already spread out inside, the staff examining the rooms on the ground floor. Dayton came toward him now, said, "This should be a suitable place, sir. Turns out Jefferson Davis spent some time here. They seem eager that you should sleep in the same bed. Um, sir, the fellow in charge says he knows you."

"Where? I don't recall anybody here in the hotel business."

"That old chap, crippled leg. Says he knew you in New Orleans."

Sherman moved that way, looked at the old man, who seemed to wait for recognition. Sherman knew the face now, the telltale bum leg, smiled. "You old coot. How'd you get over here?"

"Could say they tossed me out of New Orleans, General. I wouldn't be lyin' much."

Sherman took the man's hands, felt the fragility of age. He glanced at Dayton now, said, "Major, this fellow's older than Methuselah. Used to run a place in New Orleans."

The old man was all smiles now, said, "Yessiree. The St. Louis Hotel. I thought New Orleans was a strange enough place for an old Vermont wood-cutter to find. Savannah's a little nicer. Used to be anyway. Rebel generals made themselves at home a bit more than I cared for. Hard to keep my dang mouth shut more than I liked. No need lettin' on just where my mama birthed me."

Dayton said, "Vermont?"

"Yep. Cold as a maiden's hind end in the winter. Old bones need warm weather."

Sherman scanned the lobby, thought of the name, Pulaski, a hero from another war. "Great deal of history hereabouts."

The old man eyed Sherman, nodded. "I'd say there's a bit more right now. They done made you a general. Knew you'd turn out to be more'n some supply sergeant. Camp cook, mebbe. You ever fig-ure out how to make coffee?"

Sherman knew he was trapped, that the stories would continue as long as the old man had the strength for it. He saw Hitchcock enter, making way straight for Sherman, and for the moment, Sherman didn't care why. It was his escape.

"Excuse me, but the army requires my attention. We'll talk later."

There was a hint of disappointment on the old man's face, but he seemed to understand. Hitch-cock was close to him now, eyeing the old man with curiosity, and Hitchcock said, "Excuse me, sir. General Geary is with General Slocum. They heard you were making use of this place."

Sherman rolled the cigar in his fingers, looked again at the old man. "You have someplace my generals can sit, have a private chat?"

The old man pointed to one side, and Sherman saw the space, the guards already standing at the doorway. He said to Hitchcock, "I'll be right over there."

He respected John Geary, had been surprised by what seemed to be Geary's show of bluster at capturing the city. But Sherman could see now that wasn't the case at all.

Slocum sat across from Sherman, Geary to one side, Slocum as businesslike as Sherman had seen him.

"Sir, it was my decision that General Geary bring his headquarters to the city first. The general has considerable skills with civilian affairs."

Sherman looked at Geary, saw a sober, straight-backed man, full of confidence, waiting for Sherman's judgment. "What kind of skills?"

Geary said, "I was mayor of San Francisco in the gold rush days, sir. Followed that by a term as governor of Kansas. I am very familiar with the operation of the civil authority. Not to suggest that there should **be** a civil authority here."

Sherman knew something of this, recalled Geary's reputation for efficiency beyond his years with the army. "There will be a **military** authority here, that will carry authority over any civil office. General Slocum, I see no reason why your recommendations should not be followed. General Geary, you are to serve as military mayor of Savannah until otherwise ordered. Not sure where those orders might come from, but I'm certain someone in Washington will insist on making an appointment of their own. I want order in this place, General. Wrecking Savannah will only embolden the enemy."

Slocum said, "Not sure I understand that, sir. Your orders were clear that we cause considerable discomfort to the enemy, including our civilian enemy."

"Orders change. Think about it, Henry. We make Savannah our new base of supply and operations, and all the while, we treat the city and its citizens with generosity, show them that we didn't come here to devour the place. They still think I'm Attila the Hun, for God's sake. But we keep order here, including those men who pride themselves on scavenging, and it won't take long for word of that to spread to the enemy's troops. Think of what that will do to the rebels' morale. There won't be any cause for revenge for what we're doing here. Nothing we do will inspire anyone to bloodlust. General Geary, you might consider this hotel your headquarters." Sherman fingered the letters in his pocket. "I am told by Major Dayton that it was you who secured the letter from the mayor, that Arnold fellow. Thank you for passing that along."

"Yes, sir. I knew you'd wish to see that. I had him purposely address it to you. He's most cooperative. As the military mayor, I believe I can work well with him to keep things quiet here. Pleasant enough chap, if a bit hangdog. When he offered to surrender the city, I thought he was going to bawl."

"There's bawling aplenty going on around here, General."

Slocum laughed now, and Sherman saw the cause, the view through the tall window, the far side of a broad square, a cluster of soldiers around a pair of black children. The children were doing what Sherman had seen so often before, a whirling dance, frantic excitement, the soldiers clapping, one man with a harmonica, trying to make any kind of music that would keep the children in motion.

Slocum said, "No bawling there, sir."

Hitchcock was at the door now, said, "Sir, there is a gentleman here, most insistent on seeing you. Claims to be British, has a generous offer for you. That's what he says, anyway."

"What kind of offer?"

"A headquarters, sir. Says he has the nicest house in the city, and he's offering it for our use."

Sherman expected something like this, well-dressed civilians coming in droves, asking all manner of favors. But he didn't expect much generosity. "What do you sense, Major? We should get a look at the place?"

"Cannot hurt, sir. He's not what I expected here, none of that syrupy Southern gentleman nonsense."

From behind Hitchcock, a voice, heavy British accent. "I say, you'd be General Sherman, then?"

The man's head protruded above Hitchcock's shoulder, the man wearing a monocle, a silk cravat around his neck. He raised a silver-tipped cane, as though attracting Sherman's attention, and Sherman saw a smile, thought, All right. Fine. Now's as good a time as any. He looked at Slocum.

"General Slocum, you may resume organizing the city as far as the encampments of your men. I expect Howard's doing the same. General Geary, you will assume your new authority immediately. Establish an office as quickly as possible, and let that mayor fellow know what we're doing. He gets out of line, remind him who has the bayonets."

The two generals stood, Hitchcock making way for them, both men eyeing the Englishman as they passed him. The man stepped fully in the doorway, made a crisp bow, removed the monocle, said, "Now, then, sir, if I may suggest, I have a potential headquarters for you that befits your station, far more than this drab old hotel."

Sherman was intrigued, heard no hostility in the man, his demeanor pleasant, as generous as his words seemed to be. "What do you do around here, sir?"

"Charles Green, at your service, sir. I dabble somewhat in the banking trade, though, I must admit, there hasn't been a great deal of commerce in this place, not for a while. Your damnable blockade . . ." He paused. "Forgive me, sir. One must adapt to one's circumstance. I'm a bit slow on that point."

"Blockade slow things down around here?"

"Oh, quite, sir. The trade with Mother England has been squeezed rather severely, I'm afraid. Perfectly understandable, of course."

Sherman couldn't help a smile. "And perfectly dreadful, as well."

Green tapped the cane gently to his head, a salute. "Admittedly, yes. However, I am no enemy of yours, and bear no great loyalty to anyone other than my queen. If you will accept my invitation, sir, I assure you of satisfaction. Plenty of room for your staff, and whatever business you have. My home is open to you, sir."

The man's cheerfulness was infectious, and Sherman saw a smile on Hitchcock's face, Dayton there as well. "All right, gentlemen. Let's go have a look."

GREEN HOUSE,
SAVANNAH—DECEMBER 22, 1864

The mansion had far more grandeur than Sherman had expected, and the wide eyes from his staff added to his own observation. He had never been comfortable with abundant pomp, but the mansion was spectacularly decorated, including tropical plants set around in enormous clay pots. Sherman studied the man's collection of artwork, various paintings and portraits, suspected there was considerable value, but he wouldn't ask that, wouldn't give the man any reason to fear him. But the furniture made the man's case, Sherman sitting down on a chair that seemed to swallow him in comfort. He saw the self-satisfaction on Green's face, thought, He's a businessman, no doubt about that. He has something to offer, and he creates his own demand.

"Tell me, Mr. Green, what exactly do you expect in return?"

"Sir? Sorry, I'm not following."

"You're a horse trader. What do you get in return for all this graciousness?"

Green nodded toward him now, another salute with the cane. "Very good, sir. I happen to be in possession of a substantial amount of the cotton stored hereabouts. I have the papers to prove that, I assure you. I was hoping perhaps your army could be convinced to permit me to make delivery to my customers. There are contracts in place, after all."

"Customers in England."

"Well, yes, certainly. No one here is a **buyer,** sir."

"I accept the offer of your home as my headquarters. We shall be as courteous as possible, and avoid any damage to your furnishings. As for the cotton, well, we can talk about that at another time."

He stood in his new room, a grandly appointed bedroom, looked out the window, the waterfront, the lingering columns of smoke from the rebel gunboats. He was drinking tea, an odd luxury, not something that usually tempted him, but it was his host who had insisted, describing his offering as something far more rare than coffee, something imported from India. Whether it suited Sherman's taste didn't seem to matter as much as the pampering Sherman had finally allowed himself to enjoy.

He studied the waterfront, his hand resting on the rich silk on the back of another outrageously comfortable chair. A nap would be most useful right now, he thought. He eyed the rugs beneath his boots, thick and lush, thought, I could sleep right here. I get into that bed, I might not get out again.

There was a soft knock on the door, and he knew from the timidity, it was Hitchcock.

"What is it, Major?"

The door opened slightly, Hitchcock peering in. "Very sorry, sir. There is a gentleman here you must see."

Sherman was annoyed, but Hitchcock knew better than to bother him with some local complaint. "Who is he?"

Sherman heard the deep bass voice coming from

behind Hitchcock with the volume of the self-important.

"He's in there? Very good, yes. Thank you, Major. I'll handle this now."

Sherman moved toward the door, saw resignation on Hitchcock's face, unusual, and he pulled the door back, saw the man's impressive suit, a gold watch chain, a shine on expensive shoes. "What the hell do you want?"

Sherman's annoyance seemed to catch the man by surprise, and he backed up a step, cleared his throat.

"My apologies for disturbing your idyll, sir."

"My what?"

"Apparently I have come at an unfortunate time. But I cannot wait, sir. There is serious business here."

"Who the hell are you?"

Hitchcock seemed eager to step between them, as though protecting the man from what Hitchcock knew of Sherman's wrath. "Sir, this gentleman came in from Ossabaw Bay, courtesy of Admiral Dahlgren."

The man pushed past the major, extended a fat hand toward Sherman, and said, "General! Ah, such a pleasure to make your acquaintance. Long journey, as it were. But your aide is correct. Well, not exactly. Being carried by Admiral Dahlgren would be a singular honor in itself. I was transported on a packet upstream, the Ogeechee, I believe. Odd names in these parts. Indian, so they say. Sir, I am

Agent A. G. Browne, here on behalf of the Department of the Treasury, Southern District. My department has determined that you have captured a considerable amount of valuable goods here. The government has determined to act on this with all haste. We're talking about cannons, rice, buildings, and most important, a considerable amount of cotton. I have come to take possession."

Hitchcock had verified the man's credentials, and Sherman sat across from him at Green's dining room table.

"You can't have it."

Browne made a grunting sound, said, "My authorization is quite in order, General."

"I see your authorization. You can't have it. Until we know just what the army's needs are."

"What kind of needs?"

"That's my concern, Mr. Browne. We have just occupied this place, and must establish a base here. I have some sixty thousand men to provision and feed, and we must see to the defense of this place, should the enemy determine to attack us. We have caused them a great deal of damage militarily and politically. They will not just walk away quietly."

Browne seemed to shrink slightly, his bluster replaced now by uncertainty. "Do you believe the enemy is planning an attack?"

"I have to assume so. That's why my men must be

provided for, before the government takes what it wants. No one in Washington needs artillery right now. We do. No one up there is subsisting on rice. We are."

Browne stroked his chin, pondering Sherman's words. "I see. Well, that does sound somewhat logical. How long will it take for you to make those determinations?"

"Till those determinations are made. There's a very nice hotel here, the Pulaski. I'd get yourself a room. As long as the enemy doesn't start shelling the place, you'll be comfortable."

Sherman knew he had pushed that as far as he could, saw a slight grin on Dayton's face. He scowled at Dayton, said, "Have a security escort accompany Mr. Browne to the hotel. Can't be too careful. Snipers and all."

Browne seemed suddenly anxious to leave, stood quickly, then stopped, a new thought entering his head. "Sir, I understand your concern. I do not wish to antagonize you. You are correct that your conquest of this place should be your first priority. To that end, sir, might I offer you a suggestion?"

"I'm listening."

"All of Washington is in something of an uproar with concern for your well-being. The news out of Nashville was most beneficial to the mood of the capital. News of your success would do as much or more to boost spirits. Might I suggest that you pen a note to President Lincoln?" Browne looked to the side, a small Christmas tree at one end of the room, perched upon a small table. "That's it, sir. Perhaps you could offer a celebratory note to him, something that would resonate well in the newspapers."

"I don't care much for 'resonating,' sir."

"Oh, but this is perfect. Perhaps you could offer the president a gift. Say, the city of Savannah?"

He sat staring, his eyes not seeing beyond the pane of glass. The cigar was set to one side, the newspaper draped over his lap, and Sherman ignored both now, tried to see the image of the small face, the baby he had never seen. He had often imagined what the infant Charles might look like, if he had his father's red hair, his mother's softer gaze, the sad eyes. Behind him, Hitchcock's voice came, very low.

"I am terribly sorry, sir. There was nothing in the mail. Certainly she will write you."

Sherman nodded slowly, no words. He looked down at the newspaper again, said, "Where'd this come from?"

"Came in on a packet with the mail today, sir. We were shocked, certainly. I searched for a letter from your wife, but the postal authorities say that much of the mail for the command was sent in error to Nashville."

Sherman ignored Hitchcock's explanation, looked

again at the paper. "He was barely six months old. I never saw him. Won't ever know what he looked like. He might have smiled at me. Imagine that?"

Hitchcock backed away, and Sherman was suddenly afraid of that, a glimmer of panic at being alone. He turned in the chair.

"Major, if you please. Your company is welcome."

"Of course, sir. Anything I can get you?"

Sherman stared at the paper for a long while, pointed to the side, one of the soft chairs. "Sit down, Major." He couldn't fight the emotions any longer, blinked through tears, and after a long moment, said, "I do not handle tragedy well. My own, or anyone else's. It happens all around us, every day we face the enemy, every day someone falls ill. Most often that kind of pain is inflicted on someone else. But I am not immune. This is a horror no one can prepare for. There is no greater loss, you know. None. This is twice for me. I have lost two sons." He paused. "When Willie died, I thought my world had ceased to matter, that nothing I could do would allow me to move past that. My career, even my marriage. But then the war came back, all of that duty, the damned rebels. They nearly captured me, someplace in western Tennessee. That was a help to me, in some way I cannot explain. I don't expect this to make sense to you, Major."

"It's all right, sir. I do not know how to respond to any of this. There are no useful words I can offer."

"No, suppose not. But still we must try. I will write Ellen tonight. My brother John . . . I should write him as well. He will offer comfort the way a brother can. That is a valuable thing. A necessary thing."

"I'll get pen and paper, sir."

"Later. Just sit."

"Yes, sir. Sorry."

"Ellen will accept Charles's death as the Hand of God, the same way she got past Willie's death. She has no other understanding. Her mother did that, gave her that marvelous gift." He glanced toward Hitchcock. "I know you believe me to be thoroughly anti-Catholic. Perhaps I am. But I recognize the value of comfort, explanation, understanding. She will seek that, and no doubt she will find it. For me, it will be as before. I will gain more by doing my job. Rather pathetic, is it not?"

"No, sir. You are a hero. You are revered among the men. The entire country will salute what you've done here. Because you did your job."

Sherman pictured Grant in his mind, tried to move past the image of Ellen and her tears, the misery of what his home would be, black draperies, black wreath on the door, black everything. The thought suddenly struck him hard. "It's Christmas, for God's sake. I should be there. If not for Grant's confidence in me, in what he expects of me, I would go. The right thing to do. But you are right, Major. There is the job. And we are not yet finished."

GREEN HOUSE—CHRISTMAS EVE, 1864

The letter had come by packet, the way most of the mail was reaching the army. He knew from the Treasury agent, Browne, that the faster boats could reach Fortress Monroe in only a few days, and from there the telegraph wire could reach anywhere in the North the messages needed to go. More important to Sherman, those messages could reach him the same way.

He read it again, let the words boil up inside him, felt energized, the full fury at the enemy building. The staff had gathered, and he knew they had read the dispatch already. But they seemed to wait for his response, watching him as though expecting a volcanic eruption. He twirled the cigar in his fingers, held tight to the smile, felt suddenly playful, toying with them, keeping them in suspense as to what might happen next. After a long moment, he burst from the chair, faced them, held the paper out toward them.

"Do you know what this signifies?" No one responded, the staff knowing when not to interrupt him. "This, gentlemen, is a Christmas present. My commanding general is, after all, generous. He is also wise."

He saw their smiles, and Dayton said, "Sir, there is much to do. Should we not issue orders . . ."

"Oh, good Lord, Major! There will be orders aplenty! It is Christmas, after all. Is it not enough that our commanding general has demonstrated faith in this command? Might I revel in that for a small moment?"

Dayton seemed overwhelmed with Sherman's boisterous response. "Certainly, sir. At your discretion."

"Yes! You put it precisely, Major. At my discretion! Grant has made it official! This campaign shall continue, at **my** discretion!" He looked at the letter now, pulled out the words he was searching for. " 'You shall make **another wide swath through the Confederacy**.' And that, gentlemen, comes from the pen of Henry Halleck. It seems that General Grant is capable of admitting his mistakes, and convincing others along the way! Now, with his permission, we shall join his army in Virginia the way I prefer, overland, driving this army through the very heart of the rebellion. We shall unite this army with Grant only when we have completed the task still to be accomplished here. This war began in South Carolina, gentlemen. I expect that this entire army will welcome the opportunity to pour salt in **those** wounds."

CHAPTER TWENTY-SEVEN

HARDEE

CHARLESTON, SOUTH CAROLINA—DECEMBER 29, 1864

"How will you protect us? Do you not see why this place is as important to the Confederacy as any yet confronted?"

Hardee tried to focus on Magrath's words, but the weariness was overwhelming him. "Governor, I understand your concerns."

"I do not believe you do, sir. I am aware of what took place in Savannah. You abandoned those people without so much as a sword raised in anger! That will not do here, sir. It will not do at all."

"Have you made that complaint to President Davis?"

Magrath sniffed. "Sir, it has long been understood that President Davis attends to matters close to his own priorities, which do not include any army that he himself is not managing. I have beseeched the president to consider what the rest of us know very well. Charleston is the true center of the Confederacy. It was here that our rebellion against outrageous tyranny began, and it is here that we must stand tall! If this war is to favor us with its outcome, it is here we must drive home the sword. Sir, I was witness to the first cannon fire that drove the trespassers out of Fort Sumter. If there is justice to our cause, sir, I intend to witness cannon fire anew. General Beauregard has referred me to your office, to plead my case before you. As their governor, the people look to me, and I have no choice but to look to you. Are you willing to do the right thing, sir?"

Hardee was even more exhausted now by Magrath's bluster. "Governor, there are realities of which you are not aware. I may not always agree with President Davis's methods, or his strategies. But he is my commander in chief. And, sir, it is not necessary for you to lecture me on the wisdom of the orders I must follow. General Beauregard and I agreed that preserving what forces we could withdraw from Savannah was the correct decision. Sacrificing those men to Federal prison camps benefits no one. I do not fault you for your loyalty to your home state, but South Carolina is one of many states still fighting for independence."

"But, General, despite all your army's best efforts, the war has now come here. There is no great campaign being waged on any other front. General Lee's army is under siege at Petersburg, and General Hood is nursing his wounds in Alabama. Is that not accurate, sir? I do cast my eyes beyond the borders of this state."

Hardee leaned his chin into one hand, closed his eyes for a brief moment. There is no argument here, he thought. He just has to make it feel that way, as though no one else could understand this war like a politician can. He looked at Magrath now, the man's arms crossed, no change in his defiant tone. "Governor, I do not disagree with your assessment of our military situation. There is little doubt that South Carolina will become the next great battleground. I would suggest that you put your energies and your influence to finding me some troops with which to defend your state."

"And what would you do with those troops, sir? Retreat, as you did all across Georgia? I have spoken with Governor Brown. He is incensed, sir. Incensed! He had been forced to recall his small force of militia to act as a last line of defense against any further invasions by that devil Sherman."

Hardee sat upright now. "He has done what?"

Magrath seemed pleased with himself, that he

had knowledge of something Hardee had not yet heard. "Well, sir, Governor Brown has ordered his militia to return to their side of the border. Someone has to protect what those people value most, if your army will not do so."

"I find it odd, Governor, that you seem pleased with Governor Brown's actions. With such an act, he has only weakened the forces in my command. We are losing men to desertion as it is, without the governor of Georgia making it official that those particular men should return to their homes. There is still a war, whether or not Governor Brown approves." He was furious now, knew too much of Brown's reluctance to involve Georgia in any part of this war beyond its own borders. "Possibly, Governor, you are not aware of our situation as precisely as you may believe. If the Georgia militia has marched away, that leaves us with little more than twenty thousand troops to defend territory from Charleston inland to Columbia, and possibly farther than that, should the enemy choose to make their march in a more westerly course. I am charged not only with protecting Charleston and Columbia, but every rail depot, every line of communication, every significant intersection. Until General Beauregard or I know just where Sherman intends to go, we cannot form a united front. That was true in Georgia as well. Hindsight tells us we need not have protected Augusta or Macon. Hindsight, Governor. Unless you can offer me perfect insight into Sherman's thinking, I must make do with the forces I have on hand."

Magrath seemed to calm somewhat, weighing Hardee's words. "There are troops on the march from Augusta, I believe."

"I have included those men in my calculations, sir. As I have included the brigade said to be moving southward from Virginia, courtesy of General Lee. Those are North Carolina men, and though I welcome their muskets, and their enthusiasm for what we are facing here, I am quite certain General Lee sent those men with considerable regret. There are no pleasant ways to explain this, Governor. Mathematics has been a crucial part of every fight in which I have been engaged, and that has not changed. We have won many fights where the numbers were against us. But the scale continues to tilt toward the enemy. No amount of wishful thinking can change that."

"Yes, I suppose I understand that. Can you not state your case with such clarity to Richmond?"

Hardee looked down at the floor, let out a breath. "Sir, Richmond understands mathematics as clearly as I do. President Davis can only provide us what is there to provide. I regret the loss of the Georgia militia. Even those few men could have added something to our unfortunate equation. It is not my place to protest the governor's decision, but I do not believe the state of Georgia faces any further threat from General Sherman. It serves no purpose for the Federal troops to linger in Savannah, and the only logical direction for Sherman to advance now is north. He outnumbers what I have on hand by at least three to one. Governor Brown may have pleased his voters, but he has done nothing to assist you."

Magrath walked slowly across the room, seemed to reclaim his air of self-satisfaction. "It is possible that we greatly overestimate Sherman's willingness to tread on this soil, as I believe you overestimate his strength. There is a determination to the people of South Carolina that he has not yet encountered. I predict a bloodbath of epic proportions, sir."

"Have you ever seen a bloodbath, Governor?"

The question seemed to throw Magrath off track. "Well, certainly not. That makes little difference."

"A massacre then? A one-sided assault that crushed a defensive line? A volley of muskets that obliterated a foe?"

"You mock me, sir."

Hardee had endured all he could of the governor's speechmaking. "When you instruct me on the business of waging war, no, sir, I do not mock you. But I will not accept advice or counsel or instruction from anyone who has not led troops in the field, whose experience with artillery is limited to the 'glory' of pulling a lanyard. If you do not know of the horrors of war, sir, then perhaps you understand this. My family is in Charleston. My wife, my children. I withdrew from Savannah because there was no alternative beyond sacrificing my entire command to the earth, or Federal prison camps. General Beauregard understood how foolhardy it would be to stand up to a force as powerful as what Sherman brought against us. You wish me to hold the enemy back, then provide me with the means to do so. If you cannot do that, allow me to fight this war according to the orders I am given, and the resources I have available."

Magrath seemed to know he was outgunned. "I will leave you now, sir. I understand fully that you have enormous responsibilities. I shall once again beseech President Davis for reinforcements to assist your efforts. I pledge to you, sir, that I shall endeavor to raise at least five thousand more good South Carolina men, fit for your command. If there are more to be found, I shall find them."

Hardee felt like Magrath had more to say, but the governor made his exit without another word, his bluster disappearing with him. Hardee was relieved, sagged in the chair, his thoughts rolling toward anger. Brown was willing to surrender his state to the Yankees, he thought. Now, instead of assisting us, he calls his own troops home. Somewhere that would fit someone's definition of treason. Richmond, certainly.

"Are you alone, my darling?"

Her words rolled through him like music, and he

turned toward the far doorway, Mary peering in, cautious, never to intrude.

"Yes, he's gone. Please, come in. Sit with me."

Mary moved with a soft grace that made him ache to touch her. She leaned in close to him, the aroma of her perfume washing the staleness of his mood away. He looked up, expecting a kiss, but she slid away, teasing him, sat in the chair, the perch where Magrath had first warmed the cushion. She adjusted her dress now, offered just a hint of one leg, another tease, said, "He seems to be a dreadful fellow. His voice carried all over the house."

"Andrew Gordon Magrath has been governor of this state for exactly a week, but you would assume that somewhere long ago, someone had appointed him lord high potentate, with the wisdom to match. And all I did was insult the man, show him so much disrespect that it could cost me my career. If he was friends with the president instead of a rival, I'd be dismissed from the army before the sun set." He paused, his voice trailing away. "The war has been merciful to South Carolina. But that will now change. There is no safe place, not anymore. And Magrath knows I'm right. That has to gall him even more. No amount of politicking can change what is about to happen. All those 'powerful' men are finding out they have no real power at all. It is something I have seen before, my darling, both in and out of the army. Men with power either trumpet to everyone just how powerful they are, or they use that power effectively by keeping quiet about it, and going about their duties. I regret he is the former. This state will not benefit from imaginary bravado. It has never worked. Not anywhere."

"Why must they condemn you so? Forgive me, my husband, but I could not avoid his awful assaults on you. I don't care if he's the governor. He has no right to scold you. I did not mean to listen, but he was just so . . . loud."

"There is nothing that happens in this house that you should not be audience to. The girls, either. My son, well, perhaps that would be different. He hears the kind of dressing-down I just received, and he'd stand up to anyone, governor or not, to defend my honor. He's too young to understand that an enemy's sword is likely as dangerous as his own."

"He will fight, you know."

There was more to her words than a simple boast.

"What do you mean?"

"He thinks I won't tell you. A stepmother has no real authority, of course, so I cannot convince him of anything. But he still intends to join them, Terry's Rangers, is it?"

Hardee closed his eyes, one more wave of despair.

Willie had insisted on joining the army while still engaged in his schooling, something Hardee had strenuously objected to. The boy was only sixteen, Hardee with no desire to see his only son becoming a soldier. But in the chaos of the fighting that rolled around Atlanta, Hardee's attentions were too focused on the war to deal with the administrative concerns of his son's schooling, and Willie had quit the school in Athens with the exaggerated fantasy of joining the 11th Texas Cavalry, known as Terry's Texas Rangers. The romance of that was obvious, but Hardee of course knew the realities of the war that his son had never experienced, and Hardee had taken steps to ensure that his son would not carry a musket for the Texas Rangers, romance or not. But the school would not accept his return, and so Hardee had been forced to keep Willie close by, the only way to know just what the boy might try to do. He had placed the boy on his staff, allowed him to serve as an aide-de-camp, kept mostly out of the way from Hardee's daily routines by the efforts of Major Roy. During the Atlanta campaign, when Hardee had been banished to Charleston, Willie's ardor for combat seemed to cool, but now, with the war fully engulfing Hardee's command, Willie had once again pushed for a position facing the enemy.

"He promised me he would go back to school. I should have taken him there myself, laid my sword on that headmaster's desk."

She smiled now. "And when did you have time? He has no use for school right now. Look at all that surrounds him, all those soldiers, all those muskets. He will not be satisfied until he fights. Like his father. Is that not the lesson you've taught him?"

"Not on purpose. That's why I wanted him gone, doing something worthwhile with his brain. Let this war end, and he can do whatever he pleases. I do not want him shooting at anyone. Or, worse, having someone shoot at him."

His felt his heart beating in hard thumps, stared at the floor beneath him. She knew his moods, kept silent for a long moment, then said, "My husband, how much longer will it be?"

He looked at her, felt a sad wound from the beauty in her young face. "You assume I know the answer to that."

"Yes, I do. More than anyone around this country. I read the newspapers. I know how badly things are going for us. There was a time when we could read of victories, off in some distant place, places I never knew existed. But there is none of that now. Now the papers speak only of the enemy, of Grant and Sherman, and all the terror we are likely to suffer. I read of what Sherman did to Georgia, how he murdered people in their homes, burned the land, destroyed everything in every place his army marched. You said yourself, to the governor, he is coming **here** now. If you believe he cannot be stopped, then what are the rest of us to believe? Your daughters are working still with the doctors here, learning how to dress wounds, how to care for the injured. They are preparing for what will happen next."

"I don't know what will happen next. No one does."

"Do not treat me like you treat Willie. I am not

so young I do not know what you endure. I know of your friend, my friend, General Cleburne. I know of Bishop Polk. It is what wakes me every night, begging God not to take you, not to see you with some awful wound. And now you believe that Sherman is coming here, will bring his war to Charleston. Am I not allowed to be afraid?"

He stood, moved toward her, put a hand softly on her head, felt the fineness of her hair. "We are all afraid, Mary. We cannot be victorious. No great speeches, no lies in the newspapers, no fantastic dreams that we hear from our president, nothing changes the truth. But I do not believe Sherman is the devil. I do not believe he rapes the innocent just for recreation. My brother is still in Savannah, and I would not have allowed that if I thought Sherman would abuse him. I cannot accept that a career soldier, a man from West Point, a **professional** . . . I cannot accept that Sherman is simply a beast. He is fighting this war to end it. He is better at that than I am, than Beauregard is, Bragg, Pemberton. And he has something we will never have, something we lost long ago. He has the army strong enough to do his bidding, to execute his strategies, to fulfill his tactics."

He paused, looked at her, saw teary eyes staring up at him, her words coming in a soft cry, "Then why can **you** not end this? Before it gets worse. Before it comes **here**."

He let his hand drop from her hair, moved away.

Because I am a soldier, he thought. But he could not say that aloud, felt suddenly foolish, telling her that he was helpless to his duty, to obedience, no matter the wishful fantasies of his president, of Governor Magrath, of anyone above him who still believed in victory.

"The men we brought out of Savannah . . . they're being positioned in key locations, including the defenses outside of Charleston. They are protecting the railroads, the intersections. I am told by General Wheeler that the columns marched north from Savannah with considerable despair, that the men lack shoes and proper clothing. But **still they march**." He looked at her again. "You must understand that. They continue to serve this army, this cause, they continue to hold their muskets, to man their artillery. They are still an army, and they have not yet given up this fight. How am I to tell them they are wrong? My son still wishes to join them. His father, **Lieutenant General** Hardee, prefers that he goes anyplace else. But I cannot fault him for wishing to stand up with the men he admires. Perhaps Magrath is correct. Perhaps the men of South Carolina will stand up in a way the men of Georgia did not." He stopped. "Now it is I who am dreaming."

"So much has been lost, my husband. You saw what Christmas was like here. It rained all day, the people were in terribly somber spirits. Can you imagine what it was like in Savannah, or Atlanta? So many places the war has already destroyed?"

"Yes. And I imagine it was a joyous, festive time in Washington and New York and Philadelphia. And in Sherman's camp, they sang songs and worshipped and prayed and celebrated, no differently than we would have, if that were my army."

"And you cannot make Richmond understand, to make this stop? You cannot convince that horrible governor?"

"They see what they choose to see. And right now, they choose that I should form an army the best way possible, and protect all that we have fought for."

She stood, wiped at her eyes. "You mean, all that **remains** to fight for. And what is that?"

He put his hands on her arms, pulled her close to him, felt the warmth, the softness. "My darling wife, what remains is the war. And it will be up to others to stop what we are doing, to say that we have done all we can do, to order the men to return home, and their generals as well. All I can do now is the very thing I have trained for my entire life. As long as there are men to lead, I must lead them."

CHAPTER TWENTY-EIGHT

SHERMAN

SAVANNAH—JANUARY 5, 1865

"Sir, there are women in the parlor. Two, in fact."

He looked up, saw the pleasant smile on Green's face, the Englishman still the congenial host.

"I assume they're here for me? I've had enough entertaining for one day. After two dozen Negroes, I've run out of politeness. One can only be gracious for so long."

Green laughed. "I must say, they do show a level of affection and respect for you that I have not seen. Not at all. The outpouring of emotion alone is quite remarkable. From what I have observed, there is nowhere in this city you can go without attracting considerable attention. It must be enormously flattering."

"It is. Can't say I expected that. Never thought of this campaign as one of liberation. Now, those women?"

"Oh, yes, sir. Perhaps you could spare them a moment? They're quite well known to me."

Sherman let out a breath. "There are a few who wish to become quite 'well known' to me as well. It is best that I avoid such temptations. My wife is rather particular on that point. I've learned to keep an arm's length from that kind of trouble."

Sherman heard a woman's voice now, older, the undisguised hostility he had heard so often before. "Mr. Green! I do not wish to make acquaintance with the general! Not for one second would I set foot in the same room with him."

Green slipped out of the room, his low voice still reaching Sherman. "My mistake, madam. I thought—"

"I came here to see you, Mr. Green. We are quite put out with all this soldiering business going on throughout the city. It is shameful, and a disgrace."

Sherman sat back, was entertained in spite of himself. He leaned out, tried to see the woman's face, Green blocking his view. Green kept his words low again, said, "What may I do about this, madam?"

"I had hoped, sir, you would be of such influence as to invite your English friends to right this horrible injustice. Surely there are warships or some such off the coast here. With so many Yankees hereabouts, there should be targets aplenty."

"Madam, I cannot, er, rather, I do not have such friends. We are living here in peace, as a courtesy offered by the Federal army. Are you certain you do not wish to meet General Sherman?"

"I would sooner stab myself with a knitting needle, sir."

The voices trailed away, Green leading the woman to some other part of the house, still the patient host. Sherman sat back in the chair, looked over toward Hitchcock, who sat waiting with a pad of paper. Hitchcock kept his eyes toward the doorway, and Sherman smiled, said, "Not all of these people are friendly, I suppose. Some of these ladies have charms that aren't especially appealing. Quite a difference in attitude between that particular damsel and Mr. Green."

"Oh, yes, sir. Quite."

The voices returned, Sherman catching the words from Green.

"I am happy to offer you a tour of the residence, madam. That room up that way is the abode of the general. I have made him most comfortable, in my own bed."

The woman's voice came again, more gruff than

before. "If you were a true patriot, sir, you would stick a thousand pins in that bed, and torture the general as he has tortured us!"

Hitchcock stood now, a show of concern, and Sherman waved him back, said in a whisper, "Let her say her piece. There is a great deal of bark to some of these people, but I am not so concerned about their bite."

Hitchcock returned to his chair, pen in hand, Sherman trying again to focus on the letter he was preparing for Henry Halleck. The voice faded away again, and Sherman heard the loud thump of the front door, Green appearing with a look of profound apology.

"Oh, my word, sir. I'm terribly sorry. Awful woman. Mrs. Grizelda Moodie. Her daughter is somewhat more refined. They are rather upset that Mr. Moodie's business has been closed down by your security people."

"What kind of business?"

"He runs something of a gambling establishment. It is said that he features charms of a feminine sort. To those willing to pay, of course."

"Of course. Gambling and prostitution. One of your more aristocratic families, no doubt."

"Ah, well, sir, I have always aimed to do business with anyone, regardless of their place in our society. I am a businessman first. Be assured, however, I did not offer her any promises."

"I can offer her one myself, if she lowered herself

to speak to me. There is corruption enough surrounding any army in the field. When possible, I have tried to eliminate it. I would promise her to enforce that order to the extreme, in her husband's case. 'Torture' works both ways."

Green laughed, just a bit too much enthusiasm. "Ah, why, yes. Very good, sir."

"Please leave us, Mr. Green. I have correspondence to put to paper."

Sherman knew that Green understood protocol, that he was not privy to any kind of army business. "As you wish, sir. The cook is preparing a fine repast, for six this evening?"

"See you at six, then."

Green was gone now, and Sherman tried to sort through his thoughts, the message he was trying to convey to Washington. Any note sent to Halleck would certainly be spread through every official channel in the capital, and possibly the newspapers as well, a lesson Sherman had learned long ago. The greatest lesson was in choosing his words so as not to cause yet another controversy for anyone who supported his efforts in the field, especially Grant.

"Where were we, Major?"

The interruption came again, Green slipping in quietly. "Very sorry again, sir."

"What the hell do you want now?"

"Somewhat of a different circumstance, sir. A Mr. Hardee is here. Claims you know of his brother."

Sherman looked at Green, curious, saw nothing to show that Green was playing with him. "Mr. Hardee, as in General Hardee?"

"Quite so, sir. Mr. Noble Andrew Hardee."

Sherman looked at Hitchcock, said, "Put the pen away, Major. Go find Dayton, bring him in. McCoy, if he's still out there. This might be interesting."

"Y̶ou are most generous, sir. I am here only to express my gratitude at the respect you have shown the people of Savannah."

Sherman did not expect this kind of graciousness, the man as sincere with his thankfulness as Green had been with his hospitality. "You are older than your brother?"

"Oh, yes, sir. William . . . General Hardee is a bit more than ten years my junior. We are most proud of his achievements. Though, of course, my family would prefer his situation to be somewhat more positive."

"That's not likely to change, sir. Your brother is leading a force that is in rebellion against this nation. My duty is to stop that any way possible."

"Oh, yes, General, I quite understand. But William has offered you something of a gesture, wouldn't you say? My presence here, when there were ample opportunities for me to take leave, should convince you that William bears you no ill will. His is a show of faith that I admit took some convincing for me to accept. But, here I am. At your mercy."

"That you are."

Sherman had already met the wife of the rebel general Gustavus Smith, the woman proving to be another of those prominent Confederates who chose to remain in Savannah. He knew that Hardee was correct, that if the rebel commanders had expected a savage rampage through the city, none of these people would have remained. So, he thought, I am not quite the barbarian the newspapers insist I am.

"General Sherman, I am a cotton merchant by trade, as is your host, Mr. Green. There are a great many of us who are well aware that throughout this war, maintaining trade with British merchants has proven unwise, and unprofitable. Profit is a tempting prize, sir. I admit that. The English have been a disappointment, to say the least. If they had valued our cause with as much passion as they enjoy our cotton, this war might well have been different in its outcome."

"There is no outcome yet, Mr. Hardee. As for the English, I suspect they never intended to enter this war unless they were certain you were going to win it."

Hardee seemed to appraise Sherman, who kept his stare hard into the older man's eyes. Hardee said, "I fear your opinion of the English is correct. As for the outcome of the war, allow me to disagree with you, General. There is only one outcome, no matter how much patriotism rattles through the hallways of Richmond. I know how the Southern army has fared of late. And, to be frank, sir, it is only by the grace of God, or rather, by your grace, that this city survives the torch. We are all certainly aware of the price you could have exacted from us. I have friends in Atlanta, sir. I know how a fire can devastate. I commend the discipline of your men."

"Actually, Mr. Hardee, my men have become fond of Savannah. Creating a base here offers something of a respite from the campaign. The men have been on the march for many weeks. Savannah is a pleasant diversion for them." Sherman could see something unsaid on Hardee's face. "I am rather busy. Is there anything else you require, Mr. Hardee?"

"I believe it is a fair question to ask, sir, if you intend to remain here? Clearly, no cotton merchant can ply his trade with his best customers as long as those customers are kept away by your blockade. It would suit all of us well if we could resume that trade with our **other** best customers."

Sherman appreciated the man's candor, smiled, twirled his cigar in his fingers. "**Northern** customers, you mean."

Hardee shrugged. "A paying customer is a paying customer. Many of us care not what flag flies over his ship."

Sherman was curious now, wondered what General Hardee would make of his civilian brother's duplicity. "So, you are not a Confederate, then?"

"I admit that we had leanings in that direction, when it seemed the South would prevail in this unfortunate affair. It is quite clear to me, and to many of us, sir, that the outcome of this war is an inevitability we must plan for. As I said, sir, I am a businessman. I must consider the future."

Sherman had suffered outpourings of righteous indignation from various English merchants, some of those based in Savannah, or others who had somehow evaded Admiral Dahlgren's net, the very men who put currency into Hardee's pockets. He was still surprised that Hardee didn't seem to share their hostility toward Federal occupation of the city.

"Your English friends are not as polite as you, sir. I've had to endure all manner of protest over my confiscation of their cotton. Some of that must surely belong to you."

"The future, General. We must assume that this year's crop is simply lost, all of those bales now guarded over by your soldiers. We must regard that as we would an unfortunate turn in the weather. The results would be the same. I am already in contact with several large plantation owners, encouraging them to put their energies toward next season. Surely, the market will be a healthier place."

Sherman studied Hardee, saw only sincerity, a surprise. "It is a shame, sir, that your brother is not so eager to put this war behind us."

"I assure you, General, William shares my sense of what is real and what is fantasy. He is in something of a trap. I'm sure you understand that. You are both soldiers. Certainly, you do not always agree with the instructions handed down by your superiors."

"I obey my superiors, as your brother does. Perhaps one day we may discuss just what kind of people our superiors are."

"Perhaps very soon, then? I would expect your army to begin its march toward Charleston. Perhaps you are waiting for a bit better weather?"

Sherman felt a bolt of caution, could hear a change in Hardee's voice. But the man's expression seemed pleasant enough still, and Sherman realized clearly he was in the presence of a man used to making a sale. Sherman smiled, said, "Mr. Hardee, my army shall resume our campaign in due time. There are military considerations which I cannot discuss with you, or any civilian here. Charleston shall be cleared of any stain of this rebellion when the time is right."

"Well, sir, I for one shall welcome the time when this unpleasantness has passed. Truly, we are grateful that Savannah is no worse by your occupation. Your soldiers have added considerably to our well-being, not just by their gallantry, but by their willingness to spend money. Regrettably, prices for even the most basic goods have escalated. I saw a merchant offering a bushel of apples for fifty dollars."

"American dollars?"

Hardee laughed. "Oh, very good, sir. I believe he would have accepted either scrip. Some still hold out the hope that their hoard of Confederate currency shall sustain them. I do not happen to share that view. As I say, once this unpleasantness has concluded, and we return to the Union, such matters will be swept away."

"I disagree with your description, Mr. Hardee. There is no 'return' to the Union. As far as I am concerned, and my president as well, Savannah, the state of Georgia, and every other state south of the Mason-Dixon Line never left the Union at all. A few state governments made particularly idiotic decisions, and as a result, they cost the lives of a generation of men that this nation can never replace. My job is to put that outrage to rest, so that the same flag flies over your city as my own, the only flag that matters. I have no idea what anyone will do with their Confederate scrip, but I assume you will find **dollars** as useful to your trade as the British pound."

He walked through a blustery wind, Oliver Howard beside him. As usual, the two men were escorted by Sherman's guards, and behind them a scattering of staff officers who held back several paces. Sherman kept his gaze to the front, had eyed the prominent monument for several days, finally had the time to stroll closer. He moved toward the enormous shaft of marble, could see the figure of a woman at the top, what he assumed to be a representation of Lady Liberty.

Howard showed little interest in the statue as yet, seemed lost in thought. After a few more steps, he said, "So, he believes we're marching to Charleston?"

Sherman slid the cigar through his lips, nodded. "Absolutely convinced of it. They have to believe that. The rebels, I mean. This was a plum like no other in the South, and Charleston would be one more. The citizens, the newspapers, hell, even Richmond has to believe I'm down here dancing with delight at my great conquests. Naturally, they would assume I want more. Charleston is the most logical place we would strike them. The navy would be there to help, certainly. Hardee's there, as far as we know, and I'll wager he's got every man who can lift a shovel putting up earthworks."

"His brother tell you that?"

"Didn't have to. But Mr. Noble Andrew Hardee came to see me for more than a show of good manners. All that talk of how peaceful our future will be, how he yearns so for the end of the war. He came to me on a fishing trip. Curious, though. I'm not sure how he'd get word to his brother if I had told him anything useful."

Howard chuckled. "Word travels in many ways,

General. You know that. Rebel cavalry is poking around anyplace they can. There are unfriendly eyes watching us even now."

"I'm counting on that. This is no different than the campaign through Georgia. I would rather avoid a major confrontation on any ground of their choosing, so it's best we keep the rebels guessing. Spread the word yourself, throughout your command, any way that seems helpful. Tell everyone who'll listen that we're preparing for the march, and we intend to move up the coast."

Howard was gazing skyward toward the monument, said, "That won't be difficult. The troops have made many new friends hereabouts. Bound to be some fair ladies who think of themselves as loyal to their cause, who are plying our boys for secrets."

"I thought you didn't approve of such goings-on, General Howard."

"For myself? Certainly not. But the morale of this army is as high as it has ever been. The boys are enjoying themselves, and much of that has to do with the hospitality of the ladies. I am realistic, sir." Howard turned, called out, "What's this square called?"

Behind them, one of Howard's staff responded, "Monterey Square, sir."

Sherman saw the courthouse off to one side, admired the scene for a brief moment, massive live oaks down the far streets, the monument standing taller than many of the nearby buildings. He continued to walk, moved out into the square, the guards spreading out well past. Down every side street, soldiers were appearing, coming closer, word of Sherman's presence spreading quickly. He stepped closer to the base of the statue, saw the ornate designs all along the stone facing, said, "Impressive as hell. A true hero, this fellow."

Howard still cringed at Sherman's cursing, something Sherman knew would never change.

"Quite right, sir. Here's a vignette of the man himself. The moment of death, it appears. Casimir Pulaski, died 1779. Four score and five years ago. Ironic, isn't it?"

Sherman examined the details along the base, another look skyward to the female figure high above. He stood with his hands on his hips, the cigar planted between his teeth, said, "What's so damned ironic about it? Died fighting the British. We'd have all done the same."

"Well, certainly, sir, but look where it is, where we are. This is a magnificent symbol, a monument of a fight for liberty, planted here, amid a city whose very existence owes so much to slavery."

"Not anymore. It's the one thing Mr. Noble Hardee said that made sense. The smart ones, the businessmen, they're already thinking of a world without slavery. Curious, though. With all his talk about the future, he never once mentioned just who is going to pick all that cotton."

SAVANNAH—JANUARY 12, 1865

The packet boats and merchantmen continued to flow into the city, the waterways finally cleared of any dangerous obstacles. Much of that work had been done by rebel prisoners, and Sherman knew there would be criticism of that, most of it certainly coming from the rebels themselves. But casualties had been few, the labor effective, allowing the navy's various craft a far more convenient passage into the city than the lengthy excursion up the Ogeechee.

The most valued cargo many of the ships carried was mail, and Sherman had received the expected notes from both Ellen and his brother John, heartfelt praise for his accomplishments, tempered with the overwhelming sadness of the death of his infant son. Other letters came as well, lengthy offerings of guidance from the War Department, wonderfully generous congratulatory notes from President Lincoln. The mail went both ways of course, men able to write their loved ones for the first time in many weeks, each one with great tales to tell.

Supplies had begun to arrive, fresh uniforms, shoes, all those goods that kept an army healthy in the field. Already word had gone northward of the plight of the citizens of Savannah, that the city was seriously squeezed by the army's presence, food growing more scarce, the needs of the army taking priority. Sherman had made efforts to provide for the civilians, but resources were limited, some of that by the destruction of the railroads which Sherman had ordered himself. To Sherman's surprise, a movement had seemed to erupt in the North, a spontaneous outpouring of sentiment for the plight of the citizens, that no matter if their city had been a crucial port for the rebellion, they were being viewed as innocent victims. The word had come to Sherman from David Conyngham that **The New York Times** was trumpeting a drive to raise funds to assist the civilians, an effort that was surprisingly effective. From what Sherman had been told, enormous stores of foodstuffs were being prepared for transport, from Philadelphia to New York to Boston. He didn't completely understand why the Northern populace felt such pangs of remorse, or were encouraged to offer such generosity. But if ships bearing such assistance were actually to arrive at Savannah's newly repaired wharves, Sherman knew it would make his relationship with the people of Savannah that much more positive. There was no fault to be found with that.

On January 11, one of many smaller ships arrived, bearing the usual mail, other goods bound for his army. But this one carried a cargo that was unique, and to Sherman, a complete surprise. Embarking at the wharf in a hard chill came a handful of officials, including the greatest surprise of all, the secretary of war, Edwin Stanton.

GREEN HOUSE—JANUARY 12, 1865

Stanton appeared ill, wheezed repeatedly into a handkerchief. Sherman sat at one end of the large parlor, Green making the visitors welcome. If Green was impressed by his new guests, Sherman couldn't tell. He was too impressed on his own.

Across from him was Montgomery Meigs, the army's quartermaster general, a man who carried enormous authority over the army's vast supply network. There were others as well, various officials who worked directly for Stanton. The entourage that had accompanied the secretary had included civilian officials from a variety of government offices, men who were already spreading out through the city, escorted by General Geary. It was clear to Sherman, and to Geary as well, that military control over the city was soon to pass into the hands of various government agencies, those men already laboring to merge their civilian offices with the structure Geary had established for the operation of the city. To Sherman, the flood of bureaucracy was overwhelming, a great herd of men in suits, each one offering him a brief show of politeness, as though Sherman was simply in the way.

Stanton was unshaven, wore small, round glasses, looked at Sherman with a hard stare, the handkerchief clutched in one hand. "General Grant insisted I make this journey, difficult though it might be. He says the air here is good for the soul. Not sure why Southern air is any better than what I was breathing in Washington." Stanton coughed now, heavy and wet, the handkerchief over his mouth. "I'm not breathing very well, to be sure. You've heard from Halleck?"

Sherman had received a number of letters from Henry Halleck, most of them easily ignored. "Certainly. Is there one in particular you're referring to?"

Stanton paused, seemed to gather himself, as though his words were rehearsed. "I am most delighted to be in your presence, General. You are a true hero, in every sense. There is one concern which has surfaced, which I must address, and the opportunity to nurse this ailment seemed appropriate. Halleck wrote you about our fears that you might be sending the wrong message to those who see this war as a struggle to free the slaves."

Stanton's bluntness caught Sherman by surprise, the letter from Halleck now coming back to him. "I told General Halleck that there is no substance to such rumors."

Stanton kept his stare on Sherman. "Yes. You described the matter as 'a cock and bull story.' Well phrased. And, possibly, not completely accurate. I have beseeched you repeatedly to offer more assistance to the Negroes who have been liberated by your campaign. There is considerable talk in Washington that you have manifested an almost criminal dislike for the Negro. It is estimated that some

fifty thousand slaves have welcomed their freedom by flocking to your army, and that you drove
most of them from your ranks. There is considerable
talk about the unfortunate incident at Ebenezer
Creek, that General Davis showed a hostile disregard for the well-being of freed slaves who had entrusted themselves into his care."

Sherman never expected this, his mind already
churning through the names of the men in his
army who would offer such a story. He thought
now of the reporters, those men so eager to send
home their dispatches, wild tales to enhance their
reputation. Damn them all.

Stanton sneezed, made a low curse, the handkerchief coming up, and Sherman said, "Sir, I have
discussed the Ebenezer Creek incident with General Davis. He maintains with perfect sincerity that
his primary task was to retrieve his pontoon bridges
in a timely manner. I had no reason to carry the
matter any further."

"You should have. There was considerable dis-
agreement among the Fourteenth Corps's commanders, and some of that ill feeling toward General
Davis's actions has found an audience in Washington, eager to seek punishment. Not only toward
him, but toward you."

Sherman sagged in the chair, his hands working the buttons on his coat, a hard cold stirring
through his chest. "Because I did not eagerly accept
the added baggage of tens of thousands of Negroes,

who would have been an encumbrance to my army, I am construed to be hostile to the black race? And I would be punished for that? Is no one in Washington paying attention to what has been accomplished here? General Grant did not approve this campaign as merely an expedition to strip plantations of their slaves."

He pulled back on his temper, saw Stanton still eyeing him, and Stanton nodded now, smiled, another surprise, said, "Yes, well, I have done much to deflect such criticism of your command. The president has enemies who will seek any means to undermine his popularity, and right now, you may be the most popular man in the Union. The president has been most public in his praise of your achievements, and so, any blemish on your record creates one on his. I regret it is that simple."

Sherman closed his eyes for a long second, thought, I despise politics. "How do I answer these attacks? Am I to be punished?"

"Easy, General. I came here to calm the angry voices, to satisfy those who seek hammer blows when a mild switch is sufficient. I should like to speak with General Davis myself. I am aware, according to his staff and the word of several who brought complaints against him, that he operated outside of your orders. Though his command is your responsibility, his actions in the field can be judged as they are."

Sherman realized that Stanton was playing the

game so familiar to anyone whose power is granted by others. I am an asset to the president, he thought. If there is fault to be found, it will be found somewhere else. "I shall send word to General Davis to meet with you at the earliest opportunity." He paused. "I must suggest, sir, that General Davis is an excellent soldier, and I do not believe him to harbor any animus toward the Negro."

"I should like to hear that from him. I would also like to have a meeting with the local Negroes, the most influential among their number. I would imagine that to include clergy, possibly merchants."

"Negroes? Might I ask why?"

Stanton wiped at his nose again, adjusted his glasses. "Simply put, General, I wish to know what they think of you."

CHAPTER TWENTY-NINE

FRANKLIN

SAVANNAH—JANUARY 12, 1865

He had been hired to work for the commissary officers, a hearty recommendation given him by Captain Jones. The business of the army had gone mostly to drill and preparation, the distribution of supplies, not only to the army, but throughout the city as well. Like many of the soldiers, Franklin had begun to wonder if the army was staying put, if Savannah was to be their new home, what he learned was called an army of occupation. There had been work on the various rebel forts, strengthening some, obliterating others, as though the army was confused as to just what they might be ordered to do next.

Nearly all of the rebel artillery pieces had been spiked as the rebels left the city, a piece of iron jabbed into the opening that prevented the powder from being fired. But Franklin had watched Sherman's engineers, patient men who had experience reclaiming cannon. Franklin couldn't avoid the concern that these guns might be used again, this time holding back what some said was an inevitable assault by the rebels to take back their city. But Jones had assured him that the rebels were most likely going the other way, pulling away from the enormous amount of power Sherman had anchored in and around the city.

Among so many new experiences came the notion of wages, that Franklin would be paid for the kind of labor he had once done with no other reward than the absence of punishment. He understood Jones's promise that the army would pay Franklin for whatever task they might require of him. The only real scouting mission he had performed had been the dangerous foray into the town of Millen, alongside the newspaperman Conyngham. For that Jones had given him a pair of five-dollar gold pieces. But Franklin felt guilty accepting anything for that adventure, Franklin fairly certain that the army didn't benefit at all from anything he or Conyngham had done. The greatest benefit to Franklin had of course been Clara. She was reward enough.

Franklin knew that he was one of the fortunate ones, that a new problem was confronting the former slaves who had stayed close to the army. So many of those people were discovering a world none of them could ever have imagined, still learning just what freedom might mean. And with that freedom came a new reality. They had to eat. Those few slaves who had come into possession of Confederate currency learned quickly that a great deal of that was required to purchase anything meaningful, especially food. But there was one other problem. If there was a limited amount of rations to be given out, a single sack of rice, a single basket of whatever fruit might be available, it was the white man who got first priority. If there was anything left over, the former slaves might get a share as well. The freed Negroes in the city were more cooperative, but even then, the supplies were thin.

Franklin knew that gaining the respect, and even the friendship, of Captain Jones had been an enormous blessing. Jones had made it clear that Franklin could always find a meal at the camp of the 113th Ohio. But Jones could do little else to put hard currency into Franklin's pocket. And so the opportunity had come elsewhere, a commissary officer who required labor, Jones pushing Franklin in that direction with a hearty endorsement. The job included hauling crates or cloth sacks from the wharf to various warehouses, labor requiring muscle and stamina, which Franklin found simple enough. To his amazement, at the end of the day he would be handed a greenback, or if the greenbacks didn't come on time, the officer might add to Franklin's meager gold hoard with the addition of another small coin.

He kept Clara in a Negro camp close to the 113th, Franklin wary of seeking shelter among the Southern civilians. Many of the slaves had seemed to disappear into various neighborhoods, gathering with freed blacks or by themselves, finding a place to sleep anywhere some white landowner didn't object. Very few found comfort in a home, and so, in the parks and larger squares, small villages of canvas had sprung up, most near the army's newly established distribution stations, where commissary officers handed out surplus rations. But there was danger in those places, and the elderly or those with ailments were often pushed aside by the greedy or others even more predatory, some from the city itself, who preyed on the slaves for whatever kind of booty they could steal.

As he and Clara became more accustomed to this strange new life, he had been surprised to learn that Clara had very little knowledge of the church. He had assumed that every former slave had been schooled as he had, but Clara could barely read. Franklin's surprise at that brought out a reaction of shame in her, something he deeply regretted. But even if she had no formal religious training, he knew the church might offer her the opportunity to learn at least the fundamentals. He had sought out a place of worship in a mostly black part of town, attended by freed Negroes, the congregation now increasing by the addition of so many from the countryside. The minister was an elderly black man, Garrison Frazier, who welcomed the couple with the understanding that Franklin was asking for more than just a Sunday sermon. Frazier had obliged, offering Clara reading lessons, lessons in simple mathematics, as well as the spiritual guidance she seemed to yearn for. Most of the slaves seemed to have some kind of roots in the church, any church, depending on what kind of leanings their masters had. Some were familiar with Catholicism, some spoke of the Presbyterian Church, but many more seemed schooled in the gospel of the Baptist or Methodist church, as Franklin had been. He had no idea that religion could exist in such variety, but Frazier spoke less of the differences between the churches than he did the similarities, lessons that Clara absorbed with the eagerness of a small child.

The church was small, a tall wooden spire that supported a tiny cross at the peak. If there had ever been a coat of whitewash on the building, that had been done long ago, the walls mostly faded or bare, the inside colorless, makeshift benches, small windows of plain glass.

But there was warmth to the place, most of that flowing up from the personality of Frazier, a man Franklin liked instantly. Frazier had no real idea how old he was, but age was evident in every move the man made, the lines in his face, the crookedness of his fingers, the curl to his back, the small patches of white hair that survived on the man's bald head. When Franklin wasn't working, he spent most of his time with Clara at the church, the most welcoming place he had found outside the camps of the army.

"You sure you won't be sleepin' here? It's fine by me. There's room in the back. No one will mess with you."

Clara kept one arm on Franklin's back, a self-conscious gesture she seemed always to make in the presence of any other man. She looked up at him now, said, "Is it all right? He doesn't mind."

Franklin had resisted the preacher's graciousness, couldn't avoid a feeling of intrusion into the limited space the old man was offering them. But there was genuine kindness in Frazier's eyes, the same kindness he had shown them from their first meeting.

"I suppose, sir, if it's truly all right. I don't wish to intrude on your house."

"My boy, this is the Lord's house. If I could make room for every freed slave around here, I would. But I have another motive with you." Frazier laughed now, a low cackle. "You're a workingman. Good strong arms, hard hands. There's repairs to do, everyplace you can see. I'll see to it you'll earn your keep."

The question rolled into Franklin's mind again, and he fought the hesitation, his curiosity pushing through. "Reverend Frazier, were you a slave?"

Frazier smiled, moved away, pointed to a small room behind his meager pulpit. "That's for you. Both of you. I'll be assuming to marry you formally afore long." He paused, serious now. "Yes, son, I was a slave. Bought my way to freedom. Had a good master. Generous man. Grew old, feeble, said if any of us could put something of value together, anything at all, he'd accept it as pay for our freedom. I think he was trying to teach us to look out for ourselves, to learn how to live in the white man's world. The old man, Mr. Kile, he was close to dying. I gave him a sermon, right there in his bedroom. Most proud thing I ever done. Gave the man peace, felt like I was handing him over to the Almighty with a smile on his face. He freed me right there, last words from his mouth. His boy heard it. Thought I was gonna have a problem with him, maybe not as generous a soul as his papa. But he was all busted up, crying, missin' his papa already. Didn't stop him from making me work for it. All told, cost me near a thousand dollars hard money. But he done it, and I had no cause to complain. I got my papers, and went on my way. Didn't have no place to go, so I started preachin' on the street. Got a following, even a few white folks. Some of 'em built this place for me. They don't come in here, most times, the white folks. But still got the following. You've seen 'em. Some of 'em feel obliged to make an offering, maybe bring me a handful of corn, a pocketful of rice, all they can spare. But still they come. Mighty grateful for that. I'll be too old for this, one day. Maybe soon. You oughta consider doing this, Franklin. Doing the Lord's work."

It was a phrase he had heard before, and Franklin absorbed that, said, "I heard that plenty of times from Master Cobb. That's what he said the Confederates were doing. 'The Lord's work.' I don't know what that means, Reverend. I think, for now, I'd rather be doing General Sherman's work."

Frazier smiled, nodded. "Just don't go shouting out about that, and keep a watch out for who's behind you. There's folks here who don't quite see the Almighty and General Sherman in the same light."

"You?"

"That's easy. General Sherman's doing the Lord's work, too. Not saying your master Cobb was wrong. It's all the Lord's work. There's plans working here. The Almighty ain't gonna tell us about any of that while we're still on this earth. But you've done seen what General Sherman's about. He's freed you. He brought you and Miss Clara close, and brought you both here. Sounds pretty much like the Lord's work to me."

The old man laughed again, and Franklin felt Clara hold him tighter around the waist. She looked up at him again, said, "He's right, you know."

Frazier stooped low, picked up a small piece of trash from the wooden planks of the floor beneath them, stuffed it down through a small hole to the dirt below. He stood slowly, looked at Franklin with a curious tilt of his head. "What's your whole name, anyway?"

"It's Franklin, sir."

"No, the rest of it. You got another name?"

"Do I need one?"

"You plannin' on marryin' this gal? There's laws about such things, even for coloreds. You got to have a name, case there's a baby."

Franklin felt suddenly horrified, as though he had made some awful mistake, that all of this might suddenly be taken away. "I don't know, sir. I don't. Honest. My papa never called me nothing else."

"What was his name, then?"

Franklin searched his memory. "He was just Henry, most of the time. All I ever heard. A few cussed names, from the overseers."

"Well, some people goes by their master's name. Seen a lot of that. I don't think that would be you."

Franklin shook his head. "No, sir. Rather not do that. Cobb is his name, belongs to him. It would be like stealing."

"Maybe. Well, I'm gonna believe that Franklin is your last name, family name. You got to come up with what you want people to call you by. What about you, Miss Clara? You got a family name?"

She spoke in a soft voice, said, "Yes, sir. Like you said, I was given my mistress's name. They told me it was Davis."

Frazier grunted. "You need to marry this boy soon enough. Don't care for that name a'tall."

The door behind them opened, and Franklin turned with a start, his hand on his pocket, fingering the knife, reflex. He saw a blue uniform, an officer wearing glasses, the man removing his hat, a slight bow.

"Pardon me. Sorry to interrupt you. You would be Reverend Frazier?"

The old man stepped closer to him, said, "I would. Who might you be?"

"I'm Major Hitchcock, from General Sherman's staff. The general has asked me to seek out the most respected Negroes in the town, and your name seems to be more prominent than most. The general has a favor to ask of you."

"A happy favor, or a sad one? I can do both, if need be."

Hitchcock seemed confused by the old man's response. "Actually, I'm not really sure which, sir. The general has been entertaining the secretary of war, Mr. Edwin Stanton, who has come all the way from Washington City. It is hoped that you might gather up several others, freedmen and all, for a meeting with the general and the secretary."

Franklin had seen Hitchcock before, felt an instinctive kindness in the man, something to be trusted. Franklin said, "May I ask, sir, the purpose of the meeting?"

Hitchcock looked at him, studied for a long moment. "I know you, don't I?"

"Could be, sir. I worked with the 113th Ohio. General Morgan's camp, mostly."

"Yes, very good. Well, I can't really offer you an explanation. I was ordered to find a number of prominent Negroes."

The old man put his hand on Franklin's arm, said to Hitchcock, "I'd be pleased, sir. Might I bring this young man with me, since he seems to be prominent in his own way?"

"Oh, yes, certainly. The general is seeking the meeting for tonight, at the Green mansion, the general's headquarters. Do you know it?"

Frazier laughed the low cackle again. "Major, every man in Savannah knows where General Sherman's living. You may tell him we accept his invitation."

GREEN HOUSE—JANUARY 12, 1865

There were nearly two dozen black men, young and old, many of them from the other churches around the city. Franklin knew a few of them, some friends with Frazier, others from the work he had already done for the army, hauling food to various neighborhoods. He was surprised to see several of the men who had come along with the army, former slaves who had begun to stand tall among their own people, whether by their education, or their instinct for leadership. They sat scattered around a large room, some in chairs, Franklin on the floor, near a small chair where Frazier had sat. To one end of the room was a large table, where three staff officers stood, alongside two men sitting. One of the men standing was Major Hitchcock, the seated officer familiar as well. He carried the mess of short red hair, the rough, unkempt beard. It was General Sherman. Beside him sat a white civilian, an older man, round-waisted, peering at them all through small round glasses. Franklin kept his eyes on Sherman, as much curiosity about the man as there was about the purpose of this gathering. Sherman seemed uncomfortable, fidgeted with his coat, rolled an unlit cigar between his fingers, and when the group had seemed to settle, Sherman said, "It would be good if one of you was to speak for the others. Not completely, of course. The secretary here has some questions for you. There is no reason for any of you to be concerned or afraid. Mr. Stanton has made the journey here to learn of your condition, as well as the condition of my army."

Franklin looked to the civilian, saw another unkempt beard, a hard weariness on the man's face, one hand holding a handkerchief, a quick wipe across the man's nose. Across the room, one of the older men spoke out.

"General Sherman, we don't have no one I'd call a leader among us. Not like you, sir. But I believe Reverend Frazier here is the most knowledgeable among us. Most respected, too."

All eyes turned to Frazier, who said, "Thank you, Mr. Hawley. I accept your praise, but I will allow myself to speak for us for one other reason that seems to matter more to me. I am by far the oldest man here."

There was low laughter, and Franklin kept his stare on Sherman, who said, "If you will permit, sir, the secretary, Mr. Stanton, would like to ask you some questions."

Stanton spoke up now, said, "Any of you, please do not hesitate to respond. Is it Reverend Frazier, then?"

"That it be, sir."

"Yes, very good. If you don't mind me asking you, sir, what is your understanding of the Emancipation Proclamation?"

Franklin felt concern, had heard the words, but had never been clear on its meaning. But Frazier did not hesitate, spoke now in a clear voice.

"Sir, as far as I can understand it, President Lincoln gave an order to the rebellious states that if they laid down their arms before January of 1863, all would be well. If they did not, then the slaves in those states would be lawfully freed, henceforth and forever."

Franklin saw a slight smile on Frazier's face, a hint of surprise from Stanton.

"Reverend, will you explain what you understand slavery to be, and what freedom was offered by the president's proclamation?"

"Sir, slavery is the execution of irresistible power of one man over another, and not by his consent. The president decreed that freedom would remove the yoke of bondage from any man so abused, and would place those people in a position where we could reap the fruits of our own labor, and be responsible for our own welfare. We would have the power to take care of ourselves."

"How would you accomplish that?"

"It would be best for most of us who worked the land to have land of our own. Others could find employment with skilled men who would be willing to teach any of us a trade, in a mill, a factory, some such place."

"Is it your preference to live among whites, or would you prefer to live in colonies or villages with your own race?"

"I do not know if it is proper for me to speak for my brethren here. But for myself, I would choose to live by ourselves. There is a prejudice against us in the South that will require years to pass." Frazier scanned the room. "Please speak out, if you disagree."

There were nods of agreement, one man raising his hand. Franklin didn't know him, saw youth, another of the preachers from the town.

"I am James Lynch, sir. I believe it is in the interest of all peoples that we shall live together. I do not
foresee such a thing without difficulty. But I would
hope we can all see ourselves as one people, as we
are in the eyes of the Almighty."

Frazier looked again at Stanton, said, "We cannot
decide our fate, no matter how honorable our intentions might be. Much has to happen, and you,
sir, have more to say about that than any of us."

Stanton seemed to weigh the responses, wrote
something on a pad of paper, Franklin now burning with curiosity. He looked up at Frazier, who
glanced toward him, a brief smile. Franklin felt
overwhelmed by the entire scene, looked again
toward Sherman, who sat with his arms crossed,
staring at Frazier with wide-eyed surprise. After a
long moment, Stanton said, "General Sherman, I
would request that you leave the room."

Sherman reacted slowly, looked at Stanton, and
Franklin caught a strange gleam in Sherman's ex-
pression, a hint of anger. "You wish me to leave?
May I ask why?"

Stanton coughed into the handkerchief, wiped at
his mouth, said, "Please, General. Just for a time. It
is the best way, under the circumstances."

Sherman stood abruptly, moved with heavy steps
across the room, his staff officers following. They
exited through the large wooden door, the door
coming closed with a loud thump. Stanton seemed
to exhale, folded his hands under his chin, said to

Frazier, "Sir, would you kindly tell me your feelings about General Sherman? What exactly do the colored people in this community have to say about his command, or his actions?"

Frazier did not hesitate. "On that I can speak for all of us, sir. We feel inexpressible gratitude to him. I believe him to be a gentleman, and a friend to our race. Some of us called upon him in this very house, and were met by him with no less courtesy than he must certainly have greeted you with, sir. By his military campaign, he has allowed what must be an entire nation of enslaved men to walk free. We have confidence in General Sherman, and we believe that our concerns could not be in better hands. He is performing God's work here, sir. Of that I am supremely confident."

There were murmurs of agreement, Lynch speaking out. "I would caution myself not to judge the man, having known him for so short a time."

Franklin could not sit still, stood up beside Frazier, felt the words building up inside of him, a hot nervousness in his gut. "I have known of General Sherman since he visited in my father's house, on Master Cobb's plantation. I have walked with his army since that day, and if it is allowed, I will walk with his army until they are no more, or there is no call for his army to march into the field."

Stanton kept his eyes on Franklin for a long moment, then scanned the room. "I admit, I did not anticipate this kind of reaction to the general." He looked at Frazier now. "You are not only a well-spoken man, you are possessed of more intellect and can speak on the subject of race with greater eloquence than most in the capital. I commend you, sir. I commend all of you. You have performed a service for your country." Stanton coughed again, and Franklin could see the tired eyes of a sick man. "I shall recall General Sherman, and determine if he has any further questions of you. I for one am satisfied that this meeting has been most fruitful. Most fruitful. You may leave at your pleasure."

The meeting went on well into the night, two hours or more, seeming to end only when the secretary's strength gave out. When Sherman returned, Franklin could see a visible scowl on the general's face, undisguised by the formal politeness he saw between Sherman and Stanton. As they filed from the room, Franklin held tight to Frazier's arm, the old man as tired by the questions as Stanton had been by asking them. They reached the street in a hard chill, Franklin pulling his thin coat tightly around him, Frazier doing the same. The others offered their quiet respects, some taking Frazier's hand, kind words that Frazier seemed to appreciate. Franklin had his own hand taken as well, knowing smiles from the older men, the young Lynch the only one among them who seemed to feel any dissent to what was said.

Within a few minutes the crowd had gone their separate ways, Franklin still beside Frazier, moving in rhythm to the old man's slow gait. After a long silent moment, Frazier said, "You did real good in there, son. I believe we surprised a few folks."

Franklin thought of Stanton, the questions that thoroughly intimidated him, answered with perfect ease by the old man. "You surprised me, Reverend. I ain't never heard any one of us speak to white men in such a way. You answered every question he had. You think General Sherman and the secretary think different of us now? If they want to know anything about any of us, I hope you'll be there."

"I can't say what they might think. But I hope to be around long enough to see the end of this war. I have to have faith that the Lord won't call me away too soon for me to see what will happen next. I have faith in General Sherman, faith in President Lincoln. If they want to know where we belong, what we feel, how we expect to be treated, all they have to do is ask."

CHAPTER THIRTY

SHERMAN

GREEN HOUSE,
SAVANNAH—JANUARY 13, 1865

He hadn't slept, a long night of cold darkness, staring up at the plaster ceiling, nursing his fury toward Edwin Stanton. But with the daylight had come the business of the army, the senior commanders knowing that instructions would be coming their way soon, what part their troops would play in the next phase of the campaign.

The breakfast offered by his host has been a grand feast, far more than Sherman's tender stomach could handle. He tried to walk off the effects of that, felt at least comfortable enough to sit at his desk. The meeting with the Negroes had been both a benefit and a lesson in the subversive motives of the secretary of war. From the first day's march out of Atlanta, Sherman had experienced little or no problems with the Negroes who followed behind his army. Since reaching Savannah, the outpouring of affection toward his command had grown to astonishing levels. There was nowhere Sherman could go in the city without being engulfed in joyous celebration. In the Green house, the front doorway seemed constantly to be opening for some new admirer, white or black. There had been of course the occasional grumble, the hostility of those who continued to dream of life without the Yankees. But the devoted vastly outnumbered the angry, and in every case, Sherman had offered as much politeness as he knew how.

He ran his hands over a sheaf of papers, requests from various commands, letters from townspeople, letters from Washington. He eyed the one from Halleck, new meaning to that one now, the arrival of Stanton bringing home to Sherman just what kind of conversations were taking place in the capital. *He came here to stir up trouble where none exists,* he thought. *They expect the worst of me, and Stanton came here to document that. General Davis and his clumsiness at Ebenezer Creek gave them all the fodder they required. But damn it all, I cannot fathom that Davis simply hates Negroes.*

He eyed the letter from Halleck again, the meaning much more clear now.

Some here think that, in view of the scarcity of labor in the South, and the probability that a part at least of the able bodied slaves will be called into the military service of the rebels, it is of greatest importance to open outlets by which these slaves can escape into our lines. . . .

Sherman tossed the paper to one side, his mind poring over the motives of Edwin Stanton, just why he needed to counsel with the Negroes, and why Sherman had to leave the room. He was angry again, tried to ignore the stirring in his stomach, said aloud, "What the hell do they think is happening down here?"

Dayton appeared, said, "Sir? You require something?"

"Get in here, Major. I can't go making speeches to myself. People will think I'm touched in the head. Those that don't already. I just figured out why Stanton came here. Halleck says there is the opinion in Washington that the slaves will take up arms for the rebels. We already know that to be utter foolishness. He also says that we must make every effort not to block the avenue of escape for the slaves from their plantations."

"Sir, have we not allowed any who would come—"

"Yes, by damn! Did you hear those colored men last evening? They understand exactly what this army has accomplished, and just how much benefit has been given the Negroes in our wake. For whatever reason, Washington seems completely oblivious to the fact that this campaign has been a success, in every part! Last night, the secretary interrogates the most prominent Negroes hereabouts, no doubt expecting a condemnation of my character. This, aimed at the general who has commanded sixty-five thousand men through four hundred miles of enemy territory, who has captured cities, destroyed railroads, with barely any loss. All of this while allowing tens of thousands of slaves to find their freedom. And for that, I am construed as hostile to the black race."

"Sir, I don't believe Secretary Stanton believes you to be against the Negroes."

"The hell he doesn't. That's what his little show was about last night. If those preachers and whatnot had given him the ammunition, if they had spoken out against me, the next thing you'd have around here is an order for my dismissal." He paused, saw Hitchcock at the door. "Enter, Major. Join the festivities."

"Sir, I heard . . . do you require anything?"

Sherman stood, moved toward a tall window, hands on his hips, turned now, stared at both men, said to Hitchcock, "What did you think of our gathering last night?"

"I thought it was extremely positive, sir. That preacher, Frazier. He has to be the most well-spoken Negro I've ever seen. And he wasn't alone."

Sherman moved again to the desk, an unlit cigar waiting for him. He snatched it up, stabbed it between his teeth. "I am a fool, gentlemen. It seems I take myself and my command too seriously. It is easy to believe, when you are in the field, out from the eyes of superiors, that the world belongs only to you. You make a small mistake, you can fix it. When you achieve victories, you enjoy the satisfaction. No one else matters, unless you fail, unless you suffer some massive defeat. But there is another kind of war going on in Washington. Men are maneuvering themselves for what happens **next,** for what winning this war will mean, for who might get rich, who might gain power." He paused. "I trust the president. Didn't always agree with him, but I believe him to be an honorable man. I don't trust a single soul he has dancing around him, including our secretary of war. I have handed them a great prize, just as Grant did at Vicksburg, Farragut at New Orleans. Happy times for all. And then the politics begins. Generals become an inconvenience. We're in the way. All those minions who came along with Stanton, they're out there scampering all through Savannah staking their claim on their territory, how much authority they can add to whatever power they had up north."

"There's more to it than that, sir."

Sherman didn't see McCoy enter the room, turned toward him. "What do you mean?"

"Sir, I've been talking to Mr. Conyngham, for one. Several other newspapermen. They gather around here every morning, looking for something new to talk about. This morning there was something new, Conyngham in particular chewing on something he had a hard time swallowing."

"Get to it, Major."

"Sir, word has spread that there is a movement afoot to give the Negro the right to vote."

Sherman dropped his arms, the cigar hanging loosely from his mouth. He waited for more, but McCoy seemed to have nothing to add. Sherman pulled the cigar away, felt strangely deflated, emptied of the fury. "So, that's it? It's not about me, and my supposed prejudice? It's about pleasing the Negroes, so that one day, Stanton and his ilk will gain their vote?"

"Seems possible, sir. The reporters say there is considerable talk in Washington about bringing the Negro into the . . . um . . . Conyngham called it . . . **enfranchisement**."

Sherman felt suddenly very tired, the lack of sleep finding its way into his brain. "No one will ask me what I think of that. That's a machine far larger than any influence I'll ever have. To be honest, gentlemen, it never really occurred to me. Half these people we brought in here can't even read."

"Yes, sir. That's why they're ripe for promises and such."

Sherman had a clearer picture now, the meeting, Stanton offering so much graciousness. "They'll remember all of this, one day. Those men last night. They'll be grateful for the personal attention of Mr. Stanton, and so they'll remember **that** when they have a ballot in their hands. Once, of course, he tells them who to vote for."

Behind McCoy, an aide appeared. "Sir, begging your pardon, but there is a letter here from the secretary."

"Read the damn thing."

"It's fairly lengthy, sir. His aide said it was important for you to act on this before the new campaign begins."

Sherman saw the paper in the man's hand. "Give it to me. Where is the secretary now?"

"He was in his quarters on the cutter this morning. His aide said he was not feeling much better. He is said to go visiting with various townspeople, merchants and whatnot, later today."

"You mean, voters."

The aide seemed puzzled, and Dayton said, "That's all, Sergeant. You're dismissed."

The man was gone quickly, and Sherman moved to the desk, sat slowly, his eyes fixed on Stanton's letter. He read for a long minute, then said, "He is suggesting, if that is the word, that the government stake claim to what is defined as abandoned lands, now in our possession by virtue of this war. This land is to be used for the settlement of Negro colonies."

Hitchcock said, "What land, sir? Savannah?"

"No. Abandoned farmlands and plantations, all along the coast, as far down as Florida, as far north as the existing settlement at Beaufort, South Carolina. He is appointing an Inspector of Settlements and Plantations, General Rufus Saxton."

"Saxton! How did he get that job?"

Sherman looked at Dayton. "Easy, Major. Saxton may not be a favorite in this camp, and he may not have accomplished a damned thing on a battlefield, but he's just the kind of squirrel to do a job like this. Has a talent for paperwork, and this sounds like mountains of it." Sherman read further. "There's more. The secretary is insisting that we begin encouraging the enlistment of able-bodied Negroes as soldiers into this army."

McCoy said, "We have a great many already, sir. Teamsters, laborers, sappers, carpenters, all manner of service."

Sherman read further. " 'Negroes so enlisted will be organized into companies, battalions, and regiments.' He means for them to fight."

Hitchcock said, "Is that a problem, sir?"

Sherman put the paper down, thought for a long moment. "There are colored regiments now, throughout the army, some under Grant, some under Thomas, other places. Some of those units have acquitted themselves well under fire. Most

haven't had the opportunity. In the past, I have expressed reservations about that. They proved me
wrong at Vicksburg. Put up a hell of a scrap along
the river." He ran his eyes over Stanton's words,
thought a moment, said, "We've got a whole new
flock that's come along with this army, men who
probably hate their former masters, maybe hate the
South. If some of those want to carry a musket,
we're to give them the chance. Whether or not they
can fight . . . well, maybe Stanton's expecting me to
shove them up to face the first rebels we run into.
Not going to do that. If Washington wants to interpret that to mean I'm against the black race . . .
well, hell, what am I supposed to do about that?"

On January 15, as Sherman was preparing
new orders for his commanders, word
came to Savannah that offered an even
greater boost to morale.

Fort Fisher, which guarded the mouth of the
Cape Fear River, near Wilmington, North Carolina,
had long been known as a rebel strongpoint where
blockade runners had a reasonable chance of reaching safety. The fort was considered a serious thorn in
the side of any effort to unite Sherman's army with
Grant's. In an attempt to eliminate that problem
once and for all, Ulysses Grant ordered General Ben
Butler, with a force of six thousand troops, to attack the fort by advancing down the coast on board

naval vessels. The army would be assisted by gunboats commanded by Admiral David Dixon Porter, the man who had been so enormously cooperative to Grant's efforts at Vicksburg two years before.

In early December, Butler had landed his troops in the sand dunes within sight of the fort. But the rebels had anticipated this move, moving a force roughly matching Butler's on a march south from Virginia, to reinforce the garrison already there. Pressed hard by Grant to get the job done, Butler attacked without adequate preparation and adequate reconnaissance, a combination that breeds failure. After fruitless assaults, a frustrated Butler had made his last-gasp attempt on the fort by positioning a boat packed full of gunpowder nearby, hoping the explosion would destroy the fort. The boat exploded on schedule, doing no harm whatsoever to the fort or its occupants. Discouraged, Butler convinced himself the fort could not be taken, and he abruptly withdrew his troops, and returned them by ship to the James River. Disgusted with Butler's failure, Grant ordered many of those same troops to return, reinforced by another two thousand men. The expedition was led this time by General Alfred Howe Terry. With none of Butler's self-doubt, and considerably more ability in the field, Terry's expedition pushed hard against the fort's defenses. After three days of naval bombardment and a determined assault by Terry's troops, the fort was secured. On January 15, the last gap in the Federal stranglehold on the South's Atlantic seaports had been sealed.

Sherman's initial reaction to Butler's failure was that the fort might best be left intact, that leaving a rebel garrison there would ensure that a sizable number of the enemy would be kept separate from any force the rebels might bring into South Carolina. But now, with Fort Fisher in Federal hands, Sherman realized that the city of Charleston had become nearly indefensible. Hardee would have no alternative but to withdraw his troops well to the north of Sherman's new march, or risk being surrounded.

As Sherman accepted the wisdom of Grant's strategy regarding Fort Fisher, another piece of news brightened Sherman's mood even more. Fresh from the overwhelming Federal victory against John Bell Hood at Nashville, General John Schofield was now moving an entire corps of George Thomas's army eastward. Schofield was transporting an additional thirty thousand men to Fort Fisher, to be added to the sixty thousand that would march again with Sherman. No Confederate army remaining on the continent had the strength to match what Sherman would now command.

JANUARY 19, 1865

General Geary had relinquished his duties as military mayor of the city and rejoined his troops under

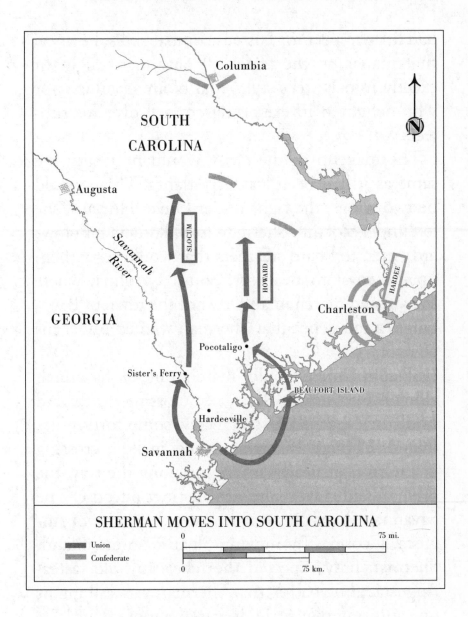

SHERMAN MOVES INTO SOUTH CAROLINA

Union
Confederate

0   75 mi.

0   75 km.

Slocum's wing of the army. The city was now placed
under the umbrella of John Foster's Department
of the South, the city to be occupied by the Federal Nineteenth Corps, troops newly arrived from
Grant's command on the James River. If Sherman

had little respect for Foster's combat skills, he knew that managing the affairs of Savannah might fit exactly into Foster's style, that of an administrator who delighted in exercising control over his subjects.

The makeup of the army would be nearly the same as it had been leaving Atlanta. There would be two wings, the right under Oliver Howard, the left under Slocum. Sherman issued orders for Howard's men to board steamers that would ferry them up the coast to Beaufort, South Carolina, where they would march inland toward the town of Pocotaligo, a rail depot that Sherman wanted under his control.

Slocum's men would march out of Savannah along the Savannah River, not crossing northward until they reached Sister's Ferry, some forty miles inland. Though the army could make a crossing of the river at nearly any point along the way, the drive inland served one very distinct purpose. The Savannah River ran straight toward the city of Augusta, Georgia. By moving Slocum so far inland, Sherman fully expected the rebels to hold fast at Augusta, anticipating that Sherman was still intent on capturing that prize. It was one more feint.

If the rebels couldn't be sure of Sherman's intentions, his own commanders had no doubt. The orders he issued had been specific. Both wings of the army were to drive toward the next city Sherman considered important to his campaign. With the state of Georgia now under their belts, every man in the army knew that South Carolina would be their next target. Sherman had spent the final few days in Savannah measuring the mood of his men, feeling out just how much passion they had for the next phase of his campaign. He was not disappointed. To Sherman, South Carolina was a strategic goal, one more step on his plans to unite his army with Grant. To his delight, sentiment among the men was that South Carolina bore the blame for this war, and thus should be punished for it. To that purpose, Sherman had ordered both wings of his army to converge on the state's capital city, Columbia. Even if the war was not concluded by its capture, putting Columbia under Sherman's belt would be a wound to Confederate hopes from which they might never recover.

CHAPTER THIRTY-ONE

FRANKLIN

SAVANNAH—JANUARY 19, 1865

"I'm not sure that's the best idea."

Captain Jones peered over his shoulder at him, then turned back to his work, closing his small trunk. It was the last bit of Jones's baggage, the rest of the tent bare. As Franklin watched, the captain completed the task, buckling his sword, putting on his hat. Franklin stood just outside Jones's tent, still leaned in, held his own hat in his hand, waited for the right time to speak.

"It's the best idea I got, sir. This has caused me some considerable argument. Inside, I mean. Clara, she says to do what I have to do. I swear to you, sir, there's a powerful notion that I've got more to get done than hauling barrels. I appreciate the job and all. Really do. Got thirty dollars in gold put away. Give it to Clara, for holdin'. If she has any trouble, she'll be able to pay for food, anyhow."

"You gave your gold to that girl?"

Franklin saw the frown on Jones's face. "It's not what you think, sir. Truly. We'll be married when this is done with. I know that. She's right now with Reverend Frazier. She'll be stayin' in the church. He says he'll look after her. There's other women, too. I've done give her my sweetest goodbye, sir. It's done."

"I can't tell you your personal business, Mr. Franklin. I can tell you that the army has sent down orders to bring in any Negroes who wish to serve. But there can't be any kind of uniforms, weapons, anything like that, not yet. There's no time right now. We're already moving out of Savannah, and this unit will be on the march in a few minutes. It'll be another long one. The new colored units can't be sent out until you have the training, drill, formations, bugle calls. And, if you're lucky, marksmanship."

"You mean, can I shoot a musket?"

"Shooting's easy. Hitting a target's a little tougher. Killing a man . . . that's the hardest thing of all. Believe that."

Jones paused, moved out of the tent, seemed to gather a long breath. He stared off, where already a thick column of soldiers was marching on the wide roadway. He looked at Franklin now, a hint of sadness, Franklin not sure what that meant.

"I'm sorry, I done interrupted you, sir. Maybe it's a foolish thing, me wantin' to be a soldier. But I swear, sir, it's pulling me. Clara understands, she truly does."

"Let me tell you something about being a soldier." Jones paused. "God looks you square in the face when you pull that trigger. I've seen it. Shot a man with my pistol, right through the forehead. Chattanooga. He watched me do it, stood there, like he was expecting it. That's something I'll never forget, the look in his eyes. It was God looking at me, right through the rebel's eyes. The man fell, blood everywhere, no time to think on it then. But I know what happened, what it meant. Since then, I've shot at plenty of men, maybe hit some. Never had one so close, close enough to watch me kill him. You sure you're ready for something like that?"

"If he be a rebel, I think so."

"Got nothing to do with that, Mr. Franklin. A man is a man. Even rebels got family, a wife maybe. Children. You're telling me you're ready to rip the life out of that man? That if God's watching you, you can put your musket into a man's face, put your bayonet into his heart? That's what you have to believe to be a soldier. That you can do any of that without thinking about it, without stopping to think about what God thinks about it. Don't know of too many men in this army who don't think about that some."

"There's killing aplenty, Captain, sir. Must be some folks in this army got the feel for it."

Jones nodded, looked again at the road. "It gets easier, some say. Most of that is just talk. What makes a soldier kill without thinking about it? Panic, Mr. Franklin. A line of troops marches straight at you, and you see all those bayonets. You're scared so bad you lose your pee. Pardon me. But that fear's what makes it easier to pull the trigger. You see a line of troops facing off, a hundred men, a thousand men standing face-to-face in a field, I promise you, there's not much aiming going on. They march up close in big fat columns, and any man pulls his trigger, he's just as likely to hit somebody by pure chance. That's when men run away, that first volley. You stand there with an empty musket in your hand, and if you don't keep your head, reload like you're taught, like these men have drilled a hundred times, you won't stand up to those bayonets. You'll haul your bottom out of there, running like the devil himself is chasing you, running till you drop."

"I won't do that, sir. I'd never run off."

"Every man says that. Every one. You ever heard a musket ball sing past you, Mr. Franklin?"

"No, sir."

"The wings of death. You might hear it coming, and if God moves it just right, it'll miss you, clip off a piece of your ear, maybe take off your hat. Or it'll slap into the man next to you, drop him like a sack of potatoes. You can't pay attention to any of that. The man on the other side of you's still standing, still trying to fight, and he's counting on you to stand your ground."

Franklin absorbed what Jones was telling him, said, "You're trying to scare me outta here, make me glad to be going back to Clara, to Reverend Frazier, to hauling barrels and sacks for the commissary. I respect you, Captain, but I ain't as dumb as some folks want to think. Nobody knows what it takes to be a soldier until they done it. Even you. Every man has to learn all those things you just said. Now, they done learned it. That's all I'm asking, sir. I come this far because I needed to do something to help you. Never really thought about that until I met Clara. We're gonna get married, I promise you that. Maybe have children. And we can do something for ourselves, work the land, learn things, all because of this army. No matter all those terrible things, I can't just watch you march on out of here and make a fight with the rebels, just so I can stay here and be safe. That ain't fair. You say the Lord maybe judged you for killing a man. Well, He'll be judging me if I just take the good you've given me, and don't pay nothing back."

Jones put his hands on his hips. "You're a good man, Mr. Franklin. But I can't give you everything you want, not right now. In time, once this campaign has ended, they'll be forming up new regiments, creating camps for drill and instruction. All I can offer you right now is that you come along like before. Old Poke is gone. Sick, I think. We need some help with the horses, with a great deal more around the camps. Like I said, no uniform, no musket. When the time comes for the new camps, if you still want to do this, I'll send you off with a good recommendation. I give you my word on that. You need to give me your word that you'll not run off just because you start missing that girl of yours. That can be a mighty strong pull, Mr. Franklin."

"We talked it over. She cried, that's the truth. But she's safe with the reverend, got plenty to do, can sew, cook. Reverend Frazier already got her working some in a boardinghouse. Long as I know she's not in trouble, that nobody's messing with her, I'll be fine. She's done seen me off, said a long prayer for me. I'm ready, sir. I got to do this."

"You can write her, you know. We should have mail going back here, at least for a while."

It was something Franklin had never considered. He had never actually written a letter before. He thought a moment, said, "She's learning to read pretty good. That'll help her. That's mighty kind, sir."

Jones laughed. "Don't give me credit for delivering mail. It's just what the army does. Helps a man to know how his family is doing, helps them back home to hear from him, make sure he's all right."

Franklin was amazed by that, that a man so far from home could find a way to reach out, that the ones he cared about might do the same for him. "This is one strange world, Captain. You got ships hauling goods from someplace out past the edge of the earth, you put men to marching on roads that don't ever seem to end. Towns and bigger places just seem to appear, rising up in some place where it seems like nothing could ever live. This army . . . you got men shooting at you, hating you, trying to kill you every day. You walk through mud and sand and the coldest days I ever seen. You sleep on the ground, and eat something my papa wouldn't give a plow mule. And then you write letters to folks at home, telling 'em about it."

"And you want to come along."

Franklin smiled, nodded. "Yes, sir. I reckon I do."

"Well, our orders are to march out along the Savannah River, probably be on the move for a couple days. We're traveling pretty light again, just like when we left Atlanta. General Sherman's orders. Not likely we'll find much in the way of rations in this country, at least for a while. Rough land. Rice and oysters, until we get clear of Savannah. Then, just rice. We'll be sending out bummers again, pretty sure of that. But we'll be in South Carolina, Mr. Franklin, and I'm pretty certain those people will be even less accommodating than anyone in Georgia. And rebel cavalry will be waiting for every foraging party, trying to ambush 'em down every trail. You can ride in the supply wagon. Go on over to Sergeant Jordan." Jones pulled a scrap of paper from his pocket, a stub of pencil, scribbled a quick note. "Here. Give him this, tell him I authorized you to move out with the commissary wagon. Then keep that in your pocket. You get separated from this unit, it won't do for some green-eared lieutenant to toss you aside. Remember what I said about rebel cavalry. I can't give you a mount of your own. Wouldn't look right yet to have you ride along with my aides."

Franklin looked toward the road, a thick column of blue moving past, colors and horsemen leading the way.

Jones called out to one man, "Bring my mount. Time to go."

Franklin knew the face of Sergeant Jordan, colorless man, no smiles, no talk at all. Franklin moved closer to Jones, said, "Uh, sir, pardon me. The soldiers got no choice but marching. If it's all the same to you, I'd just as soon walk with them. I'll stay back, keep out'n the way."

Jones's expression was changing, something Franklin had seen before. His eyes seemed distant, a long stare out past the road, far past the camp of his men. The regiment was in formation now, by company, filling an open field to one side. To Franklin, it was a glorious parade, the muskets up in neat rows, the blue uniforms mostly clean, the officers moving among their men, straightening the lines, sergeants calling out their usual curses.

Franklin thought of the captain's descriptions of war, what he had seen of fighting, of the enemy, of death. He felt a glimmer of understanding now, that if you wanted to be a soldier, you had to accept that this was not just some grand spectacle. Out there, across the river, there were rebels still, and for all the happy talk in the city, for the laughter and games and festivities, there was still a war, and some of these men, the men he saw now, might not survive. He looked at Jones, thought, That's what he's thinking.

Jones climbed up on his horse, his eyes on the road, the color bearer riding up, holding the flag of the 113th Ohio, the young man now close beside the captain. There were drums, another unit moving past, the captain seeming to wait for his place in the larger column. Franklin stepped closer to the road, closer to the field of men, familiar faces, some of them laughing, the jokesters, others staring ahead, nervous eyes, impatient to begin. He saw a flock of horsemen moving up across the road, a larger flag, the Stars and Stripes, officers, one in particular, familiar, the grim stare of General Morgan. A gap appeared in the road, the trailing end of another regiment, a pair of artillery pieces now moving past, hauled by caissons, their crews mounted up, some on the caisson, some on the horses, hearty cheers, raucous shouts going out toward the foot soldiers.

The general rode closer, said something to Jones, then backed away, and Jones moved his horse into the road, the color bearer out beside him, now another man holding a bugle. Jones made a sharp wave, a bugler blowing a quick rhythmic call, the voices in the field falling silent, the jokes past. Franklin saw Captain Gorman, Company A, a hard salute toward Jones, another toward Morgan, Gorman leading his company out into the road. He stood, held his sword upright, the men falling into line, the column four across, filling the sandy road, and immediately they began taking the first steps forward.

Jones spurred the horse, led the way in front of his own column, looked back toward Franklin, no smile, a hard, cold stare.

"Fall in, Mr. Franklin. Route step, forward march."

CHAPTER THIRTY-TWO

SEELEY

NEAR POCOTALIGO,
SOUTH CAROLINA—JANUARY 21, 1865

He had watched Hardee's withdrawal from Savannah from a stand of pines, the cavalry spread out as protection, should any of the Yankees attempt to interfere. Throughout that dismal day, his men had shivered in silence, matched by the gloom of the column of soldiers as they passed. There had been no Yankees, nothing at all to prevent Hardee's troops from making good their escape across the river, and they were now moving farther into the South Carolina countryside.

At Pocotaligo, many of those men had boarded railcars, would add to Hardee's new defensive position in Charleston. Others would move out to the west and north, anchoring new garrisons at anyplace Hardee or Beauregard had considered ripe for attack. Wheeler had simply followed orders, what remained of his horsemen doing the same. There was little energy in the troops, some of that from the lack of decent food. The horses were no better, mounts dying in every camp, others barely strong enough to bear their riders.

If morale was sour enough among Wheeler's men, there had been the infuriating visit by Inspector General Alfred Roman, sent specifically by Beauregard to investigate rampant rumors that Wheeler's men had lost all effectiveness as a fighting force, and worse, that many of the troopers had become little more than bandits, raiding and stealing horses and any other valuable commodity the local populace might present. Roman's report had gone back to the generals, claiming that Wheeler's men were displaying "a brutal interference with private property. Public rumor condemns them everywhere, and not a few do we find in Georgia as well as in South Carolina who look upon them more as a band of highway robbers than as an organized military band. Had I the power to act in the matter, I would relieve General Wheeler from his command, not as a rebuke, but as a punishment. . . ."

Beauregard's reaction to Roman's infuriating report was to offer the War Department in Richmond a recommendation that dug hard at Wheeler: "Unless Wheeler's command can be properly organized into divisions, under good commanders, a large portion of it had better be dismounted forthwith. Its conduct in front of the enemy and its depredations on private property render it worse than useless."

Wheeler was, naturally enough, outraged, and he responded with a letter of his own, claiming that there was "positive proof that the country swarmed with organized parties who do not and never did belong to my command" despite the fact that in nearly every instance, those roving gangs identified themselves to the civilians they plundered as being Wheeler's men.

But Wheeler had one hard and fast friend: William Hardee, who countered Beauregard's dismal assessment with at least a hint that Wheeler was an asset that the army could not afford to lose. Hardee added to the fray by telling Richmond and Beauregard that "the reports of its disorganization and demoralization are without foundation, and the depredations ascribed to his command can generally be traced to bands of marauders claiming to belong to it."

To Wheeler's enormous relief, any suggestion that his cavalry was to be disbanded was, for now, ignored.

Inspector General Roman was long gone, but the sting of his report still gnawed its way through the men. Seeley knew as well as any other commander that, whether or not his troopers had decent horses, the men themselves were lacking even the most basic weaponry. In Seeley's most recent command, three hundred men had dissolved to barely a hundred, many disappearing from the various camps, presumed to have deserted. As he inspected his men every morning, Seeley could see for himself that those men who could ride were often missing pistols, and a third had no muskets at all. Uniforms were a thing of the past.

At Pocotaligo, the rail depot and telegraph line that ran toward Charleston had been untouched by the Yankees, Hardee keeping as close communication with Wheeler's positioning as possible. As reports from the various scouting parties found Wheeler, he had wired Hardee that his first priority was farther inland, close to the Savannah River. There was no secret to what Sherman was attempting to do, a significant march along the river, which aimed itself straight toward Augusta. Wheeler had responded by riding that way, accompanied by a sizable portion of his command, keeping close to the northern banks of the Savannah River. Wheeler's decision had far more to do with another report his men had offered, that Kilpatrick's horsemen were accompanying that column, would likely lead the way into the city of

Augusta, or, if Sherman changed course and made a crossing of the river into South Carolina, Kilpatrick would certainly cross first, ensuring a safe passage for the infantry across Sherman's pontoon bridges. It was no more a surprise to Seeley than it was to other officers in Wheeler's command that if Kilpatrick's whereabouts could be confirmed, Wheeler would do everything he could to stand in his way.

Seeley's own men seemed not to care just what duty they were assigned, whether they were in close pursuit of Yankee cavalry or just guarding the rail depot. It had been many weeks since there was a fight of any kind, the Federal surge into South Carolina close to Savannah seemingly just for show, to prevent any Confederate forces from adding to the men Hardee had kept in the city. Now, with Savannah fully in Sherman's hands, Seeley had expected a rapid advance northward, knowing full well that the columns he had seen, Hardee's men, numbered fewer than ten thousand. If there had ever been confusion before as to Sherman's numbers, that uncertainty was gone. With so many camps spread out in and around Savannah, Wheeler's scouts had confirmed more than once that if Hardee was to be attacked in Charleston, he would be outnumbered at least five or six to one.

The land they rode through was flat, mostly featureless, miles of sandy ground, flat grassy fields, cut through by low bottoms, cypress patches, bog holes, and mud pits. The ride had misery of its own, but today that misery had been compounded by another change in the weather. They had grown used to the cold, the lack of any threat from Sherman allowing the men to settle into camps where the fires stayed high. But now the hard chill was punctuated by rain, the sandy roads deepening, the weakened horses struggling all the more.

The orders had come from General Dibrell, passed along to him from Wheeler, that care had to be taken that Sherman wasn't merely feinting toward Augusta, that Charleston could still be the primary target. Seeley knew that General Hardee would need every piece of information the cavalry could give him, that if any significant column was suddenly to appear along the coast, Charleston had to be made ready.

He kept his gaze downward, water flowing in a cold stream off the bill of his hat, soaking what was already soaked, his seat and legs rubbed raw by the rough cotton of his pants, every move by the horse scraping his skin. Up ahead, the road narrowed, thickets of pine woods pushing together, a small farmhouse to one side, no sign of the farmer. No, Seeley thought, he has more good sense than to do anything in this weather. What would he do, anyway? What grows here? They say rice needs plenty of water. Well, there's that. And snakes. And every kind of bug the Almighty set on this earth. Maybe too cold for those critters. Just as well. There's enough misery right here.

He pulled to one side of the road, looked back to his small column, the men stretched out, great open gaps between them. He held up his hand, stopped the lead horsemen, called out, "Hold here. Let them group up."

He looked again to the front, had none of that itchiness, the sharp sense that, up ahead, maybe in those trees, there might be a threat, an ambush. He hadn't seen any Yankees in weeks, beyond those he had scouted in their camps from a perch above the Savannah River. Yankees may not be any smarter than us, he thought. But they surely got enough sense not to go marching on roads this bad, in weather that could drown a fish.

The column was drawing up closer now, the faces of his men showing him more misery than he felt himself.

"Keep up, boys. No straggling. This ain't a place you want to get lost in."

No one responded, even the old man, Gladstone, keeping his curses to himself. Seeley rode back into the middle of the mushy sand, heard a voice behind him ask, "Where we going, anyway?"

He turned again, saw one of his lieutenants, Gibson, a man younger than he was. "We're going where we're told to go. General Dibrell sent us to scout down closer to where we can see Beaufort. You heard the order, just like I did. You have a problem, tell him."

"How much further?"

There was no playfulness in Seeley's mood, his words coming in more of a shout than he intended. "Have you seen me with a map? You got one? We'll know we're at Beaufort when we see Beaufort. You confused about that? Look for a whole passel of tents and a thousand colored soldiers. Ain't you been paying attention? Yankees took that place long time ago, put a whole pile of Negroes in there, figuring nobody'd mess with 'em."

"We aimin' to mess with 'em?"

"We're ordered to scout them, make sure they're sitting tight. That too complicated for you?"

He turned away, spurred the horse, tried to calm himself, the rainwater sliding down the back of his wet shirt. He yanked on his raincoat, the rubber and canvas doing nothing to keep him warm. He knew they'd follow him, had gone through far worse than this, but his patience was gone completely, no time for talking about it, no time for discussions about just how futile this duty might be. Just do the job, he thought. We get close to Beaufort, there's gotta be somebody nearby who's got a roof we can crawl under. And if they wanna complain about us to General Anybody, they can go right ahead.

He rode closer to the hourglass of trees, the road

piercing through tall, thin pines, a muddy pond visible to one side, surrounded by a stand of cypress. He stared that way, his eyes dancing with the sleepiness, more water streaming down from his flopping hat. There was a flicker of motion, a dark figure in the distance, then more, and now he heard the sound he knew too well. The musket ball passed overhead, and he was jolted awake, stopped the horse, stared that way, searching the rain, the thicket of trees. Now another ball came past, closer, in front of him, and Seeley held his stare through the driving rain, searching the distant trees, felt strangely disconnected, as though this were unreal, an odd dream. The men were gathering up behind him, no one seeming to hear what was happening, and more musket fire came, the hard **zing,** a wet slap impacting a man behind him. Now the men responded, aware, the man tumbling from the saddle, the others calling out. Seeley waited a long moment, still couldn't believe it was happening, that there would be Yankees out here. Our own men, he thought. Has to be. Another patrol, lost, probably. Panic and stupid.

"Hey! We're your own! Hold fire!"

The rain drowned out his voice, more zips and hisses from the musket balls, Gibson calling out, "Sir! Pull back! Take cover!"

"Gotta be our own men! Damn fools!"

The men were backing away, seeking shelter on the backside of the trees, and Seeley felt raw anger, would find their officer, if there was one, scream into the man's face. He jerked the reins, the horse pulling back, stumbling in the deep sand, Seeley falling to one side, hands grabbing for him, Gibson, others. He righted himself, more musket fire coming, the air buzzing like so many bees, and he jerked the reins again, said, "Pull back! Let's find out what's going on. I'll stick that officer's sword where there's no sunshine! Take cover, till they find out how stupid they are! Who's hit?"

Gibson called out, "It's Simpson, sir! Not bad. Slit the top of his shoulder."

"Dress it best you can. Damn their souls!"

The men were down, the horses pulled back, and Seeley crouched low close to the road, his ankles buried in wet mud. He looked back, saw Gladstone spitting out a brown stream of tobacco, a smile on the old man's face. Yeah, you think this is funny. How about this?

"Sergeant! Take three men, move out through these trees. Get as close as you can, find out what kind of jackass is in charge out there. If you can call him off, do it. Tell him who we are! There's gotta be some kind of garrison keeping watch on Beaufort. They got nothing better to do than shoot at anybody they see."

Gladstone didn't complain, had been with Seeley too long for any arguments. He pointed out three men, groans coming fast, and Seeley pointed the way, Gladstone doing the talking.

"Leave your danged carbines here! You ain't had dry powder all the blessed day! We're just lookin'!"

Seeley watched as they moved off, Gladstone standing tall, the others crouched low. They seemed to sink into the deep grass, disappeared quickly into the pines, and Seeley watched the road in front of him, felt a burning need to slap someone with the broad side of his saber.

The minutes passed, the rain in his face, burying any sounds. He strained to hear any more firing, voices, but there was nothing, no sign yet of Gladstone. Behind him, the men were grumbling, and Seeley thought of rations, knew there were none, that even hardtack was becoming rare. He looked out through the trees the other way, saw clusters of palmettos, had heard talk of eating the roots, or something else that grew in the thickets, what someone called swamp cabbage. Or maybe, he thought, those boys out there brought backpacks with something to eat. That'll be a good lesson. You shoot at me, and you can hand me your grub.

"Sir, what's that?"

He saw Gibson point ahead, down the road, looked that way. Far past the narrow passage through the pines, there were more dark specks.

"It's men. They're coming in some kind of hurry."

Seeley stood now, eyed the figures, a slow jog toward him, three hundred yards, closer, dark shapes draped in raincoats. He felt a cold stab in his stomach, had seen this before, too many times before, his hand moving to his pistol, reflex, and now he heard a sharp cry to one side.

"Get mounted up! Get going!"

Seeley saw the three men who had gone with Gladstone, a mad scamper through the wet, sloppy grass. They reached the road now, bent over, one man wheezing the words, "Gotta pull back! They's a flock of 'em!"

Seeley looked past them, saw Gladstone now, making his way with slow, methodical steps. He felt suddenly helpless, furious, baffled, could only wait for Gladstone, looked again down the road, saw the men coming closer, slowing, in line, spaces between them. **A skirmish line**.

Gladstone climbed out of the grass, breathing heavily, a broad smile on his face. "Well, now, sir, we got a report to make to General Dibrell, or anybody else what cares."

"What report?"

Gladstone saw the men coming at them down the road now, nodded, pleased with himself. "That, sir, is the advance line. There's more down in the woods thataway. Seems the Yankees done decided to take a stroll thisaways."

"How many Yankees?"

Gladstone shrugged, his eyes on the road. "I'd say maybe a million or so. There's another road, out through those trees, backside of that pond, maybe a quarter mile or so. Better road than this one. They's marching heavy, full column. Flags and whatnot. Rain don't seem to bother 'em none."

The musket fire came again, the skirmish line moving up to the cover of the pines. Seeley heard the sharp zips again, knelt low, saw the men tending the horses, a hundred yards to the rear.

"Time to go, boys. Get to the mounts!"

The men obeyed, quick, sloppy steps through the deep mud, no one making himself a better target by staying up in the road. Seeley followed, kept everyone in front of him, saw the wounded man, Simpson, holding a bloody cloth on his shoulder. He moved that way, close to Simpson, said, "You can ride, Jack?"

"Yes, sir. Hurts like the devil, but it'll be all right."

Seeley waited, watched as the men reached the mounts, climbing up quickly. Now they waited for him, and he scrambled out into the road, jumped up on his own horse, looked again at the men back in the trees. The flashes of fire were scattered, no more than a couple dozen skirmishers, and he thought of making a charge, knew that Wheeler would think of that first, would try to drive them off. Not our job, he thought. We're out here to scout. Well, we scouted.

The rain had slowed, the men now moving away, pushing the horses as hard as the ground allowed. Seeley eased his horse off the road, a lower profile, stared out to the far woods, where Gladstone had been. He heard it now, unmistakable, the steady rhythm, adding to the pounding in his chest. It was drums.

"I done tole you, Captain. There's a column over that ways, and if you look real good, there's one back thataways, too."

Seeley looked again toward the skirmishers, far behind them, saw the flicker of a flag, men on horses. He thought of Wheeler, chasing the Yankees upriver, far from this place, wondered who **these** men could be. The skirmishers were still peppering the air with their fire, and Seeley felt himself pulled back, a hand on his reins, Gladstone.

"Best not linger hereabouts, Captain."

Seeley nudged the horse, followed his men, a steady retreat, retracing their steps through the watery sand. His mind raced, thoughts of the enemy, and Seeley stopped, pulled out the field glasses, stared through wet lenses, blurry images, the colorful flag, the unmistakable flicker of the Stars and Stripes. Gladstone said the words as they flowed into Seeley's brain. "Ole Sherman did this in Georgia. Split up his army, drove 'em two ways. Guess he's done it again."

"Guess he has, Sergeant. We best tell somebody about it."

CHAPTER THIRTY-THREE

SHERMAN

BEAUFORT,
SOUTH CAROLINA—JANUARY 23, 1865

The boat trip had taken most of two days, including a brief stop at Hilton Head, for a council with General Foster. But the journey was made far more miserable with the change in the weather, with the kind of seas even sailors had learned to dread. For the army, men who had rarely if ever been at sea, the journey was an education in the frailty of the human body. To Sherman's amusement, tempered with concern, most of the soldiers who accompanied him had become seasick. As the affliction spread, though, any humor had faded, and

Sherman understood that weakening his men at the start of a campaign would provide one more reason for delay. He had run out of patience for delay.

The surprise at Beaufort was that the town was a healthy, vibrant place of businesses and merchant-men, peopled by both black and white who seemed barely to notice their differences. Some of those were soldiers, the colored regiment garrisoned there after one of the few successes by Federal troops dur-ing the first year of the war, those men acclimating to life as just another part of the whole. As a result, throughout the war, the town had been virtually free of any real conflict, the Federal government going so far as to emancipate the slaves in that area, an act that seemed to affect no one beyond the town's bor-ders. But Beaufort had not been ignored altogether. Recognizing the town as something of a sanctuary, escaped slaves found the means to reach the town, not even the most vigilant trackers wishing to deal with the possibility of a confrontation with the regi-ment of colored troops. Thus did Beaufort continue to grow and thrive. It was the one port along the southern Atlantic coast not affected by the Federal naval blockade, adding to its prosperity.

For Sherman, the only really disagreeable aspect of the town was the weather. The storms that had so plagued his troops at sea continued on land, and de-spite Sherman's orders that Howard's wing make rapid progress marching inland, the roads had become riv-ers of swamp water, what so many of these troops had seen before. As the army had learned on their approach to Savannah, the low country was fit for little but growing rice and the occasional field of sugarcane. Sherman's supply wagons were full for the most part, the ships ferrying goods to Savannah now supplemented by transports and steamers that pushed up the various waterways that flowed past Beaufort, supplying the army even as they marched closer to their first objective of Pocotaligo. But the rains had swollen every waterway, flooding roads so severely that not even corduroying the surfaces provided much help. On the left wing, the Savannah River was now swollen to dangerous levels, Slocum's men unable to make any significant crossing with the pontoon bridges they had on hand. Sherman knew to be cautious, that pushing his army too far too quickly in these kinds of miserable conditions might create a problem of his own making. In this kind of dismal country, supplying the men had to be a priority. For many of the troops still in and around the town of Beaufort, an old staple was found in abundance, oysters, something many of the men had come to enjoy. The cooks had become as creative with the bivalves as they had with the rice, both a hearty alternative to hardtack. But not everyone accepted the oysters as a treat.

"What's the matter, Major? You not hungry? You didn't appear to suffer too badly on the ship."

Sherman couldn't help smiling, watched Hitchcock prod one of the open shells, his fingers dip-
ping slightly into the fleshy meat of the oyster.

"Really, sir, I don't see how anyone considers this
a delicacy."

"Not sure they do around here. The people along
the coast probably eat the things pretty often. When
there's an abundance, take advantage. You prefer them
cooked, perhaps? In Savannah, I had them fried in
oil, something quite different. Makes them a bit
crunchy, rather than . . ."

"Gooey. That's what they feel like, sir. Goo. My
apologies to the fine-dining culture of the South,
but this is one journey I cannot make."

Sherman reached over, slid Hitchcock's plate
toward him. "You don't mind, then, do you, Major?"

Hitchcock motioned the plate away with his
hand. "Please, sir."

"Perhaps you'd prefer a taste of this sugarcane. A
little hard on the teeth, but worth the effort."

Dayton sat at the far end of the table, said, "Yes,
go ahead, Major. Just chew on the stalk."

Hitchcock held up a short piece of cane, the
outer husk stripped away. He sniffed it, took a short
nibble off one end, the frown disappearing. "Well,
quite tasty, I admit. Like a confection."

Dayton chewed on a stalk of his own, said, "That's
where confections come from, Henry. They boil
the stuff down, I think, pull out the sugar. Didn't
they teach you anything at your fancy college?"

Sherman put one hand on his stomach. "Not sure I can eat any more of this. Major Dayton, be sure our host is aware of our gratitude. I have always said there are two things a soldier must do anytime there is the opportunity. One is eat. The other is write letters home. I shall now do the latter." He watched Hitchcock struggle with the sugarcane again. "Enjoy that, Major. But a word to the wise. When I was in Louisiana, I learned to partake of that treat in moderation."

Hitchcock peered over his glasses. "Why, sir? Pretty tasty."

"Yes, and as well, I found it can provide some rather energetic stimulation of the bowels. That can be of benefit, on occasion. Though when we begin moving by horseback through swamp country, the benefit might become more of a hazard."

Sherman heard the laugh from Dayton, his eye still on Hitchcock, who withdrew the cane from his mouth, stared at it. He seemed crestfallen, said, "Sir, you have mentioned on more than one occasion that you encourage your staff to eat hardtack. Keeps us in step with the men, all of that."

"Yep."

"For the first time in my perception, sir, that seems like a good idea."

JANUARY 24, 1865

Captain Poe had delivered the latest collection of maps, showing a myriad of roads and farm trails that sliced in a haphazard pattern away from the marshy plains along the coast. To Sherman, the line Poe had sketched that attracted his greatest attention was the railroad, the Augusta and Charleston line, the last remaining link the city of Charleston had with any points to the south. The town of Pocotaligo was the first objective, that depot astride the rail line that stretched from Savannah to Charleston, leading to the bridge across the Savannah River that Hardee's men had already burned. Northward, the rails were a tempting target, but Sherman knew that Hardee would prepare for that, would likely position a good percentage of his troop strength across that avenue. That was a move Sherman was counting on.

He began the day's ride in a mood that matched the foulness of the weather. Poe had expressed what Sherman already feared, that the heavy rains would make any crossing of the low country a challenge at best, both wings of the army certain to face delays along every flooded road, every creek and swampy bottom. He stared down at the impact of his horse's hooves, soggy splashes through soft, watery sand, the only sounds the steady rain, the sloppy steps of the horses, and the growling curses that rolled through his brain.

He had ordered Kilpatrick to accompany Slocum,

leaving only a few squads of cavalry leading the way out of Beaufort. His final order to the horsemen had been to keep Sherman informed of their location by the burning of the occasional house, a joke that played well with Kilpatrick's brand of humor. Sherman looked up across the great sea of saw grass, miles of watery plains, thought, A joke on me, for certain. Slocum's got the river to deal with, and Poe's men sure as hell better have learned about pontoon bridges by now. If this rain doesn't stop, we're gonna have a different problem. The water might rise up out of this flat country and swallow us up altogether. We'd have been better off bringing the damn boats right off the ocean with us. Rowing beats drowning.

There were riders now, coming toward him, a response to Sherman's order that Howard keep him informed of anything that lay in their path. The horsemen reined up, moving alongside.

"Sir! General Howard offers his respects and reports that the enemy has withdrawn from the village at Pocotaligo without much resistance. There were cavalry patrols, but nothing of consequence."

Sherman guessed at the time, didn't feel like exposing his pocket watch to the rain. "What the hell time is it?"

"Near four o'clock, sir."

"Any place to make camp up ahead?"

"General Blair has pulled his men into some fields at a plantation, called Gardner's Corner. There's dry ground there. General Howard has been informed, sir."

"How far?"

"Not more than three miles, sir."

"They got a house?"

"It's a plantation, yes, sir. Fine old home, though seems to have been abandoned sometime ago."

"Lead me there."

The place had fallen into considerable disrepair, the owner long gone, Sherman not certain if the man had fled the inevitability of the war or had simply given up trying to live in such a place. He stepped heavily into the parlor, water flowing off every part of him, his boots spilling water over the tops. He saw a small wooden chair, sat, pulled hard on the boots, little success. Hitchcock was there now, looking as miserable as Sherman felt.

"Major, you can offer me considerable relief if you will pull off my boots."

Hitchcock wiped at his glasses, nodded slowly, said nothing. He moved toward Sherman, bent low, a valiant effort on the left boot, which finally gave way. Water poured from the boot, adding to the puddle growing around Sherman's chair, and Hitchcock grabbed the other boot, removed it as well.

"Thank you, Major."

"Sir. You suppose it would be proper to have one of the aides do the same for me?"

"Just tell them, Major."

Sherman slid out of the raincoat, another lighter coat beneath it, removed that one as well. Dayton was in the house now, more misery, and he moved quickly, took the raincoats from Sherman's hand.

"Allow me, sir. I'll find a suitable place."

Sherman felt his uniform coat, his trousers, said, "Tell me, Major. If I had so damned much rain cover on me, how come I'm so damned wet?"

Dayton didn't laugh at the mild joke, the day's ride draining away his humor. "Don't know, sir. Can't recall rain this hard."

"I recall it plenty of times. It's never as bad then as it seems right now. And for all we know, tomorrow will be worse."

"We could hold the army here, sir. Let this storm pass, or whatever it is. One thing for certain, the enemy can't move any quicker'n we can. Not likely they'll suddenly appear to our front."

"That's why we're not stopping. I want this army inland as far as possible before Hardee or anyone else figures out what we're doing. I have to explain that? This is a campaign, not a scouting expedition. I intend to grab as much of South Carolina as possible before anyone decides to fight over it. We have to maintain our supply lines as long as possible, and once we're far enough from the coast, we'll be relying on the countryside again. I don't want anyone to get to those plantations before we do. Am I clear?"

"Completely clear, sir."

Dayton moved farther into the house, and Sherman scowled at the small lake he had created around his chair. He had no reason to be angry at Dayton, at any of them. I'm like some child, he thought. Spoiled by having it easy, everything going my way. Somebody tossed a rock into my bowl of sweets. Hell, Dayton understands. Been with me too long. He's right, though. The damned rebels aren't doing much more than we are, plodding their way through the mud, if they're moving at all. Hardee has to believe still that he's the target, that we're going to make a grab for Charleston. Damned Southerners, it's always about land and towns. Same with those politicians, all that crowing about how easily the war will end if we grab Richmond, or so much panic that the damned rebels might have grabbed Washington. Old-fashioned foolishness. Hardee's a better soldier than that, ought to understand that what matters is the **army,** those men out there who can fight, who can kill these men here. That's the target. I didn't punch a hole in Georgia just to scare civilians. I made a point, a point I'm going to make in South Carolina, and maybe North Carolina, and maybe, if we have to, Grant and I will make it again in Virginia. I'm tired of fighting a bunch of rebels who made this damned war because they thought they could play politics with our flag. I'd rather play politics with a battery of artillery, and four corps of veteran troops. We'll see who wins.

He slept on the floor, near a brick fireplace that had seen better days. The aides had found little to stoke the fire, the majestic live oaks spread across the plantation already stripped of limbs, used by his men to build fires of their own. He rolled over, the stiffness in his back matched by the hardness of the wooden planks beneath him, cursed aloud, sat up. The night had grown much colder, and he stared at the glow of a handful of embers, moved closer, blew hard into the ashes, a cloud swirling up around his face. He coughed, spit.

"Damn it all!"

A damp handkerchief removed most of the ash from his face, smeared the rest, and he cursed again, shivered, the wetness in his clothes not yet dry, even his meager nightclothes damp. He slapped his arms against his sides, shivered again, his eyes searching the darkness. In one corner of the room was the skeleton of an old bed frame, and he climbed to his feet, fought more stiffness in his knees. He stumbled toward the wreckage, bent low, picked up one end of a broken board, snatched hard to the side. The frame came apart, and Sherman dragged the broken piece out toward the hearth, jabbed one end into the fireplace.

"Too damned big." He looked up above the mantel, saw an old clock, had noticed it earlier, long broken, the small glass front shattered. He reached up, pulled the clock down, stepped away from the fireplace, raised the clock above his head, launched it downward with as much force as he could. The clock shattered at his feet, a discordant clash of metal innards and splinters of wood. There were footsteps now, voices, Sherman ignoring them, kneeling carefully, avoiding the springs and gears, shards of glass. He gathered up as much of the splintered wood as he could, stepped carefully to the fireplace, voices in the dark, "Sir! Are you injured?"

"Nope. Just cold as hell, Major. Help me get this damned fire going again."

Dayton was down beside him now, and Sherman blew again into the ash, closed his eyes, fought the cloud, blew again. The embers found the splinters, the fire growing slowly, the room lighter now. Sherman sat back, realized there were a half-dozen men behind him.

"What the hell do you want?"

Hitchcock was fumbling with his glasses, said, "Sir, I heard a terrible conflagration. I thought perhaps an artillery shell!"

Sherman looked at him, shook his head. "A clock. Gave its last breath so that I might not freeze. Now go to bed. All of you. Anybody else needs to stay by the fire, fine, but do it quietly."

The men dispersed, and Hitchcock sat on the floor, said, "To be truthful, sir, I am frightfully cold. My blanket isn't adequate."

"Then help me break up that bed frame. It should burn for a good while."

Hitchcock stood again, planted his foot hard on the larger piece of timber, a loud crack, the brittle old wood coming apart.

"Excellent, Major. You're a master vandal." Sherman paused. "You know, for all the destruction this army has done, I believe this is the first act of vandalism I've committed myself. Don't mention any of this to the damned reporters. They'll make up some kind of nasty little tale about that."

POCOTALIGO,
SOUTH CAROLINA—JANUARY 25, 1865

He woke to a bracing chill, and blue skies.

Outside, the army had formed a vast camp, and for the first day in nearly a week, the rain clouds were gone, the air crisp and dry. He stood on the porch of another old home, the owner nowhere to be found. The coffee was hot, a slab of ham waiting for him at a broken-down table behind him, and for the first time since landing in South Carolina, Sherman actually felt good.

He inhaled deeply, the cold air energizing him, gazed out across the slow motion of the mass of blue. Fires were everywhere, the men pulling down fence lines, trees, anything they could burn. He watched one larger fire, saw a platoon of men gathered close, some of them now looking toward him. He smiled, thought, You know what this means, don't you? It means I'm about to give orders, and you already know what they are. It's time to move.

He hadn't heard from Slocum, but the dry weather meant the Savannah River would begin to fall, easing the burden for the engineers. Even now, one of Howard's divisions from the Fifteenth Corps had been trapped below the swollen river, those men forced to march through the muddy bottoms and flooded fields alongside Slocum's troops. But now they can get their tails up this way, he thought. Howard will be happy about that. He likes things orderly.

For now Howard's men would gather up, ease out on the march, preparing to move at as rapid a pace as the drying roadways would allow. But there would be no great surge northward until Sherman heard from Slocum that both wings of his army were safely in South Carolina. It can't take long, he thought. February will be drier. Usually is in the South. Wonder if Hardee knows I'm aware of that? He has to feel pretty damned safe up there knowing what kind of miserable country lies between us. Well, General, you keep holding on to that thought. And keep your garrisons right where they are.

He thought of the rail line, his men already at work destroying as much track as was within reach. I should send them out a little farther, he thought. Hardee'll have cavalry scouts all over hell, watching what we're doing. That might give him just a little more confidence that we're headed up his way. He pulled out the map Captain Poe had given him, the network of roads that had become impassable. But that's going to change, he thought. Not just the weather, but the geography. We get farther from the coast, the ground rises. Better ground for marching, the farms will be healthier, good forage for the horses, plenty of rations for the men. It'll be a whole lot prettier than these damned piney woods, too. Get back up to hardwood country, away from these palmettos and their snakes.

McCoy was there now, had come up late from Beaufort, part of the staff remaining behind to ensure the commissary officers were doing their jobs, supervising the transport of those last supplies that could still be useful to his army.

"Coffee's really good this morning, sir."

"It's not the coffee, Major. It's the air. You know anything about fortune-tellers, Major, those Gypsy women that claim to know the future?"

McCoy laughed, caught himself. "Not really, sir. Haven't ever used one."

"Me, neither. But if one was here, I know what she'd say. She'd say we're due for a good healthy march, for one. And one more thing, too. She'd tell us that come February, those folks up in Columbia are going to have a rough ride."

CHAPTER THIRTY-FOUR

SEELEY

NORTHEAST OF AIKEN, SOUTH CAROLINA—FEBRUARY 9, 1865

"The crossing of the river was inevitable. I do not believe for one minute that Sherman intends to strike Augusta. But General Hardee is most insistent that we protect that place, as well as every important place in South Carolina. I have long exhausted my inquiries as to just how we manage that."

Wheeler was pacing, an unusual show of energy, the words flowing out in a steady stream. Beside Seeley, General Dibrell seemed to puff up, his usual posture.

"Sir, is it not wise of us to strike out against the enemy's flanks?"

Wheeler looked at Dibrell as though staring at a snake. "What 'flank' do you have in mind, General? Are you aware of a 'flank' that no one has told me about? I suspect if we march just about anywhere in this country we shall stumble into some Yankee position."

"I just thought we should make an aggressive move. The Yankees must surely believe they have the upper hand. Such arrogance leads to carelessness."

Seeley winced at the obviousness of Dibrell's observations, another officer speaking up, saying, "General Dibrell, perhaps you were not informed that Kilpatrick's cavalry is making a move along this side of the river. It is fairly certain he is moving in the direction of Aiken."

Seeley was surprised by that, knew nothing at all about Kilpatrick's movements. But his men had come west and south on orders from Wheeler, no explanations offered. Seeley knew that remaining closer to Pocotaligo made little sense, that his men would find themselves in full retreat every day Sherman advanced. Wheeler's order made sense for one other reason. Seeley agreed that the cavalry should act as a more united force, that spreading out in small scouting parties served only to annoy the Yankees, and not much else. With the improvement in the weather, it was certain that whatever

Sherman was planning to do, he would move more quickly.

Wheeler paced again, hands behind his back, noticed a handful of slaves off to one side of the house, watching the gathering of officers in the estate's grand front yard. Seeley kept his gaze that way, his eye catching an old man, who seemed intensely interested in the conversation. Seeley slipped away from the officers, moved toward the Negroes, the slaves suddenly dispersing, the old man moving off with a hobbling limp. Seeley reached him, grabbed his collar.

"Where you going to, old man?"

"Nowheres a'tall, boss. Gots chores to do."

"Chores like gathering up information? You talking to any Yankees hereabouts?"

"Oh, no, sir. No Yankees pay heed to this old soul."

He still held the man's shirt, felt the fear in the man's quaking voice. Seeley had no energy for this, thought, What can he tell anyone? That cavalry was here? He released the man's shirt, remembered Tennessee, Mississippi before that, the infuriating discovery that the idle slaves that watched the passing of the soldiers were just as likely offering scraps of intelligence to Grant's army.

"Hardly matters now," he said. "Nothing you can tell Sherman they don't know already. They stupid enough to pay you, you take their money. Now go on."

He pushed the man gently, had no stomach for abusing one crippled old man. He moved toward the front of the plantation house again, saw Dibrell waiting for him.

"What are you doing?"

"Those slaves were watching us pretty intently. Thought I'd run 'em off. No need to have so many ears about."

Dibrell's eyes narrowed, and he looked past Seeley, a scowling stare toward the various black men, going about some sort of labor with any kind of implement that was close. Seeley saw the counterfeit effort, thought, Yep, they were listening to every word. But he wouldn't say any more about that to Dibrell, didn't want to see the general's usual show of bravado against people who were simply helpless. Dibrell sniffed, said, "Well, you watch them close. Tell Colonel McLemore what you saw. We maybe ought to put some people around here, watch for signs of Yankee scouts."

"I'll tell him, sir."

Seeley ached to get away from Dibrell, his division commander too eager to inflict punishment on any civilian, black or white. It was one more reason why Joe Wheeler's troopers were becoming so reviled along the trails, the tendency for some of the officers to treat every citizen as the enemy. If the civilians seemed unpatriotic in their eagerness to be rid of the war, Seeley knew that punishing them with abuse would only make them more uncooperative. No one seems to know what to do about that, he thought. But whatever we're doing, it ain't working.

Seeley walked around the corner of the house, the yard spreading before him, saw a rider approaching, Wheeler leaving the others, walking out to the road to meet him. Wheeler seemed to keep the man out away from the others, his habit, receiving the latest dispatches only for himself, sharing what he felt his officers needed to hear. Seeley felt annoyed again, had grown too accustomed to showmanship.

Wheeler spoke for a long minute to the courier, then turned toward the men. "As I suspected. Kilpatrick has been sighted just south of Aiken. Finally. Finally! Mount up, go to your commands. How many effectives do we have at hand?"

Dibrell had returned, a low murmur among the ranking officers, Wheeler waiting with angry impatience. One of the others spoke up now. "Best as we can figure, sir, two thousand effectives. If we wait for a couple days, we can bring in more from the railroad, or those men you sent off toward Augusta."

"We don't have two days to play around, Colonel. Gather up your commands. We'll move into Aiken. I will plan a reception for General Kilpatrick he does not expect."

Seeley heard the shots from down the road, and as he rode closer, he could see the horses splayed out, blood on their carcasses, a dozen men standing nearby, pistols in their hands, silent misery on their faces. He looked for Lieutenant Gibson, saw the man standing far out near the tree line, away from the carnage, talking to what seemed to be a civilian. He spotted Gladstone close by the horses, said, "How many? Eight?"

Gladstone turned away from the dead animals, a grim sadness on the man's face. "Eight today. We'll have to take down a few more tomorrow. One of 'em was Old Lucy. She just couldn't go no farther. Run out of heart. Loved that danged horse. Had her for two years." Gladstone paused. "Hard thing for a man to do. Kill your best friend."

Seeley hated to see Gladstone in a foul mood, the one man in the company Seeley could depend on for a shot of morale. "Very sorry, Sergeant. We'll work hard on finding some mounts."

Gladstone shrugged, kept his eyes away from the carcasses. "Just part of the war, I s'pose. Good animal, she was. Got me out of more'n one scrap. Woulda done it again. Can't ride a bag of bones too long and expect much." He looked up at Seeley now, made a quick scan of Seeley's horse. "Dang shame what we's doin' to these critters. You ride that old boy careful. He's hurtin'. I can see it in his eyes."

Seeley appreciated Gladstone's instincts, a man

more at home in the cavalry than anywhere else
they could have put him. "I'll ride him as gentle
as I can. But we've got business. General Wheeler
wants us to ride into Aiken. Set up an ambush."

Gladstone's expression changed, wide-eyed curiosity. "Kilpatrick?"

"He says so. Reckon we're gonna find out."

Gladstone seemed to perk up, a hint of enthusiasm in his words. "Hey, Captain, how 'bout you
tell Lieutenant Gibson to find me some horseflesh.
Not sure he knows how to decide much of anything on his own. But I'd hate to miss out if there's
gonna be a party."

Gibson was approaching, a look of hopefulness
that Seeley dreaded, the young man's bright optimism severely out of place. "Sir! Been talking to a
fellow who's got a place just down the road. There's
a good-sized farm out that way. He says that place
could have some mounts. Mules maybe, but at least
we'll be able to ride."

"What fellow? That civilian?"

"Yes, sir. Fellow named Jenkins. He says he's not
on too friendly terms with the neighbor, says the
old man done let his place run to ruin, but he's
likely got all manner of goods squirreled away in
the woods behind his barn."

Seeley thought, Yes, and that would take our eyes
away from Jenkins and whatever he might have
hidden. "We know the fellow's name, the plantation owner?"

"Jenkins just called him Old Fart."

Seeley felt like laughing, held it in. "I suspect that's not his name. But we oughta go check in on him, do a little scavenging. Maybe pay a little more heed to Mr. Jenkins as well. We're riding into Aiken by tomorrow, and I want every man in the saddle. Might be heading into a scrap with Kilpatrick."

Gibson's eyes got wide. "Don't say? Well, yes, sir. Let's go pay a call on, um, what'd I say?"

Gladstone responded, shaking his head. "Old Fart."

Seeley led a dozen men along a gravelly road, saw an old fence line, the house beyond, slowed them with a wave of his hand. A man hurried toward them from the house, a pathway leading away from the crumbling porch of the dilapidated old home. Seeley saw the double-barreled shotgun come up, pointed at his own horse, reined up with one hand on his pistol. The man called out, "You keep back! Get on outta here! I got nothing you want!"

Seeley took a deep breath, dismounted, tried to keep his calm. "Sir, we mean you no harm. We are good Confederates, like yourself."

"How do you know what kind of Confederate I am? I ain't met a soldier on neither side worth his spit. What you want?"

Seeley latched on to the man's words, thought,

Don't ask him now, but someone oughta find out just what soldiers he's seen on the **other** side. He studied the man's face, thought, Might not be the man we're looking for. Doesn't seem all that old.

"Sir, are you the owner of this land?"

"Why you need to know that? None of your business, anyhow."

Seeley looked out toward the house, a sagging roofline, overgrown bushes hugging the walls, no sign of any tilled fields. He glanced back at Gibson, said in a low voice, "Not much more than a run-down farm."

Gibson didn't respond, his eyes locked on the man's double barrels. Seeley stepped out clear of the horses, both hands extended to his sides. "We mean you no harm, sir. We're engaging the Yankees shortly. We appreciate your help. We have great shortages, and are counting on your generosity."

"Bah! I got nothing here. Nothing!"

"Well, sir, I respect what you say, but we're in a desperate way. We'll offer you a note for anything we might take. General Wheeler will honor it soon as he can."

"Wheeler, huh? You'd be his boys, then? What kind of note? How much?" The man seemed to catch himself. "Don't got nothing anyway. Don't matter."

"Sir, my men do not wish to harm you, but we require supplies, and I regret that I will force you to part with what we need. I'd lower that shotgun if I were you."

The man seemed to blink, the shotgun coming down slightly. "I got nothing. You all just go on down the road."

"Not sure until we make a search. You keep that shotgun low. No need for you to fear us."

"Plenty of need. But you seem like a decent boy. Like my little brother. Ain't heard from him in two years. Had some coloreds here, too. They done run off."

The man seemed nervous still, and Seeley said, "What happened to your brother? He in the army?"

"Dang fool wasn't fifteen. Went up visiting my sister in Sandy Springs. Some smooth talker convinced him he oughta join up. Last I heard he was marching north, Pennsylvania. Ain't heard a word from him since."

Seeley thought, Gettysburg?

"Well, we can put in an inquiry with General Wheeler's staff. Maybe even General Hardee."

"No need to go bothering generals on my account. I'll find him, sooner or later."

There was no sadness on the man's face, no sentiment in his words, still a jittery nervousness. Seeley felt an itch that the man was holding back a great deal more than anything about his brother.

"You do any stretch in the army yourself? Seem fit enough."

The man hesitated, a quick glance back toward the house. "They didn't want me. Sickly. I just want to get on with working this place. Now look around if you have to, then go on down the road."

The man lowered the shotgun toward the ground, moved away on the narrow path to his house. Seeley took the cue, pointed silently to Gladstone, four others, motioned for them to follow him, motioned for Gibson to keep back with the rest. Seeley spoke in a hard whisper toward Gibson, "You hear shooting, come running. Don't trust this bird."

The man led them onto a porch, holes in the planks, remnants of four pillars that were missing completely. Seeley looked up at the ceiling, saw the sag, thought, Nothing holding this place up. Doesn't look like a soul actually lives here.

The man waved them to one side of the house, said, "You go on and look around out that way. Ain't nothing for you to see in the house here. Look in the barn. Anything you see you can have. Then go on."

The man closed a rickety wooden door in their faces, and Gladstone moved up close to Seeley, said, "He's in a blamed hurry for something. Maybe he's got a bottle in there. His last prized possession."

"Not sure. He's too anxious for us to leave. It's more than a bottle of whiskey he's hiding."

One of the others moved up close, Private Clemons, said in a whisper, "Maybe he's hidin' his brother. Maybe the young fella done run off from the army."

"Could be. But if the boy went to Gettysburg, by now he's likely in Petersburg. Either way, he's better off dead. Come on. Let's look around back."

Seeley stepped back off the porch, moved around the side of the house, saw the barn to the rear, caught a sudden glimpse of motion, the man scampering out from the back of the house, across the overgrown yard, disappearing into the woods behind the barn. Seeley jogged that way, said, "He skedaddled into the woods. Easy. Spread out. He might have more'n a bottle. He might have the whole fixings for a whiskey still back there, and he loves that shotgun."

The men moved with him, wide formation, a quick glance into the barn, what Seeley knew would be empty. Gladstone moved up close to him now, said, "You smell that?"

Seeley sniffed the chilly air, smiled. "Fresh horse piles. Let's go. Slow, quiet."

They moved around the barn, the woods thick with briars. But there was little else to block their view, the trees tall and thin, the brush mostly empty of leaves. Seeley stepped high, crushed thin vines beneath his well-worn boots, thorns finding their way through thin leather. He motioned to the others to move ahead, worked to free himself from the tangle. He kept his eyes on his men, the others struggling with the briars, slow progress. Seeley pulled free of the thorns, his glove still grabbed by a stubborn vine, yanked it loose. He was moving again, farther into the woods, and to his front, he saw the flash, the burst of fire, then another. The men dropped low, calling out, but Seeley knew what they were seeing. It was musket fire. Seeley flattened out, thorns in his face, Gladstone calling out, "Yankees!"

A few feet away, one of Seeley's men raised his pistol, fired without aiming, a musket blast answering. Seeley felt a frantic helplessness, the briars holding him in a painful grip, said in a hard whisper, "Hold fire! How many are there?"

The man kept low, shook his head. "Saw a few. Not sure."

Seeley pulled his own pistol, looked for Gladstone, saw the older man on his knees, peering up, and Gladstone fired his pistol now, then again, more musket fire coming back.

"Get down, you old fool!"

Gladstone looked at him, the yellow toothy grin, said, "We done run into a fight! Hee!"

Behind them, Seeley heard the others coming at a run, looked back that way, saw Gibson now, leading the rest of the squad forward on their knees, carbines in their hands. Seeley looked at his pistol, his only weapon, screamed at himself now, Stupid! You didn't trust that fellow, and now you're in a damned ambush!

Behind him, a carbine fired, then another, and he lay flat, still helpless, hard in the grip of the briars. There were shouts now, farther into the brush, what seemed to be an argument. There was another carbine blast from his own men, Gladstone's pistol firing again. Gladstone called out now, "Give up, you damned fools! You ain't getting out of this mess!"

Seeley closed his eyes, his heart racing, thought, Not the time for a bluff. How many are there? Not sure who's in the "mess."

To one side, one of Seeley's men stood, his pistol aimed, Seeley wanting to shout the man into cover. But the man just stood, said aloud, "That's right. Easy. One step at a time. Hands over your heads."

Seeley saw one of the men now, a heavy black coat, a scruff of a beard, hands high.

"Don't go shooting us. We ain't gonna fight you."

Seeley fought to stand, the briars tearing through his pants leg, his pistol up. In front of him, six men were moving out of the woods, hands high, one man walking straight toward him, desperate fear in the man's eyes. Seeley aimed the pistol at the man's face, said, "Slow. What you doing out here?"

"Same as you. Looking for food and whatnot. Ain't wantin' no fight. We won't be causing you no trouble, long as you treat us decent."

Seeley couldn't keep his hand from shaking, the pistol quivering, and he lowered it slightly, saw nothing that looked like uniforms, none of the men looking anything like soldiers. "What unit you with?"

"Ain't been with a unit in some time. You a captain, then? Cavalry, I guess."

Seeley felt a wave of suspicion, thought, Yankees

wouldn't know if I was a captain, or cavalry, neither. The men all looked at him, seemed to recognize authority, one of them the plantation owner. Seeley understood now. "You boys are working for Sherman, right? Done caught you scavenging. You know what's happening to men like you? Both sides done agreed on an eye for an eye. Some in this army would cut your throats. Might still. Might just shoot you down where you're standing."

He stopped, was never good at empty threats. I'm not murderin' anybody in cold blood, he thought. But his words had the desired effect, one younger man breaking down in tears, dropping to his knees. "Don't kill us, sir. We ain't with Sherman. We're South Carolina. Just going home."

Seeley stared at the man, scanned the others, said, "You deserters?"

The counterfeit landowner spoke out now, seemed to speak for the rest. "We done give all we had, Captain. This army's got no use for us, no how. We all know what you know. It's over. Few more killed, maybe. But not us. We got families. Let the generals figure it out. There just ain't no more purpose to this."

"That's not up to you. You're soldiers. You don't just up and go home."

"So, what you gonna do with us? They gonna see us hang? Shoot us down in front of a whole regiment? They's horses back in them trees. Take 'em, and maybe let us go. We woulda rode on outta here, but the only way out'n them woods woulda been straight past you. Either way, we'd run out of luck."

One of the others spoke up now. "Ain't had nothing to eat in four days. These farms ain't got nothing. This fella what lived here tried taking us on with his old shotgun. Not smart. We were hungry, that's all."

"Shut up!"

The shout came from the imposter, and Seeley felt a sick turn inside of him, said, "Where's the farmer, then?"

"Sir!"

It was Gibson, a shout coming far back in the trees.

"What is it, Lieutenant?"

"There's horses here, sir. Six of 'em. And a grave, just dug."

Seeley looked at the imposter, said, "What your name?"

"Kincaid. Don't much matter anymore."

"You're good with a lie. You also a murderer?"

The man fell silent, his eyes turning away from Seeley's stare. The younger man on the ground close to him was crying again, a low wail.

"We's gonna hang. I know it. Help me, Lord."

The others began to sit as well, the last sign of their surrender. Seeley saw Gibson leading the horses out of the trees, carrying the shotgun.

"The mounts ain't in too bad a shape, sir."

Gladstone moved forward quickly, one hand

rubbing the neck of a large mare. "No, they ain't in bad shape a'tall. This one'll do fine. Call her Lucy Junior."

Gladstone glanced back at Seeley, permission he knew he wouldn't need. Seeley motioned to the horse, said, "She's yours, Sergeant. Let's get the rest back to the camp, and these fellows, too."

Gladstone called out to Gibson, "Say, Lieutenant. I spent some mighty fine times shooting a scattergun just like that one. You mind if I have that thing?"

Gibson looked at the shotgun in his hands, shrugged. "No use to me. That okay with you, Captain?"

Seeley nodded, and Gladstone took the shotgun, aimed down the barrels. "Yes, sir. I got something for Kilpatrick now."

Gibson said, "What you gonna do for buckshot?"

Gladstone eyed the imposter, Kincaid, said, "I'm bettin' this fellow here knows where's there's plenty. He wouldn't a taken this thing if it was useless."

Seeley ignored the banter, looked at the prisoners, the six men sitting in an uneven row, one man now lying flat in the thick grass. He could see how scrawny they were, rags for shirts, threadbare coats split at the seams, their shoes an odd mismatch. He realized now, they had stolen those, and if it wasn't from this farmer, there would be others in their wake.

"Let's go. Get up. General Wheeler will want to get a look at you, maybe ask you some questions."

Kincaid seemed to perk up at the name. "Looking forward to that. He'll be proud, for sure. We done tole a bunch of folks that we ride with him. Didn't help us get anything to eat, though. One fellow near took my head off with an axe."

Seeley knew this would matter to Wheeler, that these men had never been cavalry, had most certainly made a contribution to the stories of Wheeler's abuse of the civilians. But these weren't just raiders, stealing food from wealthy landowners. Seeley wondered about the man who actually owned this land, if he had offered them anything to eat, if he had given them a plea for his life. In the end, he thought, he might have gone for the shotgun, tried to fight these men off by himself. And now he's buried in his own woods.

"Good job, young captain. You're right. These varmints have caused me no end of trouble. We'll get them off to Augusta at first light. There's gotta be a hundred more just like 'em, scattered from here to Savannah. General Hardee told me about the desertions. He lost a good flock of men who just decided to go home. Got no patience for that, Captain, none at all. Man joins up to fight, he puts aside thoughts of his wife, or anything else he left behind him."

"Sir, it's pretty clear they murdered a civilian as well. The farmer."

"Damn. You know his name?"

Seeley thought of Gibson's unflattering nick-name. "No, sir. Won't be hard to find out."

"All right, but there's no time for that now. I want your men up in the saddle at first light. I've got a reception planned for Kilpatrick. Think of that, young captain. You might be the one puts a bullet through his heart. Prefer that to be me, but I'll accept the outcome regardless. Report to Colonel McLemore, then go on back to your men. Get them ready for a good ride tomorrow."

Seeley saluted, Wheeler returning it. He moved away through the small house, glanced around, small portraits on the wall, thought, Another land-owner rooted out of his home. He saw children now, had missed them when he was called in to see Wheeler.

"Well, hey now. This your home, then?" There were two girls, younger than five, a boy slightly older. The girls pulled back, the boy standing defiant, and Seeley tried to appear as friendly as he could. "Where's your mama?"

"Right here, soldier."

Seeley turned to the voice, saw the woman in a plain drab dress, anger on her face. "Mighty nice family, ma'am."

"You can get yourself out of here right now. I might have to put up with a general, but I ain't gotta entertain no thief-of-a-horse soldier."

Seeley tried to force a smile, tipped his hat, stepped

out of the house. He was in the cold now, bright blue above him, couldn't avoid wondering about the father. Never see the fathers, he thought. Either hiding from us, or off getting shot at. He couldn't avoid thoughts of Katie, agonized over the image of his wife, that he might forget what she looked like. It had been many months, his transition from released prisoner to horse soldier far too brief. The letters were nonexistent, the cavalry too often in some place where the Yankees had cut the lines, occupied the trails. He had written a handful of letters himself, still carried them in his pocket, no faith that they could actually reach her in Memphis. God, but I miss her, he thought. He fought that, knew he had to stay in the moment, focus on getting his men fit to ride. Wheeler's admonition rolled into him now, the lecture about desertions.

"Man joins up, he puts aside thoughts of his wife. . . ."

Wheeler's wrong, he thought. I feel sorry for a man can just forget what he has waiting for him at home. Those deserters, they remembered it all, maybe too much. Killed for it. That's what this war is doing. What it's doing to me. God, I just want to go home.

He moved toward his horse, past a courier just arriving, more horsemen moving past, Wheeler's staff at work, other men carrying orders, dispatches, as though nothing were different, the war moving on as usual. He took the reins from a groom, climbed up on the horse, felt the animal sag under his weight, couldn't escape Gladstone's warning, He's hurting. Seeley leaned down, patted the horse's neck, but there was nothing he could say, no kind words that would make any of this better. He straightened, reins in hand, pulled the animal toward the side, rode slowly into the road.

CHAPTER THIRTY-FIVE

SEELEY

AIKEN,
SOUTH CAROLINA—FEBRUARY 11, 1865

They had reached the town well in advance of any Federal cavalry, Wheeler placing his men carefully. Down every side street, squads were positioned as a blockade to any unsuspecting horsemen, while along the main street of the town, Wheeler anchored a heavy concentration of his men, hidden as well as possible as a perfect ambush for Kilpatrick's main column. The ruse was a simple one, to remain hidden until Kilpatrick's men were well within the town's limits, then spring on them from the flanks. Wheeler placed his men with the confident expectation that Kilpatrick would be brazen in his foray into the town, and Wheeler had stressed to his men that surprise was their greatest weapon. No one was certain just how many men Kilpatrick led, and Wheeler had considered the possibility that his men would be greatly outnumbered. But a surprise assault was always the great equalizer, and with his men put into place well before dawn, there was little chance anyone would have the time to alert Kilpatrick to what was awaiting him.

Seeley anchored one squad to a side street just off the main avenue, an eighty-man force like so many others, staring into darkness with pounding hearts, fingering their weapons, checking and checking again their carbines, the edges of their sabers, the caps on their pistols. With the last hour of darkness came the early morning cold, the hard chill driving into the men, made worse by their nervousness. Along the main street, many of the men had dismounted, anchored into good cover, hundreds of carbines and muskets poised for that first hint of Kilpatrick's approach. On horseback, Seeley shivered along with his men, few voices, low whispers that betrayed the tension.

He was facing east, a good vantage point for observing the first hint of sunrise, a gray veil lifting slowly above the houses across the wider street. Behind him, his own men stayed close, bunched together for at least an attempt at warmth, the

horses shoulder to shoulder, some of them dancing slightly, their own brand of anxiousness. Beside
Seeley, Gladstone curled low on his horse, and Seeley looked at the older man, thought, He's sleeping.
I know it. Does this before every fight. He eyed the
shotgun, Gladstone's new prize, a sack of buckshot
hanging from the man's waist, a cartridge box filled
with blank loads, a makeshift effort that Gladstone
seemed to know well. Seeley watched the avenue
again, his horse a few yards back, flexed his gloved
fingers, the gauntlets threadbare, worn completely
through at his palms. He looked at them, nothing to
see, thought, Yankees would have gloves, certainly.
Boots, too, I suppose. The sergeant can have his
scattergun. I'll take a good warm coat and gauntlets. He flexed his fingers again, stiff and frigid, his
mind spilling over with anxious thoughts, a babble
of words that rolled through his brain. Maybe a
new pistol. This one works all right. But the Yankees have better ones, so they say. Always seemed
that way. Maybe I'll see Kilpatrick, stare him down,
my pistol against his saber. That would be glorious, truly. Wheeler would promote me for that. Or
maybe not. Maybe he wants that glory for himself. Why do they hate each other so? It's more than
Kilpatrick being a Yankee. Something else between
them, something maybe from West Point. He won't
tell stories, though. Keeps all that to himself. Just
spews out his orders and his ideas and we all just try
to do the job. He stared out across the wider street

again, saw movement on the other side, another squad of men waiting there as well, hidden as best they could be. Nobody shoots straight ahead, he thought. Ride hard, straight into the flank, use sabers first. Pistols maybe. Let the dismounted troops have their go first. We'll just pick up the pieces.

The whispers were growing behind him, and he glanced back, thought of quieting them, but that would require more noise than he wanted to make. They know what to do, he thought. Nobody's going to raise Cain with some rebel yell until we've got them where we need them.

He stared upward, over the roof of the house across the way, the daylight creeping forward, stars just now fading away. Hurry! He strained his eyes, tried to see details on the house, could make out the unevenness of the street, the gray sky growing lighter, another long minute, lighter still. He glanced back, Gladstone now up straight in the saddle, no more napping, the faces of his men becoming visible, eyes on him, some staring past him into the street. He turned again to the front, flexed frozen fingers one more time, cursed the thin gloves, curled his stiff toes inside his worn boots, flexed them as well, rubbing them against the inside of the boots, another piece of agony. Boots. I need boots. Grab some prisoners, for certain.

And now he heard the snort of horses, soft hoof-beats, the low whispers behind him silenced. His heart thundered, his cold fingers gripping the saber, one hand squeezing the leather reins, pulling the horse to attention. His senses were focused, straining for more detail, but his eyes gave way to his ears, pulling in every sound, the light clank of a mess kit, another snort, soft hoofbeats in the dirt street. The thought flashed through him, a lightning bolt of excitement. They don't know we're here! It's worked! He scolded himself now, Pay attention! There won't be any orders, nobody to tell us when to attack. You'll know when you see them, when they pass, let them go on by. Wait for the first volley, the only order that matters. His hand shook on the grip of his saber, his fingers tightening again, his heels slowly pressing into the flanks of the horse, the animal protesting silently, bouncing him, Seeley loosening the pressure, a silent apology.

The flash of a volley came well down the street, but it wasn't many, and he felt a stab of panic, too few! He eased the horse forward, tried to keep calm, heard a chorus of voices, shouts, and now horses emerged from across the street, an officer too jumpy, more horses moving quickly in front of him, musket fire in scattered volleys. He felt a burst of cold, shouted out, "Go! Let's go!"

They followed him into the street, and he saw, far down, a melee engulfing men on both sides, flashes of fire, swords in the air. He searched the side streets, frantic, more horsemen emerging, confusion, no orders, but the fight was down the way, and he pointed his saber, spurred the horse, his men following, joining in with more squads, the men moving forward in one chaotic mass.

He saw the first Yankees now, a violent fight, swords clashing, horses pushing past more horses, pistol shots from every quarter. He searched for a target, so many men seemingly engulfed in the mix, men on the ground, his horse moving past them, a man in blue, pistol in his hand, firing to the side. Seeley screamed out, nonsensical, his own piece of the rebel yell, pushed the horse past the man, his saber coming down across the man's chest, the blow nearly ripping the sword from Seeley's hand. But the man collapsed, the horse empty of its rider, and he searched for more, saw men on the ground, fists, clubbed muskets, the stink of smoke from the pistol fire. He drove forward, another man in blue, coming straight toward him, sword high, terror and fury on the man's face, and Seeley saw the blade coming down, bent low, the blade impacting his horse, Seeley pushing past, away now. More shots came, some close to him, others down a side street, men scattering, a piece of the fight driving that way. He turned, searched, saw men grappling on horseback, both falling, more pistol shots, heard a thunderous blast behind him, a familiar yell, realized it was Gladstone, the shotgun. The gun fired again, smoke enveloping Seeley and he turned that way, saw a Yankee falling toward him, coming down against the rump of Seeley's horse.

The fight continued to swirl out in every direction, a sudden surge by more of Wheeler's men, a fresh charge into a crowd of tangled troopers. He raised the saber again, felt a sharp pain in his shoulder, the sword ripped away, cried out, surprise, anger, the saber just . . . gone. He jerked the pistol from its holster, saw blue, a man aiming his own pistol, and Seeley pointed, fired, too quick, too high. He aimed again, a brief moment, clarity, silence, the Yankee turning toward him, eyes locking, the man raising his pistol, furious eyes, his arm coming up slowly, dreamlike motion, the pistol a few feet from Seeley's face, the blast, the flash blinding him. Seeley closed his eyes, flinching, curling up in his mind, the sulfur smoke blowing past him, and he opened his eyes, the man still there, the pistol coming up, the man cocking, and now Seeley aimed, shaking hand, the pistol moving all across the man's body, firing now, the man stabbed back, backing off his horse, eyes on Seeley still, surprise, terror, the man now gone.

The noise seemed to fill him again, the fight in every direction, surging horses, more firing, hard shouts, men down in every part of the street. Now men were moving off, men in blue, horses scrambling to escape. From the street came more musket fire, carbines, but the Yankees were moving away. He spurred the horse, pursuit, others doing the same, but the Yankees were prepared, a line of men with carbines of their own, covering their retreat. The musket balls whistled past him, one man close beside him falling, a horse going down, awful scream. The line of Yankees seemed to dissolve, riding away quickly, and now more shouts, close behind him, orders, a voice of calm, strange, out of place. The order came again, firm, distinct, and he turned, saw Wheeler riding forward, passing over the bodies of men from both sides.

"Pursue! No quarter!"

The men obeyed, Seeley responding with instinct, spurring the horse, the pistol in his hand. He moved with a hundred more, along the wide avenue, out of the town, the dust rising up in a cloud, the mad retreat of the Yankees. Around him, men were picking up the call, the cheer of the victor, chasing a wounded prey. The road started uphill, the horses slowing, a new sound, beyond the dust, a hard cry. Seeley saw them now, a thick line of Yankees, driving their mounts toward Wheeler's men, sabers high. He felt paralyzed, the men in blue driving closer, some firing from around him, but the Yankees came on, were there now, sabers whipping across and down, men responding, more grappling, men going down, both sides. Seeley focused on one man moving straight toward him, a hard gallop, the man up in the saddle, Seeley the target. He jerked on the horse's reins, turned to the side, the Yankee passing, turning his horse abruptly, and Seeley held the pistol, had no idea how many shots he had fired, tried to see the percussion caps, foolish distraction, the Yankee coming for him again.

"You'll die now, rebel!"

Seeley ducked low, the man's saber ripping Seeley's hat away, a dull blow across Seeley's back. He tried to turn the horse, pointed the pistol, fired, no aim, no time, the man on him again. Now there was a hard blast to one side, a burst of smoke, the Yankee disappearing, his horse moving past Seeley riderless. Seeley heard the cackle, familiar, saw Gladstone, the shotgun pointed forward.

"Pitiful. You're a better shot than that, Captain. I ain't gonna be there to save your apples every time."

Seeley felt a hard shaking in his hands, glanced at the pistol, then back to Gladstone. "Thank you."

"Yep. That's a bottle of spirits, for sure. Lookee. They're giving it up. Moving off. Done the right thing, though. Stopped us in our tracks. Brave devils. Not all of 'em made it outta here."

Seeley followed Gladstone's gaze, men writhing on the ground, more horses down, but Gladstone was right, the Yankees were pulling back, the orders flowing across the men, "Hold here! Damn their souls! Damn it all!"

He turned to the voice, saw Wheeler, red-faced anger. The calm returned, men gathering into line, expectant, more men coming out into the avenue, coming from fights of their own, down the side streets. Wheeler faced them now, a hard glare, spoke slowly, precise words, words to slice a man in half.

"Somebody fired too soon. I don't know who did it, but somebody gave it away. They were coming, sure as rain, right into the trap. Somebody got . . . excited. We had him." Wheeler held out his hand, made a slow fist. "We had him right there."

Dibrell was there, more of the senior officers, and Dibrell said, "We whipped him, sir. Drove 'em straight away! Glorious victory!"

Wheeler turned away from him, said nothing, stared off toward the Yankee retreat. The others seemed unwilling to speak out, and finally Wheeler said, "I saw him. He was the first one to ride away. He's up there on that far hill, watching us. He knows we whipped him. And he knows he got away."

Dibrell seemed oblivious to Wheeler's black mood, said, "Sir, you likely saved Augusta. They won't try that again."

Wheeler turned toward Dibrell, scanned the faces of the other senior officers. "I don't care a whit about Augusta. We had an opportunity. We just gave him the chance to do this again. Because somebody got excited."

Others began to move closer now, and Seeley saw Colonel Hagan, the Alabaman.

"Sir, I regret it was a few of my men. We were dismounted, awaiting the pass of the enemy. Some of my men couldn't wait. I deeply regret this, sir."

Seeley was surprised at the man's admission, knew of Hagan from various fights around Atlanta, a man seemingly made for higher command. Wheeler stared at him, said, "I shall condemn no man for enthusiasm, Colonel. But we shall have to confront Kilpatrick again. Would you suggest how your men might redeem themselves?"

"We shall redeem ourselves by your orders, sir. What you instruct in the future, we shall carry out. If you wish us to assault the enemy on our own, we shall do so."

Seeley watched Wheeler's reaction, could see that Wheeler had a good deal of respect for Hagan.

"That time shall come, Colonel."

Riders came in from the direction of the retreat, a squad led by one of the Tennesseans, Captain Jarvis.

"Sir! The Yankees have withdrawn to a creek crossing some four miles out. They are preparing a defensive position, sir!"

Seeley knew Jarvis, one of Forrest's former troopers, and Wheeler seemed to regard him as he had any of Forrest's men.

"Would you have us remain here and moan about that, Captain?"

"No, sir. It is a strong position, though, sir."

Wheeler lowered his head, then said, "Fall into formation. We know where the enemy is, and we shall teach him a lesson. If we cannot surprise him, we shall crush him, man against man."

Jarvis seemed to accept Wheeler's judgment, made a quick glance toward Seeley, who understood the meaning. Seeley felt helpless, had a sickening stir inside of him, that what Wheeler wanted to do now was simply wrong. But he could say nothing, looked toward his own division commander, Dibrell, who seemed to embrace every suggestion Wheeler made. Dibrell said, "We are prepared, sir. On your order. Let us teach those devils what it is to trespass on our soil."

They moved out as quickly as formations could be assembled, the urgency obvious, not allowing Kilpatrick's men to establish a strong line, or even worse, not encouraging the Yankees to pull back farther, escaping altogether. But Wheeler's efforts confronted well-prepared blue-coats, Kilpatrick's men greeting Wheeler's approach with well-aimed musket fire and the overwhelming firepower of repeating carbines. As quickly as the fight in Aiken had run its course, no more than a half hour, the confrontation Wheeler seemed so badly to need dissolved in a hail of Yankee musket balls. If there was to be another confrontation, another opportunity for Wheeler to rip his saber through the heart of Judson Kilpatrick, it would come at another time.

With complaints against Wheeler's men continuing, even Hardee couldn't prevent the inevitable reaction from the impatience of the War Department. Confederate cavalryman Wade Hampton had been sent southward from Lee's army in Virginia, had focused most of his efforts toward the protection of Augusta. In the Confederate hierarchy, Hampton carried considerable respect, and, he was a native South Carolinean. If South Carolina was to assist its own cause, the people had to embrace a hero, someone who could inspire the civilians to support their army. On February 17, less than a week after the triumphant, yet hollow victory at Aiken, Joe Wheeler's authority over the cavalry forces confronting Sherman was diminished by the elevation of Hampton to that command.

Reacting to the hammer blow of Wheeler's loss of authority, combined with the frustrating futility in their attempt to strike yet another meaningful blow against their Federal adversaries, Wheeler's men began to desert the army in even greater numbers, driven away from their cause by discouragement and despair. For Captain Seeley and his diminishing force, the orders would come again very soon, the call once more to track down and scout the Federal advance, seeking some vulnerability, an opportunity to damage Sherman's army any way they still could.

Though Kilpatrick may have been bruised and humiliated at Aiken, the defeat was no great catastrophe for Sherman's army. Despite a wave of congratulatory praise heaped on Wheeler for his success, letters from Governor Magrath, accolades from various ranking Southern generals, the victory that Wheeler's men tried to embrace proved even more hollow than they knew. Kilpatrick's men had made their advance through Aiken as part of a well-planned feint toward Augusta, one more part of Sherman's plan to keep the Confederate command guessing. Ultimately, the fight at Aiken proved to be a distraction that only benefited the Federals, who had already extended their march deeper into the heart of South Carolina, well away from any threat to Augusta.

CHAPTER THIRTY-SIX

SHERMAN

As for the wholesale burnings, pillage,
devastation, committed in South Carolina, magnify all I have said of Georgia
some fifty-fold. . . .

—DAVID P. CONYNGHAM,
The New York Herald

The trail of destruction began with the first
advance of Sherman's men, the soldiers as
aware as their commander that South Carolina was a very special place, destined for the kind
of punishment that went beyond scavenging for
supplies. Hardeeville was among the first towns
to feel the torch, the destruction there beginning
with the firing of an old church, spreading to the

business and government buildings, as well as the railroad depot. From there the devastation spread toward Orangeburg, Barnwell, and Lexington, the troops justifying their complete disregard for civilian property by the simple explanation that South Carolina, more than any other state in the Confederacy, had given birth to the rebellion, and thus should feel the greatest pain. For some the destruction was as much sport as it was military necessity, most of that kind of viciousness coming from Kilpatrick's cavalry. With the embarrassment of the fight at Aiken behind him, Kilpatrick moved his men northward, obeying Sherman's instructions to protect the western flank of the army. But Kilpatrick took Sherman's orders a step further. As his horsemen made their way through the various towns and river crossings, they probed and tested what kind of resistance the rebels might be putting in their way. But the rebels were barely there at all, scatterings of home guard and state militia, who vanished as quickly as the Federal cavalry appeared. With little danger confronting them, Kilpatrick's men followed the lead of their commander, who showed no quarter to any Southern towns along their path.

The advance into South Carolina had not been completely free of confrontation. As Howard's men moved away from Pocotaligo, they had pushed toward the Salkehatchie River, and there Hardee had established a stout defensive line along the far banks. Already, as they drove closer to the Salkehatchie, the Federal troops had been forced to slog their way through the misery of swamplands and bog holes for many miles, and the low plains around the Salkehatchie were no different. Still swollen from the extensive rains, the river was certain to tax the abilities of Sherman's engineers, the men charged with laying the pontoon bridges. Adding to that challenge was a steady dose of artillery fire from batteries spread along the rebel side of the river. But, as had happened all through Georgia, Hardee's men were too few, and Sherman's too determined to make their crossing. With a force Hardee could not match, Oliver Howard's lead divisions spread out in flanking movements, and continued to brave the rebel fire until the bridges had been laid. Once the rebels realized that their position was untenable, they had no alternative but to pull away. It was Hardee's first real confrontation with Sherman's army, and it ended with no surprises, save one. Hardee never expected that Sherman's army would use the route they did, straight through the worst of the swamplands that Hardee and Beauregard had convinced themselves would be such an impassable barrier to any army's advance. To the Confederate generals' disbelief, the Federal troops made their advance through the most miserable conditions many of those soldiers had ever experienced, wading chest-deep through lowlands that might span a mile or more across, the officers struggling to maintain a column of march in some woodlands where no roads had ever existed. On the primary routes, the engineers pressed many of the troops into the kind of labor they had never performed before, working as sappers, cutting the small trees and saplings the engineers could lay as a carpet on the muddy trails, corduroying the roads to provide some support for the wagons and artillery.

Once past the Salkehatchie, Sherman understood just how effective his feints had been. While the geography offered more obstacles to his army than he expected, the rebels did not. As he moved the two wings deeper into South Carolina, it became evident that the greatest concentration of enemy troops were still mired in the uncertainty of their senior commanders, heavy garrisons holding forts in Augusta and Charleston. Between the two cities, South Carolina lay mostly unprotected.

As the infantry wound its way in the cavalry's wake, the destruction became a contagion, the troops still scavenging for food, for loot, inspired and energized by the burned-out buildings in every place the cavalry had already been. The pickings were mostly slim, the lower part of the state not nearly the fertile breadbasket they had found in Georgia. Adding to the wrath of the troops was the march itself, the men impatient with the slog through such miserable countryside, only to find that the occasional farm offered little reward for their troubles.

If the goal of the army seemed to be punishment, Sherman held to a slightly different purpose: conquest, with an eye toward laying bare the illusion that South Carolina could protect herself from his army. He understood, even encouraged the army's animosity toward the birthplace of the war, and he had very little objection to the columns of black smoke that welcomed him into every small town. But all along the way, he studied the maps, Captain Poe's careful rendering of the roadways and intersections that would eventually lead the army to Sherman's next major goal. On February 16, while Hardee sat perched in Charleston, the Confederate commander still expected to learn that Sherman had swung his army that way, still watched for a flotilla of Federal gunboats that he anticipated would steam through the mouth of Charleston Harbor. Instead, Sherman's men continued their drive through the center of the state, and soon after clearing the misery of the lowlands, the vanguard of Howard's wing arrived on the high bluffs overlooking Congaree Creek, a small tributary of the Congaree River, which framed the city of Columbia.

As his army gathered into camps across the river from the state capital, Sherman rode forward to see the place for himself. He expected a fight, or at least some effort by the rebels to hold him away.

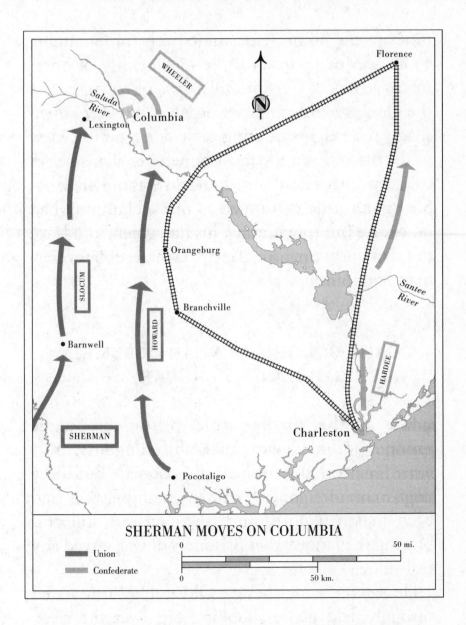

SHERMAN MOVES ON COLUMBIA

Union
Confederate

0   50 mi.

0   50 km.

The scouts told him a very different story. The city lay virtually undefended, the only defensive forces positioned there a small body of Wade Hampton's newly arrived cavalry. Despite Hampton's proud boasts that he had come south to rescue the fortunes of his home state, the citizens of Columbia could see for themselves the inevitability of Sherman's advance. On the hills west of town, across the Congaree, blue masses began to fill every open space, the heights offering each side a perfect view of the other. Even the most hopeful civilians began to accept that Hampton's bravado was only talk. As Sherman's army continued to mass, Hampton had no choice but to withdraw his horsemen, and leave the citizens of the capital city to whatever fate Sherman had in mind.

"CAMP SORGHUM," NEAR COLUMBIA, SOUTH CAROLINA—FEBRUARY 16, 1865

It was another of the former prison camps, the ground potholed with makeshift dugouts, burrowed by the hands of Federal prisoners. But those men were long gone, Sherman assuming they had been marched northward, their captors still embracing the fantasy that prisoners of war served any real value.

He sat on a log, beside Oliver Howard, stared through field glasses, looking out over the river, past the skeletal remains of the bridge.

"Burned it themselves?"

Howard glassed as well, said, "Yes, sir. Knew we were coming. It was the smart thing to do."

"The smart thing to do is surrender, and end this

damned war. All they've done is delay us for a day or so. I want Captain Poe working his pontoons with all speed. He's getting mighty good at it. I'm interested in more than this view."

There was an artillery blast, down to the right, a burst of smoke rising up through low trees. Sherman looked that way, said, "Who the hell's firing? And what are they firing at?"

Howard had no answer, the two men rising, Sherman nursing the stiffness in his hips, the ride through the rugged ground plaguing him. He stretched his back as he walked, camps spread out to both sides, all across the hillsides, and as always, the salutes poured his way, the calls of "Uncle Billy." He ignored that now, heard another blast, quickened his pace toward the rising smoke. There were shouts down below him, and he glanced that way, saw men with hats in the air. But they weren't paying any mind to him. He saw now, the shells were impacting in the city, bursts of fire and smoke. He moved quickly down the hill, any pains in his bones forgotten, a low fury building inside him. Howard was struggling to keep up with him, and Sherman called out, "Did you order anyone to start an artillery assault?"

"No, sir. It wasn't me."

It's your people, Sherman thought. But there would be time for chewing out Howard later, if there was guilt to be assigned. The cannons erupted again, and Sherman was there now, a battery of six guns, smoke rolling around them. He stopped, tried to catch his breath, saw an officer, the man wide-eyed at Sherman's approach. The man threw up a salute, said, "Captain DeGress, sir. Playing havoc with those rebels, that we are."

Sherman ignored the salute, said, "Who authorized you to begin your own artillery barrage?"

The captain slowly dropped his hand, pointed toward the town, stammered his explanation. "Sir, we have spotted considerable cavalry moving about in the streets. The intersections where we can plainly see them provides excellent targets for my men. Good training for the newer crews. These are twenty-pound Parrotts, sir. They can do the job, I assure you."

"I know what kind of guns they are, Captain. Have you not noticed that you are conducting a one-man war?"

"Sir, I believed it was the prudent thing to do. I am convinced that there is a considerable body of rebel infantry in the city, awaiting our crossing. Some of the infantry officers have confided in me that they expect a heavy fight once we push across the river. I thought it best to, um, loosen them up a bit."

Sherman looked at Howard. "Have your scouts mentioned any infantry positions over there?"

Howard was staring hard at DeGress, said, "No, sir. Captain, did **anyone** give you authorization to fire on the city?"

DeGress was clearly nervous now. "No, sir. I just thought it was prudent. The infantrymen seemed to appreciate it."

Sherman rolled a fresh unlit cigar through his teeth. "It wasn't prudent. Infantrymen appreciate any shelling that isn't aimed at them. You will stop firing immediately. We have not yet demanded surrender of the place, and shelling civilians makes us look like barbarians. If you actually see some of that infantry, you will inform me. I haven't seen any, and don't expect to. Because they're not there."

DeGress saluted again, called out a cease-fire order to his men, who had already heard the conversation, the crews gathering closer, more interested now in looking at Sherman than in anything across the river.

Sherman waited for the last of the smoke to clear, raised his glasses, scanned, focused on the large rail depot. There was considerable commotion there, reports already received by Sherman that trains had been vacating the city all through the night. He could see movement, a crowd still moving close to the place, said, "Great deal of activity at the rail depot. Those damned people can't leave here fast enough."

Howard said, "Sir, Colonel Stone's men have reported large bands of Negroes, already doing a fair share of looting. The rebels had apparently hauled a good deal of grain to the depot, anticipating its removal."

Stone's brigade had been the first troops into the

city, crossing against what little resistance the rebel cavalry had offered. Sherman knew the men had suffered for their march, the rations meager, the swampy advance preventing any real foraging for something better to eat than what they might have had in their knapsacks.

"You tell Colonel Stone we need whatever's there. Grain, or anything else."

"Yes, sir."

He looked at DeGress again. "All right, Captain, you're so damned eager to light up the place. I want you to drop a few shells near the rail depot. Scare off any of those people who might be hoping to walk off with **our** supplies." He paused, scanned the city again. "And, while you're at it, drop a few shells on their state capitol. That's something the men will enjoy."

COLUMBIA,
SOUTH CAROLINA—FEBRUARY 17, 1865

There had been some shelling throughout the night, a scattering of rebel artillery firing from well beyond the river, impacting directly into the camps of his men. With the dawn, Sherman had inspected the damage, the casualties, his anger rolling into a red-faced explosion.

"Savages! It's murder, simple as that! Killing men while they sleep. It's that damned Hampton. Despise that man. Perfect example of everything about the South that needs to be wiped away."

His staff had seemed to wilt under his tirade, though most of them had been audience to this kind of fury before. He stormed away from them, moved out to the open bluffs, saw Poe's men at work on the pontoons, the bridge mostly complete, bluecoats adding to the men already on the far side of the river. He kept walking, his boots kicking up loose ground, the rough tracks made by horses, the camps of the men, most of those shelters now coming down. He ignored that, continued to walk, venting the steam from the boil inside him.

"Sir?"

He didn't want company, knew the voice, knew there would be no escape. Sherman stopped, stared at the work on the bridge, waited for Hitchcock. "What the hell do you want with me, Major?"

Hitchcock was breathing heavily, reached Sherman now, seemed to hesitate, then said, "Sir, I'm just trying to understand your thinking."

Sherman looked at the man, a wilting stare, but Hitchcock seemed up to the challenge. Sherman leaned closer to him, said, "I'm thinking every minute of the day, Major. What the hell are you talking about?"

Hitchcock let out a long breath, adjusted his glasses, Sherman forcing himself to wait for what was coming. "Sir, the shelling last evening. We took a few casualties, to be certain. Not many, though.

I have always believed that every life is precious, of course. But I have learned that in the army, there is always human cost, and if the casualties are few, it is a blessing."

"So?"

"Last night. Was that not an action justified by our shelling the city? All along this march, I have observed a complete disregard for the well-being of the citizens. We have fired and wrecked structures of all kinds, put people out of their homes, destroyed businesses and places of worship. I admit, it took me some weeks to accept this tactic, and I understand your thinking on that score, sir. I really do."

"So?"

"How can you hold such anger toward the enemy, just for shelling our position? Is the war only to go in our favor, sir? Is the enemy not entitled to some vengeance of his own?"

Sherman knew this was the kind of question he was going to hear often, possibly in Washington, certainly from the newspapers. He stared at Hitchcock for a long moment, saw sincerity on the man's face, the question a serious one.

"I don't have time for coddling your sensitivities, Major."

"I understand, sir. I'm still learning. My apologies for disturbing you."

"Listen to me, Major. In all that burning of towns, the raiding of plantations, everything we have left in our wake, how many civilians did I order executed?"

Hitchcock seemed surprised at the question. "None, that I can recall, sir. No, none."

"In every house fire you witnessed, were any people burned along with their goods? Were there firing squads, was there butchery of anyone not in uniform? Hell, even **in** uniform? We make a fight against those who make a fight against us. The civilians have given fuel to this war, and we have used it up by the most efficient means possible. You recall the bummers we came across, those men who had been executed? Happened more than once, and probably happened more than we'll ever know. Throats cut, left by the side of the road. All right, that's the way the enemy responds to our destruction of his property. I know the bummers have been out from my control, have taken my orders to an extreme I did not intend. But their actions accomplished exactly what I **did** intend. The enemy captured some of those men, and meted out a brutal punishment. I have no real problem with that. That's war. It just means we'll respond by doing the same. I told Kilpatrick, an eye for an eye. We've sent word into every town: You shoot at us, you burn the supplies we require, we'll respond in kind. It has worked, occasionally."

He reached into his pocket, fished around, pulled out a paper. "You recall this? Letter sent through the lines by Joe Wheeler. He says he will not burn any more cotton, if we promise not to burn any more houses. That's a rebel peculiarity, clear as day. What the hell do I care if they burn their cotton? Can't eat the stuff, and we're sure as hell not hauling it with us. Let Stanton and his minions parade out here and take it to Savannah. It's all going to end up in the U.S. Treasury anyway. But Wheeler doesn't say anything about food, grain, potatoes, any of what we value. They keep burning what these men need to eat, we'll make them pay for it. That's an eye for an eye, Major."

Sherman stuffed the paper into a coat pocket, and Hitchcock scanned his coat, said, "Do you carry every correspondence you receive on your person, sir?"

Sherman shrugged. "Easier that way. Good to have your headquarters right in your pockets."

"I suppose so, sir, though part of that is my job."

"Another part of your job is to support what this army is doing. You recall how many times the rebels laid those damned torpedoes in our path? That was murder, pure and simple. If I was to salt the ground around this city with bombs like that, there would be hell to pay. Mostly in Washington. That damned Wade Hampton calls himself an aristocrat, a Southern gentleman, thinks he's fighting for the cream of manhood, or some such nonsense. So he orders his artillery to shell sleeping men."

"I believe I understand, sir."

"Understand this, Major. We're about to march

into the capital city of South Carolina. I have no intentions of torching the place, of laying waste to the city just because of what it represents. My goal is to put my people into North Carolina as quickly as the rebels will allow that. If there's food to be had here, we'll take it. If a rebel shoots at me from a second-story window, I'll destroy his house. The rebels did us a favor by not defending this place. I'll do them a favor by marching out of here quick as we can."

By midmorning, the city's mayor, Dr. Thomas Goodwyn, had surrendered Columbia to Sherman's troops. Sherman rode into the city alongside Howard, trailed by the staffs of both men, and the latest addition to Sherman's command, General John Logan, now in command of the Fifteenth Corps. With the conclusion of the campaign to occupy Atlanta, Logan had asked for, and received, Sherman's permission for a leave of absence. The reasons stuck somewhat in Sherman's craw, that Logan had pressing political needs at home, specifically involving the 1864 election. Logan had come into the army after serving as a United States congressman, and to Sherman's annoyance, the election was a priority to Logan, despite the duties of the army. But corps command seemed acceptable to a man who certainly would rely on his military résumé to enhance his political career once the war was over. Sherman had little use for political officers of any kind, but he had been with Logan since earlier in the war, Logan performing well at Vicksburg, in particular. Now, Logan had returned, and Sherman had been gracious in allowing Logan to settle into his new command, replacing the Fifteenth's commander, Peter Osterhaus, who had ambitions of his own. Sherman agreed with the War Department to honor Osterhaus's wishes for a high-level administrative post, and now Osterhaus was on his way west, named chief of staff of the Army of the West.

Already, the Fifteenth Corps had driven out west and north of the city, anchoring along the Broad River, one of the two rivers that joined at Columbia to form the Congaree. Sherman had given orders that the remainder of his army would skirt past Columbia altogether, no need to funnel so many troops through the center of town. Sherman had pored over the maps, planning the route the two wings would follow, anticipating no great Confederate barriers until they reached North Carolina. It was still a mystery to Sherman why his ruse had been so completely effective, since surely the Confederate hierarchy had to expect that Columbia would be a likely target.

There was another surprise in the town itself. For a place so steeped in the sparks that ignited the war, the Federal troops found what Sherman saw now, that life in the city was as close to **normal** as anyone could have imagined, as though there had been no war at all. Letters were already coming to his staff, invitations where he might sleep, others missives from old friends of Sherman, from his days serving at Fort Moultrie, a young lieutenant who always seemed to attract the attention of the ladies. That attention was obvious now, notes coming from women whom Sherman tried to recall, who made it known that their husbands were off in some duty other than managing their homesteads, most likely in service to the Confederate cause. Sherman tossed those aside, had no interest in such complications. But another letter caught his attention, a note from a lady superioress, who supervised a convent school. The woman had once schooled his own daughter Minnie, at a convent school in Ohio. His response was as friendly as possible under the circumstances, that a guard would be assigned, with assurances that Sherman did not intend any destruction of private property in the city at all.

His parade passed first through the scattering of corn and cotton fields that spread along the edges of the town, and immediately he saw the reception his army was receiving. The avenue was wide, the street lined with a mass of faces, both black and white. The cheers that rolled over him seemed surreal, something in a dream, Sherman reminding himself just where he was. He tried to maintain his decorum, the stiff back, eyes straight ahead, but along every block were dozens, if not hundreds, of people who seemed to welcome him as a conquering hero. He watched them, saw the nervous movements of Lieutenant Snelling, the guards moving closer to the people, a logical precaution against any kind of trouble.

He looked up, the taller buildings, windows alive with handkerchiefs, the occasional Stars and Stripes. Howard seemed as surprised as Sherman, eased his horse closer beside him, said, "What do you make of this? You would think we had just liberated Philadelphia."

"I see it for what it is. No matter what pushed these people to make war, they recognize just how much power we have brought into their parlors. The smart ones know there isn't any point in resisting. So, they're not."

"Strange, though. Didn't expect this."

Sherman shrugged, said nothing, could see ahead to a wide square, more crowds there, mingling with men in blue. He moved that way, felt a hard gust of wind, nearly removing his hat, tapped it down with a quick pat. The air was alive with more than cheers now, and as he rode closer to the square, he saw what looked like fat snowflakes, swirling past his men like the start of a blustery storm. Flecks of white were settling against his uniform now, on the horse, and he felt one, rubbed it in his fingers. Beside him, Howard said, "Cotton?"

"Of course it is. I'd rather it be snow. I've come to hate this stuff. If it wasn't for their damned cotton crops, the English would never have made so much noise about joining up with 'em."

"Doubt that's happening now."

The wind was blowing stiffly across the wide square, propelling wisps of cotton over the crowds, the people reacting to it as though it were one more part of their celebration. Sherman spit out a piece that intruded into his mouth, looked behind him, saw McCoy, said, "Major, I'd prefer we find a head-quarters as quickly as we can. I'm about to go into a sneezing fit."

"Yes, sir. There have been invitations aplenty. I'll look into it, sir."

Sherman saw an older man, rotund, a good suit, the man making his way through the nearest crowd, hand in the air. Sherman pointed that way, the guards moving closer, the man regaling Sherman with a broad smile. Sherman stopped the horse, the man approaching, a hint of nervousness on the man's face.

"General Sherman, to be sure! I am Mayor Good-wyn. Your command was most gracious in its ac-ceptance of my note of surrender. I must beseech you, sir. Please tell me what we must do to protect these citizens. We wish no harm to come to the city, nor to any one of our residents. Is there some instruction you wish followed? I shall endeavor to obey any order you give me, sir."

Sherman saw sincerity in the man's face, thought, Doesn't seem to be just about voters.

"Do not be uneasy, sir. We have no business here other than to replenish our rations, and rest my men. We shall not delay in moving on. I have no cause to injure any private citizen, or destroy private property."

"Thank you, sir. I am greatly relieved, and am completely in your service. I might suggest an appropriate headquarters for you, sir. The residence of Mr. Blanton Duncan. He is, I believe, what you would call a displaced Union man. Kentuckian by birth. I know you will be welcome there."

"I'll find him, thank you."

There was a commotion ahead, the guard coming together, and Sherman looked that way, nudged the horse forward, heard his name, a half-dozen men pushing past the citizens. Snelling was down from his horse now, other guards following, the commotion swallowed by the sounds of the crowd. Sherman kept his focus on the men, thought, Rebel deserters, most likely. No doubt they're all ripe with precious information that I should reward them for.

Snelling looked back toward him, a positive nod from his guard, Sherman curious now. Snelling led the men closer, and Sherman saw bits of ragged blue shirts, what remained of trousers. One man spoke out, a burst of tearful emotion.

"General! Praise the Almighty! You have saved us."

Snelling said, "Sir, these men claim to be our own. Officers all. They claim to have escaped their confines at that camp outside of the town. It is just as we have seen before, sir. Their guards skedaddled, and the men found sanctuary here."

Sherman climbed down from the horse, moved past Snelling, scanned the faces, gaunt, sunburned, another man speaking up.

"General, I am Captain James Otis, 5th Iowa Volunteers, sir. We are most grateful for your presence here, sir. We have freed ourselves from confinement."

Sherman studied the men, saw the childlike joy on each face, tears, thankfulness. He felt himself tightening, tried to hold it in, said, "You men are a testament to the spirit of this army. You are safe now." He turned, pointed to the horsemen behind him. "All of you, that man is General Howard. Once we have reached a headquarters, report to him. He shall provide for your comfort, and make necessary arrangements for you to accompany us."

One man pulled a scrap of paper from his pocket, said, "Sir, I am Major Byers, adjutant of the 5th Iowa. Please accept this. It would honor me if you would read it at your leisure. Please, sir."

Sherman stuffed the paper in his pocket, held out his hand, the man taking it. He felt the man's rough skin, the bones barely hidden, said, "Major, follow along with us, and present yourself to General Howard. He will give you rations. A doctor shall examine you. You are safe now, Mr. Byers."

"Thank you, sir."

Sherman moved to his horse, climbed up, Howard smiling at him. Howard said, "I yearn for these kinds of days, General. Instead of mourning casualties, we deliver men from their captivity."

Sherman nudged the horse forward, the guards moving out in front again. "I don't mourn casualties, Oliver. I try to inflict them. I would suspect that those men would agree to do the same, should the opportunity arise, especially for any rebel who stands guard in a prison. Let us see if we can provide for that."

They reached another square, the storm of cotton still blowing out around them, more cheers from civilians, many of those faces black now. Behind him, Dayton called out, "Sir, that's the depot, up ahead. Not much left."

Sherman saw smoke rolling up from the blackened frame of the building, another building beside it, and on the platform, an enormous mound of cotton bales. The wind was whipping hard at the smoldering wreckage, the fire spreading to the cotton, other mounds of cloth bags. Men were moving ahead quickly, calling out for assistance, and he motioned to Dayton.

"Go. See what's in those cloth sacks. Cotton I don't care about. But there should be some rations, grain and whatnot."

Dayton was past him quickly, other aides, more

soldiers adding to the rush. Other soldiers were there already, coats waving, low flames beaten out. Dayton held up a handful of corn from one of the smoldering sacks, and Sherman nodded, thought, Good. At least there's still something to put in the supply wagons.

To one side, Howard said, "Another fire down that street. Appears to be cotton. There's smoke over that way as well."

Sherman saw citizens gathering at the low flames, a vain effort to extinguish the windblown fire that had engulfed a full bale. There were soldiers as well, and Sherman moved that way, prepared to give them a stern order, to help the civilians. But he heard their chorus, directed now toward him.

"It's Uncle Billy! We're in for it now!"

The others seemed to stumble about the man, and he saw the jug, said to Howard, "These men are intoxicated. Damn it all! You'd think these people would hide their whiskey, or at least send it off with the rebels. I want provost guards at every main intersection. I'll not have looting from a bunch of corned-up soldiers. You understand me, General?"

He knew Howard had no tolerance for drunken behavior, could see more men emerging from a side street, another jug, one man tumbling down face-first. Howard was already in motion, orders to his staff, and Sherman pulled on the reins, turned the horse away, saw Dayton coming back.

"Not your job to put out fires, Major. McCoy should report back to us soon. I've had enough of this day. Send an aide out to find him. Every one of these damned people seemed jubilant that I'm here. I want to know if that mayor was right about the house we can use."

Dayton spoke to an aide, the man riding off quickly, and Sherman looked toward the drunken soldiers again, could not avoid the contrast to the escaped prisoners. He thought of the names, Byers, Otis. Those men have honor. They survived an ordeal most of us will never understand. And now we show them this kind of foolishness, shameful outrage. These citizens won't be in such a celebratory way if they get our soldiers intoxicated.

He saw McCoy now, riding quickly toward him, the aide riding beside.

"Sir, we have a suitable place. The mayor was correct, sir. I spoke to Mr. Duncan. Indeed a Kentucky man, most gracious. His door is open to us, at our leisure."

Sherman felt the ache in his bones now, thought, I could use a bit of leisure. "Let's go, Major. Lead the way."

McCoy moved out, Sherman behind, the staff following. Sherman scanned the sky again, the wind even harder now, the storm of white whirling above him, small cyclones, flecks blowing against every house, every shop, the street coated with a thin carpet of cotton.

DUNCAN HOUSE, COLUMBIA, SOUTH CAROLINA—FEBRUARY 17, 1865

The room was nothing like he had become spoiled by in Savannah, but the staff had settled him quickly, his first moment alone now since he came into the city. He removed his coat, the pockets thick with papers, thought of his description to Hitchcock, my headquarters in my uniform. They don't understand that, he thought. Maybe Hitchcock takes offense at it, as though I'm depriving him of his usefulness. He does try, I credit him for that. He pulled a handful of papers from one pocket, tossed them on a small desk in the room, spread them out, quick scan. He did the same from another pocket, various dispatches, notes from some of the townspeople. Discard those, he thought. Wouldn't do to have Ellen clean my soiled uniform only to find I've been corresponding with strange women. Whether or not I've actually spoken to them, or whether or not they're strange, probably doesn't matter. He pulled out another paper now, had forgotten what it was, the paper torn, yellowed, a smear of dirt. He opened it, saw penciled handwriting, the paper completely covered by verses. What the hell is this? He thought of the escaped prisoners now, the name Byers, thought, He wanted me to have this in the worst way. Something of meaning, no doubt, to him anyway.

Sherman read now, his eyes sliding slowly along each line.

> **Our campfires shone bright on the mountain**
> **That frowned on the river below,**
> **As we stood by our guns in the morning,**
> **And eagerly watched for the foe;**
> **When a rider came out of the darkness**
> **That hung over mountain and tree,**
> **And shouted, "Boys up and ready!**
> **For Sherman will march to the sea!"**
> **Then sang we a song of our chieftain,**
> **That echoed over river and lea;**
> **And the stars of our banner shone brighter**
> **When Sherman marched down to the sea!**

He lowered the paper, said aloud, "My God. This man is a poet."

He read on, five verses in total, sat on the bed, his eyes fixed still on the paper. He tried to picture the man, rough-bearded, ragged clothes. He was a major, Sherman thought. Adjutant. Well, this is impressive as hell.

"Major Dayton!"

He waited, Dayton peering through the door.

"Yes, sir?"

"Read this. Major Hitchcock, here if you please!"

Dayton seemed curious, took the paper, cradled it carefully, read, his eyes widening. "We should show this to Mr. Conyngham, sir. This is worthy of print."

Hitchcock was there now, Dayton handing him the paper without comment. Hitchcock scanned, then seemed to concentrate, adjusted his glasses.

Sherman said, "What do you think of that, Major?"

Hitchcock handed the paper to Dayton, said, "It's as perfect an example as I can imagine, sir. The men are devoted to you, and all you've accomplished. This fellow is something of a poet, no doubt."

"That's what I said. What the hell do we do about this? Man was an adjutant in the 5th Iowa."

Hitchcock thought a moment, smiled. "I know what I'd do, sir. Always room for one more adjutant. I'd put him on your staff."

Sherman took the paper from Dayton, read again. "Find him. Always room for one more adjutant."

He lay in the darkness, the windstorm battering the house, the walls seeming to shiver. Seen this before, he thought. California. A storm with no rain. Probably means something for the next few days, hell of a rain coming, or maybe snow. Infernal place, not North and not quite deep South. Caught between a normal winter and the devil's own kind of spring.

The windowpane rattled, another strong gust, and Sherman stared up, fought to push the noises away. I haven't slept through the night in, what? Twenty years? Well, maybe. Got a bed and everything, soft sheets, but no, there will be no peace. Maybe when there's **peace**. But then there'll be Ellen.

His eyes focused on a soft orange glow on one wall, and he sat up, looked again toward the window. He stood, walked that way, pulled open the sash, the wind buffeting him, the sash blowing free of his hand, a hard crash against the wall.

"Damn it all!"

He looked out, the wind watering his eyes, called out, "Major!"

It was Nichols who appeared, unexpected, and Sherman said, "What's the cause of that?"

Nichols looked toward the window, said, "There's a house afire down by the market square. Perhaps more than one."

"Go, now, be sure the provost guards are working on that. I'll not have corned-up soldiers doing damage to this place."

Nichols left quickly, Dayton now in the room.

"I saw it from downstairs, sir. Looks pretty nasty. This wind won't help the fire company, assuming they have one. Our men will no doubt lend a hand."

"If they didn't lend a hand starting it. I want the provost marshal here in the morning. If he hasn't posted guards all around this place, and all through the public squares, he'll find out what it means to carry a musket."

He lit a lantern, thought, No sleep now. There was a sudden commotion downstairs, heavy boot steps climbing up, Nichols there, breathing heavily.

"Did you run, Major?"

Nichols fought for his breath, said, "Yes, sir! It's the cotton. You recall the bales we saw burning this afternoon? There was failure to extinguish those fires, and now the wind has spread the flames to a row of houses across the street." Nichols took a deep breath. "Sir, General Woods was there, with a good number of his troops. They are working to quell the blaze."

Sherman moved to the window, stared for a long moment, the wind blowing the stink of the fire toward him. He closed the window, could see now, silhouetted by the blaze, a storm of flakes, matting against the glass. But it was not the snowlike flecks of cotton. It was ash.

Woods's troops worked through the night, aided by Hazen's division, brought quickly into the city to help fight the fires. But the wind had already won the battle, the flames spreading in one great wave from house to house, block to block. The soldiers struggled vainly, some with tools, some no more than blankets. Others moved out in front of the fire, rousing the citizens, who needed no prompting, the soldiers leading them to anyplace that was safe.

By midnight, Sherman had gone out to see for himself, could only do what his soldiers were doing, most of them helpless, the windstorm pushing the flames through the wooden homes, shops, churches, in a hellish blaze too hot for anyone to stay close. By four in the morning it was mostly over, the wind dying down, and with it the storm of ash and soot that coated every place, and every man who had struggled to hold it back.

COLUMBIA,
SOUTH CAROLINA—FEBRUARY 18, 1865

He walked through the square, struggled to breathe through the foul air, the stink of the fire now drifting through every part of the city. The staff had gone before him, seeking out the commanders, Woods, Howard, Logan, many others, the officers who had labored through the night. He stopped, saw smoke rising still, heaps of burned timbers, where a church had been. To one side, a row of homes was smoldering white ash, the citizens there already, some staring, paralyzed. He wanted to speak to them, but there was nothing to say, no promises, no assurances, all of that swept away by the towering flames that spared little in their path.

He saw Dayton, the young man's face blackened with soot, the man coughing into a soiled handkerchief. Sherman waited, felt utterly powerless, as though any authority he had in this place had been taken away by something far greater, far more powerful.

"Sir, General Howard is with the mayor, trying to find homes for the displaced."

"How many displaced?"

"A reasonable estimate, sir, is close to half the city. There could be casualties, of course, but that is not yet determined. The mayor is asking if we might remain here, to assist in the rescue."

Sherman kept his stare on an old woman, easing closer to a mound of burned rubble. He seemed to hear Dayton's words now, turned toward him, said, "Rescue what?"

"I suppose . . . the city, sir. Not sure just what he meant. They require considerable help here, sir."

Sherman felt the weight of that, the eyes that would be on him now, Washington certainly, and every city in the South. He saw a man approaching, a pad of paper in the man's hand. It was Conyngham.

"Dreadful, General. Wouldn't you say?"

"Put down the paper, Mr. Conyngham. I'll not be interviewed by you or anyone else, not now."

Conyngham obeyed, the pad slipping into his coat pocket. "You can't escape this, General. None of us can, not even me. You will be blamed."

Sherman looked toward the old woman again. "They will know. These people. We did not destroy their city."

"Of course you did. Like it or not, this is one more piece of your campaign, your legacy. Whether or not you lit the torch hardly matters. You were here. And now . . . this."

"It was the cotton. The damned wind. Maybe a few drunk soldiers, and I'll find them. We'll have inquiries. I'll talk to every damned officer in this place."

"That might soothe your conscience, General. Won't give these people much to cheer about. I would suggest you offer them something helpful. Food, certainly."

Dayton moved closer to him, said, "The mayor asked for guards, sir. To prevent mass theft, I suppose, unauthorized citizens picking up what isn't gone."

Conyngham said, "Whatever you do here, it won't be enough."

Sherman felt an explosion coming, moved away from the row of what used to be homes. "You think I planned this? Is that what your damned newspaper will print, that I burned this place, and fiddled like Nero all the while?"

"I won't. Others will. Depend on that, General."

"Who burned the cotton? Who started those fires? This is not Atlanta, there are no great military targets hereabouts. I had **no reason** to set a torch to anything here."

Dayton said, "Sir, General Woods, Colonel Stone, they said there was fire burning when they rode in. They assumed the rebel cavalry tried to burn up the cotton before we could claim it."

Conyngham moved with Sherman, a quick-paced walk. "And who will believe that? Who will want to hear that the great cavalry hero General Hampton might have begun this? No, General, this is your campaign, and your conquest, and those who believe you to be without morals will condemn you for this."

Sherman stopped, looked at Conyngham, tried to summon a fury against the man, but the impotence came in waves now, utter helplessness. He felt sick to his stomach, looked away from Conyngham, searched the streets for the route back to his headquarters, one of the few homes close to the fires that had been saved. He moved with deliberate steps, thought of the eyes, all those men in Washington and Richmond, every newspaper and every politician, every speech maker, North or South, who would take the flames from this city and use that to build a fire of their own. The thought rolled through him, spoken in soft words.

"Damn you, Conyngham. You're right."

The army remained in and around Columbia for two more days, Sherman authorizing a herd of five hundred beef cattle given to the city, the only real bounty he could offer. As well, the mayor was given one hundred muskets, with instructions to arm capable men to serve as guards, once Sherman's provosts had left the city.

On February 20, the army began to move again, leaving behind the devastation that many knew would be laid upon them. But Sherman had to keep his focus on what lay ahead, and as the men made ready to march, Sherman gave the order so familiar that Captain Poe's engineers began work immediately. They knew the routine now, the men spreading two or three miles out from Columbia in every place the rail lines ran, obeying the order they had received so many times before. They were destroying the tracks.

CHAPTER THIRTY-SEVEN

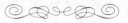

HARDEE

NORTHWEST OF CHARLESTON, SOUTH CAROLINA—FEBRUARY 26, 1865

It had rained for most of the week, adding to the gloom that spread through the army that marched with him. But the morning dawned clear and cold, the men picking up the pace on drying roads, Hardee moving along the columns talking to the men whenever he could.

Within a few days after the fire, he had learned of the extent of Columbia's destruction, what seemed to be a catastrophe for the citizens there. The harsh irony was that the fire had taken place on the same day Hardee had ordered his army to march out of

Charleston, which to the people there had been
a catastrophe of its own. There had been protests
aplenty, prominent dignitaries learning of his orders within hours of his troops pulling down their
camps. The outcries had been loud and vigorous,
tearful and angry, the women especially seeming
to believe that Hardee and his army were tossing
them to Sherman's rapacious savages. But Hardee
could offer no better explanation than the obvious.
For reasons Hardee didn't completely understand,
Charleston had been spared, Sherman choosing to
strike through the center of the state, rather than
making a grab for the port that Hardee considered
far more valuable. But he had not ever truly understood what Sherman was about, whether or not
the man was as brutish and unsympathetic to the
civilians as the rumors suggested. The results of
the campaign thus far had shown an odd inconsis-
tency, some towns escaping completely, others left
in a pile of ash.

Through it all, Hardee had been frustrated by the
inability of anyone in command above him, Bragg
and Beauregard, to devise any sort of plan or a strategy that seemed aggressive. It galled the man who
penned his own book on strategic campaigning
that he had no authority to put any kind of strategy
of his own into motion. He still answered to Beauregard, and from all he could find, Beauregard and
Bragg had their heads together, arguing and debating
over a variety of plans, neither man having enough

confidence in his own ideas to put those plans to paper.

Bragg had been in Wilmington, a city now indefensible, the number of Federal forces coming into nearby Fort Fisher far exceeding what anyone in the Confederate hierarchy anticipated. If Bragg expected a fight, he had been overruled by Beauregard, whose decision to vacate that city had been seconded by Richmond. It was a glaring admission that even the dreamlike optimism of Jefferson Davis had accepted the reality that the Confederacy was rapidly shrinking.

If Beauregard seemed to hesitate, Hardee had finally been convinced to begin his march by receiving the most bizarre of sources. A copy of the **New York Tribune** had been spirited in to Charleston, a column explaining in astonishing detail just what Sherman's army was planning to do. The reporter, who had impressive knowledge of the Federal army, had no qualms about revealing that Sherman's goal now was to march steadfastly into North Carolina, aiming to capture the city of Goldsboro by way of Fayetteville. Already cavalry reports from both Wheeler and Wade Hampton had suggested that Sherman would target Charlotte first, a logical choice, the city resting so close to the state line. But Sherman feinted again, suddenly turning eastward, and if the cavalrymen seemed unconvinced just where he was heading, the reporter in New York spelled it out with perfect precision. Regardless, sitting with several thousand experienced troops in battlements at Charleston now made little sense for Hardee at all. No matter the outcries by those who believed themselves certain victims, Hardee had ordered his army to begin their march northward.

Once he acknowledged the abandonment of Charleston, Beauregard only added to the confusion of command by ordering Hardee to march his men by way of Wilmington, what seemed on the maps to be a logical route to take toward Goldsboro. With Bragg vacating the city, Hardee had already received the last telegraph signals that the railroad there was certain to be engulfed by the newly arrived Federal troops under General John Schofield, who would certainly order the same kind of destruction to the rail lines that Sherman had perfected in Georgia and South Carolina. Hardee pleaded with Beauregard as much as decorum would allow, that he should make his march by way of the town of Cheraw, South Carolina, just below the North Carolina state line. Whether Beauregard had serious objections, or even second thoughts to any kind of plan Hardee now put into effect, Hardee had no idea. With Hardee's men on the march, and Sherman driving northward from Columbia, Hardee's means of communication were nonexistent. His greatest hope for learning anything specific about Sherman's whereabouts would come from the cavalry, who continued to skirt around Sherman's flanks, jabbing and poking at the screen established by Judson Kilpatrick. It did

not escape Hardee that the boisterous patriot Wade
Hampton had spoken long and loud about the
rescue of his beloved state. But within days of his
assuming command, all Hardee could learn was
that Hampton was riding hard and fast for North
Carolina.

Hardee rode at the head of his column,
thought of what lay behind him. They
had completed their crossing of the San-
tee River the day before, the rain-swollen waters
slowing the march in a way that lowered morale
even more.

Miles ahead, he knew the vast parade of refugees
were on the move, some using the few remaining railcars, some in wagons, every conveyance they could
find. He stared that way, knew his wife was there,
a fierce argument inside him, fearing for Mary's
safety, and the safety of his daughters, wondering
if the journey itself would prove more dangerous
than what might happen to those who kept to their
homes in Charleston. His son had ignored any of
that, of course, the boy now pushing hard to keep
with the army, still riding as part of Hardee's staff.
It was the ignorance of the young, Willie seeming
to burst with confidence that as long as he was allowed to become part of the next great confrontation, the army was safe.

The column was slowing again, Hardee crossing

a small, clear stream, allowing the men to fill their canteens. Many of the men garrisoned at Charleston had never made a forced march, and even the veterans rarely had to push through these dismal pine woods, lacking decent cover, decent clothing, and nearly any kind of rations.

Roy moved up beside him, said in a low voice, "Willie's about to drive me to desert. With all respect, sir. He keeps bragging about all he's going to do to Sherman when they meet."

Hardee looked back among the men, saw his son kneeling low at the creek, speaking to one of the sergeants, the man patiently ignoring the boy. "What would you have me do? If his mother were alive, I'd have every excuse to send him on to Raleigh, but Mary is not his mother. And he's too full of vinegar to take anyone's advice."

"You could have ordered him, flat out."

Hardee had thought of that long and hard, shook his head now. "No. He may never get an opportunity like this again. No matter how this ends, for good or bad, he has to prove to me he's a soldier. A father's curse, I suppose. He sees my uniform, has to find a way to wear it. Just try to keep him out of trouble, Tom. I can't be watching over him, and worrying about the enemy, too."

"Of course, sir. I'll keep him underfoot, as best he'll let me."

There was a rider coming forward, along the column, and Hardee saw the look, another dose of despair.

Roy said, "That's General Wright's man, Long."

"I know. Got something to say, for certain."

Long moved up close, a crisp salute, said, "Sir, I have been ordered to communicate to you General Wright's respects, and inform you that we have received a dispatch by rider, crossing the river behind us. The man was in considerable hurry, sir, and made great sacrifice to deliver his charge."

"What kind of charge, Captain?"

"Sir, the general has received an urgent plea from Governor Brown that he return to Georgia. I must also report, sir, that General Mercer has been summoned as well."

Hardee soaked up the man's uneasiness, said, "Why? In God's name, why?"

"Sir, General Wright is obeying the wishes of his state's executive. General Mercer has been summoned by General Cobb, to lead his remaining troops to the garrison at Macon."

"For what purpose? There is no war at Macon."

Long glanced at Roy, cleared his throat. "Sir, I apologize for not being better informed. All I was told is that Governor Brown has ordered the Georgia militia still with this column to return to their native state, to attend to their agricultural fields, sir."

Hardee stared at the man, wanted to be angry at him, but he knew that Long was just conveying a message that Wright himself was too sheepish to deliver in person. "Where is General Wright, Captain?"

"At the rear of this column, sir. He is assembling those units mentioned in the governor's order."

"And he did not feel there was time to inform me himself?"

Long hesitated, and Hardee saw the answer to his question. "I was only ordered to deliver his message, sir. The general regrets he cannot accompany your army farther. With your permission, sir, I must return."

"Certainly. I wouldn't want to cause any delay for Governor Brown. These men will have fields to plant in a **couple of months**."

He regretted the sarcasm, the captain absorbing it with obvious discomfort. Long began to turn his horse away, then stopped, said, "General Hardee, may the Almighty keep you safe. This war can still be won, with His blessing."

"Was that a part of General Wright's message as well?"

He saw a different look on Long's face now, sadness. "No, sir. It is my own wish, sir. I have respect for your command, and it has been a privilege serving under you."

Hardee could not fault the young man, the salute coming up, Hardee answering it as crisply as it was offered. "Thank you, Captain. Safe journeys to you as well. Should the enemy reverse himself and make another assault against Georgia, I am certain your state is in capable hands."

Long did not delay, rode away without looking back. Roy said, "What kind of nonsense is this? Forgive me, sir, but this is an outrage!"

Hardee raised a hand. "Quiet, Major. No need to add to this army's discomfort. They shall learn soon enough how their numbers are diminishing. Our greatest hope right now is that Sherman is not made aware of that."

CHERAW,
SOUTH CAROLINA—MARCH 2, 1865

He had formed a defensive position suited to the number of men still remaining in his command. As the army continued their march, stalled by more rain, and the lack of food and forage, desertions had become routine, each morning's roll call revealing fewer men in every unit. The greatest number of desertions had come from the South Carolina regiments, those men quick to realize that Hardee was marching them closer each day to the North Carolina border. At Cheraw, there was at least the opportunity for the men to find rations, to rest wounded feet and lame animals. For days now, Hardee had no real idea just where Sherman was, but with Hampton's cavalry finally making an appearance, Hardee learned that Sherman was moving directly toward him. If there were advantages to Cheraw for the Confederates, Sherman seemed to be eager to reach the town first.

Hardee rode among the workers, as he had done at Savannah, watching their spirit, the labor ongoing with a weariness he had not seen before. He knew it wasn't the march alone, that these men welcomed each morning with a miserable question, just who among them had vanished in the night. Hardee had already made the effort to reorganize his forces, Lafayette McLaws and William Taliaferro his two remaining ranking generals. Both were veterans, though neither man inspired the kind of leadership Hardee required. And so Hardee rode through their newly dug earthworks, making his best effort at inspiring the men to dig just a little faster.

The staff trailed behind him, his son Willie calling out to the men with the kind of cheerfulness that inspired curses. Hardee tried to ignore that, kept as much distance as he could between himself and his boy, knew that very soon, it might be time to yank the boy's leash with a firm pull.

"Sir, the aides report there are rations back at the camp wagon. One of the aides lassoed a hog."

Hardee turned, saw Pickett looking at him, hunger and hopefulness in the man's face. He could not hide from the rumbling in his own belly, scanned the laborers, who mostly ignored him. "I suppose we must not starve ourselves. Lead the way, Colonel."

Pickett nodded, smiling, a show of gratefulness,

turned his horse. Hardee noticed the animal's ribs, one more mount that would not survive much longer. He glanced down at his own horse, knew the animal had been given preference for the meager forage they had found along the way, a privilege of command Hardee never took for granted. He spurred the horse gently, moved up closer to Pickett, who said, "Not very much generosity from the citizens hereabouts. Their morale is about what we have in the camps. It's a terrible thing to witness."

"Defeat?"

Pickett seemed surprised at the word. "The soldiers seem to feel that. Some of 'em, anyway. The people, mostly it's hope. They were preached to for so long about how grand our independence would be, how President Davis was leading us to a Promised Land."

"You ever believe that?"

Pickett thought a moment. "I wanted to."

"We all wanted something, Bill. I wanted to lead men into battle. All I was ever trained to do. Led good men, some good fights. It was never the men, Bill. Never. Those same politicians who preached so loudly never had to face the enemy, never knew what kind of steel it took to fight. The generals who led these men . . . some of them weren't fit to lead a schoolyard of children. Maybe that applies to me."

"Certainly not, sir."

"What have I given this army lately, Colonel? What inspiration do they find by my presence?"

"Plenty, if I may say. You're here, after all. Where is Beauregard? Or Bragg?"

"It doesn't always work like that. Not every general rides at the head of a column, or charges into a fight with his men. The ones who were good at that, who enjoyed that . . . well, most of them are gone. I suppose there's a lesson in that."

He could smell the cooking pork, was suddenly ravenous, took a swig of water from his canteen. The smoke was rising from near the lone wagon, officers huddled close, all eyes on the roasting meat. There were others now, gathering slowly, drawn by the same aroma that engulfed him, a hundred or more, emerging from the trees, from the small road that led into the town. He stopped the horse, Pickett moving on, and Hardee felt sick, couldn't ignore the pain in the faces of the men. He spurred the horse, moved up close to the wagon, called out, "Officers! Stand aside. Who is the cook here?"

"Here, sir!"

He saw a familiar face, the man holding a small pitchfork, two black men behind him, stoking the fire.

"You will provide a serving of that meat to every man in the ranks who requests it. Officers shall receive theirs when the men have been fed."

"Sir, there won't be enough. It's just one old hog. Maybe a two-hundred-pounder."

"Then make the servings smaller. We find another hog, or a beef cow, or a single chicken, you will do the same."

The man looked at Hardee with a puzzled stare, and Hardee said, "Is there confusion about my order?"

"None, sir. Just . . . can't say I ever heard one like that before."

Hardee ignored the comment, moved the horse slowly away from the wagon, the gathering crowd of soldiers looking both at the wagon, and him. He pointed to one side of the fire, said, "You men will line up here." He paused, saw the men with nothing but bare hands. "Use your shirts, if you have to. It could be hot."

He glanced toward the cluster of officers now, saw undisguised agony. Pickett was back beside him again, said in a whisper, "You picked one fine time to be polite. I got spit slobbering down my shirt."

Hardee had no need to offer an explanation, said softly, "Maybe next time. These men decide to up and leave tonight, these officers will have the whole commissary to themselves. I'd rather not experience that."

The officers began to separate, audible mumbles Hardee tried not to hear. From the town Hardee could see a handful of soldiers, accompanied by a pair of civilians, the men in a frantic dash toward him. Pickett seemed to welcome the distraction, said, "What's the matter with them? Looks like something's happening."

Hardee watched them coming, thought, Everything that happens lately seems to be bad. But there were smiles from the men, the soldiers whooping, one man jumping, hands waving high.

Hardee said, "The telegraph. Must be. The line still runs north."

He spurred his horse, cutting the distance between them, could hear the cheerfulness, the smiles broken by exhausted breathing. One man staggered close to him, his hand holding a piece of paper.

"Sir! General! It's deliverance, sir!"

The paper reached Hardee's hand, the man collapsing to his knees in gleeful exhaustion. Hardee felt a nervous stir inside him, steadied his hand, opened the folded paper.

"It's a telegram, all right."

Pickett leaned close, said, "Well? Please, General. You're not gonna let me eat, at least let me in on the secret."

Hardee lowered the paper, stared ahead, his mind working, drifting, his thoughts scattered by fatigue, hunger, trying to gather what might happen now. "Won't be secret for long. We need to share this with the men. Seems our new commanding general, General Lee, has some ideas for us that didn't come out of Richmond. I doubt the president would have suggested this on his own. They hate each other, you know."

"Lee? I thought he and the president were friends."

Hardee pulled himself back to the place, the

moment, the men around him. Some were curious about the commotion, the ones with meat in their hands coming closer in a loose crowd. Hardee turned the horse, called out, "Gentlemen, if you please. We have received word. By order of the commanding general, Robert E. Lee, General Joseph E. Johnston has been named to command of this entire theater of the war, superior to Generals Beauregard, Bragg, and, well . . . Hardee."

The men erupted in loud cheers, more men running that way, the word passing with windy speed. Hardee watched the spreading joy, the sudden outburst of elation. He tried to share that, to feel the contagiousness of it, looked again at the wire. No, he thought, the president would not have suggested this. Lee knows Johnston well, knows what he can do, better than any commander in this army. Joe Johnston is a master of the retreat.

He continued to watch the soldiers, the word spreading out through the trees, through more of the camps. He glanced at Pickett, said, "You cheered by this, Bill?"

"I suppose so, sir. Old Joe coming back? That will give them, well, hope, sir. This might be the blessing we need."

Hope. Hardee said nothing, rolled the word through his brain. He searched for the feeling, for renewed optimism, but the tactician in him could only see the numbers, the plans, the strategy. He moved the horse away, would not say anything to dampen anyone's spirits, not even his friend, Pickett, or anyone else on his staff. He saw his son now, the boy on horseback, riding hard, a self-appointed messenger, spreading the word to anyone who would hear it. And they will hear it, he thought. They will see this as a sign, a symbol, that the confusion and uncertainty will be replaced by . . . what? Victory? He shook his head, moved away from the joy of his men, thought, No, what Johnston will give us is spirit, at least for a while. And when that is exhausted, perhaps we can say he at least gave us a little more time.

As the night fell, the cavalry scouts rode hard into camp, the dispatch even more urgent than Hardee expected. For a few days, there had been delay, the Federal army caught behind the high water of the Wateree River. But those waters had fallen, and now both wings of Sherman's army were marching in a rapid advance to occupy the town of Cheraw. There could be no hesitation, no futile optimism that his feeble defenses would hold Sherman's juggernaut away. With his artillery and baggage trains sent safely northward, across the Pee Dee River, Hardee gave the order to his men. The march would resume, northward, across the border into North Carolina.

CHAPTER THIRTY-EIGHT

SHERMAN

HANGING ROCK,
SOUTH CAROLINA—MARCH 2, 1865

He had hoped by now to be in close pursuit of Hardee's army, confirmation reaching him that Charleston had been abandoned, and those troops were on a route that should cross his own path. He had ordered the commanders to march with all speed, but as had happened so many times throughout the campaign, the weather had failed them. Rain-swollen creeks slowed every column, and Sherman had ordered his own camp to remain at Hanging Rock until the pontoons could be put to use.

He was traveling with his Twentieth Corps, commanded by Alpheus Williams, one part of Slocum's left wing. The other, Jeff Davis's Fourteenth Corps, had been trapped behind the Catawba River, their pontoon bridge swept away by the rising water. A frustrated Sherman could only make camp and wait, hoping that the rains that were again plaguing his army might also work to slow down the enemy.

"How long does he anticipate?"

The courier was shivering, soaked through from his ride, and Sherman tried to temper his questions, couldn't fault this man for his efforts.

"Sir, General Davis is most distressed by the lack of progress. The engineers are making use of every kind of material to reconstruct a workable bridge. The waters are most unforgiving, sir."

"In other words, General Davis has no idea whatsoever how long it will take him to cross that damned river."

The man was shaking visibly now, and Sherman wondered if it was the cold wetness in the man's clothes as much as it was intimidation in Sherman's presence.

"No, sir. I assure you, sir, the general is hard at work."

Sherman rose from the dining table, moved toward an energetic fire in the brick hearth. He had no idea whose house this was, just that the staff had found the first place they could dry their clothes. But even now, the roof above him was leaking, a steady drizzle of rainwater flowing into a hole hammered through the floor. Sherman stepped past that, warmed his hands at the fire.

"Sergeant, you may share this warmth. I will not attack you."

The man eased closer, as though not quite believing him, but the fire was too inviting, the courier standing beside Sherman now, the floor there growing wetter from the man's dripping clothes. "Thank . . . thank you, sir. I apologize for intruding into your headquarters."

"You had a job to do. You did it. No need for you to court some illness by staying out in this miserable weather any more than you have to."

CHESTERFIELD,
SOUTH CAROLINA—MARCH 3, 1865

As General Davis finally pushed the Fourteenth Corps past the stubborn Catawba River, Sherman began to move again, alongside the Twentieth Corps. But the weather was unrelenting, the roads so poor that nearly every yard had to be corduroyed, a process that slowed the army still, and drove Sherman to utter fury.

As the troops marched into the village of Chesterfield, they were met with a hard skirmish line, what was quickly identified as cavalry under the command of Matthew Butler, whose horsemen had most recently been observed around Lee's position at Petersburg. It was one more piece of evidence for Sherman that the rebels were scrambling with any maneuver they could, holding off both Grant and Sherman with numbers that likely were diminishing daily. The skirmish was brief, Butler's men moving away quickly, unwilling to stand up against a wave of blue infantry.

The staff found him yet another house, what had once been a grand plantation home, now a rundown structure whose sole asset was an unleaking roof. As the staff prepared the place, aides were sent out to the commanders with specifics on Sherman's location.

He stepped into the house on bare floors, wet boots tracking their way into a foyer, a parlor, a sitting area still with furnishings. The owner was an old man, his wife seemingly older, a frail-looking couple who stood silently to the side, acknowledging their helplessness. Sherman found a comfortable chair, the only one available, sat heavily, eyed the old couple as they eyed him.

"You have any coffee? No, of course you don't. Whiskey, then?"

The old man shook his head slowly.

"Good. Don't need it anyway. No one in this army needs it, not until they all go home."

The staff was spreading through the house, and Sherman glanced toward the window, more rain splattering against the glass. He saw riders, dreary men with rain pouring from their hats, dark, heavy raincoats. He caught a glimpse of one face, recognized him, one of Kilpatrick's staff officers. Sherman thought, What the hell does he want? They're supposed to be a long way off from this place.

He stood, more curious than he wanted to be, heard the boot steps in the foyer, moved that way, the aides taking the man's coat. Sherman chewed on an unlit cigar, said, "Captain . . . Kingsley, isn't it?"

The man saluted him, stood straight-backed, the annoying air of a man who knows he's in that "special" arm of the service. "General, it is a privilege to see you again, sir. General Kilpatrick offers you his most sincere respects, and requests that I share with you a number of correspondences that have passed between our camps and the camp of the rebels, specifically between General Kilpatrick and General Wheeler. There is an increasing amount of hostility between the two camps, and words have been passed that have, frankly, sir, infuriated General Kilpatrick. The rebels are making astonishing accusations against us, sir."

"There's supposed to be hostility, Captain. This is a war."

"Oh, yes, of course, sir. But General Wheeler has accused us of rape. And to make matters worse, sir, one of our patrols came upon seven of our soldiers, infantrymen, to be sure, who had been executed in a fairly gruesome manner, throats cut and whatnot. They were marked by a sign as having been the rapists. Again, they were certainly infantrymen. General Kilpatrick is very clear on that point."

"I'm certain he is."

"Well, sir, General Kilpatrick responded with appropriate outrage, pledging that he would execute any rebel prisoner in our possession for every Federal soldier executed by the rebels."

"You said correspondences. You have them?"

"Oh, certainly. Right here, sir."

Sherman took a leather satchel, turned away from the man, felt an annoying sense that this captain was enjoying his job just a little too much. "Stay here. One of my aides will get you something to eat. Dry off, for God's sake."

The captain obeyed, Sherman now alone in the parlor. He studied the letters, accusations of murder, flowing both ways. He scanned for the mention of a rape, saw it now, an incident not far from Columbia. Wheeler's letter was direct and specific, the girl's identity, the name of her father, the fact that seven men had taken part, said to be the same seven tracked down and executed by Wheeler's men. He forced himself to read the back and forth between Kilpatrick and Wheeler, so much of it posturing, defending some mythical honor, the captain's words coming again to Sherman, infantrymen. Certainly couldn't be a **cavalryman,** he thought. They're so far above reproach for any wrongdoing. Idiots.

There were boots again, voices, the annoying pleasantness of Kilpatrick's man, but the other voice was more familiar still. It was Slocum. Dayton was there now, said, "Sir, General . . ."

"I know. Send him in here."

Slocum appeared in the doorway, and Sherman held out a hand.

"Tell me, Henry, we still able to march, or are the men swimming now?"

There was more anger in the words than Sherman wanted, but Slocum seemed to share the sentiments, pulled off his hat, slapped rainwater in a spray.

"Miserable place, Cump. Miserable. How these people survive these winters, I don't know. Whiskey and tobacco, I suppose."

Sherman held out the letters. "Just got these, sent by that energetic captain out there. Kilpatrick's been in a duel of words with Wheeler. We're being accused of rape, among other atrocities."

"Rape? Really? Haven't heard any of that. Other things, mostly with the bummers. We're not making friends hereabouts, that's for certain. Rebels are getting more bold about disregarding the rules of war."

Sherman set the letters on a small table, said, "What do you mean?"

"Well, I haven't reported every incident to you.

Too many of them, for one thing. And, it's war. You know we've made every effort to control the scavengers, your orders, mine, every division commander we've got has nailed notices to trees, or passed the word all the way down to platoon level. Regrettably, it hasn't been very effective. Perhaps there is some benefit to what the rebels are doing about it."

"What are they doing?"

"Executing them. The cavalry in particular seems to have targeted the scavengers as a priority, and when they're caught, Wheeler, or whoever else is in charge, has taken to killing the men, and making sure we find them. It's been going on fairly regularly now. Worst case, we came across eighteen men, all with their throats cut. My men also found twenty-one others, tossed in a ravine, like it was some sort of official burial ground. Signs are showing up, along roadways, 'Death to all Foragers.' Not sure it's stopping any of our worst offenders from abusing the citizenry, but it's got the men pretty riled up in camp. There's talk of executing prisoners in retaliation."

"Have you?"

"No, of course not. That's not a War Department inquiry I would enjoy suffering through."

Sherman sat, thumped his fingers on the table. "Don't like this, Henry. Not one bit. If our foragers commit excesses, then we will punish them ourselves. But I will not tolerate the enemy judging us for what is lawful. Just because we raid plantations and feed this army doesn't make us war criminals. And we're sure as hell not murderers. Or rapists. Are we certain that Wade Hampton is now in command of the cavalry?"

"Quite. Prisoners talk about nothing else. Like he's an avenging angel. Wheeler can't be too happy about that."

"I don't give a good damn what makes Wheeler happy. But I'm not tolerating this. I'm the one they're calling a butcher, and they're massacring prisoners? Major Hitchcock!"

He waited impatiently, heard the boots in rapid steps. Hitchcock was there now, said, "Yes, sir?"

"Get your pad of paper. I want to send a letter."

Lt Genl Wade Hampton
Commanding, Cavalry Forces, CSA

General,
It is officially reported to me that our foraging parties are murdered after capture and labeled "Death to all Foragers." One instance of a lieutenant and seven men near Chesterville, and another of twenty one near a ravine near Fosterville.

I have ordered a similar number of prisoners in our hands to be disposed of in like manner. I hold about 1000 prisoners captured in various ways, and can stand it as long as you; but I hardly think

these murders are committed with your knowledge, and would suggest you give notice to the people at large, that every life taken by them simply results in the death of one of your Confederates. . . .

Within days, Hampton's reply was received.

I shall shoot two Federal prisoners for every one of my men you execute. . . .

The war of words produced no satisfying result, and Sherman had to suspect that Hampton might very well carry out his threat. Sherman had long ago accepted that this war, or any war, was no gentleman's game, that honor and dignity would be early casualties. But the foraging would continue out of necessity, no other way for Sherman to feed his army, a point he tried to make clear to Hampton. The orders went out again to the foragers, urging at least a measure of respect for civilian property, but Sherman and his commanders were forced to accept that they could not effectively govern the behavior of men sent out without direct control, and that temptation, greed, and viciousness had become part of the everyday life of a greater number of his soldiers than Sherman wanted to admit. As they marched through the raw middle of the Southern aristocracy, as they observed the lives of the masters and their slaves, as they heard the outpourings of joy that came from the freed blacks, his army had come to share Sherman's complete lack of respect for what it meant to be Southern, and just what the South was fighting to preserve.

That both sides had men who could show such barbarity was not a pleasant reality. Sherman still believed wholeheartedly in the doctrine of total war, yet he was learning the cost, that as the war dragged on, the boundaries between **combatant** and **innocent victim** were becoming blurred. It only added fuel to Sherman's fire to push onward, to drive his army as far as necessary to strangle the remaining Confederate strongholds, or confront and defeat whatever armies their generals might still command.

He entered Cheraw on March 3, making a rendezvous with Oliver Howard and troops of his right wing. The pursuit of Hardee's men had been futile at best, the Confederates traveling with far fewer encumbrances, an advantage to them only while on the march. But Sherman was quick to understand that Hardee had left Cheraw in a hurry, had likely been closer to the jaws of Sherman's army than Sherman had realized. In the town were the great treasures left behind, most of that from the citizens of Charleston, their effort to secure their belongings from the hordes of Sherman's army. But Hardee had been forced to abandon military stores as well, an enormous amount of shot and shell, artillery pieces and musketry. But one artifact was brought to Sherman's attention, one prize that the men in Sherman's command would hold dear. Among the cannons left behind was one marked with a bold plaque. It was the cannon that had fired the first shot at Fort Sumter.

CHAPTER THIRTY-NINE

HARDEE

FAYETTEVILLE,
NORTH CAROLINA—MARCH 9, 1865

As Hardee resumed his march, intending to meet with Johnston in Fayetteville, there was confusion still, an order received from Braxton Bragg that turned Hardee more to the west, with the new goal the town of Rockingham. Bragg had been inspired by rumors that Schofield's Federal troops were on a rapid march up the Cape Fear River, a path that would lead from Wilmington directly toward Fayetteville. Within a day of Hardee changing direction, a correction came from Bragg, that the Federals were not in fact pursuing

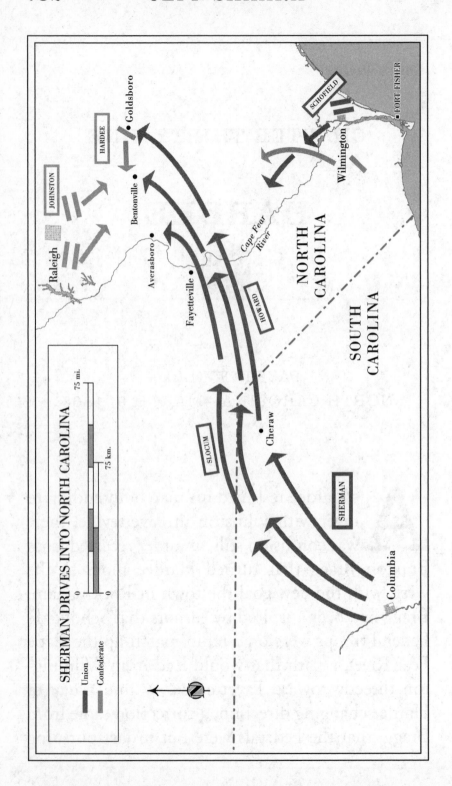

SHERMAN DRIVES INTO NORTH CAROLINA

Union
Confederate

75 mi.
75 km.
0
0

N

SCHOFIELD

FORT FISHER

Wilmington

Goldsboro

HARDEE

JOHNSTON

Raleigh

Bentonville

Averasboro

Cape Fear River

Fayetteville

HOWARD

NORTH CAROLINA

SOUTH CAROLINA

Cheraw

SLOCUM

SHERMAN

Columbia

that path. But Hardee had been too efficient for his own good. He had reacted to Bragg's order by making the most logical preparation for holding Schofield away, which included burning the bridges at Fayetteville, which would certainly slow Schofield down. Now those burned bridges proved to be a barrier, preventing Bragg's forces from crossing the river and uniting with Hardee.

Hardee stared out the window, a thunderous rainstorm lashing the house, water in sprays against the glass panes.

Johnston sat in a soft chair, read dispatches just received, notes from the cavalry, another note from Bragg. He studied the paper for a long minute, said, "He says he didn't tell you that Schofield was on the march. You misunderstood his instructions."

Hardee turned to Johnston, let out a breath. "Of course that's what he says. I've grown accustomed to General Bragg's way of conducting his affairs. If things don't turn out to his liking, he merely changes the facts."

Johnston folded the paper, put it in his pocket, and Hardee knew there was meaning to that, Johnston keeping a record of every order, and now, every mistake.

"How much did you have to abandon at Cheraw?"

Hardee hated the question, knew there would be loud complaints to Richmond, complaints Johnston might already have heard. "Sherman's army was within a few hours' march. We did not have the luxury of time spent loading a vast wagon train, a wagon train we did not have. I was fortunate we learned of Sherman's whereabouts when we did." He paused, knew he hadn't answered Johnston's question. "A great deal was left behind. The citizens of Charleston relied on our army to take care of more personal property than I would have hoped for, property they did not feel safe having in Charleston. I did not encourage anyone to send wagonloads of valuables to Cheraw. Panic is a disease. The people of Charleston had an epidemic all their own. I admit, my own family was stricken. My wife and daughters insisted on traveling north. I believe they are in Raleigh." He paused. "I am forced to admit, sir, that this army became guardians of a considerable store of every kind of goods, from wine to fine carpets. I trust General Sherman is making good use of our generosity."

"I hope your family will be safe. But I am not concerned with carpets, General. You also abandoned a considerable store of ordnance."

"And rice and flour. Yes, powder and muskets and a number of artillery pieces. I am eager to know how any of my superior officers would have rescued so much material, without a railroad, a navigable river, or a sufficient number of wagons."

Johnston seemed to soften, said, "There is no inquiry here, General. I am merely attempting to take inventory of our assets. It was my hope that by this date, I could have your forces united with Bragg's. We must assume that since Sherman seems obsessed with capturing state capitals, he is intending to march on Raleigh. There are several alternative routes he may take. Regardless, I fear that his vanguard has succeeded already in moving between our forces. We have disadvantages enough as it is. Fortunately, I do not believe Sherman's cavalry has gained sufficient information on our positions to enable the enemy to make a decisive move against any of our positions. Such a strike could be disastrous, and we cannot afford disaster in any form."

Hardee waited for more, studied Johnston, saw calm, rigidity, the kind of decorum Johnston was known for. He was a small man, with a neat arrow of a goatee, a severely receding hairline that accented a wide forehead. Hardee had always respected Johnston, even if he didn't always agree with his tactics, especially in some of the fights around Atlanta. But Hardee, and most of the army, believed that Johnston was a far superior field general to either Braxton Bragg or John Bell Hood, an opinion that Johnston seemed to share. The thought flickered through Hardee's mind.

"Is there any hope of bringing General Hood's forces eastward?"

Johnston's expression didn't change, a stern soberness. "What forces are still available to General Hood are mostly recuperating from their recent campaign. Moving those people en masse from Alabama would be a challenge. I have considered the option. Even if we could make such a move, I'm certain General Hood would not accompany them. That is, of course, his choice. The difficulty lies with the lack of railroads. South and east of Atlanta, the enemy has destroyed most of the usable lines, and any movement through Tennessee would invite considerable attention. I am pleased, though, that some scattered units have reached North Carolina by foot. Admirable, certainly. A garrison has been formed at Charlotte, another at Smithfield. Brigade strength, no more. But it is something. Others might reach us within the week. We cannot depend on anything more useful than that. Any organized march by a substantial number of troops could draw the attention of General Thomas in Nashville. Should the Federals learn that Hood's army is attempting to move in force, those men would be a tempting target, and a vulnerable one." Johnston slid another paper across the small table to his side. "I can make available to you one division of additional cavalry. Those men have been graciously sent southward by General Lee. With the garrisons now present in this theater, including General Bragg's forces, I believe we can put into the field close to twenty-five thousand effectives."

Hardee mulled the numbers in his mind, had no idea what kind of garrisons were spread out around

North Carolina. "Is General Lee able to assist us with additional infantry?"

Johnston rubbed a hand over his head. "No. The situation at Petersburg is desperate. General Lee is profuse in his apologies, but he believes he requires every man in his command to fend off the pressure from Grant's army."

Hardee weighed Johnston's response, felt a wave of despair. "Is there **any** place we are not grotesquely outnumbered?"

Johnston kept his grim stare, said, "Yes. Right here in this room. I believe you and I will make an effective combination, General. Also, I have sent an urgent request to General Lee that he order Bragg's command to be placed completely under my authority. I am concerned that General Bragg might be somewhat confused by my place here. There can be no argument over whose orders take priority. Not now."

Hardee needed no further explanation about Bragg's tendency to claim responsibility for anyone in his own camp. The fact that Bragg was still in command of any troops in the field had been a surprise to Hardee, especially following the intrigue that had plagued the army prior to the disaster at Chattanooga. But Bragg seemed to operate in a sphere all his own, and for reasons Hardee could never grasp, Jefferson Davis was a willing accomplice to Bragg's ongoing ambitions, a feeling Hardee knew he could never reveal to Johnston. But Johnston had opinions of his own, the well-known feud with the president, a gravelly relationship with Lee, who had come to command by replacing the wounded Johnston during the summer of 1862. Even now Hardee had nagging questions, wondering if the president had bowed to Lee's putting Johnston in this command only because he knew that Johnston would be the best man to keep what remained of this army out of harm's way. There was nothing about that that Hardee found encouraging. The next state border above them was Virginia.

"Sir, I must ask if you believe Sherman's intentions are to continue his drive northward, possibly surrounding General Lee's forces."

"Don't you? Nothing any of us has put in Sherman's way has proven effective. Merely backing away and allowing him free rein through North Carolina will only hasten the end of the war in his favor."

Hardee was curious now, thought, Well, yes, that is obvious. Then why are you here? He stood now, eyed the driving rainstorm again, dreaded the thought of a walk to his horse, a soaking return to his camp. Closer to the window, he put his fingers against the glass, felt the wet cold. He turned toward Johnston now, who was writing notes on a pad of paper.

"What are your orders, sir? I have examined the maps. I believe we can maintain a sufficient lead on

Sherman's vanguard, and I am confident that the cavalry can screen our movements to allow us to go as far as Raleigh unmolested."

He waited for a response, thought, He knows all of that. He is no doubt mapping out a route all the way to Petersburg. Or he knows that Lee is planning a move that would bring him south.

Johnston didn't look up, said, "General Hardee, you seem to be under the impression that I was appointed to this command in order to facilitate an ongoing retreat."

Hardee clamped his jaw tight, thought, Weren't you? "I'm not certain what you are referring to, sir."

Johnston looked up at him now, a hint of a smile. "Don't play a game with me, General. I am not endeavoring to unite our forces just so we can march away on the same road. I believe we have one hope."

Hardee thought, That **word** again.

"Sir?"

"Sherman's army is advancing in two primary columns, two wings, with the cavalry screening mostly to their left flank. Correct?"

"That has been his tendency, yes."

"Why would he change those tendencies? They have worked remarkably well. I have to admit, General, when I learned that he was intending to bypass Charleston by marching through those lowlands, through those horrific conditions, I thought him mad. I've seen those swamps, those rivers. I've seen what floodwaters can do to an army. And yet, he was not swallowed up. He was barely delayed at all. His decisions defy explanation, and yet they succeed. He has maintained a pace of march that I thought impossible, he has created roads where none exist. I admit, General, despite my loyalties, that Sherman has accomplished something remarkable." Johnston paused. "It is possible that one day I could tell him that. He might not be a gentleman, but he has earned respect, even from his adversaries."

"He is still our adversary."

"Yes, and for that reason, and because he has been so unmolested, I believe we have an opportunity. As he marches north, the maps show diverse routes, roads that spread out with some distance between them. Sherman has no reason to fear us, and thus he might become careless. It is the only opportunity we are likely to have."

"You mean, attack him?"

Johnston glared at Hardee now, as though he understood the insult. "Of course, attack him! It is my duty to make the best use of this army that I can. In the past, that has inflamed critics of my command, jokes at my expense, assumptions in Richmond that I am unwilling to fight. Be assured, General, there is still fight in this army. If Sherman allows himself to be careless, I intend to make him pay. If he unites his forces, and joins up with whatever troops Schofield brings from the seacoast, we have no chance of stopping him. But divided, it is a more equal fight. And, just like **you,** General, Sherman does not expect that we will assault him. But we **will**. I am quite certain that he is preparing himself for a valiant march into Virginia, already rehearsing what he will say to Grant, how they shall shake hands and embrace, and offer compliments to each other on their marvelous successes. But he is not prepared for a **fight**. And so, we shall give him one. With vigor."

They marched northeast, a straight avenue that would take them to Goldsboro. But Hardee's orders were specific. He was to keep ahead of Sherman at all costs, but at the same time delay the march just enough that he might tempt Sherman's lead columns to engage. There was one purpose, and Hardee knew it did not include any real effort to defeat Sherman's infantry. Johnston was continuing to bring together the scattered garrisons from their various outposts throughout North Carolina, a time-consuming effort on poor roads made even more difficult by the weather. What Johnston required was **time,** and Hardee's was the only piece of Johnston's army in a position to give it to him. For the cavalry, the harassment so common to both sides had turned uglier, part of that the response to both Kilpatrick and Wheeler accusing the other of various atrocities. With the armies now in much closer proximity to each other, it was becoming common for cavalry skirmishes to chatter through the pine woods and small towns on a daily basis. Whether anything would come of this was of minor concern to Hardee. His duty was clear. Keep ahead of Sherman, while slowing him down. If Hampton and Wheeler could do anything to aid that cause, Hardee had no objection at all.

CHAPTER FORTY

SEELEY

NEAR SOLEMN GROVE,
NORTH CAROLINA—MARCH 10, 1865

There were no stars, the rain clouds still thick above them, nothing to offer the men a glimpse of anything but their own horses. Seeley rode slowly, focusing on the trail, his men keeping close, no one taking the chance of straggling. For too many days now, there had been skirmishing in almost every direction, the two cavalry forces keeping closer proximity than Seeley had ever experienced. The darkness had made the men unusually jumpy, but now, with so many Yankees in so many different places, no one needed a reminder to keep his mouth shut, and his horse under control.

He stared at nothing, the pine woods around him smelling of swamp water, the only sound the low slurp of his horse's hooves. He had hoped to find Wheeler on this trail, felt an agonizing tension, thought, There was one map. One scrap of paper. Gone now. Where the hell did I put the thing? We could be anyplace except where we're supposed to be. Or we could be right where the map says we're going, and wouldn't know it until somebody opens fire on us.

The orders had come from General Dibrell, passed down from Wheeler, who now answered to Wade Hampton. Whatever cavalry could be gathered in the vicinity of the two armies was presumed to be pulling together, as large a force as Hampton could assemble. With Sherman's army advancing into North Carolina, the urgency was obvious to all of them, that the cavalry had to become a more effective arm of the entire army, and right now any kind of sharp strike on the Federal positions could be helpful in gaining time for Joe Johnston to pull together even more troops from the scattered outposts all through the state.

Seeley had been given specific instructions, ride this trail until it ended, one of a dozen just like it, a spiderweb of routes through the pine woods and farmlands. In the darkness, any ride was dangerous, the Federal troopers just as eager as their counterparts to launch an assault, with as much surprise as possible.

He didn't know of any plan, just that the rendezvous was tricky, Hampton pulling together the men not in some convenient town, but in the middle of the woods, at night, with rain possible at any moment. Seeley knew nothing about Hampton beyond the man's reputation, spoken of throughout South Carolina as one of the state's favorite sons, and since the death of Jeb Stuart, Hampton was said to be the greatest horseman in the South. Seeley had never heard Wheeler speak that way, knew that in Tennessee there would be an argument to that from anyone who had ridden with Nathan Bedford Forrest, Seeley included. But for now Hampton was in command, and from the tone of the orders, something was happening, and Seeley's men were to be a part of it.

He tried to control his anxiousness, knew that the men had plenty of their own. Keep your calm, he thought. Don't let on you're scared. He glanced out into complete darkness, a slight breeze whispering through the pines, thought, One dog barks out here and the whole lot of us is liable to skedaddle in the other direction. Don't you be leading the way. He heard a man's voice, low, indistinct, halted the horse, the others doing the same behind him, following his lead. The sounds came past a thicket of trees, a hint of open ground beyond, and Seeley closed his eyes, tried to pick out the sounds.

The voices came again, definite, clear, men talking in harsh whispers, and he opened his eyes, his heart racing, glanced behind him, dull shadows of his small column. He made a sharp hissing sound, the only order he would give them, nudged the horse forward again, pulled his pistol, the reins in one hand. The pistol was heavy, a light mist on his face, his breathing heavy, and he edged closer to the clearing, his mind trying to distinguish the shapes there, a cluster of men. Or bushes. He strained to see, had done this too many times, searching the darkness for movement, his eyes tricking him, dancing images that were nothing at all.

Another horse was beside him now, startling him, a hand on his arm. He couldn't see faces at all, but he knew it was Gladstone, the telltale odor of tobacco spittle. Up ahead, the voices were clearer now, and he felt a hard tap on his arm from Gladstone, a soft whisper.

"It's our people."

Seeley kept his eyes on the dark images, cursed the sergeant in his mind, How do you know that, you crazy old man? But more images rolled into view, Seeley could see another column of horsemen, emerging from a road to one side of him, no more than fifty yards away. They halted, one man riding forward, more of the low talk, and Seeley knew the voice. It was Wheeler.

He let out a long breath, felt like laughing, the tension of the moment passing, replaced by curiosity, just why he was there. He leaned close to Gladstone, said, "Hold them here. Let me check on this."

Seeley nudged the horse forward again, moving closer to the other column, keeping their place, while their commander moved into the clearing. He had a sudden burst of nervousness, that they might think he was . . . not one of them. He wanted to speak out, knew the orders, realized the pistol was still in his hand. Bad idea, he thought. One shot, even a dumb accident, and this whole place might become a blind battlefield. He holstered the Colt, moved closer to the head of the second column, said in a low voice, "Good night to be a ghost."

The man's horse seemed to bolt, dancing from the man's startled reaction, and Seeley pushed on past, moved into the clearing, no time for explanations to anyone he couldn't see. The group in the clearing was formed in a circle, and Seeley moved up, a gap forming, slid his horse in between two others, realized now there were close to twenty men, surrounding three in the center. One of those men said in a low voice, "Who's that, just come in?"

"Captain Seeley, sir, 4th Tennessee."

Wheeler was one of the three, said, "He's one of mine, sir. A Forrest man."

"Welcome, Captain. I'm General Hampton. By dawn we should make even General Forrest proud. This fellow beside me is General Butler. I'd introduce all of you, but that hardly matters. So far we've put together near fifteen hundred men. Your orders are very simple, and maybe not so. Simply put, we have located Kilpatrick's camp, without being detected. At dawn, General Butler will lead a column on the road that passes through the swamp to the west of that camp. General Wheeler shall listen for the first firing, and lead his men off to the north of this position, which will put him in the rear of the enemy's camp. Is Captain Bostick present?"

A low voice came next to Seeley. "Right here, sir."

"Captain, as you know, you have the enviable job of finding and capturing General Kilpatrick. The rest of this force will do what we do best, and cause the enemy as many casualties, capture as many prisoners as our surprise will afford us. But capturing Kilpatrick is our primary goal."

Seeley was impressed, thought, This is big, enormous. He searched the dark shadows, thought, General Dibrell could be here, should be here. If he's not, I'll pay for it. He'll want to know every word, and he'll blame me for getting him lost. It's just what he does.

He strained again to see the faces, to identify any of the officers, knew only the figure of Wheeler, had seen him too many times before in black darkness. The generals were speaking together, low whispers, and now Hampton spoke again, just loud enough for the men to hear him.

"Dawn. Try to rest your men until then. No bugles, no fires, nobody discharges a weapon. Kilpatrick's camp is through these woods, that direction, not more than a half mile. Dismount with your men, pass along the orders. No conversation, no jokes, no foolishness. Keep close to your horse, in the event we are detected."

One of the men across from Seeley said, "Sir, how do we know where Kilpatrick himself might be?"

Hampton whispered something to Butler, then said, "You're late arriving. No matter. There is a house, the Monroe house. Stands out. Largest around. Captain Bostick shall move directly there, and put Kilpatrick under guard. We shall do all we can to come to his support, as events allow it. No more questions, gentlemen. Seek out each other, be aware of your location, the location of the rest of this command. This is a golden opportunity, and I shall not see it squandered by carelessness. Go now, to your men. When it is light enough to see the man's face beside you, mount up, prepare to receive the command to attack."

Hampton moved out through the circle, Butler with him, the men making a path. Wheeler rode directly toward Seeley now, stopped the horse close beside him, said, "Where the hell have you been? Where's Dibrell? McLemore? Porter?"

"We made our way as best we could, sir. I haven't seen any other senior officer since nightfall. General Dibrell ordered me to follow a map to this point."

The others had dispersed, and Wheeler seemed to wait for the rest to be out of earshot. He spoke in a low voice now, but not low enough, a volume that made Seeley cringe.

"We finally have our chance, and Hampton gives the prize to one of Butler's men. If you'd have been here sooner, I might have convinced him to let you do it."

Seeley kept his whisper. "Capture Kilpatrick?"

"Yes, you simpleton. Now Butler can grab the glory. Well, you listen to me, young captain. You heard what Hampton said. Go to that large house. If that Captain Bostick gets his hind end caught in a sling, you can help him out of it. Or I will."

"Yes, sir."

Wheeler said nothing for a long moment, Seeley not certain what to do.

"Sir, I should return to my men. We're on that trail, back that way."

Wheeler turned his horse, hesitated a moment longer, waved a hand toward Seeley, then moved off. Seeley sat alone for a long minute, the quiet settling over the clearing. He absorbed Wheeler's instructions, what seemed a direct contradiction to General Hampton's orders. But Kilpatrick, he thought. I grab him, maybe with that other fellow, won't matter. That'll be a story to tell Katie. And the whole army, maybe.

He pulled the reins, the horse moving to one side, spurred the animal gently, moved back toward his men. He had questions, wondering how they had found Kilpatrick's camp, why Hampton had come, who Butler might be. I've got eighty men, and they're talking over a thousand. Maybe two.

He saw dismounted troopers, knew the shadow of Gladstone, the old man walking out to meet him.

"Well, the brass monkeys tell you how to win the war?"

Seeley climbed down from the horse, thought of Hampton's instructions, the harsh orders, the care, the opportunity. He leaned close to Gladstone, said, "Yep. Just wait for daylight. If everybody can keep quiet, we're gonna be a part of something pretty big."

Gladstone spit a stream of tobacco to one side of Seeley's leg, a low laugh. "Heard that before, Captain. Just try to keep us from getting killed, so damn close to the end of this thing."

Seeley wouldn't hear that, not now. He had nurtured too much of his own despair for too many months, realized he was a part of something enormous, a **plan**. For the first time in a very long time, he was excited.

SOLEMN GROVE,
NORTH CAROLINA—MARCH 11, 1865

The daylight took an eternity to arrive, the low clouds keeping the wet darkness wrapped around the men like a cold blanket. But the faces were clear now, and he moved through them, passing along the orders, what was supposed to happen, what kind of opportunity there was. He was surprised by the lack of enthusiasm, nearly all the energy coming from him, the men too accustomed to disappointment, assaults that too often had become frantic retreats. He knew better than to cheer them on, the kind of mindless hoorahs that Dibrell would offer. Already men were moving in the trees around him, other trails, some pushing past the thin growth, gathering on the larger roads. He saw officers now, Wheeler leading the way, a slow, deliberate ride over soggy ground. Wheeler saw Seeley's men, motioned them forward, made the same gesture to others, more columns moving out, gathering, several hundred men. There were low voices, no one speaking out, the instinct for the value of **quiet**. Seeley kept his eyes on Wheeler, saw some of the other senior officers, still no sign of Dibrell. Seeley heard the rattle, straight out through the woods, a crash of musket fire, all eyes that way. He held tight to the reins, felt for the pistol, the saber, habit, watched Wheeler, saw the man's cold stare off toward the sound of the fight. Wheeler put one arm in the air now, no words, none needed. After a long second, the arm came down, and the men began to move.

They rode as quickly as the woods would allow, the sounds of the fight growing in front of them. Seeley moved out to one flank, the woods to his left alive with horsemen, Wheeler somewhere in front. Seeley ducked tree limbs, the horse obedient, efficient, a quick glance back to his men, keeping up close, eyes on him, on the sounds to the front. To one side, men were in the woods, on foot, men in blue. Seeley wanted to call out, but the men were advancing toward the fight, as the horsemen were, what seemed like a skirmish line. Seeley pulled the pistol, but the Yankees paid no mind to the horsemen, and Seeley watched them, saw glances his way, no recognition, thought, They think we're Yankees! He nudged the horse closer to the main body, putting distance between his men and the foot soldiers, those men nearly gone, blocked by the timber. He was frantic, fought to keep the horse in a slow gait, the pounding in his chest ruling his brain, his hand finding the butt of the pistol, the voice screaming through him, Let's go!

The woods began to give way, smoke now finding them, the sounds of men, screaming, shouts, more firing. They were in the clear now, the village laid out in front of him, men in motion in every direction, many men on foot, a mad scramble through small houses, open yards, a narrow street, a wider road. The attack was utter confusion, men with sabers high, a line of horsemen, riding hard, colliding with another line, men in blue. The fights were singular, duels with sabers, pistol fire, men chasing down the men on foot. Seeley moved out into an open area, trying to find some order, glanced back,

his men still with him. There were Yankees coming out of the small houses, some barely dressed,
strapping on belts, swords, running for a corral of
horses.

"That way! Charge them!"

He spurred the horse, the others following, the men
on foot ragged, disorganized, desperate. He reached
the first man, the man curling up, his hands high,
useless shield, a sharp, terrified cry. Seeley moved
past him, no threat, and he searched, more men, one
with a carbine, firing into a group of fighting men.
Seeley jerked the horse that way, rode hard, low, the
man seeing him, the carbine coming up, the pistol
in Seeley's hand firing with a hard jerk. The man
dropped, Seeley's horse rolling past him, more men
at the corral, a mad dash to mount up, men without
uniforms. He aimed the pistol again, too many targets, searched for danger, for anyone trying to make
a fight. One man was on his horse now, held a pistol of his own, hatless, a thick beard, spurring the
horse toward Seeley. They closed the gap between
them, a hard gallop by both men, Seeley trying to
keep the pistol on the man, firing, a burst of smoke,
Seeley firing again. The man fell, the horse passing
by Seeley riderless, and Seeley searched for the man,
but there were others, too many, his horse taking
him into the corral. He spun around, shouting,
others answering his call, their own piece of the
rebel yell, driven by the raw terror, the manic thrill,
the fight boiling up in every direction. He saw faces,

bits of uniform, could begin to see more of the Yankees, some of those men dressed, many more in nightclothes. He searched, saw another heavy line of Confederates, a charge coming across in front of him, and he spurred the horse, saw a cluster of his own men, called to them, blood on one man's arm, but they came, responding, and he led them into line. They advanced together, more than two hundred, a heavy line straight through the village, a line of Yankees forming up to meet them. The two came together with a heavy metallic crash, swords and sabers coming together, harsh shouts, carbine fire, pistols, the awful cry of horses, screaming men. The two lines separated again, the Yankees drawing back, disorganized retreat, the men around him regrouping, Seeley checking his pistol, reloading as quickly as he ever had. There were commands, a hard voice, and he saw an officer, older, unfamiliar, the man pointing his sword, the line coming in close, the assault beginning again. They moved against the retreating Yankees, those men stopping to fight, but not all. There was pursuit now, some of the Yankees dropping down, hands high, surrender, Seeley moving past them, no interest in grabbing prisoners, not yet. He searched the village, frantic motion, his men coming toward him, respect, seeking orders. There were bodies on the ground, both sides, men crawling, bad wounds, some just splayed out where they fell. Seeley absorbed all he could, listened for anyone's commands, but the fight had dissolved into small battles. He called to his men, no more than half his force, "Form up here! Check your weapons."

He searched the village, smaller fights still ongoing, but many of the Yankees had gone, some still on foot making their retreat. And now he saw the larger house.

"With me!"

He spurred the horse that way, saw others, both sides, some riding hard past the house, others dueling, one Yankee leveling a pistol, the blast into a man's chest, firing again. Seeley pulled his saber, pointed toward the man, the target to guide them all, led the horses in a calm charge, quicker now, the men staying together. The Yankee saw his predicament, turned his horse, a quick dash away, and Seeley looked at the fallen man, recognition, an officer, Anderson, one of the colonels. The man was writhing, blood in a muddy pool beneath him. Seeley pointed to him, shouted out, "See to him!"

Men obeyed, but Seeley was past the wounded man, his eyes on the house. He saw a man in gray on horseback, speaking to a man barely dressed, and Seeley rode that way, saw it was a captain, tried to recall the name, Butler's man . . . **Bostick**. The captain shouted down to the near naked man, "Where is Kilpatrick? **Where is he?**"

Seeley saw the other man, nightclothes, frantic fear in the man's face. He pointed down a far roadway, said, "He rode there! That man on the black horse! He's getting away!"

Seeley moved up close to the captain. "Captain Bostick?"

The man looked at him, furious frustration in his face. "Yes! Who are you?"

"Doesn't matter. Should we search the house?"

"Too late for that. I'm going after him." Bostick looked at the man on the ground. "If you're lying to me, I'll be back here to split you in two!"

"He went off that way! I saw him! I swear it!"

Bostick moved off quickly, and Seeley eyed the house, moved the horse slowly that way, a handful of his men coming up with him. He said, "This is Kilpatrick's headquarters. We should check it."

Musket fire was whistling past them now, some striking the house, the confusion of the fight swirling around them in nearly every direction. Seeley searched for the source of the firing, but it was too scattered, some of it distant. He turned to the house again, heard one of his men say, "Captain, look, it's a woman. Dang, she's near nekkid."

Seeley saw the door of the house, the woman in a thin white gown, bare legs, a bare shoulder. The others were all moving that way, one man down from his horse, the woman calling out, "Protect me! Please!"

Seeley shouted, "Go! Take care of her!"

From behind, a hard blast blew through the dirt street, then another. He spun the horse, smoke rising, the air ripped by another shell. Men were gathering, pulling the wounded off into cover, an officer now, familiar, calling out, "Artillery! See to the wounded, then withdraw to the edge of town! That way!"

The shells came again, four in quick sequence, and Seeley looked again to the house, saw the woman, escorted by a pair of his men, pulling her down into a low ditch, a shell impacting a few feet behind them. Seeley thought now of the man he had seen, the nightclothes, searched for him, thought, The house. He should be with her. Maybe his wife. He dismounted, moved toward the door of the house, pulled the pistol, stopped at the door, felt an itch, Don't be careless. He eased into the house, saw pieces of a uniform, more, a canteen, a saber, boots. He thought of calling out, felt too cautious, looked in every corner, eyed the doorways, the staircase. The artillery was coming again, the thunder rattling the house. There were more blue uniforms, a trunk, a dining table set with china, wine bottles, a breakfast prepared.

"Sir! The lady's done told us, you gotta hear this, sir!"

Seeley looked toward the man, Private Goode, a serious, sober man, seeming to burst with words. "Told you what?"

"The lady, name's Marie Boozer. She says she's Kilpatrick's special lady. Begging us that we ought not be rough with her."

"We won't be 'rough' with any lady. Did she tell you where Kilpatrick is?"

"Just said he done left." The man hesitated, then said, "Lookee, out that way! Man's haulin' it off on a horse!"

Seeley rushed to the window, saw the horse emerging out from a small barn to the rear of the house. It was the man he had seen, still in his nightclothes, the horse at a hard gallop, disappearing now into the smoke from the incoming shells. Seeley stared that way, felt a sudden wave of nausea. He thought of Wheeler, all the hatred, the rivalry, the feud. But through it all, there was the one detail Seeley didn't know, the question he had never thought to ask. Just what does Judson Kilpatrick look like?

As the Confederate cavalry gathered up, they assessed their haul, nearly five hundred prisoners, though they lost more than a hundred casualties of their own. But the success was short-lived. The village was ripe with plunder, the Confederate troopers, many without boots or decent coats, ceasing their pursuit of the Yankees to rifle the homes for loot. The precious time they afforded the Yankees was all Kilpatrick's men required. Within the hour the cavalry returned, this time backed up by Federal infantry and artillery. The Confederates, mostly Butler's men, were suddenly faced with a heavy line of Spencer repeating carbines, a hail of fire the men could not hope to match. Hampton's troopers had squandered their surprise and had no choice but to cede the village back to Kilpatrick's men and a newly arrived force of Sherman's infantry.

For Seeley, the depressing reality was that he would make the effort to confirm Kilpatrick's description, the image of the man in his nightclothes burned into his brain. All he knew for now was that Butler's Captain Bostick had missed his opportunity, and that Seeley might well have sat on his horse with a pistol in his hand, staring down at the pathetic figure of a man in his nightclothes, who was most likely Kilpatrick himself.

CHAPTER FORTY-ONE

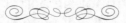

SHERMAN

FAYETTEVILLE, NORTH CAROLINA—MARCH 13, 1865

The boat was the **Davidson,** a navy tug that plowed its way slowly up the Cape Fear River, the first craft of its kind Sherman had seen since he left Savannah. For the men it meant mail, vast crowds straining against the order imposed by the provost marshals, the mail sacks doled out to the impatient joy of the men who might once more hear from home.

For Sherman, the arrival of the **Davidson** came a day after he had ridden into Fayetteville, reaching the next link in a chain that wound him that

much closer to the final confrontation with whatever enemy lay in his path. The boat's arrival meant
a supply line was now open to the coast at Wilmington, and for men who had grown weak from the
poor foraging over the past weeks, Sherman knew
the boat was a symbol of better times, that more
boats would follow, hauling every kind of supplies
his army required.

Major Byers had become a fixture around Sherman's camp, the lyrics of his poem put to music, a
pleasant surprise for Sherman's staff officers. Byers
had organized a glee club of sorts, its members
coming mostly from the former prisoners who had
shared his confinement at Columbia. More than
once, Sherman had invited Byers and his men to
regale the various senior commanders, the audience delighted by the talent of the men who carried
the tune, Sherman focused more on the extraordinary words Byers had put to paper. Already he had
encouraged Byers to pass on the poem to Conyngham, to any of the other reporters. It was a small
show of pride from Sherman, allowing himself to
feel the compliment from Byers's talented lyricism,
something he had even shared with Ellen.

But once in Fayetteville, with the river spread before him, Sherman had another mission for Byers.
When the **Davidson** resumed her voyage, moving
seaward, Byers went along. In his pocket he carried a message meant for the eyes of Ulysses Grant.
The note was simple and straightforward, none

of the anxiety about politics and the intrigue plaguing Washington. Sherman offered Grant a neat
summary of the campaign through South Carolina,
offered positive descriptions of the condition and
morale of the army. But most important, Sherman
communicated to Grant his absolute confidence
that even if Joe Johnston threw obstacles into Sherman's path, they would be overcome with a mini-
mum of effort, and assuring Grant that Sherman
was perfectly certain that "I will be in position to
aid you materially in the spring campaign."

Word had come of the embarrassing incident
at Kilpatrick's encampment, not far from Fayetteville. The soldiers spoke of it freely, information,
whether accurate or not, passed along from the senior officers to their men. Sherman waited for a
direct report from Kilpatrick, but his own staff was
picking up the tidbits as they floated past his headquarters, and whether the rumors were exaggerated
or not, Sherman was gaining a pretty clear picture
that Kilpatrick had been badly bruised. Whether
the cavalryman would ever admit that really didn't
matter. Sherman still required his services, both as
a probe to the front and as protection for Slocum's
far left flank. The rumors and sketchy reports suggested that Kilpatrick had suffered a heavy thump-
ing from Hampton's troopers, losing prisoners and
more casualties than Sherman wanted to hear. But
the teasing from the soldiers was the most annoying, Kilpatrick's reputation for luxurious accommo-

dations and the company of a variety of toothsome women bothering Sherman more than he knew it should. As long as the cavalry did its job, Sherman had little to complain about, but Kilpatrick's bad habits were becoming a distraction, if not to the rest of the army, then for Kilpatrick himself. Too many reports painted the picture of Kilpatrick caught in a compromising position, his camp without suitable pickets or any kind of defenses at all. That Kilpatrick was able to escape was testament to the man's skills as a rider. That he left a woman behind who might have provided the rebels with all manner of indiscreet information made Sherman furious.

In Fayetteville, Sherman placed his headquarters in what had been the old United States Arsenal, a facility enlarged and put to efficient use by the rebels who had commandeered it. But those men were long gone, protected by the burning of the primary crossing over the Cape Fear, what he knew had been accomplished by Hardee's men just prior to Sherman's arrival. But Captain Poe had gone immediately to work, the pontoon bridges now in place, and already Sherman was planning the next step in the advance, still intending to nip at the heels, if not grab the entire body, of whatever force Hardee was leading.

As the **Davidson** churned away downriver, Sherman stood staring at a glorious sunset, the last remnants of the latest rain clouds that inflicted a wet plague on his army. He moved back inside, saw Hitchcock at a desk, copying the letters Sherman had written, all the usual correspondence he was obliged to send to the War Department.

"You not finished with that yet?"

Hitchcock looked up over his glasses. "Almost, sir. Sorry. There will be another boat tomorrow. The **Davidson**'s Captain Ainsworth assured me of that. They are anxious to provide for us all the goods you requested. It is a gratifying experience, sir."

"What?"

"The cooperation of the navy. I had always heard about rivalry between the services. But so far, Admiral Dahlgren, the others, all seem completely willing to support the campaign."

"Suppose there's some navy men feel differently. But my experience has been a good one. Vicksburg, Admiral Porter. He and Grant made that work like a fine clock. Any navy man decides he's running his own show, remind him who's keeping the enemy away from all those forts they built on the coastline. It's not a damned contest."

"Yes, sir." Hitchcock paused. "Strange town, sir. Hardly anybody in the streets. Not sure if they're afraid of us, or just . . . bored with this whole affair."

"It's the Sabbath, Major. These people aren't what we saw farther south. Good Scotch Covenanters, mostly. Some of 'em went hard for the rebels, no doubt. But a good many just want this thing to be over with. Not especially loyal to anybody's flag. The British found that out, early in the revolution. Redcoats tried to tame these people, got bloody noses for their trouble. I've got no cause to treat these people with any punishment in mind. This isn't South Carolina. You sent that order to Kilpatrick?"

"Oh, yes, sir. A copy is . . . here. 'You will deal as moderately and fairly by North Carolineans as possible, and fan the flame of discord already subsisting between them and their proud cousins of South Carolina. There never was much love between them. . . .'"

"That's enough. Good. I just hope he can control his damned raiders so we don't burn as much of this place as we did south of here. I want Schofield to get that word as well."

"Do you expect General Schofield to meet with us here?"

"Hell, no. I'm not staying around Fayetteville more than I have to. The rebels are hightailing to the north, and I want to grab Hardee by the soft privates before he can gather up much help from Johnston. If we can't catch him, at least we'll keep him running. Schofield will rendezvous with us at Goldsboro, and if he understands how important that is, I expect to see him within a week or so. A great deal can happen in a week, Major. I want all of it to be positive."

"Sir, should I inform Major Dayton that we intend to march tomorrow?"

"The day after. The men are enjoying the rest, and they earned it. If the tugs will bring rations and clothing upriver, the men will welcome that opportunity."

"They'll march without any of that, sir. Never seen morale so high."

Sherman thought a moment, looked toward the door, the daylight almost gone. "They know what the compasses tell them, Major. This isn't a slog through some Georgia swamp, or some march to someplace no one's ever seen. Every day we move, they're a little closer to home. That's how you boost morale."

Hitchcock smiled, nodded. "Yes, sir. I understand."

Sherman moved again to the door, saw flickers of lantern light, most of it from his men, the guards close by, others encamped close to the arsenal. He stepped back inside, saw McCoy now, peering over Hitchcock's shoulder. "Question, Major?"

McCoy straightened, said, "Just one, sir. You had mentioned yesterday that we would leave this place only when the arsenal was dealt with. Do you have orders to that effect?"

Sherman glanced up, heavy wooden timbers,

wood planking on the walls. "Tomorrow, order Captain Poe to begin burning the place. Every structure, and anything left inside." He paused. "This was a hell of a well-run operation, Major. If it was practicable, I'd garrison the place. But it's not. We'll call it our one lesson to the people of North Carolina. We give you responsibility over a Federal arsenal, it won't pay you to appropriate the place. Tell Poe to blow it up with gunpowder, and knock down every wall. I intend to recommend to the War Department that they not stick an arsenal anywhere in the future where a misguided rebellion might make use of it."

By March 15, Sherman had marched his entire army across the Cape Fear River, on the roads that would lead to Goldsboro. As before, Howard's wing, the Seventeenth and Fifteenth corps, took the eastward path, while Slocum's Fourteenth and Twentieth marched more to the west. The maps showed the obvious, that if Johnston was gathering any substantial force of rebels at Raleigh, Slocum's men were closer, and would likely bear the brunt of any assault. In response, Sherman ordered Kilpatrick's men to shield Slocum's columns.

He rode with his staff, the misery of another storm soaking through him yet again, the slop of the roads bogging the artillery in front of him, men gathering in work brigades to free the wheels. He moved past cursing teamsters, ignored the work. He tried to keep his back straight, but the cold wetness had already flooded down the back of his neck, souring his mood, keeping the staff at bay.

There was a wagon now, down in a shallow ditch, a quartet of men straining against one wheel. Sherman halted the horse, tried to see past the disguise of the raincoats, looking for an officer.

"Get more men, for God's sake! Who's in command?"

One man stood straight, a salute, the telltale sign of a young officer. "Yes, sir. Lieutenant Folyard. General Sherman, it is an honor, sir."

"Shut the hell up. You have any more men than this under your command?"

"Yes, sir. A platoon, up ahead."

"Well, bring them back here and use them. What the hell do you think they're for?"

The man saluted again, and Sherman spurred the horse, cursed under his breath, the young lieutenant running past him through ankle-deep mud. The column resumed ahead, and Sherman fought the despair, an odd blanket of gloom that seemed to soak him as easily as the rain. He wanted to stop, to find some dry place, had passed at least a half-dozen small farmhouses. But the men were on the move, and he knew to keep them there, that every mile was one less before they reached Goldsboro. Damn it all, he thought. Has there ever been a campaign that survived drowning as much as this one? Is it just the time of year? I don't recall New Orleans this miserable. Where's Kilpatrick? If he's got some wayward beauty stuffed in his camp wagon again, I'll skin him myself. If there was anyone else out here who outranked him, Kilpatrick would be haying horses.

Sherman closed his eyes, fought a budding headache, struggled to see past the gloom, a mood as black as any in weeks. Why now? he thought. Is it just the damned weather? I'm just so sick of so many days doing nothing. He had a sudden thought, remembered Georgia, the approach to Savannah. We pressed them, compacted them, and so I thought there was danger in that. Interior lines, a tight defense, all of it. Hardee wrote the textbook, for God's sake. But he didn't make use of it. Or maybe he didn't have the strength. What about now? Johnston's giving him orders. What does that mean? He's retreating, we know that. Running like rabbits, with this big damned sixty-thousand-man hound dog on his tail.

He tried to take some comfort in that, forced himself to say aloud, "We're winning. Damn it all. No reason to be so down in the mud about it. What the hell's the matter with you?"

He tried to think of happier times, better places, Ellen, his children. But those memories were poisoned too easily by thoughts of his son Willie. He felt enormous guilt for his lack of feelings for the infant, had never seen him, had no idea what he looked like. That will be a problem, he thought. Ellen will not understand. She endured both of them, suffered through two dead children. God help me, I can only feel for Willie. He was me. No other way to see it. Nine years old, and he would have grown up to command an army. I know it.

He blinked away tears, glanced to the side, no one there, the staff keeping well back. The guards rode out to each side of him, Lieutenant Snelling up front, seeming as miserable in the saddle as Sherman was now. He won't show it, he thought. Most loyal man in the army. Willie loved him. Loved everyone of them. Damn, stop this!

He saw a rider, moving toward him along the side of the muddy road. The man stopped at Snelling, the lieutenant pointing back, sending the man on past. Sherman tried to focus, the headache in full blossom, the man closing the distance, the face familiar, one of Slocum's men.

"Sir! General Slocum offers his respects, and wishes to inform you that the rebel line has been driven back. General Kilpatrick is heavily engaged, but has made way for units of the Twentieth Corps."

Sherman felt a spark of alarm, stared hard at the man. "What the hell are you talking about? I haven't heard a damned thing."

The man pointed toward the front, and for the first time, Sherman heard the thump of artillery.

"Where is Slocum?"

"Just ahead, sir."

"Let's go."

Sherman turned, the staff already coming alive, McCoy and Dayton leading a handful of aides closer. Dayton said, "What is it, sir?"

"A fight. You heard anything?"

"No, sir."

"Well, let's find out what's happening."

Sherman spurred the horse, Slocum's man moving out front, Snelling and the guards keeping pace. Damn you, he thought. Wrapped up inside your own head, whining about dead children. You forget where the hell you are?

The sounds were reaching him consistently now, heavy thumps, the rain slowing. He saw Slocum, a cluster of officers, Slocum pointing, giving orders, men in motion. Sherman was there now, called out, "What the hell's going on?"

Slocum peered at him from the brim of a dripping hat. "Kilpatrick ran into a heavy skirmish line at six this morning. Stood toe-to-toe with a bunch of rebels for a while, until he called for help. I moved infantry up, drove in their line. But there's another behind it."

"You can't flank them? How many can there be?"

"The river is over that way a short hop. There's a flooded creek to the left. No choice but to drive straight ahead."

Sherman rode past the officers, stared out, the rain finally stopping. The musket fire was reaching him now, most of it out along the soggy road. He eyed the trees to both sides, thought of the rivers, the swamplands, **Hardee**. You chose this ground.

Slocum was beside him now, said, "Doesn't appear to be a large force. But they've got good defensive lines. Hardee's making use of the terrain, that's for certain."

Of course he is, Sherman thought. He wrote the book.

A courier came hard, splashing mud high as he rode. He focused on Slocum, reined up, said, "Sir! The 105th Illinois has driven in the flank of the enemy's position. Major Reynolds is moving up more of the artillery."

Sherman thought, Reynolds. Good. Knows how to place his guns.

Another courier rode close, eyed Sherman, tossed up a salute. "General! The rebels are giving way!"

"Who's pushing them back?"

The man looked at Slocum, then back to Sherman. "The First and Third divisions are in line, sir. Making a whale of a fight!"

Sherman looked past the man, the only sounds a steady chatter of musketry, broken by the heavy thunder of Reynolds's big guns. Hitchcock was up beside Sherman now, said, "Sir! Should we ride forward, see what's happening?"

There was too much energy in the question, and Sherman looked at the young man, shook his head. "Let the men do their jobs, Major. They need us, they can find us."

The fight near the village of Averasboro settled into haphazard skirmishing for several hours, Hardee's well-chosen defense making perfect use of the protection on his flanks by the two waterways. But by midafternoon, Slocum's infantry gained the momentum. Hardee's men continued to resist, and even as they gave way, Hardee kept his men together with enough organization to continue the skirmishing throughout most of the following day.

Aided by the misery of the weather, and the narrow peninsula of land framed by the two rivers, Hardee had laid his troops out in three defensive lines. The first two were manned by his weakest, most inexperienced troops, with his seasoned veterans at the rear. The front lines were certain to give way, Hardee anticipating that the stout line of veterans could absorb and rally their collapse. As the Federals struggled to advance, they confronted each line, and when that line gave way, the Federals followed their victory by a mad dash forward, only to stumble into Hardee's next line. Though maneuver was difficult, both sides probed and poked the other, momentum swinging both ways. But Hardee understood mathematics, and with more of Slocum's infantry driving into Hardee's narrow position, Hardee had only one final maneuver he could make. He withdrew.

The fight at Averasboro produced casualties on both sides, but in the end it amounted to only a heavy skirmish, the best fight Hardee could make. But there was a success for the rebels that even Hardee didn't completely understand. Averasboro forced Slocum's entire wing to delay their march, while farther to the east, Howard's columns continued onward. Instead of Sherman's two halves advancing in tandem, each wing capable of moving to a rapid support of the other, a gap had opened between them, a gap that Joe Johnston's cavalry scouts watched with great care. As Hardee pulled his men away from the fight, he only knew he had given Slocum a bloody nose. What Johnston realized was that Hardee might have given him the one desperate opportunity he had hoped for.

CHAPTER FORTY-TWO

FRANKLIN

The march had been as miserable as most, the roads sucking the shoes off the soldiers' feet, the single advantage Franklin had by wearing no shoes at all. Colonel Jones had offered to find him a pair, but Franklin had spent most of his young life in bare feet, and the effort to confine his toes inside stiff leather was at best uncomfortable. As the soldiers struggled with the mud, Franklin did what he had always done before. He just walked through it.

The promotion had come to Toland Jones in mid-February, someone in the army noting that a regiment should be led by a man with a higher rank than captain. To Jones's surprise, and the delight of every man in the unit, he had been promoted two ranks, to lieutenant colonel. If the soldiers weren't certain just how the army made these decisions, to Franklin it was one more source of outright confusion. How could a man be both a lieutenant and a colonel? The explanation had made little sense to him and for reasons Franklin still didn't understand, Jones was referred to by his men as simply the **colonel**.

Jones rode at the head of the column, the proper place for a regimental commander, and Franklin had kept in line with the men close behind, trying to fit in wherever there was space. He felt awkward without a musket, envied the men their marvelous weapons, imagined he was carrying one. He had found a heavy stick, carried it against his shoulder, mimicking them, drawing the small joke. But the soldiers mostly ignored him, nothing like the teasing he had heard the first time he assumed a place in line. They knew him now, even his name, and to Franklin's relief, they seemed to accept him for what he was, a camp servant. Officially he was Colonel Jones's aide-de-camp, a title that meant only what Jones intended it to mean at any given moment. Still, there was no uniform, no weapon, no rank. Even if Franklin functioned more or less as the regimental gofer, watering the horses, gathering forage, carrying messages to other officers when the couriers were busy, the job meant that Franklin was a part of this army. Gone were the evil smirks, the crude comments that the soldiers had aimed toward Clara. He was grateful for that, felt more than ever that leaving her in Savannah was the best thing for both of them, no matter what he realized now was the price he would pay.

Since leaving Savannah he had missed Clara with an ache that surprised him, a longing to be with her. She was his mate, but also his fellow novice, ignorant of the ways of the world, in almost anything beyond their former lives as slaves. As he observed everything new, from people to the countryside, he imagined her there, would talk to her in his mind, pointing out some tidbit that no one else around him would notice at all. At night she seemed to fill him completely, the silent conversations in his mind full of explanations and wonder, the pride of marching with the soldiers, only swept away by the daylight, the sadness of starting a new day enduring the reality of her absence. For the first time in his life, sleep had meaning for him that he had never imagined before. The dreams were pleasant, happy times with her, so very different from a boy's nightmares, chased by dogs, the sight of his father's horrible injury. Even more, the dreams offered him glimpses of some kind of future he still couldn't quite understand, and certainly couldn't predict, pieces of a life with her that still seemed a marvelous fantasy.

Since their last goodbye, he hadn't heard anything from her, no letters even from the old preacher, but there was nothing strange about that. Franklin still didn't understand the army's mail system, was hesitant to ask Colonel Jones or anyone else if he was allowed to mail a letter, or what kind of thoughts he would put to paper. He had seen what the soldiers used for stamps, another oddity, like a tiny bit of currency, what seemed to be an adornment on the letters, a decoration that had meaning Franklin still didn't comprehend.

On the march through South Carolina, he had been careful to keep close to the soldiers, though it was unlikely any of the Georgia plantation owners were extending their search for their freed slaves this far north, Franklin seeing the wide Savannah River as a boundary that meant more to him than the army's struggle with pontoon bridges. He had never known anything of this place called South Carolina, but he understood it now, that the army marched through this new land carrying a serious anger, the explanation coming from anyone he asked, that this awful war had been born here, that these people deserved to feel the pain of that.

The farther they marched from the seacoast, the more hilly the land became, the flat swamplands rising into lush forests, more fertile farms. The trees changed, too, fat oaks and tall pines taking the place of so much scrub, the thickets of cypress and palmetto bogs. He had observed all of that with a keen eye, marveled at the similarities with Georgia, had begun to wonder if the whole world looked like the places he had already seen. That inspired laughter from the soldiers, but they were eager to set him straight, the men describing to him their homes up north in very different ways. Their seriousness had impressed Franklin, the soldiers growing sad as they spoke of towns and villages, homes and family, the place they called Ohio. They pointed, too, to the trees they passed, comparing the tall pines to what they had back home, vast forests of broad-leafed hardwood trees, how those would change color in the fall, glowing orange and red, some of the men calling it God's great paintbrush, wiping across the landscape to signal the coming of winter. He had seen snow before, but not what the men described to him, powdery white, as deep as a man's waist, the lakes and ponds freezing hard, so that a man could walk across. He had been skeptical at those kinds of stories, knew that they thought him stupid, but the stories were passed between the men themselves, memories of what they were missing, where their families waited for their return. Franklin saw real emotion there, and for the first time he understood that these white soldiers felt the same kind of ache, the longing he felt every day for Clara.

There were plantations in South Carolina as well, not as many, and most of those not nearly as grand as what he had seen in Georgia. There were exceptions to that, of course, and in every case, the army marched past the mansions to cheers from a fresh crowd of Negroes, who flowed out away from the estates to follow the great Sherman, leaving behind a life that Franklin had to believe was no better than what he had left in Georgia.

He didn't see the destruction of Columbia, the Fourteenth Corps sent farther out along the river, making their crossing several miles from the capital city. The soldiers seemed angry about that, as though missing out on some wonderful victory. But there were fires still, homes along the way, smaller villages where the bummers had been, leading the way as they had done across Georgia. Franklin had seen what was left of many of those homes, smoldering wreckage, had seen the white people still lingering, buried in sadness for what this army had done to them. The soldiers had mostly ignored that, still sought out the treasures, mostly food and spirits, anything the bummers might have missed. But there was little time for treasure hunting, the orders passed along from high above that this march had a purpose, and it wasn't to end in South Carolina.

And then, the talk changed, a new excitement, and when they crossed yet another wide river, Franklin was told by the colonel that they were now in North Carolina. It was another marvel, Colonel Jones's adjutant showing Franklin a map, pencil lines in odd shapes, marked by rivers and railroads, and small X's for the towns. All Franklin could see from the map was that North Carolina was larger, but he saw for himself that the land was not so different from what they had left behind, vast woods, the tallest pine trees he had ever seen. The towns were the same as well, peopled by somber white women, old and young, and enormous numbers of Negroes, many of them leaving their homes and masters, now following behind the army. The greatest difference between the two Carolinas came from the soldiers themselves, the loud talk, the obvious thirst for vengeance calming now. The officers seemed determined to convince their men that this was nothing like South Carolina, that Sherman himself had told them to treat these people with respect.

But then, there was a different order, this one directed toward the civilians who followed the army. Not all were slaves, some of them poor whites, what the officers described as **refugees,** another word Franklin didn't know. When the army reached Fayetteille, many of those people, black and white, were gathered together, officers reading from pieces of paper, the people told that the army could not feed them, that there was a better life for them down the river. The boats were there, black smoke from tall stacks, sailors standing aside as the people were herded aboard, watched over by men with muskets. When each boat reached its fill, the whistle sounded, ropes cast off, the boat belching smoke as it swung out into the river, slowly moving away until it disappeared. From the packed throngs on board the boats to the people left waiting on the wharves, the reaction to this new experience bordered on panic, rumors spreading among the Negroes that they were being hauled back home, to face their overseers. The most frightening rumor Franklin heard claimed that the boats were going straight out to sea, only to drown the former slaves in the ocean, ridding the army of their black curse. Franklin struggled not to believe that, had heard too many ridiculous rumors all along the march, none of them true. But the fear and the cries and the tears were real, even the white refugees not quite believing that they were being taken anywhere other than some kind of prison.

Franklin understood immediately that he had been far more fortunate than most of the others. If Clara had accompanied him, the orders could certainly have applied to her, one more mouth the army was struggling to feed. And, for his work with Colonel Jones, and the camps of the 113th Ohio, Franklin had been given a choice, whether to make the journey toward some unknown opportunity or to remain with the army. For him, there was no option at all. If there was land to be provided the former slaves, a place to begin some new kind of life, he had to believe that the army, or at least the colonel, would see that he received his share. But that could come later. It was clear to him that the war was still being fought, rebel cavalry still skirting the Federal march, the men he marched with still caring for their muskets. Until that had passed, and he could go back to Clara and not fear some kind of punishment, he would stay with Colonel Jones.

NEAR AVERASBORO,
NORTH CAROLINA—MARCH 16, 1865

The musket fire had been straight in front of them, Franklin as mystified as the men around him just what was happening. But the riders came quickly, horsemen moving back along the column, carrying reports to the officers somewhere to the rear. The column had been ordered to halt, the men standing in deep mud as more riders passed by, both directions. Out front, the firing had grown louder, ambulances coming toward them, filled with wounded men, pulled by struggling horses that slogged through the mud, forcing the column of soldiers off to the side of the road. He had felt the first real fear then, the sounds of the fight rising up far more menacing than the hiss of the rain. But then the orders came, the men called back into the road, moving forward. He had gone with them at first, terrifying confusion, had finally seen Colonel Jones, but the man had concerns of his own, could only tell Franklin to stay back, keep out of the way. Franklin had obeyed, settling into some wet brush, watching as more soldiers moved forward, straight toward the sound of the guns. The ambulances passed by him all day long, Franklin feeling a gut-twisting fear that these soldiers were dying, **all of them,** that something awful had happened, something no one had expected. He sat curled up in the shadow of a gnarled oak tree, his mind spewing out questions, no answers. His fears centered first on Colonel Jones, then on the others, anyone he knew, and then, the greatest fear of all, that Sherman was there, would die, along with the others, that somehow it had all gone terribly wrong. And then, even as the rain continued, the fight had ended.

He saw Colonel Jones, a shelter-half serving as a makeshift tent, the rains still blowing through the trees. Franklin was suffering from a hard chill, moved with quick steps trying to relieve the cold in his bones, his clothes thick with icy water. As he saw familiar faces, he felt breathless relief, the sight of the colonel inspiring tears. He wanted to call out, a boisterous greeting, but Jones was speaking to another officer, serious faces, and Franklin held a clamp on his joy, knew to stay back. The adjutant was there now, a new man Jones had added to his staff in Savannah, near the time Jones had received his promotion. He was very young, seemed to carry his authority with a little more pride than he had yet to earn, served the colonel mostly with the handling of dispatches, receiving the orders that were passed down to the regiment. Franklin felt immediately that the young man regarded Franklin as a curiosity, speaking of him as though Franklin couldn't hear his words. The man's name was Hartmann, but Jones always called him simply **lieutenant**.

Hartmann saw Franklin now, moved out toward him, away from the other officers, said, "Hey! Wondered where you run off to. Didn't think we'd see you again. We had us a scrap, sure enough." He moved closer to Franklin, as though sharing a secret. "That fellow there's General Mitchell, commands the brigade. He put us straight into the fight, he did."

Franklin stood shivering, Hartmann seemingly oblivious.

"Excuse me, sir, but can I get a blanket, or maybe some rations?"

Hartmann moved away, responding to a call from Jones, who saw Franklin now.

"Well, good. Get over here!"

Franklin saw a hint of a smile, was suddenly grateful Jones remembered who he was.

Hartmann said, "Saw him lurking out there in the brush. He best be careful doing that kind of foolishness. Somebody might think he's a spy."

"I ain't no spy. Just did what the colonel told me to do. Stayed out of the way."

Jones motioned him to come in under the shelter, said, "General Mitchell, this is my camp aide, Mr. Franklin. Been with me since well back in Georgia."

Mitchell was young, stern-faced, nodded briefly toward Franklin, said, "Fine. Colonel, we're moving out in the morning. General Morgan's been ordered to lead the division along the road toward Goldsboro. He says Sherman's not too happy with our little fight. We're to make up time as best we can. Our brigade was the only one from the entire Fourteenth Corps that took part in the scrap, and General Davis wants to know what in blazes we were doing. Might cost me this star, and it's not even warm yet. I'll be at division headquarters if you need me. General Morgan expects me to take the heat from General Davis. Guess I'd better."

Mitchell moved away into the rain, and Jones seemed to wait, then said to Hartmann, "Get Mr. Franklin something to eat. I was worried about you, you know. The rebels tossed up a big mess in front of us, and we had no place to go but straight at them. I got word from Colonel Mitchell—ah, **General** Mitchell—that we were needed. We were in the van of the whole Fourteenth Corps, and some say we bailed out a couple of the Twentieth's divisions by ourselves. Not sure if that's true, but I'll believe anything they want to tell me."

The words flowed over Franklin, and he said, "I heard the fight. Sounded pretty bad. He's a colonel or a general?"

Jones laughed. "Mitchell? Just made him a brigadier general in January. I've always called him colonel. Have to get used to that. He still calls me captain
once in a while. The army has its ways, especially in
the middle of a war. I try not to think about that."

Franklin was completely confused, didn't yet understand the distinctions about rank. Hartmann
was there now, handed Franklin a wad of hardtack.

"Here it is. Best we got right now."

Jones said to Hartmann, "Go to the 108, talk to
Captain Jordan. Ask him if they've got anything
better to eat. Most of the men are worrying more
about our wounded than what we're having for
dinner."

"Yes, sir."

Hartmann seemed to sag, pulled his collar up
tight to his neck, splashed his way out through the
thin woods.

Franklin said, "Wounded? You done lost some
men, then?"

"We took casualties. Problem is, there's no place
to leave 'em. Anybody goes down, we have to carry
'em with us. We're still in rebel country. North
Carolina's not turning out to be what we were told.
The high brass thought these people would rally
around us. I guess Sherman thought North Carolina is mostly Union in sentiment. Doesn't seem
that way. I get hit with a musket ball, I don't want
anybody leaving me with these people. Where'd
you spend the fight? Hide out?"

"Just sat by the road. Found a tree, kept some of the rain off. I never heard a fight before, not like that. Scared me, sir. Didn't know what to think."

"It wasn't all that bad. The rebels put a roadblock in our path. Stubborn bunch. It took some doing, but we pushed 'em away. But headquarters is spitting snake venom our way, saying we need to make up for the lost time. Not sure if we're chasing those same rebels or if they took another way out of here. All they tell me is get these men in the road and go, soon as daylight shows."

"Where we going?"

Jones removed his hat, ran a hand through wet hair. "They don't tell me that. We follow the folks marching in front of us. If I want to know where we're going, I can ask once we get there."

SOUTHWEST OF BENTONVILLE, NORTH CAROLINA—MARCH 19, 1865

The sounds of musket fire drifted toward them, digging into Franklin like a knife blade, the same cold-chested fear he had felt at Averasboro. The troops seemed unaffected, continued their march on the soggy roads, the only change the number of riders that moved alongside the column. But with the riders came orders, and Franklin kept his place close behind Jones, a color bearer to one side, the adjutant Hartmann just behind. Most of the horsemen had gone on by, but now, one man reined up, Jones responding with a salute, both men dismounting, a quick jog off the side of the road. Franklin stepped out of the column, unsure what he was supposed to do, moved closer to Jones and the other officer, the man showing Jones a map, one hand motioning toward the front of the column. Jones called out to his adjutant now, a hard edge to his voice, "Lieutenant, pass along the order to the companies. There's open ground ahead. Move out to the right, keep in contact with the 108. We're to position on their right flank. Vandever's brigade will be to our right. Move, Lieutenant!"

Hartmann seemed to animate, raw excitement in the young man's face. He spurred the horse, spinning in the muddy road, shouted, "Yes, sir!"

Jones returned to his horse, ignored Franklin, another officer moving up, a handful of aides, another flag, larger. The face was familiar, the man Franklin had met in the camp, and Jones said, "General Mitchell, just had an adjutant from General Morgan here, placing us to Vandever's left."

"I know that, dammit! I've been with him for a half hour. The rebels are in strength all across our front. Carlin's moved the First Division to the left of the road, and he ran into a hornet's nest. Make tracks, Colonel! We don't yet know what we're facing. But it's no skirmish line."

The sounds from the fight were growing, seemed to be closer, Franklin staring that way, nothing to see. Hartmann returned now, and Jones shouted to him, "Let's ride, Lieutenant. We have any couriers about?"

"No, sir. Just . . . me."

"No good. I need you with me. You ever positioned troops under fire?"

Hartmann hesitated, and Franklin had seen the look before, a man too frightened to speak. After a long second, Hartmann said, "No, sir."

"Time to learn! Keep your eye on the colors of the 108. No gaps between us, you understand?"

"Yes, sir!"

Jones saw Franklin now, seemed to weigh a decision, Franklin feeling the weight of Jones's thoughts. "Fall into line! Stay close to me, if you can. You wanted to be in the army, well, I might need you. I don't have the horses to keep in touch with the other regiments. Might have to be you. Can you follow orders?"

Franklin felt a sudden burst of pride, said, "I been following orders my whole life, sir."

"Keep up front of the column. When we spread into battle lines, you stay where I can see you. You run away, I never want to see you in my camp again."

Franklin was surprised by the anger he saw in Jones's face, but Jones was looking toward the sound of the guns now, and Franklin moved up beside the horse, one hand on the animal's rump.

"Tell you what, Colonel. You don't run off, I won't, neither."

CHAPTER FORTY-THREE

FRANKLIN

SOUTH OF BENTONVILLE,
NORTH CAROLINA—MARCH 19, 1865

The fight had begun early, one division of the Fourteenth Corps struck hard by a column of rebels that their commander, William Carlin, did not expect to see. As Carlin's men flowed out into the fields, they encountered skirmishers, Wade Hampton's dismounted cavalry. Skirmish lines had rarely been a challenge for massed infantry, and Carlin ordered his men forward, expecting the rebels to back away. But Hampton was supported by infantry, a far stronger force than Carlin was prepared to assault. Carlin continued forward,

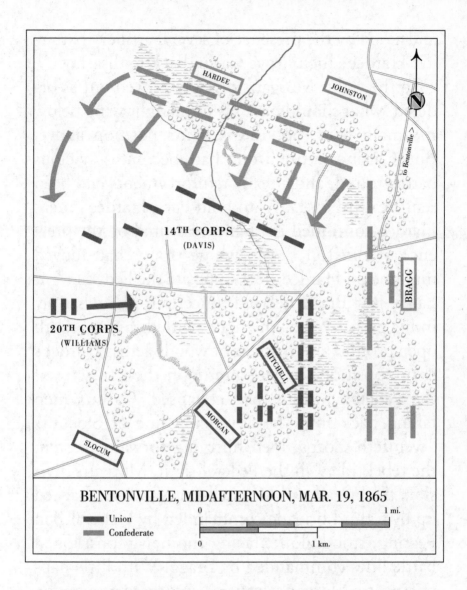

BENTONVILLE, MIDAFTERNOON, MAR. 19, 1865

■ Union
■ Confederate

0   1 mi.

0   1 km.

obeying the orders of his corps commander, General Davis, who believed that the rebels could be shoved aside. Instead Carlin drew the attention of numerous Confederate troops, driven forward by their commander, William Hardee. After a brutal fight, Carlin's division became seriously outflanked, and aided by the presence of several artillery batteries, Hardee's men drove Carlin back in disarray.

To the right, Morgan's division moved out as ordered, what should have been the right wing below the main road, opposite Carlin's position above. But Carlin's entire front had become a vicious battleground, and already reinforcements had been sent forward by Davis to hold back Hardee's men. Hardee continued the fight, reassured by the presence of Braxton Bragg, whose troops had moved into line on Hardee's left, opposite the Federal right flank. But Bragg delayed, uncertain just what lay in his path, even as the fight swirled through both open ground and thickets of woods across Hardee's entire position. By late afternoon the left wing of the Federal position had collapsed, Carlin's men falling back into the advancing line of Slocum's Twentieth Corps, men hurrying forward to stem the rebel tide. On the Federal right, Morgan's division, the brigades of Mitchell and Vandever, backed up by a third brigade commanded by General Ben Fearing, stood alone, facing the newly positioned battle lines commanded by Bragg. With little happening to Morgan's front, his corps commander, Jeff Davis, ordered Morgan's reserves, Fearing's brigade, to pull away from supporting Mitchell and Vandever and move out farther to the left. Davis's hope was that Fearing would drive directly into the exposed left flank of Hardee's rebels, which could help the Federal reinforcements he had already sent forward in sweeping the field of Hardee's victorious troops.

But the confusion was overwhelming. Fearing did find rebel troops, but those men were scattered and disorganized, making a fight on their own, a challenge for Fearing's compact lines. The rebels didn't recoil as Davis had hoped, and reacted to Fearing's appearance by settling into whatever cover they could find, content to trade volleys with Fearing's men. With the broken Federal line now strengthened by the rapid advance of troops from the Twentieth Corps, the fight settled into a slugfest, the Federals backing into the cover of heavy timber, while Hardee's rebels shoved and prodded their way into any opening they could find.

By four in the afternoon, Braxton Bragg had finally satisfied himself that his share of the Confederate front was now prepared to participate in the attack. Across from them was a line of trees, manned by skirmishers from Illinois. Behind the skirmishers stood the two brigades of Mitchell and Vandever.

"We're out of contact! Damn it all!" The cluster of officers absorbed the fury of their division commander, Morgan pacing furiously. "General Davis took our reserves, and now we don't even know what's happened to Fearing! The only word we have received is that he's taking heavy fire from two sides. I have no idea what's happening north of the road. All I hear is a storm of artillery and musketry! I haven't received any orders from General Davis, and I'm not even certain he's on the field!"

Morgan looked out to the rear of the formation, an aide galloping in, the man dismounting in a tumble.

"General! There's a gap between our left and any other troops. Except rebels, sir. I nearly ran slam into 'em. The whole world is full of rebs, sir!"

Morgan stopped moving, glanced out over the men, most of those at work creating a defensive line. "Not this part of the world, Corporal." Morgan focused on Mitchell now. "General Mitchell, your brigade is my left flank. I do not know what lies out farther left, beyond the main Goldsboro Road. Right now we cannot concern ourselves with any of that. All we know is there is a considerable number of the enemy beyond the tree line to our front. Have we heard anything from the skirmishers?"

One of the officers said, "Just that the rebels are forming into lines. They're not coming yet."

Morgan faced that way again, said, "What the hell are they waiting for? They know we're here, no doubt." He turned to the two brigade commanders again. "General Vandever, you're the right. There's two halves to this puzzle, and right now it's all we can count on. Go to your commands. It's getting late, but there's plenty of daylight."

The thunder of artillery came again from the far

left, what they had heard now for hours. Mitchell said, "They could be coming at us from that direction. Maybe that's what those fellows are waiting for out in front of us. They hit our flank, it'll be a simple matter to swallow us up."

Morgan mounted his horse, said, "There's too much firing up above the road. Somebody's holding the rebs' attention. All I know is that Slocum was sending the Twentieth Corps up here fast as they could march. The rebels don't have that many troops in the whole state. I won't speak out against General Carlin, but if his men gave way like it appears, he must certainly have run into something he wasn't prepared for. I won't have that here. Prepare to be attacked, and prepare to drive them back. And if they come again, drive them back again. It's that simple. Now, go!"

Franklin's hands were blistered, but the axe swung down hard, the tree toppling slowly, men swarming over it, trimming the limbs. To one side of him, Captain Gorman called out, "Move that up here! Stack it up. Good!"

On both sides of Franklin, men hoisted the log, Franklin setting it on his shoulder, moving in step with the others, the log placed on a stack of a half-dozen more. Franklin felt the stiffness in his back, pains in both arms, licked at the blisters on his palms. Beside him, Sergeant Knight knelt, seemed in pain, and Franklin bent low, said, "You need help?"

Knight shook his head, stood slowly, said, "Just taking a minute to rest these damned bones. These logs oughta hold back anybody. Just hope we get a chance to try it out."

When the order was passed by General Mitchell, Franklin had jumped in to help, had long known how to handle the heavy axe. With the roar of the fighting keeping off to the left, the men of Mitchell's brigade had taken advantage of the quiet to their front, had attacked the tree line for the cover it could offer. Already a hundred or more trees had been felled, a snaking line of timber now providing protection. Franklin felt the same aching weariness he could see on the sergeant's face, tried to ignore the ongoing fight he couldn't see, the sky far to the left of the line a thick haze of gray smoke. He stretched his back, saw Jones now, on horseback, the adjutant, Hartmann staying close to him, as though their horses were glued together.

"Good! If they come, we'll be ready. The whole line is strong, I promise you that! Nobody's running over this regiment, nor anyone around us."

A man came stumbling from the trees, exhausted, one hand in the air. "Colonel! The Illinois boys say something's happening. There's drums starting up."

Franklin stared that way, still nothing to see, but he heard it now, a slow, steady cadence, a low rumble now passing through the men around him.

Jones called out, "Get into position! Prepare to receive the enemy!"

The men scrambled to fall in behind the ragged log wall, muskets coming up. Franklin stood, paralyzed, stared at the tree line, ached to see what was coming, what they would look like. He felt the horse up behind him now, and Jones said, "Mr. Franklin, you had best settle in behind these logs. Could be a storm of lead blowing past you in a few minutes."

Franklin looked at him, saw fear, something new. Beside Jones, Hartmann was staring out as well, seemed to quiver in every part of his body.

"Sir, shouldn't we get down?"

Jones eyed the trees, said, "No. Our place is back behind these works. Stay on your horse. We need to keep tight against the 108, so stay close, and pay attention to anything I tell you. The 16th Illinois is to our right. Can't have any gaps there, either." Jones looked at Franklin again, seemed suddenly concerned. "Mr. Franklin, I didn't mean to put you in the middle of something like this. I appreciate all you've done."

Franklin stepped up and over the log pile, sat down in soft dirt, his eyes on Jones. He felt suddenly very cold, the fear of the moment building inside him. "You didn't do nothing to me I didn't ask for."

"Maybe. We'll decide that later. Get down, stay low. There's nothing for you to peek at. That's how a ball finds you. These boys know what to do. You don't. So I'm telling you, keep your head down in these logs. If a rebel runs over you, just let him go."

Captain Gorman was close by, said, "Sir? All the same to me, you can put a musket in this boy's hands. I'll take every man I can get."

Jones said nothing, his eyes staring hard toward the trees. The drums were louder now, and Franklin tried to obey the colonel's orders, knelt low, put his face down into a dark gap in the logs. He could hear his heartbeat in his ears, an icy lump in his gut, his fingers flexing with the nervousness. Men were calling out around him now, Captain Gorman, the gravelly voice of Sergeant Knight, "The skirmishers are coming! Get ready, boys!"

Franklin had to see, a fierce argument with himself, wouldn't disobey the colonel. But this was all new, every piece of it, and he raised his head slowly, peered through a small gap in the logs, his vision blocked by thickets of briars, low brush. The sounds came closer, the crash of men running, moving up toward him, his heart leaping in his chest. But they were wearing blue, coming in through the brush and brambles in a mad scamper toward the line. There was no shooting, the men stumbling closer, and Franklin was confused, thought, They ain't rebels a'tall. The men reached the log works, climbed over in breathless exhaustion, settled down among the men from Ohio, excited voices all along the logs.

"They's a pile of 'em!"

"Whole dang reb army!"

Beside Franklin, Knight said, "Boy, you're about to find out what the fun's all about."

Franklin kept his eyes focused between the logs, realized the line had fallen silent, no sound but the distant drums. The men around him seemed to be frozen, every man sitting still, musket perched on a log, no one speaking at all. There were voices, but far away, down in the trees, and Franklin wanted to stand up, to see, glanced down the line, everyone else down like he was. Best stay right here, he thought. Colonel said keep down. He knows more than you do.

The voices were growing louder now, blending with the steady rhythm of the drums. Now, a new sound, a high-pitched scream, the tree line seeming to erupt into some kind of demonic hell. Franklin kept his face down, tried to pray, anything he could recall, begging God for anything, his entire body shaking from the terror. The scream grew louder, all across the trees, far down where the other regiments were, a great wave rolling toward them all. He put his hands over his ears, tried to make it go away, closed his eyes, the sounds still piercing through him. He wanted to run, to escape, thought suddenly of the Sunday school lessons, the devil, the stories to terrify a small boy, terrifying him now. He dared to open his eyes, looked to the side, expected fire, flames engulfing the men, but still they sat perched behind the logs, quiet, waiting for whatever hell the rebels were bringing them. He watched Knight, the man twitching, and just beyond Knight, Captain Gorman, a pistol in Gorman's hand. Knight sighted down the musket, and Franklin looked again through the logs, nothing, brush and briars, the screaming closer still. And then a new voice, close by, a single word, **"Fire!"**

The log works came alive with the shattering blast from the muskets, smoke blowing straight forward into the thickets. Franklin felt deafened, put his hands on his ears, looked toward Knight, saw a musket handed to him from behind, Knight aiming again, the musket firing one more time. All along the logs, the men continued to fire their muskets, the men in position just behind them reloading, a continuous process, the men closest to the logs taking aim, firing, handing the muskets back. Franklin tried to see the targets, the smoke now filling the gaps in the brush, his face pushing against the opening in the logs, straining to see, eyes watering from the stink of the smoke. His ears felt stuffed with cotton, the hard crack of the muskets a steady roar, and he ached to stand, to see what they were shooting at, but the colonel's words kept him low. He felt the terror leaving him, his courage coming from the men around him, no one panicking, just doing the job, the muskets still firing, the men working together. He wanted to shoot a musket himself, had seen it done, watched Knight, the others, aim, pulling the hammer back, careful, pulling the trigger, the hard jerk against their shoulders. I can do this, he thought. I can be just like them! This is what it is to be a soldier. God bless them!

And then, another order, his ears barely picking it up, the men repeating it down the lines, the men obeying, the shooting suddenly stopping. He put his hands on his ears, pulled them away, not much difference, coughed through the smoke, felt a sudden hard slap on his shoulder, Sergeant Knight.

"Hah! They're pulling back! We did it, boy! We drove 'em away!"

Men were cheering all around Franklin, muskets held high, hats waving, the smoke clearing. Men began to rise, and Franklin uncurled himself from behind the logs, tried to stand, his knees weak, still the shaking in his legs. He pulled himself up, hands holding unsteadily to the top log, could see out through the brush. The smoke was nearly gone, the men around him still calling out, some cursing the rebels, taunts and cheers. He could see the brush clearly, realized it was flattened, pressed down by a vast carpet of bodies. He stared, mouth open, saw men moving slowly, some crawling, some just shaking, an arm, a head rising up, falling back into the briars. He tried to absorb what he was seeing, a man a few feet in front of him, splayed out facedown, arms and legs wide, and now Franklin saw the blood.

"Hey, boy, that was something, huh?"

Franklin ignored the voice, his eyes still on the dripping red, the man raised slightly above the ground by the crush of thin briars beneath him. Franklin saw the man's musket, standing upright at an angle, caught by the brush, and he was suddenly afraid, wondered if the man would reach for it, might still try to fight.

"Is he dead?"

No one answered him, the voice seeming to hide in his throat. Men were talking, jubilant, and Franklin still watched the blood, said again, louder, "Is he dead? This un, right here!"

"You damn right he's dead. Got him square in the chest. He was coming right for you, too, darkie! I sent him straight to hell!"

Franklin looked to his right, saw a toothy smile, a man he didn't really know. Franklin didn't know what to say, thought, Why would he come for me? I couldn't hurt him.

The cheers began again, aimed back behind him, and he turned, saw Colonel Jones on the horse, the color bearer beside him.

"Up and over! Search those men for cartridges! They'll come again, you can count on that. There's still a fight out across the road. Get to it! Up and over!"

The men obeyed, scrambling up across the logs, a rush into the flattened briars. Franklin looked at Jones, caught his eye now, and Jones moved the horse closer.

"Hell of a thing, Mr. Franklin. They kept in formation right up to us. Must not have seen much of us through all that brush. I waited long as I could, and when that first volley went out, they just melted. Took out their whole first line! They stood it longer than I'd have thought. But those are North Carolina boys. They'll be back."

Franklin saw concern on the colonel's face, none of the cheerfulness of the men. "I didn't never see 'em."

"Not much to see. Too much smoke. But they know where we are. There might be artillery out past those trees. You hear a whistle, you drop down."

Franklin felt suddenly exhausted, leaned against the logs, Jones's attention caught by something farther down the line. He spurred the horse, the color bearer in tow, was gone quickly. Franklin looked that way, saw another of the officers, horses and colors, looked out toward the open ground now. The men were scurrying through the downed rebels like so many blue mice, rolling men over, hands into pockets, unbuckling belts, grabbing cartridge boxes. There were cries, and Franklin saw wounded rebels, more blood, men in blue seeming to ignore that, searching for cartridges, the colonel's order. Muskets were picked up as well, men returning to the logs, climbing up, one man handing Franklin a pair of muskets.

"Take good care of these, boy. We done about melted ours, shot 'em so many times. Barrels as hot as a coffeepot!"

"Here, I'll take those."

Franklin saw Gorman, red-faced, his hand extended, and Franklin obeyed, giving up the muskets. The captain moved away, and Franklin looked back down toward the trees, could see the soldiers carrying all manner of weapons and gear. Farther down, some of the men in blue were dragging rebel wounded away, down closer to the trees, and Franklin saw Gorman again, said, "Where they takin' those boys?"

"Closer to the reb line. Make it easier for them to claim their own. We might need a white flag come sundown. Both sides fetching their wounded. Or maybe not. Rather have those fellows farther away from us."

Franklin had no idea what Gorman meant . . . white flag . . . but Gorman was moving quickly, calling out to the men, orders to return to the logs. Franklin knew when to keep quiet, could feel the raw seriousness in every man around him. Sergeant Knight stepped up through the briars, climbed over the logs, a half-dozen belts draped over his arm.

"Damn rebels didn't have near what we could use. This'll do, though. Lookee here. Got me a good knife." Knight held out the blade, broad, shining, the handle from a deer's antler.

"Can I see it, sir?"

"Sure. Don't cut yourself. Rebs know how to sharpen a knife, I'll say that for 'em. Ain't much on ducking, though. They left behind a pile." Knight paused. "Tell you what. You hang on to that thing until I need it. A man oughta have something to defend himself with. No telling what these rebels got left. I'd teach you to shoot a musket, but there ain't time nor cartridges for that."

"THE BULL PEN," NEAR BENTONVILLE, NORTH CAROLINA—MARCH 19, 1865

The rebels had come again, more carefully this time, slow and methodical, the men in blue behind the logs taking full advantage of their cover. The results were the same, a brutal firestorm where the Federal soldiers had every advantage. For Franklin, the curiosity had been overwhelmed by the sounds of the musket balls, the logs in front of him slapped and splintered as the rebels made a more determined effort to shoot their way through. But the defensive position all across the two brigades of Morgan's division was too strong, the rebels finally pulling away again.

As the sun began to set, the officers had gathered, Morgan coming forward himself, Mitchell and Vandever laying out in detail everything they had seen, concern even greater now that the men might not have the ammunition to withstand another assault.

The soldiers huddled low, as they had done before, the men now dirtier, sweating, the stink of powder in their clothes. The logs were still the best protection they had, but even then, there had been wounds. Franklin had been put to work by Captain Gorman, assisting a corporal named Jasper, carrying the injured men back away from the logs.

He knelt low beside the wounded man, watched as a dirty strip of white cloth was wrapped around the man's arm, the man mumbling something, fear in his words. The corporal said, "Here, Smitty. Drink this."

Jasper eased a small flask to the man's quivering lips, the liquid flowing slowly into the man's mouth.

Franklin said, "What's that?"

"Whiskey. Won't cure nothing, but he'll feel better."

The corporal stood, and Franklin looked up at him, said, "Ain't nothing else we can do?"

"Not out here. There's ambulances back there somewhere. Stretcher bearers will fetch him when they can."

Jasper moved away, back to the logs, and Franklin stood, looked out over the wounded, a dozen men, pulled together from all down the line. He stared to the right, what the colonel said was Vandever's men, saw colors, men on horses, more wounded men spread out across open ground.

The fight above the road had continued, no one

around Franklin seeming to pay that much heed
to that. He left the wounded man, walked back to
the logs, saw blood on his hands, wiped that on his
pants. But much of it had dried, the red under his
fingernails now a dirty brown. He wiped again, felt
sick at that, stared at it. Knight was there, eating a
piece of hardtack, said, "Don't worry about that. As
long as it ain't yours. You get used to it."

Franklin sat against the logs, and Knight pulled
out another cracker, handed it to him.

"Thank you most kindly, sir."

"You do this enough, you get used to the blood.
It don't ever seem to go away. Every pair of brogans
in this regiment's got blood on 'em somewheres.
Maybe the swamp water washes 'em."

Franklin gnawed on the hardtack, realized now
he was ravenously hungry. He saw a smear from
his hands on the dull white cracker, stopped, held
the cracker out away from him. "Ain't seen blood
like this . . . once. My papa done lost his foot to a
tracking hound."

"Good God. When?"

"Don't know. I was small. Years, I s'pose. Ain't
never cried so much in my whole life."

"Where's he at now?"

"Master Cobb's. Wouldn't come with me. Old, I
guess. Maybe a little crazy. Stubborn, for sure."

"Back in Georgia. Yeah, I remember that place.
Cobb's some big shot. Well, he ain't no more."

Franklin chewed again on the hardtack, his hunger overcoming the uneasiness from the dried blood. "Never thought of that. He was a rich man, for sure. Governor and all. Not sure what that means, 'cept lots of people come by the house. All fancy wagons, fancy people. I didn't never go in there. They'd have whipped me good."

"What about now?"

Franklin looked at him. "What you mean?"

"I mean that fellow Cobb. He's nothing to nobody now. This war ends, he won't have any slaves. Not much you can do with all that land if you got nobody to do the work. My papa had a farm, just north of Cincinnati. The war comes, and he loses all his workers. Lost me, too. Rather do this than follow a mule."

Franklin was surprised, had no idea any of these soldiers knew anything about the land. "I like it. Working the ground, I mean. Cotton comes up, small little plants, it's like the world done being born again. Corn grows up same way. Used to crawl out in the field when I was little. The overseers wouldn't pay me no mind. I'd go out week after week, and wait for the corn to get taller than me. But I got taller, too. All that went away. Learned to be scared of the dogs. The overseers, too. They didn't mind a colored child playing. A colored man, that's different. Time to work."

"You ain't gotta worry 'bout none of that. The president done freed all you folks, all the darkies. You can go anyplace you want to, I guess."

Franklin still looked at Knight, thought, Why's he talking to me?

"I didn't think you paid no mind to us people. Some of the soldiers made it plain they don't want none of us around."

"Well, I gotta say. You're the first darkie I ever really knew. If it hadn't been for the colonel, I doubt you'd be here at all. He likes you, says you're a good worker. Says you're smart. Never heard no one talk about any of you folks like that. I like the colonel. Been with him since the beginning, since Camp Dennison. Nearly three years now. He says to watch out for you, I'll do it. Captain Gorman seems to like you, too."

"I like the colonel just fine. Ain't never met a white man didn't spit on me first, then talk. Got a fist in my face every now and again. Didn't know there was white men any other way."

"Oh, we got a few. I've seen plenty of meanness in this army. You remember that idiot Dunlap? Dug up that colored baby? But it's not just that. You see those wounded men you helped? Some of them were just plain stupid. Man stands up in a storm of volleys, just 'cause he wants to get a clear shot. Thinks he's bulletproof. I've seen heads taken off. Those fellows back there, they're lucky. Might only lose an arm. Just 'cause a man's a soldier don't mean he's any smarter than a man who pushes a plow. You don't forget that."

There was a fresh burst of firing to the north,

more of what they had heard most of the afternoon. But it seemed closer, and Franklin sat up, Knight doing the same. The colonel was there now, on foot, stared that way, the adjutant, Hartmann, beside him. Jones turned, called out, "We haven't heard anything from up that way. Fearing's brigade is still out there somewhere, far as we know. You men keep an eye on those trees. It's getting dark soon, rebs might try to sneak up on us. Doubt they'll try a full-out attack in daylight."

Gorman appeared now, walking toward Jones, said, "Sir, we're ready for anything they've got. The second line still back behind us?"

Jones looked toward the rear, said, "Those New York and Michigan boys are itching for a fight. Colonel Moody's griping something fierce, said we got all the fun. Man's too eager to be a hero. But if we need help, they'll hold, or come up. That's up to General Mitchell. Just as soon we didn't need them at all."

Franklin heard a sharp **zip** overhead, the men along the line reacting, some with a mouthful of hardtack. "What was that?"

"Where'd that come from?"

Knight rolled over to his knees, looked back, away from the tree line, said, "That ways. Came from the rear."

The ground was mostly open, patches of small trees, and Franklin rose to his knees, as curious as the men around him. Men were reacting to what

Franklin could see, a crowd of men in blue, in a hard run toward them. They were closer now, a mad scramble, some of the men calling out, hands waving, "Rebs! Behind us!"

He saw a horseman now, realized it was General Morgan, waving the men toward the logs. Franklin heard a low curse from Knight, the men pointing muskets that way, the men in blue settling down, joining the men of Jones's regiment. Men were talking in a disjointed chorus, every man with a story, the officers with questions, a man close to Franklin, a fast-jabbering voice.

"They come right up our backsides! They's a whole passel of 'em!"

Morgan was shouting to Mitchell now, Vandever there as well.

"They came through the gap up near the road. Poured through like honey. Keep eyes down on that tree line. They might try to hit us from both sides. Do what you can, boys."

Franklin ducked low, his foot resting on a log behind him. He glanced around, thought of the rebels who had come out of the trees, the question burning through him. Both sides?

The musket fire came now, a sharp volley that whistled past him, some balls striking the logs. But it was all from the rear, the men reacting by lying flat, taking advantage of the shallow depression they had dug behind their log wall. Down the line, Franklin heard calls, the voice of Jones.

"Here they come! Wait for my order! Lieutenants! Keep an eye behind you! Don't let them sneak up on us!"

Franklin raised his head, glanced toward the tree line, nothing at all, the scattered bodies of the rebels still there. He turned to the rear again, the others on both sides of him making ready. Now he saw the rebels, a solid line of men, walking together, muskets on shoulders, a scattering of men in blue running before them, one man with a bloody arm. He felt his chest twist into a cold knot, his heart racing, his eyes frozen on the rebels, saw they were two lines deep, saw another wave coming farther out to the left, toward Vandever's men. From down that way, a volley fired, a storm of smoke blowing toward the rebels, and now the order came close by, Jones again.

"Fire!"

The men responded, a hard explosion of sounds, Franklin dropping his face into hard dirt, smoke choking him, eyes closed, a new terror, his brain screaming out the obvious, The logs! We're on the wrong side!

The men fired again, but there was no rhythm to it, each man loading his own musket, the rebels returning fire. The balls slapped into the logs behind him, one man screaming a few feet away, more smoke, blinding, a terrified panic boiling up inside him. Knight was firing the musket, rolling to one side, reloading, firing again, and Franklin felt the

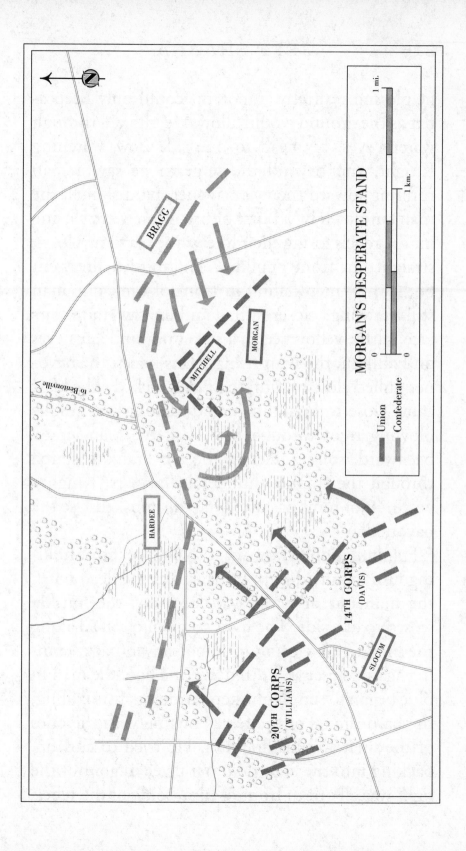

MORGAN'S DESPERATE STAND

Union
Confederate

1 mi.

1 km.

0   0

BRAGG

MORGAN

MITCHELL

to Bentonville →

HARDEE

14TH CORPS
(DAVIS)

SLOCUM

20TH CORPS
(WILLIAMS)

helplessness, utterly impotent, could only keep as flat as the ground would allow. He blinked through watery eyes, his head to one side now, watching Knight, and beyond the sergeant he saw a man running toward them, a bayonet, hard shouts, the man cut down by a burst of fire. More were closing in, the rebels losing their line, some crawling closer, straight out from Franklin. The musket fire went both ways, men falling in front of him, one man still crawling, closer still. Franklin saw the man's face, filthy, yellow teeth, a sickening smile, his eyes on Franklin, the man rising to his knees, the bayonet pulled close to him, their eyes locked. The blast came close to Franklin's ear, deafening, the smoke blowing right through the rebel, the man jerked backward, rolling, feet in the air. Franklin stared through the smoke, thunder in his ears, Knight's voice, "Got him! Bastard! Grab his musket! Use the bayonet!"

Franklin didn't know what to do, the terror holding him in a hard grip. He stared at the dead rebel, the man out of reach, too far away, the musket tossed to one side. The fight seemed to roll all along the line, rebels closing in, then shoved back, coming again, closer still. All down the line, the men in blue began to stand, muskets swinging, fists flailing, the hard shouts of the rebels mixing with the cries of the men around Franklin. He tried to curl up, backing into the logs, no other place to go. But the fight was all out in front of him, some of the rebels

blending together with swarms of blue, the men
pursuing them, then being pursued. He sat in a full
bath of terror, watched two men grappling, falling,
another man, a rebel, with a bayonet, jabbing down
hard, the man in blue speared into the ground. Beside him, Knight stood, enormous, towering above
Franklin, swung the musket, the bayonet keeping a
rebel back, the two men in a standoff, cursing each
other, a lone fight in an ocean of turmoil. Franklin
stared, motionless, saw the rebel swing the musket
again, Knight doing the same, the sergeant's gun
shattering to pieces. The rebel lunged now, missed,
backed away, viciousness in the man's eyes, Knight
backing up, stumbling into the depression, his back
against the logs. Franklin saw the bayonet coming in, the rebel hesitating, savoring the moment.
Franklin saw the man's face, a hard curl to his lip,
the man seeming to carry the entire war, the hate
and anger, his words coming in a soft hiss, "Now
you die, Yankee."

Franklin felt the knife beneath his hand, pressed
into the dirt beside him. His fingers curled around
the hard bone of the handle, and he picked it up,
rolled onto his knees, the rebel moving toward
Knight. Franklin lunged, his hand jamming hard
into the man, the rebel grunting, bending. Knight
rose up quickly, a hard kick to the man's face, the
rebel falling backward, twisting, the knife handle
upright in his stomach. Franklin leapt forward,
jumped on the man, pulled the knife, rammed it

home again, into soft belly, a splash of blood, and he pulled it out again, jammed it up into the man's neck, heard screaming, a terrible cry, his own voice, and he stood now, the knife at his waist, ready, searching, the blood running wet on his hands, his sleeve, down his shirt, the odor of the man in his nostrils, sickly sweet, the smell of death, the smell of killing.

CHAPTER FORTY-FOUR

HARDEE

BENTONVILLE,
NORTH CAROLINA—MARCH 19, 1865

The cavalry had kept mostly dismounted, Wade Hampton driving his men into whatever gap had opened. By day's end, Hardee knew it wasn't enough.

He was with Hampton, the two men still sending orders to the fighting men, maneuvering, positioning, the urgent calls for counterattacks wherever opportunity presented itself. He admired Hampton, the big man heavy in the saddle, directing his men with a fire Hardee knew was instinct, not something you could teach a man at West Point.

"I will see to that corner of the field!"

Hampton was pointing, a fog of smoke clouding their vision, but the musket fire was heavy, one hard thump of artillery.

"Yes! Go!"

Hampton rode forward in a dash, steady in the saddle, and Hardee kept back, focused through field glasses, tried to see any details, the anxiousness stirring inside him, a wave of blue emerging from a brush line. The orders flowed through his brain now, Stop them! But his men were there to receive the advance, a volley throwing a cloud of smoke into the blue line, obliterating his view. He wanted to ride forward, as he had done that morning, see it up close, direct the men himself. But that was no place for a commander, the annoying frustration of relying on officers who might not be up to the task.

He saw Hampton again, riding toward him, more slowly now, unusual, something in the man's face that caught Hardee's eye. "What is happening?"

Hampton was there now, seemed hesitant, more unusual, said, "They are driving the enemy back. For now. I've no one else to send to that part of the field." He paused. "Sir."

Hardee caught something cautious in the word, looked Hampton in the eye. "What has happened, General?"

Hampton turned, and Hardee saw a small cluster of horsemen, riding back along a fence line. They seemed to notice him now, turning toward him, and Hampton said, "I am terribly sorry, sir. He was in a bad place. The fire was heavy. It should not have been."

Hardee watched the horsemen, his mind latching on to Hampton's words. "What should not have been? What are you talking about?"

"Sir, it's your boy."

Hardee saw him now, Willie slumped over, held in the saddle by a man on either side. The horsemen moved closer still, stopping now, and Hardee felt frozen, a cold knife stabbing his chest. He forced his spurs into the horse's flank, moved that way, saw the deep red stain on the boy's shirt, his head low, the men holding him upright.

He knew one of the officers, York, one of the Texans who had tried to discourage Willie from riding with the Rangers. York saluted him, a grim sadness on the man's face.

"Sir, he is badly wounded. I fear it is mortal, sir."

"What do you mean? How could it be mortal? He's a **boy**."

Hampton moved forward, closer to Willie's mount, said something to the men in a low voice. He turned to Hardee, said, "Sir, we shall take him from the field. There is at least one hospital already along the road to the town."

Hardee kept the horse back, wouldn't see it, wouldn't lean closer, the boy unresponsive, his head still hanging low. He gripped the reins, fingers curled in tightly, closed his eyes, couldn't say anything, not to the boy, not to these men. They waited patiently, no one speaking, and now Hardee forced himself to the moment, thought, He is one of **them**. You must treat him as one of **them**.

"My wife and daughter are at my niece's house, at Hillsborough. It is not far. Take him there." He could not just order them, knew good men were being told to leave the field, just to care for their commander's son. He knew that wasn't appropriate, the officer in him pulling back from such a luxury. But they would obey him, some of them with sons of their own, and he thought of Hampton now, realized the man had lost his own son months before, another boy who would be a soldier. Hardee glanced at Hampton, saw the man's head low, absorbing the moment, and Hardee said, "I cannot order you to do this. Care for him as you will, as you are able. There is still a fight here."

Behind him, men were running forward, and Hampton saw them, waved them closer. Hardee glanced back, saw a pair of stretcher bearers, the men wide-eyed, a quick salute toward the generals. Hampton said, "Lower him. You boys will carry him to the nearest ambulance. See that he is carried to Hillsborough." The men seemed puzzled, the order unusual. Hampton seemed to catch their hesitation, his voice louder now. "Do it! Without delay! This is General Hardee's son."

Hands were on the boy now, easing him from the horse, and Hardee saw his face, ghostly white, the blood again, watched as the stretcher bearers moved into place, the boy now down on the dirty white cloth. They lifted him, began to move, and Hardee wanted to stop them, to see one more time. But he wouldn't hold them back, a voice in his mind, Every minute might save him.

One of the stretcher bearers called to him as he moved past, "God bless you, sir. He'll be just fine. We'll see to it."

Hardee saw the sincerity in the man's face, nodded slowly, waved them on, the red stain already spreading through the cloth beneath his boy's back.

He sat on a small knoll, staring into darkness, the flash of artillery marking the position of what remained of the fight. He thought of moving forward yet again, of doing anything to ignite the fire once more, to try to regain the momentum that, for precious hours, had crushed the Yankee left flank. Throughout the afternoon there had still been opportunity, the greatest chance being the attack that exploited the gap in the Federal lines that had opened up south of the main road. But there had been poor coordination, the chaos of the fight along the road too intense to permit good staff work, the couriers either lost, captured, or simply vanishing altogether.

He was furious at Bragg. But there was no time for discord, and so Hardee forced himself to hide that away. The attack against what he now knew was Morgan's division, the Federal forces literally surrounded, had collapsed on its own, helped by the arrival of fresh Yankee reinforcements, who stumbled straight into the rear of the attackers. As a result, instead of corralling an entire Federal division in a neat package, Hardee's attacking force had suddenly become corralled themselves, and Hardee had no idea yet how many of them had succeeded in fighting their way out of the accidental pincer the Yankees had created.

He rode the horse forward a few yards, the staff moving with him, kept his eyes on the artillery batteries still firing into his men. There would be nothing he would say to Johnston about Bragg's inaction, the delays that Hardee could see now had been so costly. They will do nothing to him, he thought. My men were on the march well before dawn, and we reached this field in time to crush the enemy. All the while, Bragg sat perched on my left flank, no doubt enjoying the mild weather, admiring the birds as they flitted through the trees to his front. If he had pushed his men into the enemy as we did, there would have been no escape. With so much pressure on the enemy's left, and with Bragg striking hard into the right, the entire field could have rolled up, thousands of prisoners. It would have worked. It **should** have worked. But now there is artillery, and the Yankees have strengthened their positions, and we are caught once more trying to understand what went wrong.

He knew there would be blame to go around. Delays and confusion, he thought. The maps were wrong, the generals spent too much time protecting what little they have in their commands, their arsenal. No one would move with speed. Well, Hampton, perhaps. He chose this ground, gave us the opportunity General Johnston so hoped for. But he had no strength of his own, Wheeler's men trapped back behind some creek they can't cross. And so we had no great and glorious cavalry charge, what could have swept the Federal left completely away. We gave them **time**. He suddenly hated the word. The great curse, the great gift.

By dark, Hardee knew that the Federal Twentieth Corps had pushed onto the field, adding to the battered Fourteenth, the Federal commanders helping their fight by positioning an enormous force of artillery. It was over then, he thought.

He pulled out a pocket watch, heard the striking of a match, the light quick, flashing across the face of the watch. Hardee caught the necessary glimpse, said to himself, "Eleven."

Roy was beside him, blew out the match quickly, no target for some alert Yankee sharpshooter. "Yes, sir. The men are falling back, mostly. Some units are still out there, but we'll get word to them as quickly as we can."

"You mean, if you can find them."

"We'll find them, sir. This is still a good army."

Hardee looked at him, a shadow in the darkness. "There's that **hope** again, Major."

"What else is there?"

"Victory. This was a close thing. Hampton did the job. Harvey Hill. Bragg should be shot." He stopped, glanced around for other ears.

"It's all right, sir. You're not the only man in this army who supports that position."

"I don't support it. Never will. **You hear me?**"

His voice had risen, and he stopped, closed his eyes, fought for calm. After a silent moment, Roy said, "Orders, sir?"

Hardee thought of the courier, a half hour before, Johnston's order to break off the fight. "We've been given the only order that matters, Major. For the rest of this night, it's up to the officers in the field to gather their men, pull them back as best they can, without drawing any more fire than necessary. We don't need the enemy following along with us in the darkness."

The thunder to his front seemed to slow, the artillery fire falling away. He heard voices behind him, a horse moving up slowly. He waited for it, kept his eyes on the last flicker from a distant cannon, the horse there now.

"Sir?"

It was Pickett, something deadly in his tone. "Report, Colonel."

"Sir, we have received word that your son is being carried to Hillsborough as you ordered."

Hardee felt the knife through him, had done all he could to keep that away. He closed his eyes again, dropped his head, nodded slowly, said in a low voice, "He would not obey me. He had to do this."

"Yes, sir. The surgeon examined him, says he may yet recover. I am confident, sir, he'll be in fine fettle, just a few days, sir."

"I saw him, Bill. The wound was certainly mortal. I don't need my staff lying to me."

Pickett said nothing, neither staff officer speaking. Hardee leaned forward on his saddle, crossed his arms.

"He wanted this, all of it, insisted on being a soldier. This is how we all choose to die, I suppose."

Roy said, "Sir, I'll send a courier to Colonel Harrison, ask him how this could have happened."

"Harrison will tell you that Willie was wounded in the middle of a fight. What else do you expect him to say? My boy is a hero? He was a child, and he rode like the devil right into enemy fire. That's what children do, Major. That's why men join the cavalry, so they can ride a horse and sit tall and hear the cheering. In a fight, all a horse does is make a man a better target. Nothing heroic about that."

He fought against his own emotions, anger and fear and a father's sadness, wouldn't show any of that to them. He sat up straight, jerked the horse to

the side, spurred the animal hard, the horse bolting
ahead. There was a stab of guilt, and he pulled back
on the reins, had no reason to punish the horse. The
animal slowed, moving now with a steady gait, back
through tall trees, camps where his men were still
gathering. There were wounded, the sounds of that
reaching him, the creaking wheels of ambulances,
the sharp cries of suffering men, a small house with
a soft glow of lantern light, already a hospital. He
will be at my niece's house by morning, certainly.
I will confirm that, when it is the right time. But
there is much to do right here. This army needs
its commanders. And I need mine. General Johnston will decide what happens now. Perhaps, in the
morning, we will be organized, attack them again.
Or he will do what he has always done. He will
order a retreat. To where? Raleigh, I suppose. And
then what?

Hardee knew the staff was behind him, would
keep their distance unless he summoned them. He
moved with the rhythm of the horse, the animal
keeping to a well-worn trail. He was just riding, letting the horse lead the way, no place he wanted to
be. Mary should keep clear of Raleigh, he thought.
Having her come up here is the best decision I've
made since we left Savannah. At least I'll be able
to see her, and she'll listen, and she won't judge me
for anything we've done, for what I allowed my son
to do.

He passed a small campfire, a half-dozen men

huddled close, staring into the flames, no one looking up at him. He stopped the horse, wanted to dismount, to feel the warmth on his hands, but it wasn't his place.

"You men fought well today."

"How would you know? We lost near half the company. I didn't see no officers leading no attack. Like it's always been. We're told what to do, and we just do it. Had the Yankees running scared, best thing I ever seen. And then it all just stopped. And half of us don't come back." The man looked up at him now, his dirty face lit by the glow of the fire. "You see us, right here? Three years ago, we was a whole danged regiment. Now, we's it. All what's left."

"What regiment, soldier?"

The man stared at him without recognition, the others keeping their faces toward the fire. "Ain't tellin' you nothing else. Don't trust nobody, not no more. You go on, back to your tent, or fancy house."

Behind him, Major Roy. "Soldier, you're talking to General Hardee. You watch your disrespect."

The man's expression changed, a brief flash of awareness. The others turned, at least a show of curiosity.

"Well, I didn't mean no disrespect to you, sir. But how would you feel? Six of us. Out of three hundred. No officers, no colors of our own, not in over a year. We been stuck into four other units before today. It'll be five tomorrow, count on that."

Hardee glanced back at Roy, said, "Leave him be,
Major."

Hardee nudged the horse forward, left the fire
behind him, thought, Six men. They'll be close the
rest of their lives. I should have found out more,
where they're from. He shook his head, stared
into the darkness, more campfires. Does it matter? They're the army. They're what's left. And they
know even better than I do, it isn't enough.

The next morning, March 20, Johnston
pulled his units into a semicircle, facing
east and south, as strong a defensive line as
he could mount against the troops the Federals
had now put into the field. There was fighting still,
skirmishing and forays, casualties absorbed on both
sides, strikes and counterattacks, Federal artillery
peppering Confederate positions, while the infantry made jabs and probes that amounted to little
for either side.

Whether anyone in Johnston's command held out
hope for success, no effort they could make could
counter what was coming their way from the east.
The courier came from General Evander Law, who
had maintained contact with Sherman's right wing,
the troops of Oliver Howard. A strong force of Federals had broken off their march toward Goldsboro,
and had turned toward the bloody fields south of

Bentonville. As Johnston assessed his situation, it was obvious that there was no purpose to keeping his troops in place, awaiting what would surely be an overwhelming assault by a far greater number of Sherman's troops.

Late in the day on March 21, even as Federal troops jabbed hard into Johnston's flank, his order was carried out, the troops remaining under his command withdrawing from the field, marching northward through the town of Bentonville. Each side had put some sixteen thousand men into the field, but the Confederates had absorbed twenty-six hundred casualties, a thousand more than the Federals. If Johnston's plan had succeeded, Sherman's left wing might have sustained a blow so damaging as to prevent that part of the Federal army from continuing the campaign. But darkness and reinforcements and, in some cases, simple good fortune gave Slocum's Federals the advantages they needed. As Sherman's army grew stronger, Hardee accepted what his commander already knew. Johnston's bold gamble had failed.

As the army gathered northward, expecting an assault closer to the capital city of Raleigh, Hardee learned the worst news a father can hear. At his niece's home in the small town of Hillsborough, now a makeshift hospital, with the boy's sister and stepmother by his side, Willie died of his wounds. For Hardee, there was no time for sharing a family's grief. The business of the army, the desperation of what lay ahead overpowered the emotions he could only keep hidden. There was still the war, still the effort and the skills Johnston required of him, still the hope that there might yet be a peace that would justify all that Hardee had fought for.

CHAPTER FORTY-FIVE

FRANKLIN

SOUTH OF BENTONVILLE,
NORTH CAROLINA—MARCH 22, 1865

The cleanup had begun, men searching for wounded, for muskets, anything useful. The knapsacks of the rebels carried little more than what the men in blue had, meager rations, the occasional pouch of tobacco. There were letters of course, those bits of paper the men carried with them, a photo perhaps, a lock of hair, treasures that now meant nothing at all.

Franklin followed the others, moved out through the trampled brush, not really knowing what to search for. Throughout the brutal fight that had engulfed the men around him, he had kept mostly out of the way, his head low, huddled close to the rebel he had killed. In the darkness he had watched him still, the flashes of fire from the ongoing attacks flickering light across the man's bloody shirt. When the rebel line had broken, the soldiers around him had suddenly been faced with a line of their own men, and in the darkness, there was jubilation, the rebels gathered up as prisoners, some escaping down to the far end of Vandever's line, where the grassy woods sank into an impassable swamp. There was fighting still, other parts of the field, the last stubborn positions on either side, men not willing to back away. But by midnight the rebels had seemed to dissolve, the Federal troops expecting more assaults, where no one remained to give one.

The ground in front of every Federal position was scattered with the dead and wounded, the majority of them rebels. There were dead Federals as well, hordes of wounded, the hospitals springing up in every small farmhouse to the rear. To the soldiers, it was so much the same as every fight before, the fortunate never taking for granted that they would leave yet another awful place in one piece, that somewhere **back there,** the surgeons were doing what they always did, building a pile of arms and legs outside anyplace the wounded had been taken.

But Franklin was not a soldier. He continued to help carry the wounded men back from the log works, did what he was told, obeying anyone who seemed to know what was to happen next. He went about the work with a numb mindlessness, closing his eyes to the worst of it, men missing a piece of themselves, brains and guts splashed open. Though he had heard about death, the campfire talk from men who had been through this before, nothing had prepared him for what he actually saw across the bloody ground. And as he lifted and hauled and stepped past more of the bodies, his brain would not let go of the horror still before him, the vision of the man he had killed with his own hands.

The regiment had come together, Colonel Jones blessedly safe, some of the others that Franklin knew caught with minor wounds. They spoke of one of their own, Hogarth, cursing the rebels for taking away one of the jokesters, a man who never stopped laughing, who inspired every man in the outfit by his humor. Hogarth was dead, the men who knew him well offering up bits of praise, pleasant memories, the effort to fill the hole the man had left in all of them. Franklin didn't know Hogarth well, knew only his laugh, high and birdlike, the sound carrying all through the camps, some men laughing at the laugh as much as the man's legendary jokes. Franklin tried to embrace that, the men searching for the pleasant memories, trying to erase the shock of the man's death. But through it all, he had fought with himself over the rebel he had taken down with the knife. Was he like Hogarth? Would the men he fought with mourn him, salute him? The debate inside of Franklin turned on another image, the viciousness of the overseers, of the man, Lucky, who would torture and whip a slave just for entertainment. Those memories came back as well, one part of him, a calm voice of reason, justifying what he had done to the rebel, just one more Southern man who might just as well have carried a bullwhip as a musket. But it didn't erase the blood, the dark stains on Franklin's hands still, some of that from the wounded men he carried, but not all, and he knew that, wiped hard at his pants legs, tried not to see the stains on his shirt.

The officers had passed the word, rations coming up, wagons for the 113th carrying what clearly smelled like cooked meat. The men still searching the fields had stopped their labor, drawn by the amazing aroma; others, sitting along the log wall, were rising, watching eagerly as the horses pulled the wagon closer. Franklin stood up with them, automatic response, allowed himself to feel the sudden aching emptiness in his stomach, knew to wait for the soldiers to get their portions first. He kept silent, and as he waited, his eyes drifted out over the distant fields, where more of the men in blue did their work. The men of Company A surged toward the closest wagon, laughing commotion, the good cheer that always came with hot food. He let his eyes drift to the wagon, saw one of the other Negroes, Valentine, what they called the **undercook**. The regiment carried two Negroes besides Franklin, and some of the soldiers assumed they were a trio, as though he would naturally be friends with them. But those two men wore uniforms, worked only with the cook, and he had felt a strange hostility from them, as though they regarded Franklin no differently than did the most hostile of the white men. Franklin had learned to ignore them, knew they had nothing in common but the color of their skin.

He saw Sergeant Knight now, a heaping plate of something steaming, and Knight moved closer to him, said, "Grab some, boy! They brought us a whole beef cow. Whole thing! Takes some chewing to cut through it. Must be some old bossy, a hundred years old. I'll take it."

Franklin moved forward, more men drifting toward him with plates, some with a wad of juicy meat in their hands, or cradled in their hats. He quickened his step, the rumbling in his stomach growing, reached the wagon now, saw a copper tub, one of the Negroes with a long fork. Franklin waited for the last man to clear aside, stepped closer, said, "Thank you, most kindly."

"What you want? This is for soldiers." The scowl carried a flicker of disgust, the black man standing up on the tail of the wagon, now with his hands on his hips. "Ain't no more left, besides. You go on."

Behind Franklin, a voice rolled forward.

"I knew it, you black son of a bitch! You give this man something to eat, or I'll pull you down here and show you why!"

Franklin flinched at the volume, saw Knight moving up close, one hand snatching at the copper tub. The undercook backed away, as though he knew Knight's threat was genuine. The sergeant stabbed the fork into the tub, pulled out a fat hunk of dripping meat, aimed it at Franklin.

"You got no plate?"

"No, sir."

Knight reached into his belt, pulled out the knife Franklin had used, stabbed the meat, handed it to Franklin handle first. "Here, by damn. Take it. It's yours. You earned the right to carry the thing more than me. That's the least I can do, anyway." Knight turned again to the wagon. "You hear that, boy? This man killed a rebel right in front of me. Saved my life. That makes him a better soldier than any of you!"

Franklin felt the heft of the knife, his hand squirming slightly, avoiding the touch of the dried blood, caked against the handle, smeared still on the blade. He stared for a long moment, Knight now looking at him, and Knight said, "Go on. It's yours. The knife and the beef. I owe you. Never thought I'd say nothing like that. Anybody messes with you around here, you tell me. I ain't putting up with it. You don't neither." He paused. "The colonel always said you were a good'un. He was right. I tell you what. This here cook's got a little too much gumption. I heard the captain say something about you hoping to wear a uniform. You want his? I'll get it for you."

"That's enough, Sergeant."

Franklin saw Captain Gorman moving closer and Knight lowered his voice, backing down.

"As you say, Captain. But I want it known in Company A, and anywheres else that wanna hear about it. This here fella done saved me from a bayonet. You shoulda seen him, sir. Jumped on that Johnny like a hound on a rabbit. I'd be singing with the angels if it weren't for what he done."

Gorman pointed to the pot in Knight's hand. "Give that back to the cook. Unless you intend to become the mess sergeant, let these boys do their job."

"Yes, sir."

Knight was frowning, obeyed the order, the Negro cook still eyeing him with a hint of fear.

Gorman looked at Franklin for a quick moment, no expression, said to Knight, "Get back to the log works. Scouts say the rebels have pulled off completely. Haven't heard a cannon in a couple of hours. Colonel says we're likely to be up and moving pretty quick. There's no telling what the generals want to do. We could start out pretty quick in pursuit of the rebs. Get your platoon together."

"Yes, sir."

Knight looked toward Franklin, motioned with a finger, "Let's go."

Franklin had forced himself to eat the beef, skirted around anyplace the meat had touched the knife. Along the logs, the men were mostly down, resting with their backs against the makeshift wall, some of them napping. Franklin sat, out from the wall, watched the men, all variety of snores, some of the soldiers with eyes open, empty stares, telltale exhaustion. Knight was down against the logs as well, trying to get comfortable, his eye catching Franklin.

"Captain was wrong. We're not 'pursuing' nobody, at least for now. They're letting us be. Maybe they'll let the rest of this army go chasing rebels. We done our part."

Franklin said nothing, felt a lump growing in his stomach, the meat not settling well. Knight said, "What's botherin' you? You want some more to eat?"

"No, sir. Had plenty. Not feeling too good, though. Not feeling much of nothing right now. Don't know what's happening. Ain't never felt like this before."

Knight looked at him with a slight tilt of his head. "You ever kill a man before?"

Franklin looked down, shook his head.

"You ever want to?"

Franklin looked up at the sergeant, said, "More'n once. There was some bad men at Master Cobb's place. Hurtful, mean men. Always said if I run into that man Lucky again, I'd kill him."

"Well, boy, consider that's what you did. That rebel soldier, he was just one more of them. You got to look at it that way. I killed my first rebel at Chickamauga. Shot him from about a hundred yards. I know it was me. Had him square in the sights, and busted him standing still."

"That bother you?"

Knight laughed. "Hell, no! He'd just as soon done the same to me. I learned that right off. Some can't do it, some gets a man in his sights and can't pull the trigger. Then, you see that same reb shoot a hole in the fella next to you. You start understanding what you have to do. I killed an artilleryman, too. They're the worst. Sit back behind the lines and kill men at random, by the pile. Don't never have to look at a man's face. Coward's way of fighting. Well, we run up on a battery at Resaca, and there they were, pretty as can be. Never saw us coming. I put a ball into a fellow's chest at ten yards. We captured those guns, too. For a while. Rebs came and took 'em back." He shrugged. "That's the way it happens sometimes."

Franklin looked out across the field, bodies still there, mostly rebel dead. The man he had killed was gone, pulled away from the timbers, and at first he thought it was done for him, someone doing him a favor. But he could see now, more of the dead that had been close by had been dragged farther out, to keep the men from stepping on them.

He probed his growling stomach, said, "I ain't a soldier, sir. Sounds ignorant, I know. But I didn't know what all of this was about. Didn't know what a war meant. All that marching, and the uniforms. The officers, horses. Glorious, all of it." He paused. "Nothing glorious about what I done. Still got the man's blood on me. Can't get it off."

Knight seemed to ponder Franklin's words, then said, "Listen to me, boy. I saw what you did. You didn't think about it, or debate what to do. You jumped on that fella like an animal. Like I told the captain, a hound on a rabbit. That's what you gotta do to be a soldier. It's just how it is. Think about those overseers. Maybe you answered your own wish. Maybe you killed one of 'em, just the same as being back there in Georgia."

"Maybe so. But it's done, ain't it? Don't need to keep on doing it. Hope I don't never have to do nothing like that again."

NEAR BENTONVILLE,
NORTH CAROLINA—MARCH 23, 1865

The word had come down from Slocum, through the corps commander, Jefferson Davis, that the army was again to resume its march toward Goldsboro. For now the 113th had established a temporary camp, and at least for a pleasant day's rest, Colonel Jones had his tent again, the regiment going about their duties as though none of the past week had ever really happened.

"You want to leave? Why?"

Franklin held his hat in his hands, felt as nervous now as any time in the past. "I figured out, sir, I don't want to be a soldier."

Jones sat back in his small camp chair, stared at him for a long moment. "Sergeant Knight told me what you did. Says you're a hero."

Franklin shook his head. "No, sir. I helped out when I could. Did what I had to. No telling that the sergeant might have done it, too, might have fought and took care of that reb."

"That's not what he says."

Franklin felt a wave of frustration, had a sudden fear that the army might not let him go. "Ain't I allowed to leave? I thought this army was about making people free."

"Easy, Mr. Franklin. No one said you can't leave. Actually, according to the army rolls, you were never really here anyway. But you can't just walk off somewhere. This is, well, to you, this is a foreign country. You go walking up to some farm, and they're liable to put a musket ball in you."

"Yes, sir. I know. I was hoping, you could maybe set up for me to go back to Savannah. In Fayetteville, those boats were hauling people back to some good place, so they said."

Jones nodded. "True. The government is settling Negroes on land they took from the plantation owners. That what you want?"

"Maybe. I want to go back to Clara first. Decide what we're gonna do. Maybe stay in the city. Maybe have our own farm. I ain't never had to decide anything like this before. But I want to talk to her. I think we'll be married."

"Good for you." Jones pulled a paper from a small box to one side of him. He slid the chair over to a small desk, began to write. Franklin was curious, stood patiently. After a long minute, Jones said, "Here. Take this, keep it with you all the time. It's a pass, allowing you to go through the guard posts. It has my name on it, and anybody gives you any trouble, you mention General Mitchell's brigade, General Morgan's division. It's all there." Jones stopped, seemed to scan Franklin closely. "You been paid a bit, here and there. You keep that?"

"Yes, sir. Greenbacks rolled up in my pocket. Not sure how much. Don't never use it for anything."

"That's good. Some of these boys gamble away every dime the army gives them. Or spend it on foolishness. I don't see you being that stupid. But you'll need every dollar you've got to get to any-place that matters to you." Jones stopped, wrote on another paper, signed it with a flourish. "This one you'll need me for. Let's go."

Jones stood, and Franklin backed out of the tent, said, "Where we going, if I can ask."

"You can ask plenty, Mr. Franklin. You're a free man. You can ask anybody anything you want, anytime you want. Even in Savannah, even if there's still a war. Just be smart about it. Don't go making speeches to people who might not see things that way. Savannah's still the South, and some people are still fighting mad."

Jones moved past him, and Franklin followed, said, "Then, if I can ask . . . where we off to, sir?"

"Division paymaster. You'll need every bit of money you're due. Besides your labor, I figure you earned a month's pay as a soldier. You fought in a battle, saved a man's life. That's all I need to hear. The army'll agree with me."

Franklin had no idea what Jones meant, followed him, Jones's steps quickening. The adjutant, Hartmann, came running toward them through the camp, called out, "Sir! You require my assistance?"

"No. I require your horse. Mr. Franklin and I are taking a ride over to division headquarters."

"My horse?"

"Don't be concerned, Lieutenant. We'll be back. I just need to take care of some army business. The way I see it, we owe Mr. Franklin another thirteen dollars."

CHAPTER FORTY-SIX

SHERMAN

GOLDSBORO,
NORTH CAROLINA—MARCH 24, 1865

He was surprised by Howard's anger. The triumph of what had been done to Johnston's army was muted by the complaints Sherman was beginning to hear, that there had been mistakes, **his** mistakes.

"We whipped them, Oliver. Johnston has nothing left. Surely, you can accept that for what it is."

Howard rarely showed any kind of outburst, but Sherman knew his moods, could see that Howard was doing all he could not to explode into Sherman's face. It was an extraordinary show. Howard seemed to choose his words carefully.

"I'll not debate what Johnston has remaining in his arsenal. I am not aware of those details."

"All right. Can you accept that the enemy has lost a few more teeth? With Schofield's troops, Terry's, the cavalry, we can field possibly ninety thousand men. Against what? I do not understand your concerns."

Howard sat staring away, his lone hand rubbing the side of his bearded face. Sherman saw the man's jaw clenching, even through the beard. Sherman didn't want this, had no reason to scold the man for any objections he had to anything Sherman had done. But Sherman also knew that Howard respected authority, wouldn't spray words about his own headquarters like some fountain of indiscretion. Sherman moved deliberately, pulled a cigar slowly from his pocket, played with lighting it, giving Howard time. Dammit, he thought. Say what you came to say.

"I fear, sir, we lost an opportunity to crush the enemy."

"I thought we crushed him pretty well. The first casualty counts from Slocum show we bested him severely. The rebels can't afford to lose what this fight cost them."

Howard looked at him now, seemed to summon courage, then turned away again. "I believe that possibly, some of the orders you issued were not based on adequate information. That perhaps was my fault."

It was typical of Howard, placing blame by accepting it first.

"Which orders? Damn it all, Oliver. What kind of beef should any of us have with the outcome? Johnston is in full retreat."

Howard continued to clench, shook his head. "This is not criticism, sir. But we had a grand opportunity. We made a breakthrough on the enemy's flank. General Mower had breached their left, was close to surrounding Johnston's headquarters, their wagon train. Had he been supported, we could have captured most of Johnston's command. This war might have ended right there. I had thought that was our goal."

"Mower? All I knew was that he had pushed too far forward. He could have been cut off. We might have lost his entire brigade. That's not the kind of boost I wish to give the enemy. In the last week, we have captured more than two thousand prisoners, Oliver. Two thousand! Every officer I talk to tells me those men are utterly demoralized. Whatever General Mower might or might not have accomplished, the larger picture is what matters. You disagree with my orders, fine, I accept that. But they are my orders. What more needs to be said?" Sherman hated this, did not need any kind of disharmony among his commanders, not now.

"You are correct, sir. You issued orders that had

to be obeyed. To General Mower's credit, when he was ordered to withdraw, he withdrew. I would only offer, sir, that he saw things as they were in his immediate front. With your permission, I shall advise him that he did nothing wrong, that in the commanding general's opinion, he had possibly endangered his men by advancing too far forward. There is no sanction against him."

It was as close to a compromise as Howard could come. Sherman let out a breath, blew cigar smoke toward the ceiling.

"There is no sanction at all. Not against him, or you, or anyone in this entire army. We won the damned fight. We're already past that. I'm sorry. I don't wish to insult your sensibilities, but Schofield is arriving at any moment. This will be a gratifying meeting, Oliver. You are welcome to accompany me. This is a monumental day for us. I would prefer you see it that way." He paused. "If there were mistakes made, or opportunities lost, others will judge us for it. I prefer to embrace our triumphs. Is that not acceptable?"

"Certainly, sir. I shall be delighted to accompany you. I admire John Schofield. His accomplishments in Tennessee deserve high praise."

"Good. Join me here in an hour."

"As you wish."

Howard rose, and was out the door, and Sherman was still frustrated, tore the tip off the cigar with his teeth, stared hard at the open window. Hitchcock was there now, said, "Sir, I've spoken with General Schofield's adjutant. Pleasant fellow, anxious to meet you . . ."

"Get out of here, Major."

Hitchcock froze, his mouth open. "Sir?"

"Did you not hear me? Get out."

Hitchcock disappeared, and Sherman rose from the chair, heavy steps across the room, leaned his hands on the windowsill. Outside, the town of Goldsboro was alive with his army, wagons, guns, formations of troops. He kept his gaze downward, said aloud, "We won, dammit."

He pulled away from the window, moved to the door, out into the parlor, ignored the staff, the aides, made a line for the staircase. He climbed heavily, thunderous boot steps, knew they were watching him, that someone would muster the courage to say something. To his relief, they let him go, and he walked to his room, slammed the door behind him. The cigar was shredded in his mouth, and he jerked it away, crushed it in his hand, threw the remnants in a shower toward the window. The bed was close beside him, a soft invitation, and he dropped down on the edge, swung his boots up onto the quilt, lay back, his head finding the soft pillow.

Mistakes. The word gnawed at him, burning a hole in his brain. So, I ordered Mower to withdraw prematurely? How the hell can I be certain of that? Take his word for it? No, I will not entertain Howard's griping.

He put a hand over his eyes, rubbed at his temples. *I'll be judged, all right. Mower is a small piece of an enormous puzzle, and Howard knows better than to mention that. There was only one reason we had a fight at Bentonville at all. One reason, one very bad mistake. I was arrogant, cocksure. Why shouldn't I be? What had the enemy ever done to give me doubts? I never thought of Joe Johnston as crafty or devious. They put him in command because he outranks everyone else. Lee and Johnston, the two highest-ranking men in their whole damned army. It makes sense, still makes sense. Even that lunatic Jefferson Davis must know that the end is coming, and so they put their two* **figureheads** *up in front of us, to make it official. Two possibilities. Those two generals have been ordered to lead their armies against us in some kind of suicidal sacrifice, some bloody all-or-nothing charge, or they will sit down with us and sign the papers we will put before them. Davis would rather jump off a cliff than surrender, so he needs figureheads to do it for him. It's all about symbols, gold swords and sashes, nice neat gray uniforms, so the newspapers in Richmond will say they stood proudly, forced to do our bidding only because we had bigger guns. So they can keep their honor. What's wrong with those people?*

He let his mind drift back to Howard, the unspoken words. It was the usual plague that settled on Sherman, so often, so many great fights. *You* made mistakes, and Howard didn't know how to tell you. Wouldn't just come out and blame you for anything, it's not his way. Slocum certainly knows what we allowed the enemy to do. His people got bloodied for it. So, you were careless, gave orders without knowing the details. That hasn't mattered, not since Atlanta. Johnston gathered up his people at Bentonville to bust us in the mouth, and if he had been a little better at it, what then? What would the newspapers say about that? You are still being judged, Sherman. There are men in Washington who would pay their salaries to see you fail. What would Grant say? He protects me. But if I fall on my face . . . no, it has to be more than that. If I allow too many of my men to be killed, captured, shoved off a battlefield, there is no protection, not for either one of us. He has his hands full with that damned Robert E. Lee. A siege. He hates a siege as much as I do. But Lee isn't going to roll over. I never thought Johnston would be aggressive. And that was my mistake.

He sat up now, a burst of energy. Stop this. Stop your brain from spewing out useless thoughts. You won the fight. I cannot be concerned if General Mower got lucky, stumbled his men right up to Johnston's camp. Johnston is gone, hauled his miscreant army to Raleigh. Howard wants me to chase him, no doubt. So does Slocum. To Slocum, it's about pride. He got bloodied, so he has to strike back, avenge his losses. Damn it all, this isn't King

Arthur. None of us are high up on some white horse, carrying God's sword in our hand. And none of us are faultless. If Howard doesn't understand the larger picture, he will soon.

Sherman held up his hand, stared at the lines in his palm, the yellowed fingertips, slowly made a fist. It's as clear as this, he thought. Punch your way through this war, every chance you get. Sometimes you'll miss your target. But keep the fist, keep punching. We have the power, and the enemy does not. What matters now is the rest of the story, the campaign to end this war. No general is going to scold me for some error that costs us a day, or even a week, or a hundred men or a thousand. And if they do not understand that . . . well, then, I really cannot be concerned. That's why they answer to **me**.

He stood, moved to the door, put one hand on the glass knob, hesitated. The voice was there, rising up from that awful hole in his brain, the worst enemy he had, the taunting and the doubts he could never completely escape. If Howard is right, he thought, the others, too, if they see the failings, what then? Will the men be next, those marvelous soldiers, their affection for Uncle Billy? Will they lose that? And what of Grant? I cannot betray him, I cannot fail him. Ever. So, no more mistakes, Sherman. There has to come a time when this uniform comes off for the final time, and you have to know you did this right. All of it. So, by God, let's end this war.

He had met with John Schofield, with Alfred Terry, the two commands whose work along the coast had tossed all of eastern North Carolina into Sherman's control. The railroads to southern Virginia were now held by Federal forces, the rolling stock already coming south, bringing more of the supplies and munitions that would fuel his army. Despite some calls from his commanders that Johnston's army was still the target, that Johnston be pursued toward Raleigh, Sherman would hear none of that. His plan had not changed: Add Schofield's troops to his own, rest and refit them at Goldsboro, and by the first week of April, the march would resume, a hard push toward the Virginia border.

He still kept one eye focused on Johnston, even if he said little of that to his own generals. There would be no separation of the wings of his army, no carelessness on the roads that wound haphazardly northward. His command would now extend over a force of ninety thousand men, a number he repeated to himself with silent joy.

If his generals were impatient to leave Goldsboro, the men were pushing at the gates like a rebellious bull. As he walked among their camps, he heard their calls, the morale as high as it could ever be. But he knew he should feed them first, prepare them for what lay ahead, even if he wasn't certain himself. It still impressed him how healthy the army had been, all the way back to Atlanta. The sick calls had been minimal, the men marching so many hundreds of miles through the worst geography imaginable, and yet they were aching to do it again, to seek whatever challenge the rebels put in their way. The supplies were slow in coming, though the riverboats along the Cape Fear, and now the Neuse River, which ran near Goldsboro, were alive with activity. For the army it meant that the men so accustomed to enduring hardtack would finally be made stronger by sacks of grain and herds of livestock. The railroads only added to that relief, the tracks now rattling with the first of the great locomotives that brought goods from the coast. But Sherman saw the railroad very differently from his men. The lines ran northeastward, to the town of New Bern and the seacoast, and with that pathway came an opportunity.

The strategy for joining his army with Grant's carried hazards, logistical as well as military. As he mapped out the next step in his campaign, he had to wonder if, along the way, Johnston would attempt what Sherman saw as another vainglorious assault. More important, if Robert E. Lee succeeded in evading Grant, and pulled southward from Petersburg, would Lee and Johnston combine, posing a far more serious threat? These questions had no hard answers. But Sherman knew that the best way to avoid confusion and uncertainty was to make certain he and Grant were in total agreement on their plans, no matter what the rebels tried to do. With the army rejuvenating under the capable command of John Schofield, Sherman sought out the one part of his campaign that had thus far been missing, an ache of his own that he could now cure.

On March 25, Sherman boarded the train to New Bern, and there he boarded the steamship **Russia** for a rapid journey northward. Along the way, Sherman felt his own morale rising, his self-doubts erased by the confidence that a face-to-face meeting with Grant would give Sherman a clear picture of what Grant was expecting of him, and together, what they would do to end the war.

CITY POINT, VIRGINIA—MARCH 27, 1865

The newly created harbor that spread below the junction of the James and Appomattox rivers had become a waterborne city all its own. As Sherman climbed the wharf to the heights where Grant's headquarters had been built, Sherman couldn't avoid staring back across the vast sea of merchant ships and transports, all the resources of the Union that even now were adding to the strength of Grant's army.

The greeting had been as joyous as either man would allow, a fast grip of a handshake, a brief clutch of Grant's shoulders, Sherman's nervous energy betraying his composure. The two men had taken the walk up the steep incline, to a flat bluff overlooking the water, and all the while, Sherman gave Grant details, everything he could recall from the campaign. There would be official reports, of course, but Sherman knew Grant preferred hearing Sherman's more informal version of events, his insights and opinions about commanders, his appraisal of the enemy, which might never be put onto paper.

On the bluff, Sherman saw more of the business of Grant's army, a neat row of cabins housing Grant's staff, the various departments all gathered to fuel the effort Grant was making toward Lee's beleaguered forces at Petersburg, just a few miles away. For most of an hour the two men traded experiences, offering advice and anecdotes, displays of pride and gratitude that most others in the army never saw. Only after Grant had allowed Sherman to deflate the nervous energy, something Grant had seen so many times before, did Grant finally inform Sherman that he was not in fact the most important visitor Grant was receiving that week. To Sherman's surprise, and Grant's delight, Sherman learned that President Lincoln had made the journey from Washington. It was clear to Sherman that Lincoln was just as curious as he was to see how Grant intended to bring this war to a close.

The president had arrived on the **River Queen,** now tied up at the wharf among the enormous armada Grant seemed pleased to bring to Sherman's attention yet again. Lincoln seemed content to remain on board, a gesture that Grant believed was intentional, a show of the faith Lincoln had already expressed in Grant's command.

Sherman had met Lincoln before, early in the war, had come away from the encounter without any distinct impression of the president's depth, what concerned Sherman as being a worrisome trait for a president in command of a war. Whether Lincoln felt the same way about him had not really entered his mind before now. But Grant had been reassuring, that Lincoln not only supported the efforts of his generals, but had given Grant absolute assurances that as long as Grant gave him victories, Lincoln would keep himself out of Grant's way. With news of Sherman's triumphs filling every Northern paper, Sherman had eased his own nervousness that indeed, Lincoln might offer a show of respect.

They were shown to the aft cabin of the steamer, the guard standing aside, saluting Grant. Grant made a light rap on the door, the soft words responding.

"Yes. Do enter."

Grant moved through the door, Sherman following, and Lincoln stood, the top of his head nearly touching the low ceiling of the cabin.

"My word, General, it is a pleasure as always." Lincoln looked at Sherman now, beamed a smile, extended a hand. "General Sherman, it has been some time since we spoke. I recall it well. You are quite the hero these days. There is talk I should show Mr. Johnson the door and bring you on board as my chosen vice president!"

Sherman laughed, cut it off, wasn't sure if Lincoln was serious or not. But Lincoln laughed heartily, pointed to two chairs.

"Please, gentlemen, do sit down. I am somewhat surprised to see you both, I admit. We still scheduled for a meeting tomorrow, Mr. Grant?"

Grant sat, Sherman hesitating, still the stir of nervousness. Grant glanced at him, a quick motion of his finger, the silent order, **Sit down**.

"Yes, sir. I took it upon ourselves to visit, as a social call, more than a formal meeting. General Sherman just arrived, and I thought you should be informed. No better way than to shake his hand."

"Excellent! And I shall do so once more." Lincoln extended a long arm, Sherman's hand engulfed by Lincoln's long fingers. "I offer you every form of congratulations, Mr. Sherman. Will you be in attendance tomorrow, then?"

"If you wish it, sir."

"Most certainly! As I said, you are the toast of all of Washington. It would not do for me to keep you to myself. I say, I am most anxious to hear of your expedition. I have read much in the newspapers, of course, but one cannot always believe the written word. You should see some of the things they say about me. Apparently, my grandfather is a baboon. I don't recall seeing that in him, but then, who am I to argue with the press?"

The pleasantries continued, Sherman smiling more than not, Lincoln receptive to every story, every adventure, whether any general would consider the routine travails of the army an adventure at all. But the doubts Sherman might have had about Lincoln's perception, or even his intellect, were quickly wiped away.

They sat for a long hour, most of the conversation leaning toward the social rather than the military. Sherman understood Grant's thinking, that the meeting scheduled for the following day would focus much more on the strategic, far more serious than a social greeting, which Sherman now understood seemed more suited for the protocol of Washington than anything significant to the army.

With the meeting concluded, Sherman walked with Grant to Grant's cabin, Sherman afflicted with one more bout of nervousness that he couldn't avoid. At Grant's insistence, Sherman was obliged to sit down for tea, at the behest of Grant's wife, Julia.

"So, tell me, Ulys, how was Mrs. Lincoln?"

Sherman blinked, looked at Grant, who was looking back at him. Grant said, "Um, we didn't ask for her."

Sherman saw Grant's scowl, and now a more intense frown coming from Julia. Sherman said, "Actually, I didn't know to ask. I had no idea she was even on board."

Julia put both hands on the table, tapped her fingers. "Well, you two are a pretty pair! In social circles, that is called a faux pas. You have committed an unpardonable offense."

Sherman thought, Not the first time, at least for me.

Grant said, "We shall call on him . . . **them** tomorrow morning. It is already scheduled. I promise you, my dear, we shall make amends."

Julia sat back, crossed her arms, a slow shake of her head. "Generals."

ON BOARD THE **RIVER QUEEN**— MARCH 28, 1865

They were joined by David Dixon Porter, Sherman embracing Porter as heartily as he had the last time they met, along the Mississippi River at Vicksburg, some twenty months prior. Once again Lincoln met them with a hearty handshake, a boisterous show of enthusiasm, the four men now crowding into Lincoln's cabin around a small desk. With the social niceties past, Sherman expected Grant to launch directly into the business of the army, Sherman's anxieties returning, that one purpose of the gathering was to convince Lincoln that Sherman still knew what he was doing. Grant had other priorities.

"Sir, might I inquire as to Mrs. Lincoln?"

Lincoln's expression seemed to droop just slightly, the smile returning. "I shall go for her myself! Gentlemen, excuse me. Just a bit."

Lincoln seemed to flash out of the cabin, and Sherman looked at Grant, saw a shrug, Porter offering in a whisper, "She's ill often. Don't see her much."

They sat in silence, the tumble of Lincoln's steps coming toward them, the tall man bursting through the door. He sat, seemed out of breath, said, "I'm afraid she is not well today. Please excuse her absence. But she extends the most hearty of greetings to you all. Most hearty."

There was an awkward silence, Lincoln seeming to force a smile, and Sherman waited for Grant, who said, "Perhaps we should address the business at hand."

Lincoln seemed to brighten. "Yes! Please proceed, Mr. Grant. Leave nothing out."

Grant began to speak, slowly, his usual precision, carefully chosen words, a map unrolled on the small table for guidance. Sherman already knew most of Grant's plans, the letters coming to Sherman's command filled with much of the same kind of detail he was hearing now.

Sherman was unaware that Phil Sheridan had already departed Grant's camps, a powerful cavalry thrust designed to cut off the Southside and the Richmond & Danville railroads, the last remaining supply lines for Lee's army. Lincoln seemed to know of that already, and Sherman realized Grant was offering a formality, an introduction for Sherman to follow up with whatever plans he intended to put into motion.

Lincoln's stare was intensely probing, the smile not hiding Lincoln's attention to every point either man was willing to make.

Sherman spoke slowly, careful choice of words. "Sir, I am confident that should General Lee separate himself from General Grant's army, and join forces with what Johnston has in North Carolina, the force I now have in Goldsboro is adequate to defeat them both, combined. If Lee maintains his position at Petersburg for another fortnight, I can march my forces northward, which would prevent Lee from going anywhere at all. Simply put, sir, his army would starve, or surrender."

Lincoln rested his chin in his hands, kept his eyes on Sherman. "Would he not fight?"

Sherman looked at Grant, who nodded toward him. It was clearly Sherman's show. "He could. With Grant's army and mine in combination, I would offer, sir, that it would not be a fair fight."

"Do you believe you must continue the fight? Forgive me. General Grant knows I do not interfere in your tactics. But this nation is wrung out from the killing of so many of our young men. Do you see hope that this could end without another great battle?"

Sherman looked down for a brief moment, shook his head. "The rebel has shown a regrettable stubbornness. And, they are in the service of Jefferson Davis, who from all I have read, continues to believe the fantasy that his army could whip us, the French, and possibly the Bulghars, all in one swipe. I do not anticipate Davis allowing General Lee to simply quit fighting, just to spare any more young men. If that be the case, I rather prefer the task fall upon me."

"Good heavens, why?"

Sherman saw a hint of concern on Grant's face, thought, Be careful. "Sir, my army is currently in camp around Goldsboro, is being rejuvenated by a considerable flow of supplies. They are anxious to end this, as I am. They are rested and eager. I can think of no better situation for a commanding general to find himself in."

"I am concerned, Mr. Sherman. You are here. Your army is there. Is there not some risk to that?"

"I left the army under the command of General Schofield. He is most capable. If it will ease your concerns, sir, I had thought I would begin my return this afternoon."

Porter spoke up now. "Yes, General, I am happy to provide you with the steamer **Bat,** which is a bit more seaworthy than the **Russia**. It should cut some time off your trip."

Lincoln seemed pleased with that answer, rubbed a hand on his chin. "You inspire confidence, gentlemen. Absolute confidence."

Sherman felt a question brewing, a thought he had turned over many times before. "Sir, if I may inquire, are you prepared for the end of the war?"

Lincoln seemed to ponder the question, said, "Exactly what do you mean?"

"What shall we do with those men who now call themselves the rebel armies? What should be done with the leaders of the rebellion? The political leaders, I mean. Should we allow them to escape? I'm thinking of course of Mr. Davis."

Lincoln smiled again. "No one on this earth is more prepared for the end of this war than I am, Mr. Sherman. I am most hopeful that with the arrival of peace, the rebel soldiers may return to their homes, their farms, their shops, they may begin work again, strengthening their place as a prosperous and patriotic part of this nation. As for Mr. Davis, I must be cautious what I say. If Mr. Davis was to make his way beyond our borders, I would find it difficult to be saddened by his escape. But that is not a matter I can speak on freely. The courts must decide, I suppose. This recalls an incident of a fellow making a visit to a friend. He was invited to take a drink, but declined, having taken the pledge. His host suggested lemonade, and the fellow heartily agreed. In preparing the lemonade, his friend suggested that it would be more palatable if poured with a bit of brandy. The fellow remarked that if he could do so, **unbeknown** to him, that would be acceptable. Interpret that as you will, gentlemen. Much of what has taken place in this war is likely unbeknown to me. The journeys of Mr. Davis might be among those incidents." Lincoln seemed to ponder again, looked at Grant, then Sherman. "I have occupied far more of your time than is appropriate. You men have serious work to do, and this nation is watching every action. Mr. Sherman, I hope if the opportunity presents itself, that you communicate with the people of North Carolina, and their Governor Vance, that once the rebel armies lay down their arms, and once they resume their civil pursuits, they will at once be guaranteed all rights as citizens of a common country. I go so far as to promise that their state governments, as now constituted, shall be allowed to function as they have done so for the past four years. We must avoid anarchy, and we must avoid punishment. This war has been its own punishment, and I dearly wish it to end."

ON BOARD THE **BAT**—MARCH 28, 1865

Sherman kept his gaze on the darkening skies, the sunset behind him. He kept Lincoln's words in his mind, utterly surprised now by what he had seen and heard. Though the talk focused on tactics and strategies, planning and maneuver, Sherman left City Point with an odd sense of affection for Lincoln, something he never expected. He is a humorous man, he thought. I always heard about the incessant stories, the joking, the analogies. It is nothing more than his mind at work, always turning, like the gears of a clock. Did he truly remember me? Sherman ran a hand through his rough shag of red hair. Maybe not. But he convinced me he did. And, by God, no matter what anyone else in Washington may think, whatever schemes and conspiracies are hatched by those political scalawags, Lincoln will see this through, and he has faith that no matter our failings, he has the right men in position to end the war.

He ran Lincoln's parting words through his mind, a smile on Sherman's face.

"I should feel much better when you are back at Goldsboro."

Very well, sir. Just keep your eyes on the telegraph. The news for all of us should be most pleasing.

CHAPTER FORTY-SEVEN

HARDEE

SMITHFIELD,
NORTH CAROLINA—APRIL 5, 1865

Sherman's halt had provided the Confederate forces with an enormous break of their own, a hungry, exhausted army finally rested, with at least some food gathered from farms west of Raleigh, the rail lines that ran toward the mountains still intact. With the desperately needed supplies came additional troops, the men who had marched from Hood's army in Alabama, some of those men from North Carolina, simply returning home. Whether they would fight or not, Hardee could not be certain. But Hardee was grateful for every man he could get.

With the disjointed defeat and then the withdrawal from Bentonville, the army had been diminished yet again by a mass of desertions. Hunger and hopelessness pulled men out of the ranks daily, a reality for both Hardee and Johnston that they had to address. If there was to be another fight, another effort by Johnston to strike at any vulnerability they found with Sherman, the army had to be reorganized. Hardee took the lead with that, shifting some officers to new positions, eliminating some regiments altogether, units that consisted of only a few men, just as Hardee had seen around the campfires at Bentonville. The generals were not immune. Lafayette McLaws, who had never impressed Hardee with his initiative, was ordered to Georgia, an arrangement that satisfied both McLaws and Joe Johnston. From Hood's army, Stephen Dill Lee, a capable and proven veteran, had marched along with the troops that had come back to North Carolina, and so, Johnston placed him in command of what would now be a corps, equal in status to Hardee. A third corps was formed, under another able commander, A. P. Stewart, who had served Hardee well, as far back as Shiloh, three years before. Still, with the additional strength, and the shuffling of commanders, Johnston and Hardee knew they could field barely thirty thousand effective soldiers.

With so little activity from Sherman's army around Goldsboro, Hardee had felt comfortable remaining at Hillsborough with his wife, Mary, for several days. A priority of course was the funeral of his son, a ceremony that rivaled the full military honors offered any fallen commander, a gesture authorized by Johnston. But once more, Hardee could not afford the luxury of grieving. After he had spent several days pacing about the home of his niece, his restlessness had overpowered his sentiment. It was time to return to his men.

"The Yankee prisoners have been most helpful with their information. Sherman is sitting still. For how long, we cannot of course be certain."

Johnston faced the commanders from one end of the room, his hands clasped behind his back. Stephen Lee spoke now, and Hardee detected an angry edge to his words.

"General, is it not appropriate for us to make a move toward Sherman's camps? If his army is recuperating, if they are awaiting resupply, his men will be looking more eagerly to their supply trains than to their defenses."

Hardee sat back, looked carefully at Lee. He detected a hint of hostility toward Johnston, wondered if there was animosity in the man, still lurking from the surrender at Vicksburg. Stephen Lee had been one of John C. Pemberton's senior commanders, forced to lay down their arms to a victorious

Ulysses Grant. Every officer who endured that defeat knew that while Pemberton's army was growing more desperate, Joe Johnston had been nearby with a sizable force, yet made no effort to assist Pemberton's starving troops, a move that could possibly have broken Grant's siege. At thirty-two, Lee was the youngest lieutenant general in the army, and Hardee couldn't avoid the nagging regret that had he come to the fore earlier in the war, Lee might have been one of those bright stars, a man as capable as Patrick Cleburne or Stonewall Jackson. At the very least he had survived the fights that others had not, Hardee never far from the burning question of how many battles might have gone differently had those men still been alive.

If Johnston had any prickliness about Lee's edginess, he didn't show it. He spoke instead with a calm patience, an elder schooling a novice. "General, you are referring to the kind of strategy the army attempted one time before, which eventually resulted in our catastrophe at Shiloh. The enemy was not prepared to be assaulted there, and assault him we did. But the enemy's power, his sheer numbers, stripped us of our momentum. Well, of course, I was not present." He looked at Hardee now, seemed to hesitate. "General Hardee was there, and acquitted himself in fine fashion. But such confrontations, the tactics and advantages, are not always as clear as they may seem. We know Sherman and Schofield are together. Even with the element of surprise, we would find ourselves over-whelmed by sheer numbers."

Hardee knew that Johnston was right, that Lee's youthful energy might compel him to take that kind of risk. Hardee debated saying anything at all, but the words couldn't be held back. "I admire your aggressiveness, Stephen, but there is one other consideration for keeping to the defensive. On my return to the army, it was apparent to me that the fighting spirit of these men is in a sad way. We are losing a significant number of men to desertion. Very few of those who remain have shoes, very few have been properly fed. There are barely any uni-forms, and many of the men are without weapons."

Lee sniffed. "When did any of that prevent us from striking the enemy?"

Hardee folded his hands together, did not want this argument. "I believe General Johnston will agree with me, that this army has been bested per-haps one too many times. Your command in Ten-nessee is one example, and ours in Georgia. We may believe in our cause and we may rely on the fortitude and commitment given us by the Al-mighty. But our army is a shadow of what it once was. Go, walk down the street, go to the camps not just of your men, but mine, of any place where the men gather. Listen to the talk, listen to their hopes merely to return home."

Lee seemed to puff up. "Is this defeatism I hear? I wish you no insult, General Hardee, but I know of no reason why the men outside this house cannot still whip a like number of Yankees!"

Johnston said, "If there were a **like** number, yes, perhaps I would agree with you. That, General, is the issue. Our greatest hope lies in marching this army northward, to a rendezvous with the Army of Northern Virginia. That act alone will provide a substantial boost to our spirit, perhaps for both armies. Right now, Sherman has granted us a generous gift of time. We must use that to boost the health of this army, as well as their willingness to fight. One should follow the other, I would think."

Hardee saw an aide peering through the door, one of Johnston's adjutants. Colonel Pickett was with him, both men seeming anxious. Hardee looked at Johnston, motioned toward the door, Johnston now aware of their presence. Johnston said, "You may enter."

Johnston's man, Colonel Eddy, held several pieces of paper in his hand, said, "Sir, we have received the morning's press dispatches. I cannot verify the accuracy, sir, but it is being reported that Richmond has been evacuated. General Lee is said to have ordered the defensive forces there to withdraw along the north side of the Appomattox River, presuming they will unite with his army somewhere close to Petersburg. It is apparent, sir, that the enemy has occupied the capital."

Johnston stared at him, no expression, and Hardee felt a punch in his stomach. Pickett moved close beside him, said, "It is also reported, sir, that President Davis is presently in Danville."

Hardee felt a glimmer of relief, and Johnston nodded slowly, said, "Yes, very good. I am pleased he managed to escape the enemy. I shall wire him with all haste. Colonel, see to it. I wish to know what instructions the president might have for us. I am assuming the secretary of war has accompanied the president. It seems apparent, more than before, that moving this army to unite with General Lee's is our only course."

Hardee felt pressed hard into the chair, a sick turn in his stomach. He kept the words to himself, allowed the chatter to flow out from the others, a mix of outrage and doubt, pessimism that the information was accurate at all. Pickett seemed to read him, put one hand on Hardee's shoulder, spoke beneath the ongoing flow of words around them.

"We shall await your orders, sir."

Hardee looked up at his friend, felt drained of emotion. Johnston led his adjutant out of the room, the others moving out as well, Hardee now alone with Pickett.

"We shall attempt to unite with the Army of Northern Virginia. Perhaps between our two armies, there is sufficient strength to . . ." He stopped. To do what? "Bill, I shall return to my headquarters. I presume our next order from General Johnston will be to prepare to march. If not, perhaps we should make room in our camps for the army of Robert E. Lee."

With Sherman still content to sit still, Johnston did not push the army to begin their own march northward before the men had been adequately prepared. On April 9, that changed. Scouts from Wade Hampton's cavalry reported with confidence that Sherman had finally issued orders to his men that they were to begin their march northward toward Raleigh the next day. If there was doubt about the reliability of those reports, Hardee knew that an army the size of what Sherman commanded could not merely pull down their tents and fall into column. There would be extensive preparation, enormous logistics, the gathering and loading of wagon trains, artillery trains. Hampton's cavalry had received most of their information from those who would see those preparations firsthand, the local citizenry around Goldsboro, most of those people with no love for Sherman's occupation of their town. On April 10, those reports were confirmed, Sherman's men taking to the roads, vast columns beginning the next phase of whatever Sherman intended them to do.

OUTSIDE RALEIGH—APRIL 10, 1865

Johnston led the three newly organized corps that morning, knowing that miles to the south, Sherman's vastly superior army would require more time to move along those same roads.

Hardee marched along the primary Goldsboro Road, a well-traveled avenue, where he would serve as Johnston's rear guard. By evening, what Johnston could still call his army had encamped around Raleigh itself.

Hardee's headquarters was on the main road, a small house occupied by a family named Joyce. He sat at their dining room table, tried to keep his arms away, the table leaning precariously to one side, shifting with any weight he put on it. The dinner was cold, a piece of ham that resembled old granite, his staff struggling to make coffee from what seemed to be sweet potato skins. The couple was young, the man with one leg severed at the knee, a wound Hardee had seen too often.

"If I may ask you, sir, where did you fight?"

The young man showed no hesitation, no self-consciousness about the missing leg. "Virginia, sir. Mostly. I got hit at Sharpsburg. Second Manassas, too. That's where they took my leg. Said I couldn't fight no more, so I come on home. Rode the train. All along the way, I scared the young'uns who saw me. Hated that. Never meant to scare no one. 'Cept Yankees. Didn't never expect you'd be sharing my table, sir. I am honored, truly."

"It isn't an honor, Mr. Joyce. I am an intruder. I am here because I have no other place to be. The army is on the march, and we must find accommodations wherever we can. My apologies to your wife for this violation."

"Oh, she don't mind none. She's with child, though. Keeps her in the bed most of the time. Pardon me for being so familiar, sir. She would much prefer being at our table with you. When your staff officer knocked on our door, she was as surprised as me. Didn't never expect the war to come here."

"With any luck, Mr. Joyce, it won't come here at all." He finished the piece of ham, a sour taste in his mouth, drank a glass of water, the only palatable thing he had ingested that day. "I wish I had something better to offer you for your hospitality, Mr. Joyce. This army has learned to subsist on very little."

"Oh, don't I know that, sir! I ate corn out of a horse's droppings one day. A man's hungry, he'll do most anything."

Hardee kept his eyes on the empty plate, thought, Let us hope we don't have it quite that bad.

"Major Roy!"

Roy appeared, a friendly nod toward Joyce. "Yes, sir."

"I shall retire. We must have the men up well before dawn. I expect orders from General Johnston informing us of our objective for the morrow's march."

He pulled out his pocket watch, saw it was after nine, looked at Joyce now. "Sir, I am decidedly in your debt. Please retire. The business of the army has inflicted enough cost on you. You need not lose a night's sleep, and your wife must be kept comfortable."

"No mind a'tall, sir. Kinda miss this, the marching and all. Can't say that around my wife. But if I could pick up a musket, I'd sure join along with you."

Hardee tried to smile, thought, Where is **this** spirit in the rest of the men? If he had fought for another two years, would he be so willing?

"What time is it?"

"Just after two, sir. Very sorry to wake you."

Hardee blinked through the glow of the lantern, realized there were at least four men there, Roy holding the lantern, Pickett behind him, the others, White, Poole.

"What is it?"

Roy said, "Courier, sir, from General Johnston. It's on paper."

"What's it say? You've read it already, I assume."

Pickett stepped forward, blocking the lantern, blessed relief to Hardee's watering eyes. "It's best if you read it yourself, sir."

He sat up, wiped at his face, tried to wake up, stared at the pencil scratchings on the paper. He leaned forward, the light catching the face of the paper, Roy holding the lantern closer. He read, stared at the signature, Johnston's own, read it again. Roy said, "It can't be true, sir."

Hardee stared past the paper, felt oddly calm, could feel the tension, the anxiousness from the others. "It **can** be true, Major. Until we know anything else, we must consider it to be true. Johnston will determine that with certainty. I imagine he'll meet with the president in Danville as quickly as possible. There will be much to discuss."

"I cannot believe this, sir."

He looked at the young face of Poole, saw tears, forced himself to avoid that. "Lieutenant, there will be no change to tomorrow's orders unless I hear differently. Have the men up early, prepared to march. General Johnston says here that the president is passing this along to us, based on 'unofficial intelligence.' But Johnston would not send a courier out here this late unless he believed it to be true. Until I know otherwise, we must assume that General Lee . . ." He stopped, felt a sudden pinch in his throat. He tried to hold it in, to gather himself, fought to hold back what he knew had been coming for a very long time. "We must assume that the Army of Northern Virginia has been compelled to surrender."

CHAPTER FORTY-EIGHT

SHERMAN

SMITHFIELD,
NORTH CAROLINA—APRIL 11, 1865

The general commanding announces to the army that he had official notice from General Grant that General Lee surrendered to him his entire army on the 9th, inst., at Appomattox Court-House, Virginia. Glory to God and our country, and all honor to our comrades in arms, toward whom we are marching! A little more labor, a little more toil on our part, the great race is won, and our Government stands regenerated, after four long years of war.

—W. T. SHERMAN,
MAJOR GENERAL, COMMANDING

The cheering seemed to echo for miles, word passed as quickly as the couriers could communicate to the officers, those men passing the word just as quickly to their subordinates. Already, with the fall of Richmond, Sherman had pressed his senior commanders to pursue Johnston's army with all speed, Sherman expecting that Lee and Johnston would be urgently seeking a rendezvous. But Lee's surrender was a surprise.

The march had proceeded as Sherman had ordered it, the columns marching first toward Smithfield, a ragged skirmish there with Hampton's cavalry, what seemed designed only to slow down the lead elements of Sherman's columns. Smithfield fell into Sherman's hands within a couple of hours, the columns then proceeding as he had planned, pushing closer still to Raleigh.

He had to assume that every official in the Confederacy had received news of Lee's surrender, so it was no surprise when Kilpatrick's advance was suddenly confronted by a railroad engine on the tracks out of Raleigh, bearing two officials of the state of North Carolina. Kilpatrick passed them through to

Sherman, who accepted their flag of truce. But their entreaty had only to do with a request that the city of Raleigh, along with its citizenry, be unharmed.

He recalled Lincoln's instructions, knew that Governor Vance was far less of a fire-breathing secessionist than Magrath of South Carolina. He scanned the clothing, fine suits, though both men were aged, somewhat rumpled in appearance.

"So, you gentlemen speak for Governor Vance?"

"Yes, sir. Quite."

"And you are?"

"I am David Swain, sir, president of the Chapel Hill University. This is Senator William Graham."

"I know who you are, Mr. Graham. Did you not serve as secretary of the navy, some years back?"

"Yes, sir. Indeed."

"It is a shame that a man who served his country in such ways should have pledged himself to a rebellion."

The two men were clearly aware they had no power at all, that whatever Sherman chose to do with them was Sherman's own decision. He watched them fidget, was annoyed, had expected more of a meaningful communication than merely a pleading for mercy.

After a silent moment, Swain said, "Sir, we were most abused by your cavalry. I do not offer that as a complaint. Merely that we are aware that hostilities still exist between your army and . . . the Confederates. Our purpose is to spare innocent civilians from such abuse as an army can sometimes inflict. I mention this only as a concern that what occurred in Columbia not be repeated in Raleigh."

Sherman lost any inkling of goodwill, looked around, the rail depot swarming with his men, held back by the guards. The railcar had been boarded by Kilpatrick's men first, had continued on to the station at Smithfield, piloted by a very young engineer, who stood off to one side, under guard, a show of force that was only that.

"I have been accused of many things, gentlemen. But I have been grossly misrepresented with regard to Columbia. My men and I, my own staff, worked tirelessly to extinguish fires throughout most of the night!" He felt his temper blossoming into a full red fury. "I tell you now, in the presence of God, that Hampton burned Columbia, and that he alone is responsible for it! If you came here to make accusations, you have endangered yourself to no good purpose."

He saw Graham's eyes widen, the old man extending his hands, a gesture of calm. "Please, General, we make no such accusations. We are merely concerned, as Governor Vance is concerned, that your army understand our willingness to welcome you without hostilities."

Sherman saw a column of smoke rising out beyond the station, pointed that way. "That's a house. It was burned by the rebel rear guard as they retreated before us. I've seen as much of that as I have any destruction by my own men. I want that known, and understood, especially by your governor."

Swain seemed eager to respond. "Oh, my, yes. Governor Vance is a man who understands political realities, General. He welcomes the coming peace."

Sherman regained his composure, knew there was a large audience, that every step he took now might be magnified beyond his control. "I have already ordered my men to respect and protect private property. I shall respond in writing to the governor's request. You may be assured that I will do everything in my power to terminate this war. As for any hostilities that exist between my soldiers and those of General Johnston, to that I cannot speak, other than to predict that any hostile act aimed at any of my troops shall be answered in like fashion. That is what war is, gentlemen." He glanced upward, the sun sinking low over the roof of the rail depot. "I would not advise you to make your return trip in the dark. A single railcar passing through the camps of this army would make for a tempting target. You are welcome to spend the night. We do not have the kind of accommodations to which you are no doubt accustomed. My tent can be shared with one of you." He turned, saw Hitchcock. "Major, will you graciously give up your tent to one of these gentlemen?"

Hitchcock stepped forward, an unnecessary show of approval. He nodded formally, then said, "Sir, I am pleased if Mr. Swain uses my tent. My mother was a classmate of yours, sir. Some years ago, of course."

Sherman tried to hide his annoyance, had no interest in a social gathering. "Fine, Major. See to it."

The men made their farewells, moved off with Sherman's guard, the young engineer escorted away as well. Sherman watched them go, heard the shouts coming from the crowd of soldiers now, men calling out, the usual "Uncle Billy," and much more, a chorus of cheers for what the men assumed had been a surrender offer right in front of them. He motioned to Dayton, said, "Major, pass the word among the officers present. I fear rumors will run rampant that Johnston has surrendered his army. These men smelled far too much like a peace commission. Put a stop to that."

"Yes, sir. Do you not expect that, sir? What have the rebels left to fight for?"

Sherman waved him away, couldn't shake a blanket of gloom. He caught Snelling's eye, motioned to the guards to make way toward his own camp. The rest of his staff fell into line with him, Sherman walking, his eyes straight ahead, his usual effort to ignore the cheering around him. He moved toward the cluster of larger tents, pulled out a cigar, eyed the dark clouds rolling in overhead. Rain tonight, he thought. Naturally. Is there a week anyplace in this God forsaken country where the sun is allowed to warm my bones? He spit the tip off the cigar, continued his slow march, quicker now, the need to be away from the troops, to find someplace to sit down. McCoy was up beside him, said, "Sir, if you care for some dinner, we have butchered a local hog."

Sherman stopped, looked at McCoy with a hard stare. "This is not yet over, Major. These men will lose their fire if we allow that. I sense a party here. That cannot be. The enemy is still dangerous and is still anticipating a confrontation with us."

McCoy seemed concerned, said, "Yes, sir. Dayton will pass the word, as you instructed." He paused. "Is there something else, sir?"

Sherman knew how well McCoy could read him, the young man sharing so much of the triumph and the sadness of Sherman's entire command. He thought of lighting the cigar, no energy for it, clamped it into his mouth unlit. "I wanted to be there."

"With General Grant?"

Sherman was surprised. "You know me more than I know myself, Major. That makes for a good staff officer. Yes, with Grant. I didn't know until now how much I hoped we would join these men together, that we would trample this rebellion in one great blow. I know he shares that. I can feel it in his letters, I felt it at City Point. It will not happen now."

"You said yourself, sir, we have heard nothing from General Johnston. There could still be a fight, a last desperate assault, one more defense."

Sherman shook his head. "We shall march as we planned, we shall pursue Johnston, and if he chooses to fight, we shall massacre him. He knows that. Joe Johnston is many things, but he is not a fool. Lee surrendered his army because he had no remaining options. How many options does Johnston have? That's an easy question. None."

The following morning, April 12, the officials from Raleigh were allowed to make their return journey, Sherman offering a gesture of generosity he was under no obligation to extend. The men were allowed to keep their rail engine, the terrified engineer once more driving them through the raucous abuse from Kilpatrick and his cavalrymen. Following close behind them came Sherman himself, riding through a driving rainstorm. By eight that morning, he was within the limits of North Carolina's capital.

Already the city had been officially surrendered, another cluster of well-suited officials, including Raleigh's mayor, William Harrison. Sherman expected to see Governor Vance, knew that Lincoln's intuition about Vance was certainly accurate, that North Carolina had a vocal minority who spoke out against secession. But Vance had panicked, anticipating that he would be arrested as an official of the Confederacy, and had vacated the city, escaping into the lines of Hampton's cavalry.

As Sherman rode past the fine homes and shops of the state's capital, he could see columns of smoke, broken glass from shattered store windows, his officers eager to explain that it was rebel cavalry who had looted the city, one last trampling of the citizenry at the hands of their own desperate men. Sherman paid that little mind, had no interest in Raleigh at all. Already Kilpatrick had the scent of Johnston's trail, the rebels on a rapid march to the northwest, toward the town of Greensboro, where the railroad could still carry their army the short forty miles to Danville, Virginia. Once more Johnston's weary soldiers were slopping through mud-covered roads, across swollen creeks, none of them with any real notion just what lay in their path.

Even as Sherman gathered his forces around Raleigh, in Greensboro a meeting was already in progress, most of the officials of the government of the Confederacy, bringing what they could carry from the treasury and archives of their capital. With the rain soaking through the dreariness of the afternoon, Jefferson Davis was given the dismal appraisal of the fortunes of his army, Joe Johnston offering the startling statistics that throughout what remained of the Confederacy, the combined Federal forces outnumbered any force that could be put in their path by a factor of nearly eighteen to one. Despite Davis's fantastic dreams that the war could still be won, that he alone could summon a new army from the scattered territories of his command, Johnston's entreaties to the other officials of his government finally persuaded Davis that one course, and only one, lay open.

Major General W. T. Sherman,
The results of the recent campaign in Virginia have changed the relative military condition of the belligerents. I am therefore induced to address you, in this form, the inquiry whether in order to stop the further effusion of blood and devastation of property, you are willing to make a temporary suspension of active operations, and to communicate to Lieutenant-General Grant, commanding the armies of the United States, the request that he will take like action in regard to other armies—the object being to permit civil authorities to enter into the needful arrangements to terminate the existing war.

JOSEPH E. JOHNSTON—
GENERAL, COMMANDING

On April 14, Sherman responded:

**I have this moment received your com-
munication. I am fully empowered to
arrange with you any terms for the suspension of further hostilities between the
two armies commanded by you and those
commanded by myself, and will be willing to confer with you to that end. . . .**

RALEIGH,
NORTH CAROLINA—APRIL 17, 1865

He had sent McCoy northward to Kilpatrick's
headquarters at the town of Durham's Station, to
await Johnston's response, where McCoy could
then relay that by telegraph to Sherman at Raleigh.
The response came quickly, as expected. Johnston
had agreed to meet at a point that seemed roughly
halfway between their two positions.

Sherman hadn't slept at all, kept awake by the voices
in his own head, as well as the unstoppable clamor
from the army that surrounded his camp. By six he
was up, cigar in hand, rifling through the breakfast
the staff had laid out, a meager mixture of hard bread
and teeth-wrenching meat. The staff had gathered
already, the men keeping their distance again, so familiar with Sherman's moods. Whatever was swirling
through his mind required no assistance from them.

He had ordered a locomotive with a pair of passenger cars, could see them now, the staff completing that job the night before. His hands gripped a thick loaf of dark bread, ripping it in half, one half tossed back on the small camp table, the other now in one corner of his mouth. The cigar was still there, an unpleasant collision with the bread, and he focused for a brief moment, struggled to bring his mind back from so many other places. The cigar was tossed away, the bread now between his teeth, tasteless, the effort to chew it just one more way for him to kill time.

The camps were coming alive, the festivities of the night before not preventing the men from answering the call, many of them stoking their campfires, others drifting toward the mess wagons, where the coffee already waited. The celebrations seemed muted this early in the morning, hunger transplanting the joy of what was happening around them. Sherman was grateful for the relative quiet, walked past rows of tents, stacked muskets, more wagons, more men pulling on their suspenders, coats, answering the brisk chill of the early spring. They mostly ignored him, another relief, and he kept moving, closer to the railcars, saw the guards assigned there, a detail to prevent anyone from exercising his own show of destruction. There was no reason to burn this place, no reason to burn anything now, and Sherman had been specific with his order to the provosts.

To the east, the sun was already breaking above

the horizon, a light smoky haze drifting through the camps, various smells finding him, almost none of that from the men themselves. It had been one of those luxuries sent from the seacoast, a supply of soap, the men ordered to bathe in whatever watery place was available. The commanders knew it had more to do with health than odor, that many of the men were carrying unwanted visitors, the usual plague that infested any army in the field. The cleanliness seemed to energize the men as well, some of them shaving their squirrel's-nest beards for the first time since they left Savannah. Sherman paid little mind to that, kept his short beard trimmed when the thought struck him, often without a mirror. His hair was much the same, a mat of greasy red that he tended to when the mood was right. The uniform was a different story, a high collar worn by almost no one else, the kind of officer's adornment that had gone out of style years before. He was surprised by someone's observation of that, had paid little mind to style at all, considered the high collar an aid to keeping his back straight. It was part of his decorum, what he believed to be a commander's place, to move through his men at any time, any occasion, carrying himself with the straight-backed air of a man in charge. That was negated often, of course, mostly by the naps he still took alongside the roads, some men moving past, mistaking him for just another officer who had collapsed in a drunken heap. It was the price he paid, the urgency of finding sleep whenever and wherever it would come.

But there would be none of that now. He eyed the railcars, the guards aware of him, standing that much straighter, an officer moving out to meet him.

"Sir! A most pleasant spring morning, wouldn't you say?"

"Haven't noticed. What time is it?"

The man pulled out a pocket watch, made a show of snapping it open, then closed, said, as though announcing to some sort of official assemblage, "Seven forty, sir."

"The train ready?"

"I believe so, sir. I have not yet spoken to the engineer."

"Don't. I'll take care of it."

Sherman moved past the man, returned the salute with an absentminded wave of his hand. The piece of bread was nearly gone, and he tossed it back toward the officer, didn't look to see if the man caught it or not. He felt the twist in his stomach, unavoidable, the intense nervousness he hid so well, said in a low voice, "Seventeen April."

The locomotive was getting up steam, and he watched that, always marveled at the great steel beasts, the technology that had so changed the war. So many troops can move so quickly, he thought. And, everything else besides. How much track did we destroy? Well, we crippled them. They'll make repairs, soon enough. We did what we had to.

He saw an officer stepping down from the nearest railcar, Dayton, the young major moving toward him.

"Ah, good morning, sir. She's ready to move, on your order." Dayton seemed to pulsate, arms moving, hands flexing, one foot then the other marching in place.

"You all right, Major?"

"Just excited, sir. Don't mind admitting that, not one bit. This is enormous, sir. Hitchcock's so nervous, he looks like he's going to fly into pieces." Dayton slapped his hands against his sides, as though warming himself. "Forgive me, sir. Just . . . this is a monumental day. I know we're not to speculate. But I feel it, sir. Every place in the world will know what will happen today, what you will make happen. I am honored to be in your service, sir."

Sherman looked past him, tried not to absorb the young man's show of raw energy. "I believe I shall board the train. Gather up the others."

"Right away, sir! Several of your invited guests are in the rear car already."

There was too much volume to Dayton's response, and Sherman said, "They're not guests. They're part of this army. Keep them back there. I'm not interested in chatting with anyone, and I don't want the reporters anywhere near me."

"Certainly, sir."

Sherman stepped closer to the train, eyed the thick black smoke now billowing high above. He took a

deep breath, a low curse to the bees' nest swarming inside him, stepped closer to the front car, the
guards there, stiff-backed, bayonets by their sides,
the men looking at him, unable to hide their smiles.
He moved past, stepped up, hesitated, pulled himself into the car, was surprised he was alone.

Choose your seat, he thought. Can't be that long
a trip. Couple hours, I suppose.

"Sir! General Sherman!"

He dreaded speaking to anyone, the voice unfamiliar. But the man was up into the car, a guard escorting him, keeping close. Sherman knew the man
now, the telegraph operator who had passed on
McCoy's wire. The man seemed to quiver, and Sherman felt a twinge, the urgency too pronounced in
the man's face. He looked to the guard.

"It's all right. Wait outside. My staff will be here
shortly."

The soldier backed away, was gone, and Sherman
looked again to the telegraph operator.

"What?"

"Sir, I have received just now a dispatch, in cipher, passed through Morehead City. It is from the
War Department, sir, and from the first few words,
I believe it to be of utmost importance. But I must
complete the translation. Please, sir. You must see
this before you depart."

There was nothing but sincerity in the man's request, and Sherman could feel the man's nervousness.

"I'll hold the train. Go."

The man ran quickly from the car, and Sherman stared for a long moment, a queasy turn in his stomach. He thought of Grant, some disaster, or some outrageous act by Lee's army, men refusing the surrender. He scolded himself, thought, No, you don't know any such thing. But anything from the War Department might be important these days.

He saw Hitchcock climbing into the train, the man smiling through his glasses, the eagerness of a man who understands history.

"Good morning, sir."

"Sit in the rear of the car, Major. We're waiting just a bit."

Hitchcock moved past him, Sherman not responding to the man's cheerfulness. Dayton was there again, a handful of aides, the men clamoring aboard, and Sherman saw Conyngham, down on the platform, the reporter eyeing Sherman with a glimmer of hopefulness. Sherman pointed toward the rear car, Conyngham seeming to understand his place in the entourage, other reporters following the man's lead. Sherman said to Hitchcock, "Back there, in the rear, all of you. Keep away from me. We shall wait for a moment longer."

Dayton stopped, looked at him, curious, seemed to read him, but Sherman turned away, stared out the windows to the side, men in motion all around the depot. The staff was seated now, no one speaking up, the kind of obedience Sherman appreciated. He kept his eyes on the crowd of soldiers, saw the telegraph operator emerging from the depot, moving that way, the man climbing up quickly into the car, a look on his face of raw misery.

"Sir. Here it is. You must read this."

Sherman took the paper from the man's shaking hand, saw the wire was from Stanton. He sagged, thought, Orders? Now? But he read the words, the handwriting ragged, and he forced himself through the message, felt the cold spreading down through his legs. He sat in the nearest seat, looked up at the operator, said in a low voice, with all the gravel he could muster, "Have you shown this to anyone? Spoken to anyone?"

"No, sir. I assure you, sir."

Sherman lowered his voice further, leaned close to the man, who bent low. "Then you must not. No one must hear of this until I return. It is most important. Do you understand?" The man was clearly shaken, nodded nervously, and Sherman stood again, one hand gripping the seat in front of him. He leaned out over the man, stared hard into his eyes. "**No one**. Your silence will do a service to this army. I will return here later today."

Sherman saw another short nod, the man obviously terrified.

"I assure you, sir."

"Go, now. Return to your office. I shall keep this."

The man backed away, was gone from the train,

and Sherman watched him walking quickly into the depot, no one paying him any attention. Sherman read the message again, a sick turn in his stomach. He kept his eyes down, would not reveal this to the staff, to anyone, not yet. He sat, stared at the floor between his boots, a voice now, "Sir, the engineer is asking when you wish to depart."

Sherman looked up, saw Major Nichols coming aboard, a pleasant smile, wiped away by the expression he saw from Sherman.

"We can leave now."

"Certainly, sir. I shall inform him. Is there anything . . ."

"No. Let's go."

In a short minute, the train lurched ahead, the staff behind him silent, expectant, no one daring to approach him. I must tell them, he thought. But no. Not yet. We have so much to do. There can be no distraction.

He held the translated message in his hand still, looked down, felt the emotion of it, thought, One more tragedy, one more part of this war that will inflict so much damage to so many. And I must tell them. Everyone in this command.

On the evening of April 14, while attending a performance at Ford's Theater in Washington City, President Abraham Lincoln was murdered by an assassin who shot him through the head with a pistol

ball. An attempt was made also on the life of Secretary Seward and his son. It is possible that General and Mrs. Grant are under threat as well. The vice-president has been given the oath of office as the new chief executive. I find evidence that there is an assassin on your track as well. I beseech you to be more heedful than Mr. Lincoln of such warnings. . . .

EDWIN M. STANTON, SECRETARY OF WAR

CHAPTER FORTY-NINE

SHERMAN

NEAR DURHAM'S STATION— APRIL 17, 1865

Kilpatrick had met him with the usual pomp that seemed to surround the cavalryman everywhere he went. His headquarters house was draped in flags, what Sherman saw as Kilpatrick's own particular show of celebration, far more elaborate than Sherman would have preferred. But he couldn't argue the purpose, that every man in Kilpatrick's camp was aware why Sherman was there.

The greetings were brief, Sherman in no mood for joviality. Kilpatrick obeyed without complaint, had already placed a line of cavalry in a neat formation, a salute for the commanding general. But now the more necessary parade was ordered into the road, led far to the front by an officer holding a white flag. Behind the flag bearer came a platoon of Kilpatrick's men, as much a security escort as any kind of formal parade. Sherman followed, and behind him, his staff, and most of the others who had accompanied his party on the train. Sherman ignored them, no one pushing to speak to him, even the newspapermen seemingly aware this was not the time.

He kept his back straight, his usual custom, glanced at his uniform, the grime of the campaign evident in the worn cloth, the uneven colors, the frayed cuff on one arm. He still wore only the one spur, had never considered the need for two, but as the party pushed on, the doubts began. Damn it all, he thought. Does this call for some kind of formal dress parade? Isn't it enough that Kilpatrick fills the damned countryside with his horsemen? Surely they know that if any poor dumb rebel takes a shot at me, we'll bring down the fires of hell on these people.

The noise in his head seemed to chatter on, the grip on the reins tight, his hands sweating inside of his gauntlets, a cigar clamped hard in his teeth. Is Johnston an honorable man? Did I ever meet him? Don't think so. He was in Mexico, for certain. Grant probably knew him. What the hell am I supposed to say to him? Hello, Joe. Now you can surrender your damned army. He put a hand on his coat pocket, felt the telegram. No, that's what we must discuss, before anything else. Perhaps he already knows. My God, this is a horrible day.

He saw commotion ahead, one of Kilpatrick's men riding back toward him, a salute, which Sherman returned. Beside him Kilpatrick seemed to blow out the words with the kind of bombast that made Sherman cringe.

"Report, Lieutenant!"

"Sirs, we have encountered a rider, a rebel, with a flag of truce. He says that General Johnston is close behind him."

Kilpatrick seemed to ponder a decision. "Well, perhaps we should allow him to enter our lines, as it were."

Sherman tapped his hat down on his head. "**Perhaps** I should ride forward and meet with General Johnston. We can argue formalities later."

He followed the lieutenant, the other cavalrymen keeping pace, still the itching need for security. Sherman ignored them, kept his eyes to the front, saw riders now, a small cluster of gray uniforms, the flag of truce. He searched the faces, no real need, the one smaller man standing out, flanked by a large cavalry officer. He stopped the horse, a few yards between them, saw a hard scowl on the cavalryman's face, the young officer still holding the white flag speaking out.

"Sirs, this is General Joseph Johnston. This is Lieutenant General Wade Hampton."

Sherman focused on Johnston, as Kilpatrick spoke up. "This is Major General William T. Sherman, Army of the United States. I am Major General Judson Kilpatrick."

Sherman nudged the horse closer to Johnston, studied Johnston as he knew Johnston was studying him. The man was small-framed, a distinguished point of silvery beard on his chin, a hint of gray hair beneath his hat, his face worn, tired. Sherman noticed the uniform, thought, New, probably. And look at me. Well, this isn't a dress parade.

The horses were close, and Johnston held out a hand, which Sherman took, a brief hard squeeze.

Introductions followed, both men naming their respective staff officers, the kind of formality that seemed appropriate for a review. Sherman endured that, forgot most of Johnston's staff as soon as the names were given, assumed Johnston did as well. When the introductions were complete, Sherman said, "General, is there someplace where we may meet in private? A discussion on horseback seems rather unsuitable."

"There was a farmhouse just a ways back. A short ride, if you don't mind."

"Very well. Please lead the way."

Johnston lowered his head, a hint of a smile, his soft Virginia accent framing his words with a hint of syrup. "General, I believe we should ride together, side by side. The staffs may follow behind."

Sherman nodded, was already dreading the formality of this. "Let's go, then."

They made the short ride, Sherman mostly in silence, Johnston offering small pleasantries, tossing names out from the old army. Sherman could see now that Johnston was a good bit older, possibly sixty, the hardness in his features rounded by age and experience. The road curved slightly, the farmhouse ahead, and Johnston said, "Family named Bennett, I believe. They should have no problem with our use of their home."

Sherman nodded in agreement, thought, Wouldn't really matter if they did.

The men dismounted, each instructing their staff officers to dismount and hold where they were. Johnston stepped toward the door and Sherman saw movement in one of the windows, the face of a child. The door opened, a woman, eyes wide, glancing nervously back and forth between the two contrasting uniforms.

"I am Mrs. Daniel Bennett."

Sherman said, "Madam, might we use your home for a meeting?"

The woman kept her gaze on Johnston now, who said, "Yes, if you will allow it. Only for a time. No harm will come."

"I suppose that is acceptable. Will you allow me

to remove my children? We can go there, the out-building."

Johnston made a short bow. "Certainly, madam. If we may enter, then?"

The woman backed away, a quick look into an-other room, a soft command, the sounds of padded feet scurrying through the house. There were four children, their mother escorting them in single file outside. The children eyed Sherman, and he couldn't avoid watching them, saw the eyes of one, wide, frightened. He thought of his own daughter, what this would be like, so many soldiers, an army suddenly bringing the war to your house. Plenty of children will remember this, he thought.

After a long moment, the family was gone, and Sherman thought now of the husband, glanced at Johnston, knew better than to ask. He wouldn't know anyway. But he's off somewhere, sure as hell toting a musket. Maybe right out there, part of the escort.

Johnston led him into a large square room, a massive stone hearth to one side, a stairway lead-ing to what seemed to be a small upstairs sleeping area. The floor was wood planks, a bedroom to one end, the smells of a kitchen. Sherman eyed a drop-leaf table, a pair of plain wood chairs, Johnston already moving there. Johnston sat, removed his hat, Sherman noticing the amount of silver in what remained of his hair. He felt more nervous now than any time this day, looked back toward the door, staff officers from both men staring in. Sherman focused on Dayton, said, "Major, this shall be a private meeting. Close the door."

Dayton obeyed, the room now darker, Johnston silent, and Sherman saw a hint of shakiness in Johnston's hands, thought, Even rebels can be nervous.

Sherman scanned the house, what seemed comfortable for a simple farming family, a large spinning wheel in one corner of the bedroom, another table, a large desk. He knew he was delaying the inevitable, and his fingers went to his pocket, feeling the paper dispatch. He let out a breath, said, "General, I have something I must reveal to you. No one else in my army has seen this. I do not know to what extent this news has traveled."

Johnston seemed curious, took the paper from Sherman's hand, read. His hand dropped to the table, and he shook his head, a sag to his shoulders, curling his slight fingers into fists. "This is a disgrace to the age. It is the greatest possible calamity for the South."

Sherman could see emotion in Johnston's face, was surprised, sat at the other side of the table, said, "I do not yet know what this means for us."

"Surely, you do not consider this to be an act of my government?"

That had not occurred to Sherman at all, and he said, "I do not believe that you or General Lee would ever be privy to an act of assassination. But

I admit to you, in all candor, I am not certain such can be said for Jefferson Davis."

Johnston shook his head vigorously. "I have seen the president within the last few days. There is nothing of this kind of barbarity in him. I assure you, sir. Nothing at all. This is an outrage to all civilized men."

"I agree. I have not revealed this to even my own staff, but obviously, I must do so by tonight. I dread the effect this will have in Raleigh. Mr. Lincoln was peculiarly endeared to the soldiers, and all it would take is one foolish man or woman to say something that might inflame our men. I fear there could be a worse fate than what befell Columbia."

"I cannot assist you in that effort, General. But I pray that reason will prevail, on all sides."

"I have always prayed for that. It hasn't been especially effective. General, surely you are convinced that you cannot oppose my army. Since General Lee has surrendered, you can do the same with honor and propriety. I see no alternative."

Johnston sat back, the dispatch on the table between them. "I cannot argue that point, sir. Any further fighting between our troops would be little more than murder. Can we not arrange for the surrender of all the Confederate armies? General Lee could only speak for his troops, and I can only speak for mine. I could possibly gain authority from President Davis."

Sherman thought a moment, realized this might become more complicated than he had thought. "I have recently had an interview with Mr. Lincoln and General Grant, and I believe I can speak for both men, even in this circumstance. There was consistency in their views, and the views of the Northern people, that there is no vindictive feeling against the Confederate armies. However, that cannot be said of their feelings toward Mr. Davis and his political adherents." He paused. "The terms that were given to Lee's army by General Grant were most certainly generous and liberal. Surely you can be of like mind, and see that the other armies can be convinced?"

"It is possible that overnight, I can receive those assurances from the president, and possibly the authority to act on that. But you realize that the government of the United States has never recognized the existence of a Confederate government. I am not certain how we can treat on the subject of civil authority."

Sherman stared at Johnston, absorbed in the situation that seemed to grow more complex by the second. "You agree that this war must end."

Johnston held up his hands in front of him, palms apart, a gesture of agreement. "Most certainly."

"I can, right here, offer your army the terms as given by General Grant."

Johnston frowned. "Our situation here is vastly different from General Lee's. The pieces do not necessarily fit. However, can we not pursue a goal that includes more than what you propose with my army? First, all we have now in effect is a partial suspension of hostilities. Can we not, as others have done, arrange a permanent peace?"

Sherman laid one hand on the table, tapped with his palm, felt a burst of enthusiasm, erasing the head-splitting confusion over so many definitions of civil authority. "Yes! I agree with such sentiment. I do not know of any reason why we cannot create an agreement here to end bloodshed and devastation to the land, and restore the Union. We must agree to the terms to be offered the Southern states, on their submission to the authority of the United States. I know that President Lincoln was stoutly in favor of such action."

They conversed for the rest of the afternoon, mostly pleasant, social chatter, some of it more involved with the war itself. Most important to Sherman, the relationship he had formed with Johnston seemed nearly instantaneous, a common understanding that the war had come to an end.

Sherman's only sticking point was his understanding that Jefferson Davis could not likely be included in any kind of general amnesty that might be afforded the Southern soldiers. He knew enough of Washington politics to know that Davis meant more to the United States government than any general or any other single part of the rebellion. It was that annoying focus on **symbols** again, something Sherman had grudgingly come to understand. The only symbol that might have more meaning to the Southern people would be in the person of Robert E. Lee. But Lee's surrender had made that meaningless, the man more of a symbol now of what the Confederacy had lost than whatever legitimacy the South still held as its own nation.

With daylight fading, Johnston suggested a meeting for the next day, same location, to hammer out details that could be presented to both governments. In the meantime, Johnston would seek the authority from his own government to settle so many of the nagging civil issues.

Sherman left the Bennett house with an aching sense of hope, that these negotiations would not descend into a squabble over the kind of minutiae he had so little patience for. As he rode back toward Durham's Station with Kilpatrick and his staff, Sherman knew he had one more monumental task in front of him. It was time to tell his army, his generals, and his own staff officers that President Lincoln was dead.

In every place the soldiers were camped, guards were doubled, provosts instructed with harsh terms the level of control they had to maintain over civilian property. To Sherman's relief, the acts of vengeance or hateful violence against the citizens in and around Raleigh were scarce. Instead, Sherman saw what he felt himself, that the men kept mostly to their camps, absorbing the bitter emotions, expressing the loss of their president not with guns and torches, but with tears.

BENNETT HOUSE, NEAR DURHAM'S STATION—APRIL 18, 1865

They met as before, alone, but Johnston seemed to understand the propriety of civil issues far better than Sherman. Johnston had brought John Breckinridge with him, a man Sherman knew well. Breckinridge had been the vice president of the United States under President James Buchanan. Pledging his loyalties to the Confederacy, he had served as major general, another in the long line of commanders whose feuding with Braxton Bragg had tossed him out of active service. Now he was Davis's secretary of war, a post Johnston insisted would provide the necessary civil authority to any agreement they could forge.

But Sherman felt uneasy with a man who was now a leading figure in the Confederate government, a post that put him into another sphere entirely from what Sherman felt he could address. It was Johnston who suggested that Breckinridge be involved in the conversation more in the role as major general, a compromise Sherman accepted.

After long discussions over the terms both sides could find acceptable, Sherman put the agreement to paper.

Once the terms were approved by their governments, there would be a temporary armistice, to last for forty-eight hours, what both men believed was sufficient time to pass along the terms to their respective commands. Beyond that, the more obvious terms were spelled out in neat detail. The Confederate armies were to be disbanded, the men returning to their own state capitals, awaiting further instruction, though every man would sign an agreement that he would no longer engage in acts of war.

The civil terms seemed perfectly clear to Sherman. The president of the United States would recognize the existing Confederate state governments, as long as those bodies would take an oath prescribed by the U.S. Constitution. It would be up to the U.S. Supreme Court to validate their legitimacy. The citizens of the Confederate states would be guaranteed their political rights, rights of person and property, as defined by the U.S. Constitution.

The final term was that by this agreement, the war would cease. "A general amnesty, so far as the executive of the United States can command, on condition of the disbandment of the Confederate armies, the distribution of the arms, and the resumption of peaceful pursuits by the officers and men hitherto composing said armies."

The final paragraph made Sherman far more comfortable with the civil agreements that Breckinridge had described: "Not being fully empowered by our respective principals to fulfill these terms, we individually and officially pledge ourselves to promptly obtain the necessary authority, and to carry out the above programme."

Sherman left the meeting with full confidence that peace had been restored. Unlike the awful communication he had given his army on the seventeenth, the next morning Sherman issued a far more celebratory notice: "The general commanding announces to the army a suspension of hostilities, and an agreement with General Johnston, and high officials which, when formally ratified, will make peace from the Potomac to the Rio Grande. . . ."

Early on the morning of April 19, Sherman sent Hitchcock toward the coast, to board a steamer that would carry the major to Washington. Hitchcock carried the document, as well as specific letters Sherman had written, to be delivered to Secretary Stanton, General Halleck, or General Grant. The only other restriction Hitchcock received was to keep the papers away from the eyes of any newspaper reporter.

Knowing Hitchcock would require time to make the deliveries, Sherman kept his anxieties shoved aside by reviewing his troops, especially the new units now under his command, the Tenth and Twenty-third corps, the troops Schofield had brought into Sherman's camps. None of those formalities could keep Sherman from sleepless nights, the raw anxiety that these days spent in camp in Raleigh would be his final days in command of an army.

On the twenty-third, Hitchcock telegraphed his return, that he would arrive the following morning.

Sherman made every effort to find some kind of normalcy as he waited, knowing that some miles away, Joe Johnston was likely as anxious as he was. At six in the morning, the train arrived, Sherman standing at the depot in the chill, shivering more from his nervousness than from the coolness of an early spring morning. Hitchcock quickly appeared, but there was no smile, none of Hitchcock's usual naïve cheeriness. As he stepped down from the train, another man appeared, in uniform. To Sherman's openmouthed surprise, it was Grant.

After a jubilant greeting, Sherman's surprise was crushed by the hammer blow that Grant delivered, the purpose of Grant's visit. The terms of surrender between Sherman and Johnston had been rejected by the United States government.

CHAPTER FIFTY

SHERMAN

RALEIGH,
NORTH CAROLINA—APRIL 24, 1865

They settled into Sherman's more permanent headquarters at the Governor's Mansion. Grant had insisted, and Sherman had made clear to his staff, that Grant's visit was not to be announced to the army, nor to anyone else who could be kept in the dark. Once Sherman understood why Grant had come, he appreciated exactly what Grant had in mind. He was saving Sherman's command.

General Johnston, Commanding Confederate Army, Greensboro:

You will take notice that the truce or suspension of hostilities agreed to between us will cease in forty-eight hours after this is received at your lines, under the first of the articles of agreement.

W. T. SHERMAN, MAJOR GENERAL

Grant sat with his legs crossed, smoked a cigar, read the second letter.

General Johnston,
I have replies from Washington to my communications of April 18. I am instructed to limit my operations to your immediate command, and not to attempt civil negotiations. I therefore demand the surrender of your army on the same terms as were given to General Lee at Appomattox, April 9, instant, purely and simply.

Grant set the papers on the table, a cloud of cigar smoke rising around his face. "That should suffice. You should probably issue an order to your army commanders, to make preparations for march. Once your forty-eight hours has passed, their orders should be specific, routes of march, so forth. You cannot assume hostilities will not continue."

Sherman felt his chest burning with a hard black

fury, fought to keep it inside. "There will be no hostilities. Johnston is an honorable man. And a man who understands the depth of his defeat."

Grant stared at the two letters. "The order is not merely for Johnston. It is for Washington. They must know that it is your intention to fight this war to its fullest, lest you demonstrate a hesitancy that might be interpreted incorrectly."

Sherman pushed himself deeper into the chair, fought the urge to stand, to march around the room with thunderous steps. He took a long breath, could see Grant watching him. "Interpreted how?"

Grant pulled an envelope from his pocket. "I am to give this to you, as though I was never present. This was transmitted to me by the War Department."

Lieutenant General Grant,
General: The memorandum, or basis agreed upon between General Sherman and General Johnston having been submitted to the president, they are disapproved.

Sherman stopped, held out the paper. "You explained this already. I went too far. Fine. Johnston will surrender as instructed. I have no doubts about that."

Grant pointed to the letter in Sherman's hand. "Keep reading. The last paragraph."

> **The President desires that you proceed im-
> mediately to the headquarters of Major-
> General Sherman, and direct operations
> against the enemy.**

Sherman lowered the note, looked at Grant, saw
no change of expression. "I am being relieved?"

Grant shook his head. "No. But there is talk in
the cabinet. Nasty talk. I spoke out on your behalf."

"Not the cabinet. Stanton. It's just Stanton."

"I have not communicated to you any such
thing. But the secretary is an influential man. We
have a very new president, who is hesitant to in-
sert his views, should they contradict any policies
of Mr. Lincoln. The secretary of war has no such
hesitancy."

He knew there were things Grant wasn't saying,
could see from Grant's hard stare that events had
spun wildly in a direction Sherman never expected.

"Grant, what are you to do here?"

"My desire is that I do nothing at all. I will not
remain here any longer than is required for you to
conclude this matter with General Johnston. Once
your armies have ceased hostilities, all should be
well elsewhere."

Sherman stood now, turned toward a tall window, gripped his cigar in his fist, obliterating it.
"I abhor this, Grant! I did nothing wrong! I have
no desire to interfere with civil politics. None! But
Johnston was correct on one very important point.

This is not Appomattox. His army is not as Lee's was, hemmed in a trap. If he chooses not to accept your terms, his armies will continue their march, very probably will disperse, and instead of us having to deal with six or seven Southern states, we will deal with countless bands of desperadoes. Chasing down men like Forrest, Mosby, any of them! For how long? Years? Every city in the Confederacy will become an area of occupation by our armies. How many men will that require? For **years** as well?"

Grant still watched him, and Sherman could see Grant was forcing himself not to react. Or to agree. Grant tipped the cigar down, dropping the ash to a small dish.

"You can certainly address your concerns to the secretary. I recommend it."

"What do I tell him? The United States government has made a mistake?"

Grant shrugged. "If you wish. He will tell you it's none of your business. You are a servant of that government. You do not make policy."

Sherman spun around, pacing heavily. "Damn it all, Grant. I never wanted to **make** anything. All I have done in this theater is achieve victories. This army has done so, marvelously. And now I am to be doubted? I must be slapped on my knuckles like some errant schoolboy? President Lincoln would have approved the agreement with Johnston. You know that. You heard him, as I did. He wanted forgiveness, not punishment!"

"Before you base your arguments on what Lincoln might or might not have approved, you should hear this." Grant reached into a small valise, produced another letter. "This was sent to me by Stanton a few days prior to Lee's surrender. Dated April third."

Grant read,

> **Lieutenant-General Grant,**
> **The president directs me to say to you that he wishes you to have no conference with General Lee, unless it be for capitulation of General Lee's army, or on some minor or purely military matter. He instructs me to say that you are not to decide, discuss, or confer upon any political questions. . . .**

Sherman stared at him, his mouth open. "I knew nothing of that."

"I know you didn't. Never bothered to tell you. Wasn't important then. It is now."

"So, they sent you here to read that to me?"

"Actually, Sherman, they seem to believe you already saw this. They think . . . **someone** thinks you deliberately ignored this instruction, and acted on your own. That's not a good thing for a military commander to do."

"Dammit, Grant, I didn't!"

"I know. They'll know that as well, if this continues to boil. This kind of thing happens to all of us eventually. Write Stanton, tell him you were wrong to stray into civil affairs. A foolish error."

Sherman slumped into the chair again. "All right. What are you going to do?"

Grant lit another cigar. "For now, I wish the army to be kept unaware of my presence. That would serve no useful purpose, and might convey the impression that I have come here to . . . well, to make mischief. Instead, I'm going to enjoy the comforts of this fine home, until you receive a response from General Johnston. Then I am going to return as quickly as I can back to that infuriating city."

The next day, April 25, Sherman received the letter from Johnston he was desperately hoping for. It was not merely Sherman's wishful thinking that Johnston understand his limited options. The Confederate commander accepted the terms of surrender as Sherman presented them, the same terms given Lee's army at Appomattox. On April 26, the two men met one more time at the Bennett house. The meeting was brief, formal, Johnston seeming to grasp completely the hornet's nest Sherman had created for himself. But the time for argument, for controversy had passed. Accompanied by a host of senior commanders, Sherman and Johnston went straight to the business at hand. Seventeen days after Lee's surrender at Appomattox, the two men signed their names to a document that no one could dispute.

All acts of war on the part of the troops under General Johnston's command to cease from this date . . .

AFTERWORD

In late April 1865, as Sherman prepares to leave his command, intending first to visit Charleston and his army's base in Savannah, he receives a copy of the April 24 edition of **The New York Times**. The column, attributed to Secretary Stanton, relates the entire complaint against Sherman's negotiations with General Johnston, as well as a not-so-subtle suggestion that Sherman's command is susceptible to a bribe from Jefferson Davis, which might allow Davis to escape the country. As a conclusion, Stanton writes that Ulysses Grant was sent to Raleigh to direct operations against Johnston's army, the wording identical to the order Stanton had given Grant. Sherman is outraged by the breach of military protocol, and writes a lengthy letter of response to Grant, protesting the slam against his character and reputation, including the insinuation that he has been grossly insubordinate. Sherman writes,

> **I, who for four years, have labored day and night, winter and summer, who have brought an army of seventy thousand men in magnificent condition across a country hitherto deemed impassible, and placed it just where it was wanted, on the day appointed, have brought discredit to our Government! I do not wish to boast of this, but do say that it entitled me to the courtesy of being consulted to higher authority to adjudication, and then accompanied by statements which invited the dogs of the press to be let loose upon me. It is true that non-combatants, men who sleep in comfort and security while we watch on the distant lines, are better able to judge than we poor soldiers, who rarely see a newspaper, hardly hear from our families, or stop long enough to draw our pay. . . .**

Sherman demands that his letter be made as public as Stanton's, and a war of words breaks out in the various newspapers of the day, Sherman's longtime enemies in the press delighting in the controversy.

In his memoirs, Sherman writes,

> **To say that I was merely angry at the tone and substance of these published bulletins of the War Department, would hardly express the state of my feelings. I was outraged beyond measure. . . .**

Clearly Grant recognizes the injustice done to Sherman, and by comparing the two men in his memoirs, Grant writes,

> **Mr. Stanton never questioned his own authority to command . . . he cared nothing for the feelings of others. . . . The enemy would not have been in danger if Mr. Stanton had been in the field.**

Though several newspapers take up the call for Sherman's removal, some even labeling him treasonous, he has his defenders, including Horace Greeley of the **New-York Tribune,** who describes Stanton's insinuation that Sherman had aided Jefferson Davis's efforts to escape as no more than **flapdaddle.** Secretary of the Navy Gideon Welles writes,

> **We were all imposed upon by Stanton for a purpose. He and the radicals were opposed to the mild policy of President Lincoln on which Sherman acted, and**

which Stanton opposed and was determined to defeat.

Thus is laid bare the enormous and unanswerable **what-if** of Lincoln's assassination, and just how differently the next generation of politicians might have worked successfully to heal the gaping wounds suffered by the South, instead of the policies of Reconstruction, which have dug painfully into those scars even to this day.

As for Sherman's contribution to the unhealed wounds, historians have argued over the merits or sins of Sherman's campaigns into the twenty-first century. Historian John G. Barrett writes, "Sherman inflicted wounds which would remain open for generations to come. The hatred for the North instilled in the hearts of many Southerners by Sherman's operations lengthened the South's road to reunion. . . ." But Barrett also writes, "Though pitiless in campaign and intemperate in language, Sherman was not a cruel individual with the instincts of a barbarian."

The briefest of summaries can be made by historian Ellis M. Coulter: "To him, war must be fought effectively, or not at all."

O rdered by Grant to march the substance of his army northward to Washington City, Sherman embarks himself by boat, and on May 11 he makes a rendezvous with his troops at Richmond. He marches his army through northern Virginia, passing through nearly all of the major battlefields in that part of the East, fields that Sherman has never seen. On May 19, Sherman orders his army into camps around Alexandria, Virginia, awaiting further orders from Grant. Immediately across the Potomac River are the camps of the Army of the Potomac, the men commanded by George Gordon Meade.

With his army resting and rejuvenating, Sherman visits Washington, sees Grant and the new president, Andrew Johnson, who offers Sherman assurances that neither he nor the rest of his cabinet officials were aware that Stanton intended to make public the insult to Sherman's reputation. Though Grant attempts to bridge the gulf between Sherman and Stanton with a social meeting, Sherman declines, claiming without hesitation that he will hold this grudge for a very long time.

On May 23, as ordered by Grant, a grand review is held through the streets of the capital. Meade's army precedes Sherman's. The Army of the Potomac is fitted out in new uniforms, with polished brass, shined boots, freshly adorned horses, the perfect spit and polish that official Washington expects. The following day, Sherman's army begins its parade. The men are unshaven, most in their field uniforms, and are accompanied by an enormous number of the freed slaves that still follow the army. It is no accident that Sherman offers the American public a demonstration of what a true army looks like, having just marched from the last great battlefields of the war.

Sherman leads the procession, the one notable exception in a crisp new uniform. According to protocol, once he passes the enormous reviewing stand, he leaves his army to complete their parade and climbs into the stands, joining the vast throng of dignitaries. He happily greets and accepts the appropriate accolades offered him by Grant, the president, and the attending cabinet. Then, confronted by a smiling Edwin Stanton, who extends his hand, Sherman turns away, a scene that is "universally noticed." For the following six hours, the remainder of Sherman's army, the Fifteenth, Seventeenth, Twentieth, and Fourteenth corps, passes by. Sherman writes,

> It was, in my judgment, the most magnificent army in existence—sixty five thousand men, in splendid physique, who had just completed a march of nearly two thousand miles in a hostile country, in good drill, and who realized they were being closely scrutinized by thousands of their fellow countrymen and foreigners. . . . Many people, up to that time, had looked upon our Western army as a sort of mob; but then the world saw, and recognized the fact that it was an army

in the proper sense . . . and there was no wonder that it had swept through the South like a tornado.

One soldier, of the 7th Iowa Regiment, writes,

The difference in the two armies is this: they have remained in camp and lived well; we have marched and fought and gone hungry and ended the war.

Though there are still official hostilities west of the Mississippi River, those Confederate commanders, notably Richard Taylor and Kirby Smith, recognize that continuing their own campaigns has no purpose. On May 4, Taylor surrenders the Trans-Mississippi armies to Federal commander Edward Canby, thus the final end to the war in every part of the South.

THOSE WHO WORE GRAY

WILLIAM J. HARDEE

By the spring of 1865, the man whom friends describe as boisterous, debonair, and full of cheer leaves his service to the Confederate cause a shattered and disillusioned man. Though Hardee is viewed by all who serve him as the consummate professional tactician, Sherman's overwhelming dominance of Hardee's efforts destroys any hopes Hardee has of resuming some kind of influential role in any military circle, especially his beloved West Point.

Historian Nathaniel Hughes writes,

The Army of the Tennessee was vital to the Confederate War effort, and Hardee should be remembered as an integral and able part of it. Albert Sidney Johnston, Bragg, Joe Johnston and even Hood placed great reliance on him as a battle commander, and consulted him in strategic matters. [But] limited by his reluctance to abandon outmoded military techniques in which he was expert, Hardee never rose to first rank.

He surrenders with Joe Johnston at Durham's Station and settles at his young wife's family plantation near Demopolis, Alabama, then moves to Selma. Hardee never seems to find comfort in civilian life, tries his hand at various enterprises, including cotton farming and railroading, which he attacks with a military zeal. But zeal alone cannot overcome the poor health of the economy, and in 1868 he leaves that profession.

He appeals for a pardon from the United States government, including a personal appeal to William T. Sherman. He even professes publicly that he would serve the United States Army again, should any need arise, believing that the issues so destructive to the nation from 1861 through 1865 have been settled. But the Congress is not so flexible, and his petition drags through the capital for two years before Hardee is finally pardoned.

He and Mary travel a great deal, mostly throughout the South, and make frequent visits to White Sulphur Springs, West Virginia. While at the springs in the summer of 1873, Hardee is taken ill, is diagnosed with stomach cancer. Attempting to return home by rail, Hardee dies at Wytheville, Virginia. He is fifty-eight. His young wife, Mary, survives but two more years, dies at age thirty-five, from tuberculosis.

In 1871, Hardee's daughter Sallie marries his adjutant and chief of staff, Thomas Roy.

As the war concludes, Hardee demonstrates the respect he holds for his most notable adversary, expressing to Joe Johnston that when he "learned that Sherman's army was marching through the Salkehatchie swamps, making his own corduroy roads at the rate of a dozen miles a day or more, and bringing its artillery and wagons with it, I made up my mind that there had been no such army in existence since the days of Julius Caesar."

JOSEPH E. JOHNSTON

With the surrender of his army, Johnston witnesses an act of generosity from Sherman he never expects, as Sherman issues ten days' rations to Johnston's hungry troops and orders the Federal commissary to provide sacks of seed for the former soldiers, assisting them to return to life on their farms. As a result, Johnston will never speak out against Sherman personally, or offer any condemnation of Sherman's military operations. It is not always a popular position for Johnston to take.

He tries his hand at the railroad business, but it holds no appeal, and Johnston is very much a career soldier without a career to fulfill him.

He writes his memoirs in 1874, in which he soundly criticizes Jefferson Davis, an extension of their disagreeable relationship, which goes back to 1861. As well, Johnston assails Braxton Bragg and John Bell Hood, content to leave his own mark at the expense of their reputations. Though supported in his tactical and strategic views by Sherman and Grant, the vitriolic nature of his feuds with the former Confederates diminishes his reputation. In 1870, Wade Hampton writes him, "I feel sure no good would come in any way by any publication by you raising an issue on the point [of Davis]." It is advice Johnston ignores. But after two years of brutal imprisonment, Jefferson Davis is more a martyr than villain, and Johnston's attacks on him are not well received. The memoir fails to sell.

Their feud only increases when Johnston tells a newspaper reporter of his suspicions that Davis absconded with nearly two million dollars of the gold from the Confederate treasury, an accusation that infuriates Davis and most of the South.

Johnston moves from Savannah to Richmond in 1876, and considers a run for politics. To his own surprise, he is elected to Congress, but serves only a single term, finds political life as boring as he found the railroad.

His wife, Lydia, dies in 1887, after forty-one years of marriage. Johnston is devastated by her death, and for the remainder of his life, he will not speak her name.

He serves, ironically, as pallbearer at the funerals of Ulysses Grant and George McClellan, and, in 1891, he serves as honorary pallbearer for William T. Sherman. But the brutal February weather causes Johnston to be taken ill, and he dies the following month. He is eighty-four. He is buried beside his wife at Green Mount Cemetery, in Baltimore, Maryland.

It is another of the "what-ifs" of the Civil War that Robert E. Lee ascended to command of the Army of Northern Virginia as a direct result of Johnston's being wounded at the Battle of Seven Pines, on the Virginia peninsula, in the summer of 1862. The death of Albert Sydney Johnston (no relation) two months prior at Shiloh thus took from the reins of the Confederate army two of their highest-ranking and most respected generals. Though Lee certainly excelled in the role, the question will always remain, had Joe Johnston not been wounded, would Lee have ever been given high command? And, of course, given his bitter relationship with his president, what would Johnston have done with it?

•

JOSEPH WHEELER

In April 1865, "Fighting Joe" attempts to evade capture, and, riding with only fourteen men, he embarks on a journey westward, where he hopes to join with Kirby Smith in continuing the war. But he is captured at Conyers Station, Georgia, near Atlanta.

Imprisoned at Fort Delaware, Wheeler suffers horribly, along with so many other Southern soldiers, until his release in July 1865. He returns to his home in Augusta, Georgia, where he marries Daniella Jones Sherrod. In 1866 they move to New Orleans, where Wheeler is employed as a merchant. He moves to Lawrence County, Alabama, in 1870, attempts to practice law, and settles as well into life as a gentleman farmer. He invests in what had been the Memphis & Charleston Railroad, long destroyed by Federal troops. But the railroad sees new life, and by 1880, Wheeler's investments bring him prosperity.

Drawn to politics, he runs for the House of Representatives in 1880 on a platform alien to many Southerners, that of moving past the war, with an eye only on the future, and fruitful business relationships with the North. Wheeler is elected over a man whose views are radically opposite, a sign of the times. Wheeler serves seven terms, but, even as he ages, he becomes a vocal advocate of military action against Spain, advocating a free Cuba. In 1898, the controversy erupts into the Spanish-American War. Despite opposition from his own family, Wheeler volunteers to fight, saying "if a fish had been out of water for thirty-three years, and suddenly came in sight of a great pond, he'd wiggle a little, at any rate." Because of his friendly relationship with President William McKinley, who seems uninterested in Wheeler's loyalties during the Civil War, Wheeler is named Major General of Volunteers, and his command includes a group of cavalrymen later known as Teddy Roosevelt's Rough Riders.

A year later, while in failing health, Wheeler sails to the Philippines and joins in the fighting there, but his capacity for strong-backed service is at an end. He returns home in 1900, anticipating a return to Congress. President McKinley instead appoints him to command of the Military Department of the Lakes, with his post in Chicago. But Wheeler retires within a year and settles in Brooklyn, New York. He dies in January 1906, at age sixty-nine, and is one of the very few Confederate officers buried at Arlington National Cemetery.

JAMES SEELEY

Seeley surrenders alongside General Wade Hampton at Durham's Station, North Carolina. Angered by the efforts of his nominal commander, Joe Wheeler, to continue the war any way possible, Seeley ignores Wheeler's hopes of recruiting cavalry fighters, and instead begins the arduous return journey to his home and young wife, Katie, in Memphis. He arrives in July 1865. His father, a prosperous banker, has somehow survived the war with his prosperity intact, which Seeley believes is only from collusion with the Federal powers occupying Memphis. But reality settles in and Seeley accepts the end of the war for what it is.

He goes to work with his father, becomes manager and eventually president of the Memphis Farmers Bank. He and Katie have four children.

He again befriends his first commander, Nathan Bedford Forrest, but with the latter one of Memphis's more notable slave traders, Forrest's fortunes pale in comparison, and their friendship does not move past the occasional recounting of their military adventures. When Forrest attempts to counter the policies of Reconstruction by participating in the formation of an organization to empower the South's disenfranchised white men, what becomes known as the Ku Klux Klan, Seeley takes no part, understanding that the future lies with positive banking and commercial relationships with the North. Thus Seeley willingly pledges a loyalty oath to the United States, which paves the way for the increasing financial strength of his bank, and his own fortune.

Rarely active in Confederate reunions, Seeley seems quick to accept the South's defeat as the only possible outcome, and rarely will discuss his own experiences as a cavalryman.

He dies in 1909, at age sixty-seven. Katie survives until 1928.

WADE HAMPTON

Hampton surrenders alongside Joe Johnston at Durham's Station, North Carolina. As the staffs and other officers mingle outside the Bennett house in April 1865, Hampton makes a reputation for himself by a distinctly unfriendly stance, as though unwilling to associate himself with any Federal officer. Yet, with the war decided, Hampton becomes one of the more active figures in the South in promoting a reconciliation with the Federal government. But Reconstruction sours his point of view, and Hampton reacts to the abuses of Northern opportunists by angrily denouncing Northern policies. Alongside former Confederate general Jubal Early, Hampton embraces and promotes the more mythical status of Confederate commanders, particularly Robert E. Lee. Thus does Hampton become one of the principal voices of the "Lost Cause" mythology, as an apologist for Confederate wrongs, justifying the Southern way of life.

Always active in politics, he runs for and is elected governor of South Carolina in 1877, and is elected to the United States Senate two years later, serving two terms. In 1893 he is named United States Commissioner of Railroads, a post he holds for five years. He retires from public life in 1897, and dies in 1902, at the age of eighty-four.

THOSE WHO WORE BLUE

FRANKLIN

Purchasing his way aboard a steamer, Franklin leaves the camp of the 113th Ohio and makes the journey back to Savannah. Within weeks, he and Clara are married by his friend, the Baptist preacher Garrison Frazier.

Franklin attempts to interview with Georgia's former governor, and Franklin's former master, Howell Cobb, primarily to discover the welfare of Franklin's aged father. But Cobb still holds tightly to the principles he supported during the war, most especially slavery, and only provides Franklin with the information that Henry is deceased. Convinced by Clara that his former master's reluctance to acknowledge any of his abuses is a blessing in disguise, ensuring that Franklin will never seek further employment from Cobb, Franklin instead accepts the opportunity of a parcel of land offered him by the Freedmen's Bureau, and he and Clara settle south of Savannah. But Franklin's innate curiosity makes for restlessness, and he cannot settle for life on a farm, even one that he owns. In 1868, with their two young children in tow, he and Clara move north, arriving in Washington City, where he witnesses the inauguration of Ulysses Grant as president. He accepts a job with a printing firm, but he is drawn by tales of life in other exotic cities, and so, in 1875, he and Clara move to New York City, settling in Harlem.

He seeks and finds a job at the Lenox Library, discovering the world of the written word, which he embraces with a level of enthusiasm that seriously impresses his colleagues. In 1895, the New York Public Library is founded, absorbing New York's smaller libraries, and Franklin accepts a position as assistant to the librarian, a position he holds until his retirement in 1917. But he and Clara do not enjoy a lengthy period of retirement. Clara becomes a victim of the influenza epidemic of 1918, and dies. Franklin continues a listless existence, visited frequently by his children and grandchildren, until his death in 1928. His family's best estimate is that he is eighty-two years old. He and Clara are buried in Harlem.

His oldest son, whom Clara names Sherman, serves in the all-Negro 10th Cavalry Regiment in the mid-1890s, the former "Buffalo Soldiers," made famous not only by their segregation from the rest of the army, but by their commander, John J. Pershing. It is here that Pershing receives the moniker "Black Jack."

As Franklin sought employment in the cities of

the North, it became even more imperative that he present himself with a first and last name. After 1870, he was known to all as Abraham Lincoln Franklin.

OLIVER O. HOWARD

Immediately after the war, Howard is instrumental in assisting to assimilate newly freed slaves into American political and social culture, serving as the first commissioner of the Freedmen's Bureau. In 1867, his work contributes to the founding of Howard University, in Washington, D.C., where he serves as president for the institution's first six years.

In 1874 he returns to military service, is named commander of the Department of the Columbia, and is stationed at Fort Vancouver, in Washington Territory, where he leads the government's campaign against the Nez Percé Indians, which results in the capture of Chief Joseph. He returns to the East and in 1881 serves as superintendent of the United States Military Academy for two years. Returning to the field, he commands the Department of the Platte, and the Military Division of the Pacific. In 1888, he returns east once more, assumes command of the Department of the East, at Governor's Island, New York, until his retirement in 1894.

He is awarded the Medal of Honor in 1893 for his actions at the Battle of Fair Oaks, on the Virginia peninsula.

Though Howard is faulted for his Eleventh Corps's collapse at both Chancellorsville and Gettysburg, his service to his nation both in and out of the service elevates his reputation as one of the most accomplished officers from the Civil War, and long after.

He dies in 1909, at age seventy-eight, and is buried in Burlington, Vermont.

HENRY SLOCUM

Slocum resigns from the army in the fall of 1865, becomes active in Democratic Party politics. He runs unsuccessfully for secretary of state for New York, and for a time returns to the practice of law. Finally elected to Congress in 1869, Slocum serves two terms, but fails to win reelection and returns to his law practice in Syracuse, New York.

Active in civic affairs, Slocum is appointed to head New York City's Department of City Works, and is instrumental in the approval for construction of the Brooklyn Bridge.

He returns to politics, and in 1882 is elected to Congress for a third term.

Always active in the concerns for aging and disabled veterans, Slocum heads the New York State Soldiers and Sailors Home in Bath, New York, and actively participates in the commission overseeing the construction and placement of the monuments on the battlefield at Gettysburg.

He dies in 1894, at age sixty-six, and is buried at Greenwood Cemetery, in Brooklyn, New York.

HENRY HITCHCOCK

Sherman's most educated adjutant resigns from the army in June 1865, and after a four-month journey through Europe, he returns to his law practice in St. Louis, Missouri. A fierce devotee of the law, he founds the St. Louis Law School in 1867, serves as its president until 1881. In 1878, he is a cofounder of the American Bar Association, and serves as that body's president in 1889.

Hitchcock's memoirs and collections of letters are assembled and published in 1927, long after his death. The accounts are a deeply revealing examination of Hitchcock's own concerns with and reservations about the campaigns of his commander, and especially his personal evolution as Hitchcock becomes more accepting of military realities. By the end of his service to Sherman, and in the years beyond, Hitchcock is an ardent supporter of Sherman's tactics, and is unfailing in his loyalty and devotion to Sherman and his career, writing, "To the casual observer, Sherman's quick and nervous manner, the flash of his eagle eye, the brusque command, might give token of hasty conclusions, of disregard of detail, of eager and impatient habits of thought. There could be no greater error. The atmosphere of his mind was lucidity itself. What he saw was pictured there, once for all."

He dies in 1902, at age seventy-two. Upon his death, Washington University in St. Louis salutes Hitchcock with this resolution: "His inimitable charm of conversation, his literary attainments, his broad grasp of political information, his profound learning and marked success in his own profession, and his zealous support of every educational interest, all found their origin in his undivided devotion to common welfare."

LEWIS M. DAYTON

Sherman's chief adjutant general serves his commander from as far back as the Shiloh campaign in 1862. Dayton is promoted to colonel in summer 1865. After the war, Dayton settles in Cincinnati, remains active in veterans' affairs, attending and organizing many reunions, almost always alongside Sherman.

He dies in 1891, at age fifty-five.

JAMES McCOY

McCoy serves as adjutant to Sherman from the Battle of Shiloh, promoted to lieutenant colonel by order of the president after the war. McCoy continues to serve on Sherman's staff until his death, in 1875, at age forty-eight. His funeral is attended by Sherman, along with all of Sherman's remaining staff. McCoy is buried in his family's plot at Greenlawn Cemetery, in Columbus, Ohio.

HUGH JUDSON KILPATRICK

Nicknamed "Kill Cavalry" for his impetuous and misguided assaults, which often result in casualty

counts far worse for his own men, Kilpatrick none-
theless attracts respectful attention, and he pens two
plays, which are thinly veiled references to his own
heroism. He lectures frequently and is considered
an entertaining, if not self-aggrandizing, speaker.

Kilpatrick resigns from the army in December
1865 and attempts a career in politics. He is named
minister to Chile by President Andrew Johnson
and remains in that post until 1870, when his utter
inability to perform with any level of diplomacy
causes controversy with nearly everyone he serves.
He nearly starts a war with Spain, forcing then-
president Grant to remove Kilpatrick from the post.

While in Chile, he marries Louisa Valdivieso,
whose father is an influential Chilean political figure. They have two daughters, Julia and Laura.
Laura's lineage leads eventually to her granddaugh-
ter, the famed socialite Gloria Vanderbilt, and sub-
sequently, Kilpatrick's great-great-grandson, CNN
anchorman Anderson Cooper.

Angry at Grant, Kilpatrick changes party affili-
ations, and supports Horace Greeley in the 1872
election, which Greeley loses. Always seeking the
opportunity to align himself with the winner, Kilpatrick changes parties again, and in 1876 supports
a successful Rutherford B. Hayes, who succeeds
in defeating the former Federal army commander
Winfield Hancock. In 1881 his reward for loyalty
to the Republican administration is a second appointment to Chile, but Kilpatrick's health fails,

and he dies shortly thereafter, in Santiago. He is forty-five.

He is eventually interred at West Point.

WILLIAM T. SHERMAN

Perhaps no military leader in American history is as polarizing a figure. To many, he is the finest battlefield commander of the Civil War, and perhaps ranks above any other similar figure from American military history, including George Patton and Douglas MacArthur. But to others, notably those whose ancestry lies in the deep South, Sherman is often regarded as a savage and brutal martinet, whose disregard for human suffering and destruction of private property in his campaigns in Mississippi, Georgia, and the Carolinas makes his very name a profanity.

There is no definitive argument either way, though to this day, those arguments continue.

In May 1865, the same month as his troops make their indelible impression upon the nation during the grand review, Sherman writes,

I confess, without shame, that I am sick and tired of fighting—its glory is all moonshine; even success the most brilliant is over dead and mangled bodies, with the anguish and lamentations of distant families, appealing to me for sons, husbands and fathers. . . . Tis only those

who have never heard a shot, never heard the shriek and groans of the wounded or lacerated ... that cry aloud for more blood, more vengeance, more desolation.

In June 1865, Sherman accepts command of the Military Division of the Mississippi, which eventually includes all territory from the Mississippi River to the Rocky Mountains. As such, he oversees the expansion of the West, and is charged with protecting the migration of white settlers, and extending the various railroad lines that make that settlement more feasible. He supervises various bloody conflicts with Indian tribes, though his greatest achievement with the Native Americans involves peaceful treaties, some of which assist Native Americans to regain their lost lands. Much of Sherman's reputation for brutality comes from the actions of his subordinates, notably Phil Sheridan, who, as he had done throughout the Civil War, is a far more reckless and brutal adversary to anyone who stands in Sheridan's way. Though Sherman supports Sheridan, he recognizes that the **total war** tactic both men had used during the war is not always the most appropriate when dealing with Indian tribes.

In 1866, Sherman is promoted to lieutenant general, and in 1869, when Ulysses Grant is elected president, Sherman is named by Grant as commanding general of the United States Army, and promoted to full general (four stars).

But Sherman's reign is not without controversy, and he clashes frequently with Secretaries of
War John Rawlins and William Belknap. Escaping official Washington as much as his rank allows,
Sherman relocates his headquarters to St. Louis.

To the modern eye, one of Sherman's most regrettable decisions involves the obliteration of the
free-roaming herds of western buffalo, the loss of
which Sherman believes will force the Indian tribes
to submit to government control.

He is outraged by the massacre at the Little Big
Horn, and the death of George Armstrong Custer
emboldens Sherman to increase the army's aggressive violence against warring tribes. But through it
all, Sherman continues to offer moderate views on
the expansion of white settlers into Indian lands. It
is yet another distinct contradiction that rivals the
reputation he had established during the Civil War.

In 1880, Sherman addresses a public forum in
Columbus, Ohio, where he states, "There is many
a boy here today who looks on war as all glory, but
boys, it is all hell." Thus is his most famous quote
given birth.

In 1881, Sherman recognizes the need for properly trained and educated military officers, and he
establishes what is now the Command and General
Staff College, at Fort Leavenworth, Kansas.

He retires in 1884, and lives out his remaining
years in New York City. But he cannot escape the
public eye, and is a highly regarded public speaker,

so much so that he is pressed to run for national office. To those who insist on including his name as a presidential candidate in 1884, he replies, "I will not accept if nominated and will not serve if elected." His negative view of politics most certainly is a reflection of the bitter conflicts he endured with official Washington, most notably Edwin Stanton, throughout the final weeks of the war.

His wife, Ellen, remains a devout Catholic, and his son Thomas seeks the priesthood, a decision Sherman angrily dismisses. The friction this causes is a stain on his family bond that is never reconciled.

Sherman dies in New York City in 1891, at age seventy-one. He is buried in Calvary Cemetery in St. Louis, Missouri.

In 1875, Sherman's memoir was published, which provided ample ammunition to those who supported him and those who despised him. Regardless of which side one takes (and few are in the middle), there is one indisputable fact: Through the first two years of the Civil War, the South and its generals gained advantages that could have won them the war. After the combined disasters of Gettysburg and Vicksburg, in July 1863, a Northern victory became inevitable. Though the Southern armies might have continued to fight, it was by the overwhelming superiority of Northern resources that the end came as it did. But in this author's opinion, two men, Ulysses Grant and William T. Sherman, brought the war to an end far more quickly, and far more decisively, than any other Federal commander could have done. William T. Sherman understood that war causes pain, and that the greater pain one inflicts, the more rapidly a war can be brought to a close. In that, he succeeded brilliantly.

ACKNOWLEDGMENTS

A PARTIAL LIST OF PRIMARY SOURCES

William T. Sherman, USA
Ulysses S. Grant, USA
Joseph E. Johnston, CSA
Henry M. Hitchcock, USA
Thomas D. Duncan, CSA
Cyrus F. Boyd, USA
Sam R. Watkins, CSA
John Beatty, USA
Joshua K. Callaway, CSA
Augustus L. Chetlain, USA
William B. Hazen, USA
Ira Blanchard, USA

952   ACKNOWLEDGMENTS

Dolly Sumner Lunt Burge, CSA
Thomas W. Osborn, USA
George W. Pepper, USA
Jacob Ritner, USA
George B. Guild, CSA

My most sincere thanks to the historians whose published works proved extremely helpful in the telling of this story:

John G. Barrett
Mark L. Bradley
Burke Davis
Mark H. Dunkelman
John P. Dyer
John M. Gibson
Nathaniel Cheairs Hughes, Jr.
Katharine M. Jones
Charles F. Larimer
John F. Marszalek
Samuel J. Martin
Kevin Rawlings
Craig L. Symonds
Noah Andre Trudeau

My deepest appreciation to the following, who contributed invaluable assistance and information, including unpublished, and often, previously unknown material:

John Belfrage, Pierce, Colorado
Kirk Bradley, Sanford, North Carolina
Patrick Falci, Rosedale, New York
Colonel Keith Gibson, Virginia Military Institute,
    Lexington, Virginia
Nancie Gudmestad, Shriver House Museum,
    Gettysburg, Pennsylvania
James Izzell, Bennett Place State Historic Site,
    Durham, North Carolina
Evalyn E. Kearns, Atlanta, Georgia
Emma McSherry, Gettysburg, Pennsylvania
T. J. Miller, Bennett Place State Historic Site,
    Durham, North Carolina
Kim A. O'Connell, Arlington, Virginia
Ryan Reed, Bennett Place State Historic Site,
    Durham, North Carolina
William Rutledge, Jr., Fort Collins, Colorado
Stephanie Shaara, Gettysburg, Pennsylvania
William G. Stanley, Aiken, South Carolina
Donny Taylor, Bentonville Battlefield State
    Historic Site, Four Oaks, North Carolina
Edward W. Vollersten, Monticello, Florida
Matthew Watros, Newfield, New York

ABOUT THE AUTHOR

Jeff Shaara is the **New York Times** bestselling author of **The Smoke at Dawn, A Chain of Thunder, A Blaze of Glory, The Final Storm, No Less Than Victory, The Steel Wave, The Rising Tide, To the Last Man, The Glorious Cause, Rise to Rebellion,** and **Gone for Soldiers,** as well as **Gods and Generals** and **The Last Full Measure**—two novels that complete the Civil War trilogy that began with his father's Pulitzer Prize–winning classic, **The Killer Angels.** Shaara was born into a family of Italian immigrants in New Brunswick, New Jersey. He grew up in Tallahassee, Florida, and graduated from Florida State University. He lives in Gettysburg.

www.jeffshaara.com

To inquire about booking Jeff Shaara for a speaking engagement, please contact the Penguin Random House Speakers Bureau at:

speakers@penguinrandomhouse.com.

LIKE WHAT YOU'VE READ?

If you enjoyed this large print edition of
THE FATEFUL LIGHTNING,
here are a few of Jeff Shaara's latest
bestsellers also available in large print.

The Smoke at Dawn
(paperback)
978-0-8041-9442-6
($28.00/$34.00C)

A Chain of Thunder
(paperback)
978-0-307-99088-4
($28.00/$34.00C)

A Blaze of Glory
(paperback)
978-0-307-99064-8
($28.00/$34.00C)

The Final Storm
(paperback)
978-0-7393-7820-5
($28.00/$33.00C)

Large print books are available wherever books
are sold and at many local libraries.

All prices are subject to change. Check with your
local retailer for current pricing and availability.
For more information on these and other large print titles,
visit www.randomhouse.com/largeprint.